Scratch the Itchy Teeth

Stories

Christopher S. Peterson

Fomite

Burlington, VT

ISBN: 978-1-947917-60-6
Library of Congress Number: TDB

Fomite
58 Peru Street
Burlington, VT 05439
www.fomitepress.com

To Mary J. Boyajian, RIP.

Contents

Mostro

Characters created by Carlo Collodi

His hellacious hallucinations: the surroundings with surreal, improper three-dimensional insubstantiality. Italy, 1920s. Rise of Fascism. Mussolini is in power. A rotting, pantagruelian puppet, Mostro, once called Pinocchio, has become a shambling, hideous creature with scabrous bark, green mosses, yellow funguses, and grey lichens, the transformation attributable to the many lies he has compulsively told over the years. He lives in a damp, dark cave taking care of senile woodcarver Geppetto, his creator, and spending his time stalking animals and watching humans waging war around him, threatening his routine. He believes he's been made monstrous by his monotonous existence and soul-crushing loneliness. His only friend is an insectile advisor, Talking Cricket. Clad his wretched monkish habit and torn jodhpurs, Mostro's ambling is arbitrary and accidental, politely nods to the eccentric, hulking hermit wearing rags and with ursoid eyes and bristly brows. Prehistoric cliffs. Watchtower fortress. He stomps carefully, aware of the fact he is progressing through territory with savage tribes, wild clans of predatory races, the legions of legendary giants constant menaces to them, intruding upon the venerable land, these massive, malevolent marauders quite merciless, potent and persistent as a sweeping pestilence, their antagonistic actions very much affecting everyone in the region. Such diabolical enemies to all and sundry! They seemingly flourish in inaccessible places, thrive in harsh conditions. Gambogian and sapphirine aboriginal forest is almost impenetrable. He emerges stealthily and retreats secretively on his stealing sprees. Currently, he contemplates the verdurous valley like a hawk considers taking flight over vast terrain. Leafy coppice is dimmed by fog, mountainous range obscured by distance. Military camp-entrenchments he avoids as the plague. Serpentiform slither of a sacred stream, steel-shining, its flow extending for a score of miles. Mother-of-pearl lambency. Vaporous film, rather phantasmal, hovers on a fertile expanse of a sepia-brown, well-plowed field.

He'd slaved for countless hours, sowing barley and posturing cattle for a pittance, manipulated by evil employers, his dim-wittedness and brute strength exploited. Plants veinal like seashells. Misty, shifting sky. Focusing his vision between butterfly antennae. His ligneous expression is as an immature individual's when learning he has been thrust, without warning, into the dreaded role of mature responsibility due to certain borderline dire circumstances. Native huts, these dwellings with detail and curious distinctive structural characteristics. Clouds give an ambiguous color to the empyrean and take it away. Dense virginal copse beyond. Jagged rocks. Fluctuating and peculiar phenomenon of precipitation. Sun steals up the slope of firmament, determined to reach its absolute apex. Intense Mostro has the immense capacity for uncontrollable fury, often completely succumbing to the least whim, subservient to caprice. He mixes badly with humanity, not unlike oil and water, or milk and wine. He plays hide-and-seek with squirrels and sparrows, pretends to be a noble knight who brazenly surrendered his armor to a dragon before slaying it with his mighty sword, a fighter with prestige and formidable influence, and, subsequently, uncrowned royalty belonging to a toppled dynasty locked in a painful struggle, with its fair share of crises, quarrels, conspiracies, feuds, and general inner turmoil, to regain the rightful throne. He is customarily detached and remote in his personal conduct. His unprecedented dedication to shriveled, elderly Geppetto, formerly an avid rare book collector, is on the level of lover's loyalty, this fidelity possessing an unparalleled piety, the fanatical faith of an inspired priest when it comes to God; belief without reservation, devoted as a Christian to Christ. The two have nothing in common with each other, even when Geppetto was healthy, but they have a natural chemistry, solid connection, and so are attached because of the special bond. Geppetto's superstitious. Mostro is skeptical. They were/are one another's confidante. The withered form

... deranged mind ... Harbor town in ruins and dust, result of pitiless and pathetic warfare. He gazes into the void of mental vacuity. Undulatory drizzle. Now his variegated thoughts inexplicably merge with the wavering rainbow. He muses on diverse subjects such as fate and chance, love and destiny, and the mysterious magic working in this weird world. Tranquil hush of twilight. He yearns to be in the dank, albeit peaceful, cavern with its rough-hewn stone walls. And he hopes Geppetto hasn't soiled himself. His patience in dealing with his senile father moves in slow motion, for sure. He has gone totally mad. His decline into dementia nothing short of dramatic. He had an admirable inquisitive intelligence. Tossing teal surf. Criss-cross whirls of sharp breezes. Autumnal swamp and its various shades. He mumbles to himself a strange, meandrous malediction. His piecemeal recollections of an event that'd transpired a week ago - he'd happened upon habitations of adorable and elusive elves and decimated them lickety-split with his Herculean might, an internal sardonic smile contracting like muscles in his middle. He vividly remembers the mangled remains of the notoriously private, ugly goblins months back, in the umbrageous vegetation, mutilated by his huge hands. It was a surprise-attack, a full-fledged massacre. He tore down the sturdy ramparts as if they were built of cardboard and ran amok. Images conjured in his timbered cranium, with crystal clarity, of him decapitating and dismembering the spectral enchantresses, identical ghostly figures, swaying like flags, with bony bodies, alabaster flesh, beautiful faces, large noses, saucer- sized ears, long hair, and small breasts, dressed in gorgeous diaphanous gowns, their simian gibberish driving him insane. His coal-black peepers were centered in the circumferences of the craters of his crepuscular sockets. Cinereal shoulders of cirri bore the brunt of the weighty welkin. Fresh-fallen snow steamed. He stews on his unforgivably disastrous, blasphemous decisions. He is on the verge of tears. He imagined he was pillaging a palace and ravaging the pretty princesses. Pollen's as though it's powder from crushed puffballs. Their features were distorted into impressions of fear at the initial sight of him. There was a particular poignancy to his indescribable, unfathomable wrath, raising hell in those smoky halls, commodious chambers, creamy corridors. He never fell under the scary spells of their vaunted sorcery. The revenants were alarmed by the behemothic intruder at their doorstep. The phantasmagoric sentries with ivorine skin stationed at the skull- shaped castle were easily dispatched. Eidola of swirling cumuli haunts the heavens. Constant condensation. Nothing in this universe could heal his hurt, no one can solve his problems. There are perplexities of his personality, myriad conflicts and multitudinous confusions. He admits to a chipmunk that he derived significant pleasure in the chaos, indulged in the sensation of committing coldblooded murder just for the sake of it, confesses to a raven he had no sympathy for the numerous victims' profound suffering. In addition, he wiped out their potential saviors, swarthy, stalwart, swift and youthful warriors, who'd descended on the colossal gatecrasher, waiting on the broken platform of masonry, with discretion, spears, and bows-and-arrows at the ready. They were outmatched, overwhelmed, the ranks quickly destroyed. It would be a marvelous comfort for him to communicate with a kindred spirit, to converse, perhaps connect with someone who can understand the complex essence of who he actually is, and who knows the best and worst of him. Yes! No. He would be shy and awkward. He thinks of himself as difficult yet interesting. Maybe fascinating. He's plural in personality as well as singular. Guilt wills him to stave off violent impulses, his fierceness usually inflicted on the innocent. His conscience flaps its fabulous falcon wings within him. Harsh weather, a Wagnerian sturm and drang. In his filthy robe he is a waterlogged ship with a slack sail, navigating treacherous waters, submissive to the winds and waves. Dreams of being a boy are indeed dashed. Nocturnal ceremony of tanks, trucks and motorcycles.

Mostro, all reek and creak, at a glimmering dawn, on an exploratory excursion, chases rabbits in the brumal forest when this humongous snake, Serpent, with glowing, enormous eyes, beckons to him from an abyssal pit with a singsong hiss. Mostro hesitantly jumps in. It convinces him he was born to wreak havoc. Then it disappears. He is extremely agitated, gripping the leathern neck of his empty flask, respirations coming in labored gasps. Heart in his chest is a withered reptile slinking into a safe space to avoid a pursuing eagle. He mulls over topics like love and hate, mind and matter, good and evil, angels and devils, and, to an extent, life and death. His brain is a wild bird caught in a cranial cage. Unsluiced luminosity, dammed by the plentiful foliage. Atramentous brake's agitated by avian chirps. Cogitations hover in his head as hawks. Vulpecular barking. Sky ransacked by ravens. Continuous conscious presence of the fog. Rodentine scufflings in the bracken. He has the tension of a predator about to pounce on its prey. Gusts grope their way, guttural sibilations as human speech. He has no confidence, self- respect. The umbilical cord connecting him to his country he has officially severed. Music-box tinkling of the rain turns into a maddening refrain. He pictures Geppetto meticulously washing his hirsute, arthritically angular mitts with a square of soap in the porcelain basin, sedulously involved in the daily ritual of hygienic religiosity, frontage, lachrymosely blubbered, distorted into a permanent paroxysm of grief, and murmuring to himself in olden colloquial Latin Mostro could not comprehend. He had no choice in treating him like a nurse would an infant. He's shame-stricken. At that same moment, Mangiafuoco, bald, bulbaceous and mustached, a high-ranking military officer, appears along with his men.

Discussions of administrative and executive decisions and exchanges of militaristic strategies in the campaign casually diminish. They mock him. He fumbles about to clamber out, futilely, his faculties gradually restored to him with the respite. He makes a piteous appeal for their aid, the exertion expended to climb out on his own taxing on his endurance, his psychological gymnastics putting a strain on his physical fitness. Hopeless and hungry, he begs for their assistance to get out of the trap. Mangiafuoco agrees, but on one stipulation: he must infiltrate a communist resistance stronghold and annihilate the insurgents. Mostro swears on his miserable life. He is thrown a rope and hauled out of the hole. The dominant urges in his interior have increasingly taken on a material embodiment on the exterior, accidental and absurd, an unintelligible influence on his perception. Rushing, cascading continuity of the rapids. His bloodstream, the sensation of one, feels real and unreal, and as if it's quicksilver. Volume of the vantage meadow with flanks of stumps, blurred like the scene is beheld through a liquid medium. Later that evening, Talking Cricket, voice sounding as though its throat is filled with bittersweet smoke, attempts to talk him out of following through on the "suicide mission." Mostro immediately smashes it with a buckled, polished shoe and smears its spilled guts on the cold floor. The pocked moon is a sort of sign, or signal. Embalmed animals are everywhere. He swats at a squadron of wasps, flying frenetically, ricocheting off the walls with its play of red brick, gray slate, and white stone. His hand lights on his private lever, his penile crank, only this fails to allay his anxieties. He carries his canteen like it contains the precious blood of the Crucified. Geppetto is his paterfamilias to whom he refers often with devout respect.

Deluge in the mistrals apparently goes up and down as bell ropes. Native boys have the suppleness of girls; Grecian athletes trotting in extinct oxskin loincloths. Mostro's lumbering could be mistaken for a grotesque dance. With his prodigious bestial strength he plunges animalically into the pathless undergrowth with automatic adroitness, breath quickening in nervous apprehension, pitching himself with different movements and speeds, forcing his passage with detached determination, pressing forward. He's outfitted in stolen Roman sandals, tattered tunic, beaten breastplate, and plumed helmet. He approaches the jerrybuilt fortress not unlike a cat would a mouse. His saponaceous sweat's stink stings his flared nostrils. He advances rapidly and recklessly, with a feline's slinkiness, through the brambles, accelerating through oaks' boughs and sycamores' branches. Burial mound. Overcast blackens as a scribe's ink. Perpetual screen of showers. A dumbfounded, vile and vulgar satyr's presence produces great irritation for him. And the vague abstracted countenance ... He fusses with a folded scroll of parchment. Holly bushes. Ponderously Mostro fumbles among the ferns, amid the firs, hacking methodically at the overwhelming foliage with a glistening sword. There are fungoid spots on his wrists. He shushes the snickering, gamboling centaurs in the soggy marsh. They, startled, swerve, rear up high, and kick at the saturated oxygen with their formidable hooves. He could certainly tame those asses! They're scrupulously alert, uppity and truculent, and recede like shadows. Babbling brook. Corpse of a toppled poplar, its deformed twin, in proximity, nearly bowed to the muddy ground. Prevailing chilly drafts. His foray into a hen roost, piebald with a whitewash of droppings, is whimsical and solemn. Making an ordinary and dispassionate effort to traverse the sodden territory. Exposed and elongated roots are arteries in an anatomical operated-on earth. He experiences a delicious quiver of excitement of possible bedlam, interrupted by intervals of jibing and jeering and disheveled rooks. Many sights and sounds compose incredible impressions, visually and auditorily, of unique symbols, visible and tactile, in the celestial sphere of his grey matter. At this juncture he's lethargic. Choir of songbirds. Clumps of hedges. A creek gurgles and suspires. Bubbles of fantasies burst. He pauses at the trunk of an alder in the vicinity of a divine, gliding rindle. The azure has a metalline gleam, accentuates the livid desolation of the land littered with innumerable casualties of war. A robin's yakking's incomprehensible to him. He is absorbed in his own reveries, mainly focusing on the metaphysical axiom of the druidic attitude. He regards the revolt against governmental authority as an ideological agenda of its participants, a political imperative with an independent pulse. He surrenders himself to the liberation of these heartfelt opinions. There was an abysmal chasm between his view and Mangiafuoco's - affirmation of how authentic argumentation is humanistically essential! He is merely an immortal playing his (primal) part on a stage setting of this deadly championship. He wanted a wrestling match with the captain. Coral moon. The conflict brought here like seaweed into a rockpool at hightide. He's a vessel adjusting his rudder. He relaxes as a string after an arrow has left the bow. His exultation mounts by the minute. He ambulates with alacrity, armed to the teeth with a personalized, puppetized policy of moral, or immoral, aimlessness of principles. Scruples be damned. He is (deliberately) wayward at a more leisurely pace, finding stimulus in instinctive striving, his often irrational impulses with an accompaniment of repercussions. His existential emancipation is culpability for compulsive actions, usually aggressive.

He's a bowshot of the indubitably dumbly positioned boulders. His fantastic notions come from outside Time and Space. Mangiafuoco is solely responsible for his feelings of being belittled, reduced to nothing. His vengeance will take him. He'll coil round him like the snake did Cronus and squeeze the life out of him. He will fatally choke him. Preparations for the siege are minimal. He cuts scissorishly through the woods, slips as a weasel. There won't be terms set for surrender. There'll be no survivors. No military strategy. It is an improvisational campaign. It's been a heretofore swift journey, abandoning main roads and remaining in the forest, maintaining his discipline, in spite of an unexplainable instance where he deviated from different trails and lost his sense of direction. He will bombard them with aggression. They will fucking foul their trousers. Cantering along, unsure whether or not civilians, concentrated in that specific area, will be safe. Vagaries are float in his head like dead squids on the sea's surface. He slaps a mosquito on his nape. He steals a quick snooze on a bale of straw. The moon departs and yet interestingly becomes more distinct. Construction of a tunnel has commenced. A corpulent commander of a garrison, in full maturity of his fifty years, is bafflingly affable, actuating. Mostro encounters a regiment of infantry on a stretch of gravelly no- man's land, resorts to dipping into his resources for propaganda rhetoric in linguistic theatricality. An Italian comedy. There's no physical episode, instead a verbal refrain, nothing more, nothing less. He doffs his cap and bows with a silly salute. He adeptly avoids a company of an estimated dozen foot-soldiers on a cobbled path. Men are primordial atoms skirmishing, numberless seeds engaged in combat. Musketeers, digging trenches, harass him. It is advisable to ignore them. Several traipse across a plain. At dusk, he, impossibly rugged, impervious to bullets, besieges the rebel outpost on the hill and, dear Lord our Creator, instantly recognizes faces from the past: trouble-making Lampwick, with donkey ears, portly farmer Gangio, gangling drummer Master, and anthropomorphic avian Crow. Mostro slaughters them, deftly, except for Crow, who escapes by flying away. Mostro brandishes a slingshot, flings stones, and misses the target by an infinitesimal margin. It was an honor to kill them, having a history with them and respecting them, however, he was duty-bound. Dirty work is done. With practiced aplomb. Faintest flicker of a self-satisfied smile. He scarfs a kumquat. He's a chimera of unnatural nature. Mostro stands supreme above all others. Geppetto's languorous convalescence has made his existence ... languid.

The battlefield is a theater, troops the actors. He lives in nighttime and slays in daylight. The agitators' breaches were vulnerable and slipshod. They were seized with panic, and instantaneously dispersed. He plunged as an insane Icarus bent on his own imminent destruction. Spectacular friendship among the sea, sky and earth. He exploited the surprise. They didn't have the chance to grab their weapons. He calvary-charged. Barricades collapsed from his bull-rush. Desertions increased by the minute. They relinquished the fortification. In the aftermath he, a lunatic looter, despoiled the fallen, severing a finger or ear for a ring, hacking off a hand for a bracelet. The situation was critical for the dissenters from the start, the rout on. There was no restraint, no need for reinforcements, the mayhem at full tilt, and he dashed back and forth like a madman. Thoughts of Turquoise Fairy in his brain - luminescence refracted in a glassy object. He seeks solace in her bosom, a balm for his essence. Her diamondiferous pies, marble teats, ruby lips. He is a colossal caterpillar crawling on the radiant rose of her. He's a pygmoid deformity with a glorious giantess. She is remarkably evasive, an eidolonic enigma. Voluptuous metamorphoses of her in his mind. He said there's more than enough to show a single segment of his individuality, even a small section, hinting at a larger person; the equivalent, he supposed, of seeing a room reflected in a convex mirror, suggesting a bigger space. She announced she had heartburn and a headache. Austral arc of her moue was captivating. Her voice lulled him into lullaby land. He was tempted to frisk her hour-glass figure. Would she afford him the opportunity to conduct a groping session? She was an expert weaver of silken words. He considered her elegant phrases. She was snowy, now sallow, an alien to this planet, a phantom who'd not lost her charms. She muttered as a fountain, was innocent not unlike the dove, and suppressed her suffering. His amorous obsession was her. She, the quintessence of ethereal beauty, kindled his senses. She purred as a bronchitic cat. Attraction would give birth to action. She was a divine mystery he needed to penetrate. She pretended she was in a non-place of make-believe, a void. He wanted to serenade her, but wound up sexing her in auric rays ... He eliminated them with unerring skill and savagery, swinging the sword, dull and deadly, at his adversaries. Lampwick, the stupefied scoundrel, a guerrilla jester, recognizing the bad turn things were taking, drew a pistol from his belt, the apparently proper move to prove his courage to his comrades (catastrophic mistake), pricked up his ass-ears, pivoted, prior to having one cut and hanging pendulous below his chin. He was disemboweled. His entrails spilled like spaghetti into his trousers. His valiant response attracted attention. It is worthwhile to note he did not calculate the risk. His brothers? Their brazen attack was a fine retreat. They were the vanquished finding victory in inaction, not winning anyone over by their ways. Their munitions were scarce. Mostro, not the least discontented with the Mangiafuoco contract, dodged bullets, declared he had motives, he had reasons, acknowledged the consequent development of his destiny. It was a mandatory moral enterprise. He doesn't need consolation for his deeds, for they were a handful of heretics, slothful cowards, bailing at the first sign of a fight, and got what they deserved, that is, shameful deaths. They died damned. This is a victorious chapter in his horrid history. They were thorns in his side. He was an eagle devouring mice! He already had his share of difficulties. He felt as a Christian on a crusade and they were these Protestant mercenaries. He confronted them, knowing they lacked sufficient numbers to defeat him. They were hunkered down, set on defending the region (treacherous territory) at all costs. Infiltration was child's play; he pushed through a gulley to their flanks. He hammered them with the arsenal of his aggression. He was a rogue unrestrained, completing a service, sprightly like a stripling, moved in a deceitful direction, and they deemed this a tactful error, a major miscalculation made by their enemy, and he, adept in the military arts, naturally gifted, resumed an offensive position, and they were overrun. Impromptu strategies governed his noggin. At first their dignity forbade them retreat. Allowances would not be made, even for former pals. The indolent operation progresses in his favor. Mostro, visage spattered with clotted blood, galloped, fought as a fury, was a ram battering them. He'd sacked the compound for a short duration, plundered the place, emptying it from top to bottom. He would honor the pact with Mangiafuoco, who is continuously in his cups. Possibly, with a little luck, Mostro'd be admitted into his esteemed ranks, become his go-to marionette! With them, he had the sensation of being in a den of spies, meeting and negotiating with them. His noodle is clear as it is dark. He's on his own. Nobody will lend a helping hand. There are no lines of communication to cut. Excessive emanation. He will decide his own fate. War is both a lovely and hideous thing. He craves neither condemnation nor reward, only the fulfillment of a bargain. Well-earned reward of freedom, bathing in its glow, released of all duties. He took advantage of the opportunity offered him. Sitting on the stairway leading to a courtyard. A pullet roasts on a spit in the vacant country villa. Partaking of Spanish wine, fried sausages and smoked tuna, scrounged up. Permitting himself a few scoops of vanilla and chocolate ice cream. Shadows

succumb to the lure of light. Raiding the cellar of victuals, it was like he reaped a harvest! He blows his nose
into a napkin, laps the plate, licks his fingers. A (conspicuously) choleric, conciliatory hoyden flirts with a
blanching lad, certainly a rascal, blocks his path.
Dwarvish, buffoonish castrati. Their clumsy caravan
trundles at cockcrow. Masculine and feminine cackling
(from somewhere) as hens advertising eggy provisions.
Sun is predominant. Fickle fulgor has the patina of a
polished mandolin. Vault obstinately reigns. Ossiferous
frost. Clouds, colours a medley of ruby and ebon, adhere
to it. Shoals of fish scud in a crystalliferous stream. The
chiaroscuro condenses, settles like cream. Liquefaction
of illumination, wonderfully wan. Seeing pollen, as
excited eyes encountering powder of matter. Space of
the visible. Orchard in its vivid greening crowned by
sunflowers. He summons the specter of Lampwick,
scrawny and brisk, with the humorous overbite, dumb as
a box of battle axes, elicits him inadvertently, the irre-
deemable rapscallion accomplishing a demonstration of
tenderness, and Mostro, pies catching the effulgence
like the glass of mirrors, reddened from tears, apolo-
gizes, in a typically uncivil way, for the excessive force
adopted, and is grateful for its acceptance, waxes enthusiastic with emotions conveyed with gentle dexterity,
and cultivates the necessary cerebrations which comfort
him. Using God's name in vain. Innocent kids, discalced,
rejoice in merriment, jaunty in various strains of grain.
A group of officers playing dice chuckle at Mostro,
thinking he is a comedian in mask and costume. He,
playing a role according to the occasion, mocks being a

minstrel, strumming a lute, making melodious music, whistling and skipping. They hurrah and clap. Pleasantries are exchanged in the casual encounter. His politeness is differentiated according to their respective ranks. Slice of sanguineous horizon is a neat pig- castrator's cut. He wanders as a star. He kneels and prays in an ornate cathedral, refulgence spreading over the plush altar, rickety pews and ostentatious floor. Penitent, he should be in the confessional! He had stolen the win in the warring with his chums. He'd better not be robbed of the gem of his theft! He represents the cream of the crop when it comes to killers. They were louses he smashed. He had contempt for them, like they were lice. He was an enemy inside the gates. He feels as if he's carrying the considerable weight of the Cross.

Mostro awakens from a deep sleep to find Geppetto gone. Manuscript is on a lectern. Wet rock, competently painted with an elegant antique mural of a cozy cottage and quaint park, reverberates like a submarine diving many fathoms down. Suddenly, he hears him sobbing and listens to breakers booming. From a perilous position on an awe-inspiring crag overlooking the beach, Mostro sees Geppetto, perspiry, enfeebled and haggard, with his visage lined as though it's a grimacing woodcut, hunched shoulders and halting footsteps, respirations raspy, garbed in baggy tweeds, walking on luminous sand, then wading into the glaucous water when, abruptly, the gigantean Terrible Dogfish surfaces, swallows him whole, and returns to the ocean. Mostro's agonized shriek rends the salty air, and he dives in to try and save him, to no avail. He floats on the sea, crying.

Green Fisherman, an obese ogre, catches him in his net and puts him to work on his modest boat, the Beatrice, promising him that he can use the harpoon on Terrible Dogfish if/when the moment presents itself. An ungainly, flat- bottomed barge is stranded on the steep slope of the banks. Auroral borealis of butterflies. Danse macabre of skeletal trees. Flux and reflux of cloud in the changeable heavens. Pages of a discarded literary tome flutter like loose toupees. Tribesmen, clothed in sheep's wool coats, cowhide leggings and leather sandals, are hoarse and husky, in conversation. Death-and-corruption mephitis. Pile of twigs. Cirri collaborate to form the impression of a rhinocerine presence. Heap of bones. Lachrymal dew. Bushes are as the antlers of stags. The sun's a Homeric Cyclops. Is Mostro an orphan? He'd never be able to fill the hole, accustom himself to the loss. The wound will never heal. He must bear, for the nonce, the expense for maintaining the cavern. He constructs delusions like astronomers build telescopes. Episodic digressions in his brain. Turquoise Fairy ... is she under the influence of a potent sleeping potion? He is a vein, she is an artery. He's a bone, she's the marrow. His aspirations of ardor lurk unconfessed in the recess of his core. He remarks these repressed, clandestine desires. A sinner, he wanted to violate her virtue. He wished he were a poet or phi-losopher to impress her, plumb the depths of her with sophisticated language and ideas, but he was, of course, incapable. As an alternative, he decided to tickle her bare and delicate feet, only she recoiled, facially florid, emphasized she suffered a bellyache, also said she was seized by further minor maladies, and added her ears were buzzing and her eyes were rheumy. He hoped she'd believe he was a hero who'd committed grand and noble acts. He didn't excel in conjuring epical narrative. Puppet of artful eloquence he was not. He fondled her fast as a magician performing tricks onstage. He leered, praised her. He bit into her fruit, bathed in her water. Nymphean play in puerility. His personality is a paradox, a parable, unparalleled, one that he has, inadvertently, written. He's the author of his own ardency. Cumuli manifest in varying guise. Muculent brilliance. He is an unprecedented form without pertinent matter. Nothing can harm him. No blow could hurt him. In his fervent imagination he is in the open space of a broad valley, an Atlas, bearing a global rucksack on his back, mulls over astronomical allegories, endurance waning. His pot is cracking. Hiking, he could be mistaken for a figure in the Dance of Death. He's forever harnessed to the wagon of Geppetto. A sexagenarian lapdog throws a hissy fit, complaining of malignant abscesses.

Mostro, a composition that's a phantasmagory of atoms and activity, has lost track of time. It suggests an eternity. This is an approximate, abstract calculation, naturally. He is burnt by the brine, stiff from slaving on the Beatrice. Tempest's a major weatherly disturbance. Bacchanalian storm. By a Godly merciful decree they haven't yet sunk. It finally passes and without further incident. Parasitic misery with him. He works hard, pained at every gain. His desperation, his determination to locate Geppetto inspires him to forge on, with intestinal fortitude. He's a puppety Hercules, strangling his serpentine demons. He dozes off under a variegated vista, in proximity to the rope-(Jacob's) ladder, curled like a kitten on the cordage on the soaked bowsprit. Roused from his much-needed nap, he feels rejuvenated, indeed reborn. Cycladic coruscation. Meadows of combers. He inspects the rigging, masts with the sails unfurled, the cannon at the gunport. There's artillery in abundance. Waxen light. Palm and towering cliffs are seen from the bulwarks, on an island near a broad bay vaster than a standard continent, to his perspective. Complaisant crests. In the galley an avalanche of bruisy vegetables comes down. Ambulant arachnids. Lively waves. Executioner sun's shafts guillotine the necks of shadows on the convex poop. He dreams of Turquoise Fairy, characteristically odorous, steeped in expensive perfume, the de facto love of his life, lady of his heart. Her exquisite image sends him succor in his solitude. He is bereft of her beneficence. He's afire with desire, beholding her mysterious mirage, despite his poor vision. Army of vociferant whitecaps fan out. He's a tenebrous flame consumed by the topazine ocean. Meanwhile, Green Fisherman, a scorner of the lassitudinous, slumbers, snores in his L-shaped cabin on this rocking sarcophagus, a wooden dungeon, after Mostro had applied salves to the hypochondriac captain's sunburned back. The two are, undeniably, the refuse of the seven seas, bottom of the barrel, he believes. He is a prisoner, punished for his myriad transgressions.

His weak lynxian oculi tolerate the dazzling tropical sun. A trading vessel is a pirate ship to him. Calm channel. Checking the fore and aft quarters, consulting the compass next to the tiller. His cubbyhole has a plain bunk and ordinary table with numerous maps and miscellaneous papers (covered with crude calculations) required for proper navigation, and quillpen and attendant inkwell. The decorative musket is essentially nonfunctional. Galactic rarities of maddened meteors. He's besmirched by blood and guts from bait and catch. He is an invincible menace. A rodentine squeaking from the bilge. Glaucescent brine's an alternation of tranquility and turmoil. He officially embarks on the admirable cerebral exercise of musing on life and death. Nocturnal noises: combative concert. His blood would run cold if he had any. Leaving the hull for the pantry. Pyramid of pungent fruits, prickly and scaly. Halo of tsetse flies. Eggs promise (deficiently-defended) yolks. He taps a keg with its bung-hole and gulps putrid water with drowned insectean corpses, fails to slake his thirst. Green Fisherman rescued him. He would've drifted forever. He opines a positive fortune invariably leads to negative consequences. He has refuge ... on a relic! His plans are pieces on the chessboard of his greymatter to be eventually deployed. He envisages occupying a sumptuous chamber with a canopied bed out of a fairytale. Thoughts hold their council in his skull. He envisions a coconut moon, it as manna beneath the husk of cloud. Vaguely he remembers, in a fragmented fashion, gallivanting, and fantasizing about fencing and falconry, in the vineyards in their vastity, sometimes scaring birds from ruining the crops in those farmers' fields. He'd intimidate the peasant kids. He was keen. They were ignoramuses, lily-livered, limp-pricked louts, blockheads felicitously manly, not fit to lick his balls. He wasn't their peer. He was a pariah - a fact which troubled his days and nights. He would flip arbitrarily through wrinkly magazines in the dusty library to distract himself from his worries. He felt as an aimless outlaw. Geppetto ... is he alive or dead? When he was of sound mind he, intermittently brusque in manner, treated Mostro with a kind of taciturn toughness, and would, periodically, to offset this, exude a kind of paternal pride, twirling his cinerous, bushy, walrus mustache, and Mostro's woody aspect would assume an expression of explicit pleasure. In front of Turquoise Fairy there was the improper liberation of his penial log from his pants, expecting her to be privileged by the perversion, a lump in his throat. Was he capable of realizing the gravity of this prurient foolishness? He appreciated the inevitability of a grievous punishment. She would administer a mild admonishment for his juvenile game. She always accused him of being like an ostrich hiding its head away from the world. He ensnared himself in a plight of his own engineering. His ill- concealed contentment. He refused to save face, for it wasn't worth saving, in his humble estimation. Their fluids flowed like Edenic milk and honey. He strived to be a chaste witness to her nudity. Her vagina was rich in promises to him. To her, its purpose was its purposelessness. Her backside was a hieroglyph he deciphered. Indecently he fiddled with himself. He bragged about waging war, establishing himself in the center of an intensifying fracas, as if he wanted her to bet on him, place a wager on the winning horse: him. He soared on the wings of confidence, violated her virginity. She was his personal plaything for an interminable time period. He was Adam tempted by Eve's remarkable chesty apples. His member sprang like lightning. He had clung to her by his teeth. Her first move to repel him was checkmated. They found themselves literally face-to-face. Her numerous qualities added up to mathematical rarities. Trophies of her anatomic parts. He paused, vigorously vulgar and vile, contemplated her celestial body, and for her it was a welcome reprieve. He made an immense effort to force himself on her. She, a plant planted by his bulk, resisted vehemently, wore herself out. He was tempestuously lewd. Mostro spasmed, sported a simper, climaxing. A most incredible orgasm! His mouth was as though a cannon's. He dedicates his memories to her, recent and remote recollections. Sounds of his gasping disturb the silence of a pelagic sanctum. He's sandwiched between the sea and sky in their harmonious arrangements. He braves the heat, the humidity. Weather's indiscriminate vengeance. He wants to lavish himself with the food that is plentiful, be the sole inhabitant on that looming pale island in the distance. The Beatrice pitches. The craft is a rocking cradle, the vessel a veritable jail with wooden bars, the water his jailer. The squalls show no sign of letting up. He's a hulking fetus in a wooden womb. Splendor filters through the fleecy cirri. Fish are like they're spun from colorful glass. Atmosphere decrees quietude. Waves are voltas of vortexes with curvaceous deviations. Birds exotic penetrate the course of the current and disrupt them. The tissue of his perspective is tearing. Perimeters and periphery are dimming. He believes he is wood of skin, pure of heart, a satellite in circular mobility. Thalassic sighs.

Stark contrasts of interplaying light and shadow, oblique and intersecting on the systematically tidied-up quarterdeck, organized with economy. Mostro's timorous mediations on the storm's temperamental fluctuations. Pea-green sea. He musters the courage and lowers himself through the feared trapdoor to explore the space with its stores, and his nostrils are assailed by musty smells. Curious cabinets of nautical instrumentation. Boxes of varying description in q hawser locker. The helmsman's room is reserved for other functions, in a state of unnatural disorder, transformed into a storage unit, holding hammocks, wicker cage, baskets, cases and containers. Motes swirl as corpuscles in cascades of luster. Decomposing sylvan hoard. It is an unproductive voyage up to this point. His fantasia's shoots of the plants of salacity are already taking root. To wit, Turquoise Fairy's lilial white derma layer is fulgurantly ambered. Her orchidaceous organ splits open in overripeness, revealing a puce interior. Her arms and legs are rigid not unlike carbines. His disgusting B.O. has the stink of moldering corncob. Her obscene pudendal primrose is exhibited. Her sapid cologne. Shelves support a festoonery of porcelain shells. Empyrean is an emerald jewel, measureless, teeming with rubescent stars. Her glabrate cunt has a meaty consistency and's redolent of fermented cheese. Green Fisherman's comportment a hitherto convincing absurdity. If Mostro had flesh it'd crawl. Goat-beards of clouds. Her tiny conch-shaped navel. She's an enchantress and he's overwhelmed by her cast spell. Her snatch is a purplish pomegranate, fart with a rattling sound as a child's toy.

She's lithe like a weeping willow and has cusp-shaped breasts. Paws, trunks and trumpets of flowers. Fronds in floridness. Leaves of plants could be conceivably employed as trays. His mental state provokes deliriums. Her personality precipitates elements of opium, stirring and altering his senses. He heads towards the prow. Her feathery inflection is at once audible and visual. Artifice created by her cosmetics confuses him. He's afraid he has the stench of putrefying animal. She looks like a genius sculptor's hands had chiseled her with every bit of his artistic ability. Oblong fruits of her tits with their treacly ripeness. Summer melons of her hurdies. She's contained in a cobalt cloak with vermilion hues. Ovaline droplet of sweat lingers on her nose. A couple of locks escape from her tightly wound bun. She cants slightly, rumpling her abdominal folds. His intent gaze rests on it. His tone is licentious. Her kindness is a cruelty. To savor her genitalia's spring ... Will he strike out? He'd perish in shame! Can he be equal to the task? He is a novice to the rite of seduction. He's palsied, barely breathing, dreams of digitally navigating through her mane's leonine waves. Desire flourishes in expectancy. He's struck dumb by lust. He has the stupidity of a fool. She is as a modest maiden. He feels washed away, akin to a name written with a stick on the shore's sand by the surf. He shan't feign sincerity. With her he is a bee before the honeycomb: intoxicated. He appreciates her refinements. Aquamarine down on her angulose nape. Her keister's a keg and he puckers up, putting his mouth to her bung, indulges to excess. His joints chirr like a corroded lock, ligaments scrape as rusty hinges. She's an intellectual without pedantry. Her heinie is smooth like oil. She possesses resplendence to the highest degree, has divine attributes. Indecision is an invisible blockade he is impelled to overcome. He's rendered identifiable by her, as an isle drawn in detail by a competent cartographer to be easily recognized. Will she experience the sensation of the potentiality of a serious union? Libidinous, his head spins, oculi moisten, existence evaporates. Her magnificent body's molded from a magical clay. She calls him an insolent creature. Our Creator, not Geppetto, has the power of life and death over him. Cirri perform their slow motions. His heart pounds in his breast, pleads for mercy in the torture chamber of his chest. He's a Vulcan with Venus. She has a sublime substance. Will she resolve to succor this moribund monster? He bends, nearly bows, not unlike an actor on stage for the audience, anticipating applause. He wouldn't squander these specific circumstances. He's a seashell and she's the pearl generated within him. He reduces expectations, restrains enthusiasms. He avails himself again of her anatomy. Thrusting as a knife put into a sheath. Unsynchronized superimposition of their heartbeat rhythms distinguished by their hearing. Affectionate intimacy it is not. He grins like a skeleton. He is an erupting volcano, ejaculating molten lava. Distance dulls ardor. Closeness sharpens it. He conceals his amatory motivation in his bosom as if he stole it. She exudes the essence of a figure mythological. Pyrotechnics of leven. Inner tumult during the favorable minute. Thunder's a rolling of drums. Cornucopian comet. He cannot compose sonnets for her. Cornflower-coloured firmament. He croaks like a frog. She cheeps in vexation, manhandled. Her aquiline proboscis. She comes to terms with the treatment. Chromatic scales of her screeches. His penis emerges from her vaginate funnel. He absorbs the sense of the twat's tangy aromas, whereupon he abandons her being like a warrior his valor, that is, grudgingly. She stares at him like Satan, on the verge of stealing his soul. Cloudcover silvers the skyline. With this great deal of stuff it's as though Green Fisherman is gathering evidence, artifacts collected from alien worlds to prove to schools and courts these places exist. He's caught in the grip of melancholy. Arterial throb of the precipitation.

Time passes slowly. Brilliancy's lances have the pigment of ripe wheat. Latent cumulus. The Beatrice caroms like a pool ball, mauled by the tidal waves. An eclipse blots out the sun, makes a pertinent impression, and no one underrates its paramount importance. Mostro, dressed in a cruddy cassock, playing a trumpet as a flamethrower, scorching the oxygen, spots Terrible Dogfish and hurls the harpoon. The leviathan thrashes maniacally. Mostro manages to swim into its massive mouth and discovers Geppetto has hanged himself from a tooth with kelp. Mostro considers himself a castaway in a capacious oral cavity; or a stowaway hidden in a hold. Cramped with crap, he squats and shits, the diarrheal excrement giving the aquatic behemoth the dry heaves, and it gags, retches him out. Then Mostro snaps Green Fisherman's neck and throws him overboard and natates for the shore. Terrible Dogfish is dead on the water. Mostro buries Geppetto in the thicket. Rustic fury. He is adrift in a mechanical paradise, hidden in the bowels of an Eden-esque earth. Blazing brightness impairs his vision. Bastions and hovels. Wicked arthritic claws of branches in the witchy wilderness. Dove-gray welkin. Defunct aviary is a domical, barred arena. In his fertile imagination the past is a tangible form of the present. In the varicolored garden a jay fells a gaudy bug with a blow of its beak. He hardens his heart. A flock of its similars accept flight. Cranes and herons, with prolix carroty legs, prance and preen in Indian file. Alembic apparatuses. Nature's aberrant automata. Unruly bunch of soused roustabouts don't notice him. Thankfully. He goes home. Gargantuan herdsmen wear roughened garments and wield knobby and knotty club weapons. Shrill cicadas. A standard stork, biped of nobiliary lineage, struts. Mostro, in rigid erectility like a stoic sentry, makes an indescribable gesture, his stitched sides palpitating, behavior enigmatic, the transference from them to the encompassing animalian and vegetable world, accentuating their agitation. His thoughts are far away and telescopic and close up and microscopic. Tenebrosity of twilight cajoles the immeasurable blue lid to turn into a supernal darkness. Turquoise Fairy, the sweet spirit, unexpectedly emerges and scolds him for his terrible behavior. He says, adamantly, his existence has heretofore been an injustice. Life hasn't granted him a fair trial with an impartial jury. She softly replies he's sentenced to be condemned for his countless unpardonable sins. His ligniform lineaments, in the vestiges of bronze beams made by the stumpy, soughing candles persisting in the caliginous, cavernous recesses of the residence, are directly affected by his seething emotions. He was an acorn. Now he is a tree. He's unaccustomed to her authoritative tones. With her, he has the sense he has arrived in the afterlife. He hugs her desperately. She disengages herself from the embrace. She is caressingly vocalic, admonishes him for his inarguably horrendous transgressions, anticipates his unquestioning docility. His language is disconnected. Hers is ominous. A draft has the sonance of a suppressed curse. Cogitations are coaxed from his brain as frogs from the bottom of a pond to the top by a floating petaloid blizzard. Her integument is so smooth and satiny. To her, their contact conveys the idea that it's a mistake. He is woozy like a semi-hibernating moth. His physique is beyond proportion in size. Saliva dribbles from his pendant, atrophied lips, and he accidentally slobbers on her bony shoulder, a glowworm there. And a centipede inches on his. He visualizes them strategically placing leaves on their privates not unlike Adam and Eve, pictures this vividly in his mind's eye. Their blinders chance to meet and he blushes with embarrassment. Emerald azure. Shy in this instance, she flushes. He's emotionally and physically weary. The expenditure of energy has taken its toll. Moody and drained, he could explode at any perceived provocation. She's cognizant of this possibility. Her remarks resonate as commands, castigations like orders. He grasps her chastisements. He has no remorse for the murderous violence he inflicted. He has no regrets for the vicious attacks on the rebels. They got what they deserved. The shell-like curves of her hips. He associates the seraph with devoutness. His advances are rebuffed. Intermission in his overtures. The fabric of her immaculate gown - a costly and rare material. His nasty fart sounds as a loud sneeze. Her hair is closely cropped. It used to be long, the braided pigtails like a pair of shiny and writhing snakes. Her skin is soft, sweat-slippery and silken. Disarming dimples are on her alabastrine cheeks. She cautiously struggles to register him as hurtless. His mop's a bird's nest of dark sticks woven with weeds. He, mucky like a duck in a bog, skulks as a Peeping Tom. Brick-red sky. He's besotted with her. Bats hang upside-down from the rafters like little furry stalactites in the murky grotto. He attempts to grope her. Offended, she calls him a "slimy scullion." In a rage, he overpowers her, propelling her onto the rotten pallet with its greasy, malodorous mattress. She's forever a fair young woman. She is paralyzed in a grave plenary dignity while he forcibly strips her, including her drawers, until her lissome, ivorine body is totally naked. His desire is unconquerable and unconventional. He sexually thrives, has his way with her, fondling her, experiencing absolute ecstasy. He molests and penetrates her, slides as a lizard upon her. On her, he's a brobdignagian gargoyle ornament imposed on an impeccable column by an avant-garde architect. Perfection of her bosom and buttocks. He has a poetic piety for her nude form. Sequence of her stalactiform teeth deliquescent and dripping saliva. Her ass solid like Achilles' shield. He has the might of a horse and the sturdiness (and stubbornness) of an ox. Her nates are livid mushrooms with venomous perspiration in the gloom. She is apple- ruddy with health. Her behind has a vegetal odor. Her feet are veinal leaves.

He insists he's a libertine gallant, an impure purist. He should subscribe to the dictates of sagacity, observe the rules of prudence, inculcated in him by Geppetto! Her disposition issues a calming component. He swoons. Ego, to her, is a useless encumbrance. He is not set on being an aristocrat, of whom comportment demands, avoids affectation, never destined to be a master of manners. She's redolent of lavender. Will she squirt as an eternal spring? Is she so overheated by arousal her blood will boil? Torridity and temps for the duration of the day are too much to bear. He cannot resist beating and raping her in the gloaming. Later, hysterical, Mostro summons Owl, a famous doctor, who checks her out. She has died. And Mostro suffocates, stuffs and mounts Owl on the mantelpiece. He cautiously puts Turquoise Fairy in his neatened bed and sobs. His conscience is a magnet drawing metal filings of guilt. She was an iron mount attracting the needle of his compass. Will his exile ever end? Mortuary white cloudlets. Steadfastness of opposites: sea, sky. Ground with the hue of tanned leather, tread upon by matching vagrant combatant atomies. There is an appalling mess following a bloodbath involving civilians. Sprinkles pitter- patter.

Mostro reflects, self-examines, that night, attired in bearskin longjohns and stocking nightcap, lying in the stuffy room with its fair share of purloined tapestries and gewgaws. Turquoise Fairy was a flower requiring a gardener to be preserved, the epitome of decency, pretty beyond belief and inspiring infatuation. Crotch enflamed, he worshipped this unapproachable goddess of grace. In her translucent gown she was a demure sun hiding behind a dissipating cloud. She was miraculous, living proof of a somatic sanctity. He shivers uncontrollably in frigid fire. Sickle-shaped moon. His breath has a corrosive potency. Beryl abysms of her blinkers, triumph of her tochus. He was shadow basking in her light. It was like she lay in wait, anticipating the opportunity to poetize her language. She sauntered saucily, smirking indiscreetly, and he tailed her as an inept spy. He was an animated pillar of salt in tatters. His experimental osculation and exploratory taction like they were the first and the last. He was a perverted pilgrim of her holy land. His psyche suffered a blow from her rejection. He kissed her mouth, the oral orifice as if it were a gangrenous wound receiving the correct medicinal influence for perfunctory disinfection, and touched her wrist like he was monitoring her pulse. She was sodden in a perspiry solution. Her cunny was a peony, which customarily closes at sunset and opens at sunrise. She was hot, and it was as though her bones had dried up. She was floppy. She was a corporeal ghost, a wonderful wraith with substance. Pursuing her, he was not unlike a splendrous spear, going in a straight line, and, without warning, deflected by the opposition of an opaque obstacle: her physical being, and her vocalized brushoff, indeed a cold shoulder - and deviating onto another track. Tiny particles of gnats as pieces of fresh plaster flitting. Oh, Geppetto ... Mostro had concocted a remedy for his nagging kidney stone: viper venom, toad, vitriol, liquid cow dung, and onion. Administering it forcefully, his deranged dad asserted he, his son, hadn't the requisite encephalon essential to education ... Without her torso he's a rider without a horse to mount. Dust in the dump like you'd come across in a mill. From her body that betrayed diminishment emanated the vague essence of musk. Smooching her it was as if by suction, like he was syphoning her spit. Her breath's aroma was reminiscent of jasmine mingled with mint, and elated his nostrils. His aphrodisia fermented as though a barrel of wine. His appetite for her would never be satisfied. His attraction was consuming. His brain was a prurient observatory where ideations were tested. He was an ardent wooer, a stream flowing back to its source. She reminded him he wasn't formerly invited, nor was he bidden to a rendezvous. He claimed he established her with celestial assistance. It was like there were rules of a match of flirtation regulated by him. Evidently, the (sinuous) path to her heart was a thorny one! The threads of the chance of them coupling knotted. On the threshold he delayed his departure, holding out hope the evening would be exceptional. Frescoed wainscot. Snowbanks of pillows and drifts of sheets on the cushiony settee. She suggested he get on the right track, gazed at him as if she were bearing witness to a sad spectacle. He didn't remain idle, was his reply, admitted his mistakes had significant dimensions. She coyly twirled an aqua lock and a cough escaped her. She had the wisdom of an ancient. He stood like a guard, at a respectful distance, assuming normal visitant functions. Was she (with her advice and proposed methods of living) the blind leading the blind? Feeling as though the condemned in the company of the executioner. She accused him of succumbing to his vices. He responded they were merely missteps. He committed no crimes, there were no cases against him that would disturb the judicial system. She acted like she had the power to pardon his transgressions (engendered by tedium). He could avoid the rigor of punishment through emancipation! Blots on his reputation. Would he receive vindication, be accorded unconditional freedom, for his malfeasances? Boredom was unbelievable. He carried her as a river's current the bed's soil. She shone in his wet-stony eyes and she forestalled, verbally, further overtures. He studied her like she was a problem and he was the solution. His hesitation in hugging her was solely for her benefit. He played the part of patient listener. He gained confidence, and submitted to the mellifluence of her modulation. He fixated on the ingenious modern instrumentation. His lamps were wide, ears pricked. Lunar eclipse of salacity in his coconut: the shadow of his earth fell on the face of her moon. He was afraid she'd disdain to engage him in a dialogue. They were not equals in schooling. He sought solace from her. She looked bilious. He was a devotee of his beloved. Innerly he implored the Virgin, invoked the Saints, thus abjuring his atheism. He had the urge to pour out his frustration. He avouched allusions, made pontifical pronouncements (such trite utterances), prolixity the opposite of his reputation for terseness, only it was in proportion to his determination to impress her. Should he have revised his approach? Alter his stratagem? His methods were, after all, malleable. He stank of bilge. Was it perceptible? Proof of her indifference was incontrovertible, clear as day. Their reciprocal (?) romance - he advanced and she retreated. Camomile clouds. Cranes vanished. Rain abated. Gluttonous metalline midges. She arranged his emotions as balls on the table in a game of trick-shot billiards. Her absolute disinterest retarded his progress. Hours were shredded into ribbons of minutes and torn into bits of successive seconds. Moments trickled through fissures of time. Tick-tock cadence of the old-fashioned grandfather clock. He endured a fainting spell, stumbled, like he was loaded and running on rolling logs; or climbing the rungs of a rickety ladder in haste. He was a freaky wool-gatherer. Excuses, flimsy, served as a pretext to hurry his departure. He was a heathen with a puritan. She offered appealing features beyond her beauty. His supposed confidence was abetted by her perceived coquettishness. She was energized, as if a participant in merry festivities, swayed like a reed in a zephyr. When it came to flirting he was lost at sea. He was as an astronomer who'd immersed himself in charts but never once actually navigated. He concluded there could be a congress of carnality. He never took a vow of chastity. Her laboratory was like an alchemist's lair. Fiery sun. Cerulean empyrean. Sepia water. Her derma was so anemic she could've served as a light source. She was like a docile indigene of some faery realm. His innards felt chomped on by a school of piranha. She stared at him as if he were a corrupt papist. He was fidgety, like he knew his persecutors were hot in his heels. He noticed her resistance unfolded at a steady pace. A narrow cubicle was separated by a partition. His mind floated as though it was a compass in whale-oil. He sailed with her companionship, taking the latest bearings, marking the positions of their postures, and presumed time, calculating with a modicum of assurance. She enthralled him. He would break the bread of her purity. He imagined the concavity of her pallid stomach dotted with freckles, nipples like pebbles oceanically polished, and drained the mug of flat ale. She lectured him maternally. He deemed it wise to steer the topic of conversation towards the concept of the two of them as a couple. It was a brave decision! She supplied substantial arguments against the idea. His cleric clothes were threadbare and dingy. His passage across the parlor, irregular in its plan, was noted, and he proceeded with insecure strides, telling her of the nightmare, where sewer rats gnawed on his extremities, these chubby cherubs dancing. Books lining aluminum shelves revealed a scholarly taste for erudite volumes. It was her personal museum of tomes. His axillae reeked of decomposing internal organs. Stagnant air. Salt- and-pepper beards of cirri. She completely overcame her revulsion. Implements of uncertain nature. His suspirations had the sonancy of water slapping against a hull. He was impressed by her (relative) cleanliness, the place stark of decorations save for scant photographic standards. Overall, it was a pleasant enough environment. She delighted him when she piped up with a flute, skilled in executing variations of a theme, in increasing complication, hazarding canorous complexities, notes ascending and descending in unpredictable patterns in unforeseen arrangements. From his vantage point the darkening distance created a deception of the oculi. Precip was a theater's running pearlescent curtain. Wooden structure of an organ, on its last legs, was surmounted by pipes, the bellows a bladder, on the mosaic flooring. He was trying to violate her ... in vain? His ink-drop eyes. She'd performed bodily functions in the lavatory, the door shut tight, and he imagined her shapely, milky haunches exposed while she evacuated. He surveyed the fossil collection exhibited on the shelving, glanced askance at the overflowing greenhouse. Hemorrhaging cumuli. Could he cling to her like a leech to a keel! Letters were piled willy-nilly on the mahogany desk. Was he able to bust open the breach of trust they had built? Would they create a rumpus? Would her spirit abandon her body as a sailor a sinking ship? Carpenters' tools. Could he have the run of her entirety? He was not well-versed in the seductive arts. Funereal firmament.

Laconic Mostro received significant confirmation from his companion, Turquoise Fairy, that she cared for him, expressed this with conviction. Mice, brazen, were big as babies. His operation of come-ons were set in motion, hardly a laborious undertaking. She accused him of living like a brute. Flustered, he felt attacked by a high fever. He swung at a hornet of great dimensions when its stinger jabbed his temple. Nigricant cirri. Claret welkin. Fugitives were segregated as plague victims of the horrendous phenomenon of a pestilence to avert contagion. Agents of infection? Independent thought and action. Her head was heavy, ears jangling, spectacles with smoked lenses. He was swamp-fetid. Cadaverous noisomeness. Soldiers swarmed akin to an invasion of locusts. She had powers of persuasion. Carousers in a drunken stupor around a campfire arrested his attention. They were on par with aberrant aborigines, ignorant idolators, grotesque cannibals from a heretical country indulging in a ghastly banquet. He was feeling not unlike a log hollowed out for a canoe by New World Indians. Her nether regions were worth seizing. A tank scudded over grass as a sled on snow. She showed signs of submission. Storm's portent was suggestive. He made a gesture of deference before visiting the commode. He could be peevish and vindictive. He gorged on her pears and tangerines. He was curious about the crates in the study and their contents. Ah, to broil a chicken and pop the cork of a bottle of champagne ... Profound promontoria. According to Genesis, The Almighty created heaven and earth. Geppetto made Mostro, his figure, properties and qualities, but not his tendencies. He lost track of time. Acid was a churning magma in her gut, phlegmy throat like a clogged pipe. He was larva-blind in devotion. His encephalon, dreaming of cherubim and seraphim coupling as seeds, twisted like roots, was a pond where circles of watery imaginings appear and disappear on account of dragonfly activity. Her mood was comparable to the alternating process of shine and shade. His middle was a keg of powder ignited. Concentrate of levin. Moon was a coal reddening. Luminaries of luminous excellences. Fetal night aborted by day. Quibbles tentatively detailed. He boasted of voyages on turbulent seas to Solomonic islands, lands of the Orient, a sincere Noah on the Beatrice with her Arkian amplitude, in Flood- like aqua, rain falling for forty days and forty nights, his fasting forced for a duration. Swells rose as milk heated in a pan. He sailed in that tub of a vessel along perilous routes in teeming aqua pura and their multitudes of mysteries. He'd absorbed at least a scintilla of nautical knowledge from Green Fisherman like a sponge. His celestial and infernal cerebrations. Terrain and the quick and the dead. Wind howled as wolves. Thunder roared like a lion. Lightning nictated. He used fishing rods and nets to secure plentiful sustenance. He confessed to her he was not excessively bothered by his isolation, the war zone was a staged (and bloody) story to stimulate spectators, confessed he was suspicious of all and sundry, save for her, his savior. Trust was won. Mangiafuoco, resembling a pig prepared for the oven, represented authority to which he, Mostro, submitted himself to. His power did not escape his notice. She briefly tutored him. She lavished praise on him - teacher encouraging the pupil. He described Terrible Dogfish, its tremendous corpse floating in the blue drink, skin the color of a woman's chops, fins as humongous hatchets, with rubefacient eyes, goaty muzzle, maculate belly, and tumescent mouth and teeth like nails, some sharp as blades. He auscultated the breathing of the behemoth of the deep. The sea shrugged and he periodically pitched. The craft didn't give the impression of stability. He glommed bananas, coconuts, crabs and oysters: genuine delicacies. Deck had golden glints. Surf sounded like tongues hitting against palates. Therapeutic qualities of the balmy oxygen and salty ocean. Nautics contributed to by a substantial certitude. Turquoise Fairy's collar was frilled as a cabbage. Flying foxes zipped in and out of the underbrush. Asparagus-green grass was fine like a lady's tress. He requested her (alleged) attachment to him be supported by further evidence, that even he, unapologetically aporetic, would surrender to the proof. Frequent downpours. His memories of Geppetto, old and infirm, traveled in an orbit of different breadth and progressive variation. She was punctilious to point out his egregious exaggerations. He resorted to the repertory of (flimsy, frankly) excuses to justify his anomalous antics. In example, he was invented by his pops to be inclined to error. He wiped his besnotted nose with a hankie. Her bashfulness induced him to resume contact with her, and he wanted to prove he was a loving, not harmful, entity. She was a vortice pulling the planet of him in her revolution. He wallowed in dejection, rejected, abandoned himself to the reality of failure. Perspiration pasted the frock to his torso. She was raised in a society where performing ablutions, or washing, was a necessity. She was as a cat conserving her fur's sheen. Her cleanliness consisted not only of bathing and brushing but fresh clothing as well. An oral blockade she erected between them. Sweat of his trunk like it was smeared with the dregs of a bucket. He appreciated her attractive powers. He responded to her mesmeric essence as the water to the moon's summons. He lent an ear to her songful sayings. His dome revolved not unlike a ball on a string and spun as a potter's wheel when she strumpet-sashayed. There was definite differentia 'tween 'em. She read into his apish conduct with a grain of salt. They had roast lark (her) and pheasant (him) and yams. He said Geppetto complained of thinning, graying mop, turkey wattling chin, blinding eyes, deafening ears, stiffening spine, shaking hands, and dimming mind. Moving, using the feather duster, she was like a bishop blessing the church with a censer. Igneous element of phosphorescence. She imparted a quicker pace to her progress. His uncoordinated mobility was on display. Everything about her positively exceeded his abilities of comprehension. Sea made peace with sky. Wondering on his form and function. Leafing through a brunet booklet of diagrams of cubes and pyramids, sloppy sketches of humanly and animalic figures, and notes written in arachnoid griffonage. His elocution was made of ellipses, stammers and sighs, his intensifying insecurities governing it. The sun was as a carbuncle. She would forever give meaning to his life, and still she rested in unreality, a non-being beyond capture. He slumbered and dreamt she was supine, he was prone, both supported by a hammock, and they dialogued on the mysteries of the universe. One encouraged the other's exuberance while they debated about the earth's rotations. She was like the virginal prey with a predacious seducer. Cadets were cogged together as parts of a crazed clock. To allay his anxieties, his emotional frenzies, he thought of an arboreal substance, mumbled as a machine to himself, his cogitations a lot like a litany. Mostro took refuge in the hazel-brown dusk, his preferred atrabiliar ambiance. He longed to consecrate his reconciliation with the semidarkness by beating off before her, spread as a shadow. Periwinkle-hued estuary. He was a knot in need of untangling. Winged embers of fireflies. Crickety cries. Turquoise Fairy was an enigma in search of an explanation. A bird bore a twig in its beak. She was hammered into his head like a nail. Her life was an epic poem. She, erotically fascinating and frustratingly difficult, concealed more than she revealed. He yearned to review a compendium of her clashing schizoid personalities. His musings of a hellish Paradise and celestial Hades, a set of overlapping kingdoms, and of this particular sea avian, an aquatic rara avis, its existence rife with recondite and revelatory meanings. She was a turtledove and he was the raptor upon her. Her fragrant benevolence, scented chastity. She was a deific message in its undecipherability. Moon had shone as silver, sun glowed like gold. With her he moved, and yet had the sensation he was still, as the earth in its vortex. He illustrated, to a tee, the water and illumination caressing him, cradled by whitecaps, floating there cruciform, and getting into a canine position, caught in a current, dogpaddling for the Beatrice, seeing the bosomy banks yonder. He placed his hopes in daydreaming. He swam like a frog, wouldn't defy the brine. His respiration was incorrect. Enfeebled Geppetto: because of him he had contact with creation ... Natation in an Anuran manner ... Distinguishing parrots and peaches among the olivaceous leafage ... Gauging phases of incandescence ... He was seized by carnal convulsions. Space and time confused him. He corrupted her purity. Extinction of cloud. A source of consolation? How so? In his solitariness there was a magnification of her absence. Skirmish of chiaroscuro. She was wind to his fire - fanning his feelings. He was jealous, insisting she be faithful, and his solitude stoked suspicion, the sureness that she was cheating. Chutzpah and razzmatazz were her stocks in trade. He was inhibited and impotent. Was she a bogus confidant? He feared he fell into disfavor with her, and he, vulturously poised over her, communicated to her that Mangiafuoco was constrained to authority, he was an insatiable beast to be catered to with slavish deference, his bravado galling, his strokes broad. He never showed his cards too soon to an adversary. Rarely could his diligent subterfuge be deemed pointless. Achievement offered a reward. Service was his sum. No task was too arduous. He was superb in simulating sincerity. His duplicity was undiscoverable. Sneakily smart, he taught himself to abide the dumb. The superior tolerated the inferior. He was not in the pay of employers. He choosily displayed his diabolical gifts, his talent for villainy. His grim ambition got him grudges from his peers. He successfully accomplished every unsavory assignment entrusted to him, could shift his moral course at will. His machinations weren't in moderation either. His inherent evil did not grant him respite. Nothing would afford him relief from awareness of his misdeeds. The thought of failure was a source of torment. He reveled twirling the threads of his manipulative skeins. He was legendary as the phoenix. He was a valorous fighter. His basilisk gaze with bile-black lamps ... War - the stimulus of oblivion. Turquoise Fairy's curvy hips and succulent thighs offered Mostro a dubious hold. He'd consummate his revenge on her for the repeated rebukes. He, unable to control the excess of his libido, penetrated to her place to make her the victim of ravishment. He was proud to be neither sober nor abstinent, coconut inclined, eyes impertinent. The imagistic impression of her insinuated through the meatus of his mind. Whitewashed overcast. He virulently prodded her bony ribs, poked her previously undefiled orifices. He scrutinized her private parts. She elicited his saturnalian proclivities. An exploit of this extreme magnitude, a taxing event, took him to the limits of stamina. He struck a colossus in some comedia, concedes he 'transferred' a neighbor's laundry from lines into his basket. He wove spidery strands of off-kilter themes into the narrative. Cowls of cirri. Chameleonic rainbow received every color. Glowflies created arabesques around a procession of tubulose and depilated friars discussing the mortifications of the flesh. Bevy of harpies with rouged rictuses, elven ears and bat-wings, tittered, swooped down and soared, flew in opposing directions. His brain was beclouded. With her he craved to be pleasant and reserved. An intestinal infection undermined his totality. He was a heliotrope turning in her direction. Their combatant natures were evident. Oxygen was comparable to mutton grease. He was the All Knowing's mistake. His mug was inundated by malevolence. His heated passion couldn't be concealed. It was a fire shown by smoke. The effective method of extinguishing the desire was with coital culmination. He contacted her as if to derive strength. She snapped that he was belated in motivation, quixotic in speech, swift in mercurialness, and was the Absolute Being's error. His senses strayed. He couldn't ward off her sexual influences. He was enchained by the enchantress, her angelic pulchritude imposing participation in bumbling banter. Acid reflux fermented within him and bubbled up. She was the sovereign and he was her slave. Aromatic artificial flowers in her charming chamber, a safe haven with velvet drapery and sable carpet. He couldn't endure further retention of semen and sought a remedy for the malady that dreary forenoon. He broke the bars of apprehension. She ensnared him, stole the air from his lungs. He rested as seldom as possible, didn't add up the total of his thrusting. His chest was an urn for his ashen heart. His arousal was translated into action. Would she concede a smooch to him, yield herself for an embrace? Would she teasingly present her lips only to torturously withdraw them? She looked at him as though she were Cleopatra and he was the asp. Were they two beings merging into a single person? Your narrator has numberal questions and no answers. Mostro reaped a harvest of killings sown with screams. The citadel was a massive monolith. There was an orgy of male and female mercenaries. Trusting his instincts that it was easier to hit a target going in a straight line, he zigzagged, not wishing to be picked off by a sniper. He was confronted with the dilemma of staying with Turquoise Fairy or leaving. Thumb at his belt, he sipped the julep. She had a sorbet. He was enclosed in the pantry. Confinement can weaken even the strongest of wills. She was steeped in rancor, made a gesticulation of pique, feminine hands, veinous like marble, intersecting as shooting stars, when he impulsively goosed her. He'd perish of mortification. Ferns, one imitating the other, fended off the gusts in the petrified wilderness. Deformed disembodied snout of melted candle. They composed and distributed their (improvised) satiric verses. He hovered not unlike giant hummingbird. She was beautiful above the rest, as the final work of an artistic virtuoso. He stated the obvious when he maintained the fact that Geppetto had the innate capacity for invention, like Nature itself. Spate was a coat of chain mail. She was stupendous in her comeliness, exhibited the loveliness with majesty. Vermiform wriggling of his viscera. Albinal phalli of incandescence. Cartilaginous, coralline cumuli in an amaranth azure. She was a heavenly body moving through a domestic firmament. Would she be his guide, coitally conducting him? In her masculine garb she was a supple androgyne with the movements of an oriental sensual dancer. She was an Eldorado treasure personified (fairified?). She made him feel alive. He ate apricots, carrots and figs en route to the insurrectionary blockhouse. He was bidden to bitterness. He was intent on situating himself in ambush to catch the malcontents unawares. He pined for freedom. The crepuscule brought counsel and convinced him to surprise attack. He sought out his common sense for advice. To ignore it ... he would surely be sentenced to a sterner punishment ... He pretended he was a beloved queen's renowned musketeer. Moon's viewable catacombs. It was a hive comprised of uncountable craters, to his eyes anyway. He fantasized of being a lunarian lummox living there. He thrived on thievery. He groused as a panhandler in a doorway. These bedraggled, poverty- stricken folks, with warts, pimples, impetigos and cankers, the maimed on crutches with one foot in the grave, was a wretched jumble of the dispossessed, were impecunious laureates in begging. Their animal maundering, the rank band's ranks fluctuating. Seething mass in the grove: horde of fiends, confraternity of hellions, teeming like flies over a carcass, this heinous army committing unspeakable atrocities by butchering noncombatants. Civilians were supposed to be off-limits. Permitting himself brief breaks. His nerves felt akin to dried sticks struck by a swarm of sparks. His pubic thatch chaperoned lice, and he served as the coachman. He couldn't even conceive of their insignificant, minuscular existence. Marine salinity. Solar tepidity. His guttural grunts. He was a disintegrating and evaporating planet. Would she ever consider his imperfections perfections? Effulgence was lavished on them. Cloud parted like a portiere. He remembered the marine monster - Terrible Dogfish's flaccid sleepy eye, dead and onyx, sinking out of sight, the Whale having swallowed Jonah, Geppetto, and he slumped on the sand. She was a masterpiece. Her derrière was dough he wanted to knead. Would his efforts award him the prize of her? She whetted his appetence. She made a meal of hare pie layered with egg, butter and molasses, and an attendant strata of ham, sugar and fruit, and strawberry and cheese pastry for dessert. Undulant cadence of the cirri. He went from the frying-pan into the fire, with the falsehoods ejected from his chapped choppers. He wished she'd sacrifice her purity to satisfy his needs. Her glabrous gluteus maximus was gorgeous. He would be a greedy bee in burrowing in her fanny's floweret. Frightful lab was as an apothecary's store. An abdominous eunuch, limbs short in proportion to his torso, was repugnant to the sight. She had the sensation of avoiding the noose when she eluded his hug. He was afflicted by the ailments of many mistakes. He loomed large, covered her with his enormity, providing her with her own obscurity. In the besottedness of reason he knew he had no real rationale, blackening those distracting objects from her view. Fucking her, he'd be cleansed and rejuvenated. She bid her organ close. Concert of carnality commenced. He blabbed like he was at a chantry's pulpit. Lake of molten lead. He wouldn't atone for his sins. He was an ill, she was the remedy. He was venom and she was the medicinal compound. Opaque glass. Combatants fought as atoms clashing to bear their composites. His prick was a lit wick. He reported he was Judas jailed in the Beatrice upon the open sea, and the inclement weather abetted the imprisonment. What was his betrayal? He was loyal to Geppetto! Waves lashed the boat. With her he was a dream within a dream, where neither began nor ended. He moved like he was a tortoise atop her. He accompanied her as a shadow. He quenched his thirst, drinking the cranberry juice not unlike a lamp consumes oil. Sucking an egg. Scant refulgence. He sniggered with horrid glee, had the chuckle of the damned. Lightning glitzed his vision. Spontaneous generation of cirri. Disruptions of thunder. The storm accumulated its impetus and raged. Ploppity-plop of viscid rain, an undeniable descendant of piss. Pelicans mewed. His tongue jousted with her clit. Her bum heaved with his shakers. Subterraneous stirring in his stomach. Harmonious geometry of the universe. His decadence, delirium. Cloudlets were heralds of the meteorological modus operandi whereby invisible water vapour in the air condenses into visible ice crystals. Tumefaction of

the tide. Bloat of billows. His rear released gaseous rot-
tenness. He had grazed on lentil soup, sausage and
turnip for breakfast, had dumplings with cloves and
grated bread for lunch, and lamprey with walnuts and
ricotta for supper. Faucet dripped as mucus from a nostril. Leaves, with their veiny ingots like they were made
by an expert goldsmith with adequate instrumentation,
gilded the boughs. Skeletal, German-helmeted armature. She was God's bounty, a dish for a lord. Industrious
insects in a mound of mulch. Vacuity of the vault. He
occupied a space in the nothingness of an abyssal realm,
was removed from all travail too. Was he harboring a
delusion? Was their love/lust a single line divided into
two equal parts? Was this an illusion of a play production, with him waiting in the wings? Surf swelled the
ranks and scudded onto the shore. His energy went out
as a candle that'd exhausted its substance. He thought
(couldn't do otherwise) of his remarkable birth in rela-
tion to his impending death. He was not immune to it!
He had his start and would have his finish. How much
time did he have left to live? Seconds? Minutes? Hours?
Days? Weeks? Months? Years? He lost (and was tenacious to regain) his sense of clarity, reality. He leaked
like a cask. His lineaments hung as a strap-loosened
mask. Roots complained. Skeeters multiplied. His chimerical cerebrations. Bugs went away like refuse drawn
by the currents. Armored vehicular derelicts. Florid vista
gave vigor to his volition. He discovered her characterful
cunt through his telescopic cock. Her abode's architecture and its ordered complexities, in determined
arrangements, with a special system of relational

material extensions. He ceased, could not maintain movement. Could he survive, as a pebble in The Flood? An anklet adorned her ankle, a bracelet beguiled her wrist. Din of his shpiting subsided. She, fragile as a tamarisk, lifted the shade, revived the lambency. Freaks and carnies, travestied zanies, amassed outside. So outrageous was the rigging, so outlandish were the attitudes, so inappropriate was the language. Inside. His lonesomeness ... there was no known antidote against this suffering. A few roaches scuttled, and Mostro was reminded of a worm, cut into several sections, the separate parts dispersed wildly, blindly. Turquoise Fairy enflamed and froze him simultaneously. She practically had a crane's neck it was so damn long. Reed-pipe, cylindrical stem, and narcissi were on a balsa-wood shelf. He was quite the Iago, acknowledging his bleakest offenses. Aqua pura was a liquescent lea. Branches waved like they were mimicking applause. A gibbose, pasty, feathery thing with hollow eyes was an amalgamation of fetus and raven, an abominable aberration offending the eye, the Holy Spirit's fabrication, its awkward gait underlining its deformity, stooped in a royal garden, where a fountain played, and keened horrifically, spoke in its native tongue. Mostro fathomed its homeliness. He sympathized. Reptiles had wings, avians had scales, insects had both. Puddles of wine. She dispensed sounds as silverware squeaking on a porcelain plate. He felt like solid stone, inanimate, transformed by Medusa, shamelessly exposing himself to her gaze. Chartreuse lagune was a single wrinkle in the brisk breezes. Pullulation of pools. He explained to her that to not be seen means you're intrinsically nonexistent. His respirations rustled as a vale's cane. She was rather prickly like a juniper. Line of drops on the stained, fissured window - string of pearls. A rainbow was, essentially, to him, an Asian tapestry. An emaciated kid was poppy-limp, with a drowsy head. Turquoise Fairy's dewy suspirations. Cumuli quietly commented on the cobalt heavens. A cute cupid with a roseate complexion held an umbrella while tears distilled from its crustal peepers, flittered, emitted liquefied soughs, and ejaculated a urinose rill from its itsy-bitsy member. A crested peacock's tail transmogrified into a candelabrum. A gryphon frolicked with fauns and disgorged cornucopias. He was feeling as magmized rocks, melted and fused together, and endured the calefaction. Cirri and their differentiation of motion distinguished themselves, with perceptions of themselves in the starry horizon, the passage like the occurrence of going from sleep to wake. There were his thrusts, only no counterthrusts from her. They weren't companionable compasses. Relationship in volatility. Eagerly at her bottom, he was assiduously demolishing a dome. She was a buttress collapsing. She had a bowel movement, wiped lachryma as an optician polishes a pricey lens, drowning, like by cursed Neptune himself. Pudgy, rubicund pontiff promenaded in a pall of smoke. Cutthroats scarfed victuals on a sloop. Birds swam, fish flew. She weighed pros and cons, causes and effects, sitting on the toilet, staying put. He insisted he was her and she was him, coalesced in their own macrocosm, conjoined in coition. Her vital portions stung, ass ached, splayed on the horseshoe-shaped seat. She had no notion of who she was. Moisture was pestilential secretions. She'd deprived herself of a means of escape by leaving the john's door ajar. She groaned as timber moved by a gale's impulse. Prescribed limitations of the sky expanded when clouds dissipated. Battle of the elements. Pellets of hail peppered the incompetently shingled roof. The cupola of her keister smarted. He denied mercy to it. His actions didn't provoke counteractions. He seemed to drag his shadow like it was a cloak. Forestial masts. River was becalmed as water in a basin. Obelisks proved to be scarps in the fanning haze. Tillage had the aspect of a graveyard. Anatomy exhibit of soldierly skeletons. He observed the (in)correct rite of rape. He paid (im)proper homage to his seraphic idol. He was posed as an executioner anticipating the entrance of the condemned. She resolved to render herself in an upheaval of sobs. His terrestrial traces were diminishing. A plane's plume was a scalpel clumsily incising integument. Stale air. Intestine-saffron luminosity. His hand dangled not unlike a glove. Conflation of his dick he sanctioned. There was lust in his stare, free of all love. She remarked his willy was a peg. Wan fireflies as infinitesimal waxen tapers in automatous flight. Absent moon. He went lax like an overworn cape. Upper atmosphere's clearness would never be total. She was too weak to handle the impact of any punch. Amethyst briny abundance enacted its fury, whereupon it restored itself to repose. He confused fact with fiction, acted like he was tormented by a typhoon. Cleaving to her as a tongue to the palate. Unity of celestial sphere and bounding main. Her abbreviated sibilations. His toenails were like a raptor's claws. He was the object of repulsion, not adoration. His strabismic pies, narrowed even more by discomfort, were eclipses. Her furrowed face. The cracked corners of her mouth were reminiscent of swallow prints in sand. In her decline she was still desirable. He pounded her as rollers the beach. She strived to find an egress. He informed her that Green Fisherman was really Captain William Bligh and he was the mutineer, Fletcher Christian, disanchoring the ship and ... Well, you know ... Intent on drowning his sorrows in booze, Mostro, in Turquoise Fairy's stagecoach, and with her prized Poodle at the reins, visits a tavern and is denied alcohol by the bartender, a Mastiff with matted fur. An elephantine ecclesiastic expectorates quotes from the Bible. Cat and Fox, unkempt, anthropomorphized waiters, tease him. Angry, he leaves. His sorrowful existence is a diurnal and nocturnal one. Then, two quite attractive, animated marionettes, prostitutes Harlequin and Punch, playing like the tides, pick him up on the street and bring him back to their pigpen of a place. The whores are cedarwood-scented. The humble room has scarce furnishings. Rats scurry in opposite directions. Chalice of astounding antiquity was doubtlessly pinched. He re-establishes a connection with the puppet community, celebrates a return, captivated by this marionette mysterium. The harlots are unsurpassable models. Punch produces a match from her brassiere, under her purple dress, strikes it on her knee, and proceeds to light the oil lamp squatting in an alcove in the wall, next to an artistically abstract statuette of a lion with a snake wrapped around it, probably the product of some nebulous memorial. She acts as an uncommitted companion, a precious contrivance. She hurries in the hollow gloom, hastening to cover the greasy bed with blankets, cleaning the mess, these quarters, dimly illumined, the be-all and end-all of everything to them. They are sisters-in-arms for a carnal cause. Aroused, he feels woefully inanimate, lost in Limbo, his stimulation rendered noticeable by his pitifully sad, deep-set eyes. Their movements are deliberately monumental. Harlequin, gladdened, sensuous, offers fizzy soda, moldy bread and bruised apples. He hesitates to accept, and declines respectfully. Are they, collectively, a mirage? An illusion? He issues a series of frazzled whines and abruptly leaps to his feet. He's a multiple entity, a composite creation. The apartment is a disaster area. He thinks of famines and plagues, births and deaths. Candle's fiery tongue licks the squalid joint. There is the fragrance of incense wafting in the dump, the redolence tedious and tantalizing. Harlequin, hoping to have intercourse with one of her kind, seduces him, while Punch, donning and doffing lingerie, and irritable, gets bombed on beer and masturbates. It tickles his fancy to fantasize of a threesome. Harlequin convinces him that his semen seed will produce a golden baby which will grow in her belly and make them rich when it's born. Mostro reluctantly has sex with her. The inhuman slut's mouth smacks of honey. Erratic spurts of spluttering luminescence. He is engaged in the process of devouring her, testing the limits of his libido's endurance. Whisperous wind veers. The couple rise and fall, toss and turn. He confides in her, tells her that

Mangiafuoco commanded him like a provident of Divinity, ordering him in accord with his undeniable authority, and he instructed him on the fundamental principles of the bellicose arts. He wasn't an obedient student. He wanted to postpone those lessons. He had an aptitude for pugnacity he was told matter-of-factly. Circularly speaking, his encephalon feels as a donkey turning a mill-wheel. He dedicated himself to murder, devoted to killing, to achieve the completion of a commitment. The act produced a thorough vitality of the grey matter, bestializing his spirit, but endangering the wellbeing of his soul. He didn't do it for the greater glory of God! Sleet's drops on the mucky panes are like studs of silver. He blurts out his testicles are philosopher's stones and she guffaws. She fellates and jerks him off. She is spurred on. It's as servile labor to her. She multiplies her efforts. Minutes are not unlike years. Compact strips of chiaroscuro. They redouble their osculations and tactions reciprocally. She teases, then crops up from his erectile phallus as Minerva from Jove's head. Her resistance foments his appetition. If she left would she be like a sparrow and faithfully return to her nest? If copulation is a door to be opened he prays he can push it, step inside, and slam it behind him. She's the type who says a spade is a spade. Her claws don't scratch, her teeth don't bite. He frees her from skimpy underpants she suddenly put on and picks her up, holding her aloft, like he is unloading a package from a truck, blustering on his astronomical apparatus of an appendage, rants and raves about the ferocious fish of man- eating species, the cannibalistic Terrible Dogfish.

Black and white cloudlets are ethereal, puffy nuns on the run. Spume smacks rock formations. Exactly how much time has elapsed? Unbridgeable space. He, sloshed, tries to orient himself. His appetence could move mountains. He knows he has merits and defects. The alcohol tastes of turpentine. Sky's a sieve of pores. Pulse-beats go by. Directionless gleam of glimmer. His physical strength led astray by his psychological weakness. He, a melancholic generating his own foul mood, sweats as a sponge. His misadventured mind's out of whack. His mental jibber-jabber ultimately has her cerebrally unraveling. Her pecker kissing just isn't credible. His brain is unequal to his brawn. Squishing her boobs like lemons. During the night, in a drunken stupor, Punch, active as a mechanized dummy, with the measured steps of a noctambulant automaton, and breathing like a tumid tributary, infuriated that Mostro chose Harlequin over her, taunts him. He chops both of them up with an ax and ignites a fire on the hearth, shoving aside the bulky iron cauldron, using their wooden parts as kindling. He squeezes his scrotum, genuine and fabricated, like an enemy's skull, embroils himself in will-o'-the-wisp wool gatherings. Seeking distraction, he drags furniture and fiddles with himself. Stars are as sparks from a flint. Mostro eventually passes out, nightmares, and comes to, his lower legs flaming. He crawls like a scorpion into the thicket and encounters Mangiafuoco and some soldiers, drinking, eating and cleaning their weapons. Would he die by the axe or the rope? Would they relieve him of his head and put it on a pike? He pleads for help and they laugh, raising their daggers as if to dispatch him, only they choose to cut his arms and legs off with hunting knives to better employ them as blazing torches to light the darkness. He distributes desperate, high-pitched, puzzled protests. He is in a state of shock at his idiocy, beside himself, in a blind furor, bowled over by the backwash of devastating humiliation, and bellows as though he's a stuck bull, the racket resounding like it's created in the bowels of the earth. The dismemberment is an alarming and anguishing sequence, an agonizing happening created so naturally by the perpetrators it pushes hard against the barriers of the unnatural, and the abnormal possesses the magnetic power to draw the normal towards it. His wrath will never be sated. He is doomed. He's informed of his fate and's the recipient of insults. His fears are confirmed. He is a loathsome sight, blubbering infantinely, the suffering reducing him to this state of hapless creature, at the nadir of misfortune, and complaining of nausea, on occasion. Whey- colored twilight. "Hang in there, it's not as bad as you think," are Mangiafuoco's words of nonchalant, faux-reassurance. Mostro wails, whimpers, in excruciating pain. The invader's immobility is mocked by the fighters. Burnt sienna skyline. His heart is an insect pierced by a pin on the board of his chest's wall. With Mangiafuoco (not shirking the fact that the errand would be a chancy undertaking, he'd risk life and limb, and only with a smidgen of skill and luck could he come back safe and sound), it was a transaction which saved him from certain starvation. There could be peril and glory. It was an honest exchange. A fair bargain stirs inclinations.

Thoughts increase in his noggin like splashes in water from a school of fish swimming upriver. His identity regresses into its original (fabricated) elements. Mangiafuoco yells at him as a master calling in a stentorian tone for his servant's presence. Toxical nursery rhymes are regurgitated. The azure changes, like in some organic metastasis. Pungent smoke. He thinks of tall, brusque Harlequin and small, sassy Punch. He verbalizes to the warriors that he had an insane infatuation with them, an avid curiosity for the manikin streetwalkers. He pictures Turquoise Fairy's violaceous vagina. Rebirth of an icecold rainfall. His vocalic reverberations. The men will surmount any obstacle to best torture him. Mangiafuoco's orations are as those from an oracle. Tents are stretched sails. Elms are phlegmatic custodians. Gorilline guards are stationed on the camp's perimeter. Coal-black horses munch on the frosty grass. Pack of docious stray dogs intermittently lap themselves and yawn. A bonfire blazes. A trio of cyclopes disregard Mostro. Mangiafuoco considers him sufficiently disabled. Words are not exchanged. Crow, the revolutionist, shits and perches on an incapacitated Mostro, who's muttering like he's in the throes of suffering a stroke. He is an irreparable imperfection, stone-insensible, and vermicularly creeping. Batsqueaks of boughs. His alchemical life force is neither sacred nor profane. He calculates time's course, of yesterday, today and tomorrow, and accepts destiny's invite, has no fighting spirit left. Fuck fate. Snorting, he swears an oath to his Maker never to take up arms again. He strains to delay the moment of his destruction, wants to recover, Jesus

Christ willing. Salubrious climate and luxuriant verdure. He isn't concerned with botanical matters. He feels as a turtle turned on its back, only on his front. Replenishing his weakened strength with repose. Four deceased and au naturel troopers nearby ... and Mostro is reminded of the four satellites, or moons, of Jupiter, in looking at their rumps, in occultations of illumination. His habits won't change. An octogenarian forester, in a stooping posture, near a dignified redwood, assesses him, a notorious puppet personage in these parts, has a private word with himself, and mentions beholding, firsthand, the unsettling shifting of social sands, and is buoyant like a ghost in Hades. Chestnuts and acorns are innumerable disembodied nipples. World of beasts and birds. He is pestered by the iniquities of karma. Gunshots and human shrieks echo in the just-discernible distance. His mien's a mask displaying, not hiding. He would vie to survive, having the inestimable advantage of his inhumanity. His suffering will last a millennia. He glares at his tormentors. Dizziness overwhelms him, his encephalon a roulette wheel in his cranium, and he calls himself an imbecile. Disemboweled bell's in the wreckage of collapsed chapel. The sky is in its slight motion. Civilian casualty is reduced to a skeleton, close to a stately evergreen. Monstro's not in proper working order, sedulously abused by the militant lunatics, and is prepared to pass in the clement weather, meteorologically appropriate. Throwing in the towel to despair, victimized by belief. Empyrean takes on this titian color. He is beside himself, crippled in an unidentifiable pastoral place. Jaundiced welkin. The spinney sways like seaweed on

the ocean. He's afraid he'll remain companionless, wayward in reclusion, forever. He strains again, attempts to
hoist himself up, with more failures and accompanying
curses, in a disappointing exercise. Malodorous fuel
fumes. His struggles diminish. Colder conditions jeop-
ardize his chances of success. Would he become the
figure of Christ, risen from the dead? Stumps of his
lower extremities are bent as the towers of Bolonia, and
part like the arms of a clock. He feels as an abandoned
child in the woods. His energy's not his volition's equal.
Discouraged, he tries and tries again to get upright,
regain his balance. The end of ends. Spheric moon.
Enough written. Mostro, formerly known as Pinocchio,
sticks his snoot (like a narwhal's horn) as Galilei did his
nose into metaphysics, where he pleases, in life and
death. And so on ad infinitum. Finished ... if the reader
will allow this chronicler.

Deep Cuts

The discarded lubricated prophylactic in the cobblestone driveway looks like an embryoid sea creature stranded on the shore. Burnt- eyed sun. Workers are as resurrections of Walker Evans subjects, forms that are remnants, in recognizable patterns, of a dream, in the middle of a cottonfield. Rocking chair on the unstable porch's like a stageprop. Over that slope yonder the royal palace proves to be a mere mansion, Bruce Wayne-styled, currently in a state of disrepair, a sort of happenstantial structure, one which was maybe lifted and dumped courtesy of a serious storm. Successful plastic surgeon Kilcrease Flott, suave and smooth, conducts illegal, innovative experiments on his secluded estate, assisted by his androgynous teenage son, Crum, with ruby-red lips and plump rump, who has no memories; a blank canvas on which Kilcrease does all the painting, a beautiful bird kept in a gilded cage. Widemouth of wasteland lies as a maledictory redundancy, comes away muddy after the deluge. Like a bulldozer cutting into a riverbank, the doctor slices into the meaty, bloody and ugly face of a septuagenarian patient with a scalpel. He decides he will get drunk later on with something sickly sweet. He squints, seized with exhaustion, respirations sounding as rustling cornhusks, and mops his brow, brittle not unlike parchment, with the tail of his scrubshirt. Barbaric, cold implements on the Formica countertop are as a medieval torturer's tools. Her physique's comparable to that of a shriveled tangerine. Roadmap of varicose veins. Millipedes of stitches. Curling photograph of landscape in its vastity. Ossiferous clouds in the crypt of cerulean sky. Turbulent waters. Furrowed earth. Night reeks of black. He buckles under the heft of weariness. Reading the wrinkles age wrote on her gross visage. She could conceivably pass for a surreal sculpture made out of wax. She rouses unexpectedly, ascertains who authored this operation, and slips into unconsciousness once again. His stoic calm during this long procedure. Empyrean is blued and furred by cirri. Her caved forehead, sunken cheekbones. She has a withered arm, bony fingers like hideous talons, claws of a bird of prey. He is constipated, as if he's got concrete in his guts. He uses the crippled appendage like he's performing a magic trick he's been training diligently to pull off, inserting the digits deep into his anus, whereupon he beats off. Metalline flickers of leven. Trayed surgical instruments, weird and modern and archaic, are as though they're a necromancer's demented divinations. The beefy, ensanguined frontage is a pane cracked in many fissures and mended with duct tape, it appears to him. He notices her pocketbook bulging like it is holding a powerful internal force of some kind. A car door slams. A whippoorwill calls in the dusk. Steely rime of dew. Bronte Chesser, Kilcrease's blond bombshell party girl rock star ex-wife, who has lived in Japan since the divorce, arrives unannounced, beset by clots of skeeters, the joint, in the fog, architecturally suggests a monolithic barge that slipped its moorings, the garage like a casion, to her, and is amazed at how much Crum has changed. She attributes her off-kilter perception to her altered states from the prescription pills and recreational drugs. She's petite and eccentric. She backpedals in the radical raviary as a nightmarish vision. She is also struck by the kitschy decor and pop props in the place. She wears a ruined denim jacket, tight concert tee, dingy dungarees, and flip-flops. Sable smear of firmament. Vintage camo Jeep eases up an enbrowned hill. Vaguely cobalt vapor. Homemade houses apparently built of various odds and ends. She cradles the cased Les Paul classic like she's drawing confidence from it. She feels uncomfortable when separated from the instrument, an artifact out of her youth. A family feuds. She fends through the peculiar furnishings to hug her boy proper, carries a loaf of bread and paperback book. Shale bluffs. Her charmingly cheap purse is swollen as if she's carrying the whole world in it. She promptly snorts a line of cocaine, using a dollar bill, right off the expensive and quaint coffee table and quietly confesses she feels as though life is passing her by, leaving her behind, high and dry, going its own way without her. Stabs of light. Cumuli array themselves in chaotic coalescence. Row of five-and-dime stores like neon-lit, defunct freight trains. She complains her cabdriver was hungover, was quite erratic at the wheel. A horn honks. She fixes Kilcrease a glare of mock anger in the narrow kitchen. Grove of cypresses. Because of the cosmetics, she is reminiscent of a garish ghost, rather comical, taken out of a grand-mother's spooky story. She splurges on speech. He's stingy with words. Fluorescent flashes of town. Zephyrous whispering as if issuing passwords. She is on Crum like a duck on a bug, her embrace fecund, stacks kisses on him as a mason lays brick to construct a wall. His countenance holds a determinedly bland, albeit pimply, prettiness. His ginger locks are unruly. She flus-ters about the food on the counter: fried ham, baked yams and buttered biscuits. Basketed apples. Her inflec-tion sounds corroded, a rusty croak. She accepts the sensation the joint is trying to tell her a tale, but contin-ues to tangle the narrative threads into knots. Her thoughts are pieces of a jigsaw puzzle arranged incor-rectly. Foliage fulgurantly faulted. Cogitations in her brain - veins on a leaf. Mien a gross mockery. She hon-estly feels for her sanity, insanity predaciously stalking her. Vertebral ridges wickered In branches emphasized by the emanation goldgreen. Stream snakes through the thicket. Her bracelets on the varnished desk are sun-dered manacles. She is crazier than a poorhouse rat, a feral critter he attempted to domesticate, to no avail. She extends the beat-up six- string toward her former hubby, only does not relinquish ownership of it. The two gesture as though they are mad mimes. Advertisings on the television are not unlike mysterious miracles for the viewer. Stiff breezes agitate the bushes. Day dissolves as something put in acid. Humidity has this strange viscosity. Purple evening envelopes the environment. An antique mirror throws Crum's gangly reflection back at him. Refrigerator's adorned with numerous cartoony magnets. She plunks herself in a ladderback chair, her singular- cornered smile absurd. There's something irreparably wrong with her. She led him into the misstep of marriage. Moon pulses like a pale heartbeat. He's got a grudge. She is his cross to bear. Wishing to inflict significant pain on her. Christ. He could cap her as a bird in a shooting gallery. His main goal is to kill her, swears he will do it at some point when the opportunity presents itself. She's an obstacle put in his path. He constructs a joint, strikes a match, and lights it. Lordy, he wants to box her and ship her sorry ass to Asia. His angular shadow's like a sinister second self. Telluric tenebrosity. Sand as brown sugar. Vines not unlike woven vertical bobwire on the chimney. Acacias running rampant. Boulders smothered in virid moss. Rainwet undergrowth intermittently shown in flashes of levin. Semibuckled shed, profoundly defunct, strangled by riotous creepers. Inkincision of skyline. Timbered forest with rumors of trails. Daylong downpour. Lambency swings slant. Spectral silhouettes. Void of the welkin. Sweep of mimosas. Crum, watching the tv, is hit hard by a story of a kid about his age, Sangster Lingold, who has been missing in London for five years. Confused, he cries. Thunder rumbles hollowly and ominously over the goddamned countryside. Images of an uncanny, unknown, almost indescribable adolescent chap are seemingly imprinted behind his lids. Beaded, pearlescent drencher rolls slowly on the opaque windowglass. Clouds are colorful islands afloat in the glaucescent sea of sky. He meticulously builds a cigarette, spilling bits of tobacco on the vinyl sofa, recalling a truckseat. Soaker sounds as frozen peas hitting a tin bucket. Photoelectric phosphorescence. Shack, a large relic from an older time, in shambles, square like a packing crate. Cavernous, cool and clammy room is swallowed in silence. His encephalon grinds to a halt, the universe winds down. Sinuous slate brook. He manages to sift the blow into a baggie. Luminosity achieves a measure of the Persian ruglet. He feeds logs into the maw of the fireplace, crouches on the humble hearth, hears his dad snore, his mom masturbate, the bed- springs creaking madly, upstairs. The gusts compensate to match the rain's severity, in terms of pace. Lawn goes to a lake. He steps hesitantly on the wonky stairs, long, ladylike hands clasped to his chest as if he's laid to rest in his coffin. His gait is as though he's been hooked by a tackle and is being reeled in. Wind roars in an animalic rage. Vault, blurred by cirri, methodically metamorphoses into a measureless wraith. His folks' match was squally. Slashes of precip. Oaks and hickories penitential. Territory rears out of the volatile mist. Sun's at its zenith over the riverbottom undergrowth. Squirrels forage for acorns like they're on an Easter egg hunt. Cumuli tending away. Glycerinic puddles. Spectra of cloudlets as ink in water. Bronte manifests, discalced and dressed in kinky lingerie, and he has an attitude of auscultation, dealing with her amorphous and incomprehensible monologue. Inebriated, she cradles his coconut like it's an abandoned infant. Uncovered torsos smacking sound as screen doors slapping. Slateyed, his cock throbbing like a flame, he senses he's a hop, skip and jump from defiling himself. Cicadas assail the luminescent air, music mythladen. More intoxicated, she is loud and demonstrative as a carnival barker, with melodramatic gesticulative flourishes. Fowls fluttering disconsolate in the sheets, like they can't decide where to roost. She's sozzled on popskull rotgut homebrew chartered in her asinine handbag. She tilts the flask and takes a knock of it, Adam's apple pumping as a piston. Crum's neck is like a turkey gobbler's. His halfgrown penis, expression as one you'd usually see in a mental ward. Her armpits have a feedstore smell. Her exquisite bottom's crack one of a place he would want to get to. She has dealt herself a card so high it's too wild to cope with it. Aluminum span of heaven. Lush, orangebrown foliage. Pineneedles coppery have taken a segment of terrain. He's apparently strained, like he's oaring a canoe in muck. On multiple meds and mushrooms, she has, to him, hallucinating, a shoat's paws and hooves. His desire's so acute it's agony. The two fuck, together as the essential constituents of degeneracy. He listens to her vocalized autobiography, an expert on her favorite subject: herself. Her back looks like it was scraped by a rake. His longneck bottle of a neck. She does a sitcom doubletake of astonished recognition at his genitals. Her interminable philosophical bullshit on honkytonks, blackjack and bloodhounds, sawedoffs, buckshots and beerjoints. Rotting vermiculate condom on the hardwood floor. He fills his lungs with her horrendous genitalial stink. She is damagedgoods, foulmouthed and sharptongued. And a sexy babe. Gimplegged galoot limps as a wounded monkey, makes a mandolin sing for money, harassed by virulentlooking juniors in baseball caps. Gawd Amighty. Nighflorescent fuchsia of horizon. Scorched trees from an earlier wildfire are blackish not unlike a raven's wings. His eyes are prepared to see what she shows him. At the doorsill he is perhaps waiting for specific instructions you'd probably reckon, lineaments intimating uncertainty, potential implications of standing pat sinking in, he halfturned. Suppurant gloom. Beams of brilliancy latticed. He confesses, matter-of-factly, that when he becomes an adult he wants to be a handyman or cabdriver, not a doctor, and admits his deranged dream was indeed tactile, fractured, risky and seagreen. Her tight, tensed bum is wrinkled as an octogenarian's craggy physiognomy. Cumuli smoke in the azure. Revenantial doves, collected out of the crepuscule, crisscross fulltilt in the sapphire celestial sphere. Harsh rasp of his respiring. His lust dims down as late light. Her chunks of vomit are like spatters of soup on the hardwood floor. Oxygen as a winey aroma. Her sagging stomachic crepe. She spins, lazily, as a dust devilish human being. Her integument soft as chamois. Their misbegotten amorous alliance in dimensional displacement. Raincrow glides in the castiron bluelid. He adjusts his overlaundered sweatpants with the drawstring. The door's frame bisects her buttocks at the cleft, the butt-cheeks dimpled, dented from the nervous clenching, reminding one of acidic filigrees on aluminum. Configurations of ferry lights in the marina restructure themselves in the eddying drizzle. Clouds crumble like cornbread. Adrenaline crazed, he mounts her from behind, fastens the ridiculous strapon dildo. Her chin's resting on the crook of his elbow. Her crustal, scanty pantries are rough as livestocksack fabric, soles of her feet sandpapery. He ascends and descends her spinal cord with his derrière like a ladder. She bucks as a car with the clutch popped. He has the uncomfortable feeling that hunks of his ringlets are being plucked out of his scalp like flowers from a bed. The situation is a wedge between the real and unreal. She is an afflicted omnipotent. Her absolutely vilelooking puke. Penetrating her - punching his ticket to purgatory. He keeps a smartass expression. Satin expanse of her rear end. For her, it is as if the world tilts on its axis and leans on her (somewhat) stocky shoulders. With Bronte before him, it's as though Crum's a pertinent participant in nature's arcane ceremony. Texture of her tootsies' heels like they were fired in a kiln. Cirri conform their shapes to coordinate to the contours of the azure. She is a raucous, happy-go-lucky alcoholic. Her tummy and bosom soft as speaker cloth. She fusses with herself like she found something and is figuring out how exactly to use it. The vibes have changed, as if a magnetic field's shift. Reaming her fanny before her vagina is an option he's seriously considering. Her facial dimples are like commas. Shadows are black as jet. She consistently looks for a fun time and knows where it's hidden. She scoots a smidge on the baroque balcony, rambles on the fragile dominion of his psyche, her youth sanded by age, and deepsouth taprooms. In the distinctly Caravaggio chiaroscuro she is a negative image version of herself. He has the nagging feeling of having vanished, as though a picture from a familial photo album. Separate beings, they transmogrify into a singular entity. His ears jangle like a jukebox. She stokes his fire. Jesus. She searches for his unit as if she lost it. Bodies hesitantly dovetail. Scalyskinned upperatmosphere. Cellulite on her thighs is like circular marks made by a saw on millplanks. He is indecisive and obsequious, seismic tremors running through his nervous system, skinny arms outflung to cruciform. His grey matter whirls as though it's a ceiling fan's rotating blades. He mentions to her how he addressed Kilcrease (phiz harrowed and haunted as one living under the edict of death) like he was the Reaper. She blurts something as bunkum and peremptory at his knee unbeknownst while she does it. She slugs her bourbon and rakes at her psychedelic blouse's buttons like a waitress tipchange off the counter and they go cartwheeling. Making out, it strikes you as rehearsed, choreographed. Celluloid scintillation's a casualty of the shade. Disinterested eye of the sun. He treats her with the deference you'd accord the regal. She acts, with him, like an apprentice learning the ropes of being a juvenile. It's as if she's offering herself up as a sacrificial lamb in an atypical rite. She stands reluctantly as though for a firing squad. She is accomplished when it comes to pushing nonsense beyond their limits. He has idiosyncrasies queer to him, is subject to misbehavior, and is ingrained with the impatience reserved for the young. Innumerable conjectural blackbirds congregating on a rufescent knoll. Sepia sage. He will never be the protagonist in her story. She comes clean, thumb embedded in her rectum, insists she returned to make peace with her family, however dysfunctional, acknowledges she's a part of the problem. She has an astringent tang. She is a lemon he rolls until she is full of juice. Then he squeezes her and she squirts. In one belt she empties the tumbler of rum. He caresses her scapula like to absorb her essentia by osmosis. She takes a birdlike sip of brandy from the crystalline goblet. He inhales her cuntal odor as a connoisseur sampling a fine vintage and exhales. They're down the line. Her axillae mephitis could strip paint. He is ensconced in a lawn chair. For her, behaving is beneath her. Breathily she exhorts him to drill her harder, faster. He finds her wacky past any reasonable expectation of her. She's a complex narrative unfolding itself. His thrusts are practically violent. Sections of her personal history ... alltold. Her top's tag scissored out. She is both his bane and his salvation. She spits she accused Kilcrease of being a patron of hookers, to which he vehemently denied. The inscrutability of her features point to enigmas he must solve. For him, there's a quirky connection with her that's difficult to define. Having sexual relations with her ... he can dip into the reservoir of excuses and come up with one or more to justify it. It's like gathering bones from a hundred skeletons to create a brandnew one. She's fast to get fomented and slow to get over it. He is proud as a deacon with the devout. Soapy fragrance of his pale flesh drives her wild.

His tension like he's a violin string cranked and close to breaking. Despite being comforted by Southern Comfort, he is intimidated by her. Tilting into one another they're as felled trees keeping each other upright. Her snatch is reddish like a wound. The twat's exposed and handy, as a Western gunslinger's pistol in its holster. She's still, like she's forever frozen, thanks to a photographer's camera. He is silent, bound under her spell. Climaxing, she screeches as a passenger train with countless boxcars, chugging on a lonesome track and screaming while it climbs an icy alp, the earth elevating into mountains. She claims the muggy climate suits her nakedness. She is so tiny you could tote her off in a shoe box should you fancy to. Storefront DayGlo strewn on the wet asphalt not unlike spilled baubles. Her beautiful belly is pale and flat as a granitoid headstone. His brain's revolutions like a renegade carousel. Her body odor as chopped plants. Crawly and abysmal vespers. Flimsy fencerow encompasses an English garden. She's white and weightless like dust. Her hands, mangled from incorrect playing, have crosshatched cracks you'd commonly find in baked clay, defects of lines due to blistering coruscation. Her coaxes sound as threats, or promises. She follows her self-indulgent, destructive bents. Their forbidden passion of an unreckonable magnitude happening. Blood fomenting akin to cherry wine. There is a timeless, unique quality to their mating, like they started years ago and only now he's beginning to experience a cleaving of the pin. His shrieks cut as shards of a broken bottle. She's on her hands and knees like a cute and harmless watchdog. His umbrageous emissary sends itself ahead. Thrill runs through him as heat lightning. Lodging a clump of chew 'tween cheek and gum. She turns like a paper cup in the breezes. Gleam glitters as quicksilver. She's vibrant enough that she is like the emblem of being alive. He is in slackjawed disbelief at her glorious nudity, noggin drifting as a falcon on updrafts. Her biceps thick like diamondback rattlers and alabaster as polished chrome. Moon's a dot on the vacuum of vista. She brandishes the vibrator like a club. He's sluggish as a fly caught in winter. Her teeth copperbrown from excessive nicotine and coffee. His senses knocked out, like he was dropped from a great height. She is a remembered fantasy, a darn trick of the light. His cotton trousers are coiled in the corner as something of ambiguous portent. He feels wonderfully perverse, degenerate. Albinic wigs of clouds. If Crum was coerced into taking a parental side it would basically demand a cointoss. He hems a bombed Bronte up from her armpits. It's on the tip of his tongue to inquire whether or not she maintained marital loyalty, and it's his intention to screw her. Her adorable kebs have the heady malodor of athlete's foot. They Lord. Gospel truth. She is temporarily barred by his lanky legs. He's got a wicked woody. Would she bother to drum him out of the sterile, capacious study for him begging her to roast on his spit? Would she be morose and regretful? His erect dick seeking ingress into her cranial cavity. He eases along, undulates sluggardly as riverine mud, paced by a marmalade kitty. Overcast, vasty and varied, dark like ebon in twilight. He falls to completely concocting febrile fantasies (primarily acts of careless intimacy) as a prelude to porking her. She goes with the flow to wherever it might take her. He is foreign to her. He has changed drastically, preternaturally. And it ain't just puberty doing a number, either. Her vaginal reek seems to rise out of her sphincter as well. He gooses her and she giggles. Although immobile, she, attributable to the lurid yellow effulgence in its impartial glower, is mobile, like the subject on the pages of a flipbook. He simmers on a heated burner, on the cusp of boiling. He has cornered the market on lechery. His prick is an acetylene torch in his ludicrous drawers. She's nighshapeless in the pitch. Form of her face is the sum of what he can see. His wang rousted and uplifted wholly from the ministrations of her perspiry palm. Showers as India ink. Gravity undoing her downy abs. She chugs a shot of vodka from a scalloped snuffglass, holds his dong possessively like she is charged with guarding it. He gropes her and she squeals. Racket of affection. His nose disappears into the depths of her breasts, redolent of ripening summer. Her soughs expelled in sporadic bursts. Her gorgeous body, stripped, hits him as a punch to the solar plexus. She, carefree, suffers an aversion to being clothed. He feels dumbfounded, simpleminded, tonguetied. Night obsidian not unlike sloe encompasses the geography. Moon shines as a newlystruck quarter. She saunters like a highpriced callgirl streetwalking in highheels. The event unspools before him. She can be controlled, mastered, he thinks. Massive moths, Mothra-huge, flap through the pneumatic door, propelling themselves into the commodious parlor, entrapping themselves there. Stars - spirals of sparks as litcigs spinning, flung thus, in near-simultaneity. His innards feel liquefied, lungs like a bellows stomped on, being as a mechanism misaligned. Her semimusical singsong appeals to his hearing. The pair going into the stifling, spacious attic under her lead, and to him it's like they've reached land's end, the ocean behind them. He feels as a puppet on strings. Their lovemaking looks like an eroticized Pina Bausch dancepiece. He is stonefaced, internalizing his emotions to the point of personality paralysis. Her tousled mop and boho chic are impressive. Their desperate, passionate, torrid and swift Frenching and fondling. Ravenriddled skyline. Next to her he feels as a country bumpkin with a city slicker. He and Sangster appear to be made from the selfsame blueprint. These blackbirds in the overcast and its changing incarnations are, illusorily, a curious by-product of the clouds. Her scuffed and scarred carryall, the plates and clasps battered, with a briefcase inside; a Chinese box. Crows boldeyed cluster the acreage in the voltaic dark. He has the sensation of being a leaf frozen in ice. Her gaptoothed grin. Cirri grows cancerously. He regards her nether regions not unlike talismans. He was virginal as a record that hitherto hadn't a needle put on it. Presidential profiles denominating bills on the dresser are faded like polaroids. She is less than presentable, and tolerable. He ponders her pussy as if there's encodable indicia of his existence there in that hatchet injury. He looks to be meandering in memory, standing so straight it's like he's been flatironed. Micaceous empyrean. She is as though a dream he is having. She's the anatomic affirmation of life. His bone hand (like Death's) is placed upon her fuzzy wuzzy. She's on the wrong path. He yearns to pick her up and plop her on the right one. She'd never stay where she's put. He would wordlessly dump her as an unwanted pet with an off-hand grace. The road she is on is fraught with probable perils. She, goodhearted, yens to give him advice, but holds off because her lifestyle doesn't exactly lend itself to example. She's nuttier than a cat in heat. He laps her fur burger. Her mouth has a sharp evocative taste to it. Her varicose veins like muscadine vines. Her brain's getting bad. He watches her with congested peepers and listens with clogged ears. Sun's a floodlight with a weight of white. Crocked, she lopes crookedly into the john. Claret smear of firmament. Her bedheaded tress as broomstraw. Bales of hay on a flatbed. It lurches into gear, bounces and diminishes into the smazy distance. Her foreshortened penumbrous self fluctuant. Hunkered on her heels the waistband of her skintight bellbottoms chafes her middle. She whiffs like she is smoldering. Bragging about her highdollar circuit course overrun with rednecks. He is slender as an architect's ruler. His choppers are parched, his dry derma feeling like it's drawn, as shrinkwrap. She rises like in the Rapture, worrisome stewed. Her oral cavity is a hog wallow with all the cussing. In her company, it is as if you are unraveling universal enigmas. She's a pretty (how he cares to categorize her) conundrum. He is motionless like a flag on its pole in windless calm. Eventide's as though it's perspiration darkening an armpit. Her skin is filmed with a sheen of sweat. Her pink brassiere and jockeys are crisp and clean like they were recently pressed. His diaphoresis makes him feel drenched in grease. Limegreen loungechair, wastepaper basket adjacent to it. Crum feels pressured, as a pooch put in a spot where it has to scrap with another canine over a bitch. Bronte is a lovely China doll. Just a tadbit woreout. She turns on the coquetry quickly, like flipping a lightswitch. Green cage of coppice. She grips his lean legs. Tangle of briars. Her trills sound as a creek over rocks. He appraises her form not unlike an archeologist a patch of ground that's a potential digsite. Sweat troubles his sinister pies. He clutches her keister. Virile vegetation. He feels filthy, as if some bastard spaded dirt on him. They are like ardent acolytes at some abstruse formality. Her merkin plaited into pigtails. He gazes at her wiggling wormy toes, their imperfect nails painted pink. The illumination's brightness intensifies. There's something ceaselessly ceremonious about her. His thoughts are rays of refulgence through smoked glass of his grey matter. Intercourse becrazed. She moves as though a fish swimming beneath a pond's surface. Cumuli's fanned like the hair of drowned victims. Glowflies drift gently as fulgent specks behind his eyelids. Her tender strokes, gentle smacks. Cirri imaged on the azure. Affectionate osculations and tactions. Her slenderhands are workroughened with calluses from playing guitar. Heaven shocked with lightning. Fullthroated roar of thunder. Autumnal mural is like from a Halloween print. Oxygen nippy and sere. He's out of intimate range by a decent margin he surmises. His curls are as question marks. She verbalizes her love for him. Her speech is loose. Gulls forage over the slurring surf. She declares his scrotum smells good enough to eat. They recall parts of a puzzle connecting correctly to complete the picture. Splendor seeps onto the claret couch. He is wringing wet. His cardiac organ has the thumping sonance of a malfunctioning dryer. Flash of her casabas. She labors and wheezes like an overloaded washer. She is severely tripping on acid. A Technicolor chorus line of anthropomorphic animals are singing and dancing. Cleancoin moon. In a semireclining position on the lavender sofa they've officially crossed the line with consequences awaiting them on the other side. His mental condition on the verge of ecstatic. Hesitantly, with whiteknuckled hands, he cups her jiggers. She puts a palm on her chest as an MD would a stethoscope on a sick patient's. His vascular organ knocks like something malevolent is trapped in his breast and is pounding with a sledgehammer to escape. Crum jokes Bronte is a human red flag and Kilcrease is the bull. She doesn't react. His pulse has the sonancy of a telegrapher's tapping. His elation is as a hex with a perverse spin put on it. Cloudlets scuttle, then streak. Day was intent and purposeful. Night's now a torrential caliginosity. She is grifter- clever, cunning like a con artist. The chance for them to turn back longgone. They deserve to be tarred and feathered, he thinks. They're both broken beings that cannot be fixed. Shoals of sprinkles. They merge, mother and son, into a combinent alien thing. Sourceless (avian?) din. She has a gravelly voice. Their tongues sound as oars lapping at water. She stares at him like a Doberman at an individual trespassing on private property. His rubberized, ungainly sexcalibur, with its conveyance of jumpy energy, deadcenters her frontispiece, fortuitously finds her succulent mouth. Kilcrease and Bronte, sitting on an iron cot, air their dirty laundry that had remained in the hamper for a long time. Detailed and inventive namecalling. Both have volatile tempers. Her ballbat limbs. She aims for his crotch with her chops and he offers a token protestation. Their argument approximates the apocalyptic in terms of severity. Orchestral big band swinging blasts from the stereo system. She imagines them in highwattage copulation. Contraceptive worries his wienie. Freaky fornication. She has a husky intonation. His toupee is messed into an Elvis-ish pompadour. She smiles wryly. Rorschach clouds. She judges them. Night overtakes day: ink running on a page. Roadhouse jukebox. She swiftly sniffs slim lines of coke with a tenspot off the Sears and Roebuck catalog. Heather blur of cirrus. Her pancaked acne's recollective of the ventilation holes in his wingtip shoes. She takes nauseous and pukes beige chunks. Her removed tattoos - stains leached off wood. Fireflies in the murk evoke taillights winking through exhaust fumes. Stand of sassafras. His scrotal shag is as a hirsute arachnid. Nameless birds. Her scalp's like parchment, visible through the dyed roots. Her posterior's pucker's corrugated as a walnut. Doped, reality for her is negated, doesn't exist, she is dismissive of the prospect of it, irreality a dislocating, changeful island of wonder. This depraved session is risky. What do they have to gain or lose? She feels painted into a corner. She looks through him not unlike clear aqua pura, says she ventures wherever life catches up with her, and that she craves an easygoing, simpleminded guy. She mentions she is forever saddled with cumbrous issues, old and new, she held a rowdy concert at a Pentecostal church close to ranchstyle residences ostentatious. She is nihilistic and sarcastic! With her runny mascara she reminds him of a surprised raccoon. Loud licks of a rattletrap automobile. Her modulation's smoky and sarcastic. Enormous evergreens and redwoods. Her stare elongated in entreaty. Her sobs and suspirations are unconventional counterpoints to his moans and groans. His comments acerb. Her hypnotic blinders. She has the sensation she is disembodied, disaffected, distanced from herself. She wishes she were a mole in its mound. Precipitation, to her sight, is shaped as musical notes. Weather's an implicit threat. Chinooks skitter a plain wrapper and quarterbitten styrofoam cup along a chainlink fence. Morning was dense. Afternoon was somber. She went from post office to pool hall without skipping a beat. He fesses he owns a modified sex doll, pimped out to resemble Samwise Gamgee from 'Lord of the Rings.' He'd huff and puff to blow it up until it dawned on him, at last, to employ a frigging bicycle pump! Steelwool cumuli. Gunmetal sky. She finally toes out the maryjane on the tan tile. He looks and listens at her like it's a legal proceeding being carried out. She tinkers with her hornrimmed glasses. Normally weak, he, holding her, feels strong, as if he's assimilating her strength somehow. Cattletruck in a junkyard. Pools of shadow like muddy water. Rainbow's chromatic as a carnival poster. She pictures the horses in the meadow as being unicorns. They are momentarily joined by an excitable German shepherd. Stoned, her head is filled with animated, and meaningless, hieroglyphics, written by an automatous stylus. She'd dug him long ago, in another lifetime. She misfired in the marriage, one in a historically long line of disturbing misfirings. Seasons shift but it's the same ole shit. The pour pops like oil in a hot pan. Waves require replacement. He feels like further runover roadkill. Rain strings from the rotted gutters. His desperate and increasing unease in the testy environs. Unmetered poesy of mizzle. In their wedded state, with an improper beginning and proper end, they had mutually united in this legalized mode which made them miserable. Unwinded woodland. Ash flicks from her beef jerky-long More cigarette as dingy snowflakes. The ragged easy chairs rattle, their sitters, denned up, ill-contained, like beercans in temperamental gusts in the world at large. He hugs her cautiously, as if he might break her. She forks olives onto a saucer. He hunts in her ripped jeans for the elusive feculent hole, an excremental entry into a corrupt sanctuary, for fortune nookie. She ice-splinteringly shrieks. She knew their nuptials were grinding to a halt only she didn't possess the requisite tools to fix them. She grasps his gynecoid wrist as though it is a goodluck charm. His bewhiskered chin scours her cheek like vellum. The civility he is showing her is, to her, commendable. She ostensibly conjures his pizzle by sheer will. They launch themselves from silos of restraint and explode with recriminations. Getting nowhere fast, she debates innerly whether she should cut her losses and leave. Ambery light limns them. She is lost in transit, between being high and dealing with him. His cryptic moue. He reluctantly zips his fly.

Skimming clouds. The manse is an otherworldly, albeit ornate, outpost, with them as sole survivors after a nuclear disaster. Her cozy house beckons from afar not unlike a haven that guarantees warmth and rest. Nervewracking altercation. Her abdominal ripples are as heatwaves emanating from a woodstove; or from an ill-tuned harp's strings. He's stiff like a poker in his boxers. Golden portal of sun. She inexplicably quotes a sample of Sophocles philosophy. With the hood of her sweatshirt cowling her head she is monk-semblant. The familiarity of his beaver basher is perilous. His raspber-ries sound as highcaliber rifleshots. Her quim throbs. Shorting voltage of leven-circuits. She kneels, face upraised, as a supplicant. Bronte, whitehot, is a chime-rical entity engendered out of Crum's fertile imagination. She sits on the edge of the bathtub, behaves like she was exiled from society, lathers her muscular legs, wan as bone, and starts to systematically shave, employing a straightrazor. She's a ball-busting enchantress, putting a curse on him. He listens to the faint scrape and gets an erection. His expression's like he's had a stroke of paral-ysis. She is clad in bikini briefs and tank top. He feels warm and wooden. Mistrals are as if they are alive things. She's a temptress, hot like a cookstove. He marches as though he is a lifesize toy wound up. She brushes, seductively, her sham shock of peroxided hair, fading from a botched dyejob. Her lupine visage is comely. Tar-black shade. Her hind's flattish not unlike a pool table. She explains in detail it is supposed to be orange. He ambles as an animated scarecrow in a fan-tasy film. An aura of self-obsession hangs about her like a plague. Weeping welkin. Indication of sun. Drafts have the sonance of last breaths from dying people. Sycamore colossi. Her slack jaws. She's comfy as a badger in its den. Overcast blanched complexion is like butcher's paper. She thaws his iciness. Tumorous moon. Shooting stars like flung stones. Her pert tits and perky nates are a perversion of gravity. She's gymnast- rockhard, schnoz a hawkbeak, trap a sinkhole. Her pearlgray pallor, predatory lamps. Indian summer firmament. Her athletic, taut calves. Lighting is as malfunctioning wiring of the empyrean. Copse of sumac sinks into indigoid dusk. She is translucent like ice, insubstantial as smoke, and struts, augmenting his arousal, as a hitchhiker, down the carpeted corridor, yakking about gaudy roads and neon bars and the brawls and her tinnitus and roadies and groupies male and female like armies of ants and streetlights making revelry on slick cement. Crum's parents' conjugality was a constant wreck. When it comes to relationships, he's not a capable restorer of order. His folks' connubial damage could never be repaired. She strums the strings and they glisten with melody as variegated metalloid threads. Their quarrels were elongated, fierce, frayed. To her, Kilcrease never gave his faithful wife her proper due. His nerves are redhot wires. Unstable dawn combusts. She rises like a bubble in a carbonated beverage. Dew holds. Chill lingers. Her whining is as a chainsaw. Pollen talcums the esparto. Bloodred radiance. She discloses she was once a thickset bulldog of a tomboy who relished putting on her onepiece swimsuit to tease the dudes. Random changes of weather. To Bronte, baked, she looks like a funhouse mirror's reflection. She swills the mug of brew, swivels on a stool, takes a nother swig, and wipes the foamy mustache with a sleeve. She jokes about Crum's pecker being as a cigar stub. Shivering scrub. He ingests a roastbeef sub and hardboiled eggs and imbibes tepid joe. Their verbal foreplay an embryonic commencement of an eventual cataclysmic spat? Her voice has the sonancy of a fingernail on a chalkboard. The matrimony was a coin and he saw both sides of it. She, without warning, sings like a siren, personality larger than life, living outside the law, and has no difficulty reaching the expectations others set for her, nor does she have a problem immersing herself in the role others cast her to play. He pictures entering her front door and exiting out the back. He appraises her like she is some species he has never encountered before. Her mind is mushy, as if someone scrambled her brains with an eggbeater. He jerks like he's jolted by a course of electricity. Verdurous clump. She boasts audiences surged into the clubs, every strata of society accurately represented, in expectancy of ultimately witnessing something spectacular. She didn't disappoint. Humanity jammed the joints to maximum capacity. Wasted, she appears as though she's a fox beleaguered by hounds; or like a person saved from dangerous floodwaters. Her tunes, just for the record, are punkish, jazzy, catchy, ballsy and melodically strident, her (energetic) stage presence slinky and spicy. She is apparently performing for him. The disparity in height between her and the band members (customarily cavorting as cool clowns) is interesting. Crum's porcine eyes squint. She describes in detail the phalanxes of burly bouncers on the lookout for any hint of confrontation developing in these billiard and diner establishments. She snuggles with him like she is loathe to lose the stimulation of the conversation. He immerses himself in the somatic geography of her, as if she's a chart and he's searching for a specific location to mark. She examines him in the basement's seats (like church pews) as though he is a vintage item she is contemplating purchasing. Mother looks at son like he is the Immaculate Conception. Stars flare as beacons. No avian tweets, no insect buzzing. Raindrops, in the beryl scintillation, are splintery shards of agate. Adolescents, in dishabille, a local bootlegger's offspring, like alien delegates from a juvenile alien race, actually human beings set apart, frolicking at the levee, screech and seek shelter from the window washer under a rickety bridge. The shape of sky accomplishes a cosmic corporeality, forming itself out of clouds. While Kilcrease is at the clinic and Crum at school, Bronte, potted, freaked out, fucked up, brown Crocs sloughing softly on the shiny linoleum, chances upon a secret lab in the macabre (her opinion) residence. Fighting with Kilcrease earlier: they took no prisoners, no quarter drawn, no mercy shown, no compromises made. His youthful handsome Roman profile. She bitched continuously, becoming a caricature of a shrew. Countryside was as one of a failed landscape painting. Her tongue was lubricated by liquor. With Crum, afterwards, she coasted on the rising tide of enthusiasm. She howled like a wolf. There was something about her splaying on the pristine parquet of the capacious parlor that stayed him with caution. Her pooper's pungent excrementitious reek hit him hard. She spread-eagled herself as if to right the universe for him, to set everything that's wrong with the world straight. Her inflection took on a snappy, shaky quality. He stared at her with clinical detachment. He acknowledged her impeccable manicured and pedicured nails. Her fuzzy asshole was not unlike a bur with fur wrapped round it. She wagged her tail with liquescent dexterity. He felt as though he were in the keep of her fanny. Her sensuality honed itself to insectival wings which bombinated to confirm their existence. She regarded his resistance with a dull patience that belied her horniness. His cast expressed a benign placidity. Her whoopie cake's aroma was like acrid smoke from burning rubber mingled with new leather and musky feces. He was motionless as a fencepost. Rank fishy funk of her pudendum. She had scratches on her left side like she had cuts which were in the process of healing. Drizzle was in tatters. Clapboard cabin with a sloped yard. She had lethal hairpin turns for hips. He molested her tochus bothhanded. Her silken intonation was as a disc jockey's, and it was hoarse, like a torch singer's. She fumbled a J out of a Camel pack, sparked it, and blazed the blunt. She offered him a toke but he dismissively waved it off. She noticed he had a chicken's limberneck and a lobster's eyes-on-stalks. Her derrière's cheeks separated as if she were splitting heads of lettuce. Predawn brume was like a community of apparitions in their drifting passage. Bareankled feller in a felt hat traipsed. Vista was mottled with magenta. A brunet owl landed on a dripping and dappled bough its predecessor relinquished. A splendorous shield pervaded over the featureless shacks, some untenanted. She aggressively fiddled with herself, scaring the bejesus out of him. He looked in dread of whatever the inevitable dispute with her would bring. His entirety was sleepnumbed. Shootingstars were fishtailing brakelights. Rubberbanded sportscards. Vehicular plumes were phantom plowlines. Sheet lightning as an airliner's instrument panel. Stars pulsed. She was humped against the throne, out of it. She dislocated him in time. He held her like a cop apprehending a miscreant. On a drunk, a binge for the ages, she knelt as in parodic imploration, countenance arsenical green. He inspected her critically, wound tighter than a watch. He tipped a cigar out of its case and carefully kindled it. She was a pitiful, misshapen thing, gagging. He stood like a sentinel ... Bronte suddenly discovers, in an underground hideaway, a fancy bunker in a remote part of the estate, computer files and spiralbound notebooks detailing what has transpired - Crum committed suicide, having hanged himself, cyber-bullied by Sangster Lingold, a fellow student, back in England. Kilcrease, stricken with grief bordering on the bizarre, would even the score, tracked down Sangster before the authorities could nab him, kidnapped him, and, over the course of time, turned him into a dead ringer of his late son, and brainwashed him. Sangster has heretofore fought to cling to the core of his identity. Crum would be avenged, Kilcrease promised himself. Bronte suffers a sinking sensation in the pit of her stomach. Kilcrease materializes and surprise-attacks her and beats her to death. He sounds as a marauding savage. Deceased, her face swollen almost beyond recognition, she has an expression of bemused wonder. He foams at the maw like a maddog, hardon like a fundamentalist preacher's bacon bazooka, sounding as if he's speaking in tongues. An obese codger with a caronal combover and appareled in tentsize overalls sits in a loungechair, limbs spraddled, in a parkinglot chugging a halfpint close to a woodpile, junkbox pickup truck shored up on cement blocks, and this tireless trailer, his presence popping up abrupt on the periphery of Crum's vision. The elder's halfmoon calves are tawny, sandaled, pteradactylous feet pasty, like ghosts of tans. Haybaler plaything. Serpentiform blacktop. Hammering heat. Caws of crows. Ivy-covered porch. Weight of light. Volume of it. The manor risen malign over the remainder of the immediate world. Where the lane ends the residence begins. Kneehigh weeds. Morning sucks the dew from the sedge. Spungold emanation. Slipstream of dustbunnies. He feeds the vacuum cleaner cord. Ceramic statuettes of cattle are on the pinball machine. Cloudcover as though it's tinfoil. A motley of pubescent strays mill, swag, in no haste whatsoever. Crum quaffs the remains of vodka in the bottle and vows to redeem it tomorrow. He remarks his bladescarred (slugshaped) wrists from failed suicides, forsakes the protein powder which is like mortar mix. Sixpack of canned beer resides on his knee. He grazes on tofu as placidly as a cow. Blinded by sunshine, he needs the service of a seeing-eye canine. He exhales and inhales his breath (as if he ought to acquire it) like a hummingbird sucks a nectarean substance from honeysuckle. He remembers Bronte scrutinizing him as though to make sure he met her exact specifications. Kilcrease was perched on the couch like a vulture waiting for someone to die. He left, in a demonstrative huff. She flowed as water. Fulgor through the blinds: shuttered snapshots. Blondhaired (hornetnest-shaped), wildeyed girl halfcrying in the thighdeep, probably lukewarm creekbed has fistsize knockers. Wasps are not unlike divebombers. Cattails cant in the swift current. Atmosphere is vibratory with high-tension wire humming. Finches recently quit those gaunted branches. Hovels hunched and miserable. Bronte's starkwhite hooties, rosered nipples, peepers a guileful green. She was totally tanked, wobbled as a baby learning to walk; or like a wino navigating circuitous alleyways, sputtered and choked (as if she were drowning) on yark, Crum in tow, rod blowing up like a stick of dynamite. She staggered down into the musty cellar, flinched when he touched her shoulder, as though she were scalded. She urked again. He was aligned with her like an iron filing on a magnet, his heart's pounding out of sync with hers. She gelked. His pupils were as nictating pinpricks. Bats veered in the electric gloam. Moon conspiratorially blinked in the interim cirri. It was like an obscure mystical symbol. He was mousequiet/still. She thumbbolted the doorknob. Dollhouse was a miniature museum. His kiss brushed her yap as a cue ball a corner pocket. He'd never sufficiently gotten up to sexual speed, so to speak, in bondage to Kilcrease, indebted to him. She disattired, casually and confidently, unrigged without formality, felt herself to substantiate her own authenticity. He watched her like a hawk while she chucked her

fashionable thong and bra, pirouetted as a mock ballerina on her bent toes. He practically took an eternity to
peel, and in that span a million kids ejaculated their
junk, he thought. He left on his dingy undies. Awkwardly
he pressed her solid nalgas, so they were like florets
sandwiched in between pages of the Bible. Her build
was as if she was hacked into proportion by an axe.
Cumuli shuttled like sequences of filmframes. Her gorgeous tushie adjusted itself to accommodate his simian
hands. A cock crowed. He yielded to the temptations of
the flesh. "We're as debauched hillbillies," he said, vox
with a bell-like clarity. And she didn't disagree.
Twentieth- century country voodooed by a witch doctor.
He caressed her cellulite-pitted legs like they were
printed in braille and he was typhlotic. Grand Ole Opry
on the transistor radio. Guilt ravaged his system as
malaria. He was a fly caught in amatory amber.
Misfortune had a mortgage on his soul. He haunted her
heinie, redoubled his efforts. He remembered Mom and
Dad fighting like cats and dogs. Her simper one of
rueful amusement. Police cruiser spun its wheels, stuck
in muck. Celestial sphere was a cosmical conflagration.
She was tantalizingly on all fours. Bags of goodies in the
vicinity purchased with the proceeds of Kilcrease's credit
cards. Rare minerals were enshrined behind the cabinet
glass. She brooked no nonsense, usually. Her hangered
clothes, shelved makeup, suitcased stuff. Moms staying
with pops was a case of feeding the marriage into a
make-it-worse contraption. He was a cadaverous kiddo,
cardboard flat, with next to no definition. She was intricately crafted, as a Swiss watch. There was a distinct

businesslike manner to her being, efficient and mechanical. A hunger gnawed at his loins. It was like their possible union was fiction which required his complicity to become fact. He was wonderstruck at the sight of her. Her sighs sounded as sand cascading in an hourglass. She had the hardest whiskey and buttered popcorn on her breath and admitted she had an affinity for sodomy. Her bobbing jubblies were suspensions of the laws of physics ... That afternoon Crum questions Kilcrease on Bronte's whereabouts. Kilcrease answers she had touring commitments to fulfill. Suspicious, Crum studies the security tape (Kilcrease forgot to erase it) and sees Kilcrease carrying Bronte's body out the back door. After he ditches her corpse, Kilcrease flips on oldschool wrestling on the massive HD television set, sipping an inordinate amount of cognac and feeling, in this stuffy study, akin to a mummy in his sarcophagus. Place's mazed. Bronte could certainly be meanspirited, coldhearted. He moved her carcass in a wheelbarrow. He is finally free and clear. The phosphorescence lists against the paneling. He was intimate with her cadaver, experiences postcoital despondency. Being with the living has never broken him of this perverse proclivity. Winds whip trash in a dervish. Her nails were sharp as rodentine teeth. He wasn't mourning the loss. Gusts sounded like something grieving. He'd slogged through wedlock as a soldier through war. Sky blued by a bevy of jays. Blackened clouds like spitshining military boots at inspection. In the disposing of her he was fastidious as an officer of the law working a fresh crime scene. Even divorced she kept coming back not unlike a bounced check. Her dying was drawnout for his pleasure. The thought of her is a physical presence. She resisted his initial assault, in an appalled outrage, the primitive instincts for survival insisting she fend him off. Her soughs sounded as snow falling on leaves. The red line she always imperceptibly drew he crossed like the border of a foreign country. Murdering her, time was wormholed. Pewter wardrobe. Scenery undimensioned, unfeatured in the henna haze. She was the diametric opposite of him. He dug her grave in the balmy breezes with their distinctive nosound. Perishing, she clacked as a door swinging repeatedly on loose rusty hinges, the remainder of the universe steeped in silence, his breath pluming from his mouth like smoke from a chimney. His chin pillowed her sanguineous skull. When she was alive, she was a sternfaced, exquisite exhibition, an enigmatic trophy, a splendid showpiece for his satisfaction. When he was done he smashed her cranium in with a crowbar for good measure. He could sink or swim without her. She was slumped bonelessly, her expression as an effigy's cast from plaster. His mouth had tacky saliva. She was lying in state in an expanse of merciless, windswept wasteland beyond a forestial childhood fairyland. He wrapped her in a floral quilt. Her pockmarked donk. Carillonneur tinkling of rain. He handled her with unorthodox decorum after he blew his load. Fiery air burned his lungs. Birds erupted behind him in a detonation of feathers. It poured without cessation, variation. Her pies were terror-stricken. The moon was cornea-achromatic. Hail peppered him, and ruthlessly. She was no more animate than a dummy without its ventriloquist. His psychological condition was one of disassociation. Torrent of the wet stuff fell like an afterthought. And the night deteriorated. Day was dawning as the advent of cosmic page-turning. Beeches and birches, laurels and lindens looked like gigantean ink-sketched ironwork. Analyzing her blanketcovered figure. She was as a baroness stricken down by an assassin. Bruises marked her throat. He loved inflicting the injuries on her. She was remote, at a remove from their sacrament. Their relationship bloomed evilly, family blossomed, with Crum, into poisonous flowers. Having a baby gave their relationship a validity it didn't have before. Callous constellations. Cartwheeling candy packages. She was a civilization personified which rose and fell. Sibilant enunciations of the house settling, sequenced into a whisperous monotone. He recycled excuses for his infidelities in perpetuity. Mooted moon in the cover of cumuli. Grackles cackle cheerily. Anthracitic pollen. It was to the extent that the tie that binds was of no moment for him. Her attractive aspect in life was a ruined rictus in death. Cirri are shapeshifters biding their time. There was a ton of shit he wanted to tell her but it was all beyond articulation. Blood-copper sky. Her credit cards spread on the oilcloth tabletop like a poker hand in the provisional luster. Fencing stitches the property. The countryside, in the coruscation, is as an image in a developing photographic plate. Her bubbly optimism invited scathing pessimism. His guts feel like charred rubble. Landscape's as a stagesetting backdrop. Redeyed fire detector. Vault's serene, unexplainable and expectant, caught in a caesura betwixt

clear and cloudy. Kilcrease, creeping like a coldblooded
killer, enters Crum's bedroom, warm as a womb, his
member telescoping towards him. He approaches with
dire intent, surfaces as monstrous dread. With the lone
lightbulb hanging above his head, he feels like the main
character in a comic strip when he gets a bright idea. He
walks as a boxer coming out of his corner to meet his
opponent in the center ring, and with a week's worth of
facial hair. Plush drapes on the windows are not unlike
drooping lids on drowsing eyes. Crum, perspiry rivulets
coursing down his front and back, jarred out of slumber,
stands and disrobes ... He is no longer male, is now
female, having undergone an extensive sex change operation at Kilcrease's hands. Concupiscent, Kilcrease bats
his eyes as if in hambone- actorly surprise.
Noctambulously he stumbles to retrieve the important
tube of lubricant. He flicks the switch, turns out the
light with quickened urgency, the pad plunging into
piceous relief, concedes he always wanted a daughter.
They sleep together. Carnal relations are labor-intensive.
The two plough into each other like a couple of maniacal mowing machines. Nookie with no letup. Kilcrease,
preferring the top over the bottom, looks as though he's
a shipwrecked sailor clinging to a liferaft. Crum's tummy
is soft and yet substantial beneath his own. His hair
moves outward on the mattress like ripples on water.
His harsh soughs have the sonancies of rattling shack-
les. Concussion of the coupling diminishes in intensity.
His lips as leeches. He'd permitted a previously forbidden sphincterial penetration. Charged gloominess.
Clackety-clack of a train on the tracks. Kilcrease quivers

spasmodically. Suspirations of the zephyrs. Levin is like threads of light. Semen accrues out of his schlong in spurts. He rises as vapor from a swamp, sweat-sodden, and negotiates the hellhole's mishmash of belongings to take a leak. He urinates copiously, believes Crum's orifice draws his cock like iron does lightning. His lungs feel seared. He envisages the clipped, carmine wings of his lover's tress. Vehicular cacophony. Furiously flitting bugs, conceivably enlivened by a dark alchemy, in the peach orchard, glint as contrivances of jewels. He looks like someone lost. Night's black as shoe polish. Rainwater races like quicksilver down the plateglass. Thunder thankfully faroff. Foliage opens and closes as a theater curtain. Odorous ozone. He envisions another round of lunatic hanky-panky. Crum surreptitiously spikes his drink with a sedative, knocking him unconscious. When Kilcrease regains consciousness later on, his whole head is swaddled in bandages. He unwraps them - Bronte's face has been transplanted onto his by Crum, his former apprentice. He taught him everything he knows when it comes to plastic surgery. He air-raid-siren- screams. The place, with him panting, is swelled with the oxygen released from his being. Crum gasps, runs, contained in a russet lounge romper, at breakneck speed on the winding road, leaving the asylum of an estate behind. The universe holds his destination. Cloudlets break down as cells in the bodily sky. Crum, currently calling herself Sangster, returns home. The Greyhound bus has stalled. Streetcorner magi bloviate. Pedestrians throng the sidewalk like refugees. Group of juvenescent giddy gals gallopade on the pavement. His parents, fifty-something Weldon, with a wig as a torch, sesame seed lamps, and turtle's physiognomy, and Scarlett, about his age, falconfaced and boxlike, with a carrot-colored, turban-formed bouffant, are chatting in a trendy bohemian cafe. He advances, in a polka dot cami tank, striped track shorts and suede pumps, to tell them who she is, and who he was. Let us end here.

The Ogress

O MY DEAR brothers and sisters, I have a story to tell. Jewish adolescent Fishel Akselrad, his father Israel, mother Pnina, and sister Rika, live on a farm outside the city. After Fishel's bar mitzvah, Kristallnacht happens. He flees into the frigid forest and chances upon a small, albeit stocky, juvenile girl with blond pigtails, a cleft palate and club feet and wearing a Gestapo uniform, severely injured near a tank and three dead soldiers. She is beautifully ugly, to him, her body shaped as an upright udder, with an anal aspect and hemorrhoidal honker, voice vibratory like a cigar held for a duration between your fingers, inflection sounding as a plucked nylon string. Insectean egg sleet. Impulsively, he decides to take her to a nearby abandoned barn and tends to her wounds. When she recovers she tells him she has no memories and cannot remember her name or what happened to her. He calls her Emilie. He brings her food and nurses her back to health. He's smitten, in spite of her unique appearance, and gives her false identity papers. They soon establish a romantic relationship. Enemy parachutes in midair are numerous Cheshire Cat smiles appearing and disappearing in the fibrous fog. She has a face shriveled like the scrotum of a swimmer in cold water, puff-pastry cheeks, breasts as paired (fleshly) faucets, pinchable posterior, and a sphinx's taloned tootsies. To Fishel she is pretty not unlike a Chagall bride. His spectral lust floats over her as a horny Holy Spirit. She spits out several false teeth which fall like rotten fruit. Rain secretes from the sky that's straight out of an abstract medieval painting. Petaliferous flames of the fire, its embers describing ellipses. She is graceful as a plastic ballet dancer mechanically pirouetting on a music box. Pond in proximity steams like a stew. She rises as a soul from the body, arms cruciform like the wings of a butterfly pinned on cork. Emilie somatically suggests an aged, cosmeticized fetus rudely ejected from a uterine monster. He's a morose Gulliver in the company of a lovely Lilliputian. Mournful lupine howls; pack of wolves lamenting the fact that they are on death row. Town's sad as a shelled summer camp. Physically Fishel is reminiscent of a bipedal El Greco greyhound with a brown mop. He admits he often feels like a juvenescent bronchitis infecting his parental lungs. Tangle of pines. Her metamorphosis from larval would-be Nazi warrioress to polite gal is miraculous. His diaphanous intonation. She waddles akin to a penguin and with the languidity of the obese with excessive girth. Snowflakes dissolve on his fresh face as ice-chips evaporate on the tongue. Snot on his collar a shiny snail trail of slime. Cotton candy clouds. Thunderous thudding of explosions. People have abandoned the burg - a gigantic mouth with depopulated gums, teeth taken by deranged swastika'd dentists. Minuscular shell of her navel is unintentionally exposed, fatty alabaster folds, like husks, too. Statuary as quiet sentries. Algid, asthmatoid wind. Snow soft like flour. Blowtorch- flames of stars. He blurts that with the Gestapo he feels tyrannized by tribesmen in the jungle of warfare. He is Mormon-angulose. Phlegmy tambourine-rattle when she speaks. Her carapace of crud. Could she use his dollhouse-sized washbasin! Her thick lips utter he's her guardian angel. Slush hangs from branches as translucent spiders. She thinks his schnoz resembles an anteater's snout. He paces, walks quickly, like he is a character in a silent movie. He imagines her pubic hair as being on par with fox-fur. She's draped in his mothball-smelling wool coat, sips beef broth, chews buttered bread, and confesses she's out of sorts, confused not unlike a nocturnal creature abruptly caught in the dawn. His fishy peepers swim on her. Farsighted owl-eye of moon's unblinking. His long legs are as a gull's. Cirri are faded streamers from a cosmic carnival. Large capsules of helmets. He dreams of playing backgammon, cards and billiards with her, a pool hustler chalking her cue ... She reluctantly divulges she feels like a cuckoo clock winding down. Her smirk is a developing serpentiform scar. She is firmly installed in a hollow log. His vox's husky with desire. Is she an escapee from a circus? Her intestinal

squirming is audible. He explains the boarding-school
he recently attended was basically a barracks with labyrinthine corridors. She's a mystery emphasizing the
mediocrity of everyone else. Each dinner in his depressed
home is as a Last Supper. They crouch, comparable to
quadrupeds, superimposed on the boundless darkness.
He verbally details the exterior of the house as pictur-
esque, the interior bland like the waiting room of a
private doctor's office. He is ramrod-rigid, Adam's apple
a paper- weight. Precip's the size of poker-dice. His
erectile cock stands at attention as a tin soldier. In the
frosty valley below, troops with machine-guns are devils
wielding pitchforks. He's tall and lean like a dockyard
crane, with the disappointed pies of a saint. Majesty of
frozen and distant mountains. He hesitantly tells her
Israel is planning on moving the family to Poland, to
stay with relatives, believing it will be safe. Emilie suddenly throws a violent temper tantrum and Fishel,
uneasy, leaves. Hungry, Emilie breaks into a cozy chalet
to steal food and is apprehended by the owner, young
and cinema-star-handsome Hauptsturmfuhrer Walther
Brunner, manifesting as a ghost, in order to haunt her.
He'd risen like Lazarus. His fawnish countenance displays indifference, is her opinion. He is sleek, effeminate,
with Dumbo-ears and Bambi-limbs; a Disneyfied fas-
cist. Eventually he becomes quite garrulous, despite the
situation, droning on, till his prattle is stymied to a slur,
a change conferred on it by her bold kiss. At his manor
headquarters she strikes a bargain with him: she knows
where a family of Jews are hiding and will give him the
details in return for her release. Brunner reluctantly

agrees. The Holocaust, he discloses, is a large-scale public-works program, a venture into the belly of the beast, and laughs. Brunner places Emilie in an orphanage of a bunker-like building with Speer-esque architecture. There, she is taunted by the popular Sofia because of her deformities. Her knees knock in sync with her heart's beat. Sun's a spent lightbulb. She is short and stout. Hardly thin and elegant like Sofia. Groundskeeper is a hunched wraith with sunken eyes, crooked arms and legs, and shuffling gait. Lake as lotion smeared into a rectangle, shimmering in tremulous lambency. Her bright, lemon-yellow ponytail's like a fakir's rope, pallor the very pigment of oblivion. She exhibits an abnormal fascination with death, making her fellow foundlings and the staff nervous. She shows psychopathic behavior. Smoldering rib cages of structures are unrecognizable, ruins interspersed by (remarkably) still-intact buildings. Vehicular shark snout. Pigsty of a bathroom. Successive, contradictory layers of luminosity. Pompeiian piles of rubble. Drooping manes of the ferns. One day, the sun sallow, she tosses a harmless grenade off a bridge and on to a parade, causing a traffic pileup. As punishment, she's whipped by mathematics instructor Karl Kammler, with his Buddha bulk and gargoyle's features, and enjoys it. Later, she spies on him, showering, and masturbates. She can't climax. He catches her in the act. His toenails long as knitting needles. He's a big boy drag queen, rouged and powdered, in bacchanalian glee, naked in his stuffy study. He looks to her like a bowlegged, balding version of Edward G. Robinson from Fritz Lang's 'M' film. He babbles on about property and prostitution.

Her sapphic stanzas, distinctive physiognomy, and translucent integument, enrapture him. She feels submerged, as the Spanish galleon, hallucinating ghoulish teachers, decapitated chickens, octopi sarcophagi, detainees motionless akin to figures in a wax museum, and a pygmoid witch doctor lancing her infected boils, and she cheeps like a distressed bat. Her inexhaustible charm has him, squiffy on high-octane, absinthian liquor, hypnotized. Vitric light. He possesses an anatomic knowledge on the level of Andreas Vesalius. His spiel, the bunkum alky-influenced, embellishments of (supposed) military accomplishments - embroidery, cross-stitched in the material of possibility. His piping has the sonance of bullets' trajectory sounds. Mourning veil of drizzle. His phosphorus-blue blinders. She caresses his stubbled chin. They kiss fervently, making their choppers open and close as fish's mouths. His pathetic wirehaired wig subsides on, ironically, a barber's chair. Her orifices are hurting. Blood fizzes like gin in her head. She partakes of a slice of sponge cake, feels as a kind of in-between entity, not unlike a chrysalis between a larva and butterfly. An artillery battalion rushes as a company under fire. A grizzled, quizzical medic, frail like a plant plucked from an herbarium, ambulant as an umbrella taken in a gust, copes with casualties. There are, on the first-aid post cement stairs, random piles of the beloved Fatherland's dead, like Jews prepared to be bulldozed into a mass grave at Auschwitz. Insecticide scent of incense that's lit by Karl. A number of corpses are covered as garbage that was swept sloppily under carpets. His piston-rod penis. Daybreak is a faceslap. Emilie's bottom's sort of soft like pulp. Headmaster Herbert Six, she notices, is limp as a saw-dust-filled rag-doll. Magritte azure. Intimate, upright, the lovers could pass for fencing foils. Pumice-stone sun. His metalline cry cuts into her ears like a dagger. Concentric circles of the cumuli as water when pebbles are thrown into it. Her labial lips open and shut not up unlike the petals of a flower in the evening. His bar-rel-bum with staves of scratches is redolent of a putrefying coffin. He has the expression of a naughty kid, brags he performed Peter Pan heroics on a particu-lar rescue mission. Her strength weakens, as a vampire's with dawn approaching. She has gone off the rails with the whiskey. They lurch back and forth like windshield wipers. The environment is adrift on effulgence. Coins clink in his palm as ice cubes in a glass. Their bodies are fused on the foul mattress. He slips his prick into her rectum like a tramp sneaks into a train. Her grimace is a significant weight on the scale of her phiz. Constellations of November-colored leafage. The den ship-sinks. He's currently a shaven Santa Claus in striped pajamas. He was, supposedly, a former fairgrounds wrestler. Her flaxen axillae moss. Village of conoid tents in the icy field. Is this awful sodomitic degradation a perverse reward for her many mistakes, faults, defects? Her chi-clets are rather eroded by tidal waves of sugar, he sees. Grand piano in the corner is as a Buster Keaton con-traption. It came with the place. Spur-bumps on his feet (in their chimpunity) are like protuberant bony clavi-cles. Precipitation drops, racing in greedy streamlets, glisten as diamonds on a throne. Her ass is killing her.

He gestures like an illusionist. Brief bout of sex, bereft of passion, for her, sure took its toll on her cunt and derrière. He is simply shallow, materialistic, superficial, with appalling halitosis. Emilie is amazed she remains alive and well in the world-wide warring, with its suffering, courage, famine and anxiety, as a rock unexplainably untarnished by the waves. The landscape has the definition of a Matisse. Orgasmic eye of moon. Kammler gazes at her like the head of a fish on a plate at a patron in a restaurant. She's chameleon-still. He has an unruly mustache and beard. It's incredible how much time has passed since she first met him. When he vocalizes he sounds as an orator on a gramophone record played at the incorrect speed, accusing her of being insolent and undisciplined, and having a petulant arrogance. Her incredulity is obvious. The semi-destroyed, baroque edifice is like a compound situated in an enclosure. The meatball's heavy as a foetus in her gut. Her voice is like shattered porcelain. His criticisms are as variations improvised on a specific theme. She is stationary like she is posing for a photograph. Sea, inexplicably, reeks of detergent. These supple nymphets of mixed blood (begging to be spilled) saunter, struggle in recalcitrant heels, wear dresses as deliquescent Dali clocks, and certainly rarefy the air. Her throat's sandy like a Japanese garden, gestures sinuous as a squid's arms in the ocean. His penial key in her vaginate sardine can. She's poised not unlike a shop- window mannequin. Their nude torsos rub frenetically against each other, the friction starting a flinty spark of arousal until a sciatic twinge forces him to wince and stop altogether. Their big-screen smooch, tender and yet spasmodic, and squeeze. She gently applies an herbal balm on his hirsute tailbone. Her bronchitic breathing irritates him. Her Delvaux deliciousness. Her pink pussy-curtain parts to reveal a pink, carnivorous, sinister grin. Still life oil painting of a partridge and a cactus is askew on the paneling. Her somnambular state. She stares at him as a master attempting to solve a chess problem she'd never hitherto encountered. They chatter like magpies, the two on uppers and downers. An elderly, tetchy bureaucrat with hostile blinkers harasses a cripple on crutches in the hall. Face-sitting on Kammler, Emilie is as a pigeon perched on a park bench. She's a code he swears to crack. Panzers are in a solemn procession like in a funeral cortège. Amber aureole of the ornate lamp. Caruncular condensation beads on the dermoid glass. Improbable dusk. The banal, capacious room. Her cardiac organ sounds as suppressed sobs. Glycerine puddles. Precarious tremors of her temple's pulses. Spangly vastitude of a capital city right out of Alfred Doblin in the distance. He acts like he's a parish priest and she's a charitable case. Her slightly sagging belly is as an anemic marsupial pouch. Paramecium pudendum. He, ardent, is aggressive like an armed assailant. She takes his pallid dick as an elephant's trunk does a peanut from its keeper. His authoritarian appetence. Complex web of her cogitations she is caught in. He mauls her like a starved beast. Arachnoid chandelier. She has the disgruntled quietude of the deceased. Night flower of her Fanny opens and closes on his member. Spumy crochet the tide left on the shore. Orally he wanders her appealing anatomical geography. Their epileptic flailing in tangled sheets is maybe comical. Panoramic view offered. He returns her carnal clamors as an echo in a cavern. Opacity of her skin. Her gypsy oculi. Curled up, she looks like a bread roll, backside a collapsed soufflé. Bundles of laundered clothing as barriers. His heinie is perhaps the size of a mortuary icebox. Hail's frozen chickpeas. He bows gallantly to munch on her genitalia. He's erect like the head of a yipping coyote. Emaciated olive and fig trees. Lavender empyrean. Gilt-framed acrylic, watercolor and charcoal artworks. His hard-on withdraws shyly as an antenna. He unintendedly slides sideways on her like a raft lurching off course. His jaundice-hued nails, perspiration as cod-liver-oil, midsection the size of an electric generator. His flesh has the fragrance of inexpensive soap. He puffs on a cigar not unlike a steam engine, has the aura of a (scholastic) conquistador. The luminescence bleaches them. He snorts, the sonancy as the breaths of a deep-sea diver. Her mind's aimless like a certifiable lunatic in a psychiatric ward. Her rashy, gauzy underarms. She is tentacle-coiled on the gynecological table. She shivers as if she has malarial fever. Her vocalic dirge of the dying. He ravishes her, rages like a bull in heat, blows air out of his nostrils, and butts her in the bosom. This concupiscent congress emphasizes her loneliness, shame, and homesickness, in spite of not knowing where home is. A reedy Untersturmfuhrer with a reptilian rictus slithers. She feels oppressed, degraded. Her spirit splats at the bottom of an inner well. To be fetal'd in the womb of slumber ... She is a malformed china doll in an elaborately kinky getup, her racing heart pedaling as though a bicycle. His respirating with the sound of a refrigerator motor. Walls of the lavatory with the white of an igloo. He mumbles like a village idiot. Waffen-SS honchos resemble chalk figures of cave drawings, astoundingly animated. They mingle as invalids in a sanatorium, brains mush from medication. She shoos away his mitt prowling round her hind. She's a hideous seductress. Disaster area of the bedroom. He behaves like he's on thrombotic throes. Her celestial surveying, moist with diaphoresis, yap askew, anatomy awry. He ogles her, sighs sounding as a tuberculose steer, perspiry peninsulas marking his tee. She has a dragon's forked tongue. Metalloid sheen of the reservoir. Somersaulting scraps. She snaps war is rife with "vileness, corruption and urinous (?) shrapnel." Airy fingers brush the chimes made of iced branches. Gelid oxygen. Barracks a wart on the neck of a cliff. Teats of cement mixers, pneumatic blow torches. Shades are wrinkled like the lids of the sleepless. Indecisive illumination. His meticulously polished jackboots are akimbo. He belches his salami lunch in one fell swoop. She puppy-yelps when he gooses her. Their methodical, erotic St. Vitus' dance. She wishes he were comatose, a condition induced by pills and schnapps. His indistinguishable blabbing, mush opening and shutting as a camera's shutter. Her piercing glare, ignoramus simper. Arterial splendorous pulsations. She has the inertia of a carcass. Their comet flights, judo tussling and onomatopoeic grunts on the lettuce-green mattress are humorous. Kammler's tobacco-stained saliva pools in her clavicle. His geckoid eyes. Coitus on par with a blood ritual.

Emilie's triangular platinum fuzz. She strides like a mechanical toy. He clips his sculptor's 'stache and goatee, clad in an immaculate union suit. Their coition was as creation, her stumpy legs parted like the waters, mangled avian feet clenched as fists. Expression of consent; complicity of partners. His smudgy silhouette. Her vision's blurred. He's sated. She is not satisfied. She is shriveled like a plant in the Antarctic. Van Gogh colony of crows. Infantry on the terrain are as ants on a cake. Countless crates of munitions. Spermic tears on her genitals like heated milk. Her sheer exhaustion, prominent collarbones, nipples soft as grapes. She evaporates like an echo. A wiry Feldwebel is Dracula in the daytime in the colonnaded acacias. The screwing reconciled her with herself. X-rays are negatives of interior portraits. Asleep, she's a European stony infanta statue. She's a fantastic foreign land he now occupies. Her ego has been eaten away by the acid of insecurity. Officers dining in a bombed-out funeral chamber of a parlor: Georges de La Tour supper work miraculously animated. Kammler has the introspective profile of a meditative philosopher. She possesses the distended, malnourished middle of an impoverished individual. Phosphorescent abscesses of lights illumining the sprawling encampment beyond. Her abdomen is an aquarium of derma run aground in the water of sweat. Rackety cascade of her cachinnations. Her snatch is as welcoming as a cradle to a baby. She feels detached from life, like an infant from its momma's vagina during birth. Firmament is tumescent with bruisy clouds, swollen as if from punches and kicks. Battered, humbled Third

Reich. Her stained hyena gnashers. She's impatient like a driver late for work and stuck at a red light. He extracts her from the towel and propels her facedown on the treatment table. His sadistic, viscose snicker. He performs a clever flanking maneuver on her behind. Speckles on a moth are jewels imbedded in a ring. Her umbrella ribs. She is mutely murmurous with luster. Intimate shrine-ish silence. Moon fresh as though a newly minted coin. She waits not unlike a casket for him, her suspirations with the sonance of bugs sizzling on a kerosene lamp. She surrenders herself to him unconditionally. Violet, succulent valves of her vaginous fly trap. Her stenchy B.O. testifies to her imminent perishability. Cupidity spreads, sings over his entirety, sullies his totality. Considering his girth, he looks like a gargantuan bambino. His wang in the obscurity navigates anatomically, searching for her foof in which to anchor. Rum pollutes her breath. She breaks as a wave, at once victorious and vanquished. He is wrapped around her like a boa constrictor. Odoriferous fart. His. Skeins of embers from a barrel scabrous with corrosion. Magnesium flashes of leven. A Herculean Unteroffizier advances across the crustal pavement as a great thundercloud. Her vibrating veins are taut like the strings of a violin. They discuss the imbecilic, colossal pointlessness of warfare. Her obstinate quiescence. Mangy cur. Panicked birds' wings wave in the scraggly scrub as drowning victims' arms in a frenzy of feathers because of the deafening mortar blasts. Railing's leprous from rust. Rough road, riddled with potholes, is relieved of a sleeve of snow by a plow. Her eyes are like those of a alligator's on the swamp's surface. Unscathed so far in the conflict, she feels as a section of shade coruscation hasn't heretofore reached. She pictures the fantastical flora and fauna taken out of a lush picture-book. Tools like torture implements. Her auricomous bush is as a brush. She's a bag of sugar, embraced by him. She longs for safety that's nonexistent. She is sheltered like pus in a blister. The sight of her, in dishabille, sends shivers up and down his spinal cord. She flops as a dumped sack of potatoes. Her period's painful. She unbuttons his shirt and unzips his fly ceremoniously. Vapor dissolves like incense in a church after service. Her soles are red as scorched Angolan earth. Pitch-black, malicious, rancid Gefreiter uniform is a profane status symbol, a perverted rendering of a widower's grieving garments. Environs are pregnant with the embryos of uncertainty. Stucco and plaster. She has the patience of a prostitute paid by the hour. Obscenities vented by officers are exchanged outside. Inside, the couple play chess with some poor souls swathed in bandages in the infirmary. Her idea. An annoyingly adenoidal, gangly Stabsgefreiter, content not unlike a cleric at a feast, is expelled from the slate twilight, a trembling volute of smoke pluming from his pipe. His cacchinating is absolutely ear-splitting. Nicotine-saffron emanation. Her disorienting distress and disorder, brassiere at her midriff as a fallen silken nimbus. Screaming-meemie air-raid siren ... unsettling. False alarm. Her migrainoid issues. She can no longer differentiate between the rational and irrational, reason and unreason. Her surroundings are distorted, like from a funhouse mirror. Her narcissism's a knot which can never be undone. Lucidity of her vanity. Her thrilled being is tightened in tenacious expectation. Her back's smooth as a sheet of pricey stationary. Her ineffable adorability. Their fling themselves around like they are trapeze artists. Only he is capable of stitching the unraveling seam of her essence with the threads of articulated thought, but she drives him off with her radical mood swing. Excitement spreads in her diaphragm as an eagle's wings. Makeshift nightclub has these whitewashed walls. He applies cuff links like he's stapling fabric to his wrists. Her chicken wing shoulder blades. Semenoid tears on her sternum with pellucid conjunctivitis. He is a lumbering mammoth. Her beaver is abrasive as steel wool; or stems belonging to chrysanthemums. Sequins of stars. She is supposed to be in class for midterm exams! He is privately tutoring her. Yes! Legitimate excuse. No. Lame. Their smacks sound like rubber suckers. On the dresser, its dust a domestic pollen, is a collection of dog tags as metallic sacramental bread. Her fortune nookie gushes like a burst artery. She meanders with a sloth's languor. He has the proprietorial bearing of a big boss. Her saccharine, gaseous perfume is completely overwhelming. They converge at a singular common point - smushing. She's emotionally enervated, physically energized. Bandy-legged rocking chair. Her weary person, tranquil bones, butt- cheeks volcanic rock-porous. Maintaining hygiene has evidently never been her habit. Social convention is a straitjacket to her. Resinous smell manifests. Sober AMT's cabinet of walnut wood, bay window dingy. He goes over her, diagonally, as a lobster. She's in his care like a snail a shell. He behaves as if he's protecting the pope. His uniform is cleaner than a pontiff's robe. Vise-grip of her migrainoid headache. Her ambulance-wails. She is drilled recklessly by him. She flops like a mermaid on a pier. He trots as though he's an ass, stops, and appraises her digital pincers, flabby tummy, hefty hips, and haystack of hair. Strobile heap of apparel. Harp of a fence. Japanese transistor radio. She looks into his eyes not unlike a visionary into eternity. Emilie feels, with Kammler, as if she's an apathetic acrobat, the feats of theatrical derring-do uncoordinated and unharmonious, that she's going through the motions for the benefit of a paying audience, and, without warning, she ups and leaves, ending up skating with students. She purposefully pushes Sofia, treating her like a rancorous State would an ignoble (perceived) race, the rawboned redhead with a long, delicate neck and stinking of vinegar and low tide, in the gossamer rays, falling and crawling as a caterpillar before getting up onto her blades, inadvertently heading toward the pond's thin ice, which collapses, and she drowns. Emilie stirs up a rebellion, within herself, a revolt against the aggravatingly smug faculty, refuses to submit to them. She revisits Kammler's office, with nothing on save for suede gloves, her shadow optically producing her, pounces on him as a famished jackal, beats him, snoring like a basset hound, limbs illusorily boneless, loose as tentacles, with a cudgel, smothers him with a pillow, and fixes him with the skill of a professional gelder. Halogenic light wrenches her, hunched like an owl, out of the murk. She quells the surge of bile coming from her esophagus, fades away as though breath on a pane. A cemetery quietness. Her confidence grows not unlike mold in a bathtub. She manages to evade a mandatory medical examination by pretending to have a toothache, seducing the lecherous dentist, convincing him not to extract the "infected" molar. She fellates and fingers him. She self-administers an enema, staying calm and collected, a gross, if effective, procedure, her constipation horrendous. The scuzzy toilet shakes with the flu, throwing up wads of paper after its convoluted digestion of feces, a brownish paste as squashed figs. Gobbets of skin strewed on the cobblestones. She's not one to keel over at the drop of a hat. An American soldier amputee wriggles in a schoolyard, looking like a bulbous insect whose legs were plucked by an imp. His eyes are empty windows in a burned-out building of a body. She is gnawed by appetite. The structure's evacuated before it's annihilated by allied bombs. Shit hits the proverbial fan. The campaign increases with intensity. Carnage unfurls, proliferates as a nightmare. The metropolis is a slaughterhouse. Her cranium roars like a crematorium. An adorable, lugubrious, lanky Aryan boy, somnambulant, is as a living Michelangelo sculpture. Syncopated clanking noises of malefic machinery. Her moving parts are lubricated by sweat. Money is a necessary requirement at this juncture. She can adapt without a hitch to her circumstances, advertise her services with a sultry striptease. Sobs of showers. Congelation of her spittle. She feels like a she's in a state of algor mortis, the second stage of death. Snow is settled on the sidewalk as dust on books in a library. She flounders through the morass of conflict. Toppled brewery. Combat provides perspective, stimulates the animus. Crags have transmogrified into glaciers. Her daily booze transfusion is of paramount importance. Rain comes in circular spurts, like it's sprayed from a sprinkler. Razed soccer stadium. Frilly, foamy surf. Watery sludge. She has the urge to urinate. Carcasses of beastly vehicles ossifying. Maze of a market of mayhem with its clusters of vendors and customers and confusions of wagons, with attendant mules. Gabbling guns. Citizenry threnodies. Lachrymose translucency of an onion. Degenerated facade gapes with bullet holes. Serpentine line of the dispossessed for soup (flavor of boar and manure) served at the mobile kitchen. She is cold as a statue kept in a crypt. Pustules on her like mussels a reef. An alley has the stench of decomposition. Albatrosses are in cahoots above. A youthful suicide is snagged in a shrimp net. A ripped kite roosts on barbwire. Muffin in a saxophone. Trolley rants on the rails. Nictating tip of a cigarette as a flashlight message. Vessels call from the wharf. She can't get rid of the horrific dream in which she was lost in a sawmill, these mutated salamanders and scorpions, taking on a grotesque grandeur, chasing her relentlessly. She heard amplified crickets chirping. Her visage was an automobile's grillwork. Human screaking. Quagmire of entrails. Gray, plump doves nestle and coo on a ledge. She wants peace and predictability. Actuality crushes the bones of her fancy. Vagrants yak, their reflections popping up in intervals of glass. A tilting tenement's visible remaining portion of stairwell. The moon is vigilant. A gynandrous guttersnipe clad in a baggy SS ensemble sucks on a lollipop and whinnies. Cathedral weathercock. Granitoid clouds. Moribund spruces. Harlots disguised as hussars revel with Wehrmacht members outfitted like tango dancers and flinging flowers in an orbit of halogenoid comets. Shapeless smoke. An Arado airplane's fumes endeavor to stitch up the eviscerated firmament, some of its visceral cirri having been spilled. Basilican hall with checkerboard flooring exposed. German units march. Salt-and-pepper shaker summits. Migratory movements of cumuli. Varied calls of terns and snipes. These columnar business establishments are still somehow standing, appear artificial somehow. Acreage looks like a stage set for a battle to take place. Welkin's a monotony of unfolding material. Emilie's emotions are noticeable in her expressions, like a cholera flag on a boat. Antlers of fallen boughs. Malodorous petroleum. Horizontal sarcophagus of an elevator. She is, illusively, malformed (permanently) by a lens. Blanket used as a morgue sheet. Her marmoset mien, newt's oculi, lamb-lips, spongy gums, castaway clothes. A pockmarked hobo, a flea-bitten nonagenarian, with coal-black choppers, and covered in a woolen jacket and patent-leather shoes, wallows in an archway, scuttles like a spider crab, drinks out of a chamber pot, and snorts as a shoat. Fervor of gulls. Chicken cartilage in a jam jar. Fraulein sirens, frantic, are caught in the squalls, like whip-lashes, on the beach. Squinty, unbathed stevedores. Wake-level silence. Plentiful pickpockets, streetwalkers, and police to contend with. A towheaded transvestite, hair on his head as a brush with missing bristles, and kept in a buc-caneer costume, sambas, (bagpipes played by a girthy guru), employs a crowbar as a cane, in a subway passage with its uriniferous tang. Distinguished personages spectate. Emphysematous breezes. Hair on his head not unlike a brush missing bristles. Penniless druggies and drunkards. Disemboweled ottoman. Cellophane oxygen and noisomeness of stable. Garrisons delouse themselves. Pagoda intact. The flood waters retreat as a giant sucking in saliva. Emilie's duck steps. Her breath, with its sock- bin and yeasty pungency, could probably carbonize a cockroach. Fearsome night has this black widow patience. Stony lacquered beetles. Combers sound like radios crackling. Hustle-bustle of hoi polloi. She applies an allegedly affective special ointment on the martyrdom of liver spots on her shins. Discordant capers of children. Her vascular organ reverberations. A devastated pastry shop's basement turned into a gambling den. Fetor of a dump. She is impregnated with perversion, glistening with the combustion of lechery. Savor of thyme and parsley. Steinway's as a pine box for a behemoth. Blackish buffaloes of alps. Birds' nests of her underarms. She may strike you as the type who plucks the wings off flies for amusement. Her neutral expression. She is an eye in Germany's storm. Vampirish vaudevillians in Siamese positions sip belladonna, chamomile and linden teas and nibble on croissants with the consistency of cardboard. Her heart sinks like a bucket in a well, physically and psychologically affected by the witching hour's brilliance. She's powdered and pomaded and perfectly imperfect. Solicitous swarm of the devout pass out pious publications. She feels as paper reduced to bran from bookworms. She pictures the metropolis as being an astronomical asteroid fabricated out of the imagination. She squeaks like a hamster. A two-headed preemie, swathed in sports pennants, brays in a carriage. Emilie skirts round a skirmish, goes her own way, and ends up in a Deutschland military camp, remote as a leper colony, the sinuous sandy road she instinctively took leading to this construction site surrounded by flimsy wiry fencing, where several Soviet rebels are being interrogated by the bilious, impulsive Obersturmfuhrer Irmfried Drauz, a master of combat strategy, who has the frontal of a duck-billed platypus, depilated pate, peepers, bulging like those of a riled prefect, panda'd from lack of shuteye, mouth a cruel moue, livid leer a (potentially) grimy threat, bulging gut a cushion embroidered with sutures, duff as an offertory box, body odor hovering like a halo, who is instantaneously infatuated with her. A few guards accompany him as loyal dogs. Her muteness is appreciated by him. Museum quietude. His Luciferian pies. She accurately translates the revolutionists' Russian language, deliberately mistranslating it, and, as a result, the men are executed. Afterward, she denudes herself of garments for Drauz, who's already in the buff, in his ovaline office, and they make love. Prominent redolence of decay. Lying in the raw on the bunk, he has the semblance of a white whale (Moby Dick) stranded on the sand, in the vicinity of a stolen equestrian sculpture. Mann Gottlob Best, reminding you of an ulcerated Boschian toad, talks like he's reciting text in a recondite Eucharistic ritual, modulation syrupy, oral cavity dry as the Gobi Desert. He departs with the pace of a pregnant camel. Emilie commences her apprenticeship of adaptation, drinks the amber ale out of the wine glass like it's a vial containing a nectarean elixir. Drauz touches her flaccid, downy stomach with surgical caution and she giggles demurely. She dissipates as sugar in coffee in his suffocating embrace. She takes off her holey stockings akin to a snake sloughing off its skin, bobs like a moored craft, rocks as a cradle, hugged thus. Bashed, he drivels on about ambition, victory, defeat, radio communications, metaphysics, tawdry cabarets, gastritis, and her "vegetal virginity." Whatever that means. And he, embalmed in lascivious bliss, concludes her sexual creativity has dexterity. She's vaguely absentminded, relishing her cream enhanced with nutmeg and cinnamon. Her brain is a blown fuse. Her blank encephalon makes her feel like a mental defective. She had suffered a concussion in the crash. He toddles as a pigeon. She experiences the sensation of being a toy pulled by a string. His punctured-tire-sounding flatus. He's captivated. She is mesmerizing. She withstands a cogent dread, confronting this heinous figure, clear as a childhood nightmare, oscillating and tactioning her. Her intestines squirm like a nest of waking serpents. He sedulously molests her bazoos, diligently fondles her grandest canyon. The tip of her gratitude is performing fellatio. Low tide of depression encroaches. Her pulse pounds, rattles like the loose dentures of a snoozing oldster. In the putrid place, she's as Noah in an Ark chock- full of animals. There's a sensuous quality to her strut. She, erring on the side of coquetry, sits regally in the rickety iron-wrought chair, adjacent to the Formica table. Being flirty comes effortlessly. Her diaphoresis is like lamp oil. She indulges in her combat ration of canned food. Her eyes have crow's feet. Muslin curtains are the amputated wings of archangels. His respirations with the shrill whir of a monstrous mosquito. Their elephantine devouring, in the preposterous intimacy, with trumpety blares, makes, effectively, a cacophonous concert. The crazed coupling is a hellacious upheaval, an ecstatic earthquake. He whispers his belief into her ear that war has neither a beginning nor an end, its links are forever chained to the participants, that it's a web of misery, has epic proportions, is intrinsically smoke and mirrors, ostensibly a magic trick, sleight of hand, an optical illusion, and he carries out cunnilingus on her. He frowns in arthritic discomfort. Innocuous annoyance of opera music. Prayerful susurrations of gusts. Communion wafer of sun. A prisoner, narrow as a drinking straw, rummages like a rat through rubbish. Drauz's complaints of chronic colitis agitate her. He philosophizes on hunting and fishing. He often manipulates the past and distorts the present to control the future. With her, he is enthralled and exasperated in equal measures. Orgasming, he neighs as an injured horse. His fingers close on her nipple like petals on a flower. Stars wink as embers. Lambent dribbling of a candle on the sill beside the relics of trophies. The construction has the look of a dilapidated mosque. Vulvar handkerchief on his lap. She masticates on a stale mint, mummified in a blanket. He dominates her from pillar to post. Oxygen's oleaginous like his preferred anti-venereal cream. She's rendered a Picasso subject in the flickering light. Attributable to her fluent Russian, she has become the company's cultural guide and interpreter. Drauz declares to his peers that she is their good-luck charm and hails her as a heroine. It is like he's expecting an enlightening reply from her. Nothing's forthcoming. He is a nasty piece of work, she concludes, and should be rotting in prison, or even executed, for the horrid crimes he has committed against humanity. He's amoral, evil, should be held accountable for his sins, carrying out uncountable atrocities, demonstrating he's a sadistic psychopath, eliminating the Jewish people, shooting, raping, burning them alive, and gassing them, his "business," putting food on the table, as it were, fulfilling a function, doing his duty, disagreeable as it is, completing the job, albeit a regrettably repugnant one, obeying direct orders from the proper authorities above, the powers that be, his superiors, knowing he's a link in a limitless chain of the Third Reich. Genocide, he insists, is a strictly Germanic phenomenon. He is a cog in the machine of this horrendous enterprise. Stars flick on and off like warning signals. Endless expanse. He plays a crucial role and is proud of it. He takes responsibility, feels no guilt whatsoever. His hands are stained with blood in his chosen occupation, as an auto mechanic's are with grease. He's a sociopath swatting the opposition not unlike flies, and crushing the Jews as bugs. The current of his dear nation, his beloved country, carries him along with its flow. These are dangerous times. His power, rank, social, economic and military statuses ... enticing ... he's a Black Sea she dives into and deliriously drowns in. His ordinariness is extraordinary. Sun sheds its splendor on the floor. When she resisted him initially, rejecting his blunt overtures adamantly, he behaved like a dethroned despot. Countryside, vacant, is shaped as a lizard. Milky Way's made by high-powered carbon arc lamps. Frowsy slippers. Scurvy sky with ulcerations of cumulus. Cartwheeling newspaper in a catastrophe courtyard. Fortressy boutique. Lumpen disused lot. Skull-faced, diminutive urchins have a snowball fight around a defunct gas station adjoining an active foundry. Emilie, resembles a grownup gnome, her tresses done up and fastened in a bun, following his explicit instructions, strands straggling. Drauz has a forced native- idol smile, trudging as a wounded penguin. He has butane breath, teeth grinding sounding like roach steps, dopey from opium. He thrusts into her with the propulsive energy of a combine, sounding as a thunderclap, rolling over her in vengeful detonations. She is squat like a buoy, garbed in pajamas as if she's a puppet, the bathing suit he coerced her to put on underneath too tight. She has a champagne-froth hairdo. Cannibal breath of his flatulence. Her Narcissus taciturnity. His excrement has the malodor of a clogged sewer system. Her cellulite and varicose veins spoil, for him, her chubby thighs and falcate calves. His iguana wattles. Tomato sun. She slips quick like a silverfish. Municipal urinals are being cleaned by public servants. A docile goat with a jangling cheerless bell's on a terrace. Drauz expectorates mango seeds. A Moorish, barefoot concubine, voluminous waist wrapped in a starched sheet in the listless eventide, pads as though she's a panther, flashes her raven pubic fungus, growls the Allies have threadbare spines, yammers on about frying pan concentration camps. Emile's forsaken feeling grows like vibrissae in nostrils. She gets lost in her reveries. Azure convulses with amoeban clouds. Satanic hammering of mortar rounds. Gang of thugs on an esplanade abscond. Megapolis is depopulated. Tempest of a storm plays on the harpsichord of a ship's rigging, in utter disarray. Her throat's as a bullfrog's. She coasts in vagaries. Remembrances are automatically exhumed from her grey matter; snippets of recollections from a possible past. The world, she says in a drugged glutinous coma, needs to be relieved of the weight of war. It is warm in these quarters, like a boat's boiler room. With him, she has the sensation of being as a smuggler on a ship. Mousetrap found in a cupboard. Blowing him, she gags, folds like an accordion. He wheezes. Her rear has the texture of armadillo meat, feet as jellyfish, puss protuberant not unlike a fish's head sticking out of a pail. Thalassic suspiring. He evaluates her organ as a magus the star of Bethlehem, speaks an upside-down language she fails to understand. He's on her like a parasite a leaf. Violating her, he makes numerous mistakes with his maneuvers in the bed, winning and losing, and soon enough acting as the leader of a football team in a championship match. He is a bloated clod of ludicrous dimensions.

Emilie kneels like a slave to mouth Drauz's manhood. She leans as a lily in wind. Shriveled scintillation. With stunning regularity his secretaries swarm around him like flies round a hippo. Explosive din out the Gothic window. Warped girders of a dynamited bridge. Wrecks of equipment. Self-assured sappers scour the terra firma. Artillery carriages are as crumpled tin cans. Oil slicks. Strewn debris. Sweetish acridity of smoke. Tanks are toys overturned. To lighten the mood, she traipses to and fro, frizzy-tressed, in breathtaking turquoise panties and marching garters, asinine monocle glinting, epaulettes worn as earrings, shouting "Heil Hitler!" before beating a hasty retreat into the bathroom. She is a girlish golem. Representatives of the majority and minority meet, swollen with weaponry, at this chemical plant. Magnificent moon. Taffeta-rustle of leafage. Network of canals. Plastics warehouse. Forgotten ferry. Residences in their decrepitude. Intellectual riffraff gather. Novice nun with ermine eyes sermonizes with evangelical zest, papal pomp, missionary vehemence, facial features contorted by liquor, her presence fulgurously falsified, unyielding virtue virtually tangible. Militant stomp is in tune with the temperature of the onlooking pedestrians. Razor-sharp hiemal gales. Dozers graze on bodies. Vulturine Sikh has an ancient mariner's beard. Seafarers and farmhands coalesce on the waterfront. Ash-gray escarpment. Insecure ceiling and an enfeebled heater. Sunflowers bent in the floral vase are like heads hung in displeasure. Pelagic sighs. She's cocooned in his adipose arms. She is wizened and itty-bitty as an aged pubescent; or she's a teensy-weensy adult plunged pitilessly into an abysm of infancy. Her sphincterial arbutus berry is attractive to him. Their intemperate frolicking, tremendous stimulation. Aromatic valerian. Her mallow-hued, perspiry paunch is like a dewy dawn. The queen bee is poised on her throne of a hamper. A zaftig peddler hawks his sparse wares. She is a hot hunchback, grasping her misshapen, reptiloid ankles, planispheric breadth of her prat available. His voracious libido, incessant mania for her duff. His fervid obsession tinkers with the machinery of his scruples. Bawling of senile beggars in the pea soup is interminable. He looks as a manatee with a crewcut. He was merciless in his handling of a homosexual malcontent with a case of dysentery. Oyster pungency of her nether regions. Cariosity of her teeth. She has the halting modulation of an oracle. She, dawdling at the threshold, imbibes the amniotic fluid of her mineral water, ingests a buttered pancake. Her breasts are pushed against his pileous nape as an orchidaceous clump on an embankment. Spermaceti sleet. She's simultaneously attentive and distracted. Her wayward locks complicate her countenance. He has these jailed saboteurs and looters to inevitably deal with. Wehrmacht sentinels equipped with gas masks look like sinister bipedal unicorns. An abominable smell of carrion assails one's nose. Emile and Drauz are unrecovered from the stupefaction of sex. His bulbaceous thumb traces her appendicitis slug of a scar. She bleats as a sheep. She feels not unlike a scarab in the carcass of the Fatherland. Her expression is etched by disillusionment and hopelessness. Her gadabout's feet, vermiculate toes are connected by membranes of blisters, attributed to an allergic reaction to poison ivy. Her snout has these excrescences. She strides as a wrathful cherub who lost her wings. Disoriented district, verminridden, and its indescribable disorder. Palette's like an autopsy slab when it comes to comfort. His sugarplum's stubbornness is frustrating. Cabaretists, ladies and gents, are herded as billies into a pen to practice a routine in the indoor swimming pool/gymnasium. It looks like an obscene palace soirée. Arrayed in a low-cut Turkish gown, she gazes at him as she would an unannounced visitor. Her intriguing speech impediment and florid inflection. His sound chamber intonation. Foyer is like a decorated bullring on the brink of collapse. She is an uncomely creature right out of Rubens, in an inert pose. Cyclopean eye of her bellybutton, one he wants to poke. Badly. The compass of his principles ... lost and winding up, cracked, on the shore of madness with its fugitive flotsam and jetsam. She can tell when he is lying, just as you can discern the skeleton of a cheetah under its skin. She's a mobile stuffed saurian, a landlocked aquatic monstress, an albinal golliwog, a midget cheeping like a chick. Her shape's as a sack of beans. Her fibs are spread fungally. She has the natural intuition of distinguishing truth from falsehood, an innate ability that consistently comes in handy. She goose-steps with those web-feet. She has the witty bite of a bedbug. She baas like a distressed calf, reamed by him on the tumbledown mattress, her nutcracker claws clamping on his pectorals (with the viscidity of quince-jelly) with impassioned intensity. His pot has the texture of porridge. Her bunghole's as a diseased nut. Her tootsies are snug in the orthopedic sandals. And she has the semblance of a heartbreaking, sublime, wicked femme fatale. Buzzing in her ears is like cicadas. Helmet as a model sci-fi spaceship. A charming Galician chambermaid with a ping-pong ball Adam's apple briefly interrupts. Thinking Emilie needs a mandatory boost in morale, some essential motivation, important direction, Drauz makes her exercise, au naturel, to eliminate any element that might threaten her serenity, communicating this like he's transmitting vital information. Kommando divisions are deployed. He vigorously skewers her, is furious he wasn't officially invited to the damn dance ...

Jerking Drauz off, Emilie's callused hand works ever so slowly, as one belonging to a clock. His head's a veritable boiling kettle. Enamel-whitish overcast. She's crippled in the wheelchair of wartime absurdity. He bugle-calls when he comes. She's preserved in the formaldehyde of humid air. He is still, inalterable in a prone position. She imagines Fishel, the flexible beanpole, looking like an aspiring contortionist. Her brain has independently emancipated itself from her body at this point. She is revealed, at a glance, as if Radioscopically, like an opaque object, in the violaceous irradiation. Cute commas of her facial dimples. She stumbles as an auto- accident victim for the pack of cigs and glass of muscatel. Her marmoreal flesh gleams. Meanwhile, he's an anthropoid Tower of Pisa, blitzed on pear brandy, and on the cusp of collapse. He is ponderous akin to a glutted mastodon. Bones in the damp closet like for a macabre anatomy course. Fruits of her bosoms and buttocks jiggle. Shagging with him, she's as a chameleon, with her multitude of expressions, camouflaging herself, bent not unlike a penknife, for his pleasure, whereupon they, in the altogether, play dominoes. She crams noodles into her craw as a nurse stuffing intestines back into a stomach. Stretcher-bearers load a rangy noncombatant with bandaged stumps into an ambulance. She is splayed like a frog for dissection in biology class. She believes she's bereft of sense. Luminous shafts sieve through the damask drapery. Tribal drumbeats of their hearts. Chartless venereal crossings. She feels as a sound searching for silence. Perspiration shivers down their vertebral columns. She coagulates in a chilly sweat. Bubbles in the sink are like ones in a comic strip, the text, in this particular instance, illegible. This apocalyptic atmosphere's comparable to the dawn of man. Her resigned, tense grin. Their phantasmagoric quarters. She protects herself with lies as bodily tissue does the fibrous capsules enwrapping them. Prehistoric remains of memories she, an incidental paleontologist, is compelled to reconstruct correctly to create a past for an exhibit in the present. Her mug flowering red, she is a mangled marionette manipulated by his stubby fingers. Egg white of cloud cover. Variegated smudges of her whorish makeup on his jowls. Their raunchy hara-kiri. Coital sojourn on the carpet. Igneous eye of sun. She has the attitude of a disdainful prima donna. Indian knickknacks on the designer shelves. His bulldog brow is furrowed. Her haunches are like mounds of mashed potatoes. Soaker sounds as crockery being broken. Their contentious debate is as a marital disagreement. Her dear Deutschland has become a chaotic provincial bacchanal. Not to him. Their dispute's as bland as one of a pair who were divorced by mutual consent. Tulip-shaped lamp settled on the bamboo table in the musty office. Xylophone blinds. Electric shocks of affection. Their obscene parallel trajectories meet on the couch, where the two entwine like pieces of pasta in a bowl. He fixates on her marble bust, her sphincterate maraschino cherry. A crematorium disgorges its ashes. Pops from a rifle range. Acid as a geyser in her gullet. He drills her, then smashes her into smithereens. Their spicy martial arts. He, rigid and peevish, lingers like indigestion. A pearly-haired SS Amazon with the facet of a limestone lioness that would ordinarily be posted out front of a superstructure, a caricature of a Lewis Carroll character, a Pantagruelian bitch, the repertoire of her movements having the rhythms of a waltz, the warrioress infamous for her promiscuity and brutality, patrols along the perimeter through sooty snow. Einsatzgruppen schmooze and slaughter undesirables by firing squad at the lip of an abyssal ditch.

Drauz's massages smooth out the rough edges of Emile's vehement protests when he grabs her posterior. He is an ivory elephant. She brushes the dandruff out of her thatch of a mane as you would breadcrumbs from a tablecloth. She could be the model used for a plump seraph that was painted on a fresco. The quilt preserves the imprints of their bodies. He behaves like a horse in heat. His flared nares. She snake-hisses. They writhe as eels in a bucket. Chiaroscuro quivers like vermicular death throes. Expressionistic woods are remindful of a wintry daguerreotype. She feels like a fish compromised in competing currents of reality and irreality, reason and unreason. He looks as a species of bovine. Captives are concave with starvation. Her excess of pancake and mascara thrills him. The stupid bastard acquires a nervous tic, pursing his lips rapidly and repeatedly. Elasticity of her integument. Pieta eyes. Moldering moue. Taloned toes. The galoot goes over her fascinating derma layer with a fine-tooth comb. He clings to her like a monkey to its mother's arm. Sky's embolisms. He clasps her ankle as if he is clamping an artery. Her abdomen, with its many decorative moles, is warm like toast. He's built as though he's a rugby player. Climate contracts and expands. He injects morphine into his deltoid muscle. Canteen's balanced on a rucksack. He is a recumbent living effigy. Everyone in this godforsaken place bare themselves like they're naturists in a forest. His trunk absorbs her as a rug does the sound of footfall. Pressing her to his torso like a crucifix. She sparks in him an avid flame, fanned by her long johns and woolen socks. It is a heavy- handed operation, manhandling her. Pandemonium of explosions and shouting. His mouth sucks as a plunger. Fog's smoke from a censer. Poignant dignity of a decimated brick-reddish abbey. She glares at him with a ruminant distrust. A stern sexagenarian Sturmbannfuhrer, with the physique of a hot-air balloon, belches like a blocked pipe and manducates on a toothpick. Jizz rises In Grauz's nuts as acid reflux in the throat, breakers of heartbeats pounding against the seawall of his chest, and he splooges with a cry. Voices bubble up like ill-broken-down breakfast. Emilie is a shot of adrenaline to him, the syringe's needle sticking his groin. Invasion of her orifices commences. Defiled, she has the terrible sensation of falling helplessly earthward from heaven. She assumes a vegetable detachment from the depravity, has a sickening feeling of self- loathing. She has the glossy stare of a taxidermized animal. Crescentic moon is swallowed by treetops, from Emilie's perspective. Profusion of search-lights. Drauz's bowels rumble as an avalanche. Would she, at some point, metamorphose into the impeccable insect for him? She is a filly he tames. He reigns over her. He nips obstacles in the bud. Surmounts them effortlessly. He's driven to succeed. There is no absence of ambition. There are defined goals, clear objectives. He issues words of devotion. She feels isolated, like she is quarantined. He manipulates her as a goldsmith his articles. He sounds not unlike a mad dog when he ejaculates. And he mentions the ambushes and mines he survived. Hastily discarded underthings. She assesses his societal standing with mounting envy. Shaking her hair like a maid does a feather duster. She begins to pick at herself as a mandrill at lice. There is an expensive Art Nouveau lamp. She looks prematurely old. He remarks her acneous pits. Loud orgy next door. She flutters like a perplexed moth, nauseous from bourbon, complexion greenish. He starts to stroke the rubescent rasp of her sascrotch with an ursine paw. He molds her out of the modeling clay of his imagination. She's exciting, electrifying. Troops are a plague of locusts. Light and shadow are in complicity. Her personality: miles of desert with an oasis somewhere. Forestal density of his manscape.

For some weeks she witnesses the horrors of fighting, including the butchering and plundering of civilians. Drauz, now in love with Emilie, in order to keep her safe, pulls some strings and enlists her in the elite Bund Deutscher Madel (League of German Girls, female equivalent of the Hitler Youth) boarding school, the edifice looking as a cuboid Greek temple, with chimneys like the horns of oxen, the rococo roof in dire need of repair, and commodious corridors. Clam- colored students, teens with kale-stem necks and sulky mouths, move in their chimerical canter, the flock shepherded by the stern- faced staff. She's immediately recognized by everyone, faculty and pupils alike - her real name being Herta Mandel, "The Ogress," their headmistress of "pure Aryan stock," an expert in "racial science," possessing a talent in detecting Jews, using her rare gift, Wunderwaffen (wonder weapons), that is, nipple erectility, as a dousing rod locates water. Also, she's actually forty years old, afflicted with a rare condition that makes her appear to be very young. Drauz backs off, shrugging his shoulders and nodding his head. She remembers being en route to the Akselrads to arrest them when she and her escorts were blindsided by insurgents out of the blue. She eventually discovers the Akselrads have been imprisoned in a ghetto. Ultimately dismayed at who she is and what she has done, Herta hangs herself in the thicket. And it should be noted that she thumbed her nose at nothing except the blackness before doing so.

FIN.

Rhinocerotic Woman

Hot heaven is hell on this goddamn wide world. Uncaring arciform sun in the ashen clouds diminishes. Malevolent heat and humidity. Silvergray overcast. A young boy, Friedrich, bonewhite, thin and girlish, with a brown mound of curly hair, currently like a crow's wings in the balmy breezes, shallow, hazel eyes, and aquiline nose, has recently lost his mother, Amahle, to sepsis, and thus survives alone in a quaint, dollhouse-looking mission church, an integral part of the folklore of the African region, its colorful, domical, affronted structure semiburied in the abundance of bushwillow, looming in the leaden drizzle as a veritable ghosthome, at the edge of the outlandish jungle. The architect obviously had a decided affinity for the opulent. To Friedrich, he is a ruler in his temple. His routine recycles its repetition. Stand of jackalberry, aligned and almost apologetic, enshroud the place. Curious orientoid bushes. His amphitheater of a bedroom. Probably belonged to a bishop. Wasps snarl like pistolshots. Motley of mutts apparently accrued from the afternoon itself, eventually vanishing in the fog in nature's sleightofhand. It's as if the dense forest, ripe with flora and fecund with fauna, has a quota of wilddogs and no more are allotted. He disdains the miserable weather. He wanders, wends his way through the hedgerow as though it's plucked from a cautionary tale. Taffy sky. Skirling nameless birds. Din of commerce coming from the distant town. Thunder sounds rhinocerine in its roar. Leven's miles of electrical wire strung in the sapphirine empyrean. Cadaverous cirri's like the impotent dead. Swamp warm and smoking as a gigantean gun. Windscattered candypapers are like iffy present wrapping. One evening he hears noises and, nearnaked and quiltcovered, dresses in outsize overalls and circus clownish shoes. Transportable tabletop radio out of commission, for the nonce. He sweats visibly and audibly. Tinny tones of the rain. Here is his refuge from civilization and its baffling doings. His ragged respirations. Palm cupping the old flashlight, he turns it on. Then he instinctively decides to leave the comfort of his cozy, fawnhued quarters, austere and tidy, redolent of years, solitude and decay, bric-a-brac souvenirs accumulated over the course of a lifetime, like items in a bizarre museum he regularly visits, knickknacks a chattel of relics, to investigate the source. He eats cheese and crackers and drinks soda. Waddling as a penguin because his feet hurt, rather raw with the numerous blisters from hiking. Anxiety aches inside him, twisting sharply like a knifeblade. Dwarven saplings. Sullen firmament. Tombstones capsized in the graveyard doused in beatific brilliance. Blood bombinating in his head, ears ringing as bells chiming, he, on a whim, grabs the sawedoff shotgun. Seconds clock into minutes. His noctambulant, feverish sights are like hallucinations from the far reaches of dementia praecox. A spacey impulse suddenly seizes him. His cardiac organ hammers against his ribcage. He peers to discern what manner of creature lurks there in the damp brush. Cumuli are pearlescent stains soaked into the texture of the material of welkin. Rubberbanded sheaf of papers on the muddy ground. Nervous, palsied, he feels as if he's infected by a powerful strain of virus affecting his brain and nerves directly. Gnarled trees in grotesque configurations. He abruptly discovers a wounded, yet wellfed, rhinoceros, concealed in the spinney, massive beyond his powers of comprehension, whereupon he experiences this strange separation from reality, seeming to examine the thing clinically. Tending to the beautiful beast, he attains a weird state of grace, has the peculiar sensation he has successfully wrested a universal truth from the millennia. He halts from his rhino ministrations to think of this: has he taken leave of his senses? He wonders ... Sleep takes him dreamlessly. He nurses the animal back to health. For some unfathomable reason he names it Elna. She is like a remnant of a fantasy refusing to fade. Later, a hunter, Luan, sinewy, squint-eyed, middleaged, and corpse-bluelooking, a half-crazed cartoon character, arrives, asking about the rhino, saying it trampled and crippled his wife. The son of a bitch boasts he'd slaughtered the male and young, taking their horns to sell on the black market as ornaments, and wants the female. Friedrich replies he doesn't know anything, believes he is prepared to straightrazor his throat if necessary. His lie convinces, he gets by on blind luck. His heart pounds as though it possesses an independent will of its own. Ideas roil in his mind like tissue paper in gusts. His breaths hiss as tires on asphalt. He is on tenterhooks, wound up in uncertainty, waiting for the other shoe to drop. Luan stares quite intensely, countenance harried and agitated, like he is reading the kid's thoughts. He speaks with a slight lisp, commenting on the brick wall, marble fountain, and stony statuary. His dispensed language is brisk and businesslike. He appraises Friedrich by a conceptual standard, gazes at him with an expression of bemused caprice. Shuttles of cinereal cloudlets in the void of vault. Avian shrieks, animalian ululations. Sultry twilight. Primerspotted flatbed truck's abandoned on the grassy slope. Luan's malevolent glare. Friedrich's skittery peepers. He is chilled to the core. Panic shorts the circuits in his grey matter. Communication with Luan, for him, is rather provisional, and he's indeed poised for possible flight. Dry leaves clash in the zephyrously stirred, shabby shrubs, the waxing and waning lemon light limning them. Haunted bog is as the property of a troll. Boiling sun. Luan is mean like a snake. And he glowers at Friedrich as a mentor at his protege, a sorcerer at the apprentice. Bentwood series of pews. Darkness black like the ace of spades. Friedrich feels as a mouse in the presence of a cat. His fart croaks not unlike a frog. Meanwhile, Elna is hiding in the copse's shrubs. Luan, in spite of being suspicious, departs. He struggles to start the muckslathered rattletrap pickup. It sulks, won't fire nor hit. Starter turns slowly into clicking sonances. It grumbles to life, from the dead, as a vehicular Lazarus, screams like a mechanized zombie, fishtailing, balding tires slipsliding in the slick mud, wheels semisubmerged, slewing sideways in the worst of sodden clay. He pops the clutch. Gears grind. Palms are bent as penitents. Clouds in immeasurable increments in tumultuous twirl. Contemptuous elements. Friedrich slumbers, lifts a rotten plank to see these translucent centipedes crawling. Awake, he pretends he is a prince living in exile. His great love for his mother has transformed the rhinoceros into a very lovely woman. The metamorphosis - like the magical work of a mad sorcerer who'd cast a potent spell. Fireflies are flittering flecks of iron ore.

His rapt, rodentine pies are illumined by perhaps an approximation of religious fervor, in reckoning her, an enchantress out of some sacred sect sent to maybe tempt him. She looks as a kind of freshfaced, fullfigured teacher who would undoubtedly be the recipient of countless catcalls from the studentbody, in darken devotion, on a schoolyard. Friedrich has the odd feeling that they are pieces of a puzzle that fit. Her cute carmine smile. He regards her with an uncanny speculation. Buffalothorned horizon, from his vantagepoint. As time draws on, the two become much closer. Ofttimes he'll surprise her with a sweet hug and/or kiss when the notion strikes him and she'll reciprocate; or she will occasionally find herself initiating the affection. Lightning stalks the summits in strobic arrangements. Stormbent baobabs in the flickering dusk. His chaotic vascular organ. Stars flare down the ebon vista. Levin measures it out. The joint is crept with creepers and ivy. Terminally ill, Friedrich, throbbing, perspiring, athwart the sodden, blanketed mattress, suggests some sort of schizoid carpetrider. Elna's thick, dirty, discalced feet smell of loam in the sanctity of this spacious sickroom. Limitless landscape. Broken variegated shards of stars. Wraithfield in the eddies of mist. Owls call inquisitively in the vaporous pitch. Conspiratorial sibilations of honeysuckle and its heady reek. Fragile fence gone to climbing plants. A couple of russet Eurasian kestrels wheel in the flawless azure verged with being faulted by forming cirri. His oculi are bloodred and veined with malicious malady, flesh leached into ancient, sallow parchment. He manages to reconstruct remembrances of the most adorable Amahle in his head. Phantasmagoric phosphorescence. Skyline soars through eternity. Jaundiced unblinking eye of the moon. A tawny booted eagle squawks as a rusted hinge. Maze of lala palms. Gaudy constellations alter the gloam. Slick scum, vile green, on a pond. Flocks of sooty falcons are souls raptured up into the profound heavens. Nasty weather reverts to nice. Washedout midmorning sun blazes. Skeletal marulas and mopanes. Her breath's comparable to the musk of apples. Insectan drone. Her diaphoresis like tart, winy juice. Is there a sign in his sickness? A message to be deciphered in his suffering? She is absolutely alone, burning as a solitary candle. His limbs are not unlike sticks at this point. Jaundiced pallor. He bays as a foxhound. Zephyrean spookspeak telling talltales ofttold. Autumnal verdurous grails, the precip sissing in them. Apparently sourceless lambency lists out of coagulations of cumuli, merges into a row of Natal Mahoganies. An opaque stream courses down the windowpane, creates a sketch of cleanness in the crud. Humpbacked Cape vultures contained in commiserations, or council. She is in a constant state of sorrow he brings into focus. Her drops of sweat is like beads of oil. She maintains a biblical attentiveness of maternal dedication at his bedside. She gropes for a way to exist as a human being instead of rhinoceros, struggles to live this life in the world at large. Sanctuary of pines. Sitting on the hearth in front of the dormant fireplace and sobbing. She collects herself and reads a hymnbook to him. He dies silently and her heart falls as a stone. Slipstreams of dustbunnies. She is barefoot and sleepyeyed, wearing a calflength nightgown. Horrific visions haunt her sleeping and waking. Her ears sound like horsy hooves on macadam. Riffling through a clothing catalog to distract herself. She mewls her inarticulate grief.

Friedrich and Elna had lived an idyllic existence. It ended tragically. Elna now works as a nurse in a hospital, subtly gone to seed, as a fairytale building which could, conceivably, be a gnomic residence, with its cobblestone driveway lined with tamboti and weeping- wattle. It could certainly pass for a portion of a city sacked eons ago, only never forgotten. Blacktop crossroads. Happenstantial automobiles like circus trickriders on break in the cracked-cement parking lot. Medical institution hubbub. Identical aluminum angels stand sentinel at the gate leprose with corrosion. Lilac luminosity. Misty field. Her fellow employees find her to be eccentric and she's ostracized. Luan is admitted, in the narrow hall with its chemical odor, having broken his leg in an accident. He is evidently confident he is in capable hands, calm and strapped securely on the stretcher. He recognizes Elna, and informs a doctor, Jubulani, with protuberant hartebeest lamps, flat proboscis, and canary-yellow teeth, also bald, bulky and oldmaidish, and a little long in the tooth, that Elna is, in reality, a rhinoceros, hiding in human form. Rhinos are active through most of the night, and when it warms up in the day, around 9-10 am, their eyes droop, movement is significantly slower, with moments of inactivity, and he has noticed these dramatic changes in her job performance during this time period. Jubulani believes it is on par with the Salem witchcraft trials where the outsider is the scapegoat. Porcelain jazzy Muzak breaks into shards as a dropped teacup. She has a solid, reputable position in the community! Her job performance is impressive! Luan, however, has leverage, because he has powerful friends in high places who help fund the hospital. Jubulani essentially disregards these ridiculous words, for acknowledging them would surely lend them an undeserved credence. He studies the rangy big-game hunter warily, as if he's gauging whether or not he meets the criteria he judges people by. Standard stethoscope is yoked around his bull's neck. The ludicrous allegation is beyond his powers of comprehension, past the realm of probability. Luan's ideas are like malignant cells of an embryonal cancer. His cleft chin rests on the arch of his villose, arachnidan hands, a vein pulsing as though something alien and vermiculate is wiggling beneath the skin of his temple. Elna feels controlled, as an impersonator is mimicking her and a puppeteer is pulling strings to manipulate her movements. She doesn't feel like there's safety in numbers here. Her blinders dart away, avoiding ocular contact with Luan. The nearby staff's reassuring raunchy camaraderie. Patients in the sterile, nighcolorless corridor are not unlike mourners in a funeral procession. EMTs revenantial. A blandfaced, limpideyed, stoopshouldered securityguard, stricken with a shruggy twitch, is vigilant and stationary in anatomic erectility. A stink is vaguely vegetal. Heavyset orderly converses with a dishwater-blond vendor. Jubulani, seething beneath the surface, sigh a staccato static, explains in detail about her exemplary professionalism and impeccable ethics, gives specific examples. He says speaking hypothetically, going out on a limb, for the sake of argument, supposing there is even a semblance of truth to be sought out, how could one approach actually proving such an outrageous accusation? Persistent precipitation gathers. Boughs wave metronomically.

Luan, flushed to the deepest crimson, insists he knows of an infallible test to prove he is right about Elna. Jubulani reluctantly agrees, having little choice in the matter. Elna feels anxious and clammy. Memories are for her as images drawn in chalk on a board and erased, with faint traces left behind. She feels like a form devoid of shape. Her heart taps as a blind person's cane. It is difficult for her to deal with the many differences of the universe she is presently discovering and the one from the past. Experiencing an impending sense of dread. To her, this situation is preordained, her previous animalian life was a rehearsal for this humanistic one. Luan, with his bent dagger of a nose, carved cheekbones, jaw askew like a pro pugilist's, leathern derma and amberous eyes, breath redolent of a wetland's putrescent gasses, explicates there are options and alternatives that are feasible, proffers a hand, poised in midair, to seal the bargain, and Jubulani, trembling violently, glowering levelly at him, hesitantly shakes it. Zigzag fissures in the creamy ceiling. Dimestore tortoiseshell glasses. Chairs are as mockups of furniture. Rain reeks of a rotten log. Drip drums and flute quavers seep from unseen stereo speakers and gradually work on her system in mysterious ways. Luan, snake-oil smooth, his cologne with the fragrance of curing wood, touches Elna's shoulder and she flinches, like she was burned. Flaps-of-dead-flesh-clouds dangle from the livid face of firmament. He fancies the secret blossom of her curvaceous body, irresistibly voluptuous, pleasingly plump buttocks, her slightly sagging breasts sandwiched against his scrawny chest, hearing the reap of her soughs, his respiring rattling as cutlery as he imprisons her heavy hips with his hands. Riotous growth on a rocky outcropping. Elna feels like a defendant on trial in the court of law, that Luan is the prosecutor, and Jubulani is the lone juror in this case. Jubulani isn't prepared to divine any dizzying revelation. He cannot make neither head nor tails out of this nonsense. Luan's mad as a fucking hatter. She feels like she's imprisoned in an enemy's camp. She believes in signs, is terrified of inevitability. Geometric tiles of the linoleum floor. She is motionless and mute, contained in an attitude of listening, the intricate designs of cogitations collected in her cranium dissipating. Illumination slides as illusory imaginings in a fulgent, febrile skull. Rows of phallic flowers, evoking Venus flytraps, are arranged with antiseptic precision in a high-tech hothouse nursery.

Elemental play of rapturous chiaroscuro. In the vastitude of the grasslands, at a water hole and feeding area, in lambent luminescence, Elna is introduced to some rhinoceroses. Something akin to recognition flashes in her eyes. They interact with her, communicate with her, with vocal sounds, using facial expressions and body language, conveying different messages. Jubulani, scholarlylooking, with a duck-like waddle, concludes the fairhaired huntsman is vicious and vindictive, permits himself an acute stare. Is allowing this asinine charade to continue a lapse in judgment? His physiognomy expresses anger and contempt. Deluge tinkles as chimes. He has a banker's professional politeness, intonation coarse. He appears readied for departure. His heavylidded eyes squint, sundrenched. Can he stop up the holes where her life is spilling out? He's deceptively amenable. Fear is woven into his inflection. Luan is on the verge of breeching the boundaries of civil conduct. His awkward zombie gait, his gasping laborious as a fish reeled out of water and into the air. One hunk of dialogue segues into another. Showers abrupt and absolute. His gum snapping sounds like plastic pennants flapping. He feels as a winding spring personified. Jubulani's mien is like he's stricken by grief. Brumal terrain looks as if it's viewed through smoked glass. His ponderous paunch. Vehicles in the keep of rust. Luan rambles on about his unconquerable addiction to soap operas: a daily dramatic televised pomp of entertaining crises for pretty people in perpetual flux. His homespun, shopworn tenets are redundant, not to mention irritating. She, without warning, removes her uniform and sprays urine, adds feces to a dung pile, and licks the bottoms of her feet. Luan, coldlooking in the downpour, moving like flaming fuel, tells Jubulani these bizarre actions substantiate his claims. Suddenly, Luan knocks Jubulani unconscious onto the ochreous dirt, the bulbiform MD slumping limp and ragged as a scarecrow stuffed with straw, ostensibly defying the laws of gravity and physics, and beats Elna severely on the sawdusty sand. Ectoplasmic essence of condensation. Sprinkles are rinsewater malodorous. Thread of sinuous brook. Almost audible hues of the arcuate rainbow. Her existence is a picture and she cannot completely discern the details. In excruciating pain, she caterwauls. The soaker is a vital fluid. Stray canvas tarp. Clockless time. Glowflies are as though they're miniature spirit lamps. Dispassionate chorus of the cicadas. Her suspirations are a serrate sobbing. Pond's circular and silver like a tobacco tin. Fading light. She takes to bleeding, bruising and swelling, could conceivably pass for a survivor of a carcrash calamity. Her sanguine-smeared clothes, khakis and shortsleeved shirt. Woozy, she mumbles as if she's halfwitted. Her shadow is long and short before her. Telephone wires with the residual hum of string instruments recently strummed. His vibratory, furred modulation. Snick of his switchblade knife. He stabs her once in the belly and twice in the side with the mother-of-pearl blade. She's slack like a sack of flour. Wan and homely, he hadn't shaved or washed. She is inkblack, cries as a dove. Scintillation dispelling the shade. She swallows, Adam's apple bobs, eyes bulged. Kinetic flight of waxbills from the tranquil lagoon. His deliberate walk, as though he's fording a stormswoll river. He's weary like a traveler. She is stockstill, facedown, limbs outflung, languishing in her homemade trail in the gravel from prior crawling. He drives his right whiteknuckled fist into her back, its right counterpart sent into her abdomen, and she makes this agonized whooshing sound. She had breath in her and the blow pushed it out. Unexpectedly, they scuffle, the episode reminiscent of deranged strugglers. She blindsides him, only knocking him off balance. He coldcocks her, and she falls facefirst into a fencepost. Welkin's bloodied as a butcher's paper. Tuneless whydah. Monotone of cricket. She gets a glimpse of his equine chin, viperine oculi, bovine tongue. Onecolor territory. She glares at him like he, halfdazed, broached an important code of animalistic practice, prior to passing out. The pummeling harsh and surreal. He is a stain seeping on her. A terra-cotta squirrel arcs from one branch to a nother. Nearpigmentless firmament. Stumps don fulgurous hats and doff them. Fireworks explode behind her eyelids as she begins to lose consciousness. Her visage is distorted in anguish, jaws clenched shut. Serpentiform garden hose with its metallic tongue-nozzle lies there harmlessly greenly. Pellets of hail. Taste of coin in her mouth. He revels in mixing business with pleasure. Mottled maroon empyrean. Crested barbets loop sidewise. His leonine eyes are thoroughly compassionless. His cares lifted from him with this outcome. He rips through her like a tornado tears a swath through a town. Her ticket punched by him. Was bound to happen. Her cuts recall axemarks. Crude construction of barbed wire. Kited leaves. Activities of the bateleurs, ceaseless and hardly altering. Claret cliffs create the impression of being exaggerated, and are perpendicular to them. Scruffy, semistarved, wickedlooking hyenas linger on the jutting spine of a rocky ridge, steepening by degrees, from her standpoint, their yips and yowls like from the damned souls stuck forever in Hades. Crags as slumbersome, orangebrown colossi. Frail splendor. There's no gloating attending his triumph. It is a moral victory. This was revenge. Bottom line. Dervishes of whirlwinds pluck the morose harp of mizzle. His body odor is as if it's from an ancient tomb. Zephyrian pleabargaining in onenote timbre. Sun's the clear lens of a spyglass. Date palms planted in the wrong places, she absentmindedly surmises. Her roughcut thumbnail. He relishes the sense of power he has over her. She tentatively whines, crouches and coughs. He's disappointed in her sorry showing. Red as a beat, he looks around with conspicuous concern, like a criminal checking to see if he has left any incriminating clues behind. Her lips are dry as ashes. Her garbled speech. He leans over her not unlike a baneful god over a common deity, kneeling in parodic prayer, loitering in his dominion, who refuses to do his bidding. Bedraggled unknown birds as refugees. Her pitiful whimpering grates on his nerves. Her optimism for getting out of this alive dives precipitously. Thrust into this bloodsport, her arms windmill to fend him off, futilely. Dipper in a bucket. She wails, goes boneless. Mothball-redolent plaid afghan. Would it provide a wombish warmth? Lightning blooms. Thunder rolls. Vegetation susurrates. Sleeping bats hang like velutinous fruit. Empty liquor bottle. Rain lullabies in the plenitudinous foliage. Tilted and toppled tablets, engraved script illegible, in a vinecrept, vandalized cemetery. He, a chimera made carnate, an ambulatory predator, vanishes as a rat on a sinking ship. She is wild but he didn't tame her. He maintains he's an honor graduate from the reputable school of hard knocks, and is gone like May frost, disappears like a creature of the imagination.

The image of Luan's nightmare image is burned onto Elna's retinas. He is sloe-eyed and snow-white as mashed potatoes, surly like a provoked watchdog. Raincrows dillydally in this cornfield. Bewenned burg. Her Cupid's bow chops are puffy. She feels lost in the vastity of a void, nothing even a capable compass could point to. Common cuckoos, perched in the knob thorns, are taking their ease. Her loose locks as Medusoid tendrils. Hurtling cirri. Cataracted eye of sun. She assesses it with divine fixity. Sideroad spools slowly behind her. Residences robbed of windows are rickety affairs and unsure on their flimsy foundations. Blacking out, she feels like she is plunging through a gallows trapdoor. She pictures Him clinging to her as a spider to a wall. Mocking dawn. Her leggings of dust. Kori bustards scream like meemies. Gauntlet of growth. Her face wears a perspiry film, trunk seized by nettles. Horus swifts' drunkenly whimsy. Grizzled oldster as animated statuary. Rampant poisonoak and sumac. Coucals and drongos ascend and subsequently descend like locusts on a harvest. Leafage with lace filigrees. Dreamy gingerbread chapel. Convergence of creeks. Crackerbox shanties on acreage with scarce remnants of tillage. Fruitjars and newspapers strewn. A cock crows. Her guttural pronouncements. Boulders virid with moss. Washtub and cartire held captive in deadlooking grapevines. Thesehere sedgecovered hills and hollows. Her brow is wrinkled as roiled water. Footpaths deadend. Battleship gray horizon. Spectral traces of bluish smoke. Fugitive jangles of belled goats. Hoopoes' migratory intuition approaches the alchemical. Tortured housing development of stovepiped shacks, with their fair share of climbing kudzu, architected by the impoverished with impunity. Hoarfrost-whitish effulgence. She shuffles, hobbles, not unlike an arcane crippled thing, hitherto unsighted by men, moving with such care and caution, as a marionette controlled by an incompetent puppeteer. Some squatters stake untrusty claim on them. Traumatized, tired and wounded, she trudges reluctantly, stepping gingerly, like she's treading on thin ice, on the sandbar of silt. A halfgrown housecat deceased maybe from natural causes. Stagnant puddles. Brake of cane. In the overgrown pigweed she feels as an actress making the obligatory curtain call. Huts, buckled, look to've been perhaps dumped from a significant height, aligned like a heartless sampling of the wares of the poor on display. Pewter vault encysted with sun. She is still in indecision in the sienna dusk. Oblique and deceptive refulgence. She's stiff and sore. Her countenance congested with discomfort, the planet tilting on its axis. Down the stretch of mucky path she is as a racehorse getting her second wind. She thinks, on occasion, she is going to peter out! She's in the mood for a meal of pork and beans, sausage patties, and a melted Hershey's chocolate bar for dessert! A spotted crake goes fey in the irongray celestialsphere. Quinine-bitter spate. Hushed, eerie, bewildering cosmos. Unshapen edifices. Skidmarks in muck. Gaptoothed, asymmetrical cave entrance in a quarry. Umbrageous liquiform pooling. Her mind is wholly muddy from the tatters of the ordeal she endured. Jalopies inoperable enshrined on cinder blocks. Lanes taken greedily by the wilderness. Calcified bones. She strenuously shambles. Dung matting her tangled tresses. She ruminatively chews on a piece of straw. Moltenslag rainfall. Cordite whiff like from struck flint on a broad scale. Unchoreographed ballet of baobabs, the drearyday etiolating into nightransparency. Peaky moon. Achromatized length of a rivulet. Elna miraculously transmogrifies into a rhino. She was left to die by Luan, only lives. She retains language and memory. She envisages his mismatched facial features, like his lineaments were made of clay and an unskilled sculptor took experimental liberties and left in the middle of the session. Roadmap of exploded capillaries unfolded on his schnoz. When he hit her his action was as a unisex, one-size-fits-all move he kept in stock. His jaws were clamped like a steel trap. His oral cavity was closed as a coffin's lid. She was twinned in his berrybright blinkers.

His slit for a mouth. Leantos not unlike for littlefolk, gone partially to hemlock. Disintegrated masonry. Rubescent rage flares in the vista. A pole has impaled a shanty as if a stake was rammed into its heart. Azure is shimmery and ephemeral. Lapdog at a henhouse. Concussions of polyrhythmic wingbeats heard. He was a monstrous figure out of a hallucinatory feverdream. Rising and falling cadence of his voice. Refracted moon. Pitterpatter of the spritz. Scraps of subdued vulpine barking. She collapses like a structure with its support beams kicked away. Covert snarls in the rubber euphorbia. Her grunt has the sonance of finality. Machinery gone to rust as though they are the neglected toys of puerile gargantuas. The deranged tenant of a ruin of a shack with its doorless cavity waves sarcastically. The torrent drums arrhythmically. Sun in the careless bluelid, clocking in the cumuli, tantalizing and inaccessible, at once familiar and foreign. Woods save the dark, nullifies the light. Druidic organizations of stones. Her penumbrous selves grow and shrink. These stygian mopanes. Elongated, electronic screams from demented individuals, natives nearby. Condensation has the scent of hickory shavings. Walls of the wilds close in on her. Metamorphosis, hers, was like coruscation changing from passing cloud. A bough dangles precariously. Luster banishes shadow. She envisions pone and sardines, salivates. Fortunetelling witchwoman. Sky is where the clouds hold sway. Stars candled through ligneous slashes of branchlets. Shrouded specters of ipils. She has the patience of an animal to track Luan and gore him. He, hunkered, scuttles crabwise. He is a slithering reptile. His grievances are indistinguishable, sound as imprecations of fervid faith. He quickly strokes her like an alien pet. But there's no pet in her. Sun beckons in the cirri as a promise. His physog is contorted in histrionic hambone horror, a luckless feller caught in a catastrophe. She was drawn to him like a fly to feces. He staggers in a wooden motion. Boughs creak as the saddle of a horserider. Soggy plants. Cumuli churn like spumescent gouts in a whirlpool. He checks out her blinders as an amateur astronomer charting paired stars. Fulgor doesn't have much last to it, attributed to the clouds. Disc of moon. Twilight runs like spilled quicksilver. Bluffs anomalous dominate out of the brume. In the vapor it looks as if his existence is being erased. His squawk echoes. His tennisballsized baldspot. Allencompassing verdure. He had a curious eye for her at the hospital. Skyline's stark and dimensionless. Inhabitants like archetypes out of a childhood feverine vision. Sleety stuff in the scrub sounds as the scuttling of crabs with their claws dragging. His rictus rodentially sharp. He's tense, tight like a tugged catapult. Ranges of knolls are areas of mystery. His doubles over, gut accordioned, watching her with washedout eyes. Copper wires of his hair's strands. Sable shadows writhe as though souls in torment. Freefloating cloud. He is bowed, like an aspirant in awe, the religiose kowtowing to the Almighty. He snivels as a puppy craving attention from its preoccupied master, oral cavity a lunar crater. He burrows into the soggy shrubbery like some massive mole. He is a filmic villain pushing the envelope of what separates fact from fiction. Potbellied lowlifes, with cotton moccasin lamps, cockfight, the duality of their natures emboldening them. Their voxes as icechoked backwaters. Vibrant avians. Atmosphere is pregnant with further brutality. A motley crew cheering them on, sound as a profane rustic choir. Ground bloodied, a perverse pagan's sacrificial table. A bee-eater relinquishes a rubious rock. She's committed to endeavoring to comprehend. Highpitched keening of seagulls; a bansheelike howling. Longnecked crane and varietal archaic machinery - paralyzed prehistoric beasts keeping cognizance of their existence, waiting for the weight of their cosmical sentence that must be borne in time. Eve is composed of obsidian ectoplasm. She plods with a deft economy of movement, advances as a harbinger of doom, pictures ravenhaired Friedrich, his naptousled mop, and roly-poly Jubulani, pacing like a dancing bear turned aloose, glowering at the Great White Hunter with incredulity. Bleeding, haysmelling, gaunted, Luan, aspect grim, as if he's petrified in the epicenter of a holocaust, kisser caven and ravaged, pleads pathetically for his life, on all fours, and the begging chickenshit calls her "Elna." She responds Elna doesn't exist, adds a snort, and mercilessly stomps on him, crushing him to death. She has a lukewarm feeling of wellbeing. She sleeps peacefully, her dreams vivid. She achieves a distinct remove from society, convinces the other rhinos to forever rebel against mankind ... and so onto the rounded edge of the warping world.

FIN.

Lion in Winston

Our obdurate, creatural midget, the very British Winston Reade, anatomically suggests an observation balloon mixed with a praying mantis. He has alabastrine skin, domical head, russet rug of hair glued to a glabrate pate (the scalp smooth as a pool ball), cartilaginous ears, anuran eyes (abrim with tears), cormose nose, scimitar-shaped lips, bulbaceous body, and pipe cleaner limbs. He's immaculately dressed in a tweed suit and wears shiny buckled shoes. His vision is tunnelesque. He is no master of men. Moon's at crescent. Overcast is black like outer space. Air's ammoniated with rain. The metropolis is odoriferous as a dumpster. His gait is not unlike an arachnidan scuttle combined with a reptilian slither. He was born exactly twenty years ago today. His mother's birth canal was the rabbit hole. He was born and she had died. He goes through the drizzle, floating as a ghostly manifestation. The mangled mutant, with a beautiful mind, was recently excrementitiously flushed down the toilet (place of employment). The sky's rainbow is as the (variegated) muscle-stripes on a womb's wall. He now lurches monstrously down the lunar city's street damp with blood, drool, snot, slime and sewage, attempting to ignore the harsh stares of passers-by, people swimming in their salmon flow. Overwhelming smells of fish and fuel penetrate his flared nostrils. He just lost his job as an entry-level file-clerk at the low-rent law firm, fired for insubordination. He simply could not handle the daily drudgery, not to mention the horrible harassment, from his fellow workers, any longer. It is 1938 and he is seriously contemplating committing suicide. Knee-jerk reaction? Perhaps. Jump off a bridge in cement shoes? Possibly. Hang from a sturdy tree? Maybe. So many options! Then he considers Clara Debney, the cherubic love of his life, his childhood sweetheart, her sense of humor, horsey laugh, toddlerish teeter-totter, angelic glow, dwarven proportions, pale flesh, beetle brow, ivory, charmingly chipped teeth, infantile hands and feet, and banishes these awful thoughts of self-destruction from his mind.

Winston's aural orifice aches. Was the wax made by bees? he wonders, suffering through a particularly unpleasant and unsuccessful enema, performed by an incompetent roly-poly medic with a crew cut and copious mustache, without anesthetic, in a rank tent. Failure not earning any kudos. The base is established on a magic mountain. Thoughts rise in Winston's skull like dust-motes from a surface. Exfoliated flakes of scurf drift on his stooped, stocky shoulders. He scratches his itchy nape. Division of labor distributed ... concerning his senses. He imagines submerging himself in cold and clear spring water. His stumpy neck, inflexible as steel, feels stung by scorpions. Beside him, on the dirt floor, a thin and tall recruit, recalcitrant, heroic and handsome, grim face green and wrinkled like a wet pea, gets a molar extracted and, subsequently, a boil lanced by a divine, angular, aurulent nurse. Dazzling light is like a epiphany. Cankerous clouds. It is hotter than fucking hell. A screech sounds as a raven's. Soldierly unnatural selection process is currently on gruesome display. Olivaceous land and lapis lazuli sea are stupefied by the scorching sun. The hirsute lieutenant, once a grotesque megalomaniac, visage encumbered by a pantagruelian proboscis, is dead from tuberculosis on the filthy cot next to him. Myriad military emergencies. Troublesome insects. He thinks of Clara: she can expose one's true personality as the vestal chastity of lugubrious lambency can the colours of the earth in their unspoiled state. Lord, he misses her. Oh, the mistakes he's made ... Disarmed and defeated, temporarily out of commission, he uriniferously nitrogenizes the Eden-esque shoots of grass in circular arcs. Unfathomably deep forest, viridian, beyond the muddy, cratered battlefield, retreats, at least optically, in the thick, meandrous smoke. A goat indignantly bleats. Impudent cliffs situated on the boundary of the beach, in the lackadaisical luminosity, have the insouciance to, illusorily, impiously give God the finger. Operations run not unlike clockwork, for the nonce, the warriors, ice in their veins, valiant, resourceful and resilient. Their strong wills cannot be weakened. Guards will not be lowered. Regiments of elite troops march and sing songs with virility. Little Hitler and his lunatic cohorts! Their strategy sure has its teething problems. Calculations of maneuvers based on falling dice. The Fuhrer, insane and irresponsible, is igniting Europe. Villagers, industrialists, guerrillas, intellectuals and artists cast nets to catch fish, watched by native prostitutes. Youngsters have an audience of oldsters. The kids discuss whether or not inflation is actually under control (slips of the tongue), if up-to-the-moment economics are affected by the effects of cyclic capitalism, and mention the balls and brains of war as being something of sublime beauty, basically an aesthetic conception of man's poetic soul and Olympian spirit, pretentious claptrap uttered as profound sentiments. Winston refuses to participate in the poison gas experiments and chooses instead to explore the incredible island. He's still constipated. Christ! Stick of dynamite or hand-grenade up the ass should do the trick! Jackboot. Partridge. Rabbit. German enemy's most enterprising. The English empire must expand. No laurels to rest on. He has the sensation of being pulled in different directions at once. He's got the simultaneous urges to fight and flee. Is he grabbing the opportunity to avoid perils? Ideas are dots connecting in his cranium. Lambs ingest plenty of weeds and imbibe from sparse puddles. An arid, indomitable isle. Vertiginous summits. Mercurial flights of gulls, white like virginity. Feathery smoke plumes from a brick chimney belonging to a modest hut ringed with rocks.

Broken bolts, children's toys, rusty nails, and lizards. He's beguiled by the exotic locale, and besotted by potent booze, thinks of his inexcusable foolery that put him in harm's way. Infinite hubris. Surf laps against the shore. He's in an inescapable position. His country shows him no charity. Daydreaming of the megalopolis, a pseudo-Byzantine, bourgeois town on a vaster scale, and remembering his first hire - Samson, built as Atlas, a living caricature of a giant with titanic power and leonine mane, wearing a rather silly, frilly pirate shirt, comical pantaloons, and ridiculous curlicue shoes, second in line at the cattle call held at a defunct warehouse in a gritty neighborhood. His theatrical schtick was bench-pressing a hefty human being for the impressionable and inquisitive Winston, who was quite impressed. The Grand Guignol with circus freaks was a hit with the crowds. The critics weren't as kind. Journalists savaged the production, were loud in their written attacks in the articles. He couldn't silence the press. Booms of weaponry. Verdurous Nazarene hair. A mule brays and canters. Projectiles suddenly tear the terrain. Some ricochet. He ducks, takes cover in the dense bushes. Rupert Debney is indeed a dandy, lean like a lamppost, effeminate and yet strong as an ox. He glissades ceremoniously, graceful like a swan coasting on a pond. Winston'd tried to mend fences with him, his stubborn brother-in-law, in a minute of excruciating suspense, repair their volatile relationship, in an atmosphere of hostility. The two never got along. Too many acerbic comments on his diminutive stature, nasty remarks about his disabilities. Rupert had no respect for him, felt he couldn't measure up to his cherished Clara's standards as her husband. She, so proud and willful, deserved better. And Winston serves under his command on the front lines. Rupert has a nose that resembles the brassy Damascus barrel of culverin. He is anthropomorphised accumulated ammunition. He is blisteringly intoxicated on absinthe, very high on opium. Are his addictions curable sicknesses? He has honor, esteem and bravery to spare, a Homer-esque courage the Almighty infused into him. He fails to resist the inexorable forces of his destructive habits. Not long ago, he, principles cast into a fiery furnace, personal and national integrity demolished, knowing full well Winston wouldn't survive and endure, had decided to send him on a messianic mission to capture a top SS officer, the avianish Karl Hanke, overseeing the sophisticated projects of constructing a fortification and repairing a railroad, even if he has to drag him kicking and screaming, cursing and protesting as a problematic patient. Rupert selected Winston and fitted him into the role for the sole reason that he was capable of informing Clara of the demons he's battling. He could not permit this to happen. He isn't really worried evidence could be compiled and revealed (sentencing Winston to imminent death in a veritable suicide assignment), because of his impeccable record and stellar reputation. He was able to read the plain chemical composition of Winston's apprehension. His decision wasn't met with argument, incident, impasse. Rupert camouflages his dependence like one would conceal leprosy. The clues are there to be detected. Skeletons won't tumble out of the closet.

Winston catches the current of the command and drifts with it. He gathers his mandatory Will-To-Power. With his unit, it won't be a case of the three hundred Spartans versus the five million Persians, a mathematical challenge which doesn't compute. They are, Winston and Rupert, Sodom and Gomorrah destroyed by life. Mysterious territory. Showers sputter as lit fuses. Winston is loyal to his superior, doesn't possess a Judas touch in a classic tragedy. He waddles, sweats, moans and groans with the effort of movement, a catalogue of telltale symptoms of exhaustion circumstances oblige him to summon, lips pursed like a trout's, perspiry drops, sparkling in the unexpected luminescence, dripping on his jutting forehead and countenance, crumpled in concentration and flushed crimson. Finally, a fart! Rumble, followed by a colossal roar. Boys, semi-naked on the crystalline sand, with immodesty and intemperance, dance the samba and tango, indecently and idiotically. Too damn inelegant and vulgar! Lads from an immature civilization. They consort and frolic with local ladies. Lilac and orange flame of the empyrean. He is stuck here. He can't pass the reins, or rifle, to another. He was given a sword, so to speak, by his nation, and he has to draw it. Eating anchovies and bread sprinkled with oregano and drinking ale. In this warring world he's fated to inhabit he is an alien to his race. He suffocates in a brutal environment, as a plant from lack of illumination and oxygen proper. Formidable stream of piss released. Gurgling belch unleashed from his bottom. Transparent brilliance. He realizes with increasing honesty that he's a cat among wolves. Placid pines, erect and shivering in clammy breezes, silvered by emanation. Sun's a distended, disembodied bladder. Clara, at this juncture, is an imaginary woman, a fictitious female, in his cosmos of males. In spite of their legal separation, he has a canine fidelity to her. Soft and delicious not unlike cheese, she constitutes the majority of the febrile recollections in his noggin. Memories of her are precious, pure, obscene and perverse. Diaphoresis dribbles down his kind of lardaceous torso. Remembrances of her, positive and negative, are permanently preserved in the museum of his mind. He's aberrant. An anomaly. Why did his Creator muck about in his mummy's thingie and screw with him, his development, or lack thereof? His father, an aspiring thespian, always in his cups, sort of acted as a domestic foreigner, an invader. In the home: crisis, chaos. In his division - they're in the cesspit together. Would he become the patron saint of small people? He is a gladiator prepared for combat. He can be impetuous, irreverent. He's a potato among carrots, aware of the nitty-gritty nuances of everyone's moods, acquainted with their individual body odor, idiosyncrasies, proclivities. They are immortal and invincible. Equipment hangs. Lewd tunes are belted. Trenches are dug in a downpour. Rupert struts akin to a peacock, his cockerel antics absolutely annoying. He's got this Slavic physiognomy, prominent bones, lopsided mouth, and spatulate hands. His absurd gestures, extravagant voice, and overcooked speeches can sure stretch the patience. He provides penitent presents for himself, generous gifts in the forms of amphetamines and vodka, frequently visited by dilemmas he's in denial of, arbitrates disputes, advocates for truces. Hail is like lobbed mortar shells. Panic fills Winston at an exponential rate. He'll obey orders. He's haunted by the notion of dying, even for a noble cause his stoical Captain has bestowed upon him. His patriotism and ideals are important to him. Coccyx bruised, ingrown toenail killing him, an imitation of an impending injury, he trudges, wheezes. Here's a holiday vacation with nature's amenities. If he went AWOL there could be a retirement to the hermitage inherent in the wilderness! Would his absence be noticed? No. Yes. Embroidered handkerchief. Peels of fruit. Pinpricks of headlights.

Winston wants Clara to be around him, as water an islet. He withstands a urethral infection. His heart gallops, grey matter causing difficulties for his body. Facial grimy streaks. Wracking retches. A rotund kraut is recumbent in a pool of vomit in a patch of briar and scrub, a pipe clenched pensively between his discolored gnashers. Mucal stains are on his tattered trousers. Frowning, peepers slitted, peering about himself to ensure there won't be witnesses, Winston, with extreme, inexcusable cruelty and earnest expression, suffocates the adipose Aryan (who tugs pitifully at his besmirched sleeve), with a sock, gleans malicious pleasure in the attempted murder, culls satisfaction from the killing, like a savage raping and pillaging a vulnerable village. And he isn't quick as a flash, either. The expiring victim, expression exhibiting, equally, consternation and resignation, is conspicuously incapable of understanding the distinguished cause undertaken - it's a remedy for a disease. Winston exhorts himself to the heinous act, and feels a twinge of disappointment for his paucity of regret. The poincianas shudder, sympathize. Conclusive refutation of his conscience to plummet into guilt. He saunters exaggeratedly, carries his culpability like St. Christopher our Savior across the river. Caffeine and tobacco call him. Sagging barbed-wire fence. His acute dehydration. Heaving a mock sigh. His unhealthy renal functions, gait as if he is imitating an ape. The insistent itch for Clara is tantamount to a wound healing. She is a lemon he wishes to squeeze the juice out of. He's a slave to his appetite, masturbates as though a monkey, in the copious shrubbery. He muses on the scoundrels Lenin and Mussolini: parasitic bacteria in a utopian gut. He, in a clearing, mulls over a Tarzan film. His pies glow like valves in the mesh of a radio. Adjusting his spectacles and swabbing a trickle of blood from his temple. A grungy whippersnapper pets a mangy spaniel. Insufferable calidity and mugginess. Ah, for a siesta in a hammock in the evening's grasshopper concert ... Grim and ominous quietude. Kerosene barrel, pine cones, kindling pile and sharp boulders. Cirri huddle over mesas. His glistening lachrymous tracks, chubby chest thrust forward. He feels helpless, filled with rage, like he's bound and gagged as Clara is violated by sadistic rapists; or that he's a sunken ship, torpedoed by a submarine. She is an uncrackable, impenetrable code. His previous job in the military was as a motorcycle messenger, capable and reliable, demonstrating quality on a daily basis, until Rupert lead him into danger, delegating him to rescue a corpulent corporal, James, held by rebels in a watchtower in no-man's land. He'd received, while chainsmoking, a bible-thick packet of dogeared orders, maps, diagrams and photos, delivered personally by Rupert. He was chosen to do fishy business. He had no choice. He was neither important nor special. In fact, he knew he was expendable. He accepted his responsibility with suspicion, aware he was being sacrificed for the greater good, a supposedly lofty interest. It was a question of personal and military salvation. Whirlwind was in his noodle. Stiffness was in his backbone. Superstitious, he confided in his lucky charm, depended on the rabbit's foot Clara gave him. Scouting, he was efficient and enthusiastic. Duty is a sacred thing and he was compelled to do his utmost. There was a firefight and fisticuffs. Action commenced, the pandemonium was cathartic - distraction from demented thinking. He was vigorous, desperate, valorous, and dealt with distress. His popping-up goosebumps, peals of flatulence. The insurgents were compromised by inebriation. Owl-shrieks of insurrectionaries perishing. Godforsaken region. There was bloodshed and glory. Winston and James escaped, crashed into a mighty oak, and hitched a ride on the back of a damaged tank and returned to HQ. His life didn't matter much. It was a successful operation. There was no medal ceremony. Winston was quickly transferred to latrine duty. He is not obsequious. He's no sycophant. He would never brown the nose. He respects authority, has no impertinent attitude. Chewing hastily cooked octopus on a shipwreck-strewn beach and watching dolphins slicing through innumerable serrate smirks of waves. He pictures handling Clara with solicitude. She's sensual, scantily contained in lace and pearls topped with a conical paper hat, bum bared. Her bulbiform buttocks, flesh like velvet, are identical halves of a melon. She is nun-garrulous, hedgehog-snuffles. Stench of the corpses stuffed in a well. He's got a penile banana and scrotal rash, holds his head high. A thorn is embedded in his swollen ankle. He looks as an athlete about to throw a javelin. His shadow cowers. A public toilet would be comparable to a bishop's throne to him at this juncture. Vaporous spectres disappear as unaccountably as they'd appeared. Anxious, anticipating more carnage, he yearns to bury himself in the earth's bowels; or be sealed in a monastery's sarcophagus. Rainbow's a prodigy of wondrous hues. Labyrinthine subterranean cisterns are contaminated. He squats for a second, turmoil in his sternum. Mummified cadaver. Emaciated wild hare. Stars nictate an intricate micaceous semaphore. Leaves, sere from summer, rustle in the stands of figs and planes. Teenagers in bathing suits, hysterical, flail and convulse in the encroaching tide. Winston, exhilarated, scrutinizes them. Sparrows and warblers flitter and squabble. Daisies and poppies sway almost in unison. Plangent tones of his flatus. Line of elms are recollective of epileptics. Shells like metalloid butterflies. A rubicund priest, in ecclesiastical distinction, gibbers and squawks to himself, wandering, biblical quotes sounding as nonsensical nursery rhymes blurted out by an inmate in an institution, whilst he lugs waterjugs and washbowls. Knots of fishermen in pastoral merriment. Buzz of their chatter. Shuffle and jostle. Voluble conversations. He's afflicted with trepidation. Soldiers swarm as bees. Species of susceptibility.

Ripples of expressions pass through his phiz like those found in a pool, caused by a tossed ball. Intolerable sticky calescence. In an interregnum of lucidity, he puts together the mnemonic pieces of a Clara jigsaw, a source of flirtation, in a royally subdued posture of supreme regality; or a regression of self-inflicted incapacity, and he trembles and weeps. Kaleidoscope of refracted brilliancy. Hill surmounted and grove traversed. Tinnitus chiming as goatbells. Rain's a glistening foil fluttering down. Ambrosial adolescents play a mandolin and bagpipes, making music which emerges from opposite ends of the melodic spectrum. He jumps like a grasshopper, sports an insuppressible smile, conjuring Clara, the grin producing proof of his excitation. Choir of nightingales. Posse of pubescents, garbed satirically in outrageous getups, dials daubed, in metaphysical alliance, quarrel. Other juveniles and their polyphonic ululations, intractable anarchy. Polkas and waltzes are efficiently executed. Adults are capsized. Firecrackers are tossed. Pirouetting and cavorting cuties. Bedraggled Winston numbly appraises, with blurred vision, his befouled breeches, snickers with mirth at the revelers. Gloom gathers itself. Gibbous moon gleams metallically in the spate. Unidentifiable stink. Traipsing, his backside bellows as a bull when it's taken by the horns. He dumps his rucksack and slumbers seraphically, taking advantage of the poignant jungle's hospitality ... Waking, he invents reasons to interrupt his inadvertent imaginings of her. Insectile carpentry. He is filled with an insupportable mixture of happiness and sadness.

Slight strangulation of her customary mellifluent

modulation. His heinie wauls not unlike a tomcat. Fulgent filaments through shutter- slats of plants on the precipice. In absentia, he experiences the pleasing pressure of her weight, her anatomy assailed by the invasion of an incubus, Winston, ashen-faced. Naked as Adam and Eve, they are entwined in an embrace, their palpitations palpable, both nursing hangovers, bodies with unexplainable abrasions, in a tranquil idyll, tongues furred, suggestions of salacity ironically disguised. Although imperfect, he is circumspect, humane, patient. She'd annihilated him, blushed and stammering, in a backgammon match, and he took evasive action. Absorption of a matted marten, squeaking and ruminating on a path's curve. Imposing mounts. His solitude is appreciated. He surrenders, on a peak, to the enemy that is his obsession. He is enslaved to the master of his fixation. He's wayward, in a pall of dejection, in balletic pointless business to offset the void of Clara. His cumbrous totter, raucous renditions of popular ditties. He steams like a warship, feels as a meager plaything, discarded by Her. To hear her euphonious language again … One hundred meters (or more) distant, a paterfamilias Poseidon wades into the aqua pura, teal and shifting, with, presumably, his nymphean progeny, au naturel, the family as ephemeral dream-creatures, and they reel in a crescentiform net with a plentiful haul of aquatic life. An asphyxiating argent fish, an animated, scaly blade, flops on the sienna sand. Dorsal fin carves its way along. Hotness and humectation having a ferment which amounts to vindictiveness. His delirium, desolation … To return to private life … is this even possible? These diamondiferous stars. Moon, covered by a cumulus, is like a monocle misting over.

Weather turns against him. Serenity's shattered by sirens, shouts and explosives. Lurid pigments of the firmament, impregnated by cloudlets. Winston squints. His frontage looks like it was scratched by a psychotic kitty. Multitudinous exclamations. Bombs blast. Winds whoosh. Owls hoot. Strategic points are visibly occupied by opposition troops. His testicular discomfort'e nagging. There is no escaping the escapade he is embroiled in. He'd deftly severed lines of supplies and communications. He expects to be dead in due time. He isn't straining on a leash. He feels isolated, betrayed. Rupert's plot was preempted by legitimate events. Winston was sent off to die with insufficient provisions. He heeded the instructions. There was no resistance, defiance. Victory was snatched from the jaws of defeat. He treks across treacherous mountainous ranges, lives off the land. He is not AWOL. He's demoralised, disaffected, imbued with incalculable weariness. Pubes squirm with lice. He dredges up the top-secret training camp where he was chiseled into a commando, taught by lantern-jawed instructors with comical moustachios. He practiced the art of infiltration and sabotage, schooled in initiating 'incidents.' His first solo errand was eliminating, adroitly, a transformer. The second was assassinating a general. He felt as if he were David who defeated Goliath. Third was to encourage the population to destabilize their leaders' territories and to revolt against their oppressors. Fourth was to protect, with a handful of greenhorns, a frontier post. A demobilization effort was ordered and he was left high and dry with no hope for reinforcements. Fifth, degradingly, was burning propaganda pamphlets. He was promptly congratulated for "outstanding contributions." The victories were gratifying. He guessed. Sunny, secluded, no-name island and its amiable inhabitants. He roams unopposed, slogs through the mire, stunted limbs swinging, struggling, feet subsiding in the morass. A battered ally truck carrying artillery bogs down in the clinging mud, is beslimed by it. Rank ulceration. Gangrenous mephitis. Distinctive yowls of amputation. Winston repines, compulsively steals stale biscuits, fisherman's sweater and raincoat (khakis are encrusted with dirt) from the squalid hovel of a roofless cabin and steps over fly-infested carcasses of sheep. He had rummaged like a pig in a trough. Gory scraps of human skin dangle on scarred evergreens' trunks. He spots ghastly German ghouls swiveling. He whirls as a dervish, has no support, pivots, arms and legs feeling like leaden shillelaghs. Coruscation quivers with life. Pack of dogs aimless. He yens to see a congregation of his comrades, those glorious, granitoid gladiators. His rifle's rusted. Ambushes, lunacy, enfilades. In the copse he's a wick threaded through a cork and languishing in an emerald lagune, floats as though in a bowl of olive oil. Flying in the face of the normal. He is an impassioned automaton. Resting, regrouping, intermittently. An English battalion gets muddled up in crude chasms, monstrous ravines, enveloped by an accursed storm. The tempest is the equivalent of a Titan's fist raining down punches. Shrapnel gouges deep notches into the outmaneuvered platoon.

Thankfully, he's not participating in the fray. His regimentals are adamantine-hardened with filth, derma layer not unlike cardboard. Corroded, pathetic hulks of panzers sucked into the muck. Mortars snap. Tired bones, tummy void of nutritional sustenance, brain made maniacal, being beaten. Incarnadine ground. He journeys in a daze, evolving in a continuity of emotions, flounders on the bend of a road where warhorses and reservists hump with haversacks, in a homogeneity of mind and disposition, huff and puff, look as if they've gone through the gates of hell. He's seized by a mood of compulsive determination to continue with a ferocity which amounts to violence. He diagnoses his symptoms of depression, doesn't need a medic visitation. He was instructed to embark on improbable militant pursuits that were unfeasibly challenging. Jerking off is a prophylactic against horniness for Her. Bismuth for the syphilis (got, at port, from copulating with a porcine brunette with a brushing of flaxen down on her upper lip and a penchant for buggery and booze and narcotic predilections and skill for torpor and inertia) he copes with is pertinent. He had drilled her admittedly polluted orifices on a stack of cushions, and skewered her, sprawled, on a sheaf of papers on the shady balcony of a baroque brothel. She had brown moles on her floccose, flabby nates. The ebullient and eccentric madam was in the old-school mold. She could be an unmitigated tyrant, he found out. There were argumentative whores. It was like a family feuding. Machinations resulted in such merciless in-fighting. He peruses the medical encyclopedia, a massive volume, as a Muslim does the

Koran. Welkin is the indication of the generality of a red line of demarcation between healthy and infected areas of the flesh. Rupert's uncannily cunning as though he were Odysseus. He, sociable, stoned and soused, went on about his civilian private life. His preoccupation with himself is deplorable. Winston lies on the faultline that separates him from Rupert. He sniffs the stagnant air, cock erect. Clay's coated in a carapace of dried blood that once drenched it. His genitals smart. Noisomeness is enough to banish Satan. He discharges nuggets of turds in tulips slathered in claret membrane. Barrage of coughing machine-guns scares the buzzards away from their potential booty of bodies. Tunic sanguineously soaked. Envisaging a long slow descent into his demise and envisioning an ascent into heaven. Gigantean rodents. He doesn't participate in the triumphalism of a British conquest of a German encirclement. Prismatic humanoids armed. A hermit's congealed cascade of mop, the vagrant breathing stertorously and phlegmily, neck bound in hematic bandages, having the reek of ancient dung, enough to disturb the deceased, ill-aspect camouflaged in fuzz and crud, roves in a fluidic and elliptical fashion, an islander with the aura of an infidel, skinny as tripwire, locks carrying a cargo of nits, integument hanging in sheets, ribs and spine protruding, an apparitional wreckage with much pus and scab. Winston analyzes him like he's a problem to solve; or cattle he's thinking of purchasing. Haggling cranes. Thunder sounds as the voice from a throat contracted in the grip of polyps. Stutters of levin. Vault seems to suppress a succession of spasms. Clara is a pristine icon whose image will nullify the lousy sensations he's experiencing. His foot decay is like the Argonaut Philoctetes's. His eczema is exasperating. The ritual of inspection of his penial ailment is a daily rite of passage. Lightning's wriggling yellow maggots. Thunder growls as the ocean in a squall. Carmine nodules on his chunky thighs aggravate. For some zinc and/or sulphur! Bug bites on his calves, scabies on his equipment. He curses himself for his presumptiveness and prognostication. Scrupulous examination of his stools. He feels mowed down like corn, diminished, sustaining indignities. His love is sinew that binds him to comely Clara as muscle to bone. His groin's pings and pangs. His loins surge. Umbral form dims his vision. His twittering heart's a bird flailing futilely in a cat's jaws. He is not worthy of her. Why she left him. He's not good enough for her. He hates himself, in spite of his sacrifices for his country, fighting for it with everything he has. With her, he can be salvaged, remade, renewed. Chaffering cicadas in the marsh. Strain and malnutrition. Azure is clogged with chaotic clouds. Flowers are bursting into bud. Rubescent hawk soars over a pellucid cataract. Slipping on shale and scree. Peaty water. Lynx, pigeons, deer, bats. A withered hag, bowed and bent, with a cavernous maw, this senile crone kept in rags, the shriveled scarecrow seeping with sores, caws like a crow. A bombardment of acorns out of the blue. Soil's soft as a blanket. He dreams his prick is an instrument of conflict. Malice and caprice of the vespers. Laid to waste by wartime, nothing else matters to him except Her. Chastity of the coppice. Shreds of his uni. Fatigue a fog. He is a flame snuffed out. He's like a spirit of the dead. Sparks swirl as souls of diffident seraphim. In the mist, foliage is veiled like a virgin. Blazing magnesium sun. Sky is as an omen of disaster. A   derelict hut, scrawled with swastikas, is acrawl with cockroaches. War sloughs its skin and reveals itself as insanity. The taste of everything left behind rolls on his tongue. He cleans the components of his pistol. Winston Reade looks like he's knocking at death's door and walking on water as Our Lord. For lentil soup and sausage! His vibratory jowls. Skeeter stingers like thumbtacks. His mouth curls at the corners as aged parchment. He feels roasted on a spit. And he doesn't agree with Plato that death is only a 'change.' Finding himself is like lifting a mat beneath a table and opening a trapdoor to discover who he is in a cavity. His infirmities abate a bit. Physically he's improving. Psychologically he believes he is devolving into a state of infancy ... apt punishment for his atheism? In a despondent stupor, he is desperately worried about his degenerating status, being reduced to a condition of dependency. He innerly dramatizes his self-imposed exile, and demonstrates his self-deception. He's motionless, as if he's rigid in rigor mortis, passive and speechless, his brain disowning his body. Purgatorial panic ensues, surrounds. Winston ravenously manducates the slivers of garlic he'd chanced upon in a ragged knapsack, facial expression eloquent of extraordinary relief, sweating on account of the harsh hike, the region tricky to navigate. MIA was Rupert's booming voice. Usually his vox would emerge, tone quavery, fluttering like a swallow youngling that had fallen from its nest, in a confidential sibilation, abysmally chafing. Automated movement of brilliantly-colored cotinga rotate as though a wheel of cogs. Lyrical passages of clamors from the dying, like romantic poetry, in geysers of sentiment, overflowing onto the page of oxygen, he fancies, and his heart flies with the angels. Time stops. Drone of planes. Dismal morn and aft. He's forlorn. Looking Glass celestial sphere and unit of parachutists as subsistent shrooms, observed through a leafy canopy of the stout evergreens and redwoods. He furrows his brows and purses his lips, Charlie Chaplin-goose-stepping. He abides abject distress, the sources of bravery and sanity draining rapidly. His being is broken. He's morose. Uncontrollable bougainvillea. His will hollow, volition a vacuum. He wrestles with his demons as Hercules with his serpents. Curfew patrol. Weather here can be tempestuous. Now, it is beautiful and balmy, despite the torments of strife. He's incredulous, grateful for these atmospheric conditions. The place gives him the impression of an Arcadia inundated with mother-of-pearl phosphorescence. Lads are rowdy, resolute in their amusements, mimicking everything soldierly, delighting in the well- deserved respite, their entertainment consisting of harassing the populace, singing rousing, resonant tunes in mock falsetto, baritone and tenor, pants rolled at half-mast. Winston resists any urge to join in. His eyebrows are raised at the chaps' barmy antics. He feels routed, vanquished, stepped on by the heel of oppressive occupation. A British battery stands at attention. Appalling fetor of communal defecation. Details of a siege are enhanced by storyteller Rupert. Winston's livid resentment of him he cannot hide, lurch of dread of meeting with him, anticipating an encounter with tremendous trepidation, bracing himself, squaring his shoulders, prepared to grunt mollifyingly while the grandiloquent dick gesticulates like a maestro, the officer possessing a conqueror's hubris, his smug profile tilted at a proud angle. Amphibious aircraft reconnaissance. A scrawny, scowling private makes notes with a blunt pencil. Orchidaceous Clara grew on the pile of shit of his life. His mitt made an exploratory pinch of her posterior, in a leap of faith, resigned to being rejected. He refused to turn tail. She would lose respect for him. Their trains of thought were running on the same track. So he did kneel, craftily penitent, begging for forgiveness. Squiggles of graffiti script on available walls, quirks of individualized handwriting exhibited, the wobbly, loopy letters cohabiting in these insulting messages to the Jerries. Reptiloid moribundity. Cartoon of Adolph committing an obscene act on himself has Winston chuckling. He would give anything for a scalpel to get rid of his corns. Disabled jeep. Fucking Fritzes. He wanders as Odysseus. His dedication has dried to dust. He feels like a flea. A blast influences him to roll as an apple off a shelf. A sizable sergeant partakes of spinach pie and rice, pleased with the inauguration of his appetite's satisfaction. Winston savours the scents, suffers from these venereal infections, haemorrhoids, and anxiety disorders. He has the luxury, the fortitude, to indulge in his illnesses. He had dwelt lovingly upon the alabaster scoop of Her tit, satiny, like it belonged to a sylph, as she, in her malachite bathrobe, robustly chopped onions and peppers at the counter in the quaint kitchen, irresistibly fetching, with her tresses in disarray, his endearments emitted with heartfelt sincerity, fondling her with a virtuoso flourish, sane in his insanity. He appreciated the articulation of her bust as he would've a Rodin masterpiece, lyre-form, soles texturally reminiscent of rosewood, a whiff of rosemary in her ringlets. They had hugged, spontaneously, like siblings rather than lovers. He was a wound she staunched. He landed in her as a spoon into a cup. Her tootsie- wootsies stank with perspiration. His cardiac organ was a reverberant bass, arachnoid shaker crawling on her haunch, symphonic expressions performed on her puss, paws clasped together like in prayer. Vibrant vagaries. He snatched her slack belly as breath from the throat. A ragamuffin announces his intention to eavesdrop on a conversation, tears rising unbidden in his blinders, muffles a cry, wraps a towel round his waist, and sweeps out. It's abominably stifling and sticky. A slug is a wiggling disembodied digit. A peasant with a tousled shock and garbed in remnants of raiment, rolls a tire from a maimed armoured vehicle undone by potholes, waves in casual greeting. Precip's needle-sharp. An ovaline organ-grinder, oculi flashing fire, with his matted monkey, neither witty nor charming. Everything is upside-down. Eagles soar. Pile of manure. Fish leap. Clouds recapitulate in relief the line of vista they emphasize. Can of ham, bottle of pickles, chunk of salami. Hairpin turns. Unholy racket. He dwells upon Rupert, surreptitiously monopolising the supply of morphine, making a sour face, drawing on his smoke, the clandestine ransacking offending the honour and decency of his rank. He sipped steaming sewage-coffee on a pallet. The day desiccates not unlike an autumnal, dried leaf. Multicolored cirri are as the creations of an expert craftsman. A violin plays a Paganini piece. He's halfway between sleeping and waking, makes advantageous adjustments of his nether parts. A thrush trills on a branch. Guitar and viola perform a pizzicato at a fast pace. Rupert behaves as if he's a mythical figure that indicates the potentialities of human achievement. Excrement smeared on a Nazi flag. Is there any plan or purpose? he questions in retrospective fright, reprisal for the hiatus. Britons, with elan and grit, dismantle viaducts ... convoluted hidden agenda of a lofty concept? Winston is, overtly, a lost soul, held together by gravity. Churning oceanic masses. Sun abolished by cumuli. Gust stuns the derma like a contusion. He purloins a Luger from a lodge in disrepair. Thoughts intermingle in his coconut as though an echo's variations of the same sonancy. In a testy mood, his cardio ratchets lower and he has a taste of rancid butter in his oral cavity. Each stride is like pulling a stitch out of crochet. Bloody mess of brain and bone. A pulpy octogenarian with a brittle mane, resembling lengthy knitted rope in swimming trunks, blinkers Aryan blue, bleeding mouths of bullet holes in his back, yelps, stumbles on striated rock, and, with tightlipped effort, sounds as if he's endeavoring to explain abstruse arithmetic, holding a bedroll for a mattress, has a mangled leg with an aborted foot ... If caught stealing drugs, Rupert, pretend-co-operative, would claim to be a hypochondriac (self-generated-and-permeated), hence the need for the medications for his manifold mysterious maladies. Morse code signaling of the stars. Songsters, apparel sandy and askew, and gipsies, plastered with cosmetics and nude, with a glamorous gossamer gloss, tawny tans, moues automatic, swish and sashay with parasols and balloons in the silken shallow water, scrubbing, squealing and splashing, showcasing, demonstrably, their seductive repertoires of arousing athletics. The girls are heliotropic flowers, lithe-legged and with perky pouchy bobbies and pert butts, muffs trimmed, lissome arms akimbo like those of Protestant preachers welcoming the newly religious into the fold. They are in high spirits, vertiginously spinning, sweet and silly, not having a care in the world, comely occupations for the gaze. Boys, some, are polite and submissive, others seize up as though mechanisms; or they're masters of disguising their ferment. They glare at him like he is a ne'er-do-well; or they study him with expressions of scientific objectivity. He pretends to ignore them, this designed for the annulment of his ardency, grows abashed, and darts through the thicket as a fish through weed, shoved hither and thither like refuse by the surf. Troops are transported as cattle. Clarinet concerto. Aloes, hyacinth, coruscating warmth. Rupert often brags of being an aficionado of the opposite sex. His pomposity is overblown and overbearing, like some Wagnerian classical composer's would be. Winston has judiciously rehearsed the already well-versed hypothetical vitriolic speech (one of three versions) he will in the future inflict on him, the delivery in a contemptuous storm of righteous rancor, fairly confident his vocal aim would strike the intended target. He cannot tolerate his incorrigible uppityness, his galling patronizing. He would thrive on hitting him in that outthrust jaw with a cast-iron pot, only it would be counterproductive and lead to a horrendous penance. The idea's novel and unacceptable. He's cognizant of the repercussions. He would put himself in the proverbial frying pan. The expensive red wine is satisfactory and consolatory. His raspberries as delayed reactions. Heaven has a shade of puce. Bulbiform bombardier babbling about perfunctory brutality of foreign power-fueled engagements. Winston thinks of Him, scribbling furiously, a heap of paperwork on a makeshift desk consisting of vacant anti-aircraft shell crates, the requisition forms designated for the British military bureaucracy. The sky is cleansed, purging itself of moisture. His reveries dynamic.

He leered like a satyr. She was composed. There was no resolution forthcoming in the standoff. Neither side budged. A smile played tug of war with the corners of his mouth. She was enlightened and knowledgeable when it came to these stalemates. Stygian Spring night in the Big Apple. Drifting drapes of smog. Scarlatti sonata blared from a neighbor's apartment. His hands scraped together as shingles during a storm. He inspected the progression of her posture, like she was posing, and he surmised it bespoke uncertainty on her part. She was adept at diversionary tactics. Phrasing and harmony were inherent in her humming. Traces of natural affection and physical attraction. His voice would rise an octave if he had the occasion to speak. Silence removed pleasure they were mutually entertaining and augmented the anguish. Her coquettish pop-eyes, long-ish fingers with pink nails, gourds of her rump. His gazing caused her to shoot him a witheringly accusing glower. Absence of contact was a presence. His lubricious, corrupt imagination was fervidly active. Her winsome image lured him, and suggestively. In fantastical fairyland, he kneaded the nape of his neck, an eidolon in Elysium, with a bulging pyramid in his pants. She smirked coyly. He fantasized they copulated, as if in a moment of crisis, confounded by the intransigence of their connected configuration on the plush carpeting. His tumescent state. He sliced through her not unlike a knife through watermelon. With puppy adoration, on all fours, she wagged her fanny, tongue lolling, hands pressed together beggingly, and wuffed, plaintively whimpered, and they cachinnated at the infantine, humorous charade. She was Gwen Glenister, a freckle-faced, carrot-topped, bewitching ugly duckling beanpole with floppy elephantine ears. When he first met her, she was stroking a vintage cello with a fraying bow on the sidewalk, her playing (knock-'em-dead-aggressive and orgasmic) tremulous and rhapsodic, the poignant piece, a proteiny platterful, rising to heights of sublimity, attributed to her crafty wizardry. His immersion stopped short of hysteria. Her strawberry-blond mop flamboyantly whipped around her head, furs flouncing, skirts hitched, muscled thighs vising the priceless instrument. He couldn't disregard the ecstatic sexual component for the life of him. She fearlessly performed, playing with volcanic emotional abandon, summoning, sensuously, deep and mournful melodies, enduring and transcendent. To cease, for her, would be like a dereliction of duty. He felt as though he were an automaton of a one-member audience. He had a limitless hankering for what he was hearing. Her peerless, flawless, precise technique, body movements unconventional. He was on her akin to a parasite a potential host. Winston's marriage was in shambles. He was depreciated to a crabbed, unprepossessing assemblage of grunts and shrugs, a creature-of-habit hubby, with Clara. He was cast aside as shells, the eggs scrambled. A divorce would be a blot on his reputable name. He was prospering with his sensationalistic production. Taken with her tremendous talent and odd beauty, he hired Gwen for a European tour. On the road he had an affair with her. A Japanese photographer took a picture of the two kissing in a packed nightclub. There were adverse reactions to their mixed-race relationship in America, with racists picketing the theatre. The place was closed after damage was done to the building's structure and because of the continual confrontations between the protesters and the troupe. Clara separated from Winston after seeing the photo of him and Gwen in the paper. Devastated by the losses of his relationship and business, he returned to England to enlist, and was posted to the frontline trenches to join an infantry company awaiting an imminent German attack, serving under Captain Rupert Debney. Winston was worried Rupert would find out that his sister left him and Rupert was concerned Winston would discover he had serious drug and alcohol dependencies. Rupert was contacted by his superiors: there would be no reinforcements available and to hold the line at all cost. He, afraid Winston would catch on to the fact that he's an addict, selected him to lead a surprise operation to assassinate a German officer, knowing it's a suicide mission. Discomfited, Winston felt like a naughty schoolboy reprimanded by the headmaster, the recriminations relentless. Rupert preached ethical principles, illimitable ideals. Winston, fit to explode, looked on in disdain, ruefully regretted not having castrated the cunt when he had the chance. They were in agreement that there's abundant apathy, misdemeanors and atrocities in the ranks, zero rules in a harrowing game of dishonesty and barbarity. A code of conduct must be adhered to. Clara told him Rupert, in puberty, sought confrontations without provocation, plucked the wings of flies, bullied fellow students, taunted teachers who reproached him for resisting authority, pulled gals' pigtails and pinched their tushes, and had no table manners, on top of it all. Winston was not surprised. In addition, Rupert was a paranoid delinquent, a madman and pathological liar who withstood a stint in a mental institution. As an adult he became a wine merchant, but soon went out of business because he was drinking large quantities of the stock, the beginning of him indulging his worst impulses. Later on, he earned a living tutoring pupils in philosophy and got supplemental income as a fortune-teller. After this, being a renegade and racketeer, he opened an arms manufactory next to the premises of a dissident newspaper, enforcing an despotic domination over his employees. There would be no unions or strikes. He wasn't in any kind of shape to run the company. He wouldn't buckle to working-class aspirations, supported slave-labor. He acted on his own initiative to be an opportunist, was undeviatingly decisive, inculcated in his staff members a spurious consciousness of a crony continuity to maintain organisation, an imperative to preserve solidarity, strict discipline, keep their eyes fixed on the prize - the job. His tirades were irrational. What it boiled down to was they were expected to obey his orders. The workers were coerced into swearing oaths of obedience ... Cows browse in a pasture. Riotous party on a scarp. Fly-blown, rotting horse. Pulsing stars. Gwen said he, Winston, was "incomparably distinguished." "Beauty is in the eye of the beholder," he replied, and thought she had cataracts, or was myopic. Confidence leaked by capillary enterprise into his head. She was a neutral ship he torpedoed. His semen spewed like lava from Mt Etna. Rupert's motives are petty and vindictive. He shows his adaptability when it comes to an opinion on the war, flip- flopping on advocating it and opposing it. The single thing missing from his redundant speech-ifications is a podium. Napoleon Bonaparte-level leader he ain't. He's a virile dictator, with a feral radar for detect-ing the terminally ignorant. Disastrously inexperienced selectees are sheep following the lion Rupert into the slaughterhouse. His sesquipedalian jargon delivered as revelations from a saint. Applause/responses from the company are like they are from prompt-cards. If anyone questioned him, they'd be deemed disloyal and untrust-worthy. He vowed to pass on the benefit of his wisdom. Army of amateurs led by a donkey. Winston feels as a low-wattage bulb in the power station of the division. He yawns in boredom, weary of the dumb discourse.

Beliefs are diametrically opposed. Irreconcilable struggle within him. Busted toy soldiers. The masses will not be emancipated. They're musicians in Rupert's orchestra and he's the conductor. Motorized units on the move. Spritz sounds like fat sizzling in cinders of a fire.

Reddening sun's hoisted over foggy hummocks. Clouds are in competition with each other for variegation of construction. Unnerving booms. It is hot as a fiery oven. Winston yields to temptation and defecates in tangles of asperous shrubbery in order to preclude the eventuality of soiling himself. He has been reduced to skin and bones. His eyes have grown wider, registering both terror and wonder. A scraggy septuagenarian with a prophet's beard and wooden staff, his weatherbeaten mongrel's head hanging dolorously, tail waggling between its legs, the epitome of canine fealty. The little person's flaming lamps roll in a manner intending to signify more crap is coming. And he, Winston, recognizes, with resignation, the likelihood of this happening, infinitely subordinated by intimations of insecurity. Blasts make everything rumble and shake. A tank at a Hun garrison chokes and splutters. He touches an incipient scrape on his shin, dabs at the graze with a kerchief. Bitter cataclysm of bile. He sways backwards and forwards, whistles to himself like the tune in his belfry will abate his sense of peril, the ringing notes implying a melody of grace portraying peace. Intractable sores on his heels. Earthquake tremors in his entirety. His encephalon sloshes in his skull, leathern tongue feeling as if a razor was stropped on it. Torrid breeze. Nausea wells in his gullet. Vascular organ a kettledrum in his breast. He shuts his eyes ashamedly and despair-ingly at his compromised physical and psychological condition, stews on the cycle of his partnership with Gwen as being a curve through a problematic perdition of palliative excess and periods of self-loathing, the self-revulsion winding around his psyche as though a snake. Leafage drips with dew not unlike the Arethusa spring. Callous, granular gusts. Inordinate deluge. Arrivals and departures of Brit bombers. Supernatural strength of the soaker. Legions of abominations of par-tisan whoremongers; the corrupt doing iniquity. They sing and swim in the sea, teak-tinged by the vivid beams of the searchlights. For them, it's a costly luxury and regrettable necessity. They are paralytic in contorted, prurient positions. Cicadas make shrill droning noises. He stops as if hitting a stone wall, rooted to the spot, looks at them like they are invaders, occupiers. Crickety chirrings. False alarms. Abandoned derringer. He treads as though he's got an urn propped on his shoulder. Gwen's arch and knowing grin. She refused to smooch him, like she'd perpetuate a poisoning. His horny palms were on her pear-shaped hind. She reproved him for his admiration. Final and consummating osculations and tactions. His urges required resolution. Her chompers were sparkling, looked whitewashed. He was wistful and waiting. She made moving and exquisite sounds, pointed a wavering finger at him. His frailty engendered by his addling. He wanted to grab her by the throat and throttle her! She fussed over him and pampered him. Their frenzied and avine clucking and screeching, supine, sexing, the darkness imposing itself on them.

War-cries in sensual combat. They acquitted themselves with ferocious courage, frogmarched on the floor. She complimented him on his entrepreneurial acumen, barrel chest, bandy legs, and the fleshly protuberances of his precious possessions. Overjoyed, his face was tear-streaked. Undulating tresses of kelp on an aquamarine ocean. Her birthmark was as a horse chestnut on her narrow right hip, her intonations tentative and trebly. Froth and scum on a pondlet's surface. Peacock empyrean. Struggle of cirri. His supper of foul poultry, mucilaginous gastropod and pilaf. On the windy coast he, in the buff, comes across a spherical, semi-revealed landmine, with rusty bristles and a deceptive air of harmlessness, spiny-sea-urchin-semblant. In time it was cordoned off and exploded with dynamite by a seasoned sapper in the vicinity of a sandcastle's crumbling rampart in ochrous slush on the broiling beach. Effulgent gouts of debris rise in momentary majestic efflorescences, the chromatic billowing clods creating a sloppy rainbow of materials, from a sudden enemy airstrike, the pat of earth sticking like sugar icing, smacking and singeing folks, making modified minstrel makeup on countenances, glops of sod in perilous arc, splinters stinging as though they're the stingers of hornets. Contagion of gagging, plague of puking. Winston is guillotined by light. Hurricane of dismay in his heart. Recreational escapades of sweaty Sikhs, in the raw, playing a football match on a pitch of loam. Megalithic phallic trees. He perspires and pants. Dandelion seeds are powdering mites, ingratiating themselves upon him, quixotically clinging. His satellitic head orbits this world. Changing stalls obliterated. Floundering, he reminds one of Igor from a Frankenstein film. His tinnitus ... bells bonging. Basso profundo of his gaseous cough. Rupert setting him up - would he be demoted for reckless endangerment? Receive a severe reprimand? Put on a charge for conduct unbecoming to an officer for acting on his own initiative without permission? He'd weasel his way out of it, bribing his superiors with boxes of contraband Cuban cigars; or presenting them with mercurial sluts, a sorry gaggle, from an impoverished quarter. Drencher ticks, metronomic, tempo perfect. Gun pops sound as these backfiring exhausts. He's white-knuckled with terror in the hazardous adventure. Smells of honeysuckle and moss. Suspicion of a shadow. Sprite-forms, expelled from above, in webbing and cord, creatures from a different dimension, float below beige mushrooms of parachutes, nice cloths, of the Allies. Luxuriant brush. Colony of bats. He's bitten to death by mosquitoes. The midge's parched throat is like it's got buzzing bees in there. For Chianti, honeyed ham, mozzarella cheese, jelly doughnuts and plain yoghurt! In agonized paroxysms he has the sense of being plundered in perpetuity. He has an inkling he's disposable property, pushed over the precipice by his peers. Would there ever be an accommodation between himself and his afflictions? He's not in denial: the clinical symptoms have been diagnosed and confirmed ... His provision crisis is dire. Contemplations haven't clotted into a set of solid ideations, and he can't add any constructive congealed coda to these considerations. The dissection of his reality has banished the conjury of

his irreality. Gwen burlesqued him into dramatic oblivion. She, an expectant expression playing on her cast, in
a tasseled cap and ruby slipper with a pompon, offered
herself and he accepted with alacrity, snickered with
anticipative delight, raised his eyes to the desirable deity.
He diddled her and by consent. She was outstandingly
towering and had indefatigable abilities of endurance.
Frivolous with bourbon, he could be depressed or sentimental, wearing a tragic grimace of maximal expression
and minimal activity. Going at her bosom he looked like
he was milking a nanny goat. She claimed he was a
marvel of miniaturisation, weighing in at a paltry nine-
ty-eight pounds sopping wet. A simper was on her
succulent lips when he brought her Armenoid confec-
tionery. She talked tartly. His enthusiasms were inflated
and deflated. He was at her beck and call. She could be
admiring one minute and aloof the next. She was girlish, he was gallant. She reveled in his saccharine
uncertainty, relished heaping piping hot coals upon it.
She repented of her rude sassiness and inspired to sincere sportiveness. He'd erupted as a volcano and subsided
at last. Promulgation of promises of eternal devotion
were expressed. He kissed and caressed every nook and
cranny of her. Is he capable of being with her now?
Unlikely, as his infirmities (medical sordidities to him)
are antitoxins to arousal. Love to him is lust deliquesced.
He would never forget her. Acquiescent amnesia is
non-existent. His rosy recollections will never wilt. He
has the merit of being English and the demerit of being
deformed, honing his skills like sharpening a blade on a
whetstone.

A tributary swerves, and sluggardly, through the boscage as a runlet of tears through grime on a soldier's
face. The enervated blokes gamble, using found ration
cards. With Rupert, Winston, battered and tattered,
bearing with sunstroke, dysentery and jaundice, trap
moving as a fish stranded on a dock, tinkering with the
modern motorbike, feels like an organism on the slide of
a microscope; or a mouse caught by the tail. Red Cross
field hospital, ragged and mournful, the well-trained
staff misdirected. Firmament stirring as the sea. The rain
like surgical wire, rattles as slack strings on a mandolin's
frets. Separation and deprivation. Unspeakable waste of
life. Vitriolic with anger, he should wring his hands and
watch his improbable cockerel of a commanding officer,
an actor and imposter, fall apart, or go for the jugular
vein. Rupert's rank brings formidable firepower. The
buoyant bon vivant could dump a ton of explosives on
his existence. There's a cold war on 'tween 'em. It is abysmally clear. An Iron Curtain has dropped. Tension on an
unimaginable scale. Winston's confidence (what little he
had in the first place, accrued from mission successes) is
waning. He receives the stench of cowardice and treach-
ery. Gwen stated that without music she'd be as a flower
denied light. She had a nightingale in her voice. He
asserted control over himself in order to avoid losing it,
determined not to act on impulse and instinct. With her,
she gave him impetus, culture, whereas without her he
was impotent and frustrated. He waxed delirious with
gladness when he met her. He circled her like a lionet
and pounced. His matrimonial union kaput, He fell into
a deep depression and wept bitterly and seethed with

self-disgust, impelled into inaction by his unappeasable pain, the burden hastening his inertia. Welkin's black as an oven. His indefinite image, reflected in a saponaceous puddle, is like that of a warped wraith. He would prefer to confront doom than dishonour. His blisters bubble, ooze and burst on his soles. Without Gwen or Clara, he's a dismasted, dwarven man-o'-war. Amens drift from aliens. Surf scavenges the cratered shore. Multitudes of fighters with fatalistic eyes and vanishing dignity are condemned to a grisly demise, sallow with fluster and distraction. Batsqueaks. Battles wend to and fro, hither and thither. Apocalyptic swelter. Air-headed inmates of a bagnio, women with their artificial aspects and beautiful bodies, hope (in vain) to be bought by occupants of a cavalcade of armored cars. One vehicle lurches to a halt. Men do elaborate drills as if obeying the laws of nature. An interlude of invigorating ocean gales. Wafture of alky. These minesweepers make headway. The Master Race will lose. They are not invincible. They're inferior, not superior. They don't stand a chance in this conflict. He is sick and tired of incompetents, lunatics and fools, the senior officers deciding his fate. Looting and slaughtering. There is no clarification of intentions in the campaign. There needs to be resistance ... he grinds to play an ignoble part in the half-baked military hierarchy's nonsense. Talons of consternation tear at his ribs and spine. Being born as he is, he is sentenced to hellfire and brimstone. Rupert has apparently aged, and drastically, in a space of weeks. He sits on his hands in the safety of a bunker waiting to catch the next brainwave. Pointless calamities. Aromas of aromatic oil, sweet cordite, and warm steel. Tiger tanks are in formation in an expanse. Air support. Munitions pour in. Infallible furor of his conviction. He believes he is a subjugated sycophant. He's dishonored. Would anyone have sympathy for him? He wants to expunge the shame. Humming a lilting, lulling cradle song he remembers from infancy. He's felled by disgust and fright, beholding American corpses heaped onto a pyre for cremation. Vile stink of burning hair and flesh. Innocent victims are bound blindfolded and lined against the wall to be executed by a German firing squad. Winston always fights for survival. He jumps for a low- hanging pineapple like a pup leaping for a snack, and flows, seemingly subterraneously, through the donnybrook, praying he'll spring up in a spectacular spout of water somewhere else. Unprecedented barrage. His raging adrenaline is not an impediment to inaction. Unparalleled turbulence. Horrors witnessed. Boats bob like birds. Soldiers drop as trappings from bashed strumpets in the fracas. The sogginess impregnates itself into the environs. Salvos of weaponry. He shudders, blenched, terrified, ears ringing as field telephones, creeps like a cat going off to die, drifts into suicidal lethargy, knuckles blanched. No sanitation, sanity, sustenance. Infantrymen prepared to the last degree. Disoriented, Winston yanks his rod as the stock of his rifle, feels not unlike stone blasted to dust, a palsied rabbit held in the headlights of an automobile. An epicene, lovable major, studded with fragments of shrapnel, at death's door, is left to the crows in a ditch. Seagulls graceful in the air as tracer bullets. Tragic tangled remains of the deceased. An undermanned outpost. Thunder sounds like sticks tapping on a bass drum. Cinders as lightning bugs. Residences are gutted dolls' houses. He trusts no one. He wouldn't confide in a cadaver. The enormity of the fray breaks him. Refugees ramble. Village is razed to the ground. People clog the confined streets, carts exacerbating the congestion. Hyperbolical blizzards of Churchill and Eisenhower's messages of encouragement on the radio. Marmoreal muleteer. Buildings of import are reduced to rubble by mortars, not preserved for posterity. Resinoid pungence. Charred bark effluvium.

Planes, to Winston, optically, are as eagles released by Zeus. Nazis are microbes spreading their infections through the marrow of humanity to the veins of the world. Grace-notes of rain. Nature in nostalgic silence prior to wreaking revenge on warring men. Overcast whitens like a skeleton. Winston, porcupine-scurrying, waiting for sunshine as an opera fanatic for the over-ture, heart thudding like hooves, wishes to shake the abominable visions as a pooch does drops of moisture. Skyline's like a vaportrail. Rupert can't appreciate the beauty of this place, has an aesthetic allergy. A clash sounds as amplified crockery clattering and cutlery rat-tling. Pins and needles prick his cartilage and sinews. Wind laments a wrongdoing. He stumbles, falls like he's chopped down by an axe, makes an obeisance to the terra firma, wiggles as a worm, toboggans on his tuchis down a crusty hillock, dodging a catastrophe, the blasts not unlike blows of titanic fists, and he gets upright, shivers as a palsied Christ, inflection tinny. Menacing cacophony of thunder, having the sonance of cascading pots and pans. Such a direful clamor! Lightning winks. Tarantella of squalls. Dizzy, he rocks like a boat's mast. Fibers of his brain are aflame as the wicks of candles. His trepidity dissolves. The land is changed by mankind, its demolition disheartening. He is in disbelief. Jade grass is clad in crocus, lilac and viola. Storm's a titan with a taste for malice. He's embellished with filth and diaphoresis. Evacuations of casualties via spluttering helicopters. Transports and earthmovers parked in a courtyard. Thickset, cardinal-red nuns make their rounds. Makeshift hospitals are constructed on the fly by foreign-aid workers. Youths, credulous, play hide-and-seek, kick-the-can, tag, and cops-and-robbers in the community of a shed-city. He has lapsed into listlessness and purposelessness. Stench of rotting organic matter. Meals are unpalatable, but keep starvation at bay. He feels goddamn worthless. Ground is juddered by quake-tremors. The earth inhales and exhales. His single refuge, spot of safety, is in his head. He feels helpless, like a fly in a cyclone, conviction cudgeled out of his being, lost in a morass of self-loathing and remorse, burdened by the weight of memory, a compilation transforming into a composition of fundamental philosophical opinions. An aimless pilgrimage. Existence an eternal penitence. Pulse-stopping shrieks. Dead bodies in distorted positions appear to serve the increasing impression of being life-sized dummies. Bursts of shells. Snaps of guns. Bedeviling grief. Bullets smash bones. Sizzling skin. Trembling hands. Volleys. Tear-filled eyes. Salvos. Silver chains. Gold teeth. Photographs. Loveletters. Watches. Pens. Coins. He feels as if his essence spits and shrivels in a fire. Waves splash on rocks like blood during battle. He economizes effort, acknowledges the eventuality of his extinction. Redolent concoction. Yammering of machine-guns. Timpani-sounding explosive projectiles. Detonations of his derangement. Disapproval obvious. His optimism cannot relieve his pessimism, his gaze zeroing in on infinity. Crackles of pistol-shots. Despair emanates from his person as illumination from a lamp's shade. His mission is hopeless like the task of Sisyphus. He spares himself the details. Insectile, metalloid scrapings. The heavy dew as though it's a saline solution. Sights enough to make you queasy. Nocturnal critters. Arachnidian chaos of his handwriting. He is Atlas supporting the globe. His spirit feels trampled by a stampede of oxen. The cosmos is a mirror reflecting the distorted. His Hellenic beard. His teeth have lost their resilience and his gums bleed. Interlude of quietude. He's sustained by a dispensation of a luck intent on shining on him. He pictures himself being on Clara like a film of oil on water, relating stories of close-contact combat and near-capture to her. To chat about the past, present and future with her! Their love hardened, by degrees, as calcium forming into bone. His groin is contracted. His sardonic, mirthless smile. A nonentity, he is faithful to the Empire, and forgotten. Will everything be tickety-boo? Slicing sheets. Vindictive clamminess. He slogs his nomadic way. Draftees' virility, bonhomie. The universe has forked on a path that is misty. Rupert's a burner of midnight oil, with vulpine charisma. Livid cicatrice on his triceps. Rape of the cay. Resentment, antagonism hang like a residual stink, the smell sporadically reaffirming itself. Longing for his ex-wife turns in his gut as the twirl of a bayonet, and cuts his chest not unlike raptor's claw. Aquaplanes are automata in reconnaissance. Marlene Dietrich recordings played on a gramophone. The Reich are adept in the arts of atrocity, pillage and oppression. Cadavers of dissidents thrown into mass graves. His health usurped by hunger. Arthritis afflicts, indiscriminately, specific joints. He is temperamental as a bear whose hibernation is disturbed. His unarmed appropriation of animality, of unaccountability. He is destined for the void. Weariness, emptiness. Breath labored, like he's giving birth. Throat constricted. Rucksacked recruits ebb into the encampment. He is now stirringly obese, shuffling, with lachrymal eyes, spout of beard on dangly turkey jowls, spongy, capacious breast, scalp bursting with a toupee, in ungrudging service to his country, in spite of his handicap, fumbling for relevancy, furtively fighting for his nation. His midsection ostensibly swelling, seasonably, as if pregnant, womb gaining a wee indweller. Multi-colored flowers are as though samples of foreign currency. His halitosis is noxious. Statuette of Pan, at a drunken angle, playing his pipes at a stack of stones. Felines mew. Winston's expressions are like tragedians' masks. Skeletons of fish. Eclectic emporium of emollients, salves for sunburnt Britons. Repertoire of his prestidigitatory survival methods. He wants a time-machine to take him back to the glory days of Clara, a bedlamite with her babel of languages and floral bombardments, applying her cosmetics with painterly gestures, and a grin spreads ear-to-ear on him. Pasty puddle's as a congealed prophylactic. Record-player's winding handle. Tin box in a wartime knapsack. Holey sock. His past is present. Prodigal sun shown stereoscopically in lenses of brackish pools. He was chosen for the assignment on account of his sniping abilities, aim ofttimes accurate. He's an unfinished poem, or painting. Crashes and bangs of thunderous kettledrums. Aftershocks in the azure, abruptly and unpredictably. Filaments of web.

Sap-yellow, orbiculate luminary in the cold blue vault vacant of cloud. In the immeasurable orbit of the universe his consciousness is an organism, stirring with spirit, in connection to a cosmic soul, passionate, subliminal and superhuman, a splendorous system with its vibratory waves of magnetic forces, a powerful physical and psychic energy with appreciable intensity, beyond space and time, becoming, alas, turbulently diabolically divine, good and evil, in a mysterious manner, in the vastness of the world that is in Winston's brittle cranium. He looks in equal parts a human being and sea- creature, stress writ large on his features, nature his unreliable companion, the weather bringing him down a few pegs with its demonic malice, effectively enhancing his agitated state. He's constricted in the strain of tenseness, in a confluent maelstrom of cogitation, marching in the fern-fronds and horny bracken as an army ant into the fount of life. His personality is gorse-prickly, existence embryoid, in a miraculous egg. He butts his way against the balmy breezes, complexion like it's lichen-whitened, facial clock turning gradually filthy so he's, illusively, a carved, cracked Cupid that'd been burned in a fire. The environment is a stock-still, low- lying snake waiting to strike at the throat of man. His frozen memories melt. He's as an obstinate, blind beast who goes by scent, redolent of peat, long blank stare a singular pulse on this jeopardous earth. He misses playing upsidaisy with Gwen, his eyes gimletting through her beauteous being, both eating rhubarb pastries and creamed unripe raspberries and drinking flasks of port on those drowsy days! Quiver of combined air, flame and water in his somatic core. Pair of knolls are like virginal breasts. He patted her with unembarrassed satisfaction. To obtain what he now visualizes ... Their spoken philosophies sounded as a chant. There was a hitch in his respiratory rhythm from the muscular exertions. She sported a foxy smirk when it came to his Don Quixote idealism. The ecstasy of his mood was embellished by their discourse on the threshold, enabling his insecurities to escape. The two left the asparagus bed for a barley field. Her sensations were in exact parallel to his. Glossy texture of the hill. Her limbs were rudimentary stalks. In a magical rapture, the flushes on his face were like patches of moss on a shed. Her fantastic fundament was like the exposed belly of a fish. His blush was the color of oxidised iron. Larks' canticles. His shilly-shallying she found humorous when he divided the delectable viands. She watched him as a hawk. His wrists were weary, and he was whispering an abracadabra in its abstrusity. The liquor was a libation to their love. Their smacking and fondling rendered their feeding intermittent. The couple were filled with electricity, like hair. Her peewit's cries, unanticipated and awkward, fingered and licked thus. Silence as calm as the bottom of a valley at dawn, or dusk. He experienced a dew-sweet and rain-bitter shame, molesting her titties, like cups of water-lilies, his nerves responding to his loins, until her hands intervened, accompanied by a stormy reaction, formulating her thoughts of uncertainty into speech. His lineaments were limned by a liquiform lambency, as if he were lit by a subterranean luminosity. Cirri were aquatic denizenry, natating in a dilatory ellipse. Winston was possessive of Gwen, disturbingly and provocatively, in predatory pursuit, part of an erotic courtship rite, driven by primordial venereal intuition, in voltaic, primitive livingness. He recalled a thievish orphan. Dried kelp on rock, blowing feebly in the gales, were locks of a head thrust out of a casket. He, a lecherous cormorant in his covetousness, groaned like a forsaken, perishing bough. The broad staircase had an attitude of strenuous expectancy. His mind was an inner sanctuary, an abstract Arcadia, with its phantasmagoria of flourishing fantasies. She had the flesh of a newt, pellucid and flaccid. Shabby domiciles. His arteries felt atrophied, as though the ones of a dreadful corpse. Lazily he swerved, like seaweed sways, flowing with the tide. He surveyed her as a botanist a fine plant. Her modulated voice was like a tweety mead-pipit. The quiescence as decomposition, silence confining like coffin-boards. His derma layer was as raw clay. She was carcass-passive. His lascivious urges were hard to suppress. Atmosphere like it was in eternal rest. He took a pinch of snuff, had a Homeric view of death. Pretentious furniture pieces filled her place. Surf seemed to carry the seal of prophecy. She had quaintly indented crevices in her lacteal thighs, indications of impending cellulite. Give her an inch and she would take countless kilometers. He was poised with pontifical gravity. They were quietened as flowers doused in light in a conservatory. Saccharoid comestibles reposed on dishes on the carpet. Her gipsean pallor (in the crepuscular corner), with its seductive softness, could've attracted him from many miles away. Placid, sub-human susurrations. He had the steady gaze of a stalwart harpooner, at alert attention. She was provocatively supine. No one could dare deny her the epithet of lovely. His gut was feeling like a termite-chewed plank, held her as a priest the Black Book at Mass. Her precious presence was like the result of an ecclesiastical bequest. Her pasty feet were white as a jackdaw's droppings. There was a profusion of properties, inhabited and uninhabited, plenty of plots and parcels of land. Empty vista was devoid of glory. Her soughs were like drips from a broken cistern upon stone. Forlorn dandelions and daffodils. Wilting hyacinths. He felt as if his life was a mutant octopus, events leading to his misfortune hooks piercing the tentacles and destiny easily reeled him in. He could not endure this image with equanimity in his adventurous mind. His brain was a meteorite traveling through the space of his skull. They swam in the blue-green ocean as though they were water rats. His existence was a scintillating stream, his decisions the motes flickering from within. He had an unrefined rictus from some Venetian picture, acted like a rustic rogue. Her intonation was penetrant, and she was fragrant with heliotrope. Branches gave these scolding shakes, twanged as bow-strings. Purple vase with withered perennials was deposited on a pink ottoman, like it was something symbolical. His emotions were painfully visible, as bloody streaks from his heart. Opalescent vapor. Odorous draft. He averts his nose with alacrity. Straight boughs are like antique spears.

Humidity's as eel slime. Winston cautiously debouches from the lea of marigolds. Air is like flour-dough blended with cotton-wool. He's partial to ginger beer and treacle, tap-roots to tantalizing satisfaction. A hen screams in newborn reeds. Sky's sorrow is comparable to his own. Filament antennae are extensions of his personality. Aromatic annuals. Feathery javelin flung from a weedy estuary. He gives himself up to protracted thinking. His serpentine nerves, with venomous fangs, bite his inner being. Where is Gwen now? What's she up to? There was significant excitement for the amorists, their erotic encounters making a thrilling phenomenon, exceeding traditional passion and normal sentimentality, the pair whinnying as wild horses. Performing cunnilingus, he'd hoisted her and trotted, and they were transmogrified into a salacious centaur; he was the lower half and she was the upper part. One nibbled on the other like capering ponies. Sodomizing her, his rod was a rudder embedded in mud. His semenoid bilge-water under her stern-seat. His entirety was sensitized by the angry and tender sex. His erection was an arrow released from the bow of Sagittarius. He stared at her, wrought up, as a look-out man in a crow's nest at the horizon for a sign of a storm. Alchemistic union of physical labor, consecrated by desire, the love-making a euphoric toil, in an ardency of oneness. The perversity had a tempestuous gentleness. Joints creaked not unlike wooden dolls' limbs. The downpour has the salted taste of spilt blood. Swirling cumuli as water churned by a boat. Splendid alders. Kingfisher zips like a dragonfly. This paradisiacal place is the vision of a restless god, and Winston has, inadvertently, imposed himself upon the immortal woolgathering. Confusing mutter of mosquitos. He had hemmed and hawed, weighing his words carefully during a portion of their conversation and she got so annoyed she wanted to box his ears! He was straight and sober. For the totality of his tramp through the fen (which carries a token of events of carnage from a clash, the heavens with their abhorrent complicity), he has been fortunate not to come under fire, in the wide open. Celestial sphere is a withheld secret in the clouds. He has a self-preservative instinct, as that of a fox, sensing the gaining hounds. Night terminates day. Level area gives the scenery a curious character. He bolts like a dace, propelled by desperation for cover, dancing to the jig of grenade blasts. Reverberations of his heartbeat. His deep-drawn breaths, lineaments entangled in an extraordinary expression. The magnetism of their avidity flew, with incredible speed, as a luminescent meteor entering the earth's atmosphere, and his appetency encircled an atmospheric planetary circumference, the fantasies soaring into higher dimensions, creating stellar constellations, his person, with a primal power, turning into a supplicant of space. There was an impulsive imperative for the duo to be intimate, floating in the central nucleus of concupiscent causation. His bodily voltage was visible, like spider webs. Chiaroscuro was verdurously waylaid. Their mental intercourse. Moonlight is intercepted by shadow. Viewless migratorial, minute saurians in the nocturnal nebulosity. His cast is contorted into a vintage tragic mask, eyes with entranced inquisitiveness. War's villainous decay. His head aches evilly, heart hurts like it was punctured by a poison dart. Vastitude of chemical substratum of ether. Colours of the rainbow are as an artist's pigments. Sun reaches its apex of appropriateness. The jungle and its neutrality of demising tinges. His trauma is transmuted into a foreign celestial element. He's aware of the achievement of the automatism of his actuating. A dull thud proceeds from a portion of his malformed skull. He is a humanoid clock, each and every step striking pain. He's appreciative of the necessity of stopping. His respirations travel further than his pace. Crude violence of his anxiety. Darkness is dominant. He is at the end of his tether with stress. Pesky insects perish out a part of the abyssal wood, the twilit bush having independent thought beyond the infinitesimal existences of these bugs. He feels like a revivified goblinish gargoyle from a segment of Notre Dame; or as a stone lifted, his soiled life beneath revealed. His profile's like the caricature of a gnome. Weather surreptitiously substitutes rain for hail. He's overawed by monoliths of crags. They are phallic symbols blaspheming against God. He clutches his crotch. Prehistoric trilithon of cliff. Wind gasps forth spit, gives vent to humectation. Sounds of dying men: cross between porcine grunts and vulpecular barks. Obstacle of a cyclopean boulder in the obscurity.

He believes the mistake of self-enlisting, putting on the disguise in the role of soldier, is equaled by his stupidity. His sharp pings and pangs. He's liberated from the burden of libidinousness (carried with him in the inmost core of his self) by wacking off, with a protean fluidity. Detonations make him move, and he could be, conceivably, mistaken for a zanily gamboling, imbecilic clown. Immemorial rock and its menacing bulk, in its taciturn enormity, formidable and sacred, imposing upon the tract with implication. He imagines his asshole being made of sandstone, feels deficient of intuition. He is in the throes of a religious-type trance, and he rocks as a ship on a stormy ocean. Sabine shore is inundated by the ravisher tide.

Rambunctious children bereft of attire. Mystic moon portentous in its passivity. He gathers his licentiousness like a lightning conductor draws electricity. Remnants of radiance in its remoteness having no rival. Terrestrial bodement.

This Paradise is Purgatory. Rupert's Machiavellian gift of persuasion was undeniable, assaulting Winston's mental constitution, and also effecting him environmentally, the words a poison infused into his bloodstream, the actuality of authority shaking the foundation of his nature as a soldierly individual. He unmasked Rupert's motives and saw something monstrous. Scraps and fragments of this reality are filtered through him, roving in a nirvanic Fourth Dimension. He refused to be a laughing-stock, the butt of jokes. Feeling, in the humectation, akin to an aqueous beetle. Reeking of dry-rot. His ill- gotten cigs will go for a song! Rupert, a religious fanatic, was disciplined in military matters not unlike a dedicated pupil in a seminary. He stirred the pot, made sport of situations, rank permitting untrammeled license, the cockney orator frequently speaking in sarcastic tones. Atmosphere is unsympathetic, depressing, ill-omened, disturbing, and unpleasant. Clara had a somnolent petulance, clicked her tongue peevishly, sat bolt upright, physiognomy meditative, exuding a gynic narcissism, toying, teasingly, with her blouse's buttons, limbs rounded, visage momentarily rendered uncomely by the coruscation, fair locks loosened into wispy strands and looping upon her pale-broccoli ears. She'd gone to the mark quicker than was her custom to be cross with him, preparing to lambaste him for his unforgivable indiscretions, and, in a protracted ritual, rummaged in a drawer, seeking stockings, appraising, rejecting and finally selecting a pair. Her tress was a chromic cirrus. He was mute and awestruck before her. She glided as the ghost in Punch and Judy. His lackluster peepers looked at her like a professional beggar would a potential pedestrian donor to his personal cause. This maimed bluebottle was a jumping jack on the walnut dresser. His hereditary temple- twitches. The spacious sewing-room had a mystical significance, as Rome. Chestnut-brown lucid shafts. Cassiopeian constellation. Sputtering adversarial airplane turned topsy. His inflection was deprecatory, spasmodic, his spirit heated, like a soul in Hell. She was a gentlewoman with style, dignity and grace. He grimaced as if a spike were stuck into his celiac plexus, intonation sounding as though his oral cavity was crammed with sponge cake. She was a domiciliary truant, attentive to passers-by on the curb. It was a chilly evening. It had been a mild morning. In her company he was a tealeaf and she was the lukewarm water poured on him. She evaluated him like a fox would a badger. He was a black sheep with hypnotized pies. She was a mistress of ceremonies. She tantalized his senses. Belting in the bathroom, she sounded as a quacking duck in a farmyard. He was an atheist, only he believed in her. His mind-pictures like they were mirages made by Merlin. Sleet was as frozen peas dumped out of a bag. She took on the demeanor of a taskmaster foreman. He had an attitude of wearied apathy, speciously a tragic figure, withstood the sensation of his stomach fish-leaping. He was irritable and restless. She was complacent and impervious to the bad vibes. Brick structure of several storeys, age interpreting its instability, peeling paint and material substance bearing myriad stains of weather. Dilapidated gate. Loamy clay and leafy promise. She roosted like a fowl in the upholstered armchair. She'd slipped as a sack of flour into it, proceeded to prop herself up. Her singsong monotone. She was combative. He wouldn't budge. She would not flinch. He had pins and needles in his instep. She blew her stack and slapped him. His disconsolate sobs ended. His shame stayed. His shambling gait. She was his rosebud, nearest and dearest. Issues were complicated attributed to his disgrace.

One time he'd ravished her, and she called his dong "Arthur's sword," asserted it was a "dagger taken from its sheath," said she felt like a piece of pudding kept in the refrigerator for him to conveniently dispatch in several gulps, her disappointment communicating itself to him, cherubic cheeks flamed in indignation, oculi oriental and flashing. It was the last straw on the heap. Fuddled by spirits, she modulated her mechanical vox, precipitated herself, a vague blur of a mushroom, into the pantry. She was an unpossessive, incorruptible devotee of his, through thick and thin. He was unequivocally adulterine. Gwen. Lord. She pretended he was invisible and inaudible. The experience for him had a noticeable impact. Hurly-burly of striking factory workers. What a hullabaloo!

Execrable memories torment Winston, the scenes of such sadistic viciousness, these intense images, phantasms in forms of suffering, taking possession of him, haunting the chamber of his skull, the pictures psychologically beating him until his physical being bears the bruises. He sobs as a lost spirit. Clara was squat like the Queen of Spades playing-card, had a Euclidean Square head, volubility of voice, a bullfrog croak, twig-eaved eyebrows, ursiform snout, retreating chin, and a geometrical center. Her forehead was creased with curious corrugations, compelling the contours of her countenance's wrinkles to comply with Nature's design. She devolved from fine and dandy dainty dwarf to cantankerous shrew. They went at it as rabid wolverines. Their merry-go-round of unholy doings. His queer proportions prominent. He felt like green scum on a castle moat. Their love was lust, both born to belong to one another. Their intimacy had an animal intensity, reckless and shameless. She was lumpish, original and interesting. Unfortunately, his affection lost its savour, a dilemma that's normally difficult to resolve. They were entoiled in the entanglement of separation, a travesty of a situation, and, subsequently, divorce. He was at fault. He was to blame. He was grossly and inexplicably unfaithful. Deliberately and willfully did he cheat on her. He remained irretrievably irresponsive concerning the affair accusations leveled at him by her in a grave and unaffected tone, shawling her shoulders with a cream-coloured cashmere sweater. Winston studied the cyclopean brooch clasping her bodice, and, at a loss, ceased to speak. He couldn't counter with anything even remotely substantial, managed a "fiddle-de-dee!" This unexplainable blurting producing silence, as if the two were upset by the spectacle of universal disorder. He had the sensation he was a minnow in fresh water suddenly polluted. There was a mutual crisis of confidence for the couple, a valid unbending. They had an indirect manner of communication. Hemispheres of Clara's buttocks comprised the planetary globe of her gluteus maximus. Pastoral country, an expansive receptacle, laden with ruins in the roiling vapor, was like relics of drowned ships at the bottom of the sea. Pterodactylously beaked precipices. Gulls, keening querulous, voyaged over neolithic immensities of erections, with unique qualities, stimulating to his sight, beyond description. The two were outpourers of passion, coition with brutish purpose and heathenish hostility. He was red as though he was a turkey cock. Miasmic smaze. Their attraction was an electric essence extracted out of the atomic atmosphere of wanton appetite. He nipped in the bud the flower of their marriage showered in the pesticide of mistrust ... Winston is lulled by the security of his bombastic brethren, nerved up by rotgut, in whom bravery has found notable habitation. Grassy ridge sepia-brownish like leaf-mould. Breathings and mumblings of the stifling evening. Landscape's character's changed by cloudcover. Funk of death visits his nostrils. He feels as a sheep taken from his flock, and pasturage, and brought to a shearing place. Schlepping on ground so hot, he is like Othello wading into a gulf of liquid fire. Etheric environment. His built-up ardor for her, Clara, concentrates itself upon the policy he would resolutely follow, one of restraint. He took satisfaction in the extracurricular activity (during March winds, August moons and November rains), independent of the possible calamitous outcome, Gwen arresting his attention. Conversing with himself, here, in the lumber, there are but mammalian and insectile eavesdroppers to contend with. He is unsoothed and uninspired. English company's in blustering camaraderie. Weather has an envenoming ferocity. Uneven floor with a confused series of depressions interrupting his way. Celandines glossy and glistening. Ineffectual dam. Rampant destruction. He was walking on eggshells in the encounter with Clara. Her accusations were obstacles he had to surmount. It was her who gave him the impetus to start his own radical theater company, and he took the stimulus from there, combining circus, soapbox, and Shakespeare. There were clashes with local authorities and rabid protesters because of controversial content (with the subtlety of a ten-ton truck), threatening the status quo.

She was fashionably piquant, dominating his vision at the mullioned panes, endowing his eyes with a halcyon excitation. It was her ideas for the lion, tiger, bear, equestrian, magic and acrobatic acts. Cement and glass caves honeycombed the rancid port megalopolis reeking of fish and fuel. Ultramarine empyrean. Her perfect bobbies were meant for more than infantine suckling. He emitted surprising shishing sounds as those from some separate species. They'd planned to purchase a cottage, like a doll's house, with pollarded windows, sloping roof, fascinating flowerbed, a wickerwork garden table, and picket-fencing covered in discolored fungus. The firmament was a fabulous Finis to the fabulous final act of the afternoon, visually written by a visionary playwright. He wore corduroy breeches. Living his life: a triumph of will. Every birthday should've been a celebrated milestone. He pretended her allegations of infidelity were products of puff-ball foolishness. She approached him in the paltry pantry as a gamekeeper in pursuit of a poacher. Stars shone not unlike sequins. Thunder roared as Polyphemus. Her whiteness was nearly phosphorescent. His farting dispensed flute and oboe notes, the odors composed of undefinable elements. He wanted to crush her like a currant moth. Suppressing the tempest of his temper. Welkin without cumuli was an unconceiving womb. His nerves convulsed in his animosity. He missed the times when they were frisky lambs. His gullet sounded as a low-toned threshing machine. He imaged to himself the direct cause of his downfall - the nosy, androgynous reporter in a fedora and scarf snapping a picture of him in a seedy rathskeller with

Gwen perched on his lap. When he met her she was virginal, and she permitted him to (carnally) conduct her, like Helen of Troy, allowing, on the tower's wall, Aphrodite to guide her. She had yielded to his advances. His euphonious overtures were convincing. She played the role he wrote for her. She was purged of brumous resistance by the resplendent lances of his determination. Sun's motiveless malignity. She was jumpy as a pet when its name is called by its master. His hydrocephalic head was bowler-hatted. His built body was hardened from the heroism of labor. Clara had a gas-jet burning sensation in her middle. His face was illuminated by wickedness. Molasses-sticky oxygen. Moon's a heretic. Winston is dead and buried.

Bugs bombinate. Sky's fungicide-mauve, then turning a gentian violet. Winston's earlobes are as wattled chins. Clara maintained he was the manifestation of her nightmare, only enmeshed in the intestines and not the grey matter. To her, he was a scary shrimp with special needs. With her he felt safe, like a kangaroo in its momma's pouch. He was a heinous homunculus. The sodden air swelled as yeast dough. Asphalt driveway and rusted rooftop. He was still stirred by her bizarre beauty, in the sterile atmosphere. He vomited an acrid substance into the sink. He had this customary caricatured tendency to crying. Posters, strikingly prismatic and dramatic, were pasted on the concrete walls and frosted glass of arched windows, advertising the troupe's productions and previews. Insect-infested bleachers, sawdusty stage not unlike from a three- ring, with specialized scaffolding and jungle gyms for props (inspiring creative choreography), and, lest we forget, safety net. Cobwebbed platform, fluorescent tape marking its perimeter, above a (usually) electrically charged audience. No expense was spared. Long ladders and radical lighting rigs. He even introduced monkeys into the act, against his better judgment. The performers stayed in these monkish quarters on his dime, encompassing the bland first-floor office he occupied, a dump that stank of dirty laundry, cancerette smoke and blocked toilet. He had the distant attitude of a detective at a crime scene. Cleaners brought a level of confusion to the labyrinthine corridors with their carpet-vacuums and floor-polishers. He was the proprietor and proud, being his own boss. He had admiration for the critical crowds, who appreciated the crazy invention, the carnivalesque incorporated into the melodramas, making a (mechanical and manipulative) theatrical circus: Shakespeare meets P.T. Barnum! Although he remained behind the scenes, he shone as a star. He detested the press. He hated the reviewers. Too ignorant and unimaginative. The group contributed to the culture of society, complicit in this influence. He rubbed the ticket-buying throng, burnished the belief in themselves. He had mounting debts. His invested capital earned him a respectable, if negligible, sum in return. With her, his head hung like a rag. His heartbeat sounded as a burglar's footsteps. He was a limpet stuck on her life. His calm outside showed no indication of the chaos inside. She was soft like a sealion's underbelly. The marble-white nubbins of her feet. His fleshly pectorals. Tombstone toenails. Hurt, her tonality was sharper and nastier than barbed wire. He lost her and Gwen. Clouds

clearing in the azure - an image forming on a sheet of
photographic paper in its liquid bath. Picture's overex-
posed. Indigenous inhabitants abandon the mangroves,
mudflats. Hollyhocks and snapdragons. Life, to him, is
a theft. It was taken from him from the get-go. His guts
feel heavy as lead. Winston Reade is more alive, dead,
than when he was living.

FIN.

Girls Will Be Boys

THE SUN IS a dragon's egg hatching in a nest of cloud. Shadow's in its quivering rectangularity, timorous and lengthening. Quaint coastal town. Ramshackle clapboard house. In the dilapidated garage, chock-full of a motley of junk, with apple trees, breathing and dripping, planted around it, hermaphroditic, juvenile delinquent Faunia Nolot, built like a ballerina, with a brown pixie bowl cut, elfin ears, bulbous nose, cranberry mouth, and freckled face shining as Danish china, an aspiring tightrope dancer, white like a water-lily, voice a quirky combo of bat squeak and adenoidal honk, smokes weed and drinks booze with adolescent, puffy, bipolar buddy, the gangling Louis Cals, with his russet tousled mop, pointy proboscis, broad, bashful smile, and touching tics, the twitches as lightning strikes. Starry, shimmering evening. She's diminutive and implausible, not unlike a mischievous sprite, shaped as a wisp of fog, sits in a shabby chair, spumescent words spraying like sea foam, intonation clanging. She is dressed in a tie-dye, mesh, hooded shirt, mid-rise, distressed, ripped, patched skinny jeans, and trendy, sparkly tennis sneakers. He's attired in no-name navy jogger apparel and faux-leather, sporty slides. They've been partying from dawn until dusk, on their backs and bellies, high and drunk, pampering and petting each other, fooling about and playing tricks on one another, mortal boredom kept at bay, their many problems having left lickety-split. She'd found this old manuscript, entitled 'Lady Flowers,' a strange hodgepodge of erotic writing and pornographic pictures, stashed under a canoe. She peruses a provocative passage, sounding as if she is casting a spell, glimpses the hallucinatory doodles in the margins, and her viperine innards squirm in the pit of her stomach. There is heed on the part of readerdom. She apprehends the typed pages with ravishment, discerns editing was accomplished, distinguishes the corrections scrawled in red ink, suggestions and instructions made to the author in spidery shorthand notes, both tender and bitter. The smutty opus (making the Marquis de Sade seem milquetoast) was submitted to a perishing publisher, going by the letter used as a bookmark. Prose and phrasing are polished. Some sentences are even spectacular. Words of the writings fecundate the loins. Sticky, sanguineous river. Friendly, foreign foliage. Tempestuous, turbulent weather's on display. Her waxen flesh, runny with perspiration, like a drowning candle. The two continue to enjoy a splendid time.

With him, she has the sensation of being a criminal he assisted, with ingenious methods, in breaking her out of prison and guiding her, surreptitiously, into the free world. She is unfathomably adorable, possessing a wondrously subtle smell of moist moss. And she abruptly feels sick, as though she's succumbing to serious scarlet fever. She is so relieved to be here, staying, for the nonce, with transsexual aunt Pauline (formerly uncle Paul), roly-poly, mild- mannered, and with hair like a loaf of gray bread, distanced from that dirty, humiliated house, suffering with her pathetic, abusive parents (dad physical, mom psychological). She feels driven into exile by a vicious dictatorship in a crazy country, Pauline, who warms the cockles of her heart, granting her sanctuary. The place had a predilection for torment, a blemish on an otherwise charming street. Somber, withered woods. Her mount-imposing father and passive- aggressive mother made her life miserable. Livid with rage, Dad, fists Bolshevik hammers, would make mincemeat of her, Mom complicit by doing nothing, for an ambiguous malfeasance. He pounded her and she disintegrated. Her aunt's kindness fails to dispel her melancholy. Faunia loves her weirdly mellifluent modulation, at once feminine and masculine. She carries a cargo of regrets. Currently, Pauline is working at her needlepoint, sipping lemon tea and nibbling on toast with jam, in the cozy parlor belonging to the clean cottage situated in a rural area. Electricity occasionally goes on sudden strike in this region. Faunia, apparently sleeping while standing, remembers Dad, a tilting tower and reeking of tobacco and alcohol, Mom, during a pensive period, obviously cooking up something. Home was jail, Dad the warden, Mom the guard, and she was the inmate. She was constantly caught in a kind of hurricane of foul language and harsh treatment: part of a family tradition. Deciding to defect was easy as pie. Domestic bubble finally burst when he, dressed in bathrobe and slippers, slapped her for a nebulous transgression and, with the proficiency of a professional wrestler, got her into a bear hug and swore. She struggled and whimpered, the stage for submission set. His long growth of beard, limp mustache. His bald pate was seemingly fashioned of modeling clay. She stared mistily straight ahead, avoiding his penetrant gaze. Now - dingy towels and stout ropes. Vacation pamphlets. Chamber pot. Scummy, enameled tub with a couple of cockroach corpses residing in it. Cylindroid water heater. In the cobblestone driveway the car's hood-wing's raised mid-flap. Filthy mattress on the cement floor. Her skin gleams with sweat like a damp leaf, scanning the wilted book, dazzled and dizzy from a steamy bit, in a sort of mercurial delirium. Her moods are customarily changeable. Carnations of cumuli. Spectral rain. Drainpipe rattles. Frenzy of her fainting fugue. Rolled brocade rug. Velvet casket of piano bench. Diamondiferous drops of precip. Hanging with Louis, his B.O. a combination of mushroom rot and damp hay, she experiences an enraptured equilibrium bound by harmonious laws. All is unified in the universe. Everything is equivalent. Exterior dove-silver, interior reverberant. Glossy metropolitan mag. Vein-blue sky. Her elongated hands and feet and sharp elbows. Her senses as sensitive insectean feelers.

Louis strokes her nape and kisses her clavicle. Then she glances at her downy wrist, the glittering bracelet, gives a shivery shrug, laddered by golden light. They are roots twining into the entire earth. Leathern wedge of bike seat. Minuscular fetal shavings. Cafe au lait puddles. He caresses her silken shoulder blades, touches her Armenoid (swollen) ankles. Intricate interplay of dust-particles in a chance patch of orange lambency. Oblique silhouettes. Pubescently-lanate haze. Powdery pollen akin to crushed chalk. Violet mud. Louis sings a pop tune hit, whereupon Faunia passes out ...

... AND COMES to in the boat, floating down a satin stream, languid and serpentine. Is she waking in the middle of a mysterious and humid dream? Salmon swim on the surface. She has mollusk-mauve eyes and almond-petal lips, inert in the flickering luminosity. Eventually, she winds up on a freakish tropical island with these penile trees, testiculate rocks and vaginal plants, the location of a prison colony for juvenescent boys, run by the androgynous, gracile, Dr. Moreau-ish headmistress, Arielle Bejo, assisted by rodentine scientist Dr. Dubius, gigantean guard Querelle, a eunuch, in maroon scrubs, and shitpile sidekick, the anthropomorphized Mr. Merde (with a fly-fro), who gets around on a trained Italian pig, Pecorino. This godforsaken locale is plucked out of a lush, albeit nutty, Freudian fairytale. Phallic volcano, in its erectility, spews semenoid lava. Arielle, who originally hails from Siberia, asks about the fascinating 'Lady Flowers' volume and Faunia answers she has no idea. Faunia and the other youthful inmates are put to backbreaking work. Vertiginous crags. Blindingly white illumination. Greenhouse is constructed out of bamboo and churchy stained glass. Hot ochreous sun. A fox terrier, this plump bitch, trots through scabious florets. Later, the bonging of a gong summons the young, cacophonous captives to a sensible and substantial supper in the kaleidoscopic cafeteria. Arielle's brick-hued office is quite cramped. Dead bumblebee and a jaundiced newspaper on the windowsill. Abandoned tapioca pudding, raisin biscuits, and hard candy on a tray on the oaken desk. Faunia's spirit is a toboggan and it is nudged by circumstances to proceed downhill. Querelle, a timid giant, probably transposed into this clime, routine accepted and habitual, is indeed at a loss as to what to say, verbally bumbling, prunes the iridescent, alien bushes. He has limpid peepers and a villose mole contains his cleft chin. Mustard and ketchup stains on his sailor shirt and slacks. His gait is like he's traversing a vivid nightmare, gestures rather fussy. Arielle's the taciturn benefactress of the reform school. Her conspicuously fake lashes flutter as she rummages through her vinyl purse for certain cosmetics and compact mirror. She knits her brows, palpably flustered. The main building, ovaline, is a perspiry drop in the cleavage of mammary mountains, circumscribed by firs disembodied by blazing radiance. Her integument is translucent and she is very tall and oddly animated. She confesses she has tried her hand at numerous dreary trades, failed in countless occupations, such as sales clerk, bartender and farm slave, for examples, felt like her life was wasting away to nothing, circumstance a sore eating at the septum of her existence. She is a vulpecular, sensual woman, rides the crystalliferous wave of cocaine, reveling in its rubberoid bitterness, enchanting iciness, relishing the ethereally miraculous effects, at the dimly lit buffet on the varnished teak. Her irises are now submersed in lachrymose iodine. Her tress falls as a flag (furtively flapping) when gusts diminish. She roots through the vanity bag, speaking in a lilting vox, takes a moment to munch on a ham sandwich, mixed vegetables and honeyed bun, scrutinizes Faunia like she is a master endeavoring to solve a chess problem during a championship match, her opponent giving her the fits. Lugubrious lawnmower grumbles past. Hills with heather. Avian ascent in reception of the empyrean. The teenage jailbirds wear uniforms of cotton tees, denim shorts, and gladiator sandals, perform laborious, eccentric exercises and recite enigmatic text, belly-down and imitating frogs in natation, and, upright, floundering like awkward birds fighting for flight. Canary-colored rainbow. Oral cavity of the fireplace breathes an ashy aroma. Boards in the billiards room next door squeak as fingernails on a Times page. Faunia's a tooth and Arielle's the needle pricking the nerve, nasally informing Faunia she's officially being held on the severe charges of "moral turpitude" and "existential ennui." The case won't go to trial. There will be no judge, jury and prosecutor. Sentence will be swift and harsh. This judicial system is effective. Faunia's a soap bubble popping in slow motion, nostrils dilating. Zephyrean sighs of relief. Arielle's life is a shop's row of panes exhibiting her sensuous wares. She's an abyss sucking everyone in.

Sugar-glazed summits. Paths flow like terra- cotta hair on the slumped shoulders of knolls. She is sleek, and with a sheeny Dutchboy bob and caprine pies, chops a torrid titian, her equine profile carved by the Creator. Little bridge leads to a hyaloid kiosk. Her unexpected flatulence pops as a toad flattened by a tire, irresistible, modelesque image reflected in the meticulously polished parquet. Mosquitoes look like they are yanked on imperceptible threads with puppeteer precision in the vastity of a vaporous field. Querelle on the vermillion veranda cyclonically sneezes, trumpeting into his sleeve, grunts gently with a lyrical smirk. Gaseous chords engendered by farted notes, his bowels with musical ears no doubt. Flies buzz in alder and shrubbery. Horns of handlebars on dappled sand. Butterflies, spotted and striped, wings palpitating, flit. Querelle, hump of snout flaky, bull's neck rigid, cap flopping, rushes headlong with a wheelbarrow, gathers momentum. Variegated drops, on the wan grass from the sprinkler, are bulging demon eyes. Heat's scalding as snow. Gaudy stars of dandelions silently scream. Oxygen bombinates like telephone wires. Cocoons hanging from gaunt branches are as Swiftian swaddled newborns. Pellicular air. Faunia, in the psychedelic lavatory, vibrantly imagines Louis, with his parchment pigment, covering her, a precious illustration. Mosaic of mutilated dolls. Breezes have the sibilant soughs of train brakes applied.

Pipes gurgle. Querelle in a narcotized torpor, balances an apple on an entranced, florid-faced, angulous, bronze-tanned lad's blond skull like William Tell did on his son's head, in a pyramid of penial perennials. Muscles in Faunia's jaws ripple as a pond with insectival activity alighting upon it. Chromatic kids float not unlike Japanese lanterns. She resists sliding down the slippery slope of sleep, muses on the crazy events that have transpired, wild encounters, with intolerable, nauseating regularity. In the bunk she grabs a mildewy pillow and studies the lunar ceiling, mulling over her options. Aunt Pauline must be worried! Can she contact her? Is there even a fucking phone here? She'll write a letter! Wait ... is there a damn post office? Christ's sake! Sparks spiral in her lamps. Criminal quarters with much snoring and mumbling. Funereal atmosphere. In her baggy, pink pajamas, she ponderously tiptoes on bare feet, meandrous in the maze, her heart, with its hollow pounding, thumping as a carcass against an abattoir's wall, in the ornate hall, to investigate these surreal premises. Multicolored cirri swirl like paper streamers in the firmament's festival. Metalliferous mountains. Scent of pine. In the catastrophic kitchen, Arielle's lachrymal oculi sparkle as frost. She has a potent fragrance of mingled perfume and roast beef, takes off her teal top, and Faunia notices the supple undulations of her slightly flocculent stomach. Faunia is immediately aroused, and awfully ashamed, cardiac organ a sheep repeatedly tumbling over a fence, pulse throbbing in her temple sounding like a lock clicking, smells lavender. In the puce vestibule an oriental band drums, strums, toots, drones, wails, instrumentally performing the classics. Floor's cool as marble. Arielle offers jellybeans and circus peanuts, to which Faunia refuses. Rowdy cries. Sounds of a scuffle.

Querelle, hollering above the din, restrains the funsters, the whippersnappers would-be (cutie) combatants, gagsters purply and full of pep, in a calamitous crush. Twang of country-influenced guitar. Oh, to be supine, dream a fluffy flying ... Bizarre scene: Arielle, "articulating" in pig Latin, nares flared demonstratively, inspecting the collarbone of a meaty, cherubic urchin, a muzzled Great Dane flanking her, threatens, and limply, to poison him with strychnine, emits a hearty ha-ha, reveals ivory chiclets, sneer penumbrally stretching, and Faunia recoils in unbearable horror. Chilly aquamarine corridor. What is going on here? What's exactly happening? Angelic guttersnipes in sweatsuits galopade with inspired vitality, passionate perseverance, and impetuous laughter. Faunia's diaphoresis is like ointment. A sarcastic smile fleets across Arielle's pancaked physiognomy. Faunia yawns, slouches in her starched pjs, doe-eyes widening, pouting prettily, swaying groggily on the creaky staircase. Gelid, clammy climate. Arielle's leechy blinkers stick to Faunia's. Faunia leaves, roams as Bacchus. She'd imbibed a really lethally inebriating concoction of gin and tonic, and ingested muculent oysters, foisted on her earlier by the indisputably disgusting Mr. Merde. Insecure, she has a hunchbacked stance. The edifice with a steeply roof is bowed, like in anticipation of receiving a blow from above. Eagles, enormous and boisterous, with their lacerating screeches, are a feathery tempest in the air, aboil in summer. She is posed as a sphinx, oculi myopic-looking, grinds her gnashers, in proximity to the walnut wardrobe with its funny-mirrored door, her fatigue oppressive, a jingling in her ears like sleigh bells, her umbrageous doppelgänger an indigotic plume. A sinewy, balding, ruddy oldster, the capable cook, flabby, pilose arms akimbo, mouth a cerise arc, countenance a plaster mask, lacquered cane vised in knocking knees, converses vivaciously with a collection of toyish crims, wound up, a few bouncing on a trampoline, crucified in midair, bodies naked, in proximity to the Pompeiian atrium. Pelicans and their perpetual pilgrimage. Nocturnal murk. Mercury-ish deluge. A violin infantinely shrieks. Gilded gondola. A towheaded, wilyeyed, skinny, tender teen wrangles a clucking, scrawny, white hen, dispatches it to the vacant land of a backyard, their shadows scudding, terra firma receding in the emanation. The codger of a custodian has a lupine phiz. Open graves of irrigation ditches. Porous fossils. Bathtub is as a sarcophagus. Commonplace commode. Is this lockup a figment of an unstable imagination? Drencher completely ripples - a harp in its vastitude. Long-necked spire of the temple of modest proportions. She snorts and reclines on the mat for yoga in a purply leotard, as per Arielle's explicit instructions, assesses the stands of cypresses, lindens and poplars, their trunks in wire netting like a cage, surveys those spiderweb-cloudlets. Scintillation through the muslin curtains are reminiscent of Chinese ambery arabesques. She feels swollen, like someone evil secretly filled her with hydrogen for a prank. Puddles of molten molasses. Clitter-clatter of dishes in the chaotic kitchen. Cicadas chirring, the sonance as scissors clipping. Cobalt brook slithers. Odoriferous dew's redolent of wet galosh. Fair weather holds on by a meager thread. Querelle, out front of his squalid shack, doffs the waistcoat and dons a panama, derma with an incrustation of grime, grooms his walrus mustache, in a state of solar intoxication, thriving in his idle solitude, plays a hurdy-gurdy. It's heated and humid like a hothouse. Metalline exclamations in the aromatic acacias, and annuals, close to an emerald lagoon. Faunia's thoughts as though they're shooting stars. Leaves wave like they're fanned by a big bellows. Gargling gaggle of ungainly teenagers. Her expelled lingua franca the linguistic equivalent of hormonal rage. Sinuous creek. Windowpane with its beadwork of raindrops. The crapulent heap Mr. Merde castigates Pecorino, who squeals. A middle-aged man is a grotesque gargoyle. The rodential Dubius, eyes squinted, sourpuss twisted pugnaciously, with a squeamish grimace, chews out Querelle; a cabbie urging his nag.

Cruciform, diverse laundry dangles on clotheslines. Brotherly Italian acrobats soar on trapezes. Garish sky. A podgy ventriloquist below sings barcaroles with his crass dummy. Clown stunt cyclists pop wheelies and burn out. Spaniels in bowlers skip through hoops of fire. Sisterly Spanish aerialists do their thing. Gasps of wonder from the crowd, elastically tense, seated on fold-ing chairs in the dimmet. Iron grille of the window winks in the fulgurous shafts. Predaceous hostility of the swelter. Bengal brilliance. Arielle's voice peals as a tram. Birthmark on her tummy is like a little scar from a smallpox vaccination. Upstairs, clodhoppers' footfalls clop-clop. Wigwam of toolshed. Vitric arachnidan chandelier. Faunia's sad shadow's a humpback whilst she, clad in an outrageous auburn bikini and apron, prepares frankfurters at the stove in the kitchen. She is discalced, soles roast beef-roseate. Arielle, without warning, seizes her and violently tickles her and probingly pokes her in the ribs. Furnishings frigid in trepidation. Darkness is a measureless bruise. Arielle gives Faunia's bulbiform bottom a rub and she cringes and cries out. Drab facade. Protrusion of balcony. Medical journal on the coffee-table. Coal-blackened clouds. Hallway of considerable dimensions and smelling of carnations with a wardrobe. Moroccan slippers roach-browny. A toucan swoops upward like a swing's seat. A lanky, taciturn teen, Death's neophyte, throws a javelin into birches and beeches. Bland van is a coffin with tires. Stocky smithy with a shaved head. Brocade of plantage on the riverbend. Clayey banks are surmounted by oleander. Stridulatory grasshoppers. Arielle tugs at Faunia's rubiginose axillae tufts as if they are pigtails. Faunia pouts and Arielle pinches her bum. Anger pounces on her. Extraordinary florae and faunae. Boughs pendulously swing. Typhlotic zephyrous chimera. Shutters are shields. To extort 'Lady Flowers' from Faunia, Arielle announces she has kidnapped Louis, threatening to put him in Dubius's menacing Metamorphosis Machine, a "mechanoid cocoon,' for a sex change (without the obligatory operation). Faunia finds out that Pauline stole the magic tome decades ago to thwart Arielle, who was determined to use it for nefarious ends, and, in addition, learns her aunt's physical alterations were forced on her. Avalanche of argumentation ensues. Arielle taunts her. Sonorous spate. An invisible cape of wind passes in daytime's courtyard. Moan of a maimed cello. Breakers pound. Faunia's deliberate impudence is ineffective and premature. Tangy malodor of ammonia. Magic-lantern slides are shown 24/7 on hung sheets, poetry, protracted, read aloud in unintentionally comical narrative tones, accidental vivacious accents, inflicted on the works. Universal topsy-turvying. The whole introduction is a tedious affair to Faunia. She squats on her haunches. Lateral porch. Leonine- legged park bench gardenward. Toothbrush of a caterpillar. Peregrinations of personages unfamiliar, Faunia at a loss to guess what their function is in this funny farm. Coral splendor. Tricycle, organ and decoy duck reconcile themselves to the property. Duskening copse. Penumbras are latticed, attributed to the lacey leaves. Ovoid owl, head and body oneinthesame. Males and females, nude, and with excellent pallor, merge in the broiling jet- black gloam. Gales are volatile. Faunia's ears ring like glass. Her lineaments are distorted, visions piercing and pellucid. She is wobbly as though she is a chariot's wheel loosening from its axis. Terse oaths of the breezes. Paradisal cirri. Zigzags of leven. Arielle's organ's fuzzy like a tennis ball. Reposing adults in bathing suits. Multitude of placid rhododendrons. Drowsy gusts. Faunia feels as if she's coming apart at the seams. Weak-willed, here, she is the wrong daub of paint on a radical painting, and yet sold for a respectable sum nevertheless. Sumptuous sofa. According to Arielle, her stay, or incarceration, is a linear continuation of a lack of social skills. Faunia does not pass Arielle's muster. A cheerful, tiny hellion with a simian frontage and rusted braces is anatomic white lightning. Water in the birdbath is like imperial stout. Robust, indeed rapturous, game of rugby is contested in a glorious grove, the match for the fallen angels with its delights and distress, the participants positively splendiferous hues on her optic nerves, definitely making impressions. Arielle, divested of her frock, kept in lingerie and heels, narrows her peepers, muttering as though she's a monk taking monastic vows, respiration resonant like a coppice. If she had a bushy tail it'd be erect. Stench of decaying vegetation. Carousers croon. Leaves lap the panes. Faunia's feeling as if she's enduring an auditory mirage, recondite hearing acute, the acoustic hallucination … The black sheep are flattering to Arielle's vainness. She swigs barleywine ale, paying tribute to her vice, sprawls seductively on the lilac-colored chaise longue. Faunia endures an inner ardent torture. Her flat chest heaves not unlike a steamer's boiler. Whiteheads on Arielle's downy back as though bird droppings on a marble monument. Dozing treelets. Faunia is petrified in the harsh luster, glare sharp as a lancet, vexation excruciating. Cliffs of Dover materialize in the mizzle. Rhubarb-pinkish welkin. Querelle, squinchy and wretched, has a massive coconut like a watermelon and bulldog aspect, a revenant infrequently manifesting, a fearsome apparition with a totally blunt personality. Grapevine has it he, in a former life, was a brawler and souse, a pauper who dwelled in the sticks, on the outskirts of the wastes of a blue-grey burg, slaved at a local haberdashery, became a loyal, indispensable employee, considered himself a "strapping seraph," an ex-cavalryman who fought bravely in the Civil War, an expert in leading midnight forays, clandestine attacks against the enemy, later relieved of duty for insubordination in a conflict with a superior officer who wore a monocle. He was a boil excised from the skin of the campaign. Arielle sashays and gulps rich port from a tumbler, babbles nonsense, and plops on the peacock ottoman, melodramatically hysteric as a fortune-teller, pies like ink-drops on the vellum of her cast. Faunia is sullen in her incomprehension. A cumulus unwinds as a ball of yarn. Marmalade light. Bric-a-brac in an urn and chrysanthemums in a vase on the mantel. Arielle prattles, and calmly, with her capricious disposition, slinks along in duck bootees, and seal-fur coat, cigarette crooked and smoldering, in the garden, indistinct in the spritz. She swats a midge off her columnar neck, shuts the sash, gazes flirtatiously, with concentrated gusto, at Faunia, who is reverently ogling her. Pools are like coagulated plasticine. Faunia's remote and anxious, has a cupola-cranium. She is wide-hipped, gymnast-muscled, lovely legs ill-shaven. She deals with queasiness. Turbid waters. Her impressionability is transparent. Hem of her velour, ruffled miniskirt hiked up high, modulation (pleading for familial assistance) an evanescent adumbration. She retreats into her nook of self-deception, her cranny of denial. Wrappers shuffle in the quixotic drafts. Profuse greenery. Gossamer showers. Skyline's basically a stormcloud. The condensation is a fringe of film on coffee left too long. Arielle is a habitué of casinos. A sacrificial offering of her shadow with the lamp turned off. Vestiges of her handsome visage. Her articulated acrostics accordionized by her palm. She stutters something about the past being the future, only in reverse. Her nasalized sighs sound as if she's sipping a slurpy through a straw. She stammers on a concept that dying is synonymous with living. Here is an uncanny place for curious souls. They are the dregs drained from a societal drink. She spews garbage like a sewage pump. Conoid conifers. Faunia finds the common denominator of comeliness here, behavior a parody of puerility. Everything gets blurry, because of her streaming tears, as though she's a submerged swimmer looking up through aqua pura. Stuffed skunk over the conventional hearth. Hawk hoverings over suburbanized hedgerows. Octopus of the prison squeezes Faunia with its tentacles. Jig-like flights of blowflies. Beck's gorged with reflections. Celestial chart is as a Chinese-checker board. Management's jocose imbroglio, lethal jokes innocuous. Porcupine quills of the soaker. Cacti like they are out of a pictorial ad. Sand as sawdust. Chinchillan cloudlets. Trap doors of tidal waves. Dazzling mosaics of the mesas. Mist like mineral matter. Birds ascend, and the sky is won; others descend, the losses minute. Mr. Merde, the excremental, fly-infested mound, chastises the puling Pecorino. Faunia, on the hopper, plans to release Louis. She's quiet as a mouse. And she moves with mincing steps. Hystricomorphic liriodendrons. Venerable Lazy Susan. Ripe quiescence. Clouds meet the celestial sphere on equal terms. Overcast is a sheet of rice paper covering the expensive etching of the blue lid.

Night puts an end to the nonsense of day. Dr. Dubius and Mr. Merde are absorbed in a verbal duel. Dubius says "fiddlesticks," to which Merde replies "poppycock," and claims Dubius is ancient like a Renaissance cenobite, and, out of charity, changes the topic. Dubius is a Monopoly maestro, availing himself of his fecal adversary's competitive nature, would intermittently distill a calmative into a canary-yellow coffee cup, mephitic mastic pervading his lab coat. He, in a somnambulant trance, played Faunia, incorporated into an amaranthine maillot (at Arielle's behest), who was adept at outsmarting him, zestfully gaining an advantage, and he deftly dived into these humiliating depths of deception, cheating to win. Naively she trusted him to participate fair and square. She was replete with a sense of the doldrums. Precip's globules, rainbow-lit, are ornamented, Xmas baubles. Querelle, insolent and servile in even doses, neglected his chores, did the crosswords in the paper, held as a banner. Oxygen murmurs with various species of bug. There's tremendous sogginess, too. Bandy-legged Dubius's grey folliculated corona, his hirsute hands not unlike a monkey's. Fleshly curlicues of his grannysmith peelings. Fake suede couch. Plunging into the wicker chair at a railing, he enkindles a khaki pineconical cigar. Merde is diarrheally runny at this juncture, and bluebottle- smothered. Ashen scales flit from the seegar. A mongoloid youth with an ill-formed build delivers a telegram, scarfing a meat patty and smoked herring. Faunia, hidden from view, on a snake of a trail, with leafy canopies, experiences the sensation of being an apostle apprehensive about stepping onto the water's surface. She coheres with her surroundings. Yielding to temptation, she jells with the meteorological character. Dubius sips cider from a goblet, prepping to partake of gambling arrangements, scheduled like a virtual dental appointment, predetermined as a planet's revolutions. Dubius, the betting astronomer! Mars with a deck of cards! The waging event marked on the calendar like an inexorable examination, routine repetitive as digestion, the necessity firmly linked to a cosmic regimen. The stars, in simpatico, stir. He adjusts his pince-nez, has gross excrescences on his nappy nape, baldspot like a pallid skullcap. Scintillant spurts in an interstice between the jail and john. Scent of myrtle. She eavesdrops on their confabulation. Lacunal spaces between sentences. At the clink, a tepid cooler, from her vantage point in the gloom, she remarks Querelle's gigantesque shadow. She's flabbergasted (and fortunate) he doesn't notice her. She thinks of a prolonged kiss and hug from Louis. Dammit! She imagines Arielle's displeasure, glower of glacial derision, fathoms the disastrous repercussions, should she get caught. Rats squeak as a bather's toes on the tiles. She bites her lip and shudders, expertly picking the cell's lock with heroic effort, her (breaking-and-entering) expertise paying dividends. She's panicking inside. Desperate measures are taken to rescue him. She has an inkling something is not right. Builders' skeletons of scaffolds. Viperous mouth of drainpipe. Plebeian miscreations in a private soliloquy at a cafe, morosely dawdle and take tablets. Parked sable sedan like a Steinway with wheels. Windowpanes are shaken by thunderclaps. Terra cotta tusks of headlights. Deadish pub. Querelle's outside, whistling, puffing on his corncob pipe, during the jailbreak. He makes his nightly rounds, after preliminary pushups, a ginormous guardian archangel performing purely perfunctory duties. He has hitherto lived an indigent, disorganized life. His mind is a mine he digs and drills in as a darn son of a bitch. Ascertaining all is well. It is perfectly peaceful. Rumor has it he has a steady diet of mold and bats, cranky on cognac. He's got a crimson countenance and grubby gemstone toenails. Celestial antique of a dirigible, an obsolete airship with a rigid structure, is inoperable on the front lawn. Her suspirations sound like gravel crunching under soles. She takes the plunge. Her vascular organ whomps rapidly. Dulcet tones of hail. Arborescent ferns. Her butterfly-ears are listening. Veinal vee on her forehead while she focuses. Is the plot featherbrained? Foolhardy? Insane? Suicidal? She feels as if she is awakening in a crate, and draped in a pall of frustration. Stewing on the obstinacy of chance, musing on the infallibility of fate. Her face's contorted by a frantic expression. She thinks of demented, damaged Arielle, admittedly a flexible and fascinating amazon, with a malleable, double-edged personality, the perpetrator of her distraught status, who wants to split her like a walnut, desiring to inflict a defeat on her antagonist, toying with her as though she is a cat with a mouse, calling her a "vile, spoiled brat." Faunia felt like quarry cornered in a hunter's lair. Cockatoos fling themselves as boomerangs. Fragrance of kerosene. Ghostly plaster and stucco on the distinctly European ceiling. Febriferous eventide and its mephitic turpentine and tar. Her vulturine eyes sting from the sweat, being blazes like a bonfire. The corpulent chef's chow provokes her gastric Mayday. She is lost in the haze and hum of panic, breathing spasmodic in the grim progress, blood a niagara in her skull. Divine Louis is asleep on a carpenter's bench with assorted afghans, head resting on a portfolio of prints. Ping-pong played emphatically by wrongdoers in the game room, the blind-white plastic ball whacked across the fractured table intersected by a flimsy net with sand- tinted paddles by the exquisite, ethereal, junior convicts. French window. The haggard, boneless galoot of a gardener, a high strung fellow, anemic as a fetus in alcohol, lives in reclusion when not on the job, a modest lick of achromic filament athwart his scalp, schnozzola like a sea urchin, and he clucks his gangplank of a tongue. He's a notorious regular at the suspect taverns and popular whorehouses (in an industrial city with its manufactory smokestacks, age-old epic poems of plants), with a penchant for hardworking streetwalkers with chiseled cheekbones and their incomparable beguiling artistry executed with mathematical precision. He venomously burns with incessant lust, lumbers as if he's (partially) incapacitated by a hernia, furbished in humble raiment. Stalactiform umbra. Dour moon dislodged from the stygian sky by clouds. Sun was teasingly peek-a-booing like a coin trick. And her eyelashes were peacocked in the colorful rays. Cirri is in a radial arrangement in the firmament. Spruces and eucalyptuses are dressed up for the occasion of the season. Cumuli are passports to the Elysium of the empyrean. She visualizes the world through the prism of this place and its multitudinous alien problems. Fleshly menisci of her nostrils. An adipose accountant, a crusty crank, statistically crackers, with coarse-textured integument and its stalish emanation, and coily, bunned tresses, striation of vibrissa under her rubescent potato- proboscis, a dumpy groundhog with perforated earlobes and a fondness for spiritualism, manila folders armpitted, looks like a stranded manatee on the woodchucks. Brunet penguins of anthills. Thunderhead-blackened shade. There's a ripple effect Faunia experiences with the prisoners, the losers intrinsically circles diverging from her center. Plumbing is made out of organ pipes. A shiver of uncertainty brushes her coccyx as though it's a dry mitt in the midst of a surge of inspiration. She has the sense she's an eyeball rolling in a universal socket. Louis rouses, stunned, clambers, clumsily, like an alarmed lunatic. He gapes, limp as a rag doll, rubbernecks her, licks his chops, fillings of his teeth flashing. His hands are hot irons on the gourds of her dimpled buttocks and stout thighs with their cellulitic dents, endearments dark and delectable. She has the mug of a madonna. Printed programs on the tabletop. Wild dogs exchange barks in the foggy distance. Chiaroscuro collapses as empty vestments. Inanimate objects you'd find in a country home. Carpet feels like lichen. Star-stained welkin. Bearing the brunt of the heavy humidness as if burdened with a cumbersome trunk on her back. Her expressions change like a deck of cards repeatedly reshuffled. Insect chirps with the sonance of a comb going through ringlets. She whisks him (glimming like a blanched worm and redolent of wild game) off as though on wings, both moving like they're escaping from an enemy, staggering as individuals impregnated with beer with numerically high ABV percentage. Torrential downpour. Restroom as some Gothic cathedral. Transpicuous feathers of frost. Irate guttural winds. Like in bootcamp, the hoodlums march in single file, Merde the reluctant drill sergeant. For Faunia, it is unexplainable why they pay the crop- haired, portly valet's salary when there are no visitors. This joint's a fragmentary, nonsensical nightmare. She discovers the boys here were originally girls, and that Arielle's main goal is to control gender population world-wide. Querelle, with plethoric lungs and glum, parchment-complected, a freight train chugging along a downhill track, no pussyfooting or tiptoeing, catches them, hiding in the jungle, and promptly scoops them up as a nurse would sibling babies. Their coos are characteristic of doves. Louis's blinkers dilate, are screwed up, in his grasp. Faunia's mind goes round like a circus elephant. Hitting him, she could be mistaken for someone smacking a mosquito. Arielle reads her the riot act in a castratoid delivery.

Querelle, repressed in velveteen trousers, teaches pugilism, fencing, and gymnastics on rosined linoleum, by a blockade that's basically canyons of cabinets, the lessons redundant and rigorous. He mauls a vivacious, nondescript, chalk-pale, carmine-eared young 'un with an impediment to his speech (who'd caustically badgered him) on a Turkish divan. Faunia visualizes herself leafing through the stashed copy of 'Lady Flowers.' She is snub-nosed, mad-eyed, slope- shouldered and broad-minded, with acidic wit, to all and sundry. Her ensemble's in disarray. Her lips are as incurved chrysanthemum petals. She has grown weary of Arielle's bogus facades, deceptive enterprises. Majestic boudoir. Arielle, restricted in a rhinestone teddy, securely ensconced in the soot-dark loveseat, blathers on to Faunia, who lingers at the gentle-graded staircase, about the monumental progression of her fiscal system, and describes the pathetic-looking Russian novel, with its subject of incest, as being "sheer piffle." Situations happening to Faunia - she feels like the penitentiary is the equivalent of an electric field, occurrences as lines of force situated in planes which pass through the vibrator of her essence. Zoo-ish racket. Arielle's a stunner with sunken cheeks. A fiddle weeps a hint of a hymn. A non-entity vulgarian, an interlocutress with reptilian blinders and lorgnette, world-weary and heavy-hearted, freedom of movement hindered by corpulence and dungaree, is compliant in a contest of wills with Arielle in the bathroom with enameled flooring, voluminous not unlike a subterranean station. Luxury object of a crystal paperweight on a buffet in the cloakroom. Faunia hears the clarion of kookiness here. Occasion of a grand concert, olympically theatric, with a charitable agenda, held on the golf course. Rufescent heron flies into the horizon like a fish in an aquarium tank. Arielle, with emergent zeal, gropes Faunia, who grips her own fanny, flinches, frowns, and, subsequently, pictures 'Lady Flowers,' its spine cracking deliciously, and she dips into the titles in the table of contents, leisurely sifts through the soft paper, such fancy pages, between finger and thumb. Arielle's narcotic, urgeful intonation crepitates, complaining of "slander spread by competitors," and, amiably, accosts Faunia. Her overtures are shameful, advances odious. Skyline's spruced up with stars. Incoherent sibilances. Piebald satchel. Cacophonic hubbub. Arielle scissors her celebrated legs. Uvular ululations. Her toned arms are folded crosswise, swathes her torso in a sleazy towel, grills Faunia on who the artist is responsible for the cruel caricature of her that was passed round at main recess today. Faunia responds she hasn't the faintest. Her vermicular guts squiggle. She's a nut Arielle's intent on cracking. Arielle quaffs sweet wine and engorges pistachio parfait. Tenebrosity is total. The servant, with a paunch, starched collar and cuffs, initiates a hasty cleaning rite, scrubbing the stove with a soapy sponge. Faunia's angst and awe in the rotten-Rivendell utopia. Her emotional floodgates burst and a rush of tears pour forth. Her brain's preoccupied with problems unsolvable. Eidolonic reflections in the grated prison-panes. Tumult of sobs from the recreation entrance passage. Dopey, orally laggard, Arielle sits as a sack in the pretzel armchair, a picturesque quality to her stationary status, grand shadow in pierrot mimicry. Pack of sniffer canines. She rises like a fist to dispatch an uppercut to a jutting jaw and palpates Faunia's waist. Faunia's protests overshoot their mark. To be dislodged from this bughouse as ash tapped from a cig ... Oceanic booming. Lifers wrestle in the buff. Chest constricted, she draws a deep breath. Arielle's metaphorical, mystical mumbo jumbo. Thalassic rote. Camel-humpy surf. Membranous air. Faunia, captive in these confining quarters, perpetually under construction, in the light and shade, wards off the molestations with pertinently trivial thoughts, images as half- finished sketches. Her nipples are bilberry-ripe. Arielle is whitish like death, immersed in the improvisatory (and icky) preoccupation. Her mouth, ajar is like a black hole. Pelagic lactescence. Preeminent escarpments on the shingly beach. In a onepiece swimsuit, Faunia swills her cooled cocoa, venter trembling as a jellyfish on the sea's surface, incisors catching the chiaroscuro. Her socks are like mittens. Essaying to recapture her peace of mind. Storm of impending doom. Arielle is a ball-buster, kicking them as hacky sacks. Auditive talons of acoustic keyboards rake her ears with avian accuracy, lacerating mercilessly. Asymmetrical archipelago of Faunia's nether regions are carnally conflagrant. Arielle's enigmatic expression and eloquent smirk. Paradisian imperfection. Domed silos distinctive. Enclave's contours emerge from the cadaverous vapor, evolve an aurific glow, a forbearing gleam, those outlines significantly fledged. Clouds overtake the vault. Rapscallions play hopscotch in the raw. Corollas are Lilliputian parachutes. Lithe lifeguard has on a Red Cross armband, unbuttoned rayon tunic aflutter, pitches projectile-pebbles into the amethyst drink. Plenty of pratfalls from the darling cons. Everything in the cosmos filters through Faunia's person. When she was going up in the generic elevator, she felt like she was in Jack's beanstalk as it quickly grew. She's not on intimate terms with the fraternity of yardbirds in this clink, does not confide in them when it comes to her fancies and fears. Arielle arouses detestation in her. Chills ripple on her spinal cord as fingers tickling the ivories. It's frightfully frigging hot. Her swimwear is a clingy, clammy compress, her discomfort acute. She slits her lamps, so appallingly alone. Dwarfish furniture. This psychiatric hospital is a vein tapped out, a broken record played for years. Penumbrous fumbling on the mushy ground. Her eyesight is dulled by the dim dusk. Her deliring gray matter, cafe-au-lait tan. She's roasting alive. Her flavorless peppermint gum flag-snaps. She absentmindedly scans your standard postcard. Shelving with horned shells. A gale blows harder than its predecessors. The dear internees: a ragtag collective stuck in a rut; an inescapable cycle of social disconnection and familial dysfunction. The senescent, tubulose tutor, who resides in a bungaloid cabana, has an enviable devil-may-care jauntiness. Her being brims with unresolvable dubiety. Her personality shows through her physicality like a watermark. Hoosegow chokes her as bindweed does a column. Iambic tetrameter of the windowwasher. She's snagged in this snare, bogged down in the quicksand. Her opaque pallor. The author who wrote 'Lady Flowers' ... his/her pen must've fountain-flowed. The bricklayer's chunkiness has a piquancy, flesh with the tint of ham, kneeling in the imploring illumination. Bumblebees go berserk. He's got cornflower oculuses. Frog-eyed rhymster with patina of tan and poppy-hairy ass-crack, position recalling Rodin's 'Thinker,' with nightingale trills, recites, from memory, a futuristic sonnet, with inerrant flair and pomposity of romanticism, the remoteness of royalty, verse with rolling cadences, lyricism foreign and meaning occultic. Arielle'd cultivated a peacock pose in a fading snapshot, her lashes fringes, derma layer lacquer-looking. Her contralto inflection.

Surroundings with pretentious fabrication. Nauseating noisomeness of her self- complimentary combustion. Husky plaints skirting the cemetery. Outdoors, a critter is squashed, like it was ironed. Weeping willows wail their sorrows. Croquet hoops. Waterlogged raft is a deflated bladder. Fetor of refuse. Stairs creak as snow. Arielle's oral cavity gapes like a gramophone horn and Faunia surveys her palate, uvula, and puny promontories of ginger gums. Her china-doll lexicon. Riotous lags. She possesses an abstracted vacuity. Faunia has a risky devotion to Louis. She cerebrally notes Arielle's additional eccentricities, perceives the uncommon in the other commoners. She feels as a toy tree, unstable on its support stand. Arielle scopes her triumphant tokus, the futtocks like twin boiled chickens. She bores as effulgence through a door's chink, unwinds inside like a spiral. Beer bottles as tenpins on the duvet. Faunia settles there, like a bag of flour. Trumpet blare of her raspberry. Listless greenery's omnipresent riffle. Granitoid gloaming, imperturbable and immutable. Serpentoid jeep's tracks in the dirt. Striplings are summoned by the messy Merde, four members of the chain gang singled-out. Barracks ... a dresser, portico the drawer left open. Elongated structure in the lunar twilight. Dubious darkness. Valet has a wiry figure, cupboard can, trapezoid mustache, and spaced chiclets. Alcohol burner. A landscaper with evasive eyes, beefy voice and meaty body. Faunia, the ingenue, had spurned Arielle. She sniggers exultingly. Did she make a critical mistake by rebuffing her? Nevertheless, she chooses to internalize the celebration of an admittedly vulnerable victory. Arielle's constitution is a virile void. Deluge's oblivion. Her playacting on the particularized platform is cobbled up on the conventions of traditional dramaturgy, in compelling courses of action, dramatic trifles spontaneously discarded, the production bearing her personalized trademarks, themes threadbare, vocabulary with its peculiarities, in a Nordic singsong, with auxiliary accents, answering a thespian calling. She settles on the hassock. Her cryptic loquacity, peripatetic moue. Faunia, the gamine, once the sweet apple of her eye, is now sour fruit. Whines of the wafts. Shimmering panorama indicates an undeveloped pic. Arch of herbage. Faunia exists on an unearthly plane, her life a functioning organ, Arielle the fatal tumor. She feels comparable to a superfluous prop, a cardboard backdrop that could fall flat, lacks the confidence to convince herself otherwise. Arielle is the star of the show. Faunia's a marginal stagehand, plays her invisible part conscientiously. Arielle reestablishes contact and Faunia rebuffs her, relief for doing so lurking in the folds and furrows of her totality. She doesn't anticipate receiving a reward! She has an inner satisfaction in the rebuke. Her entirety is warmed as water by sunbeams. She's treading on quicksand! This hellaceously suffocative atmosphere doesn't agree with her. Her cardiac drumming. She is exposed like a heart by a surgeon's scalpel. Arielle's MaxFactor greasepaint. Horny nails. Blethering on about yachts and champagne. She and Faunia are parallel lines crossing. Cheeping of cicadae. Anglican church. Jaundiced brightness. Antiseptically white walls. Hobbling feet. Air's oilyly gleaming. Membranaceous moonlight. The husky bookkeeper, with a derelict character, Roman muzzle, and leathery lids, is window- washing industriously in a canvas chair, in a beret, polyester slacks and espadrilles, the sparse getup on his bulk intimating license of the scalding temperatures. An anorectic idler on the promenade. Menagerie malodor. Provincial gymnasium. Metamorphosis of Faunia's mind. Her ears are aflame. Her shadow expresses her essence. Notions embedded in her brain. From each locus of its periphery her libido (always on active duty) follows a radius to the center of her (imagined) cunt. Bungaloid abode. Classroom blackboard. Arielle strokes her collarbone in actressy automatism.

Faunia gives a fling to preserve an ounce of dignity, independence. She no longer resists, is drained of strength. Her head spins, reminding you of a weather vane. Brisk breezes. Querelle's a brutified rackmaster. Murmurous bunkum ... incantational palaver ... something about a card trumped ...

Silence sepulchral. Fertile chamber. For Faunia, the footprints of assurance have tiptoed off, leaving no traces of tracks. Her daily dreamery includes diablos, plucked out of a low-rent carnivale, the warty midgets, slathered with Vaseline, like hominid toads, cinerous rotters lumpen and tumorous, this phantasma of membraned clods twisted versions of characters from Anton Rubinstein's 'The Demon' opera, a perverse parody with the orgasmic orgies described in graphic detail in her mind. The reformatory rack's iron and she serves as the magnet; or vice versa. The bitty bites on her back are from the mattress's unwanted buggy bedfellows. Arielle noshes her liverwurst, glares at her like she is a traitress, or a cunning crook, caught in the act. Systematically manic glimmer. Sappy sibilations of the crests. Combers sound as if they're touched by red-hot pokers. Oriole-gold empyrean. Tortoises have these hag-like necks. Cirri as though they're hurrying cripples. Above each cot hangs a lithograph with text printed in microscopic type. A dependable and debonair teacher, most manly, has derma layer sugar-white, graying temples symboliz-ing middle age. Gossip maintains he was originally banished because he'd exposed himself indiscriminately to the young and old. Arielle siphons soda pop with a candy cane straw. Demolition of a granitic bathhouse, rubble cleared for its structural successor. Plenitude of racemosa and nosegay. Hazy morn. Pheasant and ante-lope in refulgent lances. The firmament has a sudden center with the moon's appearance in the cumuli with their widening intersecting circular motions. Vaporous gauze. The unsociable, spindly seamstress whirls, waist flexed. Arielle seasons Faunia's mouth with sacramental saliva. Concertinaed wire. Spurs of stars span the welkin. A trail of tepid snot jiggles from Faunia's nostril to her chin. Splendorous shaft is aslant. A flunky cockerel, breeched on the bright bay, with side-whiskers and stored-up secrets, rides the mower jockey-style, sopping in onion sweat, nibbling on sunflower seeds, is in desti-ny's sniper-scope: he will contract typhus and be executed in a firing squad for treason. Seashell ashtray. A dainty damsel (Glen is now Glenda), in a daze, in the artless aft, shunned for stuttering, is inordinately fond of badminton. Purity of her profile. She is leading her life into a blind alley. Geometric grin is inscribed on her lovesome lineaments. Her upper thighs are strung with varicose veins. Parcels loaded in a phone booth. Party with punch. Cloudlets perform calisthenics. Querelle's an uncultured beast with a portable gadget, that is, hearing aid, a deviceful apparatus, its whistling inexistent in the inept garret, in its semiobscurity, and yokelike necklace, walking draggingly. He is limited by his deafness (ideally, dealing with Arielle, the human harangue), and has diabetes. Faunia's an extinguished star in this dark space, an unfinished sentence in an incomplete chapter. Arielle's lengthy legs, denuded of pantyhose, open not unlike a nutcracker, and Faunia's breadbasket is lit up as a soundless explosion. Her BVDs hug her behind as dead leaves would a wet roof, crotch hotly alight. Being a hermaphrodite, for her, is like climbing a set of stairs with a flickering candle and the shadow manifests on the wall. Bonbons in a basket. Lamp's luster passes through its shade as water a medusa. An araucaria's in its isolation. Cavernal pantry. Is the badly worn, oilcloth-bound volume that brought her here ... safe? Strip of heathscape is transmuted into an elongated backbone, the mechanics of the metamorphosis unknown to her. Any certainty is eclipsed by uncertainty. Tenacious toiler out there. Gnats do figure-eights. Somnambulically she steps into an insensate microcosm, like a pants pocket, a caliginous zone, and a mo of muddle ensues, her external sagacity internal, countenancing the identification of these cramped confines. Breeze is sated with moisture. Heebie-jeebie-inducing householdry. She projects departing, wisely, briskly and ably, dashing with vertiginous speed, the bastille a blankness shaped in her image. Her jockeys conceal the meek disgrace of her "genitals." Arielle's pancake foundation is plentiful and exaggerated, boysenberry mouth lopsided. Her luscious lips retain their smile, that, at last, gets replaced by a sulk. After lounging, as a mummy, she moves to and fro, senses like a second sight. For a sec she suspires, and entreatingly. Cloud on sky - ink-mottled blotter. Halves of the saloon swinging door reunite. The light changes its position as a person slumbering. Babel of a kiddie quarrel curls up like a wispy pillaret. The miscreants are linked by lawbreaking and justice's fairness. Life here's a humble ritual. Impersonal crush of the caf and its racket and shifting juvies. A useless nonpracticing lawyer, getting over a battle with typhoid fever, in a funky fedora, serves them, deformed feet in smart shoes, observing the minute evolutions of cliques with neglected eyes, communicating with the dingy flooring. His pupils flash hither and thither. Bees ministering to debris of florets, incidentally mowed. Melleous aroma. Hawthorn bushes. The chalet- fashioned public toilet is occupied by a hefty harlequin for hire. Uncomplicated transformations of the cirrus in the hospitable heavens. Arielle Frenching Faunia: a sparrow feeding her fledgling. Parlor is a Pandora's Box of ill-will. Faunia's in a trance, her visions with irrepressible, incredible components. Arielle infects her anatomy with a blistering ardency, a savage salacity. Plagued by the disease of desire, Arielle takes off her cantaloupe brassiere to refresh her bosom. After her sustained siesta, with its divine amusements, there were roars of guffaws; a horrific hilarity. She tries on a taupe tankini, a prevalent nightmare, lapses into thought, and consults the mirror. Close-shaved convict skull of moon. Her vox in its crystallinity. Faunia feels like an embryo that was scraped out of the womb. She psychologically soaks in the salubrious salts of sureness that she will see her aunt again, the puckered forehead, those triangular eyebrows ... Arielle addresses her "bovine beauty," and "skittish mannerisms." Polychrome cushions. She brings up, unbidden, her flop of matrimony, the marriage, to an insurance company drone, following a prearranged pattern of dating disappointment, the disastrous denouement imposed by a clash of personalities and the collusion of circumstances, the core of their conjugality a liquiform ooze, the connubiality rife with misfortune and failure. Her robust rump, concave palms, emery-paper heels. Faunia ransacks the refrigerator and can't find a morsel of sustenance, optimism, only the mold of pessimism. Morbid ballads in her retentive music box. She's vibratory as a belfry in bronze throes, whacked by the bell-ringer of a situation. Her lemon-and- lime tonic flat like a lame joke. Showers smell of something burning. Origami of a fawn. Plopping sounds of the sprinkles. Arielle is pseudoefficient in prepping the borscht. She's as a culinary stalwart attending to the project with enthusiasm in a central period of drama, and taking the initiative to intrude on Faunia's privacy, who's on the pot, like it's a piece of urgent business, why she's barging in on her, compelled to convey the news of exceptional importance, Arielle instantly identified, and without approval, articulating in monotone, stalk-ish arms gesturing, the process of peeking at Faunia on the foamy horseshoe affording her meaningful pleasure. Faunia cannot disentangle herself from the web woven by Arielle, the gaper, chicly sexualized. Faunia, dizzy on a sorry-go-round on the prison's playground, looks at her suggestive trap like she's lipreading; or as the victim of an auto accident. Plane trees, juniper shrubs, rococo rocks. Saliferous solution of precipitation. A Dalmatian parts the glistering stream of a beaded curtain. Rivulets in the gutter. Her skin suffused with heat. Slate-blue horizon. Potted plants, jealous-green, are dying a thirsty death. Elation channels through Arielle's veins, her nerves receptive. A thrush whistles. Environs with an essence of effluvia. Maritime panting, pulse of rain, velocious colors of the rainbow. Arielle, vignettes adorning her yap with substance, clutches and cherishes her, Faunia on the brink of breaking down. Framed pen-and-ink etching of a feathered Indian lassoing a hatless cowboy on the dry plains. Faunia weighs the sophisticated similes on the scale of uneducated understanding. Her feet are fiery hot. Luminous lengths of Arielle's arms. She plays parlor games with her own issuances. Her candor like it is dutiful. Faunia gets lost in her manic maze. The overcast of her doldrums is changed by the sunburst image of Louis. Clouds are billowy as swollen snow. Equestrian statue in the taciturn twilight. Theme of storm starts out at sea. Amputations of aspens.

Faunia holds an improv session in the court of her conscience, and calls a halt to the make-out get-together with Arielle, quite collected and carefree, a weaver of words, her mockeries poisonous, inventions of her insults unsurpassable, verbal venom squirting like a sliced artery, prodigious puns as stained glass, language whips she lashes, tornadic vocalizations spinning like tops, leaving barren land and felled trees in her wake. She has a spacey disposition, cosmetics a decorous disguise. She derives ghoulish fun from creating her lingual convolutions on the fly, taking 'em out for test drives on suspected dummies. Behaving as if she is a basic proprietress of a reputable establishment and the adolescents are the fundamental clientry. Her primary gag, a smashing gift, is the nascent ability to gab, and with a certain celerity. The pair's finely tuned string instruments. Querelle's pharaoh's phiz and cranial chip. Halation of his cigarillo smoke hangs. Epileptoid applause of the ocean's whitecaps. The juveniles' hustle-bustle of geniality, with an abundance of handshakes and backslaps. Aroma of jasmine. Windswept golflinks. For a stretch Faunia lived in the margins of Louis's life, hardly affecting the text of his existence. The sunset shadow of separation (casual affairs the main culprits) haunted their relationship for a stint, and yet their staunch friendship remained unimpaired. A Doberman pinscher snoozes in the steam-warm spinney, it rather cowardly, shrinking. Thunder sounds not unlike housemaid-thumped-out carpets. The nighttide rolls, raves on. Faunia's bunched belly is a burlap roll. The two are atoms appetently recombined. The sentimentality, discord, gibberish (unrepeatable) and futility a major mishmash. A tomato-nosed old- timer, bone-white, with a basilisk kisser and salamander eyes, in hobnailed boots, is fidgety, discussing scandalous adventures with his alter ego of ghostly transparency, the surroundings seen through him, with complacent, barbarous conviction, in a stream of consciousness, the communication automatic and alchemical. Hilaration. Jubilation. Theirs. Poorly-pressed silhouettes. Lassitudinous laurels hencluck. Arielle tactions and osculates Faunia, modest and mild, as though she might detonate. Cockscomb-cerise vault. Flowers exhibited in the latest seasonal fashions designed by nature. Countryside's shaped like a greyhound. Cherry stone of Faunia's mushky. She ceases (puckering up), as air retained in the lungs. The meadow's stubble. Arielle moves like a silverfish, bites as a bloodsucking insect. Her stony oculi, caressing inflection. Umbral hobnobbing. Partitionless, stagnant office. Mandolin musical on the relic transistor radio. She has a devilish dexterity when it comes to doling out punishment. Oxygen is like olive oil. Her vacillating gaze, flesh with a goddess glaze, gait and gestures offbeat, poles apart. Lad/lass bawling. Ocular panes with operculate shades. Hunting lodge shambly. Inn tumbledown. Light and shadow ... correlation of contrariness. Fairytale forest road. Rainy asterisks. Graphs of lightning. The lakelet, a shiny silver spread, can't settle on an expression. Irrigated islet. Faunia feels as a food particle lodged behind a molar. The sanitarium with its (paradoxically) variety and uniformity. There are aims and methods in Arielle's merciless lust for power, reordering a disordered world, with a profound spiritual potency. She doesn't give a hoot about the welfare of the inmates. She deserves derision and destruction! The discernible divinity (an indispensable condition) enwafting her has not diminished; nope, it has been, in her stark state, enhanced, confirming her celestial status. Her machinations are not minuscule. This prison is destined to undergo upheavals. Field laborers, coal miners, mountain shepherds. She's a perfidious lover. She coos. Dubius is the helve, Arielle the business- meaning end of the axe. Stress runs off her like water off a goose; remarkable, considering the multitudinal matters cluttering her mind. She's unbearable to the point of asphyxiation, an ailment to Faunia. Her absinthian awfulness is concentrated, undiluted, the bottle of her sealed. Her banal credos: chaff fed to Faunia, who's fed up with the admonitions and restrictions. The mellifluent maxims are repeated in different keys. Freedom is granted, as, for instance, the capacity to crap is insinuated by the fact of having eaten. Drab dejection of the workstation. Faunia's phrenic nerves flair into a fiery pain. She mentally grasps the sordid details of Arielle's personality, recognizing her character like she would an octopus by its tentacles. This scurrilous shit is getting stale. Her stylistic affectations too. Dubius's Caesaroid baldness, armature of dated bifocals. He yowls as a cat in heat. Faunia wishes for a retraction of herself from this scenario, reap the benefits of a scene retake. The halting visual speech of the ink-bluish vista. Gusts have the sonancy of a sidewise whistle. Jagged joy of the jailbirdies playing a soccer match on a wildflowery pitch. Demonic howls of the nasty nocturne. Arielle has her system of courtship, her amatory habitude, behavioral tendencies. Wordiness of her verselets. Faunia bitches that it was a kidnapping, insists it was an abduction, elicits visible signs of worry, tear-blinded in this spheric bleakness. Shovels, hoes, stack of lumber. An electrical jolt of terror from scalp to sole. Inescapable songs over the loudspeaker; an auricular formality for festivities. Is there an unimaginable distance between her and Pauline? Is she near or far? Endless starkly-lit, neutral corridors with a succession of locked doors. She has the sense she's being watched by secret agents of incalculable proportions. Fanfares at the crossroads; general jubilation. Her heartbeat is a basic unit of time. Arielle's diabolical manipulations. She insists she's affected by insomnia, insanity is inflicted upon her. The juicy intonation ... She doesn't call all the shots. Running the entire shebang isn't required. Possessing the requisite managerial skills ain't necessary. A marine general does not have to be a crack sniper; a navy colonel should not have to be a stupendous swimmer. Wacky sequence of her involuntary facial expressions. Anecdotes about her progenitress, a thickset woman with a beehive hairdo and a penchant for substances illegal and a talent for invention, making gewgaws till cockcrow, living an insular life after the paterfamilias passed. Servants' quarters. Her mush's a crooked crease, regaining her composure. Reaching these new heights of realization, Faunia has achieved a bird's-eye view. She fancies an exorcism of imprisonment. Seedy masseur. Doddering tailor. Barber's an embittered invalid. A woeful wench, of the loosest kind, a fugitive figure with puppety jerkiness, blunders into the thicket. Leven's cracks sound like clothes ripped. Tigroid stripes of umbrae. The regime of jailers is hardcore, but still performing their tasks with dedication, engrossed by their duty. Arielle is always reviewing groundbreaking methods of effective incarceration in her independent and, in part, unsatisfactory solitude, emphatic in the conviction in coming up with irrefutable ideas. She ponders plans to flourish further in her position, and strives for institutional prosperity. She dines frugally on a blueberry bun, immersed in administrative meditation. Her servile assistants and weakling interns enter with quibbles, queries and reports, and exit. She listens to accounts of meetings. Corny counselor Faunia deems to be dangersome, a potential pedophile. One scorching midday, he quacked and pecked her on the snout. Crickets' agrarian canticle. Faunia's spinal cord is a suspension bridge, chills the cadenced steps of those crossing it, the rhythm coinciding with her cardiac palpitations. If Arielle's the ruler, a dictatress, Faunia mulls over tyrannicide. She, Arielle, is a monstress that must be eradicated. Submersing in musing. She has to hire a lawyer, or get a petition for clemency. Her nerves snap as guitar strings. She knows Arielle will suppress sedition. Fragmentary impressions from the past combine with the ones in the present. Doomful stillness. Gala affair with donors in attendance. The drencher has the sonance of a death rattle. Her slippery cogitations she cannot grip, like trying to catch eels using chopsticks.

The lowering sky seems to sag from a significant spacey weight pressuring from above. Arielle's habitually overwrought voice resounds. Faunia refuses to obey her oppressive influence. She knows she's got to get on all fours before she can get on her feet! The on call nurse, a bloated broad in skimpy scrubs, a moralizing moron with wrinkles on her bulging brow as hurdles, jelly-jowls, the amplest abdomen, and vestigial whiskers (after the electrologist's unforgivable mistakes) drifts like a sleepwalker. A survivor of a police-inspired massacre of plant-strikers when a riot broke out in a hyperborean region, she discharges a salvo of sneezes. Maniacal mosquitoes prevail. Arielle's critique is a stake impaling Faunia's chest. She feels as a beast getting butchered. Groggy murkiness and its insectoid inhabitants in aimless amnesia, winged commas forgetting their destination. Inverted exclamation mark of a linden. Arielle is Jezebel out of Jean Racine's play. Her breathing's like from an overtaxed engine. Pebbly beach. Interchange of fulgurant values. Shuddering mewl of an opening door. Faunia has the sensation of being yanked out of her own world and forced into a liquid medium, polar waters, in which she wades, arms and legs belonging to other individuals. Companionable clouds. Dust is as frost. This insulation-muffled sheltering. Steps plod along a passage. Creamy swellings of falcate, frothy rollers, informative and serviceable for the surfers. Phosphorescence gives a longer lease to the shade. Lampshade coronates the albinal light. Penknife scarcely manageable for Arielle, explaining, licking her susurrous lips, she is in charge of her, Faunia, a newcomer, breaking her in as a baseball glove, declares habiliments hamper her movements. Hitch and hesitation in her stride, modulation slenderized, unrestrained by raiment, divulging she has to wheedle slumber on a nightly basis.

For a good old fashion snore! A billow distends the briny not unlike a suspiration does the ribs. Luminous geometric gems on the wooden floor besprinkled with cinders of sand. Querelle, pottering in the orientoid garden, on savorless soil, dips his mitt into a baptismal pickle barrel. Cirri bosom the blue. Rhomboids of radiance. Gales sound as respirations of somebody with sick bronchial tubes in the prison of their person. Limping daddy longlegs. Bumpy ball of tinfoil. Arielle vows to spank Faunia if she continues to be rude to her. If she is nice she will be secured in a snuggle. Not a pleasurable prospect! Queer oxidation odor. Licorice sticks. Faunia's brave peepers probe Arielle's slim build, lording over her, boldly barefoot in the bedroom. Arielle, with a shrug of contempt, is an executrix binding her to the block. Brightness bejewels the widespread chamber with its simulacrum of a lounge, immodest as it is untidy. It's been a harassing hour with no hiccups. A Swede/ Dane sow of a curiosity-seeking seeress with impossible pies and awareness, a wonder-working fortune-teller in a comedic towel-turban, shrewd when it comes to parlor games, with the support of imagination and its inquiry, functions at her best in her native element of tension and its varying fluctuations. She's eloquent and engaging, at the hydraulic elevator out of commission, looks like her skeleton was removed by some crackpot surgeon. Porcine squeal of her frump. And another poof screams as a woman during painful childbirth (attaining ultimate limits of anguish), gastric vocal chords straining, turning into a murmurous medley; or like a man when given the news of a sweepstakes win. Her bowels engender shit to her slacks. Oleander and stardust in the hygienic eve. Fireflies dilute the darkness. Rhythmic plashes falter and fade altogether. Convulsive exertions of crows. They heckle and hail Querelle. Rich rhymes of the winds. Arielle's pearlescent vernacular purls, language, delivered in dulcet tones, with limpidity and luster, casts a brilliant spell. She, meretricious, crouches Turkish fashion, eschews a conventional cheerful smile (to which she is characteristically prone), and offers a capacious hug. Faunia overcompensates for the rusted reluctance of the railing. Her heart pounds as a galloping of eager pursuit. She hems and haws. Her capital punishment for going along with this farce - committing suicide. Her expression's like she is coping with a subliminal calamity. Harsh irritation of the illumination. Loud convo. Arielle blazons she had careers in these fields: librarian, translatress, bookbinder, and typesetter. Her backend blowout has the dominant notes from a human throat, the flatulent hurricane howling bearing the imprint of her personality. Varicose veins on her thin thighs are like traceries in India ink. Parenthesization of her cut arms, bracketed in expectancy of an embrace. Ornate vignettes, Germanized and Russianized, with a caromish coordination. Shivers of sleet pellets are as ball bearings. Forget-me-not gray overcast. Tombal stink. Dodo-like, garlicky groundskeeper with a tawney tonsure apologetically salaams to Merde. Cadaverkins of kiddos, their teeheeing with the sonance of tearing cloth. A disincarnate woodpecker. Nutshell, toenail, lottery ticket, and thingum on a glass-topped bistro table. Equivocal sundown. Hail is the size of cuckoo eggs. Desiccated flotsam and jetsam. Faunia's chogey is as an aberrant ape astray in the air and with the foulness of stewed rutabaga. She has lessons after the mandatory luncheon. She is heavy of head and light of loin. Hippopotamus hide of the celestial sphere. Arielle's verbal caesura; she's apparently stunned, like she's deliberating on diagnostics of superhuman discovery, in studied simplicity. Stylized splendor of her hairdo. She is unsure whether or not she will succeed in sneezing, holding a hankie, and in a benevolent fuss she buoyantly achieves volitional substance. She's tense as a cocked pistol. Humdrum schoolroom. Her resilient willpower, mien of kind insanity, mounting to the lav. Her disposition's like she is a monkey in mimicry of thinking of an idea, ordered to do so by her trainer; or her demeanor is as an anthropoid, in total recall, remembering shorthand notes. Thoughts play a game of leapfrog over her grey matter. She snaps to her senses like from an electric charge, regains a hold on relative reality, with its ipso facto truthlets and falsities, and remains in the sphere of earthly dimensions. Her elongated hand conforms to the concavity of Faunia's gut, and the curvature of her scapula. Faunia has tingles in the tum. Expressiveness of her physique is enveloped in trappings. Lust is the corpse of love, she believes. Orangeade puddles. Skyline contains a concrete indication of impending storm. She's a wild critter pet-domesticated. The situation demands a deliberate veneer of concupiscent complicity. Is she a disruption in this province? Pinpricks of incandescence in her retinas. A river runs out of bed. Alpinic niagara. Arielle's interested in her intricate fruit, says Merde's harebrained idea to patent and mass-market gallow poles is more than cockamamie. Ablutionary wet stuff. Snow-owl cirri. Truncated melodies of her talking. Ticktack of the wallclock. Mica fillings a leaden load in her oral cavity. Praying mantis ironing board. Unduly punctual forenoon. Grill on the patio is the shape of a stag beetle. She makes a mirage of the chat. Her cheeser tattles about its presence. Dun den, greenhouse-heated, has an untenanted appearance, highbacked armchairs, and ogival windows intrusive. Saddle-creaking floor-boards. Horsey whinny. Bitter rain comes like a belch after supper. Her slick skin is greasy as a chicken bone. Honey-brown, leather-legginged fella, emitting supple-mentary suspirations, in the honeysuckle with a creeping of coruscation addressing the verdant awning. Soapy scintillation seeps. Tenebrous trigon. Denticulate grille of a vermilion convertible. Obsolete appliances. Merde, in submission to his ignorance, is situated in the sidecar of a motorcycle, ridden by Dubius, a complacent com-rade, efforts in merging a monologue with detailed descriptions of inventoried blunders on the job futile, fusing, failingly, a fairly sufferable litany, impoliteness an impediment. To Faunia, Arielle is a minor (malignant) tumor. Arielle, going on about her abundant amours, volume moderated, is a sorceress, is bewitched by Faunia, following a reflective abeyance, and whisks her off like a hat from the rack. Faunia bobs as a wave- thrown barrel, an amphibian submersing herself in head trips. Arielle butts in with customary delish unconstraint. She is the key to the constellation of kids. Her rear, encased in cotton, radiates health and fitness. Her imperious intemperance. Tempest's not unlike a malevolent manifestation of witchcraft. Zephyrs with conciliatory tones. Canna curtseying. Dragonflies skim. Nacreous lid. Cocoa ruts in the road. Hocus-pocus of the weather.

Nausea wells within Faunia, managing the vibe she's living in a Hall of Mirrors, the glass version representing the real reflection of who she is. Series of stepping-stone rain-beads. She hums a catchy melody. The pop song is the sentimental medium for her spirit, especially effective when she's moody, and she often finds an adrenaline kick, a torrent, or nostalgic solace, an eddy, in the tune. Oceanic sororities. The encompassing grounds: Technicolored and sonorized, out of a motion picture. Oafish Querelle, the lecherous cur, with his lichenian mind, in civic hermitage, wearing a woolen waistcoat, hams kid-gloved, with a propensity for strenuous fantasies, expresses perplexity in hooking up the hose. Ra-ta-ta machine-gunnery of his butt-blasts, the prune-flavored stench all- pervading. And he rears as a steed. Arielle's entourage's frolics, the intelligentsia mighty and merry, literati with calendric indifference, savants finding nourishment in their opuses, links in a long chain of service to Arielle, with malleation in their mentality, recruited from a backwoodsy hamlet. Their publication is circulated effectively, thanks, in part, to Arielle's connections. The baby of the paper was conceived by her. She is negligent in strictness when it comes to her scruples. Her brittle rhetoric's dispensed. She has stained principles and spotty character. Cumulated cumuli. Desolate orchard. The difficult-to-define operation here blends stagnation and fickleness. Veggiemongers and fisherfolk protest against the frozen levels of pay and prices in the agronomy. Furuncular mamillae of shrooms. Infra-red rays. Hard labor in a mud bath for the juvenescent felons. A punchinello has a freckled crown. Rufous water. Every event is strange familiar to Faunia, and she suffers from amnesic shock every time, snagged in weird circumstances. Is youthful inexperience to blame? An irrational interpretation implied ... The central-cooled, bogus study, with its fictitious furnishings, is comparable to a stage's setting. She can't sufficiently get past the nagging sensation that this is an enterprise she, as an instigator, (erroneously) initiated. Cosmetics embellish Arielle's fortunate face. Her soily inflection. Faunia pricks up her ears. Broadcast voice. The empyrean is so close it's like a picture that was taken at point-blank range. Symptoms attending her cramps suggest the shade of her period. Astute peasant playwrights, scripts a mishmash of melodrama and folklore, spray-paint their scrawls of graffiti on a barn. Stars reminiscent of suspended snowflakes. JDs trample the alfalfa, sandaled feet stomping. Merde, the versatile spy, is unconscious on Pecorino, snout buried in the trough, from an overdose of chloroform. Arielle confronts the countless conundrums (cysts upon her brain) in her organization, with its fluctuations of double-crosses, and the formidable parties within, collaborating with them and receiving their danger money. They supply her, eager for consumption, the funds. Her faithfulness to the cause is insufficiently appreciated. Her reputation distinction and academic credentials as well. Physically and personally, there's not a shortage of attraction. She cups an elbow with a palm. Problems (one dovetailing into the next) have been sprouting as poisonous mushrooms. A bearish, popeyed bastard, looking like an elderly homunculus with a clipped mustache, threads his way among the stately trees, picking at a baloney-and-cucumber sandwich. Asynchronous sea. Dovegrey cloudcover. Jelly-cold fog bank ruffles the sober dusk. Moribund maples. Arielle makes a Vulcanoid mind-meld with Faunia, finds out she lived in a place above which cinematographic pictures were shown, the interior dull, exterior haggard, its deplorable rooms speciously ransacked for resounding argumentation, with her deserter dad (who had inflicted indescribable tortures on the household), and mousy mom (who died of an obscure blood disease), and Faunia got improved editions of domesticity at Pauline's, a sun-and-moon-splashed copper-colored cottage on a leafy lane. She integrated herself into the ménage as a sculptor his genius into a subject. Arielle, ostensibly aquatic in the lilac lambency bequeathed her by breaking cloud, can be a ruthless grande dame, but now she wants to cling to Faunia, a teen-aged organism surviving in the midst of the obligatory occupation of living, seeing color at the end of the tunnel, like a vine to a trunk. Quetzals and lorikeets and their abortive flutters. Apterous bugs. Petrified perennials. Customs and complications, prudery and prejudice abound. Landfill synthpop is dished out through the unseen speakers. Velvet-dark valley. Scaraboid golf carts. Faunia sees no humor in any of this. Her funny bone ain't broke, side isn't split. It's no haven here, only Hades. She feels as a question mark in an illegible sentence. Swishing herself into a slicker on the ugly steps and slipping on the landing. It's pouring cats and dogs. Fabricated charges. No legal grounds for the "prosecution" to stand on. Court of law? Judge? Jury? Witnesses? Hello! Her solar plexus is udder-warm, crossing the verdigris vacuum of the kitchen in quest of cookies, in spite of a molar maddened with flaming agony, these confections consolation prizes for Arielle's come-ons. Blindman's bluff played by her instincts. Arielle disses her orientation. Soaker has the sonance of gargling latrines. Peacock-feather fan. Saturation acts as a laxative to ease the atmospheric constipation. Hooded hill. Anemic annuals. Fudge sauce of mud puddles. Shell-hollow mutterings of the mizzle. Ways and whims of the weather. Breathless whispers of the drizzle. Wind has the sonancy of whirring propellers. Cloudlets are the viscera of the firmament. Asterisks of stars. Wallpaper is gangrenous. Arielle's patient like a petitioner, hypertrophied nether lips dampened. She treats Faunia, gruff as a convalescent, with trifles. Metalline warble of cicadas. Spray of water rears its head from the dated sprinkler system. Faunia clarifies her surroundings through the prism of her vision. She, erect in carriage, is sulky, stout like a pro mover. Disharmonious drafts rip the vaporous veil. Plinth with its rotatory potentialities. Recurrent rains. The environment is impaired by Arielle's ardent antics and vanillic intonation, a chink in her composure, digits spread claw- wise, and she launches an elocution as a lecturer from her lectern, ochroid arms waving not unlike wheat.

Her linear eyebrows, labial clamminess. Reading a reactionary rag for the substratum of civilization. Floriferous field. Arielle is poker-faced and glittery- inflectioned. Mellow salon. She resents Faunia's resistance to taking the party line, speaks on the sororities of bridge-and-book clubs in her previous life. This joint is reminiscent of a Punch and Judy show, an abstract dimension, an evil hive of pestilential activity. Gnats describe a parabola. A galoot, with a simian stoop, drool salivary tusks, complexion botched with rosacea, rictus a mask-like grimace, bareheaded as a bowling ball, lollygagging in the mangled brookside florets, supping on vealish victuals, is in a nightgown and overcoat. The institute is understaffed. Faunia's cardiac organ feels like an unfledged bird, wounded in the wing, struggling in a miry substance after having fallen out of its nest. She has the sensation her every thought and move are index-filed for future reference. She's a weed and Arielle's the farmeress. Appraising her ocular amalgamations. Tulip-shaped reading lamps on a collapsible board. Informal contact between plane, flying in mixed velocities, and welkin, with its complex system of motions. Toylike taxis, motors running gamely. Raven drapery as mutated bats' wings. Dummy (plastic) candies and flowers. Crackles of woodwork. Molluskan nightlight. Spate's a constant strip of cinematic film. Umbral stalking. Tots, snuffling and shivering after a swim, revolve around Querelle, his jaw grimly set, dusky from carbon, like moons about Jupiter. They drive hoops, employing wands, traipse through the densest dogwood as pilgrims in the pictures. Misshapen Judas trees along the radius of a dike are negotiated by a band of brume. Mealy dirt, its distinctness provided by Faunia's superposition. Walloping water gleaming like a sea lion. Arielle's frail neck, waggly behind. Sun of yellow ivory. She exhibits a Polaroid of a doll-faced double- baby, Siamese twins with perse cutis and Pygmean skulls, as a marvy amphibious animal out of a visionary fantasy, sweet like shed tears, connected by a flap of flesh, tissue of integument, the infants' peculiarities of condition wonderful, corporal components wrong, rubbery flesh right, the bantlings, quite the bundle, delivered under a balsam by a Turkish hunchback physician, capably directing her in anguishing birth-giving. At first, for her, there was terror and despair, which turned into gratitude and adoration, faint disgust transfigured into tender pride. Their duplexity, enforced union, was fascinating, these dwarfs in compromised conjunction, the common polyrhythms of their nervous system sometimes a drawback. They'd floundered, in broad daylight, their respirations sounding as wheels rasping. Pedestrians pitied their plight, very crooked and connected forever, hobbling in monsterhood, duologue the equivalent of leaves coasting in a stream's current. They lived under maternal protection, until cancer claimed them. Surf falls flat on its face. Tide gropes the shore. Squall sounds like a sonorous shell. Frenzied flight of a flock of cockatiels. A rheumy bubbler. Moon is a lamb's liver.

Faunia, recovering from the scarifying nightmare, in which she was a mannequin, perched precariously on the emerald isle of a pool table and bayoneted in the straw-stomach by an aluminumal stranger who'd packed on the avoirdupois, in a loo as a caboose compartment, but with a scrubbed sink and toilet, sizes up this institution, on the Galapagos-ish island, as Captain Nemo the ruins of Atlantis from his submarine, the Nautilus. She's a burner of bridges, any restoration inconceivable. In the dank basement (with a pungent odor of disinfectant) - talismans, trinkets, and curios in a display case. Cellar's littered with bags, cases, boxes and cartons. Genus of yellow jacket. Fabulous fish want to venture beyond the boundaries of their fishbowls. Pupae remind her of miniscular bundled toddlers. Impressive treasures of religiously themed Renaissance oil paintings. Dual-gendered, she feels like a log being sawed in two on a daily basis. Faucet drips. Unseen iron entrails of plumbing burble. Sisses from the orifices of pipes. Merde is a paralytic flibbertigibbet, grey matter fecal matter, vegetating on poor Pecorino, with his small, timid steps. Morphos, fluttering flashy flaglets, mimic their shadows on the flaxen terrain. Counterfeit opacity of the smaze. Stone effigy of a bulky bishop under a canting trellis, like you'd find in a chapel's niche. Chocolate-coated biscuits, notepaper and playbills in the library. A horn blares. Attic's filled to the brim with garbage. Cherubical waxworks. Her bristly shins. She must shave, and pronto! She has been devastated by insomnia, and naps, snorts. Gutter's gulps: sobs stuck in throats. Orpheus obelisk. Magic Lanterns and killing jars. Fountain pen as a wizard's wand. Browning automatic. She conjures up Arielle's short hair, not unlike the Venus de Milo's, these alien eyes with movements as a watch's wheels, and goody-goody moue. Her speech is euphonious. She's dressed in a sparse slip, singing, with a gypseian voice, consulting her Rolex while being groped by a pack of young rascals, listing like she is suffering a fit of paralysis, witchy cackle a wicked mockery. To add spice to the lewd scenario, the bunch of scoundrels smack her flabbying fanny. Her personality is practically indescribable, language nearly untranslatable. Higgledy-piggledy game of backgammon is in progress in the stuffy study, in the waning luminosity, which ascertains itself. She is an epicurean swan, has the mechanical carriage of an automaton, and the physique of a Greek statue. Ivy strangles the gate. Antibacterial soap expectorates from the pneumatic dispenser. Regulation blanket and coarse, sable sock on a hotel featherbed. Blur of the average yard. Ninny, with a bleached buzzcut, is on a platform, circumscribed by a palisade. Luminescent lozenges on cinnamon sand. Paws of palms. Deer antlers on the wainscoting. Pondlet's as asphalt. Sky reminds one of an inadequately developed photo. Faunia feels estranged from her own existence in this place. Her turquoise bra and hue-harmonious panties fit snugly. Paneling's paint peels in geographic patterns. Pistol shots of the floorboards. Stridulations of crickets. Crepuscular creatural cries. Bleary panes. Breakers like huge shards of kelly glass. Foliage with foxy tints. Watery fan of the sprinkler. Arielle, cruel and obstinate, had deftly reprimanded and gratuitously whipped Faunia, Louis thrown back in the slammer. Faunia's weeping choked her. She coped with an absence of balance, reeled, Arielle bunny-hugging her, conveying affection with a soothing sincerity. Faunia strove to cut the connection with her, permanently. Arielle poked her in the navel as if tamping tobacco into a pipebowl. Faunia recoiled. Arielle's nerdy specs. Spritz tinkled like instruments fussed with by an MD during an operation. Moon on high was a train's taillight in a tunnel of cirrus. The whole meeting with Arielle had taken an improper turn, and Faunia was perturbed by her indecent tweeny coyness, the coquettish grin rending her full mouth, startling Faunia, as though a fist sucker-punched her. Emanation through the overcast - urinous, saffron slashes in a snowbank. Ligneous scarecrow of an umbrella stand. Garnet log cabin like a mutant snuffbox. Tangerine brilliance. Weighty animalian wails from the laboratory. Cabinet with sliding drawers. Battered valise. Oblong mere. The corpulent, consumptive electrician, with a preposterous wig and jolly paunch, disengages an alligator arm from the fuse box, rictus reddened with agitation, flaps wires as reins. He slurps brandy on the sly, respirational rhythms like those of a child, has an impromptu consultation with a checkered bedslipper. Unremarkable dining-room's grandfather clock ding- dongs. Her calluses are chitinous crusts. Branchlets against the window: abrading condescension. Arielle, to Louis, is a "vulgar mediocrity," a "card trick personified." He, a tightly coiled spring with a mean scowl, tells Faunia she bragged she was a mineralogist and manicurist. To him, she was anaemic, as if she were drained dry. Silvery sound of the showers. Beached shipwreck has a frigate's frame. Acclamations sound like typewriters. Polite, bowlegged, African American porter, dachshund-looking, and on crutches, out on his mandated vigil, savors his smokes in the anteroom and its middle-class trappings. Splendid cake is impaled by festive candles on a bookless shelf. Charred savins. Arielle, wearing scrupulously clean undies, obsequiously smirking, in a chunk of lingering brilliancy, suggests they play dominoes and indulge in ginger soda and kidney pie and Faunia declines the offer. Her mind goes asleep as a leg does. After the rain, there's a reverberation, like when a pianist finishes a piece and keeps his foot on the piano's pedals. It is masterly magic how Arielle can, with sinister glee, convince. Her armpits have the aroma of baked apple. Her gall is vexing. She curls as though she's a cat on the love seat, her gown a gossamer turret, has a nip of bourbon, fiddles with a ribbon, skin translucent like water. And her wiglet concludes a covert arrangement with her scalp. She recognizes the idea that Faunia is a hindrance to the realization of her innovatory plan, a delightful obsession, to manipulate gender and identity, in simultaneity. Faunia hates her, the tease, despises her, furiously. Faunia, splotches imparted to her neck, feels as a lamb led to the slaughter, squashes a lump of a yawn, squishes, suppresses an unfinished humpy one with a spastic swallow, and Arielle dissolves into tears. The detention camp commences its flipped-out phase, Arielle looking at her like in parental pride. Vindictive visions are formulated. Chamois rag. Package of graham crackers. Wilted petunias. Merde's stertorous torpor on a country lane. A crippled mamzelle (?!) looks like creative nature had a brain-fart when making her. Avian twitter. Faunia, in promptitude, vamooses, and the weather welcomes her warmly. Coppery bodies of bathers, skinny-dipping, illusively modeled out of apricot brightness, make a ruckus, swimming. Faunia decides to discard the jersey and sheds her trunks and, dishabille, reclines in the shade on a slope, bordering the banks, optic umbilicus looking heavenward, witnessing a caravan of cumuli-camels. Nettles, elder. Line of hale banyans. She's harder, rougher, with a rustic tan and increasingly candid, twinkly eyes. Mouth of sun greedily glugs the perspiry pearls gushing out of her pores. Beak of her droll pecker droops on her linty pudendum. Surf maned with spume. Daedalian vehicular purr. Aeolian and fluvial sediments. Vocal ejaculations. She must quench her thirst. Her alabaster abdominal folds. Beetle- blackish aqua pura. She overgorges herself on the fine weather before she is razzed by the other inmates. Quiescence of the day resolves itself in a series of creatural screeches. Stars in the clouds are eyed wings staring serrately.

Faunia, heart jumping as a compass needle, pulled into the lab by Querelle, the beastly fella, a rogue, rover, dedicated to lepidopterology and stamp collecting, is coaxed into the Rube Goldberg-esque contraption by Arielle. Faunia thrashes, straitjacketed, like a fish on a jerking line, having bitten the bait, and is getting reeled in. Unable to handle her hermaphroditism, the thing explodes, destroying the building. Faunia awakens in the ruins and skedaddles with Louis, velocity decreasing, stamina not up to snuff, through the brambles, blazing vascular organs burning through chests, sprinting as if competing in a race, run switching into a jog, one inciting the other, spurring each other on, stealthiness increasing, rasping like trolleys, in a bed of pansies. She is confident (a gelastic gratification) in her invincible idea of emancipation, knows it in every part of her frame, however, for Louis, doubt hinders the (probably) perilous endeavor. Her inflamed imagination. His veil of irrational furor, through which he glimpses rationality. Insatiable soil sucks at them. There are lip-smacking sounds. Repetitious undergrowth. Astringent juice of the dampness. Anomalous amphibians in the steamy swamp. She's not prepared to allow uncertainty the slightest loophole. Her head spins, throat burns, ears hum. Their respirations are rhythmical as a seesaw. Babbling streambed. Fascinating insects in the thick bush. They lunge, in unison, into the canoe. It slides like a sledded carriage, slips as a soul's passage into the hereafter. Then Pecorino spiritedly plods after them, making these sniffling noises, underlip pachydermously protuberant, trudging past a succession of shops: tobacconist's, bakery, fruiterer's, and delicatessen. The can has transcended the limits of Faunia's perception. Quickening their pace in the misty mass of vegetation. Waterfall is muffled in the wildwood. Hoary chimps are Shakespearean jesters in thin porphyroferous cedars and medley of iridescent inflorescences. Sluggish and velvety swelter. Refuse bin. Mr. Merde winds up as a feculent, fly-smothered skullcap surmounting a woodpile in a pulsing semiphantom of phosphorescence, a dunnish, splattery abridgment of an excremental mound, sick soul affected by alien pseudo-sins, spirit floating not unlike a piece of furniture in a flood, claws curvaceous as those of a bat. Bouquet of forget-me-nots. More intriguing bugs. Baggage rack. Twigs crack like finger joints. Flurry of claptrap. Vines dangle as unfastened suspenders. Her left hamstring and right kneecap hurt. Her fellow residents' ace-of- spades sloe silhouettes scatter, accelerate in leaps and bounds. Billiard cloth of a front lawn with a saponaceous scent. Klaxon blast. Sky shines like the back of a sodden seal. Querelle, badly cut and contusioned, struts as though he's a tomcat, berates the broiling temps, drinks like a whale. Berries are the size of prunes. Decrepit pram next to a slate motorcar. Illumination infuses the fogginess. Rude yelling through a megaphone. Orangepeel goldfish swim in the glassbowl. Arielle, injured, wrapped in her resplendent robe, wounds life-threatening, reclines on the rubble, free as a fowl, milks the quinine. Cannibalistic natives, berserk, dance. Glade's reeds are like drawn swords. Stars are as insectival specimens, smoke-blue, pinned to the setting board's cork of azure. Frivolous twilight. Lurid cacti with prosthetic pricks. An aria of casual abstraction blares from a phonograph. Corneous arcades of turtles. Bees buzz like doorbells, insistently and irritably. Brumal chrysalid. Sparks of rain. Leaving the asylum, Faunia feels akin to a floweret peeking out of thawing spring snow. She swoons, mind going in circles as a moth around a lamp. Her intestines are as overstretched rubberbands. Inflamed octopus oculus of moon. She strikes a match, coddles the flamelet, a cobalt crown, lights a joint, takes a drag, fiery tip nictitant, and burns the dilapidated 'Lady Flowers' manuscript, its ashes flittering like snowflakes in the Rembrandtesque chiaroscuro. Bobhaired, her bangs make her appear to be a boy actor, drably engaging, playing the role of a girl, improvising in the performance of a play, script instinctually banished. She's got a mean expression. Famished, she scarfs sausage and sauerkraut. Louis unexpectedly strips (surprising, for he is customarily morbidly shy), gets naked as a bulb, in the voluptuous rosy light, and cries with visceral force, male genitalia falling off (cosmic castration?), the pink clump of private parts starboard, and female breasts growing. She stares at him like a hound a hare, her lips compressed, and, impulsively, she pinches his ass as a crab. It is soupy. The cock and balls lay lifeless in the tumbled duds. She gets a thrilling contraction in her solar plexus. Internally he chides himself and offers a deprecatory grin. His tortoiseshell glasses are wonky. Whereupon he shakes, retching bile and blood, sobbing for breath. He lures her, indeed encourages her, to get nude. He's visible, special. Words are insufficient in describing her bearing. Unearthly fulgor. Her gaze goes up and down as mercury. He was moderately endowed. Loneliness had left her with a receptive void in her vagina. She's dying from the heat and humidity, regains her composure, navy shadow accompanying her. When the pair were separated it was painful for her. With him, she's at ease. Her assiduous pout in a tawny beacon. She casts a glance at the prick dangling off the taut scrotum. Cramps are established in her belly. Twinge in her groin. She maintains control of herself. Hormones riotous. They kiss one other at random, from head to toe, stroke each another, as if to substantiate their authenticity. His hurried intakes of oxygen. Her head rocks like a boat tempest-hurled. She involuntarily thinks of Arielle's artificial moptop, mascara-laden lashes, visage distorted by excessive makeup, sedulously applied, the cut-glass cheekbones, her properties and dangers. The hideously unpleasant asylum is at last behind them! Line of communication's finally severed. Emotions are disclosed in her features. His unassuming prettiness, unhitched member and testicles participate in enthralling her. Having extricated himself from the civvies, he reminds her of a moth hatching from its cocoon. Departing from the archipelago, the pair are as an orchestra in the pit and drawing breath to play for an eagerly awaiting audience, readied for the conductor's cue. Ordeal over, he contemplates his anatomical metamorphosis. He has an apish aspect, complexion like lucent grape, redolent of boiled cabbage and dead leaf, wiggles his disembodied unit as if to test its condition. She giggles, countenance crumples not unlike a handkerchief. She devours a strawberry tart. The canoe drifts as vapour over tea. Bananas are affixed to boughs. Water's ripples like vertebrae. She clenches her champers. His hoarse intonation, eyes like fake jewels, draftsman's triangle of pubical fleece. Her convulsive, sepulchral inflection. They experience the giddy lightness of liberation. Even detached from the retreat she has the sensation of being attached, as though she's a tooth, pulled from the mouth of the cooler by a demonic dental practitioner, the quadruple roots of Arielle, Dubius, Querelle and Merde still stubbornly connected to her. Her heart beats, blood circulates, lungs swell. Porcelain bowls of his nates. Her puzzled expression disappears and she recognizes the signs, grabs her companion, hands with a pianist's agility, and they sexually savage each other in a sloppy session, saturated with opulent coruscation. Done, they uncouple like streetcars. They feel as shoes revived by a shine. With him, she's a book, a special edition, with solid binding, her pages gilt-edged. His ribcage are like pipes of a steam radiator. They bask in the Jack London freedom! She is the tepid getting hot with him. He suits her to a T. He encloses his bust in available plastic wrap. Decorous modesty. His. He's engagingly ladylike. His mesmeric hind with a gelatinous translucency. It is getting extremely toasty. She snaklily sloughs the skin of the adolescent penitentiary. His caressive, muliebral voice, heaped-up hairdo. Their fling's a romp. An enforced separation has inspired a robust romance. She's atingle following their getaway. She daydreams of a chorus of stillborn babykins. Ravishing day follows a rough night. Stony caviar and abacus beads. This will be a hard, hemorrhoidal voyage, she opines, and fesses she's not on speaking terms with her folks, who can tipple as troopers. The duo sail away in the keelless boat like a leaf catching a current. The two suspend their osculatory contacts to concentrate on rowing, mutually dismiss the giantess Arielle and her numberless troubles. They want to put the shattering experience behind them. Flying the coop, they are as fillings having fallen out of rotted teeth. The past and present for them's somehow interwoven. His back is tennis court-smooth, butt-cheeks like soft- boiled eggs. They, firm filmland lovers, Z-wise, merge and melt. Their footprints in the glossy sand have filled up with water. What happens to them afterwards is none of our business. No concern at all. They dissolve, depart forever from these pages, reader, liberated from this virtual keyboard. The narrative closes, or does it vanish? Louis's image will become immortal and replace him altogether for infinity, an eternity, unendurable, for one Faunia Nolot.

'The sea awaits you here, as vast as love
And love, vast as the sea!' - Aleksey Apukhtin

FIN.

Wastes Of The Never-Never

Dancing lightning split the indigoid sky like a dream rends the membranaceous barrier between sleep and wake. Overcast empyrean visually corresponded to a silver scythe sitting on a deep sill. Gin-clear lake. Treffyn Craze, a temper-prone twit, brain a patio with intervening crabgrass of ideas, was a flute-voiced, brittle-boned brolga with a rust-brown nest of hair, crinkled pigeon eyes, beaky nose, crooked teeth the color of burnt toast, twisted rubber band-neck, bow-and-arrow mouth, ramrod spinal cord, limbs as winding waters, and shallow scoop of a stomach. He was a youngster who happened to be a solitary prima donna, more at home in the animal kingdom than in the human one. It all began when he was eight-years-old, and he was drawing in a sketchbook with crayons at the ovaline table in the cramped kitchen with its floury fog bank and smelling of bakery, lit by a single pathetic candle, his showy, jug-built mother, Josephine, jellyfish-pale, with a fat, freckle- and-poker face, rosy anemone-lips, and tennis ball-breasts, a dervish with a duck-waddle walk and an inflection on par with a shrieking kettle on the heated stove, fussing with the fuse-box, the power system faulty from the sudden storm's sheeting, striking leven, when his loud, ruddy father, Douglas, his breathing hissy, sounding like stew overflowing from a pot and spilling into a fire, a professional butcher and camel- countenanced carouser, wiry and bearded, with horny hands, firm believer in brandy, entered with a surprise present for his son's birthday: a spotted, stubborn, slightly lame gelding named Tommy, bought at a fair price from their warrener/barber neighbor, good old grizzled geezer Bill Kelly, quite a big bruiser. Anyway, it was, without a doubt, the greatest gift he'd ever received! They ate scrambled eggs, apples, cherries and raisins and drank sweet tea together that evening. The family's shoe box of a shanty, located close to the railway and grey sea, was practically a lean-to made out of sticks, shiny and green as a laurel leaf, the place pretty much mulch-damp most of the time, the meager yard but red soil with a pitiful milking shed (Tommy's residence) and compost heap. This property was rather valuable. In actuality, they were rich (the parents were proprietors of a successful rubber factory), and yet lived like they were poor. The main reason - they were goddamn cheap. They were on the same page with the approach. Treffyn was fragile and fidgety, a drama queen only child, an oddball, outcast, misfit, rejected by his scholastic peers as the surf sends flotsam and jetsam back to the shore. He was, at that moment, for some reason, stock still, creatural kisser carved and custard-creamy, and wore his lavender night-gown and rumpled stockings, stroking and smooching his new pet. His cabbagey ears were constantly hot, like he took blows to them. He couldn't shake the nasty habit of scratching his leathery, wrinkled scrotal pouch, with its sharp bristles, when it didn't itch. Protoplasmic mist. Clouds swarmed as feeding fish, then splintered not unlike shattered glass. Pearlescent sand. Amoeban ocean. Moon was a lid set firmly on a purple cliff. He bore the expression of what could easily be considered contentment. He gobbled plum pudding and glugged orange juice. His gravel-rough respirations, the sonance as if he were puffing on the bellows, intestines feeling like coiled tarred ropes, calluses on his abnormally long feet's soles yolk-yellow, thick and tough as chicken gizzard. Douglas, so sinewy, with schoolboy skin, was apparently singed somehow. His birdy-hoppy-skippy gait was unintentionally comic. In the turbulent, wet air he recalled some rawboned Neptune drowned in dusk. Reader, welcome to early twentieth-century Australia. Duggan, to be exact.

Treffyn's cranium was a bucket brimful of wild thoughts, such wacky flights of fancy! His temples pulsed exactly when Douglas' sciatic nerve pinched. Fragrant fuch-sias, ferns and myrtles. Mud like glue. Russety hawks soared over the sump of the county. He slumped as a sack of turnips on the mauve couch. Flea bites and bitten nails bothered him. His busy brain generated reveries as his blood oxygenated. Rock wall, skillfully constructed, was choked with lichen and moss. A few bare, aromatic elms. The modest house was sparsely furnished and had an inexplicable permanent sappy scent. This was an earthly paradise to Treffyn. Douglas, snow-white, ruby-cheeked, sported a death's-head smile, in his silly socks, on tiptoe like on a tightrope, sipped his stale coffee in the honey-hued, teeny-weeny bathroom, the clogged drain gurgling as though fluid in a lung sac heard through a stethoscope. His spade-shaped beard he brushed, and stared, with limpid peepers, at Treffyn's soft, velvety physiognomy, transmogrifying in the Renaissance chiaroscuro, like he was a sacrilegious symbol scrawled on the sanctity of the Cross. Stone bridge overgrown with ivy above a crystalline stream. Patchy hedges. Tommy grazed on the balding lawn. Sink-hole of the village rotted in the distance. Roos and mozzies. Douglas stuffed his pipe and pissed. Try as he might, Treffyn could not make hide nor hair out of his folks' bizarre behavior. Nothing they did made any sense, plain and simple. Josephine jounced and jiggled, as if she were playing hopscotch, discalced, as was her wont, contained in ill-fitting, transparent lingerie, all bosom and bum, plucked poultry in the smoky haze of the paltry pantry. She abruptly sat on a wooden bench. Her cordiform frontage was crimson. Her nipples were reminiscent of fir cones. Douglas dragged his heels. Rain clicked on the churchy windows. A breeze blew. Caput mortuum sun. Mango and bracken vaporously steamed. Cirri sundered, scattered. A gust sounded like it was issued from a giant's exposed windpipe. Treffyn, muscles in his jaw spasming, was dressed in greasy jersey, knickerbockers and scuffed boots, laces very frayed, whereupon he sprinkled sugar on porridge and poured syrup on sausages. Douglas, an aggro alkie and rabble-rouser, somewhat stooped, with a floppy fringe of mane, grabbed Josephine and groped her. She giggled and squirmed in his embrace. Their whisperous conversation was graphically adult. Treffyn suffered a terrible anxiety, knees knocking, watching his nutty papa and mama, a couple of will-o'-the-wisps, hugging. Was Douglas a ravenous wolf in sheep's clothing? He wondered. He was a capable chameleon, every new character a fresh disguise to inhabit, depending, of course, on the individual he was engaging with. Deluge reeked of pencil lead. Willy-willies and billabongs. Ink-smudges of cumuli. Forking, mucky path was lined with hawthorn, maple, pussy willows, and oaks, with some briar and bryony interspersed in the direction of the dripping coppice. Vegetable garden. A stocky shepherd with straight fair mop, stringy from sweat, went in a fast stride past a stray shovel and rake on the sopping, flaxen grass, crossed a wide meadow sown with oats. The hamlet was a huge heart beating. Tommy pee-peed and poo- pooed in the bushes. Treffyn sang songs and they acrobatically shagged on the vibrant rug. Their sticky argument was as though it was a taffy pull. To distract himself, he pictured badgers, moles, fungi, spores, butterflies, spiders, beetles, worms, and so forth. Thankfully, he was shortsighted. Christ Almighty! With those two he felt like he was a sandcastle they razed, that he was a blind kid bruised from bumping into their walls, a mold on the ceiling of them (combined), or, for that matter, a tomato, and they were aphids. His mind spun as a top. Purse of his ball-sac had two testicular bits held in it. His prim and proper chops puckered. A toothache took possession of his oral cavity while he nibbled on lettuce. His narrow chest ached. Odor of alien alcohol. Douglas, illusorily, had dropped his trousers and donned breeches almost simultaneously. His originators screwed athletically and meticulously on the maroon sofa, devoid of springs, and soothed themselves with shots of sherry. Oxygen was sour with sex and perspiration. Checked blanket. Frying pan. Pennies filled jam jars and classic novels were on metalline shelves. Treffyn blushed, repulsed, chewed his bread and butter, balanced himself on the edge of eternity, scrubbed his skull sedulously because of the breadcrumb-dandruff. Musty cellar redolence. His raw elbows. Towers of books tottered. His sickness was a pink parasite gorging methodically on his vulnerable guts, the vermilion flush spreading swiftly. Remarkably, his procreators played cricket, naked, in the disastrous parlor, and discussed, incredibly, botany. Nutters! Soiled handkerchief. Cast-iron oven. Opaque glass. Wattle walls. Saucer with gooseberries. Zinc ladle on the counter. Downpour was wood shavings. Treffyn was a gormless goblin, a neurotic scarecrow, to the majority.

Aboriginal Louella Cheshire was a teenager like Treffyn. She was boisterous and he was tentative. They met on a carmine crag following a swim on a sweltering summer afternoon. She relished his male tics and quirks and he reveled in this female force of nature's nooks and crannies. She was brisk and eccentric. Corn-yellow lambency. Clammy morning. Winds whooshed. Uninhabited hut and unused shed. Abandoned canoe. The two skinnydipped in the olive lagoon. Specks of cinder swirled in a ray of radiance. Violet firmament. Their hurried steps were measured through the rich, tangled thicket and its surplus of gnarled trees. They clambered up the clayey banks of the trickling creek stained with luminiferous motes darting amidst the verdurous canopy. Finally, he managed to tackle her, circumspectly, at a healthy Bartlett Pear. She had on her dust-dull Wellingtons and khaki-green raincoat. She was otherwise nude. She ran a tortoiseshell hairbrush neatly through her unruly shock. Her loose, lanate belly contracted and expanded, his blanched knuckles resting on her knotty navel. Her tummy was charged with electricity, as if she'd scrubbed her feet repeatedly on staticky carpeting. Her rushed breath's emanation reminded him of tangerine peel. Her bulging buttocks were not unlike overstuffed hessian bags. She was burly, built as though she were a blacksmith, ludicrously beautiful, bolt-upright, had a Cro-Magnon brow, ebony pies, broad proboscis like a fighter's, plump, passionate, Turkish Red lips, bone-white gnashers, bull's neck, derma layer toffee-tawny, intonation tenor or alto, depending on her disposition, the center of his universe. She was a tease. And he was smitten. She totally registered the interest he had in her. He was a pump, she was the primer. He was madly infatuated. Emotion was expressed on his aspect as ripples on a brackish puddle created by a zephyr. He was vulturous, with a plucked-chicken neck. They shared pea soup, crouched like lower primates, napkins draped on their laps, heads bowed as in a form of prayer, amongst the nettles and raspberries, having sought shelter from the drencher under an awning of foliage like cattle would seek refuge from a storm. Outrageous plants cast lopsided shadows. The couple flirted and frolicked tangle-footedly, kissed honestly, frantically, tongues fervidly at war with each other. Soaker had this chloroform aroma. His ripping love for her was exhibited. She diligently fellated him. He clumsily performed cunnilingus on her. Her tumescent middle. He was tangle-toed, excitable, with a kooky crop of hair, his fantasies with spiraling heights, moods with vertiginous depths. Cormorant surfaced as a cogitation. Tornadic gnats and midges. His ears were like summer-heated seashells. His ladylike, fineboned, violinist's hands warm as a pastry cook's. His mind complied with the needs of his body. She enveloped him like a straitjacket. He wriggled akin to an eel in an eagle's claws. She rode him hard as a hobby horse. Daisies and jonquils tied in bunches. Gale in its salinity. Garish dragonflies zigzagged. He held her slab-siding like a rolling log in a flooding river, endeavored to finger her in the fanny, and futilely. He settled for fondling her chafed heels, molested the mangoes of her knockers, felt her blubbery hips. He was entirely bowled over by her brawny, curvaceous form. Her cast was crushed as a sheet of stationary deposited in a basket, lachrymose deltas developing on her chunky cheeks. Her chubby chin was anointed with gristly snot. He looked like a colt attempting to regain its balance. She was stooped, condensed, legs as logs, bunched paunch resembling a stack of unsawn firewood. He was eye-whites wan, in terms of pallor. Her bottom's cheeks like dragon's eggs; or paper bon-bons begging to be ripped apart. His dangler over her beam was thrusted outwards as a dagger. Her appetite had to be served. She was the queen bee and he was a worker. Her needs had to be met. She knew she was important, as a product commanding a market. He tried to be an integral part of her life, to be included, to not be a pair of muddy shoes left at the door, however, he didn't want to push his luck, either. She was like a cat, demonstrably in heat, practically meowing, rolling, rubbing against his calves, lifting her tail, purring, kneading, and arching her back. It was a come- hither performance. Courtship dance. Rosellas and lorikeets were a streetwise, independent lot. His high- cracked voice. Her beetroot-reddish trap and brown blinders. She boiled over with brashness. Her speaking was a relaxing strumming. He was a captive audience in the cabbage leaves, spoke carefully, like his words were pearls he didn't want to drop. They pushed and pulled. His cock didn't protest against the constraints of her cunt. He glanced askance at her dormouse-pink bung-hole. His heart was the hub of a wheel with spokes of affections. Their love-making was as a balloon ride. To wit, they were never sure where they'd touch down next, and the view was unreal from their upper atmosphere. His crustacean hands skittered crabwise on the trunks of her thighs. Her looming stature, squareness of shoulders he adored. He dramatized his stagefright in the sexual spotlight, cardiac organ a sledgehammer smashing his ribcage. He playfully pinched her posterior as if with a pair of blunt-nosed pliers. Her genitalia, unexplainably, seemed willful. His molten glass tears. His shakers were spiders on her middle. Her exposed anus, with her splayed on her front, was an circular stain left by spilt claret. His brain looped-the-loop like a pricked balloon. His expanding erection. Her pudendal keystone. His penile lynchpin. She received him as land accepts water. His penis was an undulant, crawling caterpillar. It drove into her vagina before doubts could deter him. Dinghy of his dick was moored. Poison- blue luminosity. Jumbled bush. Sand was as though it was brown sugar. Her black behind was spreading shade under a stranger's hat's brim. She would've thrived at Rugby! Leafage refracted luminescence. His mitts were on her tits like they were grabbing for bobbing apples. Her steam-boiler rump. His masculine organ's toadstool was introduced to her palm and it deliquesced as in a dream. His chup leaked like a pen. He spat globular spittle. Her susurrant verbiage pumped as the gunk from his gonads. Semen spurted. Carnal crescendo. Diminuendo. Done. He scrambled for his clothes, scurrying like a thief, the mucoid spunk, with its essence of flour and water, sticky on his dimpled knee. She was a magician and he was the apprentice. She was wicked in tempting him, cutting him to the bone as Arctic winds, told him fibs. Pallid keens of gulls at the quay. A flowering ti-tree, leaning at an acute angle, offered camouflage for their amorous rendezvous. His cricket shape was an advertisement he hoped she wouldn't read. Clumps of canna lilies and creamy

carnations were akin to chucked ball dresses. Cloudlets
farewelled the moon to the welkin. His bones were frail
like a quail's. They were billing and ooohing, a prelude to
another wild whooping legging over. Jubblies and
knackers jiggled. Line of his mouth turned squiggly. His
spirit was lifted as polish from a table from dumped
toddy. Without warning, David, her sturdy and robust
dad, barefoot and attired in an immaculate tweed suit
and incongruous fez, manifested perhaps by way of
alchemy, swore like a maniac, waved as if he were conducting an orchestra, fascinating, scarred countenance
screwed up, vast forehead furrowed, and scooped up
Treffyn as though he were a father welcoming back the
prodigal son, slammed him into the dirt and kicked him
twice in the ribs, the sound like a walnut being cracked.
Treffyn's nose was bloodied. Gummous spit caked the
corners of his mouth. He was stunned and sad. He
looked as a rotten carrot. He was bewildered and disappointed. David was the murderous Devil upon him.
Treffyn, half-cowed, grabbed his leg like a sailor would
a mast on a sinking ship. Louella visibly shrank, scared,
petrified. The fear on her phiz was as obvious as print
left on your hand after reading the newspaper. David
ingested vanilla wafers and imbibed barley water, was
Jesus raising Treffyn, or Lazarus, from the dead. Treffyn
was a doormat to him. She completely lost her composure, screaming at David, who had a stock-taker's oculi,
vascular organ raging like a warrior, his visage suggesting melted chocolate, clawing and kneeing him, to no
avail. They were forbidden to ever see one another again.
Beams of brilliance. Louella and David seemed to be

sucked by some unseen otherworldly entity into the dense woods. From a fetal position Treffyn leapt up, went over a flimsy boundary fence, plunged into the copse, lunged over ditches, charged through a swamp, past quinces in the marsh, headed for home. In the violent aftermath he thought she was a wicked witch with a wretched soul, their romance was a joke. The well from which his desire was whetted had dried up. He would slough off the memory-skin of her from his snaky grey matter. She was the whale and he was Jonah. He took a break for minute, gasping, clenched his fists, balled his foots as cartridge paper, his hatred for her drifting like volatile gas, anger fizzing on his noggin as the tide on the beach. His baggy, filthy shirt was a sail on his scrawny torso in the drafts. He envisages David's prick as being Moses's rod changing into a serpent in Louella's burning bush. Envisioning a cataract of blood, plague of frogs. Watercolor rainbow was a relief. Blatant butterflies zipped along. That uncommon outhouse could be seen as a glorious cathedral. Sun on the azure was a red dot on a black widow.

Douglas and Josephine had died doing what they enjoyed the most: fucking. Mutual heart-attacks. He'd initially paddled her bulbiform, goose-pimpled derrière with an aluminum spatula on the warm hearth in proximity to the burning lantern. Thwack! He stank of barroom and limestone. He drilled her while she washed dishes in the scummy sink, screwed her when she bathed in the small tub. Dying, in the pigsty dining- room, one attempted mouth-to-mouth resuscitation on the other. Treffyn was twenty-five and was, naturally, devastated.

Tears flowed like water from an overfull pitcher. When he received the awful news that they'd croaked in person from a fat priest, he immediately vomited his scone, customarily theatrically hysterical. He acted as a sick hen, felt like a miserable monster in an old fairytale, and convinced himself that they were agents for change, conduits for a new existence. He inherited the factory and promptly sold it and bought a horse farm (twelve solid acres of pasture) with the money, purchased at a fair price. His financial situation was fine. Lordy, did he miss them! He had a talent for farming he found out, reading and learning a lot from agricultural journals at the local library, using weather, seed and manure, and so forth, with excellent results. Having assistants who were experts on the subject in his employ hardly hurt. Advice from others in the know helped as well. He was no soil scientist, but he was competent enough. The paddock proved to be productive. There were good and bad seasons, only the expanse prevailed through thick and thin. Tommy had perished peacefully of natural causes. He never had flair for the dramatic, save for speaking in a human voice as Balaam's ass. Treffyn was horrendously lonely until he met him. He saved his life. And he loved his fresh-pulled celery! When he went, Treffyn was feeling like his soul was secreting sorrow as a body suffering from illness produces waste. He was so sorry to see him go and grieved greatly for him. He shat a turd of inconceivable dimension out of his rectum, an excremental monkey fetus aborted, abandoned in the bowl, and it was flushed. He tinkered with the accordion on the toilet and sobbed profusely. His crapper was relieved.

Battle-grey heaven. He put away soggy cereal, trifles and jellies. Eating Louella out, he looked like a friar-bird driving its beak into a crab apple, his ligaments creaking as bedsprings. She was cat-bird whimpering. Combined, they ran rough, akin to a motorcycle with too much choke. They revved, opened the throttle. His heart was a budgie in its cage. Her bombastic fart could move brass chimes. Air was like ointment. He had an alien physiognomy, which was brick-damp. Her vox was vaporous. She had a bulldog's forehead combed by drizzle. She was a wave pushing one way, and he was the tide pulling the other. Plantation of eucalypts. His being hummed as a tuning fork. She had banana on her breath and Velvet soap on her flesh. His diaphoresis was not unlike melted frost in a valley when the temperatures climb. Her frontal was flinty and she waggled her hinder as a bool-bool does, hams on her tail like bookends. Sugary glaze of their sex. Explosions ... emerged from them. Her vertebral broomstick. Was he barking up the wrong tree? Her modulation sounded rather strangulated. His midsection was as a dissection board. Her yap's tickles were blackberries, that is, succulent and stubbly. His kielbasa was a genie released from the dungaree vessel. Her personality was an opal once you split the rock of her attitude. Her arm got around his neck and squeezed it like a python. Her avid approach was one of deception, sleights of hand, the portion of a routine in the entertainment arts. Cirri as torn newspapers. A hatchet-mugged labourer sawed and hammered. A prophet- eyed, orientoid fortune-teller, build like a gravel-crusher's, plucked a duck and worked an abacus.

He took a break to nosh on his pork porridge and noodles, foreign features (with a harmonious relationship) appearing somewhat sinister in plenty of light. Cow country. Showers were sheets of falling aluminum. He was stiff and sore and his mouth tasted disgusting, brain and body in opposition of each other. Chipmunks scrounged for morsels. Bells sounded like cans clanking, far off. Goldfinches and chooks dallied about cattle's dung-pats. A cart was stranded as a whale. Soiled cumuli. Milk bar. Fruit stall. Cathedran canyons. He was smooth not unlike liquid, mop current-tumbling, had baked beans, waffles, fried eggs and raspberry lemonade, pacing himself as a runner during a marathon, ready to go the distance. Dazzling diamonds of brilliancy. A silver estuary was a limitless scaly fish. He opened and closed the window like an eyelid. His testicular pouch had the stench of minced liver. An ogress, in her obesity, was on a lounge chair on the seaside camping ground. A puffy-lipped smarty-pants clarinetist in a bow tie had on a cloying clove perfume and smoked reefer in the sterile murk.

Treffyn was tired enough that he was tempted to prop his lamps open with matches. His was a cautiously constructed world, unraveling as a ball of yarn. He was exceedingly weak and suffered in silence. Picturing fuzzy-faced, strong-armed, bulky-bellied, ham hock-legged, horse-heinied Louella ...

Meanwhile, many miles away, in a dilapidated orphanage (running rampant with ragamuffins), tipsy in the very quaint, populous colony of Nursey Fig, which looks like a cardboard life-sized town out of a child's pop-up book, Babs Gilhooy, a petite, pixie-cute, flat-chested, slim-waisted hoyden, her bowl-cut essentially a ginger mat, argued with her mom, Janet, almond-eyed, rigid, stout, supple, and barrel-chested, with a consumptive's complexion, chin whiskers, keister the size of a parish's poor-box, and keen voice, looking like an old-maid matriarch in a Victorian novel. She had on patent buckled shoes. She, scatterbrained, prickly as an acacia, a part-time herbalist and cantankerous like a rattler, temper deadly as a taipan's, apparently a grande dame in her gay finery, was thinner at the top and thicker at the bottom. Windowpanes in the bleached effulgence were like whitened molars after a dental procedure. She wiped her stubby sneezer. She had an overactive thyroid gland and general constipation. Rarely did she beat around the blush, was a chatterbox, and loved creme de menthe. Her portliness reflected her steady diet (a hymn to health) of meat and goodies. She had a tendency to skepticism, could wax lyrical. Her parchment-dry integument was so translucent it was like the transparent skin of aquatic life where you could discern the internal organs. Her breath had the must of forever-filed index cards blended with perished plants. Her cheeks as a china doll's. She was a tumor in Babs's life. She vowed to remove herself from it. They were butting heads not unlike rams for hours. What happened? They used to be like sisters for Christ's sake, swimming, tickling, fishing, reading, cuddling. The place consumed Janet. It was cacophonous with the urchins. The foundlings were white. Blacks were not admitted. They weren't allowed. Their bone of contention. For Babs, it was unacceptable. To Janet, it was mandatory for survival in a crowded market. She insisted she wasn't a racist, merely a realist. She regressed into sentimentality and mediocrity. Babs wasn't buying what she was selling. She was, in Janet's opinion, a fantasist, a wool-gatherer with pies-in-the-skies beliefs and living in a fairy realm. Babs was stonkered from demolishing cranberry muffins. Her lap was napkined. Her head throbbed and her mouth was parched. She scorned her greedy stomach. A cart lurched, turtle-slow. Japanese umbrellas were as an armory's weaponry. Outrageous cypresses and saplings. Lazy doodle-lines of levin. Thumping thunder. Horrid humidity. Wheat had to be harvested before it ruined. Buzzing blow-flies. Remington typewriter. Pollen like sawdust. Public park. Wallabies mated in the scraggly shrubs. Extended feuding. Janet could be cold and callous as a surgeon's tools, shuffled like a tourist sensing a thief on her backside. Babs was a food bin and Janet the mouse plundered her/it. There was resentment, bitterness. Sanity, once a surplus, was now in short supply. Babs accused her of reaping the reward of parentless, impoverished, innocent kids. Open society was really close-minded. Mosquitoes were microscopic sprites. Staying on board to assist, for Babs, was a thirst she couldn't quench. Janet partook of a sherbet sweetmeat, required respect, and Babs refused to give it, at least in this particular instance. Babs was determined, had resolve, was resourceful. She was a door Janet had shut. She slept in a rustic bed in the barn's hayloft. She is the round hole to Treffyn's square peg. She muses on the illumination refracted through the sprinkles, how it made a spectroscopic watercolor. Her oralcavity was a rosebud. She thinks of her dad, Peter, pensive as a prisoner, a polite and shy bog-pole appareled usually in ostentatious togs and toppers, a fellow with a frightful wig, mutton-chop sideburns and ugly Adam's apple, a chap occasionally taciturn, dedicated to his grilled turkey and golden ale, an undertaker who was an impulsive drinker (he had a dangerous habit of dispatching a quart of any alcohol in a single sitting), and compulsive pickpocket, contracting influenza, and was eventually claimed by cancer. Intoxicated, he could be peevish or petty, face boiled red from the inebriation. Janet was a poacher's trap personified, set to ensnare her. And she tore at her like a stupid kiddiwink at stitches in the flesh. Their relationship was loosening as a rotten tooth in decayed gums, bent at a bad angle, sent crooked by quarreling. There was much upset, the situation unchanging. Bustling littlies. Field with heaps of mulch. Dewy, winter-grey heath. A fox terrier crapped. Janet's bland office was a chilly, empty study, like a jail cell, with a plain desk, ash chair, collapsing cot, pile of cardies, dacks, undies and flannies, and a tray of disorganised dinner. Janet glared at her as the religious would at a prostie, so steeped in sin. She often gazed at her as if she were dumb. She wasn't academically distinguished, but she could certainly cerebrally hold her own, excelling at mathematics and marine biology. Her train of thought chugged on the mental tracks. Domical public library and botanical garden. Janet could cool her heated system with a steady stare. Intensification of weariness. Babs was restless, the reservoir of her energy reserves dammed. She quaffed her booze in one gulp, packed her suitcase, and left, intent on responding to an ad for a job she recently saw posted in the paper: Equine-trainer wanted for work. Her specialty! Her flatulence sounded like a sail ripping.

The interview went well for Babs. She guzzled jasmine mint tea out of a floral cup, was ferret-featured, straw-sweet, boots fouled in excrement, and had the voice of a steam-whistle. Her dial was creased in explicit concentration. Out of the gate he stared at her suspiciously, like she was a species smuggler, or a bookie even. He could've been mistaken for a maitre d' in his seersucker. Lithographs loaded the pricey paneling. He was limp and liberated as a marionette. His clothing was pressed impeccably, as a priest's frock. He put away scotch. Was she a dowdy dullard? Brushstroke of cloudcover. Hostile humectation. Cinereal sheen of smoke from farmland hedgerows burning. Hail was like mothballs. Kingfisher-blue celestial sphere. Throat of chimney belonging to a ramshackle warehouse hemmed and hawked a clot of soot. His den was somber, contained countable curios and had a boilerplate oil painting of a eucalyptus. Her dainty wrists were flexible. With her, he was a snail that had lost its shell, yet was protected in the carapace of her company. She was direct, called a spade a spade. She was inelegant, enchanting, cast a spell of voodoo on him. The substance of her character knew no limitations, her depths undeniable. And her complexities were infinite. What did he do to deserve her? He hired her on the spot. In time they became friends. With her, he felt as comfy as a kitten curled in an armchair, confided in her, confessing he hadn't the necessary funds to sustain the patch. She admitted she had a gambling aptitude, a gift given to her from God, and convinced him to let her enter a race with one of the horses, preferably Eeler-Spee, a muscular, fast Brumby, and to wager what he had left on her. What did he have to lose? Everything. It was an important financial matter which needed to be rectified relatively quickly. A bank loan would not have done the trick, just temporarily plugged the leaks. The track he found out was a weird kingdom of bookmakers with moneybags and pathological lowlifes shooting the works. Different sections were divided like land of Israel for the various tribes. Barriers and birdcage, ruck and tumble, were rude with hooting hooligans and roughhousing ruffians. A tow-headed hunchback clergyman with the body odor of putrid oyster had a jarring jauntiness of manner. Booming whooping. A rogue ticket- taker's sigh sounded as shuffled cards. Carousing jackasses thronged. Sun with clouds was hanging maggoty game. Treffyn's to-ing and fro-ing about whether or not this was the right or wrong approach to solving his fiscal crisis was aggravating Babs. She was drawn to him like a staple to a magnet. She worked her backside off for Janet, and for peanuts, was alone and lost, till, alas, she found him. Confusion of racket. It was a crushing crowd. Jester jugglers and mime acrobats, dishabille, performed admirably. Din of coaches, omnibuses. Treffyn was a foreigner here and not friendless. He hesitantly, stutteringly placed his bet. It was an enormous risk. He ponied up to tempt fortune in a shot in the dark. Roosters strutted around the dog pit. Cocks fought in a makeshift ring. It was hot as hell. A bullshitting swagman patrolled like a cop on the beat, a grotesque with squeaky dentures, swung a sack with objects as an ignoramus burglar. Corrupt clientry were in a feeding frenzy. Rabbits kept in rusted enclosures. Fillies and mares capered, not in competition. Pheasants and llamas wandered. A bleak-finished invalid, a moustached magus, sat in a wheelchair on a gangplank and chitchatted with a frowsy, buxom blonde with a supercilious mien out front of a lofty saloon ornate with oriental motifs, its exterior grubby, interior plush. Cabbies, grubby, posed. Treffyn could hardly wait to burn the "social" bridges with the riffraff he had met. An emu promenaded. A lank somnambulist sported a beneficent smile, cupped his cocoa and quoted verse, had a permanently depilated crown and peculiar hobble. Soaring mesas. Hallooing drunkards. Squirrels scurried. A tubular barker with tawdry jewelry had a Pomeranian puss, stood perfectly immobile, had the stink of wet dog, cheroot and cleaning rag. His flatus echoed the breeze. Her system was foolproof: her. Eeler-Spee gallopaded, warming up, trotted, wheezed and passed gas. Babs, posing as a boy, possessing a satanic loveliness, masculine and feminine, riding him, looked absolutely insecure in the saddle. She signaled to Treffyn, fretting, like he was a sentry, managed to abide a misogynistic squash-eared foundryman, grossly Falstaffian. Treffyn was worried, completely oppressed by humanity here. He was afraid he'd lose his lot. Eeler-Spee whinnied, irritable, and galloped. He neighed, pranced, reared. Was he a show horse? Treffyn studied the sleek beast, experienced an extraordinary excitation, his high on the level of opium, his thrill as an animal insisting on being fed. Babs lost. By a whisker. Came in close second. Eeler-Spee was tripped up, boxed in by Blackie Baby at the rails and couldn't get clear. Treffyn fainted like a hambone onto a hillock of slippery pebbles, revived in a jiff by a pipsqueak in shabby vestments and with a wistful smirk and a lumpen, brilliantined larrikin with an Irish accent, brogue sounding exaggerated, shilly-shallyers surrounding them. Babs took picturesque pleasure in castigating the nosey parkers. Her spirit was feeling pitched into everlasting hellfire. They got breakfast. He was enervated and agitated, pronounced horizontal lines on his forehead not unlike scars from surgery, encephalon aswim with stressful thoughts, being reduced to paralysis. Her failure damaged her. She was diminished, as a sheep rendered into tallow. She was tired of being a tomboy! She was outfitted in her fine frippery to impress him. Prior to meeting him, she was pinned by solitude, paranoid and alone, trusting no one, feeling like each and every person had his agendas, her ulterior motives, people were busybodies, traps to be triggered, predatory types preying on the erratic fool, hoi polloi lying as cottonmouths in aqua pura. His wisps of locks were secured by ineffectual clips, strands struggling against the tyranny of pins, some scot-free, hair pardoned for a period from the sentence of the scissors. He had a pumpkin head and prominent cheekbones. He, off the cuff, in the uncaring weather and restrained gaslight, his gait wobbly, like he was striding on abused timbers of a wharf, told her he was suffering from a terminal illness and had decided to donate the stable and horses (he lost only the acreage in the venture) to Janet's orphanage. So, the prefabricated piebald stable was to be dismantled (with the help of hired hands, jackeroos Kevin and Roy), and packed in wooden crates for transport.

It was the sabbath and Treffyn felt thoroughly vulgar, vile, for permitting his employees to mingle on the mattress, redolent of dank cotton and spoilt herring, with conspicuously adolescent prostitutes, their respective flamboyant wardrobes ridiculous, artifices of tresses worse, in the splendid drawing-room. The whores were fraudulently fawning adoration. He had drawn up the detailed contract and the hirelings signed on the dotted lines. He paid them each a wad of currency, a bonus in store if they reached their destination intact. Abrasive poverty engulfed them. They came from humble origins, evidently. Kevin was swaggering and Roy was cunning. One was a matchstick, the other a mount, one serious, the other a joker. Kevin was cadaverous and light, with curly hair, and Roy was dark and heavy, with a bald spot. Bellowing cows and puling pigs. Bleating billy goats. Gusts made whisk sonances as a sweeping broom. He had an unhealthy liver and kidney stones. Babs, bless her dear heart, did not press, would not pry, and let the issue go, like a fisherman putting a rare lobster back into the brine. They discussed their fetishes and phobias. She was plucky and twitchy, precise, self-critical, and animated, offered her opinions in globose dollops. She was his armour. Their nightcap, a thimbleful of vodka, consummated their coalition. She was relaxed in the intimate confinement of the sitting room. With his lurching, in fits and starts, he was as a robot missing an integral part and operated defiantly despite his maker's ineptitude. Her arousal snuck up on her like a nimrod in the gloam. They were a hydra, an organism, together. His hands were thrust in the shallows of his linty pockets. He was dreamy and dazed, hilariously angulose and gawkish to her, made no concession to fashion whatsoever. She took to him as a duck to water. He removed his rimless spectacles. Her feet, he noticed, were cracked like bark. Her raspberry shrieked as a plover. He noted the convexities of her filthy toenails. Higgledy-piggledy knolls of duds. They toasted with extra-bubbly champagne. He admired her, wanted only to look and not touch. She had the sensation of being a fish hooked and dangling on his line. Would he reel her in? Her eyes were cast around like she was searching for a swatter to best smack a fly. Knots in her gut were numerous as butterflies in a net. She spun stories of spider webs that snagged his attention. His tales were, visually anyway, comparable to mistakenly fixed photos that faded faster than they should've. The cubbyhole setup was vibratory with his nervous energy. He was a puzzle she failed to properly put together, a riddle she couldn't solve. His inflection was like fingernails raking a blackboard, and he was ghastly-complected, as if his countenance was a mask carved out of wax. A moue budded on his mouth. He nipped a Cuban cigar. She was direct like a pistol. He was a twig-limbed, uncombed, disheveled simpleton, all bony angles. His peepers were pouchy. He was feeling as though he were a pioneer. Would his treacherous organs hold up for the trek? His cuke-sniffer protruded from his pasty clock. They were queer companions! An empty coal skuttle supported a cane basket. Brussels settee upholstered in viridian velvet. Tissue paper cirrus. Lilacs bunched in a crackle-glazed vase. Luscious myrtles. Perfumed shrubs. Precipitation smelt of mineral oil. Lightning flickered like fault lighting. Thunder thunked as donkey engines. Gloomy halls, an untidy tangle, and bright alcoves with artistic decor, sufficient for his minimal needs. Library and laundry had chromos of caricatures in these grand gilt frames, esoteric gewgaws and radical knickknacks. White blossoms of hyaline cumulus bloomed. Ultramarine vault, incarnadine moon. Vessels plied the coastal trade. Excess of ill-matched assortment of furnishings. The chandelier hung like multitudinous vitric flying foxes. Canine barking. He announced he was an atheist when they played cribbage, in wing-back chairs with chintz surfaces, at a walnut table and by a Dutch lamp, slugging cinnamon punch and scarfing syrupy dumplings. She confessed she too was irreligious. They were winsome abstractions of humans being. Remembering finding her disrobing in the guest room, her prat pronounced in her cerise underwear, breadbasket flat as an ironing board, titties not unlike globular eggs, nates, with abrasions, reminding him of stained porcelain basins, scratches on her cresentoid calves like they were made by a vicious bandicoot. His brain locked, an outlander in his cranium. Brightness was sewn through his ocular material, a familiar fabric, threaded with splendor. She was driven by the mysterious current of concupiscence, her ardency an agonizing knife-thrust into the canvas of her cunny, an intolerable torture, just unbelievable torment. His arms flapped, legs jigged. She was an intriguing figure in a delirious daydream, laid before him as a gorgeous garment on a white sheet, smell of her juices at once subtle and insistent. Her pies were burgeoning stars winking in her heavenly features. He scrutinized her, suspiciously, like a customer would a potential robber in a bank. His eyes gaped, jaws slacked, instinct an obedient servant to his scruples. Applying his principles with an intuitive industry. She was constrained by the corset of the cosmos. His conscience was his communion with his humanity. Carrying his stamp collection in an album, feeling as a ding bat, he retreated and, ashamed, solar plexus a confused ball of string, masturbated into the dunny. She was feeling lousy in the Grecian anteroom, didn't know how to react. She was an obliterated tart, a cork tossed into the rapids, anguish blown out of proportion. Preparing for the potentially perilous journey, he was like an adventurer on the verge of exploring hitherto unmapped territories. The Aboriginals were dispossessed of their land and driven into the country. Was the expedition prepared for such an incendiary enemy? Their plan was pottery: wet clay and plaster mould - separate ideas brought together. The proposal of the procedure was a project, and, as a result, a blueprint was created, a schemata. He was cautiously confident, trusting in the collaborative process and what it can possibly produce. Were they exiting from civilization and entering chaos? Dusk was dreary; a symbiotic Gargantua/Pantagruel nightmare. His sough sounded as air pressure relieved by an open valve.

She marched like a wind-up toy soldier. Her moist blinders were as colorful stones in an aquarium. They drank and danced. The celebration was harmonious. His veinal claws clutched her swiveling laddish hips. She looked like a daredevil, he a sleepwalker. She was a suitable candidate for a confidante. She sneezed as a walrus. He was mynah bird- gregarious. They fit together like parts of a jigsaw, he felt, talked of Indigenous people being marginalized, bastardized, ignored, used and thrown away. Her larynx sounded constricted, her articulation hoarse. Was she an intrusion on his privacy? Their blinkers played cat and mouse. Clangorous fuss of clipper siren. Roy, a moose, and Kevin, a weasel, with their au naturel juvenile mollies, constructed a bodily house of cards on a chaise-longue. They were not sober, boasted they were the creme de la creme of laborers, proud perfectionists. To Treffyn, they were morally dubious and had a drop of liquor too much. They had an unchristian comradeship, tradesmen's hams hooked onto frayed belt-loops, indulged in Tuppenny, racquets and hoops. Their revelry restricted his repartee with Babs. Crikey, the participants in the rampage were oblivious and, to Treffyn, responsible for the haphazard harmony of their discourse. His mien was wreathed in winces. He caught her glance before it could land. They were parties to the salacious shenanigans. He was reedy-voiced when he informed her, language spat out like it was hot pepper, that he was apprenticed to the noble trade of wheelwright, only the work was all wrong for him, and he had a tremendous olfactory sense, slurping his consommé and engaging with his corned beef, verbally hacking away, as a hiker with a machete in the jungle. Thunder cracked like a string of firecrackers. She downed her burgundy. Vocally he pressed on, erratically pushed on, unsure of where his next spoken step would lead. Moon was wedged into a mass of cloud. Fireflies were silently screaming stars. Bats swirled as shadows of doubts.

Horses rounded up: Andalusian, Appaloosa, Fjord, Friesian, Gypsy, Holsteiner, Palomino, Quarter, Shire, and, last but not least, Eeler-Spee. Ponies: Dartmoor, Haflinger, Highland, and Welsh. Hailstones ricocheted off the dirty panes. The group was readying to embark on the trip across the Outback. Babs was a caterpillar, shedding one getup for another. Treffyn was a Montague beneath the window of a Capulet. His fate was a reef he could not navigate. She was the current which pulled him. Insectival whizzings. Prismatic clouds were medusae. Vista was lasiandra-florid. Outside, hungover, his eyes were bloodshot, earlobes hot, waiting for her. He, owl-blinky, inhaled and exhaled ozone. Inside, he was stumble-footed, suggested a peasant with long lashes rendered by Velasquez, limbs branches. He suspired like an opera singer preparing to pipe up, perambulated where furniture dictated, looking as a skeletal choirboy puppet with tangled strings, stiffy (conjuring Her) like a throbbing mainmast of a ship anchored at sea in a severe squall. Criminee! She was arrayed in long johns, engaged in a dice game with Kevin and Roy by an unnecessary amber lamp atop a cherrywood bureau, the business of a blush on her face. He was flushed in frustration, lips compressed, eyes blank. She feline-purred.

He recognized he was not mirrored in her, realized they were polar opposites. He was as an emotive clockmaker, the cogs and springs comprising his feelings, the parts of this mechanism lubricated. She was ecstatic as a lady who'd trapped a grasshopper in a bottle. He was Ulysses strapped to the mast of her. He gazed at her like she was a rodent carcass smothered by devouring ants. To him, life was a waltz and they should be (platonic) partners. Her cackles sounded as cracking knuckles, exposed a disordered row of discolored teeth. Pings and pangs were pronounced in his vital organs. Surf slapped the rocks. He experienced anger and alarm equally, fell into a swoon, gaping like the scene was a scandal committed on his premises to a disappointing degree. Mephitic links in a chain - cologne, oil, bran, oats, pollard, astringent soil, noisome humus, and pungent sand. Cedar flooring in marmalade coruscation. Pair of paraffins. Pine door with scratchy injuries from previous animalian tenants. The sparkling blue lid was a spectacle from a visionary's prophecy. He was a quirky stork with subdued feathers. Cleft-chinned Kevin. Warthoggish Roy. They'd slept (passed out) in a carrot-hued hammock on the decayed deck in the sultriness. Both had a rural air about them, a transparency in their fervor to live to the maximum, the vehemence acquired piecemeal over the years no doubt. Treffyn's peripheral vision of the debauch was too much to see. He gave them the distinct impression of sweaty timidity, china-white, aquiline-nosed, starch-cuffed, having an aura of cultivated culture. Fluffy cloudlets were mutated moths crushed and smeared on the hyaloid horizon by the nicotine-yellow thumb-end of sun. He passed wind and water. He beheld his whole soon-to-be bankrupt estate. His noggin blazed with musings. A bullying gale blew. Sky was in its volatility. Once, an androgynous relative said to him love was as livestock: don't leave them because when you return they could be gone. He pictured perky Louella, dear Lord Almighty, cheeks puffy not unlike a trumpet player's, amble bossy, brash and brisk (his bearing was mechanical, as if he, garbed in a cobalt corduroy suit, wool tie and polished boots, was an automatic construction at an exhibition and departed of his accord) on the plateau. Hail was cast-out coins. She was a hot press on his cool skin on that promontory. His loins were stirred like habiliments in a copper. She was a Bible-basher, had a bellows-belly, vaginate vibrissae as though it was wood splinters. She diddled with herself, respirations warming him like beer. He did precious little to deter her, didn't attempt to arrest the prurient process. His was an ostrich-face of languid intelligence. When they were not together he was a wound and she was the bandage unwrapped from him. She was a burning fuse.

Reddish patches on his eggshell-whitish cheeks. Her kisses were squalls playing on a craft's rigging. He, with her, metamorphosed ... a grub into a butterfly. They ran as troopers under fire. Their intercourse was tinder, the passion sparks from flint. Her tongue was a flick of the whip cutting through his verbiage. His orgasm was like a delayed reaction, as a sharp-razor slash, a slight sting followed by surprising pain, and, before you know it, blood seeps. She was a rock under the wheel him. Her beat he couldn't catch up to. He was guided by the compass of instinct, glided on the winds of impulse. He was embarrassed, indecisive. She observed him like fan-shaped fungus on a ceiling. She was all bust and duff. He admitted his adolescence was a miserable gauntlet of assaults and humiliations, he was a target of mocking girls and mean boys, his juvenescence had pariah status. On all fours, she was as a cow prepped for milking. Laws of physics were obeyed: his willy followed the line of least resistance to her quim - water on an inclined roof. Steely gray upper atmosphere. Peach blossoms were prettily in bloom. In the snapdragons, rhododendrons and pansies, they coupled, and he withdrew from her, limp like a rag doll, quicker than he could cut a cockerel's throat, wished to flee, for he climaxed to soon, and willed himself to stay. She sulked, seemed disconsolate. His squeaky comments. He diminished himself, felt faded, as a dismal drawing leached by condensation. He'd come and gone like a chilly pocket of air near a stream. She had a weightlifter's powerful build, at the jewel-bright swimming-hole. Treacly trace in the environment. She had orang-arms and sausage-legs. The shutters of her hindquarters were screwed shut. She was a brawling beaut with a porcine snout and baritone voice. She stuck out her bovinely tongue to sample the rain, and he got a glimpse of tonsil, a peek at epiglottis. A grin insinuated itself. Her suet jiggled as custard. He thought of his serpentiform schlong and its poisonous sperm. Her girth was perspiry. His body was red and raw, alive and aching after the copulation, like heretofore neglected gums scrubbed with a brush with zest, back striped with sweaty stigmata, chemicals surging in his system from fornicating. Raucous crows. She was lightning in his darkness. Lust was a considerable commodity, a burden he could bear. Indentations on her rear were reminiscent of flies spotting a window. A canal was a burnt-black handle of a saucepan. Nectarean swelter. Apart from her, he was a punished saint in an Italian painting. Precip had the scent of iodine. Ochroid sirup of light. Delft-blue brook. Cockatoos skrieked and tottered on scabrous boughs. Mustard-yellow phosphorescence. He was smooth as rice paper. Phlegm clattered in his throat, sounded like panes rattling in sashes during a storm. His stomach collapsed as overworked putty. Cirri were piglings going for the teat of a sow-sun. Parrot-pigmented rainbow. Saporific fragrance invaded his nostrils. Sticks were scrapes on the dun earth. Shrilling lumber mill. His collar was like a secular one, or as a harness. Banksias of cumuli. His self-inflicted bite-marks were lady-lips. He was in a fractious state, on friable loam, viewing Kevin and Roy, hyper and garrulous, studied them like an entomologist the varieties of beetle. He was rabbit-nervous. He wanted peppy Babs' company and conversation! His heart sank as a painter's drop sheet. He was a ventriloquist's dummy and she was his operator. She was the moving magnet and he was the following nail. He looked forward to the pleasure of her companionship, as a smoker lighting a cig and smoking; or a drinker pouring one and gulping. He yawned and stretched. His heart had harsh edges, like a busted rock. She was point-blank as a driven nail. His intestines ... like a mesh of a skein. He was all elbows and knees, believed he was inadequate and inexperienced, his insecurity about as unappetizing as unsauced spaghetti. Sonancies of hammering and sawing. Racks of roosts were strung as beads on the necklace of road. Chests like sarcophagi. Kevin's lineaments appeared out of whack, features of independent character, as if he were a practicing pugilist and his mug was permanently imbalanced. He partook of coconut maroons and played a game of rummy with Roy. They behaved not unlike barnyard animals, pecking at each other as if they were breadcrumbs. The workers slovenly and unshaven, yet suitable, capable enough to employ. They came highly recommended, had a respectable reputation. The two were worthy of respect and he granted it without reservation. Sun was a butter spot. Treffyn's nerves were tight, like tense fishing-lines with catch tugging. Boxes were as though they were caskets out of a bedtime nursery rhyme. Kevin could have easily passed for a fiend and Roy sounded like a shrew as they quarreled. There was a humorous mishap, with Roy dropping a toolbox on Kevin's foot and he, Kevin, hopped as a kangaroo. Roy was in a stoic stance, scowling, like he was inconveniencing him with his idiotic poltroonery. Not even a smidgen of solidarity. They were prehistoric, cavemen, anthropoid apes. Treffyn did not have confidence in his authority. He was stunned that there was no mock-laughter accompaniment to the accident. Kevin ooh-ed and ouch-ed. His facial capillaries were scarlet cobwebs. Treffyn made it a priority to pack his moth-eaten, musty-malodorous journal to document the expedition in explicit detail. Brass spittoon too. Clement weather was appealing to set out into. Babs, sick as a dog, cleaned the dear and roasting joint from top to bottom, the duster flicking, broom sweeping, bucket jangling, mop slapping, brush scrubbing, et cetera. She reminded you of a begging gypsy on the street. He was adamant in convincing her he wasn't as frail as he looked, his skeleton was a steel armature. She could be cold as ice! Translucid traceries made by bugs in the stagnant oxygen. Drone of crickets. Flounder-white clouds. Impressive glassworks smokestacks. His heart skipped like a stone on a pond. Babs gesticulated at Kevin and Roy as a conductor at an orchestra. They were transporting a stable (a dandy, by golly!) in crates on a cart! He was gawp-mouthed. The venture was a risk worth taking. Would the sharp object of reality puncture the spinning tire of irreality? Reality was a saw-toothed savage that could rip the dream to shreds. He was a withered flower (grown in an exotic locale). His essence was a canting stem. Her dubiousness about his participation was the stake in his heart. To him, the crossing would be like a diver descending into and ascending from the deep. He could cope with the travel. He was wearied and depressed. The tension with the crew was excruciating. He knew the expectation was he wasn't capable of making it. He vowed to prove them wrong. He wanted the gang to be allies, not enemies. Her revealed umbilicus was a critter coming out of its shell to sense the ambience. It was balmy and the rain fell as a muslin curtain on its rod. Jacaranda and frangipani sprouted. Murmurous creek. He gauged their progress in wrapping and sealing the main columns like a critic amateurish theatrics. Why did he feel bamboozled? He drew diagrams and made calculations in his notebook, his demeanor calm, posture formal. Was he biting off more than he could chew? Was he bearing a burden surpassing his stamina? Feeble fulgor. Kevin and Roy were rogues. This was a plus, not a minus. They were inclined to cause a ruckus. He would not ignore his intuition. He didn't want brown-nosers, arse-lickers. So they were impudent fuckers and gamblers. Whoop-de- do! He could not tolerate incompetence, tosspots, dogsbodies. They weren't caged birdies! They were battle- tested. Their tans were bracken-brownish in the straw-tawny scintillation. Their lives were chock-full of turbulence and upset. Natty gents they weren't. Who cared? He carried his poor health as a hull does a limpet. Would he slow them down? Was he an insurmountable obstruction? If the odds were against him ... he would make darn sure they'd swing in his favor somehow. He imagined Louella's hamhock arms, muttonchop legs. He stuffed the trunk with the fastidiousness induced by habit, bound it with bands. His existence was a cruel instrument of sacrifice. Saliva like tartar sauce. He, on a whim, rose from the rung-backed chair and closed the venetian blinds. Then he filled and emptied his chamber pot, remembering Louella's haunches, recollective of potter jugs.

The cargo was in order. It was packed and prepped. It took twelve hours to load and was securely tied down in the wagon. Lids on the crates were numbered (1,2,3,4, and so forth). They were as gigantean gifts, presents wrapped for Gargantua's Christmas. The lovely thing was as a massive model, or a jumbo jigsaw puzzle, to be constructed at a later date, in a different place. The harnessed horses, Eeler-Spee in the lead role, snorted and shuffled, rearing to get hoofing. Treffyn's life was, for a while, making lists. He noted Babs's slender wrists and ankles. His erectile ridgepole was under the canvas of his pants. To Kevin and Roy, he was a pencil-thin girlieboy with a choirboy's voice, he'd guarantee. His entirety was feeling empty, like a beast's bladder in an abattoir. He refused to permit his courage to depart him. He wouldn't allow it to vamoose under any circumstances. He made pancakes (batter runny) with cream cheese and had buttered shortbread and turkey with gravy on the side. The harlots had scrammed. They'd thrived in his home as parasites in a porker's viscera. His mop was most unruly. He was a goose in a gown, ensconced on a stool, digital tweezers manipulating a fork. Louella: she was compact, eyes red-rimmed. His petaliferous sentences fluttered, drifted into her hearing. Her sinuses swelled, inflection had a tremor in it. Incertitude bubbled up like marsh gas and popped in her stomach. Her tootsie-wootsies had the whiff of bacon fat. His buttocks were flat as slices of French toast. They gamboled. He was the hare and she was the tortoise. She had the physique of a kookaburra oven. Moles dotted her ass as cribbage pegs a board. He was strung across her like a fisherman's net. Her bulbaceous bobbies were hefty as paperweights. She was overripe fruit and he was the yielding stalk. She was on him like a rabid wombat. Her intonation quaked, tummy shivered. Her pelvis pressed against his crotch, his penis hardened. One was inside the other, as spoons. He plunked himself in the low-slung sewing chair not unlike an actor on stage. He was extremely edgy in his eviscerated bedroom, its devastated condition emblematic of his freedom. Potted plant on a workbench. Would his participation in this odyssey be stillborn? Did he even have the requisite manpower? The niggers were butchers, and the party was advancing into a lion's den, in its vastitude. In the blacks' territory - they'd be multicolored threads caught in an ebony carpet, burrs snagged on sable socks. Those riverine snakes ... He was destined to be a traveler in an obscure parable. It was not a rash decision to go. Fiddlesticks! Would he be relentlessly ridiculed? A laughing stock? Figure of fun? The men could be cruel as death. He refused to be baggage in the brush. He was frantic, riddled with angst. Could he trust these dangerous, unpredictable fellows to guide them? Could a leash be put on the vicious guard dogs? Did they think he was a niggardly marm with an incredible inheritance? He had endeavored to convince Babs he was fine, but he felt like a thespian improvising his dialogue, changing his performance, adjusting for a specific audience, and grappled with the demons of his fakery. He was unraveling as a cloud. To Babs, he was funny-looking, lanky, had a nice laugh. The outfit was to contend with water, deal with mountains. He had his limitations and he promised himself he wouldn't become a liability. Optical sun had a cirrus-cataract. Scintillation stung the salmon-silver runnel. Kevin trumpeted, the blast nothing but noise, and Roy hoorahed. They were ravingly soused, were engaged to deliver the haul. Kevin was the carpenter, Roy the muscle. The departure was nothing short of dramatic. Treffyn, in no time, was saddle-sore, had hemorrhoids which bled occasionally. And his head span. Whale-blubber flavour of the air. Sleet was icy needles drilling. Paths were illimitable innards in a slaughterhouse, and stretched on. His sweat was a viscous film. Feeling like a lab rat, subjected to a jolt from a charge of a voltaic cell. The tenacious wagon, a moving monument to their zealous madness, lumbered as a lummox, squelched in aqueous muck, thumped on puce soil, banged over rubicund dirt, its rhythms haywire, equipment making a racket. It was like a scarab slogging through animal guts in the dense scrub. Filigrees of vinage. His visions twisted as a vivid corkscrew. Goannas slunk. Grass had a flax tinge. Natives, a tribe identified by Babs as Narcoo, watched them like a fantastic float in a parade. Bullocks and billies defecated in the tea-trees. Kevin and Roy downed grog, got into a tiff, chests thrust out as pelicans'. Roy had an aura like he was a captain on the bridge. Kevin was listless as a sunbather. Treffyn had a nightmare, in which they killed Babs with a wheel, like Catherine. She poked him to command with sincerity, as an auctioneer's rouster prods a horse with a rod, and his diversiform orders were obeyed, albeit grudgingly. He was displeased and disturbed. They rocked and rolled on a pebbly ridge. His hair looked like an exploded feather-pillow, peepers feeling as blood-bloated ticks, shape like a warped pipe. She held his elbow and he yanked it as an abscessed tooth, crab-scuttled away from her on the unforgiving wooden seat, reduced and irritated. Brakes squealed. His flesh was flaky, peeled like bark from a trunk, conflagrant shock a cocky's crest, face, burnt garnet, a crumpled page of annoyance. Shit's sake, for a sugared johnnycake ... Jazzy firmament was as an illustration out of a fabulous fable. His locks flapped like manila leafage. Babs had a knife-neck with visible vermiform veins, emerald pies, and chestnut bowl-cut. Raindrops were chips of glass. He was, inexplicably, feeling unencumbered, the dead weight of battered, useless armour of insecurity discarded, as a knight who fought and won on the field. His uncertainty shriveled akin to an annelid put in salt. His certainty was brought into clearer focus. He would acquit himself with integrity, maturity, dignity. He wouldn't bend. Buckle. Cave. His chicken-neck was rigid, possum-eyes glistening. His innards were tree roots alight in drought country, brain a smoldering brushfire, mouth filled with smoke and ash. It'd be a long jaunt. He was Santa Claus, horses the reindeer, wagon a sleigh! He knew he was hawk-beaked, Babs-bought kit made him feel like a turkey trussed up for Thanksgiving. Empyrean was gory as boner's steak. That pitch night, Kevin and Roy danced a drunken jig round the spitting, dwindling fire in the campsite. In their cups, speech slurry, Kevin sounded like a braying donkey, Roy as a whip-bird calling. The smutty talk was the auditory equivalent of doors slamming. "Frigging blow me," said Roy, wielding his roger, and Kevin mock-recoiled, replied, "poppycock!" The rascals got rowdier. Members brandished. They ate like primates. Treffyn kept a diary and wrote poetry. The blokes carried on. They were low-life versions of Gilbert and Sullivan. He watched them as a parent who knows the kiddies will inevitably act up. Babs was too lah-di-dah about their antics, he felt. Kevin interrogated Roy like a magistrate a knave on the stand. Slowest- witted scamps! The peter-ticklers drank from a dam, played a game of darts, skin ingrained with grime, sang intentionally off-key. They were thick as bricks. Teetotalers they weren't. The two drank Ballarat bitter and beetroot, sashayed like bower-birds putting on a display, threw fleeting shadows. Treffyn and Babs, elements of their respective personalities clashing as phosphorus and oxygen, slept soundly in the flimsy tent, slightly illumined by a lantern. Showers were ceramic fragments.

Imminent threats in those parts lived like diving beetles in fresh water. Tough crap. To Treffyn, this was a business enterprise without the business portion. Their safety was in constant jeopardy. Joy ride this wasn't. Rough tit. Sprinkles had an aroma of aged apples. They had an ambience of outlaw import, as the Kelly Gang. On the broiling blandscape they pulled no punches, let the chips fall where they may. Treffyn fantasized they were revolutionaries. Cerebrations arranged themselves like instruments in an orchestra. Dusky welkin had changed its meaning in the day. He was exhausted, as a bird that wasn't allowed to land and kept flying. Rocking-horse of his moans and groans. He felt like a naive mascot. In the condensation his dirt was turning muddy. Seesaw of his sighs and sisses. Ructions within the group were rampant and abated after extended, enervating argumentation. Apologies were surrendered, not given. The altercating was a ritual, a rite of passage. Bickering Walkabout. Roy was hoo-ing and ha-ing, reins loose on the horses. He was a bully, Kevin the bastard. Their motives were money and mercenary. They thought of Treffyn as a ninny since conception. They ribbed him, razzed him, weren't poking gentle fun either. He was a corroded wreck of a life hardly existing. They were unblunted and precise as surgical blades. He had no intention of being a stationary bullseye for their slung arrows. Roy poured forth a mantra of insults. Kevin's limbs were wrecking bars. Desert of desolation had to be traversed. They were too desperate to appreciate the dangers. They blundered and blinkered, trooped across it with difficulty, had minor problems with lice and mites. Kevin complained they were slaving at starvation rates. Days were blistering, nights were cold. The trip was all about navigation, poring over maps, strain, maintenance and stress. Eroded gully. Mellow light. A quirky coot with a folded face, cowled snoot and a plummy voice yarned with attentive bullockies. The party claimed their interest, vacated their positions voluntarily. Treffyn's hackles rose. His cogitations were refracted, like glass shattered on a picture. Wisps from his widow's peak of shock straggled sideways. Ideations blossomed in his coconut as a Japanese paper-flower blooms in water. His slot-mouth was a sudden slit. Earlobes like leaves. Babs poked his cheek playfully, as if she were butting out a cigarette in an ashtray, and waited, not unlike a raven, for his response. He surveyed her as though he was weighing the pros and cons of a certain situation. They recalled a conquering army during the trek. Dunce-cap of a church-steeple. With the muck on his integument, he looked like a hermaphroditic, doddery minstrel. His scrotal pumice-stone smarted. There was no shortage of quandongs and ripperty-guys. Hovels, made out of cardboard boxes, created a whistle-stop from a piteous fairytale. There would be no peace with the blackfellows, no treaty. The journeyers, suspecting a set trap, went through Aborigines, who'd made a manly barricade, bearing the brunt of the pitiless sunshine, as spider webs on a park's path, in a progression which had its own logic, and dodged round the women and children. Renegade bullock drivers, a dozen, give or take, swooped like predacious birds, bellowing as ruminants, surprise-attacked them on the lamb-leg bend of a cattle-path near a rustling rindle. They wore wide-brimmed hats and dungarees, shouting and shooting. Babs repelled the men, like large and frightening bugs, by throwing lager bottles. Treffyn was incredulous when Roy, at the reins and armed with a rifle, protested. The horses trotted down an electric-green hill, Eeler-Spee stumbling, whereupon he regained his balance. Knitting needles of luster. Chaos circumscribed them. It was as a scene out of the Wild West. It was a madcap, slapstick chase. Treffyn, with promptitude, prayed out loud. Kevin was too out of it to be wary of the potential consequences of such whizz bang erratic movements of the wagon. Uriniferous cascade in Treffyn's pants. His legs hung like a wasp's, anatomy stiff as a punting pole. He had a bowed head, bent bod, and cowed spirit. Regarding Kevin's cauliflower ears, greasy substance on them. Clucking and whining under duress. It was like he had ground glass in his gullet. Germs of doubt multiplied in his noodle. He was a sorry soul! He epileptiformly shook. There was no eye-rolling, jaw-clenching, arm-flinging. Fetid beck. Oxygen was sappy. Poverty was dismaying. Bankrupt businesses in a ravaged burg. A nanny goat gnawed on cackleberries at a chain-mail fence on paving stones. The factions fought with each other for a resolution as vectors of force. Without any warning whatsoever, the bushwhackers were picked off like wingless, fattened flies on a windowsill, courtesy of Louella, figure as a loaf of bread, raven mane longer than ever, and David, rugged, craggy and balding. Treffyn's stomach churned like butter. Slop sloshed in the bowl of his belly. He felt as a broken-spined book; or like a squid washed up on shore. His uttered language was as grace-notes. He got a glimpse of Eeler-Spee's scaly pecker. There was a casualty in the firefight: Kevin was killed in the crossfire and was given an impromptu proper burial and sincere service. Cumuli were curdled. Clammy air was comparable to crinkled cellophane. Louella and David were humanoid leeches - she was bloated and he was lean. They parted ways like professionals splitting apart after a business transaction went awry. Louella wanted to be with Treffyn. She was rhinocerotically mammothic. David had a sailor's stride. Magpies were singing. When Roy, wallaby-vicious, attempted to rape Louella (she was a code he impulsively had to decipher, and he belabored her being), his instincts pushing through his conscience as a bluebottle through flywire, Babs knocked him unconscious with a tome and Treffyn bound him. They were menaced by wild dogs and Roy, mauled, mangled actually, crawled like a snail, excreted in his trousers, and was instantly installed in the shade, on a jerrybuilt ligneous sled, with a Panama hat on, torn, frail form under the tree's umbrella. He was a mutilated, screeching, bleeding mess of flesh, muscle and bone. Proud to a fault, he waved them down, as a symphonic maestro does when quieting the crowd. He was sponge-bathed and the dressings were changed regularly, on schedule, Louella assisting, with reservation, emotion bottled tight. His principles could not block the signals sent from his libido, his ego, like morphine for an amputee; there was pain in the limb that wasn't there. There was resentment in her expression. She was patient, courageous, persistent, lacked self-pity. She couldn't prevent the natural disasters of flood and earthquake of rage within her person. She cared for him, despised him. He was bold as brass. Sugary sand, fine and coarse. He complained his teeth ached, hissed like a train, and, superstitious, accused her of being a sorceress, deliberately beguiling him. To better suffocate him, she seated her uncovered, molasses-drum tail on his face, sitting for uncounted minutes, and he suffered, suffocating. Her bony ankles were greasy in his grasp. He grabbed them as a golfer his clubs. Ultimately, she told everyone he had succumbed to his injuries. No one was overtly suspicious. He was a defanged serpent, his poison sac removed. The team endured a flash flood out of the Bible, reached higher ground in the nick of time, except for three horses, who drowned. Families climbed trees which were uprooted like weeds, took refuge on roofs, the homes swept away by the raging waters. Gales wolf-howled, thunder lion-roared, and levin flashed. T Model was deposited in a dried-out water-hole. Wagon wheels had the sonancy of creaky doors needing lubricant. Scum on a millpond was skin on a stew. Gangs of striking shearers sang songs in these acetylene arcs. Besotted miners, fettlers and tricksters drained drinks of dubious content at a cannon adjacent to a pavilion in a hotel yard. They mistreated a tramp, appearing innocent and corrupted, on a rattan chair, as if he was a marauding reptile. Houses were dumps. Dour streets were in decline in the neglected boondocks, the denizens dispirited. More rat-hole abodes. Saxophone left at a bus terminal. A tarred and feathered mick holding a graphophone dictating machine damaged by the demands of its owner veered off a dingy boulevard, this hag beating him with an umbrella. He couldn't fend off the crone. Indigenous zombies dragged their heels. Fire-scarred trunks in the paperbark swamp. A zoftig galoot's cough sounded like a gargle coming from a crystalline case. He was an ashen bushman, showed regard for his billiard cue and tomahawk, homesickness palpable, at a redbricked crummy pub. A cloudlet disconnected itself from the sapphire sky and revealed a slash.

The stable was assembled a stone's throw from the orphanage (the Promised Land!), and in the streak of rainbow (hues of tropical fish) it was a cuboid prism of weatherboard. Shandong-ish coastal province. Relish-green sea sucked. Louella, feral, disheveled, absorbed Treffyn (sensuously) like paper spilled ink. He was sick, sour after a palliative spree, full of remorse, beyond redemption, dry and brittle as a dead hornet.

Conceptions floated in his head as suitcases on the ocean's surface following a shipwreck. He sampled the intoxicants of his inklings and got inebriated. His per-spiry, translucent fingers were like used contraceptives. Emotions ran hot and cold. Waterside workers were a distraction. Icy daggers of illumination. Jewel-blue pondlet. She had smooth skin, pillowy lips, reckless tongue, sandpaper soles, and an Amazonian tush. She was careless and shocking as lightning. Her kisses became tender, strokes gentle. Their raiment was shucked off on to the hay bales. Unrestrained han-ky-panky. Peppercorn trees. Their repartee ventilation was crystal- clear. They shared bully beef and butter cake on the cane couch, had more plans between them than a beach has bathers in February heat. His limbs were like a water-bird's legs. He assessed her: she was plain as day The Creator took his sweet time in making her, lav-ishing attention on every exquisite, dominant, divine detail. He appraised pliable keester. Stimulation threaded through him as barbed-wire, and his ding dong was like an aeroplane gliding alone with a splut-tering engine, its propeller lifeless, and he was a pilot sandwiched in the cockpit of shame. He was trapped in mortification as though he were a mosquito in amber. Her malleable middy was, texturally, not unlike tapioca pudding. His butt-cheeks were as satiny pannikins. She was strong like a buffalo. He was a shore taken by the tide of her. She was hot as macadam in summer, a silly dill, getting brighter and chattier. She scrubbed herself on him, her perspiration reminiscent of turps to remove the paint of his derma. The lovers turtle-doved. She had shell-gritty lint in her bellybutton. She was bodily blunt like a ruminant bail. The flesh on her arms hung as the skin on roasted chicken-wing. Their tongues plunged like hatpins. He was depleted, dried as a walnut. A love-sick pair, they devoured one another with indiscriminate passion. She was sweet like lemon squash, lustrous as a pearl, to be coveted, wet strands plastered against her caveman's forehead. He was bare-torsoed, finish galah-gay, suckled on her tubular nipples, and, worn, his pleasure became pain. His system was shutting down. She was a funfair mirror reflecting the distorted version of him he didn't wish to examine. Koels called like sirens. Her tactions and osculations were as persistent as bees against glass. These were met with his approval. She presented herself at a sharp angle, eyes frog- bulged, rampant ringlets stringy. She psychologically and phys-ically overpowered him, like an expert chess player defeating a novice in a match. He ogled her as a traveler checks the contents of his suitcase, checking to see whether or not he forgot an important item. With his thumb, he traced the outline of scratch patterns on her

abdomen like wine spilled on a tablecloth. He was on her as an unwashed blanket an unmade bed. She picked him up like a groom the bride, grasped his donger as a club. Her delivery was expressed, controlled and modu-lated, like from a medium's mouth. He was weathered and whiskered. He had modesty, vanity, when she manipulated him out of his polka dot pyjamas to sponge him with a cotton towel. Her tussocky axillae had a heady musk savor. The slippery worm of his pinky slunk into her pileous sphincter and lodged there, to her cha-grin. She had the sensation she was paying the price for some ambiguous transgression. Her masculine vox sounded coated with calcimine. His was riveted with wheezed. Her bum was a grenade, his thumb the pin. His obscene fingering was like a delectable revenge taken out on her rear end. She couldn't crap. Her bottom was this coop boarded shut, the pigeons inside. Treffyn and Louella sipped their schnapps and extinguished the hurricane lamp. They were wired on the same circuit. He handled her as a cook his pans without a pot-holder, his heart knocking like a spy's knuckles on a door, rapping code to be granted admission. Winter-whitish heavens. Passerines mourned on wedding-cake edifices. Jesus wept. She had the build of a rainwater tank. His being hummed as a generator, shell-shocked by her sexuality, his anxious affectations affecting her, if only marginally. His visage was a sight gag. She was artfully undressed, untroubled by blemishes, chilblains, warts, stretch-marks, or saggings, et cetera. They were kindred spirits, two halves of one puzzle. Her blinders were enigmatic as marble eggs, with unnameable, unknowable myster-ies. His head and body were like a single unit, an angular apparatus, had virtually no independence. His posterior - planar as claypans. Her tongue was scary like a scorpi-on's tail. She went through him as spider- webbing, countenance setting in a concrete moue, tweaking his wiry frame like tuning a piano. There was a ministering quality to her caresses. She was mighty enough to wran-gle a steer bare-handed. He, emboldened by barleywine, licked the nerine plums of her nipples, lapped the merino wool of her muff. Her umbilicus was a cuttlefish shell. Rays on the canvas made a magic lantern show in the bin. Zephyrine sibilants. His desire was a wiggling demon exorcized from his esophagus. She held his carrot as a cricket bat. Her Labrador's eyes. Her naughty commentary built up in his ears not unlike an allergy, an infection, until he could no longer bear the pressure. She wrapped her words in grody blankeys and put them down the laundry chute of his throat, and his oral lid closed. By Jove, they were going too fast for him. You must crawl before you can walk! She was a massive moth attracted by the electric light of him. A stocking hat was jammed over his skull. Her pornographic pantomime was protracted, diaphoresis petrol-gleaming. There was perversion, with her pretending to be a slattern, in plentiful mascara, rouge and lipstick, scarfing his pizzle. Her hirsute, handbag pot was cute. She was punctual as a pet at feeding time. This was their inner sanctum, their awe-inspiring accommodation. Skyline was like lolly-paper. Their respective roles were defined - he was the wimp and she was his protector. They made out, early and late. His cutis was as crepe paper. Her small lineaments were painted on the large canvas of her physiognomy. Loopy by lozenges, his belfry lolled. Her cupid's bow mouth, throaty voice, blinkers the size of biscuit canisters. He was asphyxiated by the tumidity of her venter, and feeling like a bunny buried in its burrow by a mean farmer. They made a commotion in their coital communion, their male and female particulars grinding. Her rear end was as a kero drum. She poured plonk and spread herself on him like lard on a slice of bread. Her thick thighs and button nose. A thin fruiterer, sleepy-lidded, boozer-mantled, and broad-palmed, sang bawdy songs from somewhere nearby. Louella was an overly padded armchair, blew Treffyn, spoke as a ventriloquist, hardly moving her mouth to do so. Dents in her tochus were like dints in carpeting from recently removed chairs. Her wit was a weapon. His penial perennial reached slightly for the sun of her paw. He showed symptoms of vertigo when she rimmed him. His nutsack was a shrunken iris bulb. He chortled and clucked, was a rag doll with a bantam chest. He was not a pretty sight. He was peaches-and-cream complected. They propelled themselves with momentum, ran a good race. His head was thrown out of kilter in relationship to his body. He had cherubic lips and arched feet. His balls' sweat had a stale stout funk. His cardiac organ slipped as a denture plate, lamps bounced like he was optically following the flight of birds, silken shakers affecting the shape of his ladylove, as if she were made of Plasticine. She leaked into him like cotton's dye into pores of skin. She was flawlessly smooth as an egg. They fell as though they were the rapids. Going down on him, her coconut was bowed deferentially. Their sexual slamming sounded like a bullwhip cracking, sighs as shots of electricity passing from one surface to another. The digital contacts on his spaniel's ears were soft and dry like talc. Every smooch and stroke was exact and true. Her comfortable flesh was abloom with goosebumps. Without her, he was as a wilted annual in an infertile region; whereas with her, he was one blossoming in a fertile clime. She made a meal of him, feasted to fullness, asserted her feminine license. Her heavy hands silently queried his silken shins. She said, snickering, he had a leprechaun's mouth and a monitor's tongue. She held his head like she was wrestling with the wheel, anticipating an accident. Her furry brown eye was taut. He shuddered, whined, orgasming. She climaxed, coming on his torso: milky ink spattered on blotting paper. His tendons tightened as fencing wire. Tropical plants gave salutations. The conversation had its ebbs and flows, the energies eddying. They were steel (her) and wood (him). She was gravelly-toned. He was played by her like he was her fiddle. He was a puppy sprawling at the fire of her. Aqueous air glistened as gasoline. She was a bull leaning on the fence of him. On the manicured kikuyu grass, the children jubilantly petted and fed the horses. Janet tended to her veggie garden. Sun emerged on the range like a zit on a chin. Mayflies were furious in the manna gums. Sprinkles like from a jailhouse shower. Wire fencing as metalline streamers. Tatty, overstuffed horsehair sofa. Powder-blue bay. Uneventful landscape had Dubois details. A Brylcreemed blackfeller with rimless specs glowered in sheep shit. Lumber yard. Insects, buffeted by breezes, cut these jagged characters in the dank oxygen. Oil-black clouds drifted not unlike horrific nightmares. Rains sounded as coins being jingled. Rosellas sounded triumphant. Waves crackled fizzed spluttered like a malfunctioning hearing aid, its battery low. He, eaten away as a log by termites, made noises like a misfiring motorbike. He grudgingly admitted he could be fussy.

Treffyn and Louella signed legal documents, composed their wills, got officially engaged, and, subsequently, were married in one-fell-swoop by a cranky,

straight-nosed, long-chinned minister, in a joyous ceremony on the veranda. It was windy and rainy. No-hoper
Treffyn was so weak he could barely stand. Louella held
him up. Her jowliness touched him. His eyelashes were
a hummingbird's wings. He was peaky, jut-jawed,
swigged laudanum as brew. He'd gone off into a daze,
lifeless like a shadow; or a cadaver in the morgue. She
had a square fanny. The spit on her mouth - adhesive on
a stamp. Terminally ill, he resembled a baby bird that'd
fallen from its nest. He had withdrawn from society as
an Australian buffalo from the herd. His grey matter
was an over-cranked cuckoo clock going kablooey, the
parts, namely cogs and gears, of thoughts, flying as
shrapnel. He was neat as a pin, imprisoned in the tux,
but felt like a repellent yokel. Glare and grit aggravated
their eyes, blinking signals. Royal purple rivulet. Their
glances were swift as umbrageous doubles of butterflies
on a pane. She was decked out in a taffeta dress, tunic
and poncho. He was dapper in topper and tail, although
he looked not unlike a gilled, rangy sea-creature. He was
a well-picked chicken corpse, and dry- retched.
Buddhist-yellow light. Hair-trigger Janet, in mechanics'
overalls, an incongruous bowler capping her cranium, a
grub in gear, with a military mug, repeatedly blew air
out of her jaundiced cheeks. She had the face of a guinea
pig, gluteus maximus as soup plates, mumbled like she
was reciting incantations. Next to her, he was feeling as
an aviator having landed in no-man's land. With the
cumbrous bifocals, she had this owlish appearance. She
was out of temper, a participant in this wedding ceremony, and craved her forty winks. The sting of Babs's

rejection was wrapped in the bandage of acceptance. She was a mess of melancholy. Her hurt lay there like plain guano on a curb. They pressure-cooked in the discouraging heat and humidity. Petals were as confetti on the potholed lane. White-hot beach, the people boiling like lobsters. Hitched, they were eyries ruling their empyrean. Louella was pregnant. It wasn't his. It was David's. Treffyn wasn't impotent because of his condition. He simply wasn't capable of siring a child. Babs, sworn to secrecy, was equally glad and sad. Those clouds abracadabra'd the firmament. Volcanic rocks. Crickets bombinated. Moon winked as a conspirator. Waves of Treffyn's anguish: where did the pain start and stop? He estimated Louella and Babs like he would snakes that may or may not be poisonous. He had Habsburgian ears, currawong oculi and bandy legs, jackknifed in an iron bed, spewing malachite bile into a monogrammed basin held by Babs, his caterwauling fractured, discharging digestion, Louella grunting and rubbing his cool wet ashen feet. He gagged. His respirations were periodically feathery, rattly, sometimes sounding as an engine backfiring, his vascular organ a faulty plug, broken valve, distributor with dirt on it. He retched. He clasped the puke-stained pillow like a fetus would placenta in the womb. His unpronounced pectorals. He was wan, invalid-shaky, nails dusk-yellow and smoke-white. He had an odor of sweat-sour leather. Welkin's impression of ageing integument. Wracked by spasms, he writhed and moaned and groaned, withdrew his claw as a turtle bringing its head back into its shell. The devil of sickness had taken possession of him. He squealed like skidding tyres, intonation ranging from falsetto to baritone. Babs, contained in her boiler suit, gave him a sedative solution. Their honeymoon was spent in a hay-loft. It was a place of succor and nurture. She confessed she was badly educated, was embarrassed. He didn't care one whit. Her natural honesty was engaging. Her slurpy fart sounded as spitting fat. Her feces was like steamed pudding. They vented on loaded subjects such as social injustice, unfairness in their country, a nation they loved. His skin shone like peeled potato. She was wearied and worried. Her shoulders slouched as a mansion's sloping foundation, shifting in saturated ground. He sounded drawn and quartered. She warded off damselflies. Louella's nails were like coated pills. She was sheep-dog-eyed, splay-nosed, boom-voiced, jarringly so. She fantasized that he was a jackhammer inside her. Her whoops-a-daisying. The perineal measles-ish rash was making her morose. She was perfect - earthy, practical, enormous, unpretentious. He imagined her pucker was a beetle hiding in a bush and not wanting to get squashed. She was a habit he wouldn't break. Smells of seed, mud, straw, manure, grain, mint ... rich and repugnant all at once. Their bodies were rivers changing courses. Newlyweds pugnacious. Sky was chromatic as an Asian carpet. Eeler-Spee was spooked, trampled the delphiniums and geraniums. Ichorous stool, Babs's, splattered in the dunnycan. Her system was over-wrought, celiac ball of elastic unwinding, mind gone haywire. Cries were hermetically sealed in her larynx. She was dependable, like a canine, to give affection. Fuzz on her nuque was raised on end, regarding him as if she was in the presence of something supernatural. She sneezed, and spotty light flashed like the numerical dots on those puzzles for tykes. He was, on his deathbed, or, pallet, a pop-eyed specter, with a tam-o'-shanter and tailored jacket. His flesh's pigment had lost its tone, looking as an unwell baby's. His heart's beat was the diesel whump of a tractor. The countryside, through the plywood screen, was delineated by sharp lines and crisp colors. Louella's paws were hot smoothing irons, expression like she got zapped by a car battery, the jumper cables hooked up incorrectly. She was apparently in a state of shock, as though she was an individual after a traffic accident. Her dandriff was like cake crumbs. Dappled trees. Her foots had an overripe horsemeat reek. She wrapped herself around him as a newspaper a lamppost in a westerly. Her manner was amiable enough. Micaceously peppered pebbles. Svelte strays. Dismal morn, aft, eve. Her lids were gummy, blink was reptiloid, rump hissing like a dragon, mouth a red purse full of ivories, gray-green as a foxie's insides, stocky shoulders golden like a parrot's. Rufous pool. Her stockings were laddered. Her brain was a plant producing flowery fancies. Tumbleweeds glided as migrant avians, illuminated by the thunderstorm. His medulla oblongata was dream-churned, head vibratory like an ear's diaphragm. Her skull was a cubicle curtained with cogitations. He made a piercing pet-shop din, blood circulating with black-market meds, hands under the spinach eiderdown fluttering and fidgeting as nervy cockatiels, mien awash with emotions, botty moving groggily. He requested he be chloroformed. No one complied. The elongated track on her lower back was a livid watercourse on the map of a foreign country. Cacophonous cranes. He called her "honeybunch" and gave her a ping pong ball. He had the sensation he was a serpent devouring its own tail - ouroboros - in his imagination, in its febrility. He was wilder-haired, pallider, gaunter, beakier, with an expectant bearing, in sexless shorts, his lamps no longer curious, optimistic. It took him an age to go from one side of the smutched mattress to the other. His countenance was distorted not unlike a candy wrapper unfurling in flame. They conversed on marsupials. He was feeling as an emaciated eunuch, neck crepey, pointy chin sinking into his chest, shoulders hunched ... a young fella with old eyes. Was he a goody-two-shoes to her? Hallucinating, Louella was a spectacular vision, a fantastic flying saucer. He loved her thickset figure! Overcast was frosted glass. Janet was cooking a barbecue for the nippers. Hail was gems falling from a broken necklace because of an inept burglar. His inflection had the sonance as if he'd swallowed a rodent tail, peepers like ball-bearings. Dying was nasty business. He was not long for this planet. Her heart set up a cadence. She moved as though she were a murderess in a cerulean slip. Her alimentary canal was drainpipe-clogged. Wurlitzer organ departed on the Acrilan carpet. He was wheezy and had vellum-dry extremities. His afflictions were war machine merciless. His sloe pies had sunken into their shady sockets, his Bacchus-mouth chapped. He was a photo already fading. His (droningly) spoken words like they were read from a typewritten transcript. He was peeling akin to a spoiled prawn. Horizon was hued as a Persian rug. Her feelings were compressed, constrained, like a tree's roots contained in a pot. Sorrow fed on her as a Tasmanian Devil a gweela. She abruptly masturbated, whined like a floor-polisher, gushed as water roaring out a plughole. Her encephalon was coral, thoughts fishies natating in and out. Air was like it was sucked-in breath somehow. Piceous smoke as a funeral horse's plumes. Treffyn died. He had a dreamer's beatific grin; or an infant's smile when given a rattle. Babs defied his death and her despair. Louella was feeling like she was having a negative reaction to a narcotic. The girls wept and wailed. He was gone. Janet's chiclets clicked as vertebrae shifting. Louella pulled off twenty chin-up exercises. And Babs unfolded herself like a napkin.

The orphanage, attributable to the horses and stable, achieved a new lease on life, was transformed into a school, named after Treffyn, and became all-inclusive, run by Louella, Janet having retired out of the blue. Thornbills, bulbils and scrubwrens disbanded on a pinnacle as if a pertinent meeting was adjourned. Platypus, finches, warblers, pussy cats, and bunny rabbits: animal representatives of Australiana. Vegemite jars on a snazzy ruglet of exotic origin. Bunching cirri. Pea soup like a chalky smudge. Dismembered vehicular engine and bedraggled stooge in a sale-yard. Bereaved, Babs and Louella, clad in cardies and wellies, sobbed as though they were mopokes. Their enthusiasms were like struck matches in a monsoon. Pastel heaven. Gigantesque negroes, animated as kid gloves, put on a vaudevillian show on the crumbling garbage- canned curb. One, anvil-headed, made restroom inquiries, boasted he served time in the slammer, went into the barber's for a shampoo and shave. Cardboard landscape backdrop. Sleet dinged on the pane, sounded not unlike an operator's switchboard. Vapor was comparable to espresso steam. Blocks of flats with french steel-framed windows and rusty roofs and figs and chestnuts. Bulldozed Woolworths in an industrial wasteland.

Babs and Louella, accoutered in beanies, bras, panties, and brogues, flirted while they foxtrotted on the quartziferous gravel. Their titters tottered on a perch. Brume obscured the outlines of the countryside. They had shed their garb as casually as casuarinas do their needles. They shook like leaves. Pollen was as antacid powder. They were threads woven into a new and personal thing. Louella had clumped to her, clomping, now in clodhoppers, dawdle punctuated with a subtle skip. Her lips touched Babs's like a cup a saucer. She had the potent stance of a weight-lifter. Her slick skin felt of indiarubber to Babs and had an odd aroma of depauperated nasturtium. Her heels were coarse as limes, breathing having the rhythm of rain. Changing attirement. She was big-boned and humongously haunched, mass of mane needing a decent brush, flabby middle like a crumpled paper bag, legs as wattle logs, well-preserved/proportioned. She could be mistaken for a footballer, and brought out Babs's voracity like moisture does smells out of the ground. Their garments sliding off - penned sentences of a dampened letter running. Babs was self-conscious about her mild case of psoriasis, a vermiculate veinlet wiggling on her temple, and she crept as a crab in a brownout. Louella, tone suggesting intimacy, blown away by the mere prospect of it, yet overcome by confusion, admired the austerity of her boyish beauty, her sparrow-skinny legs. She was an astronomer who found the presence of a new star with a telescope. She had no shyness when it came to her drooping bosom and widening posterior. Babs, not known for timidity, dropped like a dress from a hanger, sliding into formlessness, to gorge on Louella. They rolled around on the hazel lawn as frisky puppies, perspiration greasy like vaseline, adhered akin to membranes, came together, went limp, tired, and talked intensely, personally. Corroded tricycle and five rusty forty-gallon drums in the green oranges. The couple commenced grinding on each other like boulders in swollen and raging waters. Louella had a splitting headache. She was confused as a person in an unfamiliar environment. Was fooling about a grave mistake? She was bored and lonely, forced the issue with her. They had drunk lethal wine and eaten peculiar shrimp and got dizzily carefree. Babs tooted like a taxi in her raunchy bedroom, on the cusp of coming again, amid rejected underpants, among discarded outerwear, on cobweb-covered scrapbooks, bursting open as passion-fruit, squirting her juice and seeds. Louella was a healer, Babs the bullock. Louella's polished toenails were decorated seashells. Babs had the expression of a woman patiently waiting for an unpleasant experience, such as a gynecological exam, to pass. Her vision was tunneled. The sheet flapped like a spinnaker. She had honey-hued hair, window-shutter-flat chest, tabular midsection, snare-tight heinie, supple arms, lissome legs ivory-smooth, drawing-board back, pleading eyes, pussy hairs as the tiny feelers on prawn shells, feet sweet like sandalwood, spuds of breasts soft as jeweler's tissue paper. She was feather-light, navel like a gasket cork. Genitals were rubbed raw. Fingered, her fringe-'do flopped. Their teeth clinked as utensils, oral cavities welders' torches. They sounded like they were smithing at the forge, screeched as cockatoos. Kisses like cannon shots in the chaos of warfare. Splendor suffused the place, pervasive as oxygen. Louella was a sexy sow in nylons and leg-of-mutton sleeves, a digital litter eagerly at her nether regions. They had gone to the matinee together. Babs, sweaty, was difficult to grasp, like mercury. They went up and down, huffed and chuffed and puffed, going down and up. Their humping was homicidal. It could have been mistaken for a barroom brawl. They drank each other vampirically. Impaled by Babs's thumb, Louella was as motionless as a boar on a slaughterer's hook. They'd passed fluids between each other, turning like corkscrews. Cumuli in the azure: ash smudges on a tea towel. Atmosphere was broth-thin. Wild lantana, smidge of clover, and morning glory. They wolfed casserole. Louella filled her own skull with rubbish - Babs was good and she was evil, considered rude realities. The two disposed of pork and oysters, lamington cakes and spring water. Babs gripped Louella's acneous hind (junk in the trunk!), beheld her as an animated double-exposed photograph, teased her by calling her Miss high- and-mighty. The pair were side-by-side, like chess pieces on the board, fresh peals of laughter echoing. Louella cut a striking figure, as someone famous, her tread like she was passing through a turnstile. She was Mary ascending into the Heavens, massaging Babs, who purred as a pussycat. Her pinkie invaded her orifices, tight cavities to be sure, like sedge grass sacred grounds. She espied Babs's centipede appendix scar, played this little piggy went to the market with her toes, went through her as a heated knife through a lardaceous block. She was held like a flapping, captive dove. Gnashers clicked as telegraph keys. They were on each other not unlike voracious army ants, made filigrees of plaintive sighs. Babs had blisters on her soles and a nasty rash on her nape. She was obviously perplexed, as a youth trying to solve a Euclidian algorithm. Their fling was ructious. Babs had slipped through the sexual minefields Louella had laid for her. Louella flattened her like a flapjack, kiddingly reprimanded her, rapped her knuckles, paddled her nates, hammed it up with these funny faces out of a comedy routine, tongue a nonlethal weapon. Babs, gooey-eyed, mouth an "O", girlishly giggled. Gorilline Louella acted like she was in a cage with imperceptible bars, managed a somersault, scaring the bejesus out of Babs when she executed a triple cartwheel, tripping and teetering, and receiving a whack across the butt, round as a river rock. Her actions were so simian she could've been the real McCoy. Her flesh's streaks as tear marks. Babs flicked her fan. Curried lamb on the cherrywood table. Skylight. Drawbridge. The duo looked like they survived a cyclone; or appeared as flies crawling over the lineaments of parched land. Their bellies, slapping, made the sound of jam intermittently smacked on plates. Babs, atop Louella, was a boat on a barrier reef. They were uproarious like teenagers in summer solstice. Babs was insomniacal and Louella was her intimate instructress. They were appetently armed for battle. Louella was a torpedo sinking the vessel of Babs. They were marooned in the middle of the room. Rice cakes folded in banana leaf, bottle of Aspro, cheap baubles. A liner and tugboat progressed in the harbor. Waft of exhaust pipes. Jinker parked in the lumpy driveway of a nearby manse. Malodor of slipping clutches. An illegal immigrant tollkeeper spoke disparate languages. Aboriginal wolf-packs mingled with a hen-party of caucasoid hoidens. Smeary vault. Caravan of cabaret performers had a distinct variety-show vernacular. Noxious weeds in imperfect illumination apricot-colored as a seagull's legs. Leghorns dilly-dallied in the wheatfield in summertime's soup. Binding wires of the fencing were so tautened you could pick them like a guitar's strings to play a tune. Babs certainly was loud and opinionated. She was a jack of all trades. Her breath stank of rancid butter. Louella's hands were large and tough as if they were a farmer's. She had chipped cuticles, the taste of something synthetic that was burning. Louella's limbs big like battering rams. Fat feet in fluffy slippers. Stretch marks on her generous abdomen. Her central finger was a key, only the door to Babs's fundament was locked. Endearments made sotto voce. She seemed to be a wounded child wronged by a once-trusted adult. She deemed her character flawed. She, wearing nothing but a turtle-neck sweater and desert boots, mouth puckered as a birthday gal's in blowing out the candles, was feeling disgust, guilt, anger. Her tongue clicked like a wind-up gramophone's needle, profile glowing as though it was an electric radiator, razor-sharp fingernails like brush-hooks. She flared her nostrils, ate meat pie and crepes Suzette. Her eyes watered, swelled. Her hips had the curves of harps. She looked at herself as a low form of life. Her disposition could be both itchy and scratchy. Her approach to fucking was like a hacksaw. She was in a tizz, obstinate as a root refusing to be excavated from soil. Her knurled nut of bellybutton, scalp-white, broad behind, tootsies the size of telephone books, stomach swagging. She was koala-furry, bottoms of her feet rough-barked. She struggled to convince herself they had a future together, like forcing yourself to believe in the afterlife during a seance. They'd moved as those miracle American mechanical fishing-lures. Louella noticed Babs's mop was auburn, her asshole resembled a possum's pink nose, and she gawped, by Jiminy! There was a jacaranda-purply abrasion on her backend, put there by Louella, like an infamous bandit leaving a taunting mark for the authorities at the scene after committing a crime. Sweat showered, and in the phosphorescence it could be misconstrued as sprinkling sparks from a train's locked brakes. Armpits had the stench of moldering laundry. Oxygen was limpid like tank water. Babs rose, a realistic rendering of the Assumption of the Virgin. Constellations whirled in her cranium. There were drip-feed make-out sessions. Peepers spit-bright. They were avid acrobats. Aqua pura clear as ice. Funereal blackish cloudlets. Louella had drawn a line in the sand that Babs never saw. Moon, ember-red, was muscled, shone like a disembodied heart. They were sated (sexually) as gluttons. Their closeness was measured like prescribed medicine, where a small dosage was essential, a large one excessive. Louella lay tumescent as a well-fed python. Her voice was quavery. Babs, although satisfied, mused on events, was transfixed, coconut cocked like a tailwagger hearing a sound at a high frequency beyond human hearing, became distracted, as a student in class mulling over options for recess. Her cogitations circled like midges round a carcass. Her face was aflame and her tresses were clipped and amberously flecked and she spoke in a throaty contralto. Louella was bumptious, to a degree, looking as a brawler confident in her fighting skills. Her breadbasket was marshmallow-mushy. Hell's bells. She had imploring pies and beseeching pout. Babs ignited a Lucky Strike and took a drag. Louella was ambitious, conceited, hardly complacent. They dressed quietly, clumsily, got their clothes, previously in disarray, into a suitable state, then dined on pork chops and cocoa. Oh, there was tangible silence, suspense. Babs and Louella had rollicked in awkward sex and agreed afterwards never to get involved in a committed relationship.

Babs, pretending to be a man named Bob, became a successful jockey and gave most of her winnings to Louella for the youngsters' college educations.

FIN.

Hobgoblin

GLAUCESCENT WATER HEAVES like the back of a person sobbing. Serriform massif. Clouds fold over the moon as fingers over a palm. Ernst Boe, his presence an absence to many, this stocky, bosomy, gnomic, auricomous boy in his late teens, has a crewcut, beetled brow, cauliflower ears, brown whirlpools for eyes, bulbiform nose, hircine face, confused olivaceous teeth in a moray eel mouth, jaundiced pallor, double chin, cordiform posterior, and a dromedary hump on his back. He wears an indigotic boiler suit and scruffy combat boots. He feels like he's in a state of ferment without turning into wine; or as a needle taken out of its compass and thus cannot accurately point. He terminates his time searching for mines laid under the desolate beach and runs like a streak, gait a simian shamble, becoming rigid as a harpoon, breathing sounding not unlike surf sucking, forehead lined as a steamed prune, body smelling of rancid oil, expression a mask of mock tragedy, mumbling to himself, voice sounding like it is issued from mud. Laura Sandholt, his psychotherapist, materializes, dressed in a cerise blouse, matching skirt, and high heels, nibbling on a raisin-studded scone, and kindly receives him into the bland office of a building that resembles a gigantic pharaoh's tomb. She's quite cordial, has a vixen's peepers, pointy proboscis, china-cheeks, milk-white flesh, glossy, curvaceous blond hair, and needle-like gnashers. Her inner glow reflects her outer aura. He is an open wound she seals up. With her, he's healed and healthy. A dart of desire, tipped with poisoned pain, stabs a vital organ. She permeates his core, his essence. Silence sighs on them. Should he take off his drawers? His courage increases geometrically. He revels in the reverie of being a traveler visiting the land of her anatomy. He has the impulse to races as a rabbit. Surf smacks the shore. Scintillant spear of leven flings itself from the jet-black sky. Waves with frothy manes and ravenous mouths growl like a pride of territorial lions. Membranaceous light. Ectozoon activity in his pubes. A spark of lust dashes across his tightened scrotum. His intestines feel metallic. Ameboid cirri. Cephalate gulls. Decrescendo of corkscrewing, apparently crisscrossing breakers. Stars are fulgent chicks under hawk-wings of tawny cumuli. Reflective screen of moon. He flotsam-floats, anserously waddles. A vagary hangs in his head as a rifle in a hunter's cabin. Denmark, April, 1944. His nickname is Hobgoblin and he hates it intensely. He is a spy sent from a secret organization to assassinate the infamous, avuncular, gorillian Josef Mengele, Laura's lover, for his countless war crimes.

Out the diamond-mullioned window a flock of bean geese make a pearlescent blur in the slate-gray empyrean. Cloudlets mute the shine. Soldiers stomp synchronously. The sun contracts like an active lung, shivers into splinters. Ocean is striated with ripples. Spumescent combers, bulging in staggering increments, are fists thrown at the shore, the mountainous ones compounding over the cement wall and crashing on a serpentoid road, flooding it. Iron-ore red coruscation. Sapphirine firmament. Muck's matted with kelp. Whisperous tide. Flies draw an airy lariat. Laura's sweet and good, composed and serene, indeed a bright light shining upon him, her professionalism and knowledge beyond bounds. Rigging of libidinous fantasies hang in the gallery of his head. A tallow candle. Her pupils and irises are illumined. His pies are ember-warm, heart a burning coal, tongue a fiery ribbon. Blood flows into his face as a flash flood. She inflames him, and vice versa, he thinks, staring at his bowleggedness and scratching his itchy temple. Nothing in heaven or earth could come between them. Sweat oozes from his scalp like blood from a crown of thorns. Hail drops from the welkin as leaves from a ginkgo. Shiva shadows. He eats a cucumber pickle not unlike Cronos ate his baby. He has the physique of a sack of pumpkin seeds, has chunky hands and foots. A beam of brilliance, made by cosmic devising, embraces the ethereal curve of her neck. Her soles in those horrendous shoes must feel as rough grain of wood. The sun announces its ascendancy, then declares its descendancy. With his gaze, he calibrates it with consideration. Edgeless and expansive brine, storm-cloud grey. Ships are spawned. Spume like scraps of sail. Sea marries the horizon. He assesses the precious contents, namely contraptions. Swells have the sonance of sliding satin. If smooth was a sound ... Slashes of the rain. He beholds life in the mirror-eye of moon. His cardiac organ feels fixed to the tip of a bayonet. His will is powdery and the breeze of her breath blows it away. She's calcium in the bone of him. Her care-carved visage. He looks at her as a cannibal at a fresh corpse. He pictures her seated on a sofa, torso naked, legs cloth-covered, stomach rumpled like the ocean, his penis athwart her vagina as a dog who'd fetched a stick for its master. Gusts send slurs of sand. Handsome shrubs shield the structure, sieve the wind. She brisks her palms together. She informs him that people who suffer from depression believe they are trapped in a circular maze. Ernst admits his horrible hallucinations fly like a flock of ravens, the shape constantly changing. She wraps a shawl around her shoulders and takes a corn muffin from the tray. His inflection sounds as a croaking. She grabs him for balance and gyrates, suggesting a puppet on strings, and suddenly turns scribe, employing a quill pen and ink pot, scribbling in her notebook. The corners of her mouth are parenthetical. Her lunular calves. His tousled tress feels lanolin-soaked. He's saddened to've said goodbye to his pet mouse and wasp, yet is content in knowing they're finally free. His job is extremely dangerous. Vault broods a silver spell. Cranes cavort.

Demonic sharks - Great White comets cutting through the cinereal surface. Waves batter the bulwark of rocks. Dolphins, with bow-shaped smirks, arc out of the rearing and arching aqua pura, evoking pearly, crescentiform moons. Thunder thunks as mallet on wood. Stars float like filaments, and shoot as dandelion spores. Pulsating precip. Water of whimsy. Smudges of cirri. Murmurous zephyrs. Pollen is fine as flour. Metamorphosing vista. Iridescent fish create a sparkling swarm, their scaly forms mingled into movement. He daydreams he is Perseus, Mengele the Minotaur, a crematorium Crete. Perseid meteor shower of memories.

The cold draft is penetrant, Ernst's blood warm while he lumbers, hard and fast, into the pitch of the ossiferous woods, thorn bushes catching his crusty clothes, on his way to pay Gitte the witch a visit. He hopes, no, prays, she can cast a successful spell to make Laura adore him. Quixotic behavior of the bustards are on display. He is a dazzling streak, like Halley's Comet. Leaves on the crystalliferous brook are as mini cradles. Crows chatter on vines. He jounces through the dense forest, a timeless realm, bedecked in its flamboyant autumnal splendor, Fall in its grandeur, dons a coat and cap and doffs the scarf, confronts his fatigue, lurches cross-country, schools his stamina, plunges into the bleak thicket like a fish into obscure depths, brittle moss on the felted floor firing from underfoot. He baptizes his boots in the puddles. A haughty mockingbird scolds a toddling badger. Chipmunks scurry. He ferrets through the foliage, aflutter with tension. Working his way through the coppice as a pebble through the lining of a jacket for some secret compartment. He's weary, in body and spirit. His grey matter is a cooked onion, falling apart in concentric, pellucid peels. And his lips are parched, parted, panting heavily, like the huffs and puffs are engraving the atmosphere. He is compact and powerful as a compressed spring. A caravan of Tiger tanks are reminiscent of Chaucer's pilgrims. Determination keeps him on the trot, on the sizable hike, seemingly a sheep wandering. The many miles ... cruelty of conditions ... He traipses, wishes the egg of this planet would crack! He feels like a rabbit pursued by an impalpable hound. The bitterness of his heretofore brutal life festers and sours. He grudges with tenacity. His teary snail trails. He has a case of the dismals, slave-driven all day, sedulously sweeping the sand with his trusty metal detector, blood screaming in his veins. He is still reeling, reader, in a tailspin after his German shepherd, Albert, was blown to bits last week. Ernst stood as a broken statue on an amber hill, in the fury of a storm, tumult of gales, the tempest the wrath of God, momentarily mesmerized by the natating whales, leviathans steep as cliffs, jaws agape, eyes like stars, the animals not unlike animated islets. Turtles were buoyant. Porpoises jumped. He accidentally spilled his wine on the alabaster sand, the pencil of alcohol writing illegibly, and he read Shakespeare, slept briefly, a catnap, more or less, after imbibing and ingesting, in the skeletal shelter of craft wreckage, and he could've been mistaken for a morsel snagged in a strainer. Sky pisses. Season's temperatures obtained. Magpies orchestrate a screechy symphony. His sallow skin's shiny with sweat, his body electrically charged with excitement. He wanders noctambulantly, in a Homer-esque Odyssey. Nictating lighthouse. He pauses, regards its aloneness, aliveness. Gilted dome of a church. Jellyfish drift as children's abandoned toy boats on a pond. Whereupon he, miserable and wet, takes a break, parking on a rotted log, partaking of a meal of muscatel, bread, apples, cheese and jam, pictures beautiful Laura, a flash of a match in a dark universe. He feigned mental illness to gain access to her in order to get closer to Mengele. The pleasurable vitalizing force of being in her company ... He imagines himself shirtless, his glabrate, gibbose gut smothering her. She's contained in a pretty plaid dress, he's kept in dirty trousers, the two sprawled on the cardinal couch, and he's sucking on her gourd-ish breast like a calf suckling at its mother's teat. She ascends and descends akin to a seraph, ready to get on him as a hen its chick. She bathes him like Jesus after he was taken down from the Cross, speaks Sanskrit diligently, fluently, his malformed coconut pillowed on her downy belly. She's so whip-smart! She, out of the blue, calls him a "blessed angel," seated on his lap, the illumination as new-fallen snow. They talk simply, delicately, unguardedly. These vivid fancies fill him continuously. Octopus of the overcast discharges inky moisture, its tentacle-clouds waving in slow motion. Gitte lives in a copse-green, hellish hut with a straw roof that appears to have been built by a beaver. There's a rather large lattice of a skeletal hoopoe on the purple grass. Tree of life, filled with fruit and leafage, and doves and pigeons, is out front of the shack. Attributed to a migraine, his cranium feels like an apple with the press bearing down on it. His brains turn as the wooden blades of a mill unbraked. Dread and anxiety pour into him, a nervous nelly. Courage comes upon him, and he sends his callused, flinty-hard hand out as a probe for the piceous portal of an entrance, knocks on the oaken door, and she welcomes him. Moon in the cirri is a sanguinary, gaping wound seeping through a filthy bandage and incarnadining it. The place has the comforts of a casket. He's not really surprised, for some reason, to discover that, in all actuality, she's clearly an eccentric, carrot-topped, gorgeous gooney of a young woman, totally nude, integument chowder- creamy, with antelopean blinders, raving like a lunatic, slurping venison stew and moving quickly as the shadow of a stalking feline. With her, he acts like a soul requesting admission into paradise before a goddess. She laughs as if a cosmic joke was played on the two of them. He, innards churning, and, subsequently, grinding, like gears, gradually unscrews himself from the moorings of appre-hension and fear, appraises her rail-thin arms and legs, rocks as though he were a flimsy vessel on the vast sea. Environment's unbearable with carrion stench. Her mad whirls on the expensive Indian rug startle him. He confesses he feels like he has no past or future, just the present to call his own. His saliva is thick as porridge. Her tufted axillae have a roasting- fowl redolence. They share a slice of rich cranberry-and-nut cake and a cup of savory plum pudding by the antique Argand lamp bal-anced on a bar stool in the cramped, crepuscular parlor. She's a companion showing compassion. To him, her nature is to nurture. She is bubbling, sensual, energetic and voluble, not to mention independent and intelligent, her gabbiness spiced with gossip. He has a bulldog smile, says he's a worry wart, often makes mountains out of molehills. The dining-room is a delusion, a hitherto undreamt-of-reality, with its esoteric, exotic furnishings. Unexpectedly, she works his cock, in its vibratory erectility, like the handle of a public pump. His taut ball sack has a terrible urinose and excrementitious odor. He's ababble with anatomic inquiries. She verbalizes the experimental sexual session is going very well. She manages and guides him. His lack of experience in these matters doesn't provoke critical judgements on her part. She yokes herself to him. Boulders, mossy, are collected on the balding lawn. Rib cages of ruins. Mauve celestial sphere. Discourse on diverse topics, such as science, mathematics, art and poetry. His mind buzzes with radical ideas. She possesses a flexible mind, her erudition remarkable, arousing him with her enthusiasm. Sagging lids hood his bugged blinkers. He announces he's felt, lately at least, shackled in invisible chains, there have been restrictions put on him ... She, a bubble bobbing about, whispers here is safety and order, in a world of their creation. Furniture basically consists of several upholstered chairs, single settee, and glass-covered coffee table. She pins the velvety curtains together. A serrated edge to his intonation. A capable seamstress, she squats, measures, snips, stitches and sews. Her long, grungy feet have the distinctive stink of spoiled fruit and char from a campfire. Marvelous impressionistic mural over the marble hearth. His equilibrium's disturbed. She crouches, peruses the Ovid, scans Byron and Wordsworth, holding a wedge of rhubarb pie, and he gets a glimpse of her flocculent, roseate anus. She is aquiver, in anticipation of being put into an amorous state. Like Lot, she looks forward, but is compelled to look back. He bounces and rolls like a kid's runaway ball. Her voice has the quality of a quiet creek, offers sassafras tea, peach cobbler, and maple candy, and he immediately accepts. Her hospitality is therapeutic. Alert and frightened, still, and licentious, he tenses as if he might spring. Cumuli are decorative stitches in the materialistic skyline. Oral ocean, in its vastitude, swallows the stars. An amphibious, derelict craft coasts. Swaying seaweed. She is laundry tub-steamy, river-sinuous, frank- reddish, skinny forearms inscribed with Daedal tattoos. And she's currently slouch-hatted, flirtatiously sashays like a harlot. His trap is badly blistered, tummy shakes as a struck tambourine. He sits as a Chinese idol, sipping tomato soup and chewing on mussels, scallops and biscuits with decayed, aching molars. She, with plotting lamps, takes a trip to the lavatory. Benign sun.

She, with her entirety, swathes the injury that is his misshapen form. He succumbs to her advances. Sensations stage a spectacular chase through his person. He wonders: is this wise or foolish? He crumples into weeping, ambles the anteroom, occasionally (brazenly) adjusting obscure objects. Basket of shells. She is seemingly a Madonna carved out of plaster. Her skimpy nightie accentuates her leanness. A contusion on her sternum's like an epaulet. His nerves electrified, intestines sizzling. He is jolted from his gentlemanly reserve. Ruby red of radiance and emerald green of vegetation. Aroma of piecrust. Cranberry bog. Scrubby dell. Books by the boxload. Popcorn popper, ivory bracelet, wedding band, jar of honey, and Goethe tome on the mantelpiece. He lapses into reflection (morality being detached from humanity; souls are cast by sober shadows; war is an abysm with no bridge or bottom), and his voluble verbalizations get her to snap to attention. She was clambering up the vagary tree, climbing on the varietal branches of revery, and they snapped. She kisses him as though she's laying bait, behaving under the influence of external and internal compulsion. His member rears up like a bronco, refusing to respond to a trainer's command. Pressure of carnality catapults him into her arms. He looks marred, distorted by a bad mirror. His uttered sentences sing falsely; he doesn't listen to the voice of truth in his heart and head. Sky is separated by the span of the sun's diameter not unlike a room by a round table. He feels as a strong flower on the weak stem of her. Their association has a master and servant aspect to it. He could be child-churlish! Shadows are sketchy like chalk drawings. He is quivering as a candle's flame. Air's incense-spicy. He is pungent with cologne and dusted with talc. Fireflies flick akin to lanterns in the gloom, seen from a distance. She is a human furnace, radiating heat, yanks at his doughy chin like tugging the wrinkle out of a ruglet. Copulating, they are a two-tined fork elongated. He feels simultaneously under water and on solid ground. His buttocks bulge like twin assailants. His derma prickles with perspiration. His ardor is a long tunnel he has bored through a wilderness to reach its cumulation. The intimacy goes to its outer limit. Their lustful commingling as an interplay of glands. Her orchidaceous organ, nipples like sharp stones. A pale scar skates across her icy abdomen. His spit's as avocado paste. He's a volcano erupting. He feels topsy-turvy, helter-skelter, his talons pinning the cushions of her private parts. Rapturous, hectic is the fornication. Blue lid snaps sparks. Iodine bottle. Crenellated crematoria. His pulse throbs at a gallop. Will time move forward or backward? Her hind's pitted, like from the pox, frame slight, like a whittled stick. She is a porcelain statuary animated. She's special and rare. He can neither alter nor control the past, is enslaved to the present, and is at the future's mercy. She has expressive gestures and a sublime timber to her modulation. He's filled with the feast of his eye on her, and gulps the oxygen. Her scrawny shoulders tremble and hunch. With her, he feels as water embraced by land. She ambulates with assurance, enunciates with conviction. Cultivated garden. Tepee shed. Jungle too active to be truly tranquil. Embroidered carpeting. Dairy products situated on the quadrate table. Whiskey jug, burlap of beans, and keg of sugar on a varnished desk. Dust motes dance in a lance of effulgence, permitted in the musty root cellar with its medley of smells of vegetables. He is gaudy with gladness, blithe like a boy at Christmas, imagines plowing through her as a ship would a wave. Her long arms and fingers - a tree with down-reaching roots. Her insectoid tootsie-wootsies are rolled in pupal socks. Her armpits have a whiff of squash and scorch. Phantasmagoria of plants are frost-rimmed. She flows like liquid, fluid swishing against him as water a hull.

Raucous black and white storks in the vigilant sumacs and sycamores. His reckless, giddy gorging on greasy bacon and buttered cobs of corn and glugging of chicken broth. Stars are schools of salmon snatched in celestial nets. His thumb is a mole burrowing into her derrière's earthy den. Squinting lighthouse is a granitoid, towering totem. He, slumbersome and replete, floats like scum of soap on bath water, fesses, with his claws fingering her rear pink orifice, a poltroon's pout, a rubious rosette, Albert's was a decorous death, he'd sacrificed himself for his partner. Ernst had recited Scripture in a hastened funeral service for his friend. Creatures even assembled for the memorial. On a rectangular plank, he scrutinizes his knobby knuckles, glugs goat milk, gloms mackerel with mustard and ginger cookies, his language deformed, and remembers the rough-and-ready, lantern-jawed German soldier watching him closely, with an ironic smirk usually reserved for an orca. His vascular organ careers as a bison. Logs laid in the fireplace. Windows, smudged, are unhung with curtains. She's lean, hands and feet too, puts on a lavender sweater and color-coordinated slippers, and installs herself in the chaise longue. Shelving for a library in an enclosed cupola, walls lined in wainscoting. Rocking chair in the squarish portico. He grasps the sandalwood bannister near the plump bed, with a plenitude of pillows and puffs, to pamper them. She displays her dark arts. He's impressed. He is ravenous for her, like moisture is for nuclei needing more condensation to feed upon. She pulls his hard-as-a-brick dick: sexual seal of approval. Her hand clamps his unit as a vise. Desire is his antidote to despair. He is corpse-still, cardiac organ sounding like a casket hammer. Thoughts dribble in his noggin and a grin pullulates over his face. She presses her foot to his mouth, as if this will allow it to articulate. Her phizog is sprinkled with freckles. Her words smite his heart, her strokes a balm. Ardent two- hour tempest. She's a bean-stalk beaut. Her oral cavity is a virtual threshing machine as she fellates him. A ripeness and readiness to her. Cocoon of concupiscence swiftly spins itself around them. The ghost of Laura haunts him. A lump stoppers his throat. Something like cotton covers his craving. Fortification of hedgerows pruned into cubical shapes. Her bottom is blemished with craters. Her umbilicus is as the lid on a stove, pubic patch yarn-soft. She steals his breath and he returns it. She holds him and he is suspended like a bug in amber, her mouth on his as it would be a harmonica. Stunted, scrubby birches and lindens. Blank empyrean. The tide develops into sporadic, protracted diagonals, splash-spanks the beach, a frothy mosaic flounce in the frolicsome fulgor which has the pulse of a person. Clumps of hydrangeas. The sand's artificed by shells. Waves Apartment complex is an anomalous honeycomb. Dinghies are the incessantly winking eyes of sea monsters. Ceiling is incised with illumination, crosses as fencers, because of the blinds. He swigs Darjeeling. Does Gitte have the necessary effective potions and herbs to make Laura fall in love with him? Her existence is a rhapsody for him. She's a magnet for him. His confidence sinks beneath the water of uncertainty not unlike Ahab's Pequod. Insecurity gores his security. Abstract artifacts. Clouds cluster. He's booze-blushed. Lit candles' wicks are wiggling glow worms. Her sigh is a wisp of smoke caught in a chimney, her cry a cold in the chest. Flowers as a floppy necklace for the bed. They conclude their lovemaking with conviction. He couldn't resist. He was robbed of resolve. Silence is like the calm before a storm. Phantom SS, black as lava, march. Gitte, without warning, pretends to ride a telescope-broomstick on a chart of the solar system, and melts into the algid air, leaving behind a vacancy. He's anchored by the weight of melancholy. His camel's bump bothers him. Medieval castle is strangled by holly. The unyielding, systematic twilight ...

Laura's physical appearance ... she looks like some humanly tendril of smoke with a hurt-goose phiz. A clock bongs. Her bruisy eyes are as a raccoon's. Her serpentine neck. Hot and bothered Ernst's being encloses something special, the folds of an envelope covering his emotions. He is like a bestilled boat, desires her with all his might. She raises her omnipotent gaze from his body to his face. And he swirls as a hat in a vorticular cyclone. He feels exposed, barely concealed. Regaining his composure. In his existence, he's blindly blundering through an abyss. Brief pause intervenes. He touches her with the intense instinct the setting demands, the tension of this impulsive process mounting, the stillness, circumscribing them, spreading, her body, in expressive sensitivity, unfurling like a burgee in a blowing breeze; or as an overpowered victim capitulating to a perpetrator, both tinged with the color of love. His intentions are sincere, these gentle forces beyond humanistic control. He's stifled by circumstances, so it's like sweltering in a sauna and, with her, a window is lifted and a refreshing gust is admitted. They are clouds of joy, carried away in moderately accelerating velocity. Refulgence dribbles lachrymously, altering the deck chairs. He feels as if she is a masterpiece, in animateness, and his presence before her is interrupting the allure of the sumptuous oil painting. They stare at each other as though this is the first time ever making eye contact. Their psychology calls their physicality into play. Would she cut him down to size? He deems himself an indescribable inhuman creation. They're separate trees connected by the same root; a shared condition. The activity could be mistaken for an accident, sweetly suffered. Attentive and amiable, he submits to her sentiments, like light to shadow, suppressing suspicions of potential insincerity, his adoration playing not an inconsiderable role in this stance. The affair is alloyed with something else entirely. He is a dead individual … awakened. The Almighty is an artist who, in the ebbing flow of creation, inspiration with its up and down swells, left a portion of Ernst unfinished. The fine lines on his forehead are perhaps made by an engraving implement. Love brightens him, lust darkens him. In this extraordinary environment, sensations are refracted through the lambency in a fixed sequence, an exceptional emanation. Gestapo, with comic distress, ramble as lunatics, on the razor's edge, with their warders distracted by oppositional complications in the asylum, the arrangement in the institution otherwise in unqualified harmony. Superb architectural structures, Speer-esque, the edifices maybe evoking an enchanting eloquence, of design and execution, for eternal ages. She strives to impart a semblance of control to their questionable conduct. They split like a pair of compasses. Passion rises as fumes from a particularly potent potion. He goes ahead of her, like film ahead of a billow. His manhood rises as mercury in the thermometer tube in a scorcher. The surfeit of his exuberance inundating his system hasn't found an outlet. Her concupiscent caprice lacks a nucleus. Language of hankering is soft like a kiss. She's a pearl in the oyster shell of her country. Constellation of their discussion, a nation-oriented conversation, shoots in all directions, as a fire. They are Apollo and Venus. He turns his mind into a monument. Their lingua franca is a magic formula. He emerges from her embrace like Jonah from the belly of the whale. Their mutual agreement to pursue their pining manifests itself in gestures of the flesh. Selves are stripped. The radiant self is resonant as a voice. Her tummy is tender and full like the stomach of a youth after having scarfed too much confection. There is a candy box-resembling crematorium. The illusion closes as a curtain. His dreaming has the zigzag flight of a swift. Sensations pierce his perception. With cautious courage, he opens his very center like he's unsealing a crypt. He lands safely on her shore. He is laid low before her. Sweat sings as frost. Senses vacillate betwixt a couple of twinkling stars. Adoration pours not unlike gloaming's silver over spruces. Foretaste of an imminent union is prominent in the corporeality of the crepuscule. Ecstasy respires upon them. Anatomies, with assertion, find association. Their hugging is a surging experience. Words acquire will. Without her, his marrow is reamed out. Her drop-of-blood-reddish rectum is irresistible. A mirage of meaning in her sphincter materializes, displayed as a cockscomb, and elevates existence. Kindness is fatiguing! Subjects arrive and depart in swarms in their parley, in its concreteness, with its transitory deviations, unplagued by inhibition. The climax of their dialogue has the impression of inspiration, a luminous clarity, the conclusion, where he explores and discovers himself, like a scientific procedure, information gained from the surface and depth of experience. He feels leveled, his paunch a lava'd crater in the rumbling volcano of his trunk, heart hesitant, as a river reaching the sea. He's actually apprehensive, sends out circumspect reconnoitering glances at her, a sensuous, heavenly vision, the luminescence toying with her lineaments, and the elements of the environs, lending the surrounding shapes a fullness of life, a curious incidental association with the animate, and in the blink of an eye everything, irreplaceable and unforgettable, returns to normal, illusory movement, in secret deviation, like a transition of imaginings, having vanished without a trace, leaving tangible content intact. Reality, important and unpleasant, arises, and kills, in cold blood. He is a tangle she straightens out. Her saliva is a sleeping potion on his lips. He wishes to hear her inflection as a youngster wants to hear a bedtime fairytale repeated by a parent for the hundredth time. They are the Last Mohicans of the millennium! Dreams come to fetch him. He is a knob on the flagstaff of her. His hankering, with its plus and minus sides, advances and retreats militarily, has its strengths and weaknesses. Transported to an intermission of sensuality, she lengthens and rocks like an occupied hammock. With the accuracy of tide tables, his problems have piled up. A duologue of sound and silence. Alongside her, he's a bloated balloon with a beauteous butterfly, hovering as a rainbow. A suprasensory shiver. His. Will he be reduced to a humble backdrop from her valuable viewpoint? There is attraction and repulsion ... obstacles to overcome? His feelings for her have the clarity of a rill. He perspires his passion out through his pores. The bounds of her body are emphatically marked by his mitts. An SS soirée's racket is diluted by heat and humidity and shallowly streams. The Nazi's sky-high arrogance exhibited. Their crudely intrusive noise and high-wire-act activity, hectic hurrying. Company of troops load prisoners onto a police wagon. Empyrean dissolves in cirri and's unfathomable. His head hovers like a respiration between inhalation and exhalation. There is no end to his yearning and no beginning, either. Their wildness is a primordial alchemy. Crystallization and fluidity of their coupling. They make mute music in the rendezvous. Their unabashed conduct continues. He abandons himself to their vocal exchange. Fruit remains on the boughs. Moon disappears as a delusion. Ernst and Laura are beside themselves, fly to the moon, in the nocturnal enclosure 'tween night and day. Fact becomes small, fiction becomes large. Their merging is a metaphor - truth, only with exaggeration. Excitement is an incomparable conception. Contradictions are accepted into the maternal, and fraternal, bosom of the situation. Droplets of cum on skin. He thinks of the beseeching raised hands of millions of

Jews, like saints. He would relish the opportunity to pummel Mengele, a sinning revenant, a bewitching seducer, with the instruments of his fists, flattening his ego with a dozer. His fantasies merit a place in reality. Due to Mengele's influence, a problematic passion with higher promise, she follows his current, cannot escape his pull evidently, withdrawing from her circle of friends, avoiding hotspots where there is potential for her to run into acquaintances, effectively securing the probability she won't endure these encounters with her social set. Dot of sun sinks as a diving bell. Glowing hues of the rainbow like stained glass. Handkerchiefs of cumuli. Ernst was delivered into a hostile world courtesy of demonic fate. The world is a wound the likes of Mengele gladly turn the knife in. The simious, gap-toothed Josef Mengele's peepers are glazed and unblinking, to Ernst. Does being evil prevent him from doing good? Is there a chance the moral part of him sometimes breaks through the immoral part? Hitler, in granting him powers, is on par with giving an executioner his tools! A scarecrow simpleton from a traveling circus is mortally injured. Stars glimmer as flames. At that moment.

Ernst assimilates cogitation to perception. There is energy in his emotion, followed by erosion, a countercurrent in the occurrence, an idiosyncratic process of the self, a system of a whole, and its parts, and he experiences an unreal psychical crisscrossing in the region of his reality, an aspect of authentic activity partially contributing to these changes, creating a selective cosmos, a personal place for human relations, in a series of states, spectacular psychologies kept in a force field, the egos, apples and oranges in their interchangeability (the difference between them like premeditated and unpremeditated murder), in connectedness, dual sides of a paper, indissoluble entities exhibiting their components, in simultaneity, in the consciousness, as notes in a melody, inside and outside, all of one piece, these supplements of sensations with alterations and modulations, resonant spheres of behavior entering into each other, identity incorporating influence, claiming a comprehensive fundamental, a linguistic property's participatory translation where something can get lost, ascribed to the shape of the consolidated factor of an event, dispositions and inclinations playing secondary roles, like reinforcements, occasionally recast as causative sources approximating actualization in ideational patterns in an interwoven collectivity, superimposed on the psyche and promising satisfaction. Students, hens milling about in the chicken coop of the esplanade, encompassed by buildings, like a prolonged cement garden, in drunkenness, get into scrapes. Bells shrill and a beggar boy, photogenic, with cherry eyes, a Jesus kid, Son of God, employs a jagged, simpering intonation on the trashy, overpopulated street and micturates, the sonance as a tinkling cymbal, while Ernst, with an alcoholic vivacity (in all honesty ... a fit of sobriety), penetrates Mengele's lair, mucky turbulence on his mind, traversing the bridge of a plan, brain paralytic like a sliced muscle, having fallen under the sway of derangement, his essence, in a neutralized state of experience, evaporating, and all that remains is an empty shell. He pictures her, experiences ecstasy, his form ripping into ribbons, tearing into shreds, in a transport of frenzy, plunging into his self-made catastrophe, a preliminary stage as personal tic, on the highest plane in a final act, his body rigidifying and then loosening up, receiving freedom, becoming a construct comprised of a cluster of interrelated feelings. Laura conveys the impression of shrinking back, fending the menace that is Mengele off, in what might be a fight or flight position, a purposive counterattack, like she's regarding him as a mugger. At that instant, she is coolly collected. He brags he's a tree, staying the same, from beginning to end. He is pathologically scatterbrained, is Ernst's conclusion. Mengele associates with her like it is a contractual obligation. He, full of venomous unrest, out to wound, shimmering as a pupil, is an abscessed tooth which should be extracted from the planetoid oral cavity. The truncated grand piano, a sound machine, in the spacious, palatial music room, is an armless and legless torso. She's white like a lie. He is an artless poem. Her gritted teeth, pipestem limbs. They're gravel and mortar mixed. He wants to share the sublime and secret innermost treasure that is his heart in his chest, but nerves cut him to the quick. Tremendous tension seeks an outlet. She inspires him. He depresses her. In a snap, she's a rodent caught in his trap. He, with an atrocious eidolon lurking in his thoracic cavity, studies her like she's a geometric proof, intentionally misuses the manipulative influence he exercises over her, subjects her, with a puckered brow, to oppressively detailed examinations, physical and mental, alarming and unpleasant, with unsettling, unbridled power, and she has a meaningful character of mockery, as the Mona Lisa's smile, and her being feels not unlike it's submersed in a bubbling spring, permitting protection. She is light as a flake of ash. With his migraine, Ernst's head's stuck on the lance of a neck above an anatomical arena. For him, with her, he is a stutterer becoming an orator, a cripple a pole-vaulter, a bowl a basin, a weak young 'un a strong hero. Her presence is illumination, independently, and surprisingly, permeating the morbid vault of his breast, this luster dispersing a glorious glow throughout his extremities, his breathing tuned to the sound of the wind. Although dispossessed, and reposed, he has a cornucopia of soulful and spiritual prosperity preserved within him. His association with Mengele (the master of environment, a lord establishing an atmosphere): an ailment that was cured and left behind a limp. She's an angel assisting a devil. Mengele fuels the propagation of neurosis in his narrow circle of quacks, influential connections, a distinguished community, with their admiration of him and their own ambition, in their respective political, scientific, pedagogical and moral organizations, on clarified summits of society, these relationships with a dynamism of a broad base. Airplane, motorcar, horseteam. Grim industriousness, visually and aurally.

Mengele, not a citizen of the world, but a creature of it, manifests like a malignant gas, through the crack of a wall, mouth a leak of light under a door in a black night, voice as vinegar in a suppurated sore, language a lubricant, perversity printed on his monkey's mien. He is, to Ernst, Beelzebub's brother, chumbling pecans and caramels, seething with baneful intensity. His temperate tones. His derogatory comments on Goehring's incompetence hit not far from the mark. Unclothed, save for socks (him), and stockings (her), they loop together on the hammock in the lab, tied into an intricate bond, with overs and unders of heads and limbs. He's a hog wallowing in shit. He has stopped belonging to himself, instead has become part of Himmler. His arguments are frivolous and unproductive, do not give her a vocalic toehold. Wiener schnitzel and dumplings are uneaten. Congress of anarchists pilfer the contents of a medical supply wagon. He, her quasi-confidant, a manual of madness, his eructated words ice bags, steps over the cadaver of reason, gives the impression of being irritated. His parlance turns up as an orphan. He rants on faith and loyalty to the Third Reich, its duration of power and identity, ascribes, with a spartan honor, every imaginable kind of importance to the cause, raves about knowledge, violence, justice, and, with semi-certainty, his personal views on her. His opinions are issued like instigations, beliefs as feet firmly planted on shaky territory, his enthusiasm the equivalent of a chest puffed out, a badge of distinction, and he embarks on a digression concerning his controversial experimentations, domestic politics, military policies, and modernization of artillery. His conscience does not bear the cross of guilt. Him: the world consists of four classes of elements - earth, air, fire, and water - Hitler, Himmler, Goehring, and Rommel; unconstrained nature. They occupy a privileged position in his mind, his brain, to her, with its colorations and shadings of insanity. Craziness corresponds to circumstances. Aristotle, or Nietzsche for that matter, he isn't. He furthers suffering, singularistic and pluralistic, doesn't hamper it. Pleasure and pain are the hee and haw, bowels and bladder, genius and species, relaxation and tension, of life. She has no intention on insulting him by disagreeing. She has no foothold on the discussion. His first tests on human subjects were small steps, and now they are big leaps! The tests are reduced to links in chains of instinctual reflexes. Overcasting of skyline. Ideas are compartmentalized in his cranium, like it is a pharmacy with uncountable labeled drawers. Groupings of relevant stimuli determine his thoughts and actions. His philosophical egg from the laying hen of discomposure. Speaking as if he's soothing his larynx. Reflection is his intention, contemplating splitting the simple and complex contradictions and their sharp contrasts, giving each other apoplexy, going back and forth, up and down, in his everyday existence, a valid goal, also considering taking his life apart and putting it back together, subordinating himself to these tasks, the particularities of his individual case substantive, compelling him to resist being yanked into commotion, the cerebral application an affect of action, thinking with the confidence a well-mulled-over conceptualization provides. He administers and receives a self-rebuke for not attaining a resolution in his musing. His predilections predominant in private and public, which paves the way for an equilibrium of his internal and external states, independent of one another, an equalization of stimuli arousing his emotions. Peacemakers, national minorities, demonstrate in a row as stored medical supplies, the pacifists most unmilitary, chant in chorus war is misfortune for the earth, accuse the citizenry of apathetic materialism. No one, armed with an inner and outer readiness, does anything rash. There are causes and consequences. People could fall not unlike dominos. They're not ignoramuses not unpracticed in issues of the intellect. Idealism and everything it entails runs its course. The Lord's ordained ordering of the cosmos is disordered. Her tresses have the irregular rhythms of reins. She is an amphibian stranded on the shore, a thread in the rug he stands on. He handles her with bridle and spurs as though he's a rider on his filly, treats her shabbily, beats her like a drum. His thumb's on her nape as a tick. With her, he looks like he's infiltrating perimeter defenses, working as a Bohemian dragoon, a Hussite combatant, the embodiment of soldiery bravery. fighting a trail to the fortification. She strips herself of the gifted nylons with delicate determination, a degree of reservation, and they look like slack scabbards of swords. There's a reverse magnetism, changeable and inconstant, of these connected poles, Laura and Mengele. She, monosyllabic, procures, with dignified composure, an imported cigar for him as a robotic machine put into motion by a remote control, carrying this service out with lightning speed, whereupon a slower tempo is imposed upon her. They are Amor and Psyche. Mengele is a power station, Laura a tiny string, Ernst a little wheel. Ernst, hidden in the closet, kneeling, with a walk-on part in this sordid production, cannot resist masturbating. He longs for her like a smoker does for a forbidden cigarette. His excitement launches as an Independence Day rocket. He is Cupid with more than one arrow in his quiver! He has a sense of foreboding, like a sailor on a ship at sea senses a storm coming. A collection of thoughtful fragments, with significant merits, are coherent in the profound privation of his noodle after he'd grappled with them. He is shocked by the fiend's even temperament, sensible bearing, placid manner, being reasonable and responsible. She distinguishes the dynamic conversions in the talkfest, the communication's conceits derived from a developing discipline, a process with its origin and form, physiology and biology. Ernst expects her to box his ears! Regaining his mental faculties, he concludes conditions are thoroughly changing. The waters of his libido rise in the well of him. Their genitalial meat is encased in twin halves of walnut shells of crotches, anguish for Ernst to witness, the agony in his groin making him afraid. She steps aside, disregarding an inner self-admonition with outer determination, like a brute brushed against her in an alley; or as an waitress eluding a patroness. Her forehead's furrowed in concentration. Shagging, fore and aft. He bangs on her, before a cabinet of curiosities, like a door's knocker on a brass plate, his lust contagious to her, the crude quarters, unusually cluttered and cramped, finished with grayish plaster, composed of inelegant furniture placed here and there, not-well-proportioned. It is akin to a crow's nest tucked under the eaves. Modulations suffused with passion significant. His gimbal in her socket. His brow's flushed as ruby port and ruffled like fringe. She is spread as a skirt. Her cries sing counterpoint to his. He turns into a wolf, maw clamped on the crook of her elbow.

Her arms are long as marlins' spears, legs lank like walking-sticks. Hysteria rises in his voice. Ernst feels as a pebble dropping into a deep well. The abnormal superimposes itself on the normal. His heart thumps like a barrel on a boat's deck on choppy waves, body brimming with a furor. His flaky flesh peels as the rind from an orange. Their gabfest becomes unhesitant, liberated - a continual snarl of wordage. She prostrates herself on the damp boards and they join together. He sobs and she comforts him. Her bellybutton is like a cinnamon roll's knot. Her skin bone-white. His knees creak as timbers. Her pubic hair's a triangular iron. He has got crosshatches of cuts, scabrous whorls, all over him. She rubs a salve on his scrapes to soothe him, spreading it like butter on a piece of toast. Her teeth are scaleddown icebergs. Confounding hospital corridor, antiseptic, is all scurry. Patients in the ward are trussed up (in straitjackets) as Danish hams. Twinkle in her intonation. Perpetual showers. Shoulder blades are the wings of Pegasus, that horse of Greek mythology. He says he's not the sturdiest branch on the family tree. She endeavors to plant the seed of calmness. Ernst's gray matter spins as a weathervane. It is as if he is starting and ending a journey simultaneously, founders like a sea-slammed craft. He's back to the beginning. Ordeal of his instability is overwhelming. Crests build and break apart. Sprinkles, nature's ablution, pitter-patter. Boundaries dissolve. Aberrant albatrosses. Indifferent weather. Armchair upholstered in a cobalt oilcloth. Spiny stars. On the coil of ropes, Mengele chews pickled herring. Cumuli are a school of cod. The horizon is tranquil and protective. Wealth of gorse in the heath. Gales possess the will to whip. The storm's Eumenides scourging pedestrians. Swoops of surf. Wild water. Breezes dig bowls of blue in the cloudcover. Sunshine turns the downpour into swarms of light. After the vigorous intercourse, they argue in the stocked pantry, comfortably unprepossessing, cast verbal stones, argot with elaborations. In the thunderous quarrel, vocalic levin lunges like it's leaping from a couple of cirri. Police hurry as ants, in a ragged rhythm, heading toward some emergency. Moon's a ghastly shimmer, a tenuous blanch. Laura and Mengele are as characters from a fairy tale. His penile pestle grinds at her vaginal mortar. He is a shoat conveying himself to the sow. Incredible intimacy. They're goat-nimble, their sexual relations having the elemental fury of fire. Inhabiting the salacious seconds together. Unilaterally thronging ragbag of riffraff. He is proud, like a minister at a pulpit. To her, he appears to be an unassertive beetle from a geological epoch. Ultimately, hers is a pudendal peony, petals opening, permitting entry. He clings to her as a barnacle to a pier. Ernst, at last meandering on sooty, cobblestone streets comprising a labyrinth, feet confiding encouragement, past a dockside inn and a series of uninhabited dwellings, sick and hallucinating because Gitte spiked his coffee with rat droppings, digs up memories from the meadow of his mind. He chooses to seal and stamp his noggin with glorious images of her. He's satisfied he has made an impression on her. Mengele is arrogant and vain, ostensibly some cricket out of the Middle Ages. His coldheartedness and conceitedness are carriages in a choo-choo chugging along. His insecurity has taken refuge behind his hubris, his being in possession of the repose customarily inherent in the aristocrat. Ernst ends up slumbering, with an accompaniment of stentorian snoring, and dusk bounces from his sloping shoulders, and when he awakens, his remembrances, once repressed, are now crystal-clear: he was a main guinea pig of Josef Mengele, the Angel of Death. He, a martyr to his own misery, writes in his diary:

Sulfanilamide Experiments

To investigate the effectiveness of sulfanilamide. Wounds deliberately inflicted on the victims were infected with bacteria such as streptococcus, gas gangrene, and tetanus. Circulation of blood was interrupted by tying off blood vessels at both ends of the wound to create a condition similar to that of a battlefield wound. Infection was aggravated by forcing wood shavings and ground glass into the wounds. The infection was treated with sulfanilamide and other drugs to determine their effectiveness. Many victims died as a result of these experiments and others suffered serious injury and intense agony.

Spotted Fever (Typhus) Experiments

To investigate the effectiveness of spotted fever and other vaccines. Numerous victims were deliberately infected with spotted fever virus in order to keep the virus alive - over 90 percent of the victims died as a result.

Experiments with Poison

To investigate the effect of various poisons upon human beings. The poisons were secretly administered to the victims in their food. The victims died as a result of the poison or were killed immediately in order to permit autopsies. In or about September 1944 the victims were shot with poison bullets and suffered torture and death.

High-Altitude Experiments

To investigate the limits of human endurance and existence at extremely high altitudes. The victims were placed in the low-pressure chamber and thereafter the simulated altitude therein was raised. Many victims died as a result of these experiments and others suffered grave injury, torture, and ill-treatment.

Incendiary Bomb Experiments

To test the effect of various pharmaceutical preparations on phosphorous burns. These burns were inflicted on the victims with phosphorous matter taken from incendiary bombs, and caused severe pain, suffering, and serious bodily injury.

Freezing Experiments

To investigate the most effective means of treating persons who had been severely chilled or frozen. The victims were forced to remain in a tank of ice water for up to 3 hours. Extreme rigor developed in a short time. Numerous victims died in the course of these experiments. After the survivors were severely chilled, rewarming was attempted by various means. In another series of experiments, the victims were kept naked outdoors for many hours at temperatures below freezing. The victims screamed with pain as their bodies froze.

Sea-water Experiments

To study various methods of making sea water drinkable. The victims were deprived of all food and given only chemically processed sea water. Such experiments caused great pain and suffering and resulted in serious bodily injury to the victims.

Malaria Experiments

To investigate immunization for and treatment of malaria. The victims were infected by mosquitoes or by injections of extracts of the mucous glands of mosquitoes. After having contracted malaria the victims were treated with various drugs to test their relative efficacy. Over 1,000 victims were used in these experiments. Many died and others suffered severe pain and permanent disability.

Mustard Gas Experiments

To investigate the most effective treatment of wounds caused by Mustard gas. Wounds deliberately inflicted on the victims were infected with Mustard gas. Some of the victims died as a result of these experiments and others suffered intense pain and injury.

She is a cliff withstanding an oceanic onslaught. Laura's occupational cubbyhole in the marred building is mainly a glorified closet, albeit a first mate's cabin-cozy one. It is a shrine for stuff. There is no exorbitance in her surroundings, nothing signifying excess, and it is unflaggingly maintained, in a sector not prosperous, only not poor. Blandness is in evidence everywhere. Fittings look at him with a glower of reproach; or glare like barrels of a gun. His words bubble forth, he, for once, having a distinct height advantage, seated in a highchair, making him feel as a tennis umpire. His physique's as a bowling ball. He gets a brain-cramp, vacant to the point of imbecility, before unleashing a flood of language. She's a lightning rod attracting the electricity of him and redirecting him from a dangersome road. He is intimidated by combat, like hell is by heaven. This is how he avoids warfare, by sweeping for mines on the beach. He has honor, valor. He's incapable of heroic feats. His trepidation, when it comes to fighting, is a natural inclination, as a caterpillar's attribute is that it will become a butterfly. A St. Elmo's Fire flush is on Ernst's face, guts churning like waves. His hair's part is a winding path through woods. Adornments of choice showpieces, vases filled with paper flowers and colorful prints: elements of unity. He imagines he is a knight saving her, the maiden, from the dragon of WW2 conflict. The severity of his shape is a stark reminder of his harsh existence. He spanks her buttocks as a trainer would a horse's flanks. Cyclopean eye of a lighthouse's beacon glints. She's spread like a sturdily-ribbed umbrella. Bodies are buckled in lovemaking, both bedbound, during a deliciously windy, warm, sunlit day. Closed books and folded garments. She is light as a leaf.

He's bleached and puckered not unlike swimmer from prolonged immersion. There's a liberation of brilliance which leaves the room astir with phenomena. The furnishings lose composure in the coruscation. Objects are connected, as in a murder mystery. He is lost in unearthly thoughts, the contents transforming with infinite slowness. Are they climbing Jacob's ladder? Does he have admirable traits? He feels like a fraudster in an allegory, desperately undisciplined, opening up to her, and fearing there will be disastrous consequences for breaking an oath. He sags as an item of sodden laundry. Her eyes rest, distractedly, and momentarily, on his deformities. And she extinguishes her exasperated expression. He cannot bring his fanciful notions out of the dark and into the light. Asperous splendors of sea and sky. Physical spells cast. Their present situation is a positive produced by two past negatives. He feels redundant, useless, superfluous. Her voice chimes as a bell. She is cocooned by him. She's an angel of mercy ... bedeviled. Hieroglyphic lightning. Thunder leaves the sky in throbs. The place absorbs them. Jokey questions and answers. They're practically fluorescent. Things are revealed and concealed. Illumination is a pool of liquescent gold. Sickle-shaped slices of melon on Irish dishes. They gently hold hands, urgently climb on each other, in impenetrable privacy, triumphal and tender. Their alliance knows no boundaries. Violets and clover. Spaghetti is spilled entrails. Spring-green yard. Daffodil-yellow sun. Birds convey ornamental notes of a lullaby. Mint and chamomile. Hoofy clip-clopping of his heart. She is eel- slippery. He tells her he views himself as

David, Mengele as Goliath. Bridal cakes of boats at the wharf. She's tall and he's small, reminding him of Coleridge's ideas in that 'Ancient Mariner,' dealing with big and little. He looks wan and sickly, is slick, with sweat, like a greased pig. With his pinkie, he traverses a veinal zigzag path on her thighs. She waxes metaphoric, peers through her spectacles in the muculent emanation. He crouches quickly, as a trunk's closing lid. Frontier crockery. He is swooped up in the scoop of desire. His manhood is forged in her vaginate smithy. His respect for her forms like a pearl in an oyster. His encephalon explodes as a squid when it is taken from the depths to the surface, where it cannot survive the pressure change. He lavishes his focus on her, his stare snipped near the eye. Her martyred expression. Their fluids flow like springs from the rocks of their beings. His integument has this cheese-ish texture. She is beeswax rubbed on the bunion of him. Her osculations and tactions touch as a butterfly's wings. Mane matted, she slaps his asscheeks like waves the stern of a ship. Their ardency's molten. Silver scallops of clouds. Sausage curls of her clumped strands. Traceries of circular lesions under her oculi. Discarded moccasins. He masticates, digests. The baked fish seasoned with paprika and breadcrumbs, cabbage and squash … delicious! Her culinary creations served on plates from Russia. Canister of blister powder. His blurry reflection's in the polished tabletop. Their vowels and consonants run as rivers. Tiger lily-orange moon. She, wearing a camisole, is gypseanly sassy, ponytail wagging like a bell clapper, has a snifter of brandy. She chomps on a pear confection as a mule on spring grass. He munches on his not unlike a stowaway rat at the corner of a crate. Blushes irradiate their features. He looks at her as Noah did at the white dove. Her physiognomy possesses an unfathomable profundity. Her melodious sentences, in ornate paragraphs, sluice as a streamlet. A porcine's bladder's semi-dissected in a vitreous dish on the clean counter. Adjoining structures hulk like monsters. Coots transmogrify into confetti. Tide fingers the beach. Lemonade weeps on the sink; bitter tears of pulp. The couple laboriously wash. Bathing, to them, a respectable regimen, is a healthy and harmless practice for the body, this modern care, with industrious dexterities, a moral and social imperative, self-attention meted out, with general gymnastic discipline, for the character, cleanliness, an ingenious treatment, one sequence succeeding another, with no break in the routine, interruptions these miasmas from which frustrations arise, the daily ablutional activity a pathological and physical liberality, necessity according enough adequate time to allot ... Her head is cloaked with hair. He's a ripped glove she mends, a broken bell she repairs. They cohere as sand particles fused into the mark left on the ground where leven hit, touch like fulgor brushing a freshet with blue, anatomies, slick and crimson, vibrating as water from leaping porpoises, juices spurting like struck sulfur matches. They are stars exploding. This congregation of children let loose and launch kites and explore the minutiae of their universe. Thinking, remembering, he feels as a squirrel excavating nuts buried by others of its type. He drinks her like wine, rejoices in reconnecting with her, at her disposal, conversationally. Her demeanor changes as a cloud passing over the moon. A scant robe swaddles this precious woman, and she glissades, in the evening's suspirations, exciting his entirety into spirit. Her tootsies are heated, fleshy flatirons, hindquarters like bulbaceous lightning bugs, head screwed sideways. He insists Mengele is appallingly amoral, intent on inflicting physical and psychological injury on innocents, with an absurd arrogance, obsessing over details, handling himself as an opera singer taking care of his pipes, his base nature affronting humanity. He wipes Jews away with an iron mop. Is she Lucretia who will skewer herself, or a Judith who would hack off the head of her oppressor? She makes him feel better, takes him away from his problems, but it is like having a cold and medicine alleviates the irritation in the throat, only the cough persists nonetheless. She's seductively prominent to his senses. She raises an army of emotions in him. He is lying to her. He wants to tell her the truth, he's faking a mental malady, working undercover to assassinate Mengele, and has the sensation he's wearing a mink coat, the fur inside instead of outside, and cannot shake it out! A bead of conversational bliss turns into a cloudburst of venereal satisfaction. The victim's tears are drops of oil that lube his willpower. He feels weary, as one with a fever and his temperature has subsided, and is removed from reality, like a door taken off its hinges. It is as if he's in a dream which has departed from night to linger into day. Monotonous, melodic lullaby sounds of the rainfall. Block of margarine on the bureau. She shimmies into an oatmeal-colored shirt. Zephyrean death-rattle.

Minutes, hours pour like the drencher. His oculuses are identical dead planets. The two are intricately intertwined. Saccharine scarves of her cigarette's smoke. Her fleshly genitalial fruit, swelling and sweet, slices itself for him. Clearheadedly he realizes she has gained control over him. She's the beneficiary of his attention. Her limbs are pillars of salt. They're twisting and turning as though flamingo's necks. He feels like he slept on a bed of nails, put there by hammer blows. Runny mascara lends her the look of a panda. Purplish helixes of abrasions on her side. He sees her differently, as if she is an object that has lost its composure, like he has seen her teary-eyed, and the lachryma has since dried up. Is she becoming a stumbling block ... getting to Mengele? Warning shots of avian wings. The dreary weather dampens his spirits, like rain discharges electricity in a cloud. Wet leaves shine as rubber boots. Sickle moon. Spumous troughs. He's ramrod-rigid. Lenses of his spectacles are medals of honor. Meringue foam. And he snoozes like Beowulf on his bier.

Ernst, delirious, drugged, remembers Albert bounding, minnow-swift, and barking, before blowing up. He feels like his form is a timepiece, the mechanisms malfunctioning. These nightmarish servicemen glide as ghosts. Laura's presence is realized, on the sand, achromatic like bleached linen. She's obviously hypnotized, stepping as a blind person on the dawn-lit, mine-littered beach, shock pompadoured and haloed with light, scarf streaming like a parade's banner. Her blouse is so frilly it is apparently a fountain gushing around her neck; or it evinces a shadow-spray of dangling pine needles.

Panicked, he neither advances nor recedes. He is paralyzed, stunned, as a cow hit with a hammer on the skull. His heart flutters like a sail in a squall, brain wheels as a cyclone, distress draping him like a shroud. Her gypsy-esque tress flaps as a flag. The situation defines him and somehow goes through his system. Gulls, not unlike harpies, scatter from the reeds as bursting buttons. Cumuli, whiter than snow, are like messenger doves. He burbles as a spring. Tears do not succeed in washing out his despair. His chest torch-blazes. Dismay courses through his veins. A shrill wail emanates from his constricted throat. Fuzz on his nuque like a fleece stands. His shriek, registered by everyone's ears, is absorbed into the thalassic, granular environment, and he collapses as a burnt beam, onto the scaffolding of cetacean bones. In an unafraid act, Mengele, movie-star good-looking, hair shiny like his shoes, creamy coat winged angelically in the gritty winds, dumpling-pale, nostrils flared, and with a hatchet rictus, moves akin to Christ on water; or as a sleepwalker, a falter in his step, disrupting the sand, goes through the hissing deluge, serene as a saint, actuating like an athlete, brave as a warrior, to save her. The rescue operation is successful. Ernst's speech sputters. Language has left him. He cannot communicate with them. His strength wanes, and, weakened, says good-bye to no one, gets light-headed, an ashy taste in his oral cavity. He feels like Gulliver after his travels, where everything/one is different upon his return. He decides he can't kill Mengele after all. His attempt to flee in a stolen truck merely sends him in a time loop back to the coast. Ernst Boe is Josef Mengele's preferred patient, probably always will be, part of an experiment (with the assistance of Nazi sorceress Gitte and her black magic), to see whether or not he is capable of getting revenge on him for what was done to him, and his twin sister, Laura, at a concentration camp years earlier. In spite of these revelations, his love for Laura is rekindled, rising from the ashes, as Lear's for Cordelia, and it is pur-gatory for him to confront this fact. In the cattle car, en route to Birkenau, they pretended to be actors on stage, putting on a showy performance. The thespians and their audience were matches crammed into a box. At their destination, they were stripped and showered and herded into rickety corrals, stables for horses. They were reduced to numbers, not names, with red crosses painted on their backs. Straw mattresses. Shadows of guns. Glimpses of helmets. Dogs barking, drooling. Flashes of weaponry. Initially, they had been floating fetal roses in an amniotic lagune, shared the same warm womb, their skeletal scaffolding developing naturally, one spat after the other, out of their banshee-waul-ing mother (it was a chore just to conceive them), an esteemed professor of biology. Laura meemie-screamed. Ernst was still not unlike a stopped clock, started with a smack from the massive, nappy nurse, and he squeaked. She was the best of him. He was the worst of her. Their exactitudes were inexact. Their visages fell into similarity in his fabrication. They were florets fragile. She was the authority figure, dealing with pre-and-post-pubescent peers and adults alike. She called the shots, even with those thirteen-foot-high fences circumscribing them. A recording of Judy Garland sang through speakers.

Parties took place in the luxuriant headquarters of the Einsatzgruppen overlooking a plot of land filled with and emptied of a sickening amount of cadavers with startling regularity. A rainbow claimed a disproportionate measure of sky, straddled the sawtoothed buttes. Carts held piles of spindly, shaved corpses so transparent you could see through them. Shadows of Schutzstaffel squiggled. They recalled a cortege of dusty caterpillars. He visualized a victim's tongue crawling out of her mouth and creeping as a mollusk on the slushy, frozen ground, to berate an osprey-eyed, porky Obersturmfuhrer. Mengele was a deft death-dealer, this zookeeper, a human bag of demons, his opposition, the evil enemy, a tie. Ernst feels reborn, like a bug wrapped in a chrysalis, dissolving its organs into an original jellylike substance and reconstructing itself. He is lonely as the universe, and staggers into nothingness, an emptiness in the cosmos, mind blended with being, soul bottomless, spirit vacuous, left in sensory isolation, his essence without nature.

FIN.

Pharma Bums

THERE IS A sibling rivalry between natural and unnatural light. Mountains of garbage. Decrepit city, smothered in smog, looks like Beijing, but with buildings architecturally reminiscent of menacing bunkers, pyramids and spaceships. Cracked concrete and rusted metal. Ads are living, breathing entities. Blimps parade-float. Drones hummingbird-hover. Atari canyons. Absinthial sea. Sky's the simulacrum of a smile of insincerity; or it is a lenticular poster, in its vastitude, where the image appears altogether different depending on the perspective from which it is viewed. Sitar-sounding wind. Ruins of a spa connected to an abandoned casino, a gambling palace situated in an irradiated Ozymandias-esque necropolis, a denatured agricultural noir-neon landscape near an urban Hades. Murky waters. Sylphish, terse and tetchy Leopoldine Zentout's gait is a veritable comedy routine, her every step fraught with some risk. Then she is sprightly and silent as a maid, in spite of being strung-out and hungover, sunken-eyed and feeling jellylike with anxiety and sickness in equal measures. Her features are wreathed in wrinkles from a permanent pout. Her pajamas and their whisperous satiny secrets. She paces to and fro in the parlor, spacious as a lobby, with a boxy table and spindly chairs, carpet new chick-yellow. The pillow's imprinted with her head's shape. Zipping flies. Sound and fury of sexcapades of squatters next door. Her thoughts wheel hither and yon. Migrainoid throbbing. Whizzing mosquitoes. She is surrounded by literary books and bottles of booze and primitive 3D projections of long- gone Hollywood stars. Howdah-couch is quite a chunk. Megapolis is a scrap heap; or it's a bauble, shiny, hollow, and can shatter under the slightest pressure. Clouds coast like a school of minnows. Her misaligned almond eyes are made milky by the stark fluorescent-white lambency, spoken language with a crisp lilt to it, indeed a serrated edge. Wiping her beak and beestung lips with a used Kleenex tissue. She methodically gets changed. Her slightly pockmarked buttcheeks, lifted lip, as if she bit the bait and got hooked. Her Rapunzel hair is not unlike a shock of wheat. Aches in her skull are as though they're needles breaking through material. Technicolored riot of a rainbow. Bioengineered cyan ballerina prostitutes pirouette and strut on their toes kept in ambery slippers in the megatropolis with its post-industrial decay, cultural melting pot, the brutal sprawl resembling a colossal circuit board. Patches of field with streams of stitchery.

Stones are like loaves of bread. Januslike, showy swans. Mighty, majestic ships are faring forth from the jetty. These longshoremen congregate as if for church. Those slim duffels sagging on the wharf. She's sobered by the idea that the stuff is safe. Sun's a Hindu red dot. Vehicular tires on wet asphalt are cobra-sibilant. Her burp, high-pitched, sounds strangely sped up. Mango-golden luminosity. Rough and tough streets, rainy and trashy, haunting and hallucinatory, of the dystopic metropolis. She slurps noodles and bitches to herself about her bearded, burly boss, a Miltonian conception of Lucifer, speaking in riddle-ish sentences. R-rated hologram-matic advertisements. Gaunt, garish, harsh edifices sound like malicious machinery. Flashing corporate logos on them. Wavy luminescence suggests reflections from a swimming pool. Emberous flakes flutter in the black-mirror empyrean. Prokofiev's symphonic suite for children, 'Peter and the Wolf,' plays on an archaic stereo system. Her reed-slender limbs are very sore. Monolithic sculptures. Virtual-reality commercials. Her flat is her misfortune. The apartment, jam-packed, is a defeated obelisk in a state of near-collapse, infiltrated by noises as though it's under supernatural invasion. Below her bal-cony are promenaders, vendors, beggars, shoppers and hawkers on the crepuscular boulevard of the fishing vil-lage. She is a long, stringy and pretty young lady in her early twenties, with a silky honest face, gangling russety hair with a rumor of ponytail, quick peepers, alert and gentle, vermilion in the coruscation, cucumbery nose, prominent cheekbones, chiseled and striking, flesh snow-pale, voice like the clangor of a bell combined with an air-horn, corrugated abs, and rather thin hands and feet. She's a hard-drinking-and-drugging train-wreck. Showers stain the cool air. She sits on the leonine couch, with its mane of lemon-yellow and lime-green afghan and cushions of pink pastel, and stares at the mouse-gray rug, remembering her father, the stout Claude, French-Swiss, with a steady intellect, crown-coiffure, ruddy double-chin, pinched, spluttering laugh, wearing a button-shirt with leg-of-mutton sleeves and oversized trousers, in their spacious house with its copious enameled furniture. A neighbor/trage-dienne's shouting. Someone's Studebaker is illegally parked out front. She's a bearer of burden. She was a little girl, perched on his knee, sulky for some reason, protruding lips extended into a characaturized grimace, the two beside the small harmonium, wooden sew-ing-table loaded with bric-a-brac, ornate shelves with knickknacks, and muslin-curtained window, the sprin-kles apparently an undulant waffle- iron, a breeze respiring through the autumnal leaves in the line of lin-dens and beeches, flames crackling in the fireplace. Crystal chandelier. His man-boobs were melon-orbicu-lar. Illumination waned. He was rather attentive and serious. His temples twitched while he clenched his mandibles. She was clad in only her brocade, abbrevi-ated gown, with no undies underneath. Her mop poured as tears. He smelt of bad poultry. Crescentiform moon. Urbs' din. Dissipating fog was a crumbling revenant. Mushy slush like overlooked oatmeal. The heat and humidity made her feel as if she were a specimen pick-led in brine. Abstract sanctum of his study, a lair usually locked, in the home with its arachnidan halls and serpentoid corridors, where familial sides, with the personality clashes, amoeba-split. He cut a clownish figure, especially when one considered his Punchinello physiognomy, squashy hind, and comically booming intonation, rumbling guffaw possessing the sonance of an avalanche. His career as a professional bullfighter ended prematurely when he was seriously gored. He was a mediocre matador. And he didn't handle forced retirement well. He, an alcoholic, was drunk one stormy night, and died in a car crash. Mom was a mongoose, Dad a boar. Also, he was a cream- complected snake who'd strike from a bush. It was pursuit-and-capture in their weird, clandestine campaign. Ada, her mother, was modest and mild, almost bovinely placid, hummed hymns, was pale and gawky, with her chick-pea pies, aquiline proboscis, stern jaw, harmed-anserine aspect, tremulous inflection, and lean musculature, customarily long-skirted, short-bloused, and barefoot, once a school prodigy, frighteningly bright, a nuclear physicist and religious fanatic with this commendable conviction whose faith never wavered. She is deceased. A drowning accident, witnessed by her daughter from the shore. Memories sting like wasps. Precip-pips of sleet. Fog flows as though it is blood. Pewter-toned emanation. Her steel-magnolia energy. Suddenly, she notices her flesh is, inexplicably, becoming darker, her shadow getting lighter. She gets the horrible heebie-jeebies. Livid green of snot clogs her nasal passages. Her chest is terribly congested, sinuses stuffed, so a treatment of Vick's is of paramount importance. Oh, for olfactory freedom!

She had flagellated herself with partying. Sheet lightning sparks in her blinders. Blood rushes in her head like aqua pura passing a wooden wall. Arabesques of breakers. Penumbrous zebra stripes bar the dirty linoleum, attributable to the blinds' slats. She feels as if her existence is a story and she is not the authoress of it. Smell of tar. There is no variety in the sort of ceremonious monotony of her daily drudgery. She encircles the room like a duck floating around a pond. Firmament has the crimson of a hummingbird's throat. Bevy of swallowtail butterflies over jagged stumps of savins and cedars and mossy boulders in the plum grove with its fertile soil and blades of grasses. Saffron orb of sun. Fluffy omelette of cirri. Numerous laurels and birches. Eggplant-hued tide's curdled froth. Caliginous, kind of cathedran cave. Treacherous rocks. Keening gulls. She mounts her modified motor-scooter, baggy cerulean scrubs on her slight frame as though they are sails, weaving in and out of traffic. She works as an RN at a loony bin which is a renovated oil-refinery (you need a rowboat to reach it), not too far from a lighthouse, the funny farm tipping akin to a towering drunk, in proximity to a magical mosque, a structural deformed hunchback. She is really psyched because she's got Bernard Basler today. He is bald, wasted, pallid and elderly, suffering with dementia. She discovered recently that he was a big deal shadow-puppet theater artist, traveling the world and entertaining people in his youth. The guy is a ribald hoot, a sweet peach, her fucking saving grace. When she's off, he wanders like a ghost, haunting the joint, a poltergeist possessing the staff and patients. He is the perfect antidote for her agitation. Sometimes, with the anticipation of an event, there can be disappointment in the experience. There's a congruence between them. Guano on the fabulous formation of a statue of Da Vinci's Mary. She blows a bubble with her grape gum, it expanding to exist: pregnant Hubba Bubba. Picturing herself hanging from a rafter in a barn as a side of curing beef from a butcher's beam. Her porcine gaze. Indolent illumination. Drizzle drones on. She, susceptible to the influences of stress and its potent properties, is sick and tired of dealing with the daily pin-pricks at the work-place. She has the slipperiest grip on reality right now. She finds him in his wheelchair in the glorious garden, assessing an umbilical cord, like a dead pasty water moccasin, in an aquarium filled with a chemical bath, usually stored on a stack of tomes (Russian classics - Tolstoy, Dostoevsky, Gogol, Pasternak, Turgenev, Bulgakov, et cetera) in his jail-cell quarters. A bumble-bee-black-and-yellow taxi. She kisses his bewhiskered chin and crouches, cries saline streams, telling him of an incident from her childhood, how she felt as a sacrificial lamb, to prove her devotion to Claude ... His will was unstoppable, launched an all-out assault on her, attacked her from every direction. She had no defense against his offense. Her body was a battleground and she was anni-hilated. It was desert-quiet in the immaculate den. The disease of depravity grew to epidemic proportions. Her anatomy was in a state of acute crisis. Nostril-goo drain-age. His monk's tonsure gleamed in the lavender scintillation. He was a vandal, invaded and destroyed her private places. There was an abrupt ceasefire in the warfare. His penile serpent was coiled. Spittoon-silver welkin. A glutinous stench was secreted from his glands. There was a crack in her vaginal dam and a river gushed through the fissure. She wore purple panties and color-coordinated bra. She was powerless to protest. He was a snake, she was the ladder. Bernard mumbles, meanders, passes gas. He munches on raw celery and carrots. Claude's jowls jiggled like cornflour pudding. She sat on his lap as if she was blind, chewing pistachios, under a depressive influence, her being with emptiness and sub-mission. He sighed, said she was a pubescent sensual succubus wanting to engorge his soul. Ashen tracery of furrows on his brow, network of lines on his leathery mask, a weatherbeaten sack. It felt as though her skele-ton was shattered, bones ground into powder. Picking his piano-key teeth. Issuing imprecations not unlike an iconoclast. He held his phallic (un)holy relic religiously. She gobbled sugary snacks and glugged fizzy beverages, was nervous, had the sensation of being potter's clay manipulated by the hands of her paterfamilias. Drencher sissed as riled maternal geese. The town was contained in a wintry eggshell. Portraits hung askew. Leopoldine's recollections bubble like hot springs. Her gimlet-lamps are squinty, grey matter a time-bomb about to explode. She was as a mummified corpse that algid morning, wrapped in stained sheets. He insisted they play housie that afternoon. Confetti-flurries. He jammed her resis-tance transmission verbally and with the threat of his lunatic temper. He would've thrashed the living day-lights out of her if she disobeyed. She screamed blue murder. In the Broadway production of a household - it was the final curtain for her. Smoked-glass, enigmatic windows. His mottled Punch-countenance. Moonbeams spotlighted the condiments and cutlery set on the sumptuous dining-table. Skeeter-net of mist. He was an overfed Bozo-Buddha in virtuosic buffoonery and meticulous degeneracy. Ada stood on the sidelines, careful not to overstep the boundaries, often looking like she wished the earth would open up beneath her and swallow her whole. Claude sloughed off his costume and Leopoldine was transformed into a songbird with a faultless vox and pained wings who went low to fly high, cutting corns out of his sandpapery soles using a sharp nail-file and putting the extracted verrucas on a porcelain dish for his examination. Where exactly did the chain of cause-and-effect begin and end? He was balloon-swollen, imbibed soda and ingested circus peanuts, ranted on how unfair life was, raved about existence's injustices, that he was a felled ox and his wife and daughter were vultures circling the carrion of him. Plaster was peeling. Awesome scorcher. Vasectomist conference in a hotchpotch motel about to go phutt. Aberrational Abbott and Costello imitators in a barbed wire parking lot. With the mizzle, cashew-redolent, the scenery is a cinema screen and you're up too close and the picture is breaking into dots. Sycamores and elms salaam. Her optimism is a rose which grows in the compost-pile of pessimism. Her schizoid strands. Leafage rustles as chiffon. Moon in the cumuli blinks an owl. Gusts wheeze.

LEOPOLDINE, STONED, HER high at its Himalayan peak,

with an alabaster pallor, is at once an ugly duckling and the swan, dolled up in a paisley headband, chartreuse dress, and matching heels, making her tread like she has strayed into a bed of hot coals, eager as a nympho-maniac invited to a gang bang, ermine visage crinkled akin to sub-paper, Bernard dapper in a jaunty rented rayon tuxedo, starched-pressed, his umbilical cord, kept in a formaldehyde-filled coffee urn, an umbilicized life-line, carried like a football. She could not convince him to leave it behind. Surfeit of synchronic silence. They are venturing to the opera, the vintage venue a rococo, minstery place where Giacomo Miotti, a virtu-oso counter-tenor and mezzo-soprano, is performing a sold-out show. He is angelic and androgynous, a rock star in the fast lane, who looks as a peacock junkie (according to the majority of press, he's an exotic bird in that plumage), with these incongruent Draculoid fangs, throwing some Bowie, Jagger, Presley and Liberace into his schtick, center stage in a Ken Russellish production, erotic, surreal, lavish, salacious, insane, and roman-tic. Leopoldine, manducating popcorn, is blown away, driven into a frenzy, her brain and body ignited. Bruno snores, unconscious. Giacomo poses in an elaborate chariot, beneath clashing bougainvillaea trellises, attired an outrageous Aztecean outfit, and belting, producing great range and beautiful sound, giving the swooning audience a musical orgasm. Opulent design of scenery. He is famous, idolized, talented and adorable, capable of unleashing 250 notes in a single breath, a dashing Italian Daniel Day-Lewis doppelgänger with a bit of Chico Marx mixed in. Classical groupies adore him, pursue him, the ultimate trophy. Is he merely a treasured novelty? His piercing falsetto tones provoke rapturous cheers. Flourishes and embellishments of a world-class diva. It's rumored he believes his gift is a curse, not a blessing, he has the petulant tendencies of a grande dame. Leopoldine's mind melts when, for an encore, he manages to execute a soaringly operatic version of Tom Jones's 'What's New, Pussycat,' appareled in an absurd velour leisure suit and platform shoes. The crowd goes crazy, applauding like trained seals. She and Bernard are invited to meet him in the dressing-room. There, a model-esque, atomic-blond amazon, propped on a cane chair, slaps him, saying, in an Austrian accent, he's a "creature with no nuts," he's "got no balls," their relationship is "'The Crying Game' in reverse," he's "'The Elephant Man' of gender disorders," and marches out, glaring at Leopoldine while she goes. His histrionic hissy fit in a goofy getup is hilarious, and rooster- struts not unlike Freddie Mercury, smirk slick as ice, whereupon he boots his entourage. His distinctive, flamboyant, exquisite pipes. Christ! Fans are queued in the hallway. The dim-bulb sidekick, a Hispanic, goateed agent, keeps them at bay. Bernard is freaked. Leopoldine's bewildered. He is a prima donna, at once feminine and masculine, invites her to snort and toke. Bruno slumbers on a radical stool in the corner. She accepts. They hit it off immediately, the attraction and chemistry intense. Robotic geisha metermaids ticket vehicles with menus and skip stealthily away. Haunting holowraiths in a hellhole burgal dump. Interactive A.I. phonebooths. Cyborg cops fly in spinning spheroid cruisers. Countless synthetic angels spread their wings and flit above the claustrophobic streets with crowds and clutter. Tallowy oxygen, aphotic effulgence in a harsh climate. Roborats wayward in a metro maze. Beehive of skyscrapers. A literal red desert. Grime. Haze. Poverty. Ashen snow. Gargantuan, nightmarish buildings in gritty, dilapidated slums. Pollution. Population. Turny-twisty roads. Giacomo looks as an airbrushed Jesus of Nazareth. Leopoldine is a wonder wild in the faraway. Her megalomaniacal slavemaster (also eccentric and brilliant) superior, creepily restrained, with a zen-like calm, pages her.

Leopoldine's formula for working in the madhouse is some schnapps! Her back is stiff as a board. She's fucking starving. Her stomach growls animalianly. She's concerned her seatmate, a zaftig African American fellow employee, Cheyanne, will hear. Chairs in threadbare vinyl. Lab coat-white overcast. Cavalcade of college students in the cloistered courtyard with benches, statues, stones, and plants. Her blood runs cold. She extends her arms and legs, telescopically, to stretch them, ease the tension. A chill climbs up the ladder of her spine like a daredevil for a death-defying act. Bernard's presence buoys her up, in waters troubled, as a life vest. Attendants are like apparitions. Cherubic orderlies. Her bitesize flashbacks. Ritualistic severity. A woman's sallow, swollen physiognomy is as a waitress's when she's pinched by a perverted patron. Tenebrosity of twilight blots all distinctions. Demented patients: crooked bodies, misshapen heads, decayed teeth, greasy hair - horrifying sights in the hideous institution, humanized by the deranged defectives in inescapable everlasting torment of mental illness in this abyssal asylum. In her clean cream scrubby uniform, she unboxes medications for colds and constipation, sedatives and lotions. Visitors' footfalls are not unlike drumrolls on the floor. Nurses tend to nuts as if they are executing some black comedy with poker faces. Squawking and chirping in the immense institutional birdcage. Alien avians with ruffled feathers, uncanny species on their own private islands of padded cells. Artificial annuals run rampant. Many complaints and much deterioration. Chorus of cusses. Fits of rage. Paralysis. Paranoia. Episodes made into events. Simian jabbering. Shouted obscenities. Patterns of her thoughts take shape, merge as though drops. Disturbances are sure nipped in the bud. In a blank cubic space, a brawny, brutish guy of medium height and average weight with piercing eyes and full brown beard and in a johnny, a molester and murderer, masturbates like a monkey, ostensibly an animated broken doll: a creature without comfort. These beslobbered boys mill as prisoners, a fine kettle of fish, are links in a chain. Oblivion. A grungy giant slinks like a beleaguered dog. Inmates break rank. A stocky, mustached guard's appearance evokes a shaven convict. An emaciated, jaundiced fellow with rock-grinder gnashers and festering sores moves as if he is in a zoo, barks like a drill sergeant, fart sounding as though it's blasted from a bugle. Her intestines are tangled strings of an old instrument. Sound of her sorrow mute and yet audible. Plane trees and plain pavilion. Villa-ish storage sheds. Whitewashed ward. Air's dense. The layout of reality makes her detour, and she achieves oneness with irreality. Bells ring, intrude on her ears. A clothes-horse and coatrack. These tongues of varivoiced zephyrs speak senselessly to her. Vocalizations have piano-crashing sonancies. Pastel cloudlets, in miraculous motion, marvels of material, drape the theater of the vault. Her permed locks flutter like petals of a flower. Her existence has financially devolved into a primary atomic state. Her life's an epidermic itch she must scratch. Remembrances are a heap of coiled springs. Oxygen's as dry wine. She has to shop for food to supplement her cabinets! She imagines the acquisitions strewed willy-nilly on the counter ill-equipped to hold the purchases. She hated being called away from Bernard, like Lucius Quinctius Cincinnatus from the plow. There was an unprofessional interlude, an interim phase. She felt, with him, as a war-rioress in armor of hammered iron. In all actuality, she wore a chemise, boxsies, and stockings. Clouds were impressions fragmentary. Her sensory immersion, skin irritations, shadowy doubling. Her phiz is now framed in tousled mop. She had traces of childish affectation, expressions playing a game of hide-and-seek, clothing as a costume. She was a sketch made by a master he embellished. Language of their conversation had depth, direction and weight, both tossing word-salads hither-thither. With him, it was like a yoke had been taken from her shoulders. Without him, she would feel as a bug flicked from a leaf. His respirations crackled like a fire in an old stove. Three- storey residences, with well-Windexed windows, resemble woodcarvings.

Cymande's 1970s hit, 'Bra,' is cranked on an

old-fashioned jukebox; a nictating, colorful confessional, in the tumbledown hamburger shop adjacent to a split-level chapel. Leopoldine and Giacomo had made out on a steam punk-themed rollercoaster at cocktail hour. She'd completely crimped her hair, tricked herself out with jewelry, ironed her ensemble. She looked as a cosmeticized, plucked chicken prepped for cooking. Her chops couldn't relinquish his on the DreamWorksified merry-go-round. Tinfoil stars. She wanted to play and please. Bods were oven-hot. She was waiting in the wings, doped by desire, absorbed him like a sponge, and her pores squeezed out drops of perspiration. She felt vulnerable during the febrile romancing. Her hunger, thirst for him ... In a teak booth they discuss the cultural significance of spaghetti westerns, the varieties identified, Pepe LePew, chat about Bernard 's Alzheimer's, moduli spaces, Teichmuller and ergodic theories, hyperbolic and symplectic geometries, debate Canada Dry versus Pepsi, which is tastier ... He has angularity of physique and moral dimension. His sesquipedalian onanistic palaver is unparalleled! She's a rough spot he smooths over. She envisages his penial insect crawling into the flesh-eating plant of her pussy, envisions the cunt-calyx closing around it, his cum-water running down the dewy/downy hill of her belly and into the velutinous valley of her crotch. He pulls the essence out of her as the Magnetic Mountain draws nails out of plank wood. Her internal and external peace. She is a wisp of straw. A smile slides on her icy lips. Socially seeking the path of least resistance. She's a knife whetted on the grindstone of life. Her verbalizations converge with the drift of her reveries. Her words are like large bundles forced out of the small opening of her oral cavity. The cardiac organ in her chest sounds as a mallet hammering on a barrel stave. Language glides not unlike a dragonfly. She coquettes her way through the conversation. She thinks: have we been here for seconds? Minutes? Hours? Days? Weeks? Months? She's feeling faint, has vagaries - they're two-people-in- one, marrow melting from her bones in a single stream, in a bacchantic swirl, she's a caterpillar eaten by a bird. Curious inner and outer occurrences, geometrically linear forces flooding into her being. Will reality betray her unreality? Reason is reborn from unreason. The rational collapses into the irrational. Fantasizing taking the chance of slipping into the breach of his buttocks and dropping the anchor of her fist there and leaving him as a ship, moorings cast off, in the harbor. She ponders the possibilities, gaze drifting in an optic channel in the gap of the dinnertime tumult, dreaming of her schnoz being at his heinie like a calf's muzzle at the maternal udder. She is a passionate dyed-in-the-wool lecher! She's a painting coaxing lines and colors from an artist's hand. Convictions rise to new heights. To her, he is clever and she is stupid. She's a closed umbrella he has opened. Ramshackle power station. Habitable reception room. His compliments concessions to her. She reconciles herself to the stupendous situation, in their mutual telepathic realm. Extraordinary events cohere into an element comprising an entity, arranged in abstract aspects, obscure patterns. She's charged with incredible energy, like she came in from an electrical storm.

Certainty walks unsteadily on the stilts of uncertainty. She is swept by the currents of cupidity. And insecurity bores into her tummy as a screw. She imagines her sweat-beads are poison capsules. She's heroinely excited, poised on the razor's edge. She plants the seeds of potentiality in the fertile soil of her grey matter. She is petrified, wants to flee like a rodent from a conflagrant catastrophe. Coming against the barricade of belief that she should stay. Fear fades as inscriptions on gravestones. She's got the impression she has undergone a total transformation, an inner and outer metamorphosis. Regarding the change as born of nerves. The world has hitherto been a hiding place. He is the threshold between her reason and unreason. He talks like a doctor would to a patient, his tone strengthening, and weakening her will. A hard, detailed expression upon the soft fabric of her face. Her existence's heretofore a fire, the flames of issues inching for her, life itself standing still and shouting incomprehensibly, telling her to get out, but not letting her know where to go. Her gut is a bombshell bursting. Moon's a lens misting over in the cirrus. Her saucery eyes, vegetable-sniffer, floccose nape, ouphe- ears. Zephyrean oohing and aahing. Viscous clamminess. Pimps: scum of the earth. She's envious of his enormous earnings, sublime modulation, army of admirers, enjoys his twenty-four-carat grin, his million-buck personality on display. She admits she had the best seat in the house, backstage, where he swam in a sea of flowers, the perfumed fragrances overpowering. Blooms here, blossoms there. Scents were getting more potent, fumes unbearable, as animal feces. Conversing on creativity, she feels like she's attempting to get a match out of a box while wearing gloves! She has the sensation of being a solitary star in space's infinitude. Reflections spin in her skull as a dog chasing its tail. Diseased worries in her cranium - necrosis of the bone of her brain. Using herself like bait in the dating scene, with its fluctuant tide, she usually hooks weeds and not fish. Customarily, she instinctively imposes rules of conduct on herself, regulations to secure her impulses, often rash, principles favoring the power. Matte sheen of her perspiry integument. Mini-bar kiosks. Artificial agriculture. Sumo-shaped smokestacks. Grapes of Wrath-ish solar farm. With him, she's an egg that has cracked, having fallen on the floor, exposing the yolk of her essence. Her cogitations concentrate, condensed into an oily drop of lingua franca, her confidence crumbling as a lump of coal stepped on, cast animated, moue flickering, roots of her mop tingling, blood slopping around in her head like urine in a chamber pot on a craft on the ocean, feeling uneasy, as a military officer unexplainably finding himself in an enemy encampment. The hostess, looming large and barren of femininity, with mysterious masculinity, beats a pleasant retreat, fans the flames of a familial argument. A cute tomboy, an acneously scarred teenager, ripe- cantaloupe-shaped, puffy-cheeked, like she is blowing up a balloon, thin-lipped, thick-thighed, with a crewcut, petrol-pump proboscis, dial flushed as a map, and dung-ish BO, guided by a mustachioed nun built like a tank, gums untoothed, touchingly presented him with a cloying bouquet and warm fresh loaf of bread. He hugged and kissed her, gave her free tickets. Giacomo has risen into the sky, whereas Leopoldine has fallen into the sewer, she thinks. Effluvial emissions. Chattering birds. Her coyness implies coition as a lemon peel does its potent juice. Puffins are a parade of parasols. A plane sews the seam of horizon. Cabs are like tethered canines waiting to be unleashed to race after the prey of clientry. Her heels clank as horseshoes. So many layers of considerations of him, like simultaneous thoughts written by Da Vinci with both hands! He confesses he is pleased by the concert's critical and commercial response, the seal of approval for his ability and image. She, present and absent in his presence, demurely sips her apple juice. He insists he is the victim of the virus of popularity, maintains the side-effects of fame are excessive, his stardom blinding, that he is a superhuman singer imprisoned in gilded bars. She contemplates this and replies he's more than a tad melodramatic. Yvonne Elliman's 'If I Can't Have You' blasts. Their conversation is provocative and promising. She wonders whether she, fallen head-over-heels, is a butterfly snared in his net. Penurious reek of Kashmiri- tea-pink-skinned street-sleepers slumbering on flea-ridden mattresses on the filthy pavement. His princeling aura exerts a pull that's gravitational. Their flirty glances. He kindles her fire. She articulates by trial-and-error, rambling on about her ferociously focused superior, Robin, with her steely determination, a pleasure model killbot in sharp suits, a Frankenstein mastermind in the science lab, a reject Bond villainess, and how she gets most of her meals from a vending machine, which looks as a sexualized space vessel.

Multi-ethnic clientage articulate in polyglot tongues. She's woozy in the calidity and humectation of his popularity. Peculiar whores pose, sashay. A hag, possibly a mythological crone, has a cartoonish kisser like balled paper. An urchin, directly out of a fairy-tale, conceivably taken by a malaise, crouches and urinates at a Rolls-Royce. Edifices with bright exteriors and shimmering interiors. Android actors on a CGI billboard. Her flyleaf photo lineaments. Synthy showgirls, in the nuddy except for feathers and stilettos, artificial eye-candy, wanton widgets hookerish, wander through gigantean Romanesque statues bordering a barren wasteland (from a worldwide blackout) that is a radiation zone off-limits. Rancid refuse. Profusion of rusting scaffolding. Reeking roads. Piled prayer-mats. Oat-colored cumulus. Vigilante midges. His dulcet vox unties the knots of her tension. Her deer- startled oculi are heavy-lidded as she relaxes. His broody quietude. Is she a fly caught in his web? He lights her fuse. Her goose is cooked. Fallibility of her confidence. She's fuddled in the haze of bewitchery. She realizes he's about as controllable as inflation. Lotus petals flitter not unlike snowflakes. Krishna-blue crepuscule. Harassing harlequin mimes and mesmerists throw Molotov cocktails. Her eyes are expressive, her senses stirred. She pictures herself blowing him, her head nodding as a tern dunking for fish. Her dizzy rapture. To her, he is a Greek god visiting a mere mortal. She feels like Miranda from 'The Tempest' with him, exclaiming something about the planet and its people, buzzed, a glow going through her system as an aurified azure, and she natates in a nectarean pool. She horsily neighs and shudders, the whinny having the force of a gale. They partake of a celebratory bountiful breakfast consisting of oatmeal, cheddar cheese, ham, and fried-and-baked chicken. Deluge's tiny silver bells dinging. Her Zenoid Confessions ...

Bernard, knock-kneed, muttering like he was reciting a spell, in that arcane asylum, gave Leopoldine, in wonk- rims, vascular organ's ticktocking a mule-kicking, stone-still, steel-stiff, ears as sails, rubber-limbed, silhouette black-asnight, skin white-asday, on her second shift, (O, OT) a key to the warehouse, where his equipment is stored. The depository, close to a bubble gum factory and military barracks, is like a huge treasure chest sentried by bodhi, chinar and banyan trees. She looks at it warily, as she would a minefield. She is reluctant. Nearby structures are like jutting jaws. Cat mewls. Divisions of rooks are separated into squabbling factions. Cesspit mephitis. A spire is an accusatorially-pointing finger. Insectean bombinations. Ravens' croaks come from a chutney-chromatic hillock. Jays go bluing past. She pauses, breathes. Languorous umbrage. Masses of puddles are as wads of spat tobacco. She, shrouded in a fog of apprehension, is loose-bladdered/boweled, pats her rice-pancake-flat middle. Maddening moon. Heaven's a slate wiped clean of clouds. Bangs! and whams! Trepidation scurries in her midsection like a gecko. She gains entry and watches one of his B&W silent short films. Cardboard cutout characters re-enact particular parts of her life, snippets projected on the screen. Her derma is darker, her shadow becoming her mother. She gets the awful willies, and wets and shits her pants, shrieks as a witch, panic-stricken, her cry razor-blade-sharp, dribbles, burbles and babbles like a baby. Is the mirage out of a dream? There must be an explanation for this occultic occurrence. She's benumbed. Her blinders flit as moths round a flame. She, in a frantic state of mind, not having a firm hold on actuality, brain circling like a whirligig, perception taking a pounding, departs hurriedly, and receives a call on her cellphone. Bernard has died of an aneurism. He was found by a barrel-compact nurse in the bathroom. Leopoldine finds out he was the recipient of a heart transplant, Claude, her dad, the donor. Teary molluskous slime oozes down her cheeks. She feels as if she is doused with frigid water. Stars make the celestial sphere seem obliterated. Glutinous precipitation. Her father was like a malicious minister controlling the flock of his family. The house was driftwood-pearlescent and vessel-prow-shaped. She and her mom were spokes in the hub of the wheel of him. She was a splintering pillaret. His corduroy trousers, keghead. Her cornmeal with molasses. Hollyhock-pinkish empyrean. They appeared to be a flushed, multi-armed Shiva dancing in a circle fiery. His voice sounded as pieces of saturated sandpaper scrubbed together. Question and answer of lightning and thunder. Coastal Xanadu. Hive of humanity buzzed. Harmonious sweep of granitic manufactories had parabolic reflector-panes. Her hair's strands were interlaced, illusorily, by the mile. She was grave-serious, sand gritted in her lamps. Hands and feet elongated. Cultivated veggie garden. To her, life is blubber she has to render the fat out of. Her dinner composed of lentils, biscuits and fries. Raucous eagles with cruel beaks and arthritoid-digital-talons. Compiling hotness and stickiness. Screeching cicadas. Firmament virginally blushes, clears like Mother Nature pulled off some astonishing abracadabra. Manicured lawn of a sanatorium. She is enraptured by the exhilarating cosmos. Chalky pollen. Yuppies canoodle, cocooned in the filmy, stygian murk. Foreshortened image of a cloud's captured in a pupillary-hued pool. Limpid light. Lukewarm breezes. Condensation is squeezed from the cinder-blackish welkin, complexing the upper atmosphere. Zephyrine moaning and groaning. Thunder booms and claps. Gusts roar and rumble. Nimbuses lit by lamplighters, illumining the block, brilliancy slipping like a reflection passing on a pane. Teratoid tenebrosity. She is a spindly Michelangelo seraph. Problems pile up. Her personality's enhanced by them. Laundry list of issues. Her integument is smooth as illumination, lactescently soft, and with a violet aroma. Hitch in her stride. Thunder sounds not unlike war whoops. Marks of levin. Parish bonging. Columnar factories, chutes of streets. Passers-by make progress. Thoughts of Bernard and Giacomo are bleeding cuts. It is as though her brain is a wheel and they are sticks stuck in the spokes. Her heart's a battering-ram. Waves crash like leviathans are doing cannonballs and bellyflops. A cirrus is the "footprint" of a surfacing sperm whale on the surface of an aqueous sky, moon its blowhole. She moves as a crippled kitty, netted in brume like a leg of mutton in a stringy sack.

Alien seagulls soar and skriek in a river-brownish vault.

Leopoldine got intimate with Giacomo in the sable limousine, alongside a bicycle-repair store, brick and marble, with a tin roof, which was raided by police. She wanted to have intercourse. She was shocked to find out he was a castrato. Chrissakes! Eunuchised for a vocal art! She scrammed and shot up some low-grade heroin ... Currently, her spirit feels nibbled on by rats, her soul eaten by maggots, knowing she shouldn't have skedaddled. She overdoses on daydreams. Dun sand. The beach where her mom washed up. A transparent sun is an ovate leech greedily sucking the blood out of the numerous bathers and, glutted, bursting with splendorous sanguine. She's onion-frying. Oleaginous mugginess. Scratching an itch on her cuke-sneezer. She is chick-soft and tense as a washing-line, her being beleaguered in consequence. Linseed-oil sultriness. There are jugglers, card-sharpers, poets, protesters, musicians, fire-eaters, ventriloquists, sword-swallowers, puppeteers, conjurers, kids not unlike a tribe of cannibals, and contortionists exhibited in the sweltery ghetto. Burqa-black evening's entertainments. She'd declined invitations to cockfights, chess matches, peepshows, the solicitations striking her as thunderclaps. Vespid whining as snipers' bullets. Touristy mobs are like insurrectionists. Oxygen's sibilant with a spate. These scorpion-colored shells. She ransacks her ruminations. Claude's neat and tidy library was as a suffocating tomb to her. Never were there admissions of guilt, hints of apologies, any owning up to wrongdoings whatsoever. He was nice, which triggered her red alert. His profile was pronounced in the phosphorescence. An auditory danger trumpet-blared in her ears. His armpits were turnips-noisome. She was a fly and he was the frog who had gulped her. She sobbed as a monsoon, sang to God at the gramophone. He was an enormous palm, growing in size and ferocity in the downpour of devotion. His coconuts in a pubic thicket were grenades. He pulled the prurient pins. She screeched like a jungle. He was a snaking mangrove, creaked as wood. She sought refuge, found shelter under the fronds of fantasy, surrendered herself to the phantoms of make-believe, like she succumbed to Him. He said his harmonica was an "oral organ." Prismatic thoughts, inner and outer curves consistent, arranged around the light source apparatus of her mind. His ligaments snapped as twigs. He crushed her into a pulp. Those quarters had its strident malodors of toilet and leftovers. Shrimp-opaque moon broke out. She was physically pulverized and psychologically battered. Nipa- fruit-red-milky radiance. She was petrified, like she was set in plaster. He closed in on her as a vice. His coriander cologne was pungent. She wept. A lump was brought to her throat. At the tub, she was a waterborne plaything. They looked like some mismade, multi-limbed, stop-motion-animated Kali statue. Her wet tresses hung not unlike worms. He'd unleashed a hellaceous hurricane of halitosis. When reality was too agonizing, irreality was the remedy. Smoldering ruination of the room. He was an unmuzzled, rabid dogsoldier barking, strangled by a leash imperceptible. Wreckage of his teeth. He was a Brylcreemed Beelzebub, arms akimbo after he was all lips, tongue, and hands, his constrictor's eyes grasshopper-green. Her conical bosoms, beginning-looking. Spermatozoan droplets of the spritz. On the wicker-hamper was an anesthetic mask and gynecologist's forceps. Her spittle was as paste. His tumorous toupee and hell-pit blinkers. Periwinkle-bluish water. Dandelion caps flew off. Iridescent honey poured. She walked like she balanced a basket on her head. Cakes of crests with many-layered foam-frosting. Zags of leven in rifting cotton ball representations of cumuli. He used clever strategic maneuvers, was an occupying force in her life. She was on a personal campaign for liberation from her existence. A feral child, she shook as a leaf. He was relentless and remorseless, took his pistol out of its holster. She was torn-up and burnt-out, frozen by rising paralysis, convinced she was going to die of pain. Chaunting of wheels. Irani bistro. Stars burst like tacks, pinning a wanted poster, ripped from cork. Surf's splash and dash. Her unloosed mane, nut-meg-russet, and scattered, freckles. Thunder thumps as a pump, its shaft submersed in a mucky well. A hobo is a jack-in-the- box in an slaunchwise dumpster. Solemn procession of cloudlets. Don Quixote Windmill. After the bodily bombardment, she was in a funk, dazed, drenched, ill-at-ease. Her withdrawal from the world. More noodling than in a Chinese restaurant kitchen. Destiny bided its time. Her eyes dilated as a coffee-consumer's. Her memories are blurry, like they are seen through orange juice. She's an ivory toothpick under a dove's egg sun. Her rosy and waxen flesh's as the skin of an apple. Typhoon appetence enswirls her entirety. Giacomo, ageless and sexless, his calf-clock, labial lips, king cobra-swaying. Laddered, ligneous pulpit of life-guard tower. Gaudy quilt of sky; a chromatic cacophony.

She's in a mesh microkini. Her voluted navel. Her hip joints hurt. Her problems wind as yarn on an oblong skein. Air's thicker than an elephant's hide. Steadfast lighthouse severe, serene and austere. Vertebral shells. Giacomo is incapable of fucking, but he has his share of chivalrous sentiments! Time without him ... The calendar, in its exacting detail, is a sneering specter ... She handles difficulties as if with tongs! She rarely goes against her grain. She weeds her lashes with a finger. The wild illusion of Ada's shadow, this disturbing vision of searing darkened vividness, rises like a lambent zombie on the same shore where she'd initially washed up, in a one-piece bathing suit and single Birkenstock sandal, bellyside-up, and, physique as strip of beef jerky (she once had an hourglass figure), tall like Jack's Beanstalk, curvaceous as smoke, veins on her callused feet like the ones on a leaf, with a cloud-stepping canter, takes Leopoldine's hand, giving her an electric shock, and kisses her as a holy icon. They drift like seed-spores, float as specks of dust, and disappear together, side-by-side, in the olivaceous distance, on the ambery beach, with its salty sand, and vanish like djinns into thin air. Dried mud's as crustal blood. Seagulls twirl into the idyllic vista like milkweed seeds into the earth. Cobalt crackles of lightning. Snuffling thunder. Shrilling cranes in churnish swoop. Space is aglitter with stars. Steamboat plying the gleaming brine. Gnomon of a sundial casts penumbras.

Deformed from an auto accident, a hit-and-run, whilst on a world tour, Giacomo, a recluse, composes an intricate aria entitled 'Leopoldine,' which becomes a smashing success. Reader: a bird whispers in your ear and our story ends. Beyond the shadow of a doubt.

FIN.

Black, White

Remembrance: a ruined structure the thinker is compelled, for various reasons, to rebuild. I'm Dominique, pygmoid and waxen, resembling a forty-something, Cro-Magnon Walter Mathau with a tragedy-mask expression, cricket-bat arms, lacrosse-stick legs, ass like a treasure chest (buried in chinos), garden hose- green eyes, and bulbous nose, imagined them, Suryan and Ananda, their stares direct as nails, ready like cows for milking, bruises the insignia of degradation, looking at me as slaves would their native land they were taken from. They were trophies bought, not won, claims I staked. Buzzing lasciviously, I bore into them - a bee burrowing into a flower. This was the subservience of rationality to irrationality. I attempted, vainly I might add, to keep my affection at an unobjectionable radius, not unlike the ocean is kind of prevailed upon by the stars, though without being optically drawn closer. My libidinous ailment was adamant about lingering, the antibiotic of restraint ineffective. I peeled back these layers of memories and pieced them back together to impose an interpretative adaption on them, which couldn't accommodate authenticity. The girls seemed to sort of fly above the plain plane of materiality the rest of us exist on. My thoughts weren't in sequential order; they were reflections in psychical mirrors. Their cunts were traps set to catch the careless cock. Their beguiling breasts and buttocks jiggled. They were scrawny as POWs, leaned like decayed teeth in infected gums, those plucked chickens clucking, hunched over, sharp, bony shoulders thrust forward during a urinating and defecating episode, as if they were a scroll to unroll, both dressed in a baggy, sable skirt surmounted by a flouncy, creamy blouse, crest-capsizing, one wavelet replacing another, swinging their bloody tampons like nuns their rosaries, fiddling with themselves as though scientific experimenters approving conclusions to corroborate the legitimacy of their theorems, their craniums clear as bells. The albinal twins' pubic bushes were pruned, skin pastry-flaking, countenances cute, and crumpled, like papers balled up and thrown into a basket, gesturing as theater ushers, the heavenly hydra squirming like a snail in salt, shaking in shivering light, apprehensive, afraid of my affections. My spermic ambergris was crusty on my boxers' crotch. They skittered sideways, crabstyle, scared as lambs in line for the slaughter, blue peepers gleaming, with them shifting into gear, if you will, and driving until a tire gets pebble-punctured and then there's a crash.

The two bobbed and screeched akin to crazed cockatoos, encaged by my licentiousness, voices alternately tenor and alto. In the song of sighs there was a silent bar. A sexy caesural moment. Clear cogitations on the ground, clouded ones at the top of a mountain. My recollections were people holed in the hold of a hellacious hurricane, quivering and frightened. The gals pulled language as taffy, putting words, one after the other, like dominoes, and flung them as soldiers, wounded and under enemy fire, into a trench. I likened their behavior to children who create a house of cards just to knock it down. I wanted them to settle on me as aphids on a plant. Would such an incident leave smudges on my psyche, like a newspaper's ink on its reader's fingers? I craved their company, in that torture chamber of a bedroom. I gave them a warm repulsion, and it was as if I'd unlocked something that should've been kept hermetically sealed. I was propelled by perversion, in the harsh heat and humidity, the livid lambency. I was a demented Dante in Paradise and Hell. And I rose as gas bubbles. The gamines' reveries expanded, extended through each other's brains without considerable deviation, vagaries going from one mind to the other without any modification of individuality. Drugged and drunk, my inflection changed while I carefully caressed them; instruments' strings loosened and tightened. I was a sleepy fish carried by currents. The sisters' originality was so unique they virtually eclipsed their surroundings with quirky characteristics and wild wardrobe. My conscience could not contain the centrifugal force of my libido. They were practically translucent, not unlike an illumined window, intonations procuring a melodic fidelity, the two emerging from the musty basement as though mismade jacks-in-the-box, the extraordinary blotting out the ordinary, their pale manes a flimsy, shampoo-scented facade, a fascinating flower swaying inebriatedly in lambent luminosity. Their bottoms had the appearance and texture of Swiss cheese, repartee rhapsodic, giraffe-long-and-lean legs lowering from the bed like they were somehow getting sucked into a vacuum. Their ugliness was abbreviated beauty. They comprised a parade of a bizarre, bombinating band, gliding as a monstrous, alabaster butterfly, by the chipped sill and wooden arm-chair, ambling, a rapidly-drawn doodle (as they progressed), shimmery and yet somewhat unsubstantial, like a humanized haze. Whereupon they reeled, as if suddenly stricken by a fainting fit, so significantly uncommon, amazingly unusual, liquefied by luminescence, in a radiantly repellent metamorphosis, encumbered now by clothing, ensepulchered in cotton. With automated machinery, the threads of retention, raveled throughout my life, were unraveling. I subordinated my flights of fancy to them, the mangled macaws, in my fantasies the eccentric teenagers fidgeting, unaware of their sensual potential, robustly galloping, like flamboyant witches gathering the necessary ingredients for a potent magic potion. This was their squalid, sensuous, pleasure-dome crash-pad. I heard my nerves twang. Adolescent development hadn't branded them at that point. In the glaucous coruscation, the young ladies were iridescent amphibians held in a wild aquarium; or glistening ghosts returning to their shadowy netherworld. I was a fly glued to the paper of fortuity; a victim and the perpetrator of moral paralysis; a leaf caught in a breeze. My failure was part and parcel of my attempt at grabbing them, by hook or by crook, trying tooth and nail, in their dirty panties, scuttling as though beetles under duress, me needing to cling to them like a baby's mouth to a mother's nipples. In my agogery I lost my center of gravity and never found it, their lanky arms accompanying gruiform legs, anatine feet deposited on the filthy floor erratically and with languidity, aquiline proboscises twitchy as their walk became quite a canter. My grimy pillow took a cast of my anthropoid skull while I slept. Slumber is the sequel to wake. Sleep is the causation of wakefulness. The glutted moon was a nocturnal excursionist, its brilliant beams fading in the foliage. Booming thunder, flashing lightning. Flicking stars were riotous in the tumultuous sky. A skeletal roller coaster was semi-submerged in opaque water.

Suryan and Ananda's coy smiles were an apparent amalgamation of a singular, scintillant one, foisting itself on me, smothering me, the succulent smirks encroaching on one another, blanking boundaries, suppressing demarcations, overlapping, in increments, reminding me of, oddly enough, a school of fish, collecting before dispersing, and, subsequently, coming together. Those simpers were combined by their similarity, one I was accustomed to seeing. They had many impish ideas. The Lolitas interrogated me with insistent eyes, making a weird, shifting essence that had managed to extract all the sadness in the world, alien to "normal" impressions.

Empyrean had the pigment of skin. They were seductive subjects, giving me this mingling of arousal and agony, these grotesque models enchanting and elusive, gloriously languishing in limpid illumination, flesh soft as slush, pearlescent tresses wavy, prepared for being romantically rubbed, the darlings divinely unearthly and intimate with their unconventional environment, their thinness getting thicker, thanks to me embellishing their image. I was chained to 'em: Prometheus to the rock. The kooky chicks were represented like they were conceived by an avant-garde creator who'd taken liberties with a couple of albatrosses, their homely heads stabilizing the migrations of their oddbody, tense and erect. Their mesmerizing bums and bobbies wiggled. I saw them, milling intoxicatedly swervily, figure-eighting as an untied balloon. They looked lucent, like lit from within, ebony shawls shadowy mimes. Whisperous balderdash. They wobbled, had gruesome grimaces, naked except for wool socks, in the grody coop, a gross rental, thus robbing me of mystery, and my profound appetite remained unsatisfied. The sisters signalized with the infuriation of those who've lost the function of speech, cannot articulate at all, and who are urgently endeavoring to communicate. They immersed themselves in an innocuous skirmish, in the enfeebled emanation, only it was nothing too serious. It was visual fatigue, I admit, observing them, two blurring into one, witnessing the honeys, two-in-one. A simian grin cracked my face, chiseled cheeks permitting flushes to flare on them. My desire was brought into the light in my otherwise dark being. The duo were the embodiment of an abstract artwork, in that the play of the parts of them became mishmashed, reliant, I guess, on a general design. I put my hand on a milky thigh, as if for warmth, with a tippler's finesse, my apen forehead scored, their rattly soughs coming from petalous lips and accessing my cauliflower ears. Mixing with them, it was as though I was some paranoid hawker peddling illegal wares, glancing over my shoulder for the police. Glimpsing myself in the cracked pane didn't betray this belief. I assessed them not unlike an amateurish editor studying a fantastically esoteric manuscript that's difficult to understand. I could not comprehend them. They were Aspergersly self-absorbed. The comical caked powder of cosmetics foundation concealed their fabulous visages, gave them a delicious operatic-tragedienne aspect, mouths loopholes, pies scissors, and snipping me. We sang in sentimental modulations, in insufferably insufficiently cultivated contralto, a spirited dueling duet, betokening fondness between male, female. Their adorable navels were exposed. The minxes were rigid, like they were a rabbit hanging from a wolf's jaws. The atmosphere was as a film - a false, not true, representation of reality. The optics of my perspective of scrupulosity were unequivocally cloudy. Those caricaturable facets of my physiognomy, indeed a Neanderthalic phiz, was funny, for they strove to dam the gush of giggles, censored, perhaps, by manners. I'd overvalued my hunger for the delectable doublet on account of the lofty challenge of fulfilling it. They discounted my sensitive disposition, goggling me mockingly as I ogled their genitalic geraniums in fur- frondescence. I was acres devastated by drought and the twins were drops averse to dripping. Their appealing umbilicuses were uncut crystals in luscious abdominal rocks. Abruptly, they streaked like a creepy comet, exuberant in emancipation, nasalizing nonsense, confirming their dopiness, and certainly shrill in their joking, a pair of hominal geese honking gobbledegook, uninhibited in advancing, ambulatory, sequin- blinders squinty, shoulder blades flapping like avian wings, the whole deal reminiscent of an enigmatic procession on a faulty fresco, miraculously animated, and artificially amplified, I'd guess. I gawped. They were revoltingly ravishing. Their poor posture reminded me of a camel's, fiery glares burning through me. The three of us were clad in our Pajamas, and my looks were as pebbles pitched into an abyssal pit, signifying, I suppose, my laxity in respectability. They appeared rather bewildered, as if confronted with a chunk of Latin to transcribe. The teens comprised a complex structure, height and width changing, depending on the particular vantage point. It was as though they conjured tricks; sorceresses with somatic sleights-of-hand. More murmurous bunkum. Their physical language made me feel like a surfer encountering a tidal wave, that is, I was awestruck. They were fucking thrilling. I got my abominable behavior as a boozer gets his beverages from a package store. They were haunted hellions, enthralling, autistic apparitions, suggesting, in their manic movements, toil, or triumph, marionettes of malformation, beat-red like punished juveniles, longish limbs crippled, concave tummies lacteous. I was blanched. Suryan and Ananda skipped like parrots and

stumbled as mules carrying a large load and stuck, sporadically, in mud, abandoning their breakfast bowls,
oatmeal and raisins having been devoured lickety-split,
venting, hither-thithering, palsy-walsy, a veritable enfi-
lade of farts, serves equable with volleys, as they began
to bicker, patting their stomachs and picking their bel-
lybuttons, reproaching each other for whatever reason,
nipped and tucked surgically by the splendor. Their
dumb blather continued. My ardor was a photographic
hobby. To wit, my vision was the negative, developed in
the darkroom of my deranged encephalon, realization
the finished picture. I was a dull firmament stealing
comely cirri and getting satisfaction. I accomplished
attracting their attention, and I was marred in the mirrors of their oculi. In afternoon's aqueous effulgence, and
with a viscosity of sweat, they were marine monstrosi-
ties. Vigorously I scoured my hands over this unsolved
riddle in evolution, not unlike a dedicated, diligent
digger who'd struck gold. They turned deaf ears to my
not-so-cleverly counterfeit calming palaver, spherical
eyes, orientally narrowed, imparting to their smooth,
gangly physique, serpentoidally slinking, a slight arc. I
was transfixed by the curvy hips, gelatinous guts, curlicue umbilici, beanstalky legs, scrawny arms, and duckish
tootsie-wootsies. Both of them bestowed upon me an
embryonic stare, as children often do on adults, pupils
imbued with a glistening, complicated confusion. They
evinced an electrical agitation, like hostesses handling a
customer interminably scanning the menu and never
finalizing the decision on what exactly to order. In solid
auriferous refulgence, they were seemingly carved from

marble, derma as lilies', bolt-upright as haughty Aztec princesses, and cunning like monkeys. Gracelessly, greedily, I checked them out, wishing to be on them as the antique lamp's persistent, dim glow, by a donated vase of indeterminate botanical decoration, in their nudity a blazing pallidness, surrounded by the saccharine, sumptuous horrors of the cupcakes. My avid action could be, of course, considered dangerous, but to me it was like holding a dismantled grenade. I dreamed of lovemaking. I was as a cow grazing in a pasture. Climaxing, I was like a calf crapping. They were a puzzle I had to put together. Their teeny-weeny bosoms and itsy-bitsy butt-cheeks bobbed as apples in a barrel, viperine eyes, brimming with fury, gateways to insanity. Breathing heavily, their cinerous-oyster-shell oral cavities opened and closed, the belt tying them together like a ribbon keeping an ivory bouquet intact.

They were vulnerable like turtles deprived of their protective shells. The eviscerated sofa's entrails spilled. I was straightforward as a knife. My passion was a beast demanding to be fed. I was drawn to them - staples to a magnet. My mitts shackled their sharp ankles, clawish foots. I was very remorseful. Those who countenance guilt are their own MD; they must diagnose the problem and procure the remedy. I endured the expectancy of a cure. My retrospections were cavalier, incompatible with time, so casual with chronology. In time, the strength of remembrances weakens, sustained in the conscious until fading into the subconscious. The brain's retentive slots have many variations, as the earth has sundry surfaces. By isolating the nymphean twosome in our place, inside, it was like I was criticizing an excellently rendered portrait in a gorgeous gallery, as opposed to outside, in a public lavatory. Homicidal vehicular havoc on mucky, potholed streets in the madding city. An ancient factory coughed up a coagulum of dank soot from its chimney-throat. Hail was shards of glass. Plop-fizz of showers. Fall was lying in wait, like an alligator at a watering hole. These vintage cars wove as plastered guests at a frenzied party. A bright bulb failed, missing the mamzelles like subpar stage-lighting, where the operator fixes it unexpectedly on the set design instead of on the main actors. Countless employees marched, as if during wartime, into a warehouse. With my imaginings of Suryan and Ananda, it was like I was playing music of the past using an instrument of the present. They gazed at me quickly, as though they were assassins on a mission who had hit the target, and turned to take off. They stood, one replicating the other, poised like warped jugs on a shelf. Sprinkles were spermoid organisms in a natural drama of conception. Flashbacks flashed forward. Impressions of the past retreated from the invading forces of the present. The welkin's limitless face had numerous scars, like pimply stars were hastily extracted from it. I pictured the chickadees being stripped bare. The insubstantial sky, with its mallow patina, bore the fragmentary forms of cumuli. Spring'd sprung as a spring. The damsels' husky reverberations sounded like people striving to verbalize with portending lamentation. Moon on high was a diamond embedded in velvet of the vault. I was glad. They were sad. Distress in our household was as contagious as the plague. I wanted them to be happier in my companionship, only I was aware it was ridiculous to believe this could happen, like thinking that an unhealthy person could be converted into health and fitness by hanging out with a gym rat without pumping a pound of weight, or running a quarter-mile. I called them "the Arachnid," for they were spidery and had the proper amount of limbs. I sibilated, "at the right moment you'll realize you love me," but it was as a detective finding important clues, discovering key evidence, at the wrong moment, to pronounce suspicion on a suspect who'd already been acquitted in a court of law. Oh, to provide a necessary X-ray of our potential joy (concealed by the integument of misery) ... Evening was like a Stygian, membranous, massive wing of a mutant bat unfolding and beating silently, as snow. Those downy, flat abdomens ... Winds in pneumaticity. Arpeggios of drizzle. Through ecclesiastically asymmetrical windows, the bedewed hills were furry fists chomping at the bit for a fight. Anorexic aspens shook not unlike junkies desperate for a fix; or lunatics getting vying to get out of restraints. Silver clouds moved through the immeasurable cosmic body of the skyline as bullets in slo motion. Penumbral poltergeists wandered. Gulls, distributed on the esplanade, dawdled and wailed. Citizenry fitted together like a jigsaw. The gals were square pegs. My future with them was set, as shitty silverware on an immaculate table, unused to such cutlery habitation. Their bruises, self- inflicted, were as scum-stains on a porcelain basin, their cuts like cracks in it. They were nervous nellies, muted, chopping energetically at yours truly as adventuresses in a dense jungle, making an effort to catch their complaints before they fell. They were not unlike pacing puppets with strings tangled, where the blasé furnishings dictated. I gaped as a proprietor searching for a broom to whack a mouse on his property. My fondness could not be diminished by their indifference. I flourished being in their presence. The copiousness of their consistent character regularly remodeled itself, like it was ostensibly seen in glassy pieces, all at once. In drifting towards them, it was as if I were stirring a palish pond. They assumed an air of aloofness, or, arguably, one of disdain, their scowls splashed by alabastrine strands. Was I an able artist, capable of enhancing the corporeal composition, making the bland grand, transforming the gimpy creatures into divine beings, diminishing the homeliness and filling it with handsomeness? They bloomed like blossoms in an English garden. My musings were mandatory for me. Under the suspended sickle of the moon, a crumbly cathedral, in wheeling fog, took off its remarkable religious crown. A soupy night had extinguished an unseasonably hot day. The cirri dissipated and the cerulean horizon spread as though it was a map of the sea unfurling itself. I was the type of guy who, when, in cuckoo land, produces a clear picture of countless things simultaneously, images of shapes, for instance, precious parts of perception, and forgets them when awake. Reality and areality were ignes fatui, melded, like two superimposed figures that were, by all accounts, one. My heart throbbed as a wound, and thumped, muffledly, like a hammer upon a pillow. My sorrow, a mental illness, went away, as a pain, subsiding when the correct medicine administered commences its effectiveness. Everything was vague; lost recognitions that could not find their way back. I downed wine, the exhilarative provision provided by the grape, to drown my troubles, but the bastards had taught themselves how to float! My disgrace was an injury that wouldn't heal properly. Daggers of woe stabbed me. Scintillant stigmata. Into the mindshaft of madness I plunged. I was an average overture's note carried to … nowhere. I was depressed, like when a holiday's merriment concludes. Threads of textiled cerebrations were sown by the seamster of my cerebellum into the fabric of coherence. Crimson upper atmosphere circulated as blood. The overpopulated/ caffeinated megalopolis, its myriad buildings functional, biological entities, edifices deformed and deteriorated, the results of erosion and desecration, with its surfeit of humanity in its heinous hurly-burly hubbub, technothrummythuddy in tuberculosely gasping gusts, secreting more sounds by the second, the monotonous racket a national anthem of din, traffic shaking, rattling and rolling, urbanite snails slinking beneath heaven's slate slab, the megapolis a fractured bone in this country's geological skeleton, in serous illumination. It manifests like a photo put in solution, its changes emphasized. Precipitation had the sonance of frying eggs and sizzling bacon. Radiance glimmered rimely. I invested in lucid intellections with subliminal concentration. I saw a lot, as if through an advanced stereoscope … so crucially productive! There was activity nearby, and the disagreeable vocal chamber work of argumentation, made by my neighbors, and backed-up by a chorus of childrens' cries, kidney-chillingly blared.

My guilt was a ton of weight my conscience couldn't lift. Suryan and Ananda's vaginal carnations burgeoned. My soul was in solitary confinement. I was imprisoned by regret, a far more problematic place to attempt to escape from than an actual jail. They were ripe, virginal, shrink-wrapped, prepared for Prince Charming.

Would the setup be more satisfying than the payoff? I got out of predicaments as the Road Runner; or was I Wile E. Coyote? Uncertainty was an unstable bridge above the yawning chasm of uncertainty. I climbed down the rungs of the ladder of cognizance, from the upper level of consciousness, to the lower level of subconsciousness, where authentic logic resides. In my cranial space ideas orbited ... No ... They were ephemeral corpses in a polluted stream. The phosphorescence was a transitory phenomena, shining on the familiar and making it unfamiliar. I did what most folks do when confronting reality: I avoided it. I sought safety in speculation. A malevolent dawn turned the panes into fractured faces. Morn'd inspired and aft'd breathed easier. Clammy eve - a trembling tear drying. A royal blue moon hung in crystalliferous clouds. Time had pitted day against night in some cosmic death-match, the Godardian Alphaville hennaed by the illumination. Spores of thought shot from my seedpod greymatter. The sisters were this fluttery, shrieky, hominid stork sporting oxygen-masks, acting not unlike overwrought hambones in a soap opera, tidbits of ashes as snowflakes from their cigarettes, the delirious thespians (on a sham set) destitute of technique, their big break broken already, one being reincarnated in the other's beady eyes, a boo-worthy performance by the angelic devilkins, way up there in air-space, flying too close to the sun, fast and furious, revelations rushed. Metamorphic, dilapidatedly beauteous Babylon of a metropolis. Their Wonderland-leading bung-holes in snare-drum behinds beckoned this ardent Alice as they transformed themselves into cartwheeling cloudforms in an acrid atmosphere in the highest of altitudes, a cacophonic, conjoined wreckingcrew, effeminate frogmen glissading in the birthcanal hallway, bracelets and anklets jingling atonally in improbable irradiation, their zoomy transit implausible, racing on a route without a pitstop, spiting a mysterious malady, exterminating angels in our heavenly home, drifting like candy wrappers in gusts, waves of irreality having borne them to the shores of reality, both disappearing into thin air, part of a magic trick. They were graceful as hippopotamic ballerinas. Starfish in the seasky. The twins sprouted as giant weeds, mops agitated, and the mademoiselles, busted bombshells, sticks of dynamite, drank like fish, perspiry rhinestones flickering, brimstone B.O. left in their wake. Cirri haloed the city. Umbilical rings dangled limply. The bitchy birdies, bananas ... Would they fly the coop, or grind to a halt, stop in their tracks for me? Floating as balloons. Everest-edifices bore witness to their own decline. Garish billboard advertisements were like these glossy covers of movie magazines. Suryan and Ananda were supernovas on a silverscreen. Their outsize, supernal beings fleetfootedly walked the fine line between mortal and immortal. Krishna-blue celestial sphere. They were long-lobed, udder-bellied, and lunchbox-footed, on a knockabout walkabout, abrasions caused by their antics, blinders lit as butt-ends.

I hated my past and present and feared my future. Their light illuminated the darkness. Nothing escaped their Olympian eyes and ears. They communicated In a secret tongue, roared as jet-planes, transmogrifying like Vishnu in the daylight, running out of steam, Buddha-bulky backsides wagging. Pencil-bods, eraser-heads. Breadbaskets as white jelly. Potato-breasts. Wolfing sour sweets. Blowing like a bomb and bursting into tears. They were firecrackers going off with a bang, went kaput, collapsing on the carpet, hair sticking up as icebergs. The abysmal apartment was my Mecca and harem. I was low-key and thanked my lucky stars for insomnious times. They were my guardian angels. I spilled my spunky beans. It was a gymnastic exercise. I deliquesced into them. I poured myself into their vaginate vessels. The three of us were combers colliding in a tempest, with clapping sonancies. They hardly pulled their (contemptuous) punches in the murderous verbalized beating they doled out, rendering me stupefied, not to mention black and blue. Their seatbelt- light-glinting, ball-bearing blinkers. Their chit-chatting sounded like cast spells, maundered mantras. They were forbidden foods I ate. I had a voracious appetency. I'd pop up and they'd give me the slip. Without them ... there was nothingness. Isolation. Aloneness. In the adhesive air their flesh possessed the semitransparency and texture of melting snow, these ice-queens, ever-glacial, wearing a capital-lettered DO-NOT-DISTURB sign, written in soaring script, on their chests, chunks of meat in their sanguineous mouths. My lips were dry as the desert sands of the Persian Gulf. I consumed the whisky of their heady vocabulary. By the brass genie-lamp, their diaphoresis was like coconut oil, their particular prettiness an answered prayer. They had a manure stink.

Something bulged in my drawers and it wasn't my wallet. They were our Creator's grandiose follies, unsolved riddles, now dressed in frocks, fingers fish-hooks baiting me to bite. My life was an aimless deja vu, evaporating lachryma. In the phizog of the tenement, in this pockmark of a pad, unkempt and redolent of poverty, solemn and stenchy as a mass grave, with freakshow furniture, purchased in denial of mediocre taste, trying to appease an inventive caprice, with me determined to partake in the acquiring of the distinctive, meeting a materialistic obligation, although, admittedly, lacking the foundation of utility, the impaired walls and floors giving off an odoriferous noisomeness, as relaxing as a colonoscopy, I had repaired to repose, the archaic grandfather clock tick-tocking shyly. I sat my lazy duff into my favorite pachydermoid chair, with its hodgepodge of diverse cushions, and saw myself shown in the speculum on the coffee table, my rodentine eyes vacant as an abandoned abode, my conk a queer gewgaw hitched to my chimpanzee's rictus. I became cerebrally numb, as if my brain was a body under the influence of an anesthesia, and I maintained the ability to think while the procedure continued, and I retained no sensation. With them, I was a painter enslaved to his palette, a writer oppressed by the tyranny of language. Febrile dusk. Cumuli were chubby brides. Urbane ruction. A zephyr which blew through the shabby screen had the sonance of an oldster wheezing his way up a staircase. According to my hearing, the downpour resonated like sifting sand. An octopus-oak inadvertently threw out its tentacle-boughs. Drifts of debris. Fag-ends were ash-covered Pompeii personages. On the freshly polished parquet were tumbleweeds of dustbunnies. Ramparts of moldy books, mostly obese volumes. Amnestic conundrum. Mine. Retrospective striptease: items of clothing cast aside come-hitherly, revealing flashes of skin, the aliment of allusion. The outstanding display was hazy, as though seen through smoked glass. Blur of spry rank and file cleared into singletons. Mob moved. My fart didn't survive me. Without any warning whatsoever, a band of bedraggled boys barreled through an eidolonic smoke and it dissolved. They were chased by a walrus with incisor-tusks. Glabrous gonadal structures. Rain slapped on brick. From the tumid zit of the sun seeped muciferous rays. Thunder rolled and cracked, sounding like bowling balls striking tenpins in the alley of the azure. Lightning had paparazzi flash. The lie I told the gals was so cheesy it should've been topped with mushrooms and pepperoni; or wrapped with a Kraft label on it. Their upset shocks, aggravated attire, blinding derma layer lacquered with sweat and adorned with lipstick-kissy scabs from nit-picking, in the torrential tenebrosity of their burial-vault bedroom, a Brave New World, puppet- show shadows playing everywhere. They were pigeon-toed, gorgeous goblins in the gloom, fecund Fauntleroys indulging in woolgathering. Their ideas were bred eugenically, out of sci-fi. They were special spermatozoa of supreme beings in a paint-peeled, walled womb of tepid temps, cryptic suspirations sounding as sorceress curses, calling me a snake, rotter, pedophile, chowing Chinese and cramming Mexican, lanky Trees Of Life, uprooted, schlepping, as if they balanced baskets on their craniums and had blunt phalluses pushed up into their prats. 'The Jetsons' was on the television, the pair spinning on the mattress not unlike beef on a spit, fell onto the floor as the sun diving into the sea, knocking over a radio, and rose like a gorge, swelled as the tide. Their journal held florid handwriting. They were godless recluses, wicked witches, mutants surviving, tallish Tinkerbells existing, for I clapped my hands. I monopolized them. They were a clam I prised, prized. An operatic cat-scratchy scuffle. I snooped as Peter Sellers in 'The Pink Panther.' They were lopsided stick-figures with slanting smiles, vampiresses, reclamation projects whose backs had the color and consistency of whipping cream. Cresty smirks. Binaca breath. Lanuginose lettuces of private parts in a somatic salad. A lewd cannibal, I wished to eat them alive, only I was becoming a practicing vegan. Knifely I Frenched the Oz oddities, albinotic Amazonic Wonder Women in strip-lighting. These Never-Neverland nymphets were parade floats, and I grabbed my popcorn ... and something else. A calm before the storm. Was it the start or the finish?

On the just-cleaned checkered tiling of the local zoo, dime-a-dozen, an Insectival shadow scuttled. The settings were endowed with an ethereal emerald hue. A cadaverous giantess, with a closely-cropped raven cap of hair, vibrant, vulturine eyes, vaguely feline snout, and cherry mouth, wore a burnt-sienna, JANITOR- emblazoned jumpsuit uniform and droopy-laced, brown work boots. She mechanically pushed a mop bucket with her shin - my myopic, monosyllabic wife, Mapi. We had a marginal marriage. Hearing hoof-beats clip- clopping, she spun. A zebra had gotten out of its enclosure and was spooked by her. It bucked, reared up, and kicked her in the sternum and she fell headlong into the turquoise pool. An obsidian fin sped towards her. She was mauled by a killer whale.

After the awful accident with the orca, Mapi's left limbs were amputated. In the fair-to-middling hospital, she was tended to by a number of nurses, male and female, and of significant racial variety, in garnet scrubs. I'm gap-toothy Dominique, I'll remind you, reader, with my dumb dial incorporated into a cormous skull, a fellow who failed to achieve his ambitions. I was clad in a sorrel sweater, kelly corduroys, and scruffy sneakers. Leather wallet on my knee, I sat in phony composure in the vinyl chair next to her. I sipped my cappuccino's frothy, cinnamon-freckled shroud and brushed off the crumbly seborrheal scurf (scalp-scales) from my chocolate chip muffin I got from the cafeteria. My countenance of fake concern collapsed. There was this pervasive daisy chain of smells: flatus, cologne, deodorant, toothpaste, chemicals, dentures, feet, perfume, feces, urine, vomit, food, and infirmity. Shortly after she was (slightly) recovered from the intensive operations, she pleaded with me to impregnate her, or attempt to anyway, upon perusing an article in the paper entitled 'Whale of a Tale' in bold black and white - her suffering captured in a caption. I was frozen in icy idiocy. I ponderously proceeded, like I was afflicted by sluggardly indigestion. The frame was full, arranged for us to occupy it. I felt as a river paddled by oars. My enlarged imagination was capable of harboring corrupt scenarios. I gazed at her like she was the gallows and I was the condemned set to hang. I shut and locked the maple door, watched her struggle to get out of her johnny in a lubberly jig. Fervidly I fiddled with her as a foreigner using chopsticks at an Asian restaurant. Her features contracted into a flexible frown when I pulled my bow-arched boner, a healthy hardon, out. Love is hate's umbrage. My goofy, mega-watt grin. Our kisses were kids ... provoking one another. I was impassioned, and inwardly I dragged myself over live coals. The dye was cast. The clinically cool corridor was eerily quiet. Those klaxon-blasts were hers. The sexual session was unbearable for her. Our perspiry 'stashes and beards were smeared. Coupling was an excruciating ordeal for her. She stoked my furnace. I adjusted my charm like a TV's contrast knob. She was a pet I fondled. I was a devil drowning in holy water. Fictions, for me, were absorbed in facts. Her raw-sushi snatch. Her flesh as vapor. Mapi flopped like a marionette of substandard design. I was a chameleon husband, imitating the protective pigment of dedication. Requested violation. Suspirant discussion. Her deafening keening. Her satiny, pipe cleaner limbs flailed, amatively apoplectic, her glare, a petrified ocular carrier, reaching me, and I glanced askance, as though to spare her the further indignity of remaining in my sight. Infantilely I sucked on the auburn buds of her nipples, tight titties with the silken yellow raiment of jasmine. Her twat was stale soil. Exhausted, she let out a froggy croak when I rammed her, my cardiac kettledrum pounding. With woofer- challenging volume, we puled not unlike pigs. She was Death's dong, wan and wormy, and I was his anus, excremental and puckered. Straddling her pasty stomach, massaging her concentration camper's ribs, I made a rubbery, retarded moue. I was a lad who couldn't put his plaything down. In wanting to be parturient, she wanted a (sensible) support structure. We strained as trapped weasels. I leached her warmth. She was liquid-soft. Her lids flickered similar to Dow Jones ticker tape. I wasn't the brightest candle on the birthday cake. We emitted cold sighs and controlled caws during the intercourse. Her demise was inevitable, not dissimilar to Pris, the Replicant from 'Blade Runner': a pleasure model with a built-in expiration date. What was death to me? Recovery from the illness of life. Dismal munic-ipal moribundity. Pedestrian manikins. Light through rumpled blinds was a lingering loaf of bread. Her mag-nolian muff. Contents of the stark, cramped quarters dematerialized since the evening infringed. Timpani vascular organs. I wasn't in full form in the sack. My performance in the hay was spottier than a leopard with measles. Saturnic moths with wing-rings. Our screwing was divination sanctioned by destiny. Lust is an obsti-nate tumor; it can be reduced or removed altogether, but the trace to its source can be exacting. Glomeration of my gratification was consolidated, solidified, on which I could lean for reinforcement. Satisfaction was an aspirin assuaging an ache. Mapi had injury-inflated Zorro-mask peepers, an Etch A Sketch body. She could've been shaken, erased. She was a doodle of a drawing, the lines fading, a repercussion of the pen's ink waning. I tilted, as if on a ship's deck on choppy waters, seeing land ahead. Glottal drafts. Petrol fumes. Fullest moon, olive-greenish. She glouted, sure had the glooms. She was a violin wanting to be soothed by my bow. Did she suspect that I simulated my adoration? I had drilled her hard. With her, I was a capable chef devouring his culinary masterpiece after cooking for my clientage for years, and knocking back vodka like Dracula did blood. She looked at me like I was a snake-oil salesman. She became happily, heftily preggers.

Months later, Mapi, her pies piggybank-slitted, slot-trap bee-stung pouty, supplied with her science-fictional prosthetics, wept jubilantly, cradling a bawling bundle. She'd given birth to albinistic Siamese twins, joined at the hip by a fleshly flap: Suryan and Ananda. They resembled emus, with languorous silvery manes, plan-etoid, piceous eyes, pointy schnozzes, and lesion- lips. They were secretive and sullen, and seldom silly, at least when I was around them. With them, it was as though I was doing laps in a traditional pool; whereas without them, it was like swimming across the English Channel. Cola-brownish lambency. Their grapefruit-pink yappers, punchy aromas. I pictured them split as aged pots, or like cracked shells. Rummy reservoir. I had this typhoid soul, didn't have the immunizing agents to fight the sick-ness. They were respiring lungfuls, boozily influenced, mouthwatering Ali Babas with the personalities and proclivities of forty thieves, not gazelle-graceful, bright stars blazing at me, habited in their heather bathrobes, these cross-eyed sirens tempting me, Botticellian Venuses swaddled in vermilion blankets, sleepless in the sheets. They pecked at their ambrosian desserts with plenty of shredded coconut. Tuscan-bell botties and Michelin-mams worth a mint. The two were ravishing revenants in a material world, gulping contraband alcohol. I was a blank slate. The arteries of my capers hardened, along with something else. I was a Trojan Horse's ass. And I was porcupine-prickly, for Pete's sake! The gamines were entertaining extraterrestrials glued to the boob tube, into 'The Munsters,' space cadets digging 'Sesame Street.' Scarfing Juicy Fruits, scoffing Jolly Ranchers. Protean hinds big deals. Funny fannies! Those buttocks were magic lamps. The ingenues were Bandit Queens, stealing my spirit. Their hands and feet were of considerable length. They were flightless birds in bifocals, in disrepair, with electrician's tape at the temples, and slinkily dressed, deities in our dump. I was scared stiff and feeling foolish, my scrotal sac a shriveled apple, me with my Popeye chin and Bluto buns, a sorry simulacrum of Cornelius from 'Planet of the Apes,' a ghost out of his grave. They were prepared for the worst but hoped for the best. Tea-spit spewed in kettle-whistle discourse. Peeled-tangerine derma layer. Hair frizzied into Afro-nests. Rubber band limbs. Horny hands allergic to manicure, mangled feet resistant to pedicure. Venting a quantity of cannonading flatulence. Paddle-arms rowed, gait not unlike a bitch pissing round a hydrant. I trailed 'em as a pickpocket would tourists. Both were like a Tourettic automaton rebelling against its fabrication. Their stuttering dialogue sounded as if dried leaves crawling on concrete. They were without a stitch on, having relieved themselves of a diaphanous gown, decolorizing, like a Polaroid, misshapen mannequins slipping and sliding into the bathroom, dripping into the soap-scummed tub as massive melting icicles, and soaked, stammering, mutinous tongues refusing to obey their commands, to wash, scrubbing with a discoid Dial bar, cucumber necks craned, torsos toppling into each other, the pair tittering, head-butting, shakers made into pincers, the nymphs deciding to dilly-dally at their vaginous cabbages, basking, satisfying the demands of cleanliness, the added, pronounced breadth to their anatomies accredited to the shampoo lather, my daughters becoming aware of their prominent profiles, embellished by the rich amount of suds. Figures, corporeal components, impermanently diminished, were captured in the faucet, in a position betwixt ambulation and stationary, prior to recapturing authentic, marinating relaxation. They appeared to've been comprised of disparate, bifurcated parts, unrestricted by civvies. In a shambling tread, they'd flowered out of the murk, "oddacious" incandescent beams. Indolent goddesses they were, underwear obliging their every (dramatic) action. They had starlet auras, slouched on the velour sofa, became sideways, slumped sourpusses, sexual open sesamists, palefaced mirages, to me. I was an irritatingly imitative parrot on their shoulders. They were hybridized, a synthesis, a Sartrean, shamed subject in his story if he smoked hashish. They osculated and tactioned like some honeymooning couple, with oceanic breathing. Enveloped in sweats, wrapped in a cocoon of penetralia. They took my moral prosperity and left me with disgusting perversion. These badly behaved, bewitching beelzebubs had me by the balls, and they yanked the shorthairs.

Suryan and Ananda were glitches in our Maker's system, ghosts in the machine. They slid, drivelling on, into a drowse, spreading as though a stain, having hijacked the vinyl chesterfield, the trigger-happy terrorists marooning themselves on it, their booties bombs, the aeroplane of the ottoman on a landing-slip of mosaic flooring, a troublesome tarmac, with me a hidden sniper, the ingenues in my scope. The ladies were a cobra and I was the mongoose, unaware of my surroundings. Their pudendal organs were tools of persuasion. 'Yogi Bear' was on the aerialed, knobbed television. They were sitting ducks, even on the pogo-stick, then on a unicycle. I was a waste of space. Hues of their habiliments were season-appropriate, chased by the wearers' preternatural physical deformities. I'd followed where they'd led, like a sinner into a church, their once- pressed nylon and polyester ensemble rumpled, elicited earlier unascertained activeness. They reveled in spontaneous grandiloquence, grouching with a jaunty zest, and emphasizing the pauses with zeal. Bony fingers lifted in snappy militaristic precision, solicited more syllables from one another. They were bowels and I was the endoscope. The murmurers were deep in meditation. They were having their period (to be nabbed red-handed!) ... They dandled and

I was riveted to their raiment, uselessly outdoorsy when they were indoorsy, suggesting a provincial inducement, collected on the scraggly mat. The sisters issued soprano and tenor peals, ball-and-chained to an ambiguous hilarity, in their prism of perspective, imperceptibly engulfing them in an audible chrysalis. They experience the tremulous paroxysms which precede the commencement of exaltation, in expectancy of the imminent arrival of a transcendent experience, a feeling potentially obliterating all concerns, and its explicit content expires before the extreme sensation can be felt, and in its wake is a tremendous disappointment to be endured, however, the remaining poignancy of its essence is effective enough, a rapture derived from the phrase of a glorious sonata, only the emotion is essentially eliminated by the sheer aspiration of attaining it. Their equinely neighing. They had sharper facial characteristics than their parents, as if the intangible whizbang generational carver, with a stimulating style, went crackers with a chisel, any restraint evidently evicted from the approach. I was whey-faced, surveyed them. They were white oleaceous shrubs flowering beside a couple of purply ones (their Mom and Dad) ... Would they approve or disapprove of my nosiness? I was moored not unlike a boat on the harbor of habit. Their backs were arched as though they were saplings bending because of their arrangement on the brink of a bluff. Laboriously did they linger at their quims. I was metronome-pendulant. They were so gossamery it was like they were looking through a cutis-curtain. I gandered, evaluated. Combined, they were a vagarious, wading, effeminate Neptune, in this hyaline luminescence, a splintered pour, so slumberous, lids rolling as cartoony shades. Slurry wordage was sent out. Were they virginally risqué! These innocents laughed like loons, acted as Auschwitzians coerced by a Nazi officer to make out. Whereupon they, marvelously appealing, bumbled, precariously, on fungal foots, a gyratory tangle of daffy delirium and avianistic bursts of tweets and twills, exhibiting the dim-witted fluster of fowls wildish in an inceptive phase of captivity. The multiplicity of imperfections were an acquired taste. No doubt of that. They were automatous waxworks composed of parts in ungainly participation, implying independence, engaged according to the (mercurial) whims of their owners. The synchronic, exaggerated smiles waited before affirming themselves, as if applying a pretext to do so. Expectorating burble-baloney, gurgling, grasping for grammatical form: survival of the fittest of consonants and vowels. They did have unto them an imposed discipline of fractional learning, a domestic education, although little made a mental impact. They were essentially uneducated. Daily doomsday. The duo perorated in a garbled manner; gargled lingual flurries spat in unpredictable intervals. Blind squirrels occasionally finding nuts, they hazarded to thrash out (feigned) astute expressions, shuffling pathetically, hoping the literal dollops of grabber-indicia would exonerate them in the court of law of public opinion, defending against the prosecution's (serious) charge of stupidity. I will admit (evidence admissional?) their thirst for discovery was unquenchable. Their idle, malnourished minds ... Were they starving for a feast of profane concepts? They hopped as though a rare species of kangaroo. Viscidity of the oxygen. Knickknacks and bric-a-brac were bountiful. The fruity sky's rinds of clouds peeled away. Soaker was pine-sappy-sweet like pencil-shavings. The gigantean, glandular sun secreted illumination. The celestial sphere was, speciously, of an excrementitious substance. Stencil shadows of raw-boned branches. A nictitant megalopolis knelt to pray in a storm out of the Old Testament, begging for mercy from the Almighty. Suryan and Ananda were sarcastic, snide and dismissive. I bit off more than I could chew and choked on them. My cracks at humor were lame. They were spectral sisses, brittle and unbending, with oculi oilslicks on asphalt aspects, screaming in a boiling rage, the arsenal of their anatomies holding me hostage, both gabbling in briny pitches, happily humming. I yenned to tickle them pink. Abracadabra! They'd be pacified. They signaled similar to sloshed stewardesses explaining safety rules to flight passengers, rising akin to Phoenixes from the ashes from the hassock, placing down harslets and hasty puddings, moving like seabirdie hashers waiting on clientry, charging and changing as Juniper into a bull, on a tearful tirade, uncountable cockroaches in full flight, their wah-wahing Hendrixian. They wanted salvation and I sought damnation. The babes put on a poncho, angeling apparent, belting out Abba and Looney Tunes. They wanted answers when I wanted questions. Were they a skyscrapery sight to marvel at! We, the familial trio, were the good, the bad, and the ugly. I was inexhaustible fodder ... Needed to cash in my chips ... I was dead in the water. I faithfully served the master of salacity. An imaginary vision of the utopian megapolis glimmered. In the tenebrific twilight, edifices, to me, were docked war-torn ships. Frick and Frack conversed softly, like their fragile brains would shatter if they were too loud. They were erect and stilled - an enigmatic effigy made of spun sugar. They sang a duet, a song I was smitten with, its infectious groove hidden, mellifluent themes merging into a lone ditty which hadn't entirely settled in. And it inculcated me with a paramount elation nonetheless. Meanwhile, poor Mapi plodded as a truncated nag, whether well or unwell, without a peep of complaint, strutting, or limping, like a wounded hen, or a beheaded chicken, after the protracted rehab, encased in an orthopedic corset, trusses and braces, pomaded in Bela Lugosi cosmetics, with vitality gained from an extended duration of enforced immobility, and, immersed in the routine, had gotten energy that'd turned her into a (relative) whirlwind of mobility, devoted, to a fault, to her domestic duties. She trudged on dunes of soiled duds furrowed by punitive winds. She behaved as if she were expecting to be struck by an arrow released from its bow. She ventured to guard her girls from threats by a dangerous world, with a cat's maternal ferocity. My desire for them was ripening fruit, concealed in nature's festal scheme, that is, vegetation festoonery, and falling from the boughs on its own. I grappled with my conscience and could not get a grip. Morally speaking, this was beyond the last outpost of civilization. It was like I'd chanced upon a new breed of mortal that beseeched me to explore, examine. My intention was to deprive myself of them, deny my hunger, but, of course, I knew intention wasn't constant. In most cases it was intermittent. I was disadvantaged, as though a manic depressive who'd swallowed his last prescription pill and there were zero refills. I preferred to nip my deviant aspirations in the bud, only conflagrant dreams resumed, returned with a vengeance. The gals indulged enthusiastically in an unrefined tweeny protocol of getting ready to sleep, voxes husky. My heart sounded like a comforter on a laundry-line and walloped by a baseball bat. They were going to bed, surreally content. I focused on them, in their jammies. These gooneys were God's frigging flub. The dampness enswathed us as a sodden shawl. Parallel lines their galumphing groundcovering drew, at an indecisive velocity, bonelessly floppy, and became increasingly crooked. The electricity of urge charged me. In seeing them, I was this shipwreck survivor on a lonely island and spotting a craft a minute before it vanishes. The beauties were entwined, twirly like Twizzlers twisty licorice sticks. A sneeze swelled and ruptured from Suryan's nose and strings of snot were expelled from Ananda's nostrils. The execution, I suspected, of an incestuous act was sufficient enough, a kiss, touch, or look sufficient to bring out the latent passion in what already existed. Elements of impassivity granted or attention given could be clever ignitive ploys. Those dodo silhouettes drove me bonkers ...

A blackish cirrus on the fulgid eye of the sun was as a piratical patch. The city, its terrific towers extravagantly expressionistic, with excursive geometries, variations of radical ratiocination, was a puffed, putrid pie baking in an immense, invisible oven, aroma unappetizing, rising in radiance to set. Was I detached from fact and re- attached to fiction? Were my senses piteous vics of vicious perp-hallucinations? Suryan and Ananda, my handicapped kith and kindle, tarried, pupils pierced by pins of brilliancy and bled peacock-blue. Their penmanship, in red ink, made a postcard into a bloodbath. I molded my fatherly clay depending on circumstances. You can be misled by appearance, depending on your perspective, like distinguishing shadow and not its maker. Serene skyline. In their bedroom, with its vaulty ceiling, uncomfy, untidy and untrendy, I sloughed off my union suit as a snake its skin. The prima donnas sniggered, waddled like a skunk, traversed the lunar floor. Warily, the three of us subjected ourselves to a tuneless game of musical chairs. I was a parental product whose packaging consistently changed. I was hunter and hunted. I adapted my paterfamilias posture for effect. To be tied to them as Ulysses to the mast! My involved plot had an evilly taste of premeditated murder, the last sentence, in my mind, a perfect place to dump the body. I tracked the two as a hound following foxes. I smoked a phallus-joint, a fatty to die for, flicked it, and it dived like the Hindenburg. The divas vulpecularly barked. I'd accepted defeat in battling weed in my personal War Against Drugs. I lived in a universe of instincts not governed by principles. The crapulent crash pad marinated in a mucid fetor. Benumbed, I tenderly embraced them. I endeavored to be circumspect. Did I provoke affection … or annoyance? Their fingers and toes kicked in Busby Berkeley chorus-line sync. My coveting 'em was on par with needing sustenance for subsistence: imperative. I was a relative beast of burden. In cajoling the twins, I was a politician mooting the matters of a predicted doomy end of an entire empire. The gentle cosseting was a formula I brought forth, employing it wisely. They were as the disabled subjugated. I was ramrod-stiffened, my jaw-jutted. Moments shifted gears. I shuddered as an alcoholic with the D.T.s. Suryan and Ananda made a plow of movement. Time was a lodestone pulling us towards it. They snickered, either in delight of my (brazen) bravado, or in derision of it. Their blether banished the quietude. Sound is silence winging. Sound's a refreshing interlude of silence's intense rejuvenation. I was overwhelmed by the disjointed damsels. Silence hinders, not helps, sound's transition. Silence is the emptiness of sound. In the lassies I would conduct, with my penoid baton, and the exercised-enervated orchestra of them would execute marvy melodies, nectarean harmonies, my beetled brow dashed. My organ-grinder mitts had the fluidity of wettish breezes. They shrieked like scamps. I was vibratory with an avid disturbance, crouching to defile them, but nausea instigated a stoppage. Start of symptoms of a cold and a hot that'd infiltrated my system inspired me to halt. Our intimate life was a kaleidoscope, the vivid lozenges rearranged into a new pattern, turned in divergent directions. They were slim, gawky birds that had lost their feathers. They were an acoustic studio and I was the instrument. Was it too late to change my ways? Well, an ocean, in the aftermath of a squall, will persist in swelling. To abstain from prying, as a preventative measure, I could have closed the peephole, only it would've been like removing tonsils to avoid the risk of getting tonsillitis somewhere down the road. Cause and effect: is it the trailer before the tractor, the buggy in front of the horse? A network of magenta varicose veins and cellulitic dents in their spongy thighs. The barriers my censor propped up had toppled. They gazed in cowlike passivity. To Mutt and Jeff, I was as enticing as a gynecological exam. Grimaces of dismay. Their cottage cheesey nates. Not buying what I was selling. A fulgurous fountain with its flickers and splashes. Drops on a webcracked windowpane - rush-hour gridlock on a small scale. Specks in our eyes were darting infinitesimal cherubs. Would my daughters avenge the atrocities inflicted upon them by rejecting me? That would, the rebuffing, rip me to shreds. I pictured them applying their unblinking blinders, in which there showed not the faintest acknowledgement of me. Would they spare me this ordeal? They'd never forget what happened. They couldn't nap it out. My arrow was always pointing up ... Crude ... I was haggard and hirsute, with a messy nest of beard, scatterbrained and shifty. The reserve of their resistance was nullified by my persistence in digging out a channel for the cascade of love to flow. My apologies were retarded by amorousness. Their attitude of exasperation. They were specimens on a microscope's slide for remorseless analysis. In a domiciliary hierarchy dominance and submission formalities guaranteed order. Inspecting them, in the altogether, it was not unlike seeing a completed Caravaggio, when initially, them clothed, you saw the original sketch; or as listening to wonderful Ravel music when you previously distinguished notes on the page. With precision of depth and detail, consciousness and unconsciousness were states that evolved episodically, randomly prevailing on me, one returning to retain its reign over the other with the unpredictability of the weather. I treated them with the same care I would an illness. They were indispensable to me. I was driven to control them. They watched me like hawks. They, in their birthday suits, confirmed the bodily stability of a museum's statue, ejecting these tones as cello soloists whose cues had come in a classical concerto. In cuddling with the youthful women, I was as an impaired man who is instructed to stay still, and yet I insisted on moving, even though knowing movements would hurt like heck. Their long limbs flailed as a squid's caudal fins, sighs soothing balms for my scorched spirit. They magnetised me. My sobs convulsed me. My volition was an abyssal gash. They were armatured goslings. In them, I was like a devout Christian entering Paradise. And exiting. They were hard to fathom, as a Broadway play, a stage drama so convoluted that, in order to get its plot, you must first read the programme. The abhorrent abuse on their emery board flesh was the usurpation of their purity. I refused to permit my transgressions to trespass on the property of my scruples. We were converted into triplets. It was an appropriation of organic change, like we were invalids undergoing an innovative regimen and our health was improving. It was as if I were an accomplished international terrorist on a suicide mission, and, at a packed airport, my bogus passport was stamped for approval by customs, my luggage left unchecked, and I went onward, alarmed, for it was too easy! Squirting my semen-stickum I was like a maverick virologist injecting an experimental mucilaginous virus into my patients. They gulped as though stranded fish, and strained mightily.

Opaline, spumescent ocean. Storm took a turn for the worst. Silent scream of coruscation. Jellyfish, umbrella-ish, were as though sparks from the flint of water. Cirri rounding the moon were like celestial messengers circling the Swooning Virgin. The city was a digestive tract atomizing molecules of the mass(es), reducing all to shit. It was a beehive, providing as nutrition, the hexagonal honeycombs, insignia of industry, a fortification for jillions of drones. I was a charlatan. A peon. A fake. A clown. Cat was out of the bag. I hoped my passed gas was perfume to Suryan and Ananda, both barnstorming and new-agey, with a lisping, distinctive drawl and stylistic accessories. They were hot and bothered, reminded me of survivors of some unspecified apocalypse, with smeary makeup, motion jaw-dropping feats of derring-do, the picture they drew (with magic markers) a phallic submarine sardined with hippie seamen. The heronic temptresses were immersed in creating this, occasionally interrupting each other, making these marshland mating calls. Torturous streets traveling far and wide, were taken by a catastrophe of cars, competing for the concrete and moving in mysterious ways. Was I man or mouse? They smelled a rat. The crane-like enchantresses bit their nails as coins, the underage ensnarers of my heart. Light had a noiseless lilt. Our magic-carpet welcome-mat. The two belly danced in a ballsy bikini and unwise flip-flops, body-odor spicy.

They shook and sweated and made faces, slightly fatted, still gangly bods tanning-lotioned, appearing and disappearing in tent-flaps of dungy drapes, warmer than blood, ashen ringlets knotty ropes, these bawdy bards versifying, poetesses of meager talent dispensing those odious odes, smiles sloping, unabashed, one matching the other stride for stride, their rivalrous balance of power tilting back and forth. Rhymed ribaldry. Metrical mayhem. The pen was their sword. I bowed before these omnipotent alien goddesses in our fairground temple. I prostrated myself, titillated, and imagined my manly package changing into sand and sifting between their digits. I was a runt and they were my tormentresses. Raggle-taggle gang of orphans, the foundlings on the front lines of poverty and crime. Appetition clogged my pores. I was sucked into the slipstream of their sexiness. They didn't take me seriously. We were not equals. I was of a lesser value, had a lower status. I was like a customer paying for their concubinage! I was feeling as if I had a cameo role in the exorbitant production of their existence (requiring editing), where they were the central players. Static shots of them standing. Tracking shots of them walking. Steadicam shots of them playing me. I was whip-panned. Their stomachs had the pigment of Scotch- tape. They were celebrity nincompoops. My sea-cucumber was shadow-blue. I had mental images of them skipping rope in supranormal unison in an oily alley with footprints of brackish puddles and captivated spectators of garbage cans; the sisters in ludicrously scanty floral maillots, frolicking in an effulged, argental lake. Croaking frogs leapt from lime lily pads in lemon luster to get flies. In cartilaginous cumuli, the monocle of sun fulgurated. They practised piano, reptiloid eyes winking, crustacean hands promenading on defective keys. Bag of bones Mapi was a tough tree to fell. She blazed a blunt, to fumigate her plight, smoke stumbling out with her crone-ish cackles, bounced, with her imitation extremities, as though she was on a trampoline. She didn't think much of the olla podrida, made by me, contemplated its disposal in the rubbish bin. We were in the slapdash, shoebox parlor, with its minimalist, massacred furnishings, illumination intercepting items. My wife was held in her junkie's straitjacket, that is, addiction, track mark areas optimal for the propagation of infections. Our kids executed a competent, fulsome, hilarious Liberace imitation. Susurrantly, Mapi told me "vaccinating" with heroin was "copulatory" and "orgasmic," the hypodermic pumping in and out, the venereal syringe cumming ... She was sensitive to the radiation of intelligence. For her, the pharmaceutical grazing ... Too much of a bad thing was good. She pursued her destructive delectations with fervor. She was a mad maid, clapped and cheered, our daughters dancing cheek-to-cheek, rhythmically relating to Fred Astaire's version of the ditty on the relic transistor. My voodoo doll nuque was pinned by prickles. My pulse skirred. Babel of babble. Claret welkin was the color of a killer after committing the murder. I was in the there and then. Mapi was a marsupial on PCP. And she dipped into the Ziploc'd marijuana. My mind absorbed thoughts like dirt does moisture.

Hollow-eyed, I was lying low. The twins glared beakily

at me, vengeance incarnate, in our dumbfounded dumping ground in its aridity. We were light and dark, good and bad, black and white. They were spirits of revenge. In harmonies of imperfections, they were as flowerets developing in harsh conditions, a climate not conducive to such maturation. I was a schmuck with a Norman castle schlong, and reeking of mothballs. Suryan and Ananda were this sea-monster, betrayed by the brine. My suffering was a resounding echo. They were illusions shattered, florets with panache, mutations reborn in the flax shafts, and silent like graves, phantom sights of sweet youth in bowlers and swampers. They rose 'n' shone. To them, I was a lousy dream come true in the altered state of an apartment. I was a satyric dad, a devil not getting his due. I ingested a liver sandwich and imbibed soda pop. Tartan blankets. I darkened their doorway. Their princess-soft-and-smooth skin was delightful. They were mermaids with rubberball breasts and medusan buttocks resting on my rock. Their inflections were tremulant. A digression here, with me thinking of the well-orchestrated affair, on a small scale, with Mapi, who stank of forestfloor and farmyard. In hindsight, I would've been better off concentrating my attention on the actual, my significant other, over the outre, the children. Roller coaster of my rod, medieval icon of my mien. We were ignescent substances. My game-show host intonation. I was a guinea pig, a cream puff. Countless cloaks and daggers. Discomfort and discomfiture. Conversations in crisis. Rowdy ruckus. The place, with its mushroom malodor, had the potential for tension, looked as an anonymous ward, with its institutional incandescence and conquering armies of ants. My nutsack felt like it was stored in the freezer. Mapi, mutton-coldish, was a bucking bull and I was a rodeo rider hanging on. She hollered in heartrending distress. Her monkey shrieks and parroty squawks were ear-splitting. She yowled as if in excruciating labor, in endless birth-giving pain, a Moaner Lisa. In our sexualized states, our senses surged. Frenziedly I porked away, with a runner's rhythm and cardio endurance. She made these hiccoughy sonancies, was frail like a coat hanger, and composed, although her visage was as though she were a vampiress when dawn breaks and the blinds are up, on the love seat soggy with perspiration and spilled JD, her breath redolent of peppercorn and bubblegum. Our smacks were slurpy. She was bone-white. Springs created a funky beat. Anti-war demonstrators, many protesters, at the town hall, were distracting. I dominated. She submitted. Her body received my blows. Suryan and Ananda were cassowaries in cassocks, whiffed of anise, cloves and raisins. I rastled with my emotions and was pinned. Unshelled fiddler crabs, they scuttled sideways, satellitic peepers ever-circling. Thrill of the chase. I was a miserable Merlin and they constituted a magnificent Morgan Le Fay. Webbily I wound myself around them. Here was our Lost World of wider horizons.

They put on Kermit the Frog and Oscar the Grouch jams and Star Wars waders, goatily baaaing. The tweens were crafty avians. They were an insane dream leaking into my waking life. They shoveled in shepherd's pie, accurate and timely not unlike clockwork. Once upon a time, in their changingness, they were a ponderous poplar with poison leaves in a fairy-story, mythological beings out of a campfire tale. Was it all a side-effect of stress? Peabody and Sherman were on the television. They grew, expanded on the earth of our homestead, and into the galaxy above. Flamenco-dancing, the fantasists were chalk-whitened, a prize bull in my china shop, picking at saltines, and footslogging as if they were dragging a Steinway behind them. With them passing over me, I was a footprint on a shore washed away by their tide. They were snow-whitish ostriches, larger than life, twiddling with the cold cuts, overcome by demoniasis. My pushing and pulling ulcerous ache. Paper-pale moon. My balls were boulders in my drawers. The lassies were confessions personified (admission is the best policy) of my guilt-ridden conscience. I looked my lechery in the eye. I was a cloud covering their moonlight. They had on a gabardine greatcoat, voices quavery, pantings getting through those splintery teeth, and they billy-bleated. Pellety precipitation. Their hoofy heels (with calluses), red-as-blood soles. They were cut from a different cloth, fickle and feisty. They blew their own horns when they were already loud! I concluded I was a creep, a no-goodnik in the disguise of peace-maker, tree-hugger, leaflet-distributor, planet- changer. I kept my foot on the accelerator of intensity I didn't believe in braking, but I was aquaplaning in humectation, on the highway of our hellhole.

Suryan and Ananda were a curse, my legacy. I drained glasses of cognac and brandy in the wood-paneled living-room. My prizefighter's physique, beardy beginnings, hammy hands. I was in-training to be a cocksucker. They were chimerical Azraels, recherche snow-lilies, Joans of Arc. Myth-Mapi sew-slaved, down in the dumps, at a rickety six-seater table in the (self-made) sweatshop dining-room, central AC cranked, Walkman on, singing along, raising the roof, acting as though she's in a non-smoking, first-class, reassuringly comforting compartment of a runaway railway train, in a Twilight Zone, making these crocodile-skin undies, cocooned in her creativity, an on-the-blink bombshell in lingerie, eye-liner and lip-gloss. I was laid off from my gig as a bartender/bouncer at a disco-tech nightclub and collecting unemployment benefits. The job was not my pride and joy. I was a Day of the Dead diva on laughing gas and built like a human Hummer in our odorous opera house. The sisters' tresses were restyled into hairy antlers in the winds. They were a coalition of the combined, nature's U.N.. And I was a foot-in-the-mouth fool, a full-fledged phoney in a fatherly masquerade, a rotten egg, a bad apple. Ananda's flabby arms windmilled while Suryan struggled to tie her unsuitable shoes, their mannerisms out of a melodramatic movie, pies in the yellow lances light like round tv sets with snowy pictures when programs end and stations go off the air. Radiation was resonant. They were unmeltable, un-Disneyesque ice queens, unthawable Snow Whites whose glaciality could resist the fires of hell. They were no-nonsense icebergs wearing tam-o'-shanters, feather-boas, pantyhose (Ananda), and knickerbockers (Suryan), so close together that nothing could tear them apart. Me? I was an abominable snowman who was snow-blinded by lust. They were amateur mountaineers on my peak. My Everest-erection. Lorn park. I wore sensible kicks. The Lolitas were silkies out of the ocean, clear as weather, where you could look directly through them to discern what lay beyond, in a waterfall of sunshine. I was heavy in the light. They were ghost crabs in trampy togs, bumbling, rumbling and stumbling on flippery feet. Darkness dressed a bus in blackness. It became a mourner in the funeral of a deceased conurbation. Claw-branches of mighty trees over a cab-infested curb, drivers like barkers, the street spectralized by lampposts, in the Hadean underworld, unsleeping and staring, shadows shifting as realities. My blinders were dull, sizable circular spots on wallpaper where mini-mirrors used to hang. The lasses were Grecian statues with leprose rashes, not denied animation, parts of an alien nation. Roll of sun dripped a buttery glow. They played cards, rolled dice, in the clinical waiting-roomy parlor, the furnace blasting, rainfall sounding not unlike nails hammered. I was in the granite-gray, overheated sanctum kitchen, in its simplicity, refurbished in a hurry and on the cheap, drinking vintage champagne out of a skull-stein. They arachnoidally, arthritically advanced, Desoto-derrières jiggering. They were fair and foul empresses. I was a blasphemer whose blood flowed as wine, a king everyday, a magician, and they were my tricks. With them, I was a pilgrim at a sanctorium. They were elemental entities, devils (in hand-me-downs) possessing me. With the sponge of my derma I sopped them up. Their tendril- locks. Hair pennants in gusts. They were white like clouds. Spindly legs. Eucalyptus beings. Bellies as water tanks. Flesh like melted cheese bubbling on a griddle. Conical dimensions of their knockers. Ringlets writhing as snakes. A supplicant city. Thunder babbled. Leven slashed. Drizzle giggled. Grandfather clock chimed. Mile-long snake of passers-by slank past the wicket gate. Chuckling of footsteps. The metropolis was an egg cracking. Steam rose like an inaudible song. Showers soured the street. People's heads bobbed as butterflies. Buildings were Pandora's boxes. Mosquito-net of sprinkles. Smudges of smushed lepidopteran rainbow-speckles, the differing hues brightening the lane. The girls were children of God, with newborn integument, going on chicken-runs in our rough-and-ready pigpen, defective, acquiescent avatars of angels. A witch's brew of hormones. Hungover, I could've passed for a fiftyish fella, a homely Hamlet with a tree-beard and bird's-nest mop. Enameled figurines and contemporary art on silo-shelving. Vault with levin was graph paper. Chit-chatter mumbo-jumbo from them, tinkering with the VCR like it was an erotic game, focusing on the task, pooling their intellectual resources, each rendered exotic in my virile, febrile encephalon, wet dreams alive and well, in suits and boots, all go-go and boom-boom, limbs straight and solid as iron bars.

Their intelligence was intact, surviving, in spite of subsisting on scraps, starved of education. My plan for hanky-panky was to ride them like a carpet, cover them as a creeper in that boat-bed. The bizarre floozies were worms nibbling on my lovelorn Valentine's heart. The gals were out-of-place palms in our musty museum. Spate tinkled like chandeliers. My existence without them was a maddening eczema itch I could not scratch. Hustle-bustle hullabaloo. I was a defiler of deities. Sacred mosques of their gluteus maximi. The vista was a leviathan lavender boob filled with malign nodules of stars. Halogen lamp-eyes in glycerine-light, brains without the horsepower to properly pull their thoughts. Particolored rug was beaten, ho-humly, by Mapi, in a toga, with commendable alacrity, making a granular mizzle as winter breath blown. She sang operatically during the dirty business. The duo practiced martial arts in 'Kung Fu' television show fighting- gear jamas. A car alarm chirruped. I was pin-drop quiet. They were seeds I'd planted in a diabolism of desire. Witchcraft reproduction. They bounded like lambs, only were fish to fry. My blinkers were as lightbulbs with failing filaments. Paternally, I was not the real McCoy. I was the lowest of the low, a 'Nightmare on Elm Street.' The pair were an 'Origin of Species,' Darwinian dreams realized, mutations in extremis. Their vocalizations were like they came from a chasm. My cardiac organ played as a tabla. They were ill 'Omens,' virginal-white dual-Damiens who were Thorns in my side. Spritz corrugated the slate-gray cement. Whirring of a trash-truck juggernaut. Thrum of traffic. Screech of tires. Honk of horns. Sonorous verbalizations. In evaporating fog, the megalopolis was a present unwrapping itself. These trees with matted tops were stick-figure drawings of Medusas. Engines bleated. A chopper whupped. Syncopated footsteps. The kiddies gabbed, a corny commercial on. They were not a book I judged by the cover, it was the contents I was interested in. Their theatrical cosmetics.

Were they waters prepared to part for me? Or were they an ocean to give me up to the land? A dumb denture ad involving stupid spacemen riding bikes was on. I had dam-the-torpedoes resolve. They were in an unintended pinup pose, a cheesecake position, sulky, fish-faced. Tweetie Bird-skulls and porridge-posterns. A Mercedes limousine was a colossus which stretched forever, a Scandinavian Orson Wellesian driver with pectorals at the wheel in the survivalist city. The two were ingrately genies gone puce with brew in a magic lamp. A cutesy cookie-cereal cartoon advertisement came on. Sodding-sheet skyline was in disorienting development. They chomped on pastrami and provolone on rye. Prosties and their attendant pimps were badgered by the boys in blue. Suryan and Ananda wore midriff-showing tank tops and Daisy Dukes, lady Lucifers in hellfire emanation, wiz-kid movers and shakers with pestilential breath. I was a lazybones, not Fred Flintstone hard at work at the quarry, in meltdown mode. They were a djinn bottled by my embrace, and staggered like the Elephant Man, talked as David Carradine, elongated and tubulose, movie- native ooga-boogaing, a slate I wished to wipe clean, a spike piercing my heart. Their hands sought specific body parts, with unmistakeable intent, a passionate perversion preempting mine. Mapi fanned fumes, sulphuric smoke from the toaster much as sorceries. She was a wind-up toy in a pill-box hat on a wavy coiffure. Moonscapes of roads. Melting pot place was a shitty Shangri-La. Splendor was as liquified butter.

Mapi was a horror-flick witch sweeping with her

broomstick; or a judge with expressionist tomb-stone-teeth pronouncing sentence. Suryan and Ananda were something symbolic and slopping stew on the Yellow Brick Road of the hallway. With them, I was smoke with fire, a Prince of Darkness, slap in the center of a glass- fronted cabinet, language like lava. Stonefaced, I held my horses in the internally-illumined belly of the apartment. They were as a sacrificial offer-ing. My Himalayan hardon was a mountain for them to climb. They were wiggling Beauties dismissive of this Beast. Their Wah-wah pedal voices. Snare-drum-cracking thunder, lightning. Hip-hopping, hot-to-trot Mapi was an attractive, albeit truncated, science-fic-tion video heroine out of an apocalypse, under the influence of an accent Trinidadian, a stenchy, mutey voodoo-priestess with a ghastly, guttural modulation, a revenant grande dame, an apparition of what she was. I was told, stutteringly, by her, to groom, and I took a leap for my lover. I looked as a loco creepo hobo. I was a lowdown Ghostbuster with my zany zapper of an electric razor in our Grotesk gulag-grot, a Siberian lavatory. I trimmed and she said I treated her like a second-rate side-dish. She was as a tomboyish artiste amputee, an edifice that didn't survive an earthquake, an infuriating illuminational intermediary between mortal and immortal, an arundinaceous, anemic woman with a stammer and blind as a bat, in the short-stay padded cell accommodation. Our smooches were briefer. I wanted them to be longer. She was a dragon slain by my lovelance. She duplicated a bag lady, crunching on cashews. The twins' elephantine lumbering, a connected creature with dolls' pop-eyes, in elasticated dungarees, in the anesthesia of stifling air, a whittled, lovely lummox after a marathon of crapulous combustion in the john on the billionth floor of the complex, brilliance making everything vague. M'yeah, I brought up the rear. Earth metamorphosed into sky. I was an addict of the nymphs, and blasted on psychotropic drugs. Miniaturized configurations jostled for space. In my zombine undeath, my mind was a traitor, with a shortage of brain cells. I was Icarusoid in leisurewear and flying high without breathing apparatus, so stoned, imagining them in a fashion spread, the beautiful bergs, cover girls in combination, the frosty twosome, consumed by the flames of my feverous fantasies. They were a fort prepared for an assault by an enemy force. I went with the current, but wanted to dip into their lower depths. I was a Nabokovian Luzhin with No Defense, moving pieces adroitly on the chessboard. Mist sounded like snapping electricity. The streetlamp blinked as a rabbit in vehicular headbeams on a transformed (by construction crews) serpentiferous boulevard. I was somatically reminiscent of a virulent, murderous, maniacal Brutus, with salt-and-pepper sideburns, enwrapped in a bedsheet. It was a comic-strip version of domestic life. I'd beaten off. Masturbation is not a male cumuppance. Heck no. Ejaculation is as a dam bursting. People pandemonium. Dust-specks danced jaggedly like bugs in the brilliancy. Breezes with tones conspiratorial. Mapi, a creatrix, was a disembodied spirit needing a corporeal casing and with a falcate sneezer and snowy skin, enmeshed in a web of dependency, in facepaint and headscarf. She was a shadow (of herself), in a brumal bank, crumbling as a sandcastle, her goose cooked and with no master plan. She would show me who was boss! Rejected by her, I was one of Adam's parents, toad-squat, a cry-baby with ball-bearing testicles, expelled from the Garden by the Devil. Clothing taken, my shame was exposed in my nakedness. Sun came through cloud not unlike a cuckoo its door in slow-motion; a cosmic special-effect. My compact build. I was a vampire sucking on their lives, draining them dry. An Adam and the Ants cd sat on the stereo system. The darlings' Hong Kong Kung Phooey was rob-tickling. They glugged decaf and glommed bagels. Their softscoop icecream derma layer. Sauntering woozily, ceremoniously, as if on hot coals in our Chamber of Horrors, in a periodic bloodbath, a menstrual slaughterhouse, snide curls to their mouths, looking lugubrious in the hornets' nest (not exactly a designer-chic flat), dressed in collegial attire: buttoned blazers, blue jeans, and loafers, the layabout ladies with seek-and-destroy glowers. I gave them the third degree, in an impromptu interrogation, with specific strategic points interspersed, me wanting to know where they were off to. Mum was the word, conveyed with world-weariness. A top-of-the-bill song-and-dance show-stopper of beating-around-the-bush. Would they dare to leave me high and dry?

Wifey, distraught, was submersing into a chariot-chair by the pickup truck bathtub, in a beryl burqa and rubbing her stumps in the lavatory, like she was waiting for her limbs to materialize. Hocus pocus. Abracadabra. Nada. Nothing hunky-dory there. Air conditioner was out of commission. I half-expected to see macaws in coco-palms and insectile coronas over psychedelic flowers in the tropicalized rental. I was a spider monkey on the make. Distrait Mapi. Watching Suryan and Ananda, disserting dissidents, was a spectator sport. They played on the silver screen of my gray matter, talking up a storm, sounding as bleeping signals, and thus subtitles were necessary. My infatuation was a homing instinct. They were a full-tilt heatwave, a provisional and petrifying sun, zaniest of occultists, creating these impure irregularities in my brain and body. I was a threadbare, down-at-heel dad. Their nails sparkled like nails. Their ruby slippers were too snug. Pens, to them, banging out sonnets of unrequited love, were as swords. I lived, lawless and landless. Mapi, radish- white, was defiantly undimmed. Heavy lacing and fluffy head of my malty, medicinal stout clung to the snifter like its life depended on it. Her crow-feather eyebrows. She was a using, bitter chatterbox with bees in her bonnet, sitting splay-legged on a beanbag seat and sinking, oceanically suspirant, tongue out, racked by phantom pains in her nubs, her existence as though it was a desert with dunes of problems, the sands of excuses blowing. I was a wretched loser on the euphoriants of the sisters Siamesed, prone before their mom, me engaged in ass-kissery, degrading myself, a sniveling supplicant in ulcerative discomfort, feeling like a chicken with its gizzard slit. I chewed on a pickle in its penine detumescence, my cerebellum a catacomb of confusion. I was an adept eavesdropper, deft in my listenings-in. The twins laryngitic-buzzard voices could raise your hackles. Their tambourine-sounding pissing on the pimped-out pot. Mapi pugnacious with her porcine lamps. Ascribed to her subpar vision, she claimed her daughters were superimposed shadows. I fed the monster, in a den of depravity, sequestered from the world beyond, far-flung, in dawn and dusk. I did my body-building exercises. She oiled herself and danced for me, twisting herself into a pretzel, eyes blazing. I sat silently in a wickerwork chair, which was the dog house for me, viewing her without twitching a muscle, that is until I cupped my genitals, feeling like a Nazified, bushy-bearded brothel-keeper. I whimpered. They were as filles de joie and I was their procurer. Mapi countenanced my fructified serenade, only preferred to listen to her top 40 bubblegum bullshit, professing herself bored stiff, even with my comedy routine of perfect imperfection, her uneasiness earning me a sensation of emotional waterboarding. My chest was bedeviled, my heart demonically pounding.

The sun was a thumb's print on the glassy sky. Atmosphere was inseminated by dankness. Compulsively Mapi channel-surfed with a 'Star Trek'- phaserish remote-control pointed at the set, riveted to sitcom reruns, her caliginous cave-trap opened. To coitally cohere, hold her head like Eros the globe ... Vermicular clouds fed on the rotting meat of heaven. Made-up, she looked as a mime, decked out like Prince at a bar mitzvah. I was a wound. She was the salt. With chiclets clamped, she cooled her jets, and the quarrel concluded itself. I belted a beer, garbed in an outrageous 1970s-style tracksuit, in waters uncharted. I read her as a book. The kiddos got ready for karate class, crudely imitating Kane - clones of the character, in the cocoon-cooperative. I always got double-vision with them. In the otherplanetary under-city, Black Panthers confronted White Supremacists. Fraudulent fuckers. Bluesy African American chants. Caucasian picketers. Racism flowed not unlike a river. Sweltering season. An Eastern Indian geezer got into his taxicab. Those participants acted as extras on a Shepperton Studios soundstage of a big-budgeted Dickensian London. My marital illusions were glass-shattered. My schmenzer was a pelagic thing erupting out of the sea of my sweatpants. My stupendous cock and dwarven dickbag. Mapi was a Mephistophelian partner. She patted her nauseously aggrieved abdomen, a buttocky gut, in the buff and blushed, behaving like she was making preparations for a criminal caper, Suryan and Ananda her greenhorn underlings. She was laid back, in the raw, in the arena of our apt., coping with withdrawal symptoms from the quaaludes. She was a bendy Transylvanian vampiress. She was quarantined in her interstellar space. She was contemptuous, disdained my company. Outside our waterlogged curiosity shop condominium was dryice peasoup. Inside, I chugged serpent's venom tequila, my legs parting as the Red Sea for my genitalial Child of Israel. I was a smashed and stoned Iago in full-blooded excitement and in purgatory in perpetuity. I was Punch wanting to bang Judy. This Hadrian's Wall was between us. My wantonness was set off like a fuse. Locust-swarming primal Union rioters were down on the docks. Touraco-colored rainbow. Toupees of hydrae afloat on blue-green aqua pura. The wharf had a Mapi- on-the-rag fetidness.

Underage brown sugars street-strolled in high heels. Scotch shots quaffed. The conjoined cuties, angelic adolescents, cursed at and complained to everyone within earshot; their manipulative modus operandi. I would chase the six-foot ice maidens as a flies. Roller blading, their progress painful, in secretarial trappings, they suggested spreading trees on wheels, in imminent danger of (ignorantly) inflicting their lingual intimacies, a pidginized lingo, on us. My voyeurism was vigorous. My desirousness disgusted me. I yielded to erotic rhapsodies (in/on their remotest recesses), my attraction unacceptable, as they sat on a BMX bike, taking a spin round the Trafalgar Square room and reciting a rhyme. Mapi was on the verge of a nervous breakdown, marooned in misery. I was a red-eyed, runty Crusoe, train of thought de- railing, going off the tracks altogether. Our progeny were Pied Pipers leading me to perversion with an unsavory song, a tempting tune. They were K2s to conquer. Their viscous voxes and supple skin. I was cocked and loaded. My rocket was ready to launch. The place was a schoolyard playground for them. My high- pitched dial tone tinnitus was insufferable. Parachutes of jellyfish were adrift. In my voluminous, faux Armani I was like a mini-bellhop on the bleeding edge in a lousy lock-up. Their maturing slate mustaches, cheerleader rallying calls. They were matchsticks with klieg-light oculuses in a mutinous one-piece swimsuit and orange espadrilles in a shadowland. The wind had picked up the meteorological mantle and rain had dropped. My offspring: mirror images of one another.

The road to decency was impassably obstructed by

indecency. I skulked in the gravied gloaming, my maniacal mouth opening like a drawbridge. I looked in on
Suryan and Ananda. Their baying in merriment. I was
haggard. I was flushed. They had on towel-turbans and
scarlet teddies, gaunt arms and legs waggling, lounging on the queen-sized bed and painting crescentiform
fingernails, larval toes Rockette-kicking, in a cracked
conception of an empyreal continent. Childish comical-
ity. Raucous hilarity. They pecked and petted as if they
were blind. I was not deaf to their sighs. My lust was
intensified by my love for them. It was a truly fortunate mishap, winding up with them, like a fellow who
catches fire and runs, the guy tripping and rolling, when
that is exactly the method to follow in such a situation.
Air was drum-tight. Gloom tightened and slackened. I
scratched an insistent itch on my acned cheek as block
of cheese on a grater. Nonsensical vernacular to these
hearing organs. Lunatic slanguage. Their ceremonious
discussion required a peculiar glossary for the idiosyncratic jargon. A candle's teary flame trickled upward.
Their economical movements were typical of siblings
who're connected. Whinnies. Semaphores of supplication. Shame sliced through my shriveled scrotum. Their
crotch-clouds. The evening was a dark glop dragged by a
prodigious mollusk. Deluge clicked. A storm is nature's
spectacular show. The girls caught me. I was busted.

In the cubbyhole of a bathroom, Mapi, in polka dot
panties, matching brassiere and striped stocking,
canted, as though menstrually cramped, on the toilet.
She mumbled, clipped curled, hoary roses that looked
like they were fetuses. She was a damaged organ. Our

children's cells tried to repair it/her. Her serpentine neck shivered. Liquid purling in the pipes. Footfall sounds on creaky stairs. Tenants argued. Of a sudden, murmuring, she doubled over and vomited an umbilical cord, which slithered into her vagina like a noodle sucked off a plate and into an oral cavity. She was alive with deadness.

In an incubatorish elevator, Mapi was high and drunk. She hopped and dropped onto her knee to unzip my stubborn fly. I was chilled in horny febrility. Our chemistry was a chemical reaction.

Slab of a table. Suryan and Ananda, with an uppity, dignified reticence, ate steak and drank fruit punch with the scrutable discretion of the illustrious, and deliberately ignoring me. The intrepidity of the haughty post- pubescent pelicans was impressive. Mapi, muttering, spacey, speared a cocktail's olive using a toothpick. Sun, in cirrus, was as if it was trying to be born. Fulgent funiculi. I was paralyzed by their presence, and shook as though from stage fright; or an epileptic fit. I was scared stupefied, a holey kite hanging from their stringy arms, burbles made by their vocal chords rippling outwards like stones were thrown into a stream. Drencher was as corrosive acid. Their sturdy legs were swords sheathed in cord-scabbards. Their birdie-beaked, fascinating faces, trumpety snorting, fluting flatus, the stepping desultory sequences, wine-blurred eyes glaring. Skeeters traced out a series of rhomboids. Distantness of a variegated horizon was beheld from the miscarriage of a pantry, where bluebottles made these parallelograms, my cranium migrainously bursting, feeling struck. I reeked as a wino in the gutter. I took the melon cube from a tray in the fridge. The Siamese numphets were megastars at their savage apex, thorn-bushes visible, in tricks of light, with their sick-sounding gurgles.

Abattoir of azure. Intestinal cumuli. The giant humpbacks, Suryan and Ananda, were wearing trapper hats and dressed in tweed coats, flannel shirts, hunting trousers, and Dutch clogs, and swung along the sidewalk like grounded trapezists, utilizing perplexed pedestrians as handles. With their undaunted pomposity and determination, they had forsaken lurching through youth culture - the style and slang, popular logos and pop groups, with an MTV trajectory, you know, reader, the quick cuts, flashes (in the) pans, and clueless collages, to navigate across life in their own way, mocking fads of any type. Their baggy rigging billowed not unlike sails. They ran away from our septic-smelly, soggy slump of a residence, the cloudbusting building so labyrinthine you'd go when you wanted to come and come when you wanted to go, due to my improper interest in them, and they hooked up with Cy Cinch's circus. In my corpuscle Camry I cruised the arteries of avenues in the anatomic metropolis that was atrophied.

Grainy coruscation waved as wheat in winds. Laurels and lindens were lined like weapons in an armory. A corroded camper was propped on cinderblocks, with a town of tents in the background. Umberous sky. A buxom, pilose female, an epicene Bluto, kept in a corset, played an accordion on a merry-go-round. An elfin boy in a Nutcracker soldier costume decorated beeches and birches with Xmas trinkets. An elderly, elephantoid male in an ill-fitting Santa Claus outfit, squatted as a sumo and had a BM in the tinseled shrubbery of the wide field. He grunted, crapped copiously, and pointed to this triangular window, muslin- curtained, giving me permission to go over there. Humongous reindeer humped. Suryan and Ananda were ensconced in a saggy and stitchy electric chair and strummed this Jimmy Pagean dual-necked Les Paul guitar, with an audience of a stunned motley assemblage of mutations: midgets, pinheads, hunchbacks, trolls, Rasta vampiras, gummous gargoyles, lizardine ladies, ogres and ogresses, drag queens, transvestic geeks, clowns, munchkins, ape men, and goth-chicks galore, along with their dedicated disciples. A lanate, mammoth hermaphrodite, a human Mothra, pulled on Suryan's pigtails and Ananda cried, whereupon Ananda inhaled from a stunted cigar and Suryan exhaled a cellophane pompon of smoke. Sawdust winked like little stars.

In a separate trailer, in conditions deplorable, Cy Cinch, with a combover, lasagna-complected and lantern-jawed, covered in long johns, his wattles ruddied and his goatee straggly, was, by all accounts, cyanide- saccharine, a Snidely Whiplash-esque, slave-driving son-of-a-bitch. He counted stacks of bills and coins and changed into a drab tee and sullied boxers. I saw way too much. Clouds were torn to ribbons. Tangerine- tinged celestial sphere. My gaze festered on the gals, wrestling, starkers, in a kiddie-pool filled with chocolate pudding, an androgynous referee keeping close tabs on the contest. Concatenated turnout's applause came from the stands.

Cinch was Hitler-hysterical. I was a loaded pistol with the safety off.

Thankfully, they didn't need much convincing to return home with me. As a precautionary measure, better to be safe than sorry, I narrated a sorrowful, sensationalistic story, tugging on their heartstrings, not pushing my luck though, letting them in on their mom's predicament. Grudgingly, they accepted my apologies for my reprehensible behavior, but the fire of my contaminated inclinations still flickered. I was a convalescent convinced he was cured. They were enthroned in the palace of my chest, my cardiac organ tom-tom beating. My moralistic distance from them was commensurable with my mortal distance from them. I was bound to assent to the dictates of my conscience. My soul was a smithy on a speedball. Their conker-eyes, conchoidal ears. The wacky, wingless flamingos, so solitary, deviated from the obligation of socialization. I dreamt they were split apart.

Bludgeon of sun. Quivery, atrocious air. It was a sultry forenoon. On the pier, the sisters, burning in poetical creation, contained in tankinis and sandals, abruptly collapsed. They were strapped onto a stretcher and put into an ambulance and driven to a nearby hospital.

The doctor, a garrulous grampus, wig a frightful nimbus, explained, in detail, that the twins needed to be surgically separated because of internal complications in order for one to have the best chance at survival. Split in two. I thought of train tracks breaking apart ...

Ananda died during the operation. I pictured them together when I was told she didn't make it. Suryan lost her right limbs. Mapi and I were in shock. Destroyed. After Ananda had passed, I felt assembled incorrectly, like a dinosaur's bones "restored" inaccurately by a moronic paleontologist. Was it punishment given to me by fate's justice?

In our sterile joint, Suryan was behind Mapi, chin on her mother's shoulder, as they, in curious concert, ironed clothes on the praying mantis board. Suryan become Mapi's vital component and vice versa. An at once simple and sophisticated symmetry was supplied. They were a couple halves of a whole. I evinced a Heathcliff-on-the-moors vibe. The tiny windows were squinty. I was terse.

The beach was an Empire of the Sun. Sky was greasy pork and cirri were clumps of fat. Wavering light-beams were pellucid steps leading up to serrate summits. Drafts' insufflations. Sugary sand. Partially revealed seashells were harmless landmines. Soughing surf. Kelp was vert hair. A fading Mapi and flourishing Suryan, in Palm Springs cover-up dresses, lounged on a Bugs Bunny and Daffy Duck towel, looking like maimed mannequins, or broken beanpoles. They applied numerically-high UV cream on one another. They were mutilated: a match made in heaven. Mapi became obsessed with anatomical twos - eyes, ears, nostrils, arms, hands, legs, feet, testicles and buttocks. Unreality had supplanted reality.

Mapi, in a broad band of mid-morning glimmer, breathed stertorously. Her pings and pangs were as an invisible invading horde. She stared at my nuts and vanished, leaving her coquettish Cheshire Cat (that lapped the cream) grin. Hers was a narcotized confidence. It disintegrated.

Bedraggled like a beggar, Mapi, in early-afternoon glitter, grieved. Her mush was a pathetic pasquinade of despondency, tongue in her mouth as a turtle's head in its shell. She examined the scrunch of her punani with nicotine-stained, tweezered fingers. Women have genitalic singularity. I was tripping on acid. A disembodied brain bled on the counter. The head: single-mindedness?

The cemetery was Hell on Earth. Mapi's casket was lowered into her grave. Many mourners mingled after the eloquent service. The podgy pastor's emotional bibling had masculine and feminine tones. Her injuries and illnesses had finally taken their toll. Modern medicine and science were able to buoy her for so long before she sank. The funeral was depressing. I took a hit of mescaline.

I saw my anorexic wife everywhere following her demise - a spectral version of her, posed on a mattress and fiddling with her privates, Kevlar'd roaches clambering on her triathlete-trim thigh and crescentoid calf in cribbage-peg precipitation on a pavement-board, the window washer spurting not unlike blood from a cut artery. Mapi's expression was a delicate design in a foreign fabric of features; a miniature, plasticine Mapi in a ballerina's pirouette-posture, spinning slo-mo in a snow globe, the flakes a powdery aureola; on a curb, an ursine Eastern Indian, his rhinocerine assistant beside him, piped up, and a limbless, snaky Mapi, scaly from stem-to-stern, slithered out of the wicker basket, its lid now her hat, hissing, her pink tongue forked. Her physog was funhouse mirror warped. Hither and thither I went.

In the putrefied playroom, puppet corpses and chrysalid costumes were strewn about. I paced to and fro, blasted on meth. A Dalmatian puppy sphinxianly subsided on a pyramid of pillows. It licked its sphincter and anorectic Suryan's Adam's apple - forbidden fruit. Our mutual loss was feeling as a razor's nicks, with delayed bleeding, the burning and stinging sensations after, not during, shaving. Destiny had killed two birds with one stone. Is fate communicable, like a contagion? On the Saudi Arabian rug we cuddled beneath a blanket watching the trivial gogglebox. We were buck naked. Our existence was black and white. The dictionary's definition: pertaining to, or consisting of, a two-valued system, as of logic, mortality, and so forth. I seized her pouchy tit, the abduction like a kidnapping. She scrabbled on all twos, squishy ass splayed, exposing her roseate, excrementitious pucker. She had a doc's air, that is, she was on an even keel. Was she unsympathetic? With Mapi and Ananda alive, I felt as a customer in a queue outside the cinema, waiting to purchase tickets; whereas with just Suryan, I was a VIP escorted inside and given my choice of seat. The impact of my partner and daughter's deaths ... my grief found consolation in memories. A cloud of contentment neutralized the illumination of bereavement. My hope for Suryan's total recovery was like a bum praying a wealthy person would bequeath him money. At last, I decided my new life would carry nothing from the old one. There would be a definitive divider.

I experienced a terrifying nightmare - I wept, my tears turning into unsightly babies, funicles flowing out of every somatic orifice. There were shadowy performances, and these silhouette sagas, playing out on masonry walls. I saw my reflection in a mirror. I'd transmuted into a bodiless bazoom with an acorn-nipple and eyelet- gloriole. Was there any symbolic significance to it? Maybe ...

In the zoo's aquarium, Venus the killer whale swam. She was as this surfacing sub, Nemo's Nautilus, perhaps, telescopic fin carving swiftly through the aquamarine water. The end was beginning. I was like some pitiful penguin in a tuxedo. Suryan had on a dark dress. We stripped, me in proximity to the bald eagles, and her in the vicinity of those ostriches, miserable in their cages. Pandas slept soundly. We freed only the B&W animals. Macilent Suryan put on a latex cap. She reminded me of a prepuce covered in a rolled rubber. I glanced at her pallid pot and scarabaeoid navel. I noticed the glaring contrast between her dyed ebon pubic patch and pale flesh ... Our garms made the ying and yang sign. She was the Virgin. I was Jesus. Venus was the Hand testing the pool's temperature for our final bath. Check that ... I was Abraham, Suryan my only child, Venus the Ram. Stark nude, we held each other and slid into the uterine cavity where life itself is conceived and nurtured. The orca came for us at a clip. The start of the finish. For me, white faded to black. For her, black blended with white.

Then it was nothingness for both of us. Black and white were a successful fusion. I was reborn, colorblind.

FIN.

Eye-Opener

Once upon a time, there was a Weasel who stole the eyes from children in this village so he could see the world the way they did - with innocence. One sunny day, he accidentally took the eyes of a blind boy, who had been swimming in the pond with his sister, and thus lost his vision altogether. It was a rainy night when he sought out the Devil, who had a goat's head, man's body, girl's hands, and horse hooves, living in a hut on the top of a mountain, and asked him if his sight could be restored. The Devil answered that a deal could be made: his vision would be given to him, but the price to pay would be the loss of a loved one. The Weasel agreed, his sight returned, only to watch his mother slowly die from a sickness. He went back to the Devil .... to find out he was an optical illusion.

FIN.

Big Bertha

Cloudypubic cuntysky throbs, ejaculating rainy cum. The hippo-gray empyrean thunderously rumbles, pulls on sheets of lightning, and sleeps soundly. The day breathes in and dives into the humidity. The Gehennal city is a place of crazy and congested buildings, stalactitic edifices suffocated in ashen smog. This is a wild and wicked underworld; a hive with buzzing humanity; an industrialized Twilight Zone surrounded by a vast veil of cinereal sea. The metropolis, seen from a distance, reader, resembles an immense and idling iguana. Globby sun. Glowworm drizzle. Illumination is apparently sown by a cosmic seamster. A defunct bridge appears to bow ceremoniously, as if being knighted. Amidst mountainous garbage, reeking of countless corpses, in wounded-wraith fog, and amongst a sluggard stream of almost apoplectic insects, an antennal, supernatural squall, sprawled on the dented hood of a gutted van, are two girls in their tender, wayward teens, best of friends, oil and water, basically, polar opposites in terms of personality, but both poetically poor, like gamines in a Victorian novel, down-and-out ingenues surviving in style: sweet and sort of shy Mylene, laid back to the point of being supine, customarily walking as though she's going through a swamp, her somewhat slumped posture suggesting a chided youth, sepia-skinned, fascinatingly feral, knee-bucklingly, gypseanly gorgeous, with a faddy, underfed body, pear-breasts, foxy face, aquiline nose, moth-hued, Cupid's bow-mouth, expressive brow, exquisitely Nutcracker-soldier-lined, leonine, messy mane, saucer-ears, maple syrup-brown cat's eyes, luxuriant lashes, and weak-tea-colored, crooked teeth, and very precocious and unpredictable Estelle, with numerous professionally-diagnosed mental issues, clinically mild-to-serious, a psychiatric hospital habitue, outdoorsily terra cotta tanned, bony and ugly, at once masculine and feminine, her greasy, gollywoggy mop centrally parted. They huff the heck out of aerosol cans they'd found when digging in the dump, wearing dirty dresses and cross-trainer sneakers. There are dulcimer-strings of precip and breath-note breezes. Trolleys hiss on wires. Cardiac arrhythmia of vehicular engines. Mylene's lanuginous, lovely, lean legs swing, while Estelle's mannish, beanpole-skinny ones make treading-water motions. Their nostrils look frosting-glazed. They're high as hell. Hail's brittle like uncooked macaroni. Continual urban clamor.

"This shithole is constantly coming," Mylene says, strokes the fine fur on her thin forearms. She's dazed, like she was in a car accident.

"You are wacky," Estelle replies, picking the seepy pellicular scabs on her knurly knees. She is agitated, as if she had boarded a plane and realized she forgot her carry-on bag. Arenose gusts.

"Listen - heroin from a hypo, milk a bottle, gas a hose, fumes an exhaust ..."

"Semen from a penis!"

"Yuck!"

"I'm experiencing severe adenoidal stinging."

"T-minus zero and counting into menstruous cycle sync ..."

"Aqua Net crap sucks balls."

"I am importantly fucked up."

"My, you are a babe."

"Ha! You're just wasted!"

Estelle suddenly slides off, and slowly, sensually, teasingly strips, brazenly snake-sloughing her clothes to her filthy begonia boxsies and bra. She's androgynously angular, an upright, overused broom, glides as though she's a figure-skater, mouse-peepers fastened to Mylene, flushes flourishing on her carved, argillaceous cheeks, and finally settles on an uneven stack of worn tires, the action reminding Mylene of a bee bathing itself before flying into a flower. Her sighs sound like silken articles of clothing tugged quickly from flesh. She momentarily disappears into the inky shade as a cuttlefish, and whispers, "Hold my hips ... My oxheart asshole ... Kind of ... Hurts, honey ..." And she rises like smoke from a hotspot. Mylene struggles to smile, examines her buddy as an art connoisseur would the work of a Renaissance master, blushing like she was just castigated. She's a sapling with its branches wrapped around itself, edgy laughter expectorated from her luscious lips. She swallows hard, perspires as a leaf emanating pollen, slumps like a broken ladder, voltage charging up and down her spine, belly rippling as a basin struck by a pebble, anatomic shivers not unlike itches she's got to scratch. She beams, beacon-blinds her chum, blown away as an untied balloon in wind, a fuzzy taste in her oral cavity, her whirlpool hearing organs dragging in the drowning soughs. Estelle has degraded herself in order to exhibit herself. Mylene cannot resist drifting into the perimeter of Estelle's odor of combined spoiled sardines and damp rope. She sediment-subsides on some trash bags, Mylene does, begins boldly playing with herself, expression like a juror's on a trial, gazing at Estelle, near-naked, the hoiden's boyish buttocks with their pimply, pilose, flabby orbicularities, reptilian feet with their mussel-blue veins, wide pies at odds with her narrow face. The desirable delinquent dolly and her sawing-sounding laugh! The stone of a grin breaks the perfect pane of Mylene's ocelotic countenance. Her intestinal piping burbles, blindbeggar fingers nervously, amorously reading herself as Braille. Sexy, scrawny, scarecrowish Estelle's armpits smell of saturated bark, throbs akin to a tuning fork, penetrating her bottom's rose digitally, ignoring her shadow and its fugacious fidelity. Fiddling with herself, she is like a perfumer fussing with a block of fat. Mylene, for some unknown reason, considers the anatomical truth that the anus is an exit, not an entrance. Whines bloom as blossoms on stems of speech. The muscles in Mylene's stomach contract in a passionate ache, ardently assessing Estelle's curly bush below, firm bosom above, and bud of navel in between. She imagines the impaled pink orifice behind. Excitement is a gravitational force she cannot resist.

In proximity to a defunct nitrogen factory is Mylene's cowering, claustrophobic, low-income, drivewayless house, essentially a misshapen shack, shared with her self-absorbed, shovel-and-poker-faced, diminutive, occasional father, Denis, pale as the faintest memory, looking like an electrocuted anthropoidal Pomeranian, his buzzcut partially grown in, as if he's been A.W.O.L. from the army for a bit. Mylene genetically inherited his unbelievable laziness and her R.I.P.-ing mother's implausible prettiness. She is a lost leaf hanging from the familial tree. The home's exterior has paint peeling and creeping vegetation here and there. A tireswing dangles lonelyly from an old oak. Laundry's lynched on lines. Litter hippety-hops on the khaki lawn. Neighborly noise. An ancient pineboard fence is collapsing. Rorschach shrubs. Mangled bike and rusted grill in the piebald junkyard. Windows' screens are ripped aluminumal rinds. Ratty mat on the decrepit porch welcomes visitors in fading broad letters. Acorns are shells from a fired gun. The interior is under the unshakable spell of neglect and's dank and a disaster and reeks of a brothel. Wainscoting bearhugs the coffinous rooms where cockroaches and dustbunnies roam at will. Meager monstrous furniture. It is as though the pigpen bears animosity towards its tenants. The weather is currently so clear the Doppler Radar would show probably nothing. Air has an ammonial tang to it. Clouds swirl like they are stirred by an imperceptible, huge spoon, move as material through a digestive tract. Tranquility teems with the essence of a great gasp. Then it pours buckets, barrels, the deluge an argental mantilla, rattles not unlike oxygen through an asthmatic's bronchial tubes. Now, Denis, dogged in his lassitude, disheveled in a foul flannel shirt and dingy dungarees, comatose after his regular haunt-haunting, collapsed on the henna couch, rummage sale purchased years ago, in the hideous parlor, stertorously suspires, boomingly snores, out cold, by the antediluvian television on its swiveling base. The boiler in the basement sounds as a progressive closure of the glottis. Grubby curtains are sizable dragonfly wings. He's an inert emperor in his slovenly harem. Drone of conservative talk is on the transistor radio. Her insides bacon-sizzle. Her blood fizzles. She is disappointed. Frigging furious. The son-of-a-bitch swore he'd never drink alcohol again. He lied! His erection tents his denim. Exasperated, she glares at him, traces the scratches and scrapes on her slender wrists. She wants to melt like an ice cube on a stove's burner. Bastard. She's tense as a drawn bow. He's cunning like a contagion. Her heart pumps as a piston.

The other evening, he was solidly sober, cuddled with her on the crunchy sofa, and clung to her like a limpet to a rock. An unbridgeable gap's between them. Pushpull struggle is happening. Air has an astringent flavor. In the narrow bathroom, with its framed photos of folks, Mylene, seated on the toilet, goes #s 1 + 2. She meticulously rubs her PMS-pained abdomen. She crouches, as if in a confessional, rays of lambency like the pillars of flame which spearheaded the Hebrews, the luminosity giving the dull tiling an erratic epidermis. She methodically stands, grabbing the towel-rack, distributing her weight on grungy, floppy feet. She's an extremely private person when it comes to peeing and pooping. The luminescence hacks arbitrarily. Thoughts of Estelle get up as an audience in ovation. She has power over Mylene, can command her like an officer a recruit. To a certain extent Mylene feels bad for her, as you would for a strong and optimistic individual who loves her country and goes to war for it, only to discover the cause of it is weak, the bloodshed not worth it, the price to pay too high, and returns with a negative opinion of her nation. To put it simply, Mylene was initially impressed with her, even infatuated, until she got to know her better, witnessing the bizarre behavior, watching the crime waves, affecting her overall opinion. In addition, she heard about her getting installed in various mental institutions, thus enhancing her uncertainty when it comes to her; however, she's intensely, inexplicably attracted to her, total tomboy though she is. Mylene, the prior dried up riverbed, has been refilled by the torrential Estelle, who misbehaves like a monkey, gut-instinct guiding her conduct. Her antics draw the lines of her sketchy personality. Her laugh can chill your teeth, as if you're chewing on ice-chips. And she can insult with impunity! Mylene remembers their first fling, with Estelle attempting to mount her like she was a filly who resisted being saddled, never mind ridden. Estelle was a wave crashing on the swimmer of Mylene. Her words were so calming and seductive they covered her as though kisses. She enveloped her like clothing ... Chiaroscuro scuttles as nuns in a hurry. Effulgence tugs tenaciously on shade. A fan choo-choo chugs. Sheeny mags on the horrid sink riffle because of the clammy mistrals. Unidentifiable liquid's in a Bozo the Clown cup on the shelf. Mylene has musical scores of cuts on her muscular thighs and a monitor's brainwaves on her convex calves. Her urination and defecation's copious. Hydraulically she swipes her bum, her hand like it's magnetized, her free one on the radiator as if it's on an executioner's chopping-block. She turns on the tap to wash with a bar of soap and the plumbing pules. Hawkers sell stuff. Feeling like she's splitting apart at the seams; or crumbling into particles. She recollects her parents' marriage, disintegrating into conjugal warfare, and she was the casualty. Her sorrow is replaced by anger. She sneezes and wipes her pointy proboscis, Cyranosed due to Estelle's inadvertent elbow earlier, with a Kleenex. Her down-to-earthery, tall and beautiful mother contracted a common strain of marital indifference, a resilient, virulent virus, the germs breeding quickly, creating a vicious disease she could never succeed in bringing under control. The antique grandfather clock's hands are in a position of prayer. Nature's tyranny of weather; thunder prophesies lightning. Firmament's open-sesame. Megapolis is in its gestational process. Serpentine semis slink on the blacktop highway. Soaker crackles as though a radio. Diamonds, rubies and turquoises of refulged condensation drops. Place's deodorized with Lysol spray. Denis is a soused soliloquist, a runty reprobate, down on his luck, sedentary like a pickle-jar on a shelf, with ticcy blinders and twitchy mouth, a compact Caliban fond of alky, built as a professional wrestler, laugh sounding like a niagara, monologues usually booze-affected. A good-for-nothing schlub, with that poisonous smirk, he can be a saint or a devil. A raspberry, boomingly loud, crashes out of his rectum with this accompaniment of a vinegary-pungent belch, the flatulent odor overpowering, and reeking of casualty ward. Beginning blush of a rash on her belly. Memories of her folks rise to the surface of her consciousness as sea beasts and subside back into the deeps of her subconsciousness. Cobwebs in corners. Dust on surfaces. Teak door. Low desk. She is left in a state of extreme exhaustion.

Oculi-panes are in their sunken sockets. Leven flitters not unlike lights flicked off and on by a mischievous kid. It pauses, as if gathering itself before striking again. The thunder sounds as a tub being filled fast. Megalopolis is cracked like an aged, astronomical pot. Racings of urchin, running roundandround, through the market, steaming vendors giving chase. Whirlwinds of activity. Wondrous whirligigs. Hundreds of shoppers stream, crowd through. Moon's a slowly draining blister. Mylene is sluggish, as though she is a fly winter was easy on,

listless yet limber, pulling a hit-and-run on the refrigerator, and mad-dashes up the moaning and groaning
stairs in a stompy gait, shedding her henley, corduroys
and classic clogs, left in a burgundy faux-layer crew and
fuchsia jockeys. In her attic cubbyhole of a shipwreck
of a room, sparsely furnished, hastily decorated, and
epileptic with tale-telling penumbrae, candle-caused,
she chances upon a morbidly obese (ton-plus), naked,
headless woman, 5'6" (give or take) in all directions,
with abundant fat, billowing rolls, sallow integument
unblemished, ensconced in the corner below a webby
tent pitched by some unaccounted-for spider, sitting
on her humongous, cellulitic haunches, massive leg-
of-lamb legs curled kittenishly, enormous playground
slide arms straight out like a sleepwalker's in some
melodrama, sagging stomach sopping with unguinous
diaphoresis, tiny tootsies, with their toenails bitten to
the ragged quick, encarmined. Mylene hesitates by the
mortal mesa, staring at the luminous girth, enduring
the sensation she's hallucinating, having an out-of-body
experience, respirations sounding like an auto's airbag
continuously activated, and shivering as a wet dog shaking itself off after a dip. Horrified, she wonders whether
she should scram ASAP. Instead, she covers her mouth
with a palm and dams the digestive matter from surging out. She has gotta go potty once more. Her mouth
is a heat grate. The physical disparity between them is
a hilarious humdinger. The freaky behemothic lady is
flushed, like from a recent sexual event, sweat streak-
ing the jaundiced suet, the grotesque derma layer as a
mega mound of melted wax, her bald vagina smelling of

sewer. Crickets chirrup. Mylene shrieks violin-scratch-ily. Is she crackers, belong in a camisole de force, that is, straitjacket? Her screech is one of sheer terror. She hums best-of lullaby hits to calm herself, trembling electrically, mesmerized by this thing in its gargantuan glory, not your dime-a-dozen bulk, with its nasty vanilla/carrion redolence. Mylene is migrainously tortured. Her head feels like a log chopped into splinters by a sharp axe. She walks shadow-silently, facial expression as a child's at a toy store window, the shop's wares displayed, and enticingly. Repulsed by this ridiculous monster, she spits an inept giggle of incredulity. And an echoic, gale-force guffaw erupts from it, the preposterous, pitted, infan-tinely lactescent blubber jelly-jiggling. Ever-cautious, Mylene cautiously approaches, wincing on account of the intense body odor, her heart pounding, and carefully peers through the severed neck-hole. Piously bowed, she observes a woman's platter-sized head with these sloe, sargasso blinkers, obelisk-shaped snout, simian smile showing way more puce gums than corn-yellow teeth, in a pink lozenge oral cavity, with its labial paste and salivary bubbles. She breathes laboriously, like from hay fever. Her hog-jowls, pudendal-cleft chin, chicken wat-tles dewlap, motorcycle-wheel-proportioned ears, frizzy corona of shock with a high-protein luster, bouncing as a rubber ball, cyclonically cackling in the lardy hollows. Her flabby arms warning-wave like the Robot's from 1960s TV's 'Lost in Space.' Mylene's got to relieve her bowels and bladder urgently. She wants to burst into tears. Motionless, it's as if she's moving, like she's on an escalator. Noticing the olethreutidal-browngray welkin.

"I'm Big Bertha!" The monstrosity says in falsetto, as though the announcement will render crap A-ok, her pensile throat skirtswishing, and she adds, "I promise won't harm you! Honest Injin! It's gospel-true!" "Yikes!" Mylene replies. She is stunned into submission, incapacitated by dread.

"I am a brain fairy here to help you."

"All ... Right ..."

"... Especially with your studies." Bertha harrumphs and in mellifluous tones says, "Hey, we're mere pieces in a cosmic game of Chinese checkers and -"

"I'm gonna puke." Mylene cuts her off and wavers like a straw in gusts and barfs into the porcelain throne. "Don't do that!" Bertha tilts starboard and unleashes sickening farts. "I'm aware you've since flunked out of school." More gross gaseity. "Losing your way is hard. It is harder to find it again."

Mylene's attendance has been, admittedly, sporadic. She felt as an identityless, impactless cog in the grinding educational contraption. She's utterly unique, flaky-folksy, roughly recherche, a quacky duck, and, as a repercussion, she was mercilessly harassed, persistently harried by the scholastic masses. For Christ's sake! She felt like sand sifting through the fingers of the institution. Students in the corridor were as tenpins in an alley, she the bowling ball. "Uh ... Um ... Erm ..."

"Your occasional education, learning disability, have given you much frustration," Bertha, "I will be your tourguide on the street of the straight and narrow, so stop surrendering to a slacker's lifestyle and cut the cake and get your delicious derrière in gear by cramming like crazy to graduate in order to attend college to attain a career and meet a mate and get pregnant and give birth to babies at a rapid rate -"

"But I'm dumb as a dumbbell," Mylene, who has a useless grin, as someone smiling while emailing.

"An inconvenience, darling." A juicy, stinky, gaseous detonation. Her dimpled, porcine posterior looks pellet-riddled. She sighs like a somnambulist. "You ain't bright but you do shine!" Nasty genitalic noisomeness. Mylene sniffs the whiff of possible change. "I'm about to blow chunks."

Seismic whooping. Bertha rises and lurches and the residence pitches this way and that, and she tot-toddles, huffing and puffing in the application of moving, roly-poly and pigeon-toed and waddling on ludicrously dainty foots which clash with her formidable dimensions. She jabs Mylene in the solar plexus, barely missing her cute navel. "Start studying, honeybunch, or do you wanna brawl with an elephantine, lidless lady? Do I have to crawl into your skull and peep out your lamps? Git crackin'!" She gives her a book like it's a diploma. Mylene feels as prey in the boobytrap of Bertha's silence. Stubborn, she sulks splendidly. Her superb comeliness is collaged in cosmetics, physique partitioned in apparel, limbs lyrical. Bertha's genitalial and underarm fetor is making Mylene queasy. Constipated, Bertha takes a bunch of laxatives, the tablets eventually proving to be ineffective, and she reluctantly permits Mylene to administer an enema. When Bertha's system answers the call of nature, the event is disastrous, the stench evil, fumes not unlike they're from a cesspit, the niff sharp as a sword, which ultimately fells Mylene. Following the lethal evacuation, everything seems to burgeon, sprout like crops, becoming buddingly healthier, the excrement as dung, manure that fertilizes and causes the harvest to grow, the shit with its sacred status. Her breath has the mephitis of dysentery. She claims Estelle is Public Enemy Number One. Fading, phantasmal phosphorescence unghosts them. They are engaged in a war of wills.

Sun's an arciform volcano spewing splendrous lava, and is cowled in cream of wheat cirri. A rainbow close-shaves it in a peacock arc. Curds-and-whey heavens. Thicket juts like teeth. Bulldog-scowled, Beethoven-haired dandelions resign themselves to their seasonal metamorphosings. Estelle, the tough cookie spitfire, and Mylene, stroll along the country road's gravel that glitters, crunches, clatters, and scatters beneath their heels. In the mugginess of spring, they're as fish swimming with the current. Mylene relishes the distraction, revels in it, for the Big Bertha affair has given her the willies. Is she, Mylene, without her, Bertha, a hermit crab having left its shell to wander, unprotected, to the ocean? She has a deficiency of self-discipline. Bertha's noisy nonsense could irritate deaf ears. She insists Mylene's noggin is dry, dying for its thirst to be quenched with stimuli, and has taught her a new way of learning. Bertha is like a defrocked priest pioneering her own religion. Thinking, Mylene is as a wave hitting a sea wall, forced to go higher each time in order to get over it. Estelle claws out a square of bubblegum, guaranteed 5-chewer before swallowing, from its fluorescent pack, offers it to Mylene, who nods no, and Estelle unwraps it and pops it in, chomps with snappy sonances. Mylene's attired in sassy crop bandana jamas, groovyscrimpy crisscross tank that reads 'I Have Expressionist Bauhaus Cubist Impressionist Fauvist Avant-Garde Shoes,' and adorable flipflops. Estelle is clad in a rayon halter, tweed mini, and sandals. They try mightily to be anti-trendy. The cerulean canvas of the horizon has smears of garnet and coral that a creative kid might've painted. City, densely packed, sucks for oxygen, gassed by pollution. Mylene, hugged and kissed, with vigor, by a purring Estelle, is filled with such violent pleasure that other sensations are rendered insignificant. She can't oppose the potency of her nubility. She has the lure and burr of a dangerous little girl. Her chimpy mitts grasp Mylene's wrists, tongue lunging riotously into her mouth. She gores her in the ribs with her fingers and bouncily jogs, her character modifying the environment, superimposing a beachy backdrop. Mylene gets a load of her volume, out of the industrious scintillation, like she's in front of a stereoscope. Mylene's hankering for her has trained her imagination for this event, as an athlete coached for a competition. The realization of fulfilling the desire only increases it. Estelle is ripe. Adoration can startle you, like the open eyes of a baby when they should be closed, sleeping. Mylene is her sidekick. Robin to her Batman. Estelle's a hypnotist. Mylene is entranced. Estelle has prised her eyes, so all is clear.

She's as natural to Mylene as honey is to bees. They are two sides to a single coin. In agile, amative fury, they suck and squeak, wind sinuously. Mylene devours, is devoured. They're nude, primitive savages in an obscure rite of passage. Mylene is faint with amorousness. She breathes hard. She suffocates in her ruff. Her ecstasy is like it's chemically manufactured. The endless, lapis lazuli bounding main saltily wheezes. Grainy, balmy winds. There's hammering finesse, explosive exploration, attentive pulverizing, and thwacking oblivion, with the couple. Estelle corrupts her, mashes her, lupine gnashers biting her. The inamoratas slide lachrymally, grasp each other, chortle puckishly. The pair blend as tears in a pool. Mylene sways not unlike a cobra charmed. Estelle plows through her as a combine through a cornfield. An intimate experimental encounter: Mylene's mush collides with Estelle's neck. Is it love or lust? The distinction between the two is like the distinction between raping a woman, killing her psychologically, and stabbing her with a knife, murdering her physically; or are they similar, in an abstract way, as things thought of and the very articulations of these things are similar but dissimilar somehow, if only slightly. The moment they are sharing is as poignant as the moment which follows death. Estelle is dreamy, like posing for a portrait, nullifying her masculinity, and adopting an aura of femininity. Mylene's life is alive, born again, with her. There's a rumor of instability. What is vital to acquiring steadiness? A chair. Its position doesn't change unless it's moved. A person requires something outside of herself for stability - a chair, for example. It is interesting: when you're in good company time is truant; you don't notice the hours inserting themselves as cards into a deck. When you're alone, time inflicts itself upon your awareness. Estelle is capable of cruelty, once getting Mylene bare-assed and spanking her sore. She is intermittently constructive and destructive. The duo flow, join together akin to organic cells. Estelle reeks of rancid bacon. She's scaly and Mylene is soft. She's eccentric and Mylene's conservative. They complement one another, presently separate, intent on reconnecting, rubbing and rolling in the graveyardy garden with chain-link fencing coroneted with barbed-wire. Procession of snails inch along in their spirallyshelly accommodations, near a jumbo mower with rusted rotative blades. Estelle's armpits are cowlicked and rank. Her knuckleful of silver sorceress-type rings. Fire roars from Mylene's top to her toes. On the erotic razor's edge ... Estelle is like a rocket launching from the pad of Mylene. Manipulating her as a potterer does clay. In her like grit in a pearl. Engaged in commando-type holds. Mylene's a rat before the rattler. They concupiscently cook, mix as flavors. On one hand, Mylene wants to tell the tale of Bertha, straggle-bushed, vibratorily moving like a mechanical dynamo with a quirky hum, swerving round the pole of Mylene as a skier, a wide woman with a basilisk gaze, bulky body ostensibly a battlefield with blast-craters of cellulite, with these hitherto uncounted birthmarks on her bulbous buttocks, misertight butthole, oculi like brackish puddles, having the mussed mop of a poetess, with glints of rodentine denticulation, extending the olivebranch to Mylene, heretofore adrift in the chaosmos, in the form of textbook, and, on the other side, she wants to sweep the story under the carpet. Whitened finger of cumulus points accusatorily at a saffron, shamefaced sun. Estelle is thin of figure, thick of skull, hairy of body. Frenetic friskiness. They are undulant as candlewicks' flames.

Mylene, in a domestic war with Bertha, surrenders, vows to crack down and study, appeasing her to get her off her case, and she sprouts like a plant in the nutritional soil of Bertha's tutelage. Motivation is Bertha's stock-in-trade, her calling card. Her innovation's invigorating. She can be wildly enthusiastic and aggressively persistent. Mylene is pins-and-needles numb from sitting, plugging away, the learning enervating. Burning the midnight oil, her coccyx kills her. She sort of feels as a corpse kept in a crypt of stale air. Estelle's image is etched in her retina. She muses on the climate of class, its kind of commercial ambience (all the popular brand name logos prominently on display), the teen herd, that cattle clique, ignorant advertisers, oblivious product-placers, and gets nauseated. Bertha's phonograph-record-sized coconut robotically rotates automatically, like it's programmed, blink-rate average in those undoubtedly unprescribed nerdy spectacles. With hungeredhunter peepers she inspects her cuticles. Mylene yearns to get up and go. She yens to rant and rave. Should she revolt against this concentrative enslavement? She's stylishly pouty. Bertha handles her as a tamer does a tigress. She's imposingly vast, like the sky, encompassing her as oxygen, lock, stock and barrel. Her vart is abominable. Mylene is a tough nut to crack. She feels coerced into this. She mopes. Her studious existence paces in a paper cage. She is Proserpina returning to earth. Soda's flat in its glass on the walnut dresser. Moon visibly levitates. Dead pages are brought to life by Mylene's magical fingers. She is arrayed in a vert tee (umbilicus-revealing) with rhinestone accents, cherry V-string Brazilian panty with lace and bead details, and olive mules. She left off her Levis. She is cuddly, kissable. Their personal and academic lives are joined, hook, line and sinker. The mist's opaque, like it's highbeam-lit, and could be sliced with a knife. Bertha, the humanoid road-grader, gives advice that's administrative. She is redolent of lax sanitation, or butchery. Her bombardment of burps, parchment-flesh jiggling. Her massive gluteus maximus is a map with lardaceous landlines and flush-seas and pimple-islands. Let's not get started on the cueball-clam ... Tossed dawn breaks. Ulcerous sun leaks lambency. Vista is a Vermeeresque vision. Gobs of luminosity mushroom behind Mylene's drooping eyelids. She shakes as if reflected in a lake. Dewpoints much too damn high. She pictures Denis, her dad toiling not unlike a mule. She's fed up with being economically impaired. Being poor sucks. The shoddy flooring is fulgurously mutilated. She is clipped by luminescent shears, seated at her darn distressed desk and buried between twin boner-towers of tomes smelling of moldy bread, these tornadic contents spinning around in her mind. To be bookishly brainy ... She covets Estelle's masturbatory ministrations. Frustrated at being forced to leave her to bone up, she felt as though she were a gamer in an arcade who'd used her tokens just as she was finding her groove. Bertha has assisted her in honing her thinktank to a constitution of receptivity, giving her the ability to focus effectively. And she assuages her anxieties. With the switcheroos, choosing between B&E, she's getting ADD! But she is Darwinianly adapting. Oh, for some critical adolescent hijinks! Big Bertha's steak is done to her exact specs, medium rare, and her cutlerywork is graceful. Her shart is revolting.

Estelle's tummy is like wet stone. Hot and cold palpitations for Mylene. She's a bird Estelle plucks. Estelle possesses the nimble hands of a concert pianist. They are divested of underwear plumage. Cerebroid moon's fiery. Estelle behaves as if she's pregnant and in the throes of labor. Zephyrs sedulously search them. Mylene twirls like a torn kite, the burning arrows of Estelle's fingers in her orifices. Mylene stares at her back as though in expectancy of seeing angelic wings substituting for shoulder blades. Mylene felt imprisoned by Bertha and is now free. There's licking fondling smooching pinching in glistening gales. Estelle's fist digs through Mylene like she is venturing to violate an entity beyond her body. A swarm of variegated dots flit as insects. Her cardiac organ sounds like a transmission in trouble. Estelle chants her name as a mantra, gyrates gently, and they vine-twine, embracing, lungs bursting. Their thoughts are cells of dirty ideas that come to fruition. Estelle's fingers climb the column of Mylene's vertebrae and she gets a stranglehold on her from the rear. Her breath is reminiscent of buttered toast. Their cronean shrieks of elation, skipping like amateur fencers. Estelle pats her narcissus-pale rump as a mare's hindquarters. She's a salacious squid on her. An eel, Mylene slips out. She is electrocuted by her touch. It's like her gray matter is a river and the retrospections are floating on the surface. Memory: a curator of past occasions. Their vascular organs reverberate. In the peloid empyrean nacreous stars squinch. Rowdiness. Racket. Estelle imparts her penial philosophy - "the dick doesn't matter as long as it's in you, just as the beer doesn't matter as long as you get plastered!" Artillery fire of her osculations, tactions. Her hyena's laugh. Her tongue lags behind her words. Maritime mirror reproduces a prismatic firmament, suspires like an acid bath. Light sneak-attacks. Mylene escapes from herself, Estelle her liberator. Mylene is exceptional, Estelle is unexceptional. Mylene's extraordinary, Estelle's ordinary. They're both penniless. They have this in common. Mylene appreciates living when she thinks of dying. The sprinkles have an acidulous property. A blimp is a coasting Noah's Ark. With Estelle's cheesy, charming ring on, Mylene is Frodo the Hobbit, invisible to everyone. Mylene is Alice traveling through the Looking Glass of Estelle. Clouds are buffalos roaming in the pasture of welkin. Mylene's a fly in Estelle's web. Will Bertha flip her lid when she finds out Mylene bailed? They'd locked horns. Too much chalktalk. Mylene at the end of her rope. Bertha's hams were folded monkishly, Mylene looking as if she were in a trance. It was oral guerrilla warfare. With Estelle, everything for Mylene is fresh and new, like she came out of a coma. They rastle. What contortions they wind up in! Perverse poses, innovatory anatomic narrations. To Mylene, Estelle is robust and resplendent, as a lead character in a production whom one applauds when the play concludes, a consummate actress in a part she has cast herself, becoming more of herself without a proper script, makeup, costume, props, and stage scenery. Her thespian self seeks sanctuary in herself and vice versa. Their relationship is operatic, with Mylene's music and Estelle's voice. Sometimes, though, with her, Mylene feels like she's establishing a route through a minefield, endeavoring to not step on an explosive device, that is, Estelle's temper. Her tantrums can ignite as gas jets. If shown on a chart, Mylene's readings would be all over the place. She is gesticulant not unlike a hair-stylist using her clippers. Flinging herself at Mylene as a marble from a slingshot. Mylene's heart is a beating wing. Estelle is colorful and shines like an angelic figure carved in a chapel's stained glass window. Strokes. Smacks. Estelle's fingers are petals, hands flowers, wrists stems. Mylene is a closed umbrella Estelle opens. Mylene's pulled into her as though an article of clothing. She pushes Estelle away. "You can shoot me dead on the spot," Estelle sibilates, knowing that such a dire result isn't in store for her, "but it's awesome being a slut." Hankying and pankying. She pats Mylene's downy middle with her palm, says something about sodomy.

Mylene's cogitations are like smashed crystal. She's in a demibra and thong, and sports these unforgivably goofy-yet-necessary hornrims, blind as an owl during the day. Perspiration dribbles down her bunched belly and arced back. Bertha dispenses order and disorder theories. Mylene remembers her mom, Mathilde, the loud and soft sounds she made when she slept, the strained inhalation and exhalation sonancies, attributed to her

nasal slash sinus issues, her snoring, in sum, brutal. In
the weeks after her demise there was an eerie silence
permeating the place which was challenging to deal
with as were the crucial readjustments to the routine.
Unhappiness became habit. She had magnitude of mind,
breadth of wit, and warmth of heart. She was appealing,
sociable, sensitive. Mylene indulges in an imperative
gastric interlude. Mylene gets a glimpse of the shreds
of turkey stuck between Bertha's conical chiclets. From
her person emanates a mysterious melange of odd,
innumerable odors merging by the minute. Bertha is
fair like snow. Mylene cracks the books dubiously, eyes
red-rimmed, sheetly white, and worries homonine Taj
Mahal Bertha, sentinel-stiff-and-at- attention, will tip
over and squish her flat as a pancake. Fed up and frustrated, Mylene boils like sauce on the stove of Bertha's
insistence. She swallows and digests tasteless information, loathes being force-fed. Blood in the body of
work pumps. Flustered, she presses on, perusing, despite
problems manifesting like mosquitoes at standing water.
Her lids hang as webs. Only sweetmeat snacking arrests
her progress. She's gonna turn into a plumpie! The great
machineries of her braincells are grinding. Bertha is an
adroit puppeteer, assiduously manipulating the strings.
Her squashy keister and gut, saucery pies bleary. Mylene
feels akin to a runner doing laps around the track,
cardio insufficient. The remembered components of
her mother are mnemonically broken down into these
compartmentalized parts, focusing on one fragment
at a time. A rainbow makes this peafowl-feather fan.
Polishing up is a Herculean task. Bertha's a cow kept

sacred in her bedroom. Mylene's ears ring not unlike bicycle bells. Leafage rattling as dugdugee drums. Denis asleep in the recliner before the television, remote at the ready. Bertha calls him a rapscallion, a rogue, a ne'er-do-well, to which Mylene explains he took a series of wrong turnings in life. To Bertha, his bitterness eats at him like a drought does terrain. In logical wonderment Mylene's mind's incendiarized, brain incinerated from hitting the books, her medulla oblongata cremated. It had weakened into impotence from non-use, and is now a force knowing its strength. A chain reaction of cramming. Encephalon vaporized. Her voice is giggly and lispy. Her grey matter's a time bomb ticking, about to explode. Hailstorm of ideas in her noodle. Bertha's words of encouragement are on par with a stuck record. They're boxed in by household detritus. Shadows elongate, and incrementally, on the west walls' abrupt angles. Reality strikes Mylene as a bell on that thermometer thingie at carnivals. She feels brainwashed in some gonzo cult. Bonkers Bertha's gamy backside's hiccup. She's an immovable object hit by the unstoppable force of Mylene. Another gassy hiccough. Mylene is on the cusp of dozing when Bertha dives into Einstein's theory of relativity. Her pallid corporeal slack scrolls of skin. She flaunts her intimidating IQ. Mylene gets into flare jeans and plum tunic. She's vocally weary, Bertha is. Seersucker blouse is discarded by Mylene. Bertha maintains Mylene's life is a drain and she is pouring her potential down it. Showers' pitter-patting. Bertha's sauntering belies her mass, says, "I am your open sesame to respectability." Her sentence skated on ice, viva voce prowess vital. Mylene responds she is "cognitively challenged," a "nitwit misfit, a freakoid." She has been sitting for so long it is like she has been nailed down, numbness feeling as if bugs are crawling on her. She's an living sculpture. She's staying in. She is barefooted and listens to the gulls' complaints. Blainy full moon. Bertha stinks of a goat stall. With her patience she could turn an orchard into a sea, drop by drop.

Like an MD, Mylene determines she and Estelle demonstrate symptoms of a common condition known as aphrodisia. Aphotic anteroom. Mylene's a soldierly strategist: should she go forward, press Estelle frontally with a charge, or attack her flanks? Is she preparing her own operation? Does she strive to capture Mylene? Is she a Napoleonic tactician with resources? A deft maneuver - she blitzes Mylene from the side. What is her objective in this carnal campaign? Is this approach one of diversion? The activity offensive or defensive? What's her scheme? Is she attempting to keep her trump card up her sleeve? She tries to not show her hand. Is her plan psychological, by creating alarm in the enemy ranks; or physical, by initiating a free-for-all? She pins Mylene. In the fray, Mylene, in a poly navy coverup and wedge shoes, is overpowered because of a deficiency of numbers, equipment, and fatigue also being a major factor. Estelle has on a check shirt with slits, periwinkle shorts with functional drawstring, and cognac clogs. There's a mo of relief, not unlike the cessation of a cramp, before Estelle slinks on her for a sec. They don't communicate verbally; they're telepathic, their station-minds tuned in to receive one another's thought-signals.

"Dad's going to pot," Mylene says. "When Mom died I was devastated by grief, and he became interminably idle." Her liquescent sigh. "Diving from the consciousness to the co-consciousness is like submerging into an abyss ..."

"A comet lighting out the darkness ..." Estelle returns, gets to her dotted-doggy bikini. And Mylene sees her as Odysseus saw Ithaca. With her, Mylene is nutritive dirt; whereas without, she is barren rock. Estelle tenderly bats her about like a kitty would a new catnip toy. Pawprints and tailtrails on Mylene's integument. Without Estelle, Mylene is frozen; with her, she is heated by a fire. Estelle's reptiloid tresses are as a gorgon's snaky locks. Bertha disapproves of Mylene's lesbianic predilection. Mylene respects her, but she prefers girls and that's that! Estelle's pert breasts and perky nates are desirable. Mylene kneads them like a baker does rolls. Static sounds of surf. Mylene is smitten. Her respirations have the sonances of leafage in wafts. Beet sun. The emanation is the prized product of a goldsmith. Mylene's PMS-bloated, feels as a boa that'd eaten a rat. She's tense like a neck in the noose. Her heart's feeling rag-wrung. Their amatory abandon. Mylene scritches as Punch, flattened by Judy. Roughhousing slaphappily. Estelle beelines for Mylene's behind. The flame of Mylene's resistance is doused by the water of Estelle's determination. Estelle's pinkie encircles Mylene's sphincterial wineglass, and there's a rectal ring. Mylene's core spasms. She is an insecure structure shaken by a tremor. She's analyzed like Morse code, feels unsure, as an atheist in an abbey. Hysterically funny lovey- dovey calamities are like from a Tex Avery cartoon. The couple pratfall as funambulists. Estelle starts to smooch and pet her and stops, the second one so potent that the kisses she just gave her, and the ones she's on the edge of giving her, are nearly nullified because of the promise of them, hence the necessity of more of them, to compensate. Estelle is everywhere and nowhere: an aural, resonant passage possessing no particular universal place. Euphoriants are in their private Eden. They hover like hummingbirds. Beads of sweat shine. Quintessential countryside configurations - windmill, livestock, weathercocks, wells, farmsteads, picket fences ... Estelle, the devious deity, poos and pees on a hind of a hillock. She looks clumsily cut out of some unreal rock. Cloying aroma of pine. Mercury-wings develop from Mylene's ankles and she guides Estelle's soul into the underworld. Their fires cannot be extinguished. Mylene can't resist her, as a starving person can't resist a meal. Mylene's heart leaps and bounds. The riptide of Estelle drags her under.

Mylene is exhibited in a sweet frill-seeker vintage chambray corset. Conflict with Bertha escalates. Swelter invites lethargy. Spate's a canorous chorus. Bertha declares she wants to be Mylene's confidant and confessor. Mylene's last straw-type vexed language. Her incomprehension of the materials presented to her. Bertha pretend-choke-holds her neck. Mylene cuts to the chase in asking a few blunt biographical questions. Bertha galumphs and answers retirement is looming on the horizon. Mylene has the sensation she's a lost driver on an endless highway, reading the signs for the right exit. Bertha's scrobiculate, flabbergasting fanny spreads as she scrooches. She raises a paw like she's offering absolution. Her mop is tousled, countenance crimson. She is close to Mylene, yet is mountainously far away. Cerebrations in Mylene's brain are as brush-strokes, one justifying another to make a masterpiece of memory. Earlier, she fidgeted in a shortish chair of her rabbinically bearded, cleft palated, rotund guidance counselor's subterraneous, unventilated office while he harangued the stuffing out of her for missing classes, his vitriol spurting like blood from a fresh gash. Obstinate, she wouldn't budge. She gazed at him as if he were the butt of her joke. He was a bird and she was the cat play-ing with him. Too much graffiti on the brick wall across the street. She wore a midriff-flaunting tye- dye cami, low-riding, five-pocket bell bottoms, withit belt, and sporty slides. Bertha pregnantly waddles, tushy bounces as a tubby tyke on a trampoline. Dust-specks are micro-scopic substances in test tubes of fulgurant fluid. An intellectual Rocky, Mylene trains by a lame lamp, exe-cuting cerebral exercises, losing herself in science, history, math and geography ... Bertha, the bipedal zeppelin, lumberingly rhumbas, mucho flab swinging, cellulitic dimples squinty eyes keeping tabs on Mylene when her broad back is turned, brawny arms and legs a swirl of unintentional signalizing. She administers advice. Has she cured Mylene's ennui? It's like she waited out her juvenility. Subjective acrobatics have left her tuckered. She requires a break. She's famished and sore and losing incitement. She is going above herself, as a rivulet's bank swells during a storm. She has the sensation of being a vessel without a rudder. It's like she's doing a pirouette in quicksand! With the prelims yesterday it was as if she were a patient ailing with ignorance and the doctor/teacher, a vile, boarish guy with grimalkin eyes, burial chamber breath, and uncivilized disposition, read the X-ray/test results, upon which he'd base his decision for prescription pills to alleviate her concerns. She had struggled like a swimmer in a churning ocean. In the Bertha-imposed studious solitary confinement Mylene wishes to recommence horsing around, letting loose with Estelle. She wants to resume relations. This hiatus is horrendous for her. She calls her with an unimaginative excuse. Estelle is simmering with suspicion. Absently Bertha massages Mylene's hips. Estelle tells her she's coming over and hangs up the telephone. Dial tone. Mylene's got to hide Bertha!

The mamzelles were seductively dishabille in tankinis. Estelle divided the radius 'tween 'em. Mylene was as though she were her minor-league mascot. Bertha was irate at Mylene for meeting Estelle, whom she said was like a second-rate, real-life villainess in a Shakespearian play. Mylene is under the gun (Bertha's mitts cocked-and-loaded pistols), and the bowling-over glare of an infuriated Bertha ... Envisioning the upcoming weekend with Estelle, for Mylene: an artist envisaging a sketch, drafting it, setting it aside for a while, the creator returning to it later and making the piece different from what was initially drawn. Mylene is an injury incarnate only Estelle can heal. Typhonic arousal. Her chest heaves. Her conoid, stubbly nipples are erect. She dreams, that gushing garland of imagery and sound, with extraneous shimmerings of vivid, phantasmic forms, a fabulous picture book with sonority, in which she's a chrysalis in the evolution of birth. We begin in wake, finish in slumber, as night follows day. We do not die; instead the world dies in us. The spirit is dead in in wakefulness and is resurrected in sleep. Are we wake-walking or sleep-walking? Slumber's emancipation from wakefulness. Wake (physical) - we enter a house from childhood and become that child. Sleep (psychological): we enter that same home inside us. Mylene pictures Bertha's chops protruding fleshily, egg- white in the gathering ditchy-dark dusk, the trio of her chins lapped by feline tongues of coruscation. Mylene is drawn to the candle of her persuasiveness. Bertha's charm's a sponge absorbing Mylene, who has studied with a startled-rabbit expression, guts feeling not unlike vipers coiled in a nest. Bertha's ass is as cornflour pudding. Mylene's insecurities are a many-headed monster in a bubbling cauldron of uncertainty. Her mind roams the frontiers of diverse courses until the fat fingers of Bertha's jokes tickle her ribs. Mylene is pencil- thin, has knobbliness in her knees, slenderness of hands and slimness of tootsies, and a vulturous screech of a chortle. Her tightrope-balancer stride. She's in fine fettle. Denis, lubricated by wine, throttles his Wee Willie Winkie, retreated from reality in the living room, before the small screen. Out the latticed window a symphonic rainfall orchestrates the day, and the night. Dumbbell-shaped megalopolis is circumscribed by an Arabianish Sea in sorceries of smaze. Alienness of natives. Watery time flows. A coconut, that bearded fruit, is uneaten on the pianola. Silverware on the counter resembles forceps. Mylene

sandalled and pantied and tee'd and in a cane chair is on
memorization (automatic) pilot in a rhythmic, melodious groove at this point. Whorl of her bellybutton and
its inbreeding of lint. Ratatat of spritz. She is Bergerac-
billed, her beak bruised from a recent romp with Estelle.
Pour's a rhymeless bard. She catapults herself full-tilt in
the dining room and flounces on a tin trunk, tapped out.
Her hay-hued derma layer. Spoors of conceptions exude
from the gland of her brain. She's a captivated mongoose
at the hooded snakes of scholastic subjects. Batless gaze
of the moon. Verrucas on her soles. Spray sounds like
sitars. Atmosphere palpitates as a womb. When awake,
Mylene is a closed flower. When asleep, her petals open,
releasing a refreshing scent, such a great fragrance, and
bright colors. Her fantasies rise like bubbles and pop
with transparency. Her goosebumps run rampant. She
is a spectatress before the campy Bertha, entranced by
this entertainment. She's not governed by natural laws.
Gobs of her eyeballs ooze onto Mylene as she gets
into an argyle sweater and wrinkly cargos. A park has
a jungle gym, swing set, and merry-go-round situated
on wood chips. Crows flocking are a feathery, flexuous
arm throwing a haymaker and uppercut at the opponent of azure. Mylene says Estelle's ugliness is attractive.
In vitric illumination she's a fantastic species of fish,
an aquatic creature in an aquarium and superficially
spawning glittering offspring with minerals' iridescence.
She is sirenic, lures the listener with her song, amphibi-
anly aswim in the shine, like she's doing some St. Vitus
dance. Bertha stares straight at Mylene, whose feet are
so firmly planted on the floor they could be rooted. She

licks her lips. Calm before the storm? Vulturine Estelle with her tiny head out of her bent nib and tawny bodily plumage - an avian tempter. Her phiz is as changeable as clothing, modified in movement. And her asymmetrical, asteraceous moue! To be coitionally connected to her ... the two thrashing like they're hanged ... Sleets' shards. Clotted-cream cloudlets. Wings of leven and clapping thunder. The downpour is as a drunk's passed urine.

Bertha is livid. Her farting sounds like a lamb bleating. She doesn't miss a trick when it concerns Mylene's extracurricular activities. Much bitchery. She contends Estelle is manipulative, that everyone to her is a chess piece on the board, people are puzzles she takes apart and puts together at will. Cutlery and crockery clutter the breakfast table. Denis, blurred by gin and tonic, works his crankshaft, physiognomy glowing as though it's a beacon, says the drinks are for medicinal purposes, he doesn't want any unnatural unions. He snaps his lizard's tail. Mylene's innards are not unlike crushed ice. A perverted Pied Piper, he plays his flute. Bertha denies her the benefit of Estelle's company, as if this social "quarantine" is a medical practitioner's mandate. Mylene and Estelle, the eager beavers, treat every place they fool around in like a honeymoon suite, conversations often tournamental, as though essaying to score points to win. Mylene reluctantly unenthusiastically complies. An artifact of an armchair grunts beneath ginormous Bertha's weight. She is a goddamn conqueror triumphing over Mylene.

Estelle has pride, dignity. She won't take Mylene's brush-off well. Is she capable of getting her revenge? It's conceivable. She is nutty like a fucking fruitcake. What is Mylene to do? Tell her the truth, that a headless, hugeous woman is tutoring her? Anxiety goes through her system as poison. Introduce Bertha to Estelle? Won't, can't happen. Spidery stars weave webs of luster. Mylene in a plaid chic jacket and rio jockey briefs sips a cup of herbal tea. Bertha's obscene B.O. ruins her appetite. Admittedly, she and Estelle (serpent in their paradise) had been fighting as a married couple lately. Mylene keeps thinking of her toffee knockers, chestnut nipples, umbiliform vortex. Bertha maternally advises her to disentangle herself from Estelle at all cost. The leash will be shorter, Bertha assures her. Her bull's eyes are for radiant arrows to target. She galvanizes Mylene, who does become revitalized. Although separated from Estelle, Mylene feels they are together, like the sun's light's is distributed in a variety of courses: it's spread out but is still singular. Denis is, at this very minute, bar-hopping to get drunk as a skunk. His choreographed routine - he rouses, hungover, slaves at the abattoir, gets tanked, and crashes. Rinse, repeat. Coast clear, Bertha, with a sardine and soy malodor, raids the refrigerator, holds her head like you would a flashlight during a blackout. Her plethora of suet swishes.

The veggies on Mylene's plate are as amputated anatomic specimens for extreme experimentation. Mylene swears she'll succumb to stupidity, like when a vic is about to be raped by a perp. She resists, and with application. Regarding the new regimen and disregarding the old one, only she can't block out Estelle. Mylene is the reed instrument she blows into. Thinking of the both of them: stitched-together body-parts, robbed from the graves of time, Mylene taking these portions and putting them together, from assorted periods, to better parent a Frankenstein monster of memory. Estelle cunnilingusly satisfying her ... Mylene spread-eagled on a berth of blankets ... Estelle's peaty breath ... Mylene embarrassed in the exposure ... Is there shit on her anus? Estelle sniffs at her rectum as a hound picking up an a vulpine smell, whispers endearments into her hearing, and sprawls on her ... Mylene's retrospections are meadows fertilized with rapturous invention. Remembrances petaliferously flutter. In her melon is a cometical occurrence of vision. Estelle influences her into indiscretion. Uneducated, she can be articulate in their opinionated talkfests. With her, Mylene is a battery attracting electricity. Her room's a repository for junk, stuff strewn not unlike kelp the tide forsook. She's wearing a jade robe. Bertha cajoles her. She is as a physician deciding which pills to prescribe for the affliction of distraction. Mylene's rather comfortable with her, like when you are a toothache- sufferer and are uncomfortable with an unfamiliar dentist until she performs the procedure to relieve you of the pain. Bertha informs her that if she, Mylene, passes finals, she'll be given her head on her shoulders, as an angel getting wings for doing a good deed. "Sacrifice is the infrastructure of achievement," she says.

Mylene's period is quite intense. She whines. The agony is acute. Her perineal rash stings. And the charlie horse is excruciating, too. Her alvine anguish, parked on the hopper, feet propped on their toes on the tacky laminate flooring. Excremental, alutaceous logs. She whimpers in agony, and out of her pooper squiggles this Brobdingnagian tapeworm. She doesn't know it, but it's the indication of her prominent academic fear, stress-induced. Urinous outpouring. She screams, looking at it writhing in a fecal mess in the commode. Her expression is like Janet Leigh's when a bewigged and dressed Anthony Perkins uses her as a personal pincushion in 'Psycho.'

Denis on the davenport gets bombed and watches the tube. His loneliness registers with Mylene, who is beside him. He needs escaping, rescuing. She's feeling brazen, white-hot in a bold flapper bodice and bun pant with fringe benefits, simulating an ad lib clean-up sesh. He stares and smirks. She is blissful. Next, she soaps herself liberally in the bath, picturing him at the slaughterhouse, bloodied and dirty dancing with a slab of meat. He slips on the bloody floor, only remains upright. He molests a poultry pair, which mutate into Bertha's Swiss cheesy bahuda and dirigible-bongos. He fondles himself. She fingers herself.

Mylene submits to the tapeworm, sausage-sized, the thing repairing back into her body whence it came. She skreaks, grabbing the bedposts, the creature burrowing into her alimentary canal. Her knees jab her jaw. She clasps her calves and cries. And it's over. Cleaning up in the john, she feels, with Bertha, like Pinocchia with strings attached. Bertha controls her as the moon does the surf. She once said Mylene's brains are Solomon's minds, that she is superb, and Estelle witless, a threat to Mylene's progress, a grain of grit in the eye of the process, upsetting the balance of her schoolwork. Bertha's language tumbled like dice. Carrot-and-sticking. Alpha against Omega with a dimension of duality. The residence a racecourse for academic application. They quarreled as cats, sometimes with daggers drawn. They could be boiling hot or frozen cold, and sure dig their heels in. Pacification efforts from either side proved to be consistently unsuccessful. Calling for a truce was trying. Bertha was shooting from the hip like a filmed gunslinger. Every step taken (in a dead march) was an almighty crash, fat irretrievably sagging, school bus-clattering, blubber mushrooming in her movement, and she fell on the chair as a sack of potatoes, loud not unlike a crowd, really mischievous as a problem-child, and wild like a whirlwind, their convo as a telly talkie. To Mylene, she's a reverse-Ganesha; that is, elephant-bodied. She trampled her vocally like a flowerbed, in the calm of cocktail hour, Mylene, mild-mannered, holding her peace and ground, counterfeit-cowing into submission, but not before becoming a chiquita bullfighter, taunting her with a frock. Toro, toro! Bertha, with her thyroid obesity and class-bully bravado, nasal congestion (nose bunged-up with goo) making her goldfish-gaspy. Mylene's axillae tress grown tuftily. Bertha getting a return for her investment in Mylene. Her shrilling was telephonic, heft-hobbled, vox sounding as shattering glass, astuteness quick like a flash, mouth making these frigging fishy motions. Her language was under Mylene's skin as insect eggs. Denis was a broken mule in a torpor on the canape as an invalid on his sickbed, pupils like cloudy glass, the hooch as venom in his veins, sobriety the antivenene, he a mouse caught in his own trap. Heat bee-buzzing. Gusts whizzing like electrical pulses along cabling. Footfalls squeak on the tiles, sounding as bedsprings. Mylene ice-frozen, clamped in the grip of apprehension, mango-tits without brassiere, towel unwound like a sari, bumpa plunked on the crapper. Her dump's dramatic. She bursts, backdoor a breached dam, her waste, diarrheic, spurting into the channel of the shitter, tootsie-wootsies lost in reject laundry, linen wrapped on her crown as a caul. Denis' shakers below decks. From Mount Bertha, Mylene hears commandments, and speaks to Bertha's disembodied head.

A deplorably seedy district. Curse word spray painted, medieval church with fang-pillars, serviceable stairs, and encaged in scaffolding, is in the early stages of renovation. Courtyard gleams like its asphalt is varnished. Dishwatery skyline. A sickle-shaped, vandalized emporium. Estelle avoids a series of sebaceous puddles in jumps balletic. Mylene applauds. The dudettes enter the church's glazed door with Estelle's rusty, buck- toothed key. Mylene longed for her, thus she caved. The flirting in public and private for the yatties ... so irresistible ... Estelle is a narcotic she's hooked on. Bertha is going to unload on her! She will cross that bridge when she comes to it. The bitties apply a competent burglar's stealth. Celestial contingent of holy baby beings, surely Strozzian, oil painted on the baroque, arched ceiling, these frescoes with ecclesiastical iconography and broadstroked brushwork and rich colors, a sumptuous stage where the sacred and profane are depicted. Perfume of incense. Proof Estelle peels down to her gartered stockings, soporifically stooping on an altar, candle-lit, at a pulpit, as if obeisant, for a swinish priest, wrinkled like an arthritic tortoise. Mylene peeks from a pew. His tallow torso gives off fulguration. He should be humble, devoted, but he's not; he's a lech. He looks as though he's a refugee extra from the set of 'The Island Of Dr. Moreau.' He has demonic lamps. Estelle bends like for a blessing, in religious docility. She kneels. She gives oral. They communicate companionably; or possibly conspiratorially. He comes into a chalice and instructs her to gulp it. She does. Lewd communion. Mylene's head pounds, as water on the wall of her cranium.

Bertha scolded Mylene for her nocturnal monkeyshines with Estelle. Mylene's nerves are strung out, her gray matter not mattering. She is woefully unprepared, in the monumental marrow of the crowded classroom, with its share of winners and losers, inner and outer circles, jocks, bohemians, upper, middle and lower classes, preppies, geeks, artsy types, conformists and nonconformists … All the ranking bullshit is present here. She fantasizes about pelvis-slapping, high-impact, thrust-intensive, perspiry intercourse with Estelle, imagines her hyphenic eyes, cuppy knockers, and laddish fanny, body odor reeking not unlike a bath towel used too much, Mylene's vaginate Vesuvius spewing. She glitters and gushes as a fireworks display … Sexual ah's and oh's … Copulating, they seem conjoined … Griseous abrasions on Estelle's being like she's a stoned martyr … Carious megapolis with its spoliation of citizenry. Vitreous vapor. Sky is congealed-grease-whitish-greyish. Mylene's head is tilted as a dog's when it hears a whistle, gazing at the chalkboard and its controlled chirography, the opposite of Mylene's denticulate calligraphy. She cannot make head nor tails of it. She's not a mental marvel and it may as well be hieratic hogwash. There's no rhyme or reason to it. Dealing with a question for her: like pea soup an individual goes through, and finding the answer is that traveling person experiencing relief when reaching a safe destination. She's cooking. She gets stumped. The teacher is Mr. Toy, an Asian macadamia nut with a vandyke, electricized hairdo-helmet and zombie complexion, titian tie's knot as an additional Adam's apple, talking turkey ticker-tape-rapidly on his magenta cellphone at the center of the establishment hurricane. Rumor mill has spun out that he's gay. His relic desk. He emphasizes points with his #2 pencil, like he's practicing dart-throwing delivery. And the grapevine has him calorically plagued and with a bible beltish background. The clock, connected bell, and PA speaker. Mylene puts answers to questions as cracks of a whip lashing into flesh. Will she shine like a star or be sucked into a black hole? Her approach is now or never, do or die, all or nothing ... And she daydreams of Estelle, onion-skin-thinnish, her bust and pussy: three salient points of an anatomical triangle. Seeds of cogitation are sown and germinating. She is an etching and Mylene discerns the contours, only within there is an emptiness she doesn't recognize. Her attraction's sketchy. She experiences a sensation of awkwardness, like a peasant granted admission into a palace, not knowing what to do with the muddy footwear. She mechanizedly chews on her eraser which changes into Bertha's nipple in its pilosity. The hall is a decorous riot of flashy fashion and revealed skin. Estelle hasn't rung or rapped. She swept in and out of Mylene's life as a force of nature.

The sun is a maggot wriggling in the putrefacient corpse of the blue lid. Mylene failed on the precursory tests across the board. She fell flat, and is depressed. At the dingy damask curtains she takes off her stiletto booties, rhubarb cuffed trousers, tomato ruched top, and puts on a sapphire tube, color-correlating boxsies, and fleece slippersocks. Bertha attempts to console her, envelopes her, marshmallow-derma's folds draping around her. Mylene's forearms press on the fatty loaf of Bertha's tokus, her scrunched face sinking into the rucksacks of her mams. Bertha's support is received favorably. Mylene appreciates her compliments, is wrapped in a cocoon of confection. Dejected, Mylene says she's a dummy, wiping her tears. Bertha massages her nape, hems and haws, head wheeling to try and cheer her up. Her redolence closes rank. Mylene wrests a grin from her lips to satisfy her. She puts on a hibiscus cardigan, versatile aqua skort, and papaya Sketcher hikers. Bertha bumps into her and Mylene is like a wavelet pushed by the mass of an ocean. With Estelle - Mylene's a diver dipping into the deep. Estelle, teeth caged in braces, throat manacled by necklace, scapulae peppered by freckles, in her rambustious, salacious swashbuckles, clings to Mylene like a mollusc in chain- reactive intercourse. Seabirds are accusatively shrew-shrilly. Denis is under the flickering spell of the tv. To Mylene, it is all about perspective: close to the set the images distort; step away and they are clear. Bertha, a secret kept by Mylene as an (un) woolly mammoth in the iceberg of the abode, a mentor-ess sharp like a knife, pigmentation as unctuous paper, says she should knuckle down, zero in, pour it on aca-demically. An omnicompetent Bertha's pep talk brings roaches to silent ovation. She's the chief and Mylene's the Indian. With wizardry of wordage she has purged her of Estelle, had predicted what was in the cards. She can draw the undrawable bow of sensibility. Her arm-pits have the stench of spoiled stew. Mylene has gotten accustomed to the abnormal, and the rarefied and occa-sionally oppressive air of being in her presence. Bertha is fox-wily, unpredictable like lightning, with whims as the weather's, Mylene not making top or bottom of any of it, in her stationary, studious existence having little contact with the outside world. If Bertha is a sacred cow then Mylene is a suckling calf. The daily ritual is a dis-tressing indication of the dreamy universe she's living in. Stars are engaged in a space race. Grasshopper-green grass. Catwalk driveway. Mylene's corporal contraption cannot resist Estelle's mechanical ministrations. The heets were pecky lovebirds flapping their wings in a funtabulous tumble on an unprepossessing side street, neon-lit, adjacent to an anonymous textile plant with grubby window-panes in a fishing village in its grimy decrepitude. Heaven was black as jet. Mylene jumped like a flea when Estelle, raising her non-existent chin, went for her forbidden, feculent hidey- hole, Mylene's arachnidan hand shooing her away as a fly.

Denis slices carcasses of beef, the meat morphing into Bertha's tush. Mylene, in her heather undies and banana kimono, buckles in the kitchen, her tapeworm tossing and turning in her gullet. The discomfort abates and she gets into a cheetah babydoll and hue-harmonized tanga, engrossed in an encyclopedia, at Bertha's behest, a nearby dictionary's pages abruptly animating in a wacky danse macabre. Having flunked, she feels birdbrained, like a foreigner who accidentally affronts the local custom. Bertha clips her tortilla chip toenails. Mylene might've lost round one of the exams, but the match isn't over. Not by a long shot. She is an Icarus having survived the flame-on-and-crash. This toasty twilight, she has dinner with her dad at the 'Greasy Spoon' restaurant in town. Pasta for her, steak for him. They are sick of a steady diet of junk food. He's besuited and crewcut. He missed a loop with his belt, fixes it. She has on an ivory boucle hat, mint cord blazer, perse polo, teal capris, and suede Mary Janes. Their waitress is weathered and willowy, loosened locks these loppy pulsation of luster. The eatery is akin to a puppet theater, with its extravaganza of synchronized (manic) motion. Denis swigs his pineapple juice like it's a brew, savoring it, sloshing it around. The wagon ride has been rough for him. She doesn't want the wheels to fall off. Before they left tonight, she wore a crisscross teddy with peek-a-boo detail. Credit, or blame, must go to Estelle for her eclectic wardrobe. Denis dug through the fridge for fudge as she, on her tiptoes, went through the cabinet for goodies. His rubbernecking established itself on her. She wanted his scrutiny.

“Dessert?” He sips his coffee, picks at a roll.

“I’m fine.” She munches on a cracker. Cigarette smoke innovates a warping of the powered lighting. “Rilly full ...”

“You’re a cutie.”

“Thank you.”

“My My.”

“I’m giving school another go.”

“Hey, I’m glad.” He’s been stingy with his smiles. He sanctions one now.

“I’m worried about the tests next week. What if I hit the skids so hard they hit back?”

“Have faith in yourself, honeykins.”

“Dad ...”

“My angel with broken wings needs a lift.”

“I am afraid,” her.

“Buttercup,” him.

“I know you quit drinking -”

“I’m too impulsive ... I don’t think ... Too instinctive ...”

“You are courageous.”

“Bravery is not -”

“Shhh ...”

"You're too nice," kissing her palm.

"I love you," sipping her lemoned and limed water. "What're your goals?"

"To be a commercial animator. Yours?"

"Sustained sobriety."

For her, every so often good thoughts can hurt more than bad ones. In the raunchy restroom Mylene leans on the blow dryer, weeping, the tapeworm acting up.

En route to the casa, Mylene, hot and sweaty, suddenly strips to her apricot T-string in her father's shit-box pickup. He rubs her unwashed foot. "How're you feeling?"

Her forehead rests in the crevice of his elbow while he drives. "Mmm ... comfy ..." She is a gratified gal. She wants to tell him about Bertha and can't. She has many skeletons in her closet that should stay hidden. The wet-stuff is a carwash from hell. The latest sexual session with Estelle was brutal, bestial. Estelle had the presence of a crocodile in a daycare center. She hogtied Mylene and beat her senseless. Mylene has disdain for her, only she cannot stop thinking of her. She dropped a bomb-shell on her by breaking up with her. It was a bitter pill for Estelle to swallow. Denis grips his daughter's thigh. She's so thrilled. They are doused in a redlight's blood-bath. She is Carya after Dionysus did his thing. At their humdrum shanty, the defunct barn is up in flames. An eternity is compressed into minutes. Denis has a funny clown expression when Big Bertha staggers out of the raging inferno, gobbling as a turkey, unsteady like a fawn on ice, tripping and tumbling, her head pitching as a pumpkin thrown from a porch, embarking on a parabola, snarling in mid-air, and whumping onto a u-bend of soil. She is whisked away by Mylene, spirited off to safety. She would be convalescent from a concussion. Out of her depth, she's drowning in panic. She goes haywire, flopping not unlike a fish out of water. She could pass for an organic caricature of a portly woman. She submarine-dives, naked as the day she was born, body getting a lashing from the head's tongue, noticing her nails are bitten down to the quick, and cussing. American pop songs ferret into Mylene's ears, deeperanddeeper and inandinto her mind, roundandround. Denis is stiff like a board, spellbound by the spectacle. Estelle on the scene enacts a Petrushka pantomime, speaks in a scraped voice. Mylene bears the brunt of this sight. She's in crisis mode. Denis is a basketcase. Estelle crawls and coughs. Smoke billows as signals. Fire engines' sirens ululate. Blaze flourishes. EKGs of levin. Kabooms of thunder. Fire sounds like an untuned radio, swirling as a ceiling fan's shadows. Estelle's arrested by the authorities. She is escorted to a cruiser by an effete cop. Mylene and Denis' dialogue veers so out of control a traffic officer is required to prevent a verbal pile-up.

The police department's generic office is adorned with cigsmoke. Under an intimidating nimbus of a dyalamp, Estelle is interrogated by boilerplate investigators, one wan and lightweight, the other tan and heavyset. She's like a scorpion out to sting anyone. The evidentiary gathering was easy. She committed arson. She confesses to the charges against her. She, in addition, admits she is obsessed with Mylene and spied on her. She couldn't grasp why Mylene cut the umbilical cord of their relationship. It's as one losing a relative to a common cold ... it shouldn't happen. She's upset, like she's the recipient of ridicule, and decides whether or not to retaliate. She unravels her yarn about Bertha. It sounds as the foundation for fiction, not fact. Nobody believes her story. She'd set out to slay Bertha like David did Goliath, to get revenge on her for "stealing" Mylene from her. Estelle ends up locked in a loony bin. There is a gabby commotion in the community about what happened, but the gossip died down soon enough.

Dusty tomes are stacked by admirable armchairs, the volumes as aged wine bottles beckon collectively like a Pharos. Automobiles are mutant butterflies. Bobbing festival of boats in the harbor. Mylene chills out, wearing a 'Read My Lips' sleepshirt with tail-hem. She had tackled finals that morn and aft and encountered difficulties ... until Denis' head appeared in between her knees and kissed her, whereupon everything made perfect sense. She cut to the bone of the exams. She was dressed in a mauve poncho, twill chinos, and sequin flats, content and confident, for a change, tilted on her locker, boys and girls checking her out approvingly in the three-ring circus school corridor, smelling of cleaning chemicals. She chatted with a fiendish, cologned teach in the middle of cabalistic minors. He gave her the nitty-gritty on her scholastic strengths and weaknesses. She passed. Did well. Improvements were needed. She used her noodle. The bats of befuddlement had flown the belfry.

On a busied, bright beach, on sawdusty sand bookended by rufescent rocks, the ocean as an optical illusion, Denis, in tropical trunks, chases Mylene, wearing a tangerine bikini. He catches her and they collapse on the shiny shore. The prancing tide tramples them. He tickles her tummy. She wails and flounders. He beat his addiction. They used their noggins. They learned lessons from life, and Bertha.

Peaceful grounds. The here and now. Mylene is a twenty-something and expectant and rocking in a rocker on the woodchucks, her lover, burnished beauty Juliette, behind her. They are euphorically engaged. Bertha was eventually awarded her head and became Mylene's nanny, instructor, and, after some time, her agent. What a ruthless negotiator! Mylene got her degree in graphic design and lives in magical Paris with her mesmeric Minna, her existence tuned into a fresh signal on an entirely new frequency. She owes much of her success to Bertha. Denis died of a brain tumor. He called it a temporary tenant in his building. It said hi, bye, did this and that, came and went, and took its landlord with it. And Bertha vanished without a trace. Mylene could never make any connection.

Big Bertha's body, with Denis' head on her shoulders, sambas in a slaughterhouse. All's more than so-so. FIN.

Edith In Hollyweird

A SAPPHIRINE STREAM swooned at the hill suffocated by khaki-colored foliage. The sky had a rotten-corpse-blue smirk. Heartless wintry weather with its tormenting cold. Oxford, England. She walked, went along as a hunting hound following a familiar scent, past abandoned apartment units, ravaged residences, and impassive ships in the harbor. Plain Jane pretty teenager Edith Liddell, a petite brunette, with a broomhead haircut, reptilian eyes, exhaust pipe proboscis, looking like a combination of gooney bird and Javanese doll, at a tea (the drug) party in her beautiful boyfriend's university's cutesy dorm room, was tripping badly. A voice, Colin's (her beau), with a measured dose of concern, hauled her out of her narcotics-and-alcohol-induced stupor, as a crane pulling a car out of the water. She imagined his sphincterial pucker was like a washing machine's porthole. She was swaddled in a patchwork quilt like a cadaver at the morgue, ingested nauseating stale candy and imbibed frantic cups of spiked punch. Spitting snow was as flakes of dandruff. Rain sounded like dry sighs of drifting sand. Stars shot as bars of soap out of human hands and ricocheting off tub and tile. Her brain searched for the balance it'd lost, and finally found it. Consoling coruscation. Her liquescent form seemed to spill down the creaky stairs and spread not unlike a stain on the threshold. The room was apparently a courtesan's boudoir. Spidery carousers scuttled. Rock 'n' roll on the radio carried her dancing into the algid blackness, swept away by vocals, guitar, bass, drums and keyboards into the sea of song. She could feel, even see, Colin's presence in the absence, as a bodily imprint in a sheet after the person's departure. Her heart tapped like new shoes on asphalt. The building had these catacombs of cubicles for students. Pain pounded in her abscessed molar, the ache hammering at the dying nerve. Merrymakers, with hats comparable visually to Martian helmets in a sci-fi flick, unconsciously created an intricate choreography through the pumping place. She was quite the pale creature, sucking on a striped lollipop as a babe on its pacifier. Her mind felt like a freshly dissected animalic heart miraculously still beating. She was revved as a motorcycle on the potent pills. Rioters stared at her like they were robbers and she was a bank. They nonchalantly dispensed their animalian stink. Her fragrance rather intensified with a quick spray of pricey perfume. Try as she might, she failed to shake her stubborn shadow. A frosted fern folded and unfolded itself. Dental lamp of moon. She concentrated on the spiraling cirri, meditated on her own seriously drunk-and- stoned condition. Cigarette smoke swirled hypnotically, aluminum and ceramic trays accepting their ashes. Cumuli were resurrected, roiled. Neon trees. Cellophane, icy brook. Chrysalis of her cranium cocooned her grey matter. Her pulse insectivally pulsed. She was severely hallucinating. Porous twilight. She radiated in it. Pieces of spongoid cake on the table were like fetuses. Patient textbooks on the desk impregnated with coffee smells. Air sticky as soda. Dog ears of leaves. Edith got a whiff of disinfectant, B.O., and fertilizer. Wind whistled suggestively. Somnambulant snout of sun sniffed through the slowly evaporating clouds. Main office edifice looked like a Grecian temple. Vegetation wilted as old magazines. The upholstered antique chair she sat in was like the gallows. She had the sensation of being perched, as an owl on its branch. Dentures on a stool like Dracula's falsies. Savage roar of thunder. Serpentiform wire hanger dangled in a closet. Gelatinous oxygen. She got spasms in her stomach as ripples in a well's water when a stone drops in. She reared up and whinnied akin to a horse possessed after attempting to retrieve a glass of vodka, perspiring profusely and coolly, with a pair of tongs and spatula from the Formica. A canvas bag in the corner had a smug moue. Zephyrian mewing. Precip like beads falling from a snapped necklace. Her perineal itch she was compelled to scratch. Claret cloudlets were as bleeding cotton balls in a doctor's wastebasket. Her axillae was redolent of country cooking. Seated, her middle was gathered into fleshly pleats. Rubbish bin. Her oral cavity had a rancid taste of acid. She gazed blankly at a shirtless Colin, swilling booze out of the bottle with his Neanderthalic buddies, the thin reddish thatch on his chiseled chest transmogrifying into these floccose/feathery birds, the flock squawking like an intercom and flying over the beach of his brown belly. Grenade of dope razed her encephalon. He was in heat and she kept him on a leash, reined in. She had a frightened filly's sort of fear. Her tummy was hot as a wood-burning stove. He touched her chin like a priest blessing a wafer during a churchy function. Her mind whirred as an electric mixer in the bony bowl of her head. The invisible barrier between the couple was one of safety glass. He was ravenous for her, repugnant as a result. He was a goddamn scoundrel and impossibly lovely. Prudish pallid drapes were drawn. He guillotined a cucumber using a cleaver. Lighthouse beacon leven. Tendons on her skinny neck bulged. He singsonged her name and produced a packet of crystalline powder from his jeans' pocket as a magician and wagged it in front of her. She nodded no politely and with a neutral grin. His backside was like an oil drum. His features were really sharp and steely. He sarcastically frowned in dramatic disappointment. His handwriting on an envelope was an elementary school script. Her forehead wrinkled, with her thoroughly engrossed in the batch of tapioca pudding. Her tone was humble and subservient in talking to him. She forgot to shave her legs and it felt as if they were coated in acrylic fur. Shriveled saplings. Horrendous construction site, graffiti in pastel chalk on a few trailers like cabooses. The goose of her brain was cooked. A crippled beggar, with a stench of tobacco and stew, giggled and blinked, ambled, unassailed. Her cardiac organ clanged as pots and pans. She was, to Colin, not unlike some ungainly stork in sportswear and progressed across the parlor in precarious flight. Empyrean had the pigment of the earth. Twin tramps plopped on the vinyl couch, had the fake-pleasant modulations of a tag team of switchboard operators, and were immensely aggravating. Two gawky, preppy gals, glacial princesses, with deadpan faces, feline peepers, punched-in noses, limp plasticine lips, test tube digits, toilet tank-handle wrists, and egg-white integument, argued. It was a vocalic cat fight. Verbalizations bit and scratched. Pot smoke diligently devoured them. Adorable Edith's foul anal mouth defecated steamy excremental hellos. Her skull tangled in her mane was like a seal's head snagged in seaweed. Her dirty chipped nails painted cobalt and cardinal. She needed a manicure and a pedicure! Wolfing down a steak- and-pepper sub. This was a running joke of a crash pad. Racket rose and fell. Gusts scolded harshly. She looked as though she wore contact lenses, only didn't. Sweat made her glisten like she was smeared with grease. Her pupils sure were dilated. Gobbling prescription tiny cylinders as aspirin. She vented a disillusioned individual's sough, apathetically watched the nutty antics, proceedings. Pungent odors. Pretentious tapestries. Avian fish floated in the aquarium of the azure. An adjacent edifice reminded her of the Moulin Rouge, the structure next to it like the Eiffel Tower. Potted plant and dismantled engine on the cruddy wooden floor. Her bugged oculi took an impromptu tour of his torso. Embers from a bonfire popped as pimples bursting. She chirped like a goldfinch. Heat was cranked to the point of crematory calidity. Gypsean shanties. Disfigured fountain.

Edith held onto herself desperately, as if lost on a raging sea, surrounded by spumescent, turbulent waves of anxiety. Her Pekingese eyes glowed. Ding-donging in her ears. Her pubic hair like a flaccid paintbrush. Oratory of a shed. Her flat little pert breasts, perky posterior, and bony ankles. To calm herself, she counted down as though in preparation for an Atomic Bomb detonation demonstration. Sparrows and swallows mingled with the cirri. She was stretched out on the linoleum as a cadaver about to be cut open, courtesy of a coroner. Her vascular organ drummed like she was keeping time for galley slaves. Snow's flakes like pencil shavings. Madmen in boiler suits and foaming at the maw played catch with a madly wiggling catfish. Labyrinthine town twinkled as in a fairytale. Fuzz on her nape fluttered not unlike candles' wicks. Her entirety was completely charged, as if she were subjected to an agonizing round of electric shock therapy. Plunked on, the sallow sofa squealed. Its squat legs had an arthritic stiffness, she noticed. Clots of pigeons dotted the firmament. Cavernous kitchen was a chicken coop of flurries of kooky activity. Dishwasher gurgled. Water heater belched. She peered in like a cockatoo. Sun paid homage to the welkin. Midget bushes. Beer kegs. Drizzle as whirlpools of sawdust. Stark raving lunatics were deaf-mutes signing like crazy. Soil as saliva-soaked bread. Laurel and Hardy, claiming to be legitimate Jehovah's Witnesses, were endeavoring to break into a vacant cab. Laurel brandished a flask and Hardy gave birth to styrofoam cups. Turtledoves cuddled on a rooftop. Her coconut dropped like an apple from the branch. Her abdominal accordion wheezed with gas. Fog was fleshy. Bric-a-brac was as high-tech dashboard gadgets. Rainbow had the hues commonly associated with children's drawings. Garage was renovated into a cinema. Her bombinating grey matter sounded like a malfunctioning taximeter. Luxury high-rises, cheerless and colorless. Cocksure clowns were barmy but harmless. Brume made her derma feel slathered in cream. Perverts discussed hanky-panky. Linen shop and veterinary clinic. Plaster swans became animated and waddled on the grass and gravel. Cloudless and birdless heavens. Filaments on her nuque were as ailing floret stems. Deadmoth on the windowsill. Celluloid rindle. Her burp had the sonance of a goat's blat. Unkempt shrubs. Viscera of the house was in working order, was her uneducated diagnosis. She surmised the furniture and pictures were gifted. Hedges were ratty like a hermits' tresses. Her lizardy lips were feverishly parched. Colin's mitts clambered up her slender hips as crabs climbing on rocks with the tide coming in. She was indeed under his thumb. He knew she was neurotic, a suicide. His hangman's vox, vulturous smile. He belted his brandy. Her sweetness was cloying to him. Gushing vocalizing. With fate, she was feeling like a babe in arms. A handsome redhead in tortoiseshell rims and with a whorish smirk and idiotic hairdo and in a beryl low-cut dress, flittered, absentmindedly, not unlike a hummingbird. Cheap cupboards and cabinets. Naughty and nude boys and girls created utter chaos. Wind- up cars were parked on a toy chest in the pantry. She endured a nasty case of indigestion. Crossword on the countertop. Swigging her whisky. Nibbling on a biscuit. Confusion of rings on her fingers. Innocuous penumbral threat. Her breathless angst. She coughed into a cupped palm. Naked young adults on the croquet grounds used flamingos as mallets and hedgehogs as balls. Schwagged and tired of being bombarded by the revelers' riddles, she, at last, decided to leave. She tested the doorknob like a pilot would her propeller. Sleet jingled as bracelets. A blast of her flatulence sounded as the fanfare of closing film credits. Sun was a gigantesque yellow phonograph record turning at a fast rate. Colin was irritatingly intrusive, like a cyst on an armpit. On this quaint and very leafy lane, an anthropomorphic White Rabbit, wearing a woolen vest and carrying a pocket watch, raced pell-mell, managed to avoid these acacias as a rat dodging furnishings. Abruptly, a behemothic Cheshire Cat appeared on a bent bough and pointed in the exact direction the bunny took. Then it disappeared, only its smile remained and turned into a frown, floating on the eddying mist. She impulsively followed the White Rabbit down into a sewer hole, when, suddenly, she arrived on a movie set designed to look like the 'Alice in Wonderland' world.

Edith's older sister, the viperine Lorina, was her manager, and she escorted her, intermittently, and inexplicably, pawing at her knee. She could certainly be a millstone round her neck! Her dedication to her job was on par with the fervor of Christian piety. The Volkswagen was an excessive, exuberant moving showpiece. She was behaving as the captain at the helm of her ship. Her pallor was waxen, dubious lashes aflutter like a dragonfly's wings. Her language skidded off course. She was pepped up on something more than merely adrenalin. Her feet reeked of dead donkey and rusted can. Blurry river. She had a beaky nose, double chin, big bosom, belly and bottom. Her makeup was aggressive and antiquated. Fish scales of cumuli on the horizon. A Rolls-Royce with black beetles for wheels idled in the throat of an alley, a lumpy mattress on the hood. She envied how lissome and lovely Edith was. She insisted Edith was uncooperative and unappreciative, maintained she, Edith, hit the jackpot with the role, the part of a lifetime. Edith, nervous and insecure, felt engulfed by the whole damn thing. Her oral cavity was Ali Baba's cave, she daydreamed. Her lanky arms were as a plumber's hand-snakes. There were vibrations in her noodle and hieroglyphs in her sight. She was feeling not unlike a terrorist riding shotgun with a government official; and as if she were a script's page, twisted and torn; and like a worm in an apple, in this vehicle. Pitching back and forth, going in and out of potholes, and swerving around them. Day prefaced night. She pondered Lorina as though via a spy hole. Zephyrean asthmatoid suspirations. Deformed centenarian bag lady in pajamas hobbled pathetically, had the expression of a terrified mouse. Smog crawled like mold creeping on a ceiling. Lorina pretended as if she were super-friendly tour guide. Lambency tarnished the argentate lake. Chinese vase and clarinet poked out of a knapsack in the backseat. Laundry in a basket beside it stank of mildew and

mothballs. She had a cow's countenance and was phos-
phorescently quick-witted. She pulled Edith's leg on a
regular basis. Paused for a moment at a red light, she
stared at Edith like a beaver. They cruised as a steamer.
Heat and humidity were merciless. Feculent scabs on
a wooden bench. Panes covered with slate of shades.
Veil of mizzle. Servicemen marched drunkenly on the
motorway. Fireflies drew glimmering ellipses on the
stagnant air. Closed establishments reverberated with
emptiness. Gymnastic maneuvers of the automobile.
Improbable skyline. Caustic eye of sun kept tabs on
them. The megalopolis was an immeasurable blocked
toilet. Squalid streets and sooty chimneys. Mugginess
built up as a tear welling in the eye. Oxygen like flan.
Depressing section of the city. Their conversation broke
off as a snapped branchlet. Fat fogies jabbered out front
of a defaced monastery. Edith's mind was a comet.
Her ears rang like ice jingling in a bucket. An emaciated vagrant, looking gnawed-on by wind and water,
pushed a supermarket cart as a plow through a parking lot. Statue in the square was callously amputated.
Battalion of Catholic-school pupils. Alternating light
and shadow. Disheveled biddies in their decrepitude
meandered on the trashy sidewalk. With the cosmetics, Lorina's complexion was shiny like a marble floor
of a foyer in an office building. Her sulphuric inflection. Showers polka dotted the windshield with beads.
Boulevard moved as though it was a long strip of film
in a projector. Umbrageous trapezoids on the pavement.
Edith reminded Lorina of a scrawny albatross; or a
snobby seraph. Lorina's dandruff was as breadcrumbs.

She issued these senile sounds, juggled her phone and espresso thermos, balanced miscellaneous items on her lap, fussed with dials, the entire shebang like it was a circus performance. There was an accidental comical aspect to the act. Her epileptiform twitches and diabolic blinders. The eucalyptuses and sycamores scintillated with enigma. Celestial sphere dissolved in the cirri. Edith could easily decorate the interior with diarrhea. Manducatory effort with the fruit-flavored bubble-gum. Her back buffed the plush seat. Crisscrossings of shoppers. Stars blemished the cobalt vault as warts a visage. Polar breaths of cloudlets. The two quarreled like cartoon chipmunks. Edith's hair was a coxcomb in the warm, clammy breezes. Cloudlets were as whipped cream. Luminescent rhombi on the cement. A pre-pee masturbation interlude was necessary to alleviate her ever-mounting stress. She bent her elbows and knees like she would the joints of a superhero action figure. Overcast was white as bird crap. Rundown pharmacy and boutique. Her mien was gentle and understand-ing. She was extremely patient, however, she was beside herself with frustration, dealing with her domineering sis. She was feeling like she had dinosaurian bones con-nected by wires in a museum. Alley was slavered with condensation. She scrutinized her tree root fingers. Her head swayed as a camel's hump. Her existence was a sunken ship. Her brain was a smoldering cheroot. The migrainous ache: knitting needles thrust into a ball of yarn. EKG readings of neon flashes behind her lids. She shucked her shoes like she would, undoubtedly, peas. She pictured the Pygmy-sized, spherical White

Rabbit. Liquid-hissing sonancy in her hearing organs. Fire truck sirens, shrill, sounded certainly rabid. Her navel poked out as a cuckoo from its clock. She should shove Lorina out! If she were accused of pushing her, she would have no foolproof alibi prepared. Haha! She needed to take a leak and a dump. Noisome, grim projects for the impoverished. Her lips were rolled up on her teeth like cuffs of pants on calves. Motor snorted euphorically. Sprinkles were like the threads of a moron's drool. Oppressive rankness of garbage. Gales masticated on the quietness. She rummaged through her purse as a pup rooting in the ground for a bone it'd buried. It was like Edith was the pony and Lorina the trainer. Constellations of pedestrians' physiognomies. Shadowy phantasms played on a brick wall. Cacophonous concert. Thunderous outbursts, the sound as shaken sheet metal. Lorina's blather sounded like water burbling. Her phiz was crimson and crinkled as a piece of ignited paper. Their bickering was verily in synchrony. The precipitation's nonsense continued. Chronic cough of a cab, like it was in a state of exhaustion. Aureate aureolas of streetlamps. Vista recalled, visually, cured meat. Slinking centipede of a train. Skyscrapers loomed. Murmurous crickets. Firs and oaks practically blocked a drugstore's entrance. Jittery levin zigzagged. Cassiopeia of luminosity. Fleet of buses. Teenage football players, leaning against a chain-link fence, were aligned as dancers in a chorus line. The fast food was pig slop. Crummy district. Plants' leaves hung like the tongues of thirsty dogs. On the highway, the headlights picked the shrubbery on the side as one would spinach out of the gnashers and throw it into the murk in absolute repulsion. The moon moved as a fetus in the womb. Orange illumination. The vehicle came to a screeching, embarrassing halt. Lorina, with this wild rose of a blush, suckled her cigarette, her dictatorial intonation completely grating, weeping willow of tress tousled by the gusts, was on her case like a skin disease, dispensed her customary cock and bull, derived consummate satisfaction in the dispute, and stomped repeatedly on the brakes, at the stop sign for a poor paralytic. Sepulchral glove compartment. Laryngitic sonance of the engine. It went as a lobster. Coffin-shaped bed on the curb. Boughs waved like the arms of a drowning swimmer. An ambulance's siren's wailing lament. Ruddled luminescence.

In an enormous trailer was where the Drag Queen of Hearts, with an insectan head and anorectic physique, was waiting, clad in scanty lace lingerie and fluffy slippers, with a sign on his penis, written in arachnidan scrawl, reading 'Drink Me,' another on his bum , reading 'Eat Me.' His pimp, King James, anatomically suggesting a steroidic Shaft, clothed in a fluorescent leisure suit, teeshirt, and buckled boots, sat on a wickerwork bar stool, sipped absinthe and smoked a joint. Most high, Edith stripped and had sex with the Queen, the King jerking off. Their beloved pet, a talking turtle named Elliot, clad in a checkered sweater, mocked her from the coffee table, with detective novels haphazardly situated on it, when she was DP'd. They sat, for a respite, on the quadruped of a settee as parrots on a perch. Art Nouveau lamps on a lacquer buffet. Paleolithic flooring. Jays and robins flew at random in a muddy meadow. An old buzzard of a vendor's orangutan arms swung metronomically. Auditory succession of honking horns. Cirri were like sanguine compresses. She should've fought off the Queen's amorous advances, stood her ground, laid down the law. His insipid inflection. The downpour was as the rapids. He dried his perspiry, beetling brow with a handkerchief, like he was using blotting paper on an inky page. His iridescent irises gleamed with illness. He hopped with the grace of a frog on lily pads. His acneous complexion was as pitted stone. He possessed an alcoholic's aura. Light of weed illumined his crude, spacey jargon. She slithered like a cat does before it begins raining. Her heels were as moleskins. Hollywood Hills baked. Twirled medlars as twisty barky licorice sticks. She dropped her red undies, again, as a pigeon does its shit, bowed like a reed in mistrals. His dick was dead as a doornail, whereupon it sprung, miraculously, to life. Violated violently, she barked like a dog. In his ardency, he had the adamant audacity of a rapist. She felt abducted. Surroundings were active as a turkey pen prior to a storm. She suspired, sounding like wheezing steam, whooshed as applied brakes, and screeched as a charging choo-choo on rusty rails. During intercourse, they engine-chugged. Cankered cars. Forms were smeared through her lachrymal lenses. Her shoulders were cruciform on the carpet. Miscarriage of the sky, a frightful carmine, this gross, pasty, cloudy discharge unexpectedly ejaculated. King had an obsequious intonation and stayed clear in timorous respect. Cig-butts were larvae. Crack on the wall was reminiscent of a sizable scar. Metalline creek. Upper atmosphere had neither depth nor detail. A hirsute spider took refuge in a niche in the ceiling. Rolls of thunder tumbled in unison. Dew was startled and stirred by the lavender brilliance. Her asshole was like a trapdoor, shut for eons, now forced open. Clique of film crew gossiped as maids in a kitchen. Boughs rattled their leaves. Cumuli crowned the serriform summits. She was vaguely interested in the skulking werewolves, wearing hillbilly habiliments, probably out to pull some shenanigans, in the emerald orchard. They mooed and didn't howl, scurried like baboons. Her pouty puss, xylophone ribs, gut's guttural protests. Tempest of treetops. She was squinch-eyed, moved like her skeleton was made of springs. Her heart sounded as a bloodhound scampering on floorboards. Her apprehension grew like light in the morning. His shivering-jam eyes, crooked chiclets, fingers (thin as lobster antennae), and varicose veins. He waddled like a duck and had a cockroach's determination. She was borne aloft by them, as if she were the Virgin Mary and they were the faithful; or like she was a carnival dummy and they were rousties. Livestock milled about in an olive grove. Branches as though they were conductor batons. Runaway kites swam like a school of prismatic fish in cerulean water. Stench of decomposing cattle. Sun sank into the nuclear horizon as a toilet's tank-ball when flushed. Queen's probing digits were like insectoid feelers. He nibbled on Edith's beautiful body as vermin on a binge. Empyrean had the bright colors of playing cards. Malodor of intestinal vapor. Sweat seeped from his pores not unlike the earth secretes worms. His prattle swelled as a stomach does from gas. Chandelier's lustrous tears. Cuspidate cloudlets began to show in the ginger gums of firmament like a baby's teeth. Air was gooey and putrid. Emphysematous gusts. Sun disintegrated on the distant ridge as the deceased on a deathbed. He turtledove-cooed. Employees entered and exited the vaunted studio like maggots'd carrion. Wind whistled as it would in the crevices of a water mill. The scenery was unreal, like in a fantasy. She was penetrated as a vase by a stem. An army of ants marched single file. She felt like an oyster in the wrong shell. Her buttocks were flat as backgammon boards. They were coital bumper cars at a fairground. He was avian-nimble, had a canine's damp panting. Blades of grass were strummed by balmy breezes. They drifted like a sunken ship's wreckage. Unidentifiable shapes in the trundling tide of twilight. She was engaged in a battle with herself, losing a bout with insomnia. His expression was one of poached trout. Cloudcover was as a snowy television screen, in its vastness. King's Popeyean arms. She was brutally stripped once more, slapped hard on the hind and tum, mounted like a mule, and she moaned and groaned. She tugged on his prick as a fisherman reels in a rope from his boat. Voices were multiplied, divided, added and subtracted in a mathematical maelstrom on the movie set. Drafts with brisk efficiency. She was folded in his embrace like mussel. The motorized clamor on the nearby interstate was distracting, effecting her performance. The participants were coiled as intestines. Serpentine scintillation. Her muscular, poplar-whitish legs. Diurnal gasps. A Jeep sneezed when it started. Noise bounced like a rubber ball down a staircase. King doffed his duds and donned a wetsuit. An awesome Afro usurped his scalp. He was framed by body odor, actuated, kind of hopping, akin to an ailing kangaroo. Elliot scuttled as a blind scarab. King sported a faunish snigger. He sat on the ottoman as a tramp on a church's steps. His sidelong sneer. He was built like a bouncer. Shadows moved as servants. His interminable meaningless sermonizing. Oxygen was thick and hot like new tar. Her taut integument. Spume of cirri. Esparto was dominoes. Sacristy chest. She put on a habit and had pigtails. Hazy faces floated as balloons. Tacks poked out of the rubious rug like an antagonized cat's claws.

Eucharistic modulations of the bounding main. Religious paintings and oppressive furnishings. Zephyrous bronchial swooshing. Rain dripped as a leaking pipe. Sycophantic, unfashionable mannequins situated in a nook. File folders. Shitload of paperwork. Dilapidated mansion and barren land. Patrolling producers squawked like chickens. Wispy bones of branchlets. Edith had the droopy eyes of a beaten pooch. She perceived her debasement with a nightmarish clarity. Tick-tocking pendulum clock of her heart. Overstuffed chairs. Her pulse, pounding, sounded as the fist of a person, buried alive, banging on a casket's lid. Her hollow feeling of emptiness resonated like an empty tomb. Resigned to receive punishment, she was hunched over, impassive and inert, tight, silken midsection scrunched up, bulbiform, satiny breasts hanging, as a plow-ox in expectancy of receiving a lashing from its owner. Queen waited for an exasperating eternity for her to get in a spreadeagled position. She suspired, the sonance like a siphon gurgle. His translucent intonation, lust grew as yeast. Her expression projected anxieties like streetlights do jalousies on the paneling. He swatted at her haunches as if he were chasing off gnats. Crickets droned. She screeched like an organ. Skewered, she huffed and puffed, sniveled and complained, to no avail. Her rump's cheeks moved as a frog's. Overcast was like an aquatic membrane. She was supine and he optically inspected her. Underlings huddled as football players during a game. King's facial features' contortions were unnerving. Fulgurous remora flopped. With all the drug paraphernalia, placed willy-nilly, the joint looked like a collegial chemical lab. Fount expectorated a valance of spangles. Cirri, creatures born of microscopic eggs, peeked. She was sad and still as a graveyard monument. Set designer schmucks were like the Three Wise Men. Their artsy-fartsy apparel. They subsisted on a steady diet of hashish. Her bunghole was a gaping fishmouth. Ebbing pellucidity of the emanation. Fondled, she fidgeted. The indignity, molested, was alien to her. Baroque wardrobe. Her gaunt neck, gangly limbs, hair, from the fornication, a Liszt-styled shock. It fanned out. The trailer was as a tanker. Minuscule lavatory. She was bent at the waist like Phaedra. He handled her as the Body of Christ. Technicians were attired in ostentatious impecuniousness. Her irriguous eyes - glinting questions he had no answers for. She had the sensation of being incomplete, like a clarinet with missing keys. The pair danced an intricate ballet of carnality. Slate-gray skyline. Her undertoned griefs. Wheels of his hands partook of the sinuous tracks of her legs. King lounged on cushions as a sated fakir on a mattress made of pillows. Electric hum of telephone wires. Virtual cornfield of Port-O'-Potties. Her rear's hams were like a couple of oblivious overripe mangoes. Stagnant air was as a cavern's. She dropped some acid. Brumal eiderdown. King turned on the transistor radio and flipped through the stations. Pelagic static. Snail of her umbilicus. She experienced the sense of being abandoned, like detritus on the shore left by the surf, the beach a depository for debris. Her cries echoed as if they were sent into a well bottomless. Queen glared at her like a schoolmaster a student late for class. Her ears jangled as silverware. Jazzy (attributable to the splendor) bubbles were like mini birthday balloons. He was mean as a bird of prey, pecking at her sphincterial cherry. Her hands were unexplainably paralyzed like an unwound clock's. Indistinct polygons of cliffs. Boughs stretched as sleeping arms. Orgy of sucking on mints and sipping java. Her profile was like a masterpiece painted by Vermeer. Her feet dangled as a hanged woman's, thighs open like she was at the gynecologist's, her lineaments, in impenetrable placidity, connecting its pieces as parts of a puzzle. Leaning to blow him not unlike a vocalist to a mike. She was the splayed on the chesterfield as a human sacrifice on an altar. Briefcase. Tablecloth. Teacup. Her indifferent mouth introduced to his. He inhumed his thumb in her keister, pinkie in her cunt. Cigar was the size of a tampon. Their precise (copulatory) association like in a dance hall contest. King was the recipient of the consolation prize. Broth as though it was lava. Chiaroscuro died and resurrected itself. She rose like a sunken ship resurfacing. Lemon sun rested on the pearlescent platter of cumulus. Her feet whiffed of barbecued pork. The megapolis simmered. He spanked her, the sonance as lips smacking when smooching. Voices clanged like trams, resounded from pillar to post. Niagara rhythm of the deluge. He held onto her as a baby baboon its momma. She grizzled, shed her sepia brassiere and bikini briefs like a tulip drops its leaves, was barefoot in the bathroom. Clouds hastened as revenants. His indexer maneuvered in her unsearchable cavity like a silkworm. Lightbulbs of his hindquarters were screwed tight into his anatomy. She envisaged herself metamorphosing into a butterfly. She whimpered as a gate's corroded hinges. Mop head of her hair was sopping-wet from perspiration. Fitting together like letters in a monogram. Incoherent phrases were emitted. Her stubbly, rashy armpits. Rayon and polyester straits were formed by undergarments. Animalized breathing. Corkscrewed, viciously, she yelled as a child wanting parental attention. Temps malevolent. He was redolent of bedpan. She was lost like light in shade. A gaffer, in grungy jeans and hiking boots, had the virile ruggedness of an avid adventurer. King watched him as the driver of a locomotive waiting for the signal to depart. Jesus Christ turned into Donald Duck in her druggy/ alky daze. Her fanny was a furnace. She was bestilled and had the solidity of a cemetery's cement angel. She normally strutted akin to a Siamese kitty, strove to scandalize the movie set with salacious stunts, body doubles, those stupid stand-ins, not necessary. Queen hugged her like a department store clerk wrapping merchandise.

No man's land of lawn. Collection of syringes, bottles of pills, and sandwich bags of cocaine and heroin. Her encephalon floundered as an old toad in a flooded swamp. Roman candles spilled their coruscating guts. He was a frayed bandage on the suppurating sore of her. Antiseptic savor was like insecticide combined with mouthwash. Birds roamed through the grassy hillock as lice in thinning tress. He forcibly immobilized her, bit and pinched her. Temperatures soared. His villous chin pricked her like brambles. The pond was, in all probability, lukewarm as oatmeal. The assistant DP was Saint Bernard-semblant, apparently on the cusp of kicking the bucket, had on prophet's sandals. King sat cross-legged like a practicing Hindu. Mortars of fireworks. Pitchfork as Neptune's trident. He walked cautiously, like a bishop round a communion table, and using air freshener as a censer. Mad fury of the drencher. Menstrual-reddish moon. Edith's blank countenance made her appear catatonic. Funereally solemn song came from some-where. Hail had the sonancy of castanets. King, using a plastic spoon, made a typhoon out of his vanilla yogurt. Meanwhile, Queen grunted like an ape. Scudding cirri. Soaker sounded as tambourines. Laborers millipeded on through this semi-built cottage for a shot. Retinue of techs bustled like butlers. Caterers coasted as sting-rays underwater. Scene upcoming. Her derrière was like a stick-pocked drumhead. He was a mole in the mound of her. She was poor as a church mouse and needed the gig. Badly. She felt like grub turned inside out. Sexing, they looked as a couple of curs fighting over scraps left out by a grocer. It was steamy like a sauna. Undulant, penumbrous octopus flailed. Afterwards, she was feeling demeaned and afraid.

Edith literally got a big head when she was becoming a bona fide starlet. She was cast in the role of a lifetime! To wit, playing the part of her dear sister, Alice, revisiting Wonderland as an adult! Her cranium grew to such a monstrous size that it hit the ceiling. She sobbed, her tears flooding the luxury camper. She swam through the lachrymal pool, massive cormous skull bumping into the wainscot, and wound up on the banks of a river. There, she met a blue Caterpillar, sedulously smoking a hookah and lounging on a maroon mushroom. He, in an exaggerated hambone southern drawl, said she, soaking wet, should run in circles in order to properly dry herself off. She did, got dizzy in the process. And they got stratospherically high. He offered her employment as a stripper and she declined without any hesitation whatsoever.

In her lavish condo, Edith received an anonymous letter in the mail, the threats thoroughly worded out, accusing her of tarnishing Wonderland's reputation. She inwardly debated whether or not a career as an artistic thespian was worth the risks involved. She gave it to Lorina, who advised her to ignore it. A paunchy, bell-shaped electrician, cheeks like puff pastries, tolled to his tasks. Ochery knolls. While filming a sophisticated shot with a male, angular dodo and the dapper, diminutive Mad Hatter, both babbling, on a psychedelic platform, Edith witnessed a female Asian intern opening a package, wrapped as a present, behind the scenes, and it exploded like a bomb, injuring her. Edith found a scrap of paper warning her of more attacks should she continue making the picture. She was unable to separate reality from fantasy in show business, doubted her abilities to play the part of Alice, from whom she was estranged. In spite of their differences, their distance from one another, she still loved her. The role was difficult, personal. In the ladies' loo, she was visited by Alice, who, incensed, insulted her. Their inflections were crackly and loud, as if they were put through megaphones. Alice advanced, like she was dragged, as a young bullock pulled by its nose ring. She reeked of cabbage and was excitable like a moth at an illumined pane. Her dungy dress was dated, the Goldilocks wig outrageous. Her lanky shakers flapped as the looses soles of worn shoes, ran not unlike a chicken harassed by a butcher, intent on decapitating it. She wept as a saucer in a dishwasher. Her incisor- tusks. She could be mistaken for a strung-out junkie, anorectically angulous. An alleyway was an amusement park. Vermiform apostolic tongues in the grody sink. Crowd noise nearby. Canoe props were like mutant slugs. Decayed dragon of a pickup with rusty scales and engine entrails. She had apodictic halitosis, resembled a homonine ostrich, doled out derogatory remarks and tears, possessed a gecko's quickness. Her pneumatic respiring. Edith swung at the thrown insults and missed. She narrowly dodged irate Alice's tornadic hand-swipes, had this successful accomplice's smirk. She felt as though she were a blob of butter deliquescing on hot toast; or a bug frying itself on a lightbulb. Alice's fingertip was inserted into her duff like a suppository, which made Edith want to vomit. The sleet oozed from the sky as blood from a butchered body. There were pulsations of wicked pugilism. Spick and span corridor beyond. Methadone capsules on the trash bin. Rodent droppings on the glutinous tiling. Alice turned as a tapeworm. Her long tootsie-wootsies pedaled in the air like a character's in a comic strip. Bloodbath of skyline. Edith unfolded as a jackknife, was walloped in the breadbasket. And she ransacked her book bag for a can of mace. Her solar plexus was sore. Their fisticuffs had the slo-mo swiftness of a cinematic cataclysm. Alice's booming vox of the Last Judgement. She diagnosed her chipped nail like a doctor reading the mercury level of a patient's thermometer, swathed in material as a mummy. Her burro breath. Whistle-blow of her raspberry. Her toes, displayed with the flip-flops, in the radiance, were like anemic asparagus. She was corny as a love letter, had an auctioneer's voice, struck a statuesque heroine pose. Her arms were eel-slippery. Festival hullabaloo. Her infuriatedly flared nares. Edith was patient like a huntress waiting for a partridge, limbs tense as harp strings. Witching hour umbrae. Stall cramped like a coffin. She remembered Queen's penile promontory, commented his package was unmailable. She'd studied his exhibited unit as a mutt would a bitch's proffered prat. Alice reminded you of a deranged Our Lady. She exuded her detestable dementedness. She was also infantilely fickle, her capers of the simian variety. Pressing Edith's kidney with a knee, jabbing her in the liver with a fist. Fractured mirror's fragments reflected their essences back at them. Edith was frozen like a porcelain figurine. Intimidated, she was a hunched-in crybaby. Dentiform volcano was a rotting tooth. Alice's lengthy arms and legs were as elongated flames, silhouetted profile like charred edges smoldering, togs as hand-me-down rags bought at a flea market. A portion of peeling wallpaper hung like a florid bat from a rafter. Effulgence purpled the mere. Dripping faucet was as uncalculated Chinese water torture, driving the fighters crackers. Alice clutched her with her osprey's claw, imprinted her digits into Edith's shoulder. Lightning was veins rupturing in the abdominous azure. Storm's cascade. Edith's hand was on Alice's like a caterpillar on a leaf. She gazed at her as a foreigner at an interpreter. Acid swished in her esophagus like it was pushed along by a pump. Kids' smart- ass hubbub in the hall. She stared at the cloud-covered celestial sphere on the chance of spotting the sun. Wrestling on the floor, the sisters seemed to be fucking in a frenzy. Air was thick as cereal mushy with milk.

Shaggy yard. A mastodon of a custodian with an amiable moue trudged in, slugging a shot of sambuca, and cheeped at what he saw. He was a fretting, wrinkled waxwork. Edith's head had unbelievably traded places with her foot. Haggard Alice, prodding her in the chest, was, to all intents and purposes, pinning miniature flags on a map. The janitor stomped to and fro, like a jerky marching guard. Clientage coming and going from a casino/brothel setup. Catheter bag of the blue lid trickled. Hoopoe-hued refulgence. Tea bag lily pads in the teapot millpond. Images were distorted and protracted on the scum-slick walls. Edith endured an animalistic disquietude, as in a moment prior to a quake. Alice had a carnivorous beam. Flashes died in her pupils like lighted matches extinguished. She was discalced, had the svelte, filthy feet (heels as cowhide) of a martyr in a Renaissance painting. She could not contain her furious rage, was intent on turning her into mincemeat. Her face was superimposed on Edith's, according to the polished squares beneath them. The combatants rolled like wrappers in wind on the curb. The restroom was as commodious as a jeweler's cubicle. Alice tugged at Edith's mop, head swinging like a dead rabbit. Cylindroid excrement in the toilet bowl. Edith bled as a ripped cloth doll would sawdust during the (lopsided) drubbing. She waded into the high tide of Alice's psychosis. Light was a cheap trick. This hippopotamic hostess had a convivial unctuosity, let the women brawl. She beheld them like this was a primitive tribal ritual, the rite a curious local custom. Alice hovered over her as a hornet. Her horrendous breath brought the harbor to Edith's nostrils. Edith's noddle bounced as a ping-pong ball. She felt like she was transported to another (wacky) world, and was diminished, dwindling in size, as a diving bell, gradually descending into the murky depths. She looked at Alice's exposed nubber like it was fruit. Alice had a maniacal determination to hurt her. Or worse. Leaves wagged as unwell tongues.

Cranial empyrean with cloudy brains. Kites owled. Boats swanned in the port. Alice's contralto-cackling like her larynx was a broken record, her tongue of needle stuck in a groovy scratch, making a perpetual auditory pendulum. She was grim, spastic, threatening. Sinks glistened as ceramic trumpets. Edith's joints snapped like sticks.

Her marionette's modulation. The roughhousing looked as slapstick. Water trickling from taps sounded like billy bells tinkling. The scrappers squealed as pigs. Thalassic tang of their perspiration. Edith's shabby clothing appeared to've been purchased off the rack at a clearance sale. Alice glared at her disapprovingly, like she was a tardy visitor, spoke with sarcastic verve, had a photographed smile, hand clinging to Edith's calf akin to a barnacle to a jetty, told a sob story of being goaded by these hideous-as-sin witches, dressed in sheepskin robes, into walking, as a hamster on the wheel, discalceated, on hot coals and shards of glass, wearing a Turkish towel, while simultaneously swallowing and spitting fire. She crow-croaked, in excruciating pain. In return for the crones' entertainment, they'd heal her kidney stones, cure her gallbladder issues, and unclog her blocked up bodily plumbing. She was an oddball enfolded in a bedspread. The grappling, with vigor, was like it was an act of anatomical juggling. Their grousing delineated circlets of clamor. Whirls of expletives and insults. Lean-to hovels with stucco roofs. Grass shaved with a mower by a goateed giant in sailor breeches. Celluloid firmament. All described in detail by Alice. She was gang raped by the conjurers. The stare the hags gave her was one usually accorded to a person late to a party. Their tentacles tweaked her kneecaps, glommed sacramental wafers not unlike gingerbread cookies, glugged currant juice out of insignia'd goblets, derma layer resembling tobacco-tinged drapery. Alice shucked, and left on the costume jewelry they had provided. The occultists' hut's dimness and dampness common to a cave. Light and shade piano'd the keys to herald their arrival. Bony fingers tunneled into her orifices as woodworms into planks. There was a corrosion of quiet as they pervertedly diddled with her. The cadaverous sorceresses' atrophied muscles were like diseased trees' ossified roots. They recited rosaries when she, willingly, signed the contract's dotted line, using a standard penknife, the document written in a complex code. Constellation of candles. Her gown dropped as a final act's curtain. She held up the form like a surrender flag. They, sexually satiated to the breaking point, called her a retarded wench, played Russian roulette, cawed as ravens. Stars sparkled like polished flintlock pistols. Moribund, musty environs. Threadbare furniture. Alice slurped maple syrup, behaved as a smarty-pants, twitched like a sleeping cat dreaming of catching mice, assaulted, had the expression of a stupefied invalid. Her assailants strolled as puppets manipulated by strings, scowled at her like a fantastic facade's stony gargoyles. And their integument kept changing its texture. Arpeggios of showers. Hithe was filled with caravels, cranes, and stevedores. She lounged as a languid sea anemone. She'd lain like a soused seal on the pallet, skeptically surveyed them, their tones of voices swelling and subsiding as those heard in a library. One, with a mole-tawny tan, was pregnant, with flabby teats, nipples not unlike chestnuts, flaccid middle, neck stretched as a sunflower reaching towards the sun, tapered visage veiled by a silver mane, cocked her schnozzle in the air and jumped over Alice not unlike a horse lunging over a hurdle, nestled on her face as a sick bird, and plucked an acoustic guitar like she was waving goodbye to it ... Edith destroyed the cesspit restroom, termites inhabiting it, the urinals midget-sized, stalls pigsties, in a fit of anger, with a piece of piping, and Alice, with childish glee, bounded as a hare, flew like a quail, and launched herself head-first out the open window as a reckless stunt woman. Edith followed her like a pygmy, an explorer in the jungle.

Members of the live action version of the 'Alice in Wonderland' production staff were found murdered. First, the writer was gunned down in his kitchen. Second, the director was stabbed with an ice pick in her garage. Third, the cinematographer was bludgeoned in his parlor. Edith came across evidence incriminating her, and her increasing psychological instability made her doubt her own innocence and identity.

Arrhythmic rage of rainfall. Kayaks stranded on the shore were as beached ligniform dolphins. Gravid sun. Saliferous squalls. Beer bottles roosted in a row on the sea wall like hens in a coop. A rangy gent with a curate's cast and martial gait gave Edith the willies, as if he were a figment from a disturbing nightmare. Her saliva was like jelly. She was roasting as a June bug on a lamp's high-wattage bulb. Quartziferous sand. Mammoth proportions of a cop on the beat. He looked like a moon-man with great girth in a constable uniform. She was brusque with fatigue, yearned for a snooze, and yawned. An evidently diabetic and hepatitic manikin struggled mightily to surf. Gannets were in calamitous fervor. Medusae adhered to the ocean's surface. Vinegary vapor. A perspiry channel coursed in between the sharp rocks of her shoulder blades. She was further tormented at a packed parade, taunted by Alice. Enraged, Edith, tense as a boxer before a championship match, chased her through a crowd of people. Alice came and went out of focus, like Edith's eyes were a microscope's lenses and someone was fussing with the knobs. Each conveyed syllable weighed a ton. Welkin hocked muculent cirri from its lungs (on their last huff). Alice's eyeballs bobbed in their aqueous sockets as mucilaginous embryos pickled in jars, and her jarps bounced seesawingly like a scale's pans. Her temper was detonated akin to a cherry bomb. Edith sank into her as if she were quicksand. Her venter vibrated spasmodically. Marching band's racket was insufferable. Slap sounds. She keened, was creaky like a senior citizen. Her furry-feeling tongue hung as an intellectual's beard. She gaped dumbly at her opponent. Her spittle had the sour sweetness of the juice from a squeezed daisy. The combatants thrashed like snapped violin strings. Alice, an archangel of death, hauled her as though she were a drowned woman, then gorged on her like some carnivorous plant, clenched fist held high, exhibited as a trophy. Her armpits stank of latrine. She called her adversary a "cream puff." The sisters didn't so much as drift apart in life as dash, more or less. One had bits and pieces of the other's personality. Alice drove Edith to despair when growing up. Sprinkles were like hydrogen peroxide. Special effects place used to be a quarantine station. Edith paid heed. Wizened best boy with a licy thatch had the flesh of an iguanid belly. His snail's pace accelerated into a species of jog. Precip in its purulency.

Veinal lightning was visible in the thin elderly skin of the sky. Cumuli were splotches of vitiligo on the vault. Conglomerate of passers-by, red-faced, as from liquor, were in their Sunday best. These sickos got their thrills. Arid air. Undulatory applause from the audience. Battery of thunder prefaced by serrulate leven. Pterodactylous guys. Arabic girls. British boys. Peddlers and pets were interspersed. A geezer, derma like lacteal skim, was contained in a blanket as a geriatric emperor. Transparent parade balloons were IV bags floating free from a macabre saturnalia. Edith's bleary vision. Her nerves were incandescent wires. It felt like locusts were feasting on her flesh. Her noggin was emptied of thoughts; a chinaless cabinet. Besieged, she slumped, stomped on. Alice's crepe cutis was buttered with cocoa lotion. Vista wrung a cloud like it was a wet hankie. Purring obscenities. Membranaceous contractile covering of the overcast. Bells pealed. Levin had the rhythmic movements of a blacksmith's. She returned the bludgeoning favor in concentric ripples and Alice reeled. She didn't feel right, psychologically or physically, as if she were put together wrong, her bones rearticulated incorrectly. Spiderwebbing espaliered a hedgerow. Murres, soaring, were flat like postcards. Pestle of Edith's fist was grinding into the mortar of Alice's midriff. Fisticuffs were out of control. Invective dispersion. Spectators trilled as grasshoppers and hooted like owls. Alice's beady peepers burned. Her fierce, highly wrought features were striking. Her full-bellied guffaw. She had much to hide and yet revealed a lot. Cardboard nativity scene. Ants competed for rinds. She smelled of compost heap.

Segment of the city teemed with twitters. Grindstone sun. Pharaonic statue carved of basalt. Gummous gobbets of their sallies stuck to the palate. Rumpus of the repartee. Spouted geysers of cheap shots. Razor- sharp jabs. Skyline seemed embalmed. It was as though this was the Olympiad of the odd. Alice, something of a rara avis, captured Edith's imagination ... and held it captive. Alice shaped and spun her like clay, smelted and casted her as iron, an enterprise which was potty. Her pile-driving, rock-hard knees and elbows slammed into Edith's groin. Her arms took turns roundhousing. Alice's enigmatic eccentricities weren't exactly false, however, to Edith, they didn't ring true. Horizon was mottled (with off-white clouds) like a salt pan.

Gusts griped as pelicans. Alice's fingers climbed on Edith's legs as vines on a deserted chalet. Bombardment of slurs both ways. They puled like a sitcom. Their limbs were jumbled up. Cypresses and elms were bathed in the eventide's nacreous light. Edith murmured like a heart, sciatica subsiding as a the sea, expression still like a tarantula, got an unwanted glimpse of Alice's nether regions' triangular flaxen tuft, an incipient beard. Mimosas raised their boughs like arms in a mock Nazi salute. Sprinkles sounded as beetles' eggs cracking open. Pyramidal tents. An albino auto mechanic in a bathrobe and Panama hat put on a rubber raincoat, looked like the sole lodger in a hotel in the tropics. A train sliced the town, discombobulated the buildings with its perpendicular cutting. The spider of sorrow spun its web within Edith, covered the whole interior of her cavernous chest. A trolley galloped. Alice held the absence of Edith's waist. The battlers lurched helter- skelter as cabin boys on deck in churning waters. They could be misconstrued as imitating nymphs, in an oleograph, holding hands. Scintillant splinters were not unlike crochet needles. Honeysuckles and pines cracked as spinal cords. Mishmash of diversiform dockside warehouses. Alice's toucan pies and beak, piglet eyelashes embellished by mascara. She, sighing like a tree in a chinook, appeared to be a maniac writing a memo; or one patching a tire tube. Disembodied ribcage of aqua pura was left from a drying puddle. Potentially apocalyptic storm encroached. Tram's rusty shrill. Heat and humidity boiled with duodenal lassitude. Archipelagos of foul sludge in the skewed splendor. Soon, the megalopolis would be plunged into forlorn tenebrosity. Pimps leered. Lechers ogled. Sluts swayed. Pigeons, in a pother, contended for French fries on the esplanade. Somnambulistic harlots, with watercolor makeup, stewed their uncertainties in the hot humectation, balanced in their stilettos as storks, infected with insomnia, warbled like doves, cried as peacocks. Hammer and sickle graffiti defaced an infamous flophouse. Emotion was coaxed out of Edith like a baby from a womb by a nurse. Knot in her throat. Teachers shooed students as Thanksgiving turkeys. She hankered for carrot soup and a vitamin-rich plum! Laundry baskets. She mentally flipped through the scrapbook of her childhood. The photo album was crystal clear. Jittery breaths of breezes. A glass of prune juice would facilitate her digestion. Her bladder and bowels hollered. Geometry of telephone poles. Her medulla oblongata whirled like a roulette wheel. A doorman, with a Clark

Gable mustache and vampiric fangs, wattles dangling as an accordion, perused his paycheck, whistled a familiar refrain, was hushed and attentive. Alice, asperity suggesting a terrible toothache, moving her head like electric shocks were applied to her temples, insisted Edith's zhopa was made of rice pudding. What a wingding! A stocky fella smoked cigarillos out front of a defunct printing press. Dories of monasteries. Pedestrians manifested, were fascinated by the phenomenon of these contentious ladies, and, presto, they, the strollers, along with Alice, vanished in a puff of smoke. Whereupon Edith was struck by a truck driven by Alice, and its load, these copies of Lewis Carroll's 'Alice's Adventures in Wonderland,' spilled out like an avalanche, burying her. She knew, in a matter of minutes, that this was an imagined occurrence. Defeated and distraught, Edith accepted the false as truth. She smashed a looking glass and chewed its shards to see if her pain was real or not, cutting her mouth. She went on an imperative shopping spree. Alice was spotted amongst the crew and set. Post-It notes stuck on the walls promised to get rid of Edith. Alice finally made good on her promise and tried to pummel Edith in the dressing room, only she was thwarted when Edith knocked her out cold with a club and fled the scene. She contacted the authorities. When they arrived, Alice's body was missing, causing Edith to question her sanity. Lorina, dropping her off at home, told her that her next project was a sequel to 'Alice,' but with more adult content. Edith scoffed at the idea, and kettle-whistled in frustration. Preparing to shoot up, she tied the rubber hose on her arm like one lassoing a bull's horns, gasped as wind. Leaden disc of the moon.

The watery ribs made by the sprinkler expanded and contracted, fanned and folded, in the muscles of oxygen. Lorina's turtle nose was scrunched, crayfish eyes were squinty. She had the sluggish movements of a chrysalid. Her fingers, she envisioned, chiefed, were as green beans half-eaten by caterpillars. Her noodle overflowed with thoughts like the hemorrhaging of a toilet tank. Cirri in the sky: lacework of cosmic woodworms in the amberous dawn. Her corollas of rosacea. Cogitations emerged as decor from shade in an abandoned domicile. Skeeters trilled like canaries. Pandemonium of domestic conflict. Lowing of vessels, bovine craft mooing in the anchorage pasturage. Apian zizzing. Time-corroded tenement. Breezes were as breaths dispensed in pillows. Fringe of ferns. A hammock was like the floppy unending shoe of a clown. Tinny ringing of the bellflowers. Pollen had the diabolical smell of sulfur. Cranes' carillon. Empyrean graced by cumuli. Respirations of the russety tributary. Storm instilled its threat in the air. A fir fell as a stiff corpse. Troublous public transportation. Bronchitic gusts. A branch was pointed not unlike a harpoon. An ursine geezer was rug-worthy. Gummy rain as the drool of snails. People, their voices sounding like shrieking violins tortured by vicious bows, crawled on one another as crabs in an aquarium. Vivid caterwauling of the bottle rockets. Natatorial vehicular shoal. Lorina soughed like a tightrope walker. A radiant display of a department store hiccuped hue. Distant thunder sounded as digits drumming on a steering wheel. Perturbation got her like a bat would a moth. Cathedran ships. Bus was stalled on a bridge. Metropolis was a carousel of a melting pot. She darted as if she were propelled by a spring; or like she was beating a (hasty) retreat from a civil war. Edifices ironed in the smaze. Her botty fox-barked with farts. Dunnocks winged their way. Her spasms were as the convulsions of a tuna out of water. Edith confided in her by communicating to her she was feeling exploited by the Hollywood studio system, and that she was a fruit-cake marinating in the sherry of bafflement. Magpies, swooping, merged into a singular mass. A goldfinch seemed to be inciting insurrection in the midst of its alienated avian brethren. Robins flew in a whirlwind of feathers. Sooty city was suffocated by the chimney stacks. Pamphlets with political propaganda littered the cratered roads. Swooned noisomeness of sewage. Lorina dealt with a splitting headache, felt like a lunatic sus-pended in limbo, hypnotized, treading in a trance. She was diligently, dedicatedly working OT for her sister, never shirking her duties, and yet Edith, in spite of this, was unappreciative. She was provided with a paid-for plush pad, no dinky dwelling. There was no crumbling plaster, subpar wiring and insulation, fungoid infection on the walls, cracks in the ceiling, prehistoric boob tube, eensy panes, or leaking plumbing. It was hardly a trash heap of a joint for Chrissakes! Edith behaved as though she, Lorina, was the consummate washout, utterly use-less, irremediably worthless, with a haywire career, and that she, Edith, was left wallowing in a pigpen, her life creamed by unfortunate events initiated by ... you know ... Light vied with shadow for supremacy. Blank bill-boards. Her suspirations rattled like walnuts in a tree.

Redolence of cleaning products. A delivery van idled, trembled. Plentiful poverty, rampant squalor, embittered souls. Stimulatory littoral sighs. She dug into her pricey pocket book and, presto, excavated a flask of rubbing alcohol, and took a swig, polished it off. She tunneled for another, and, bam, brought out a nip of turpentine, and guzzled that. Columned cabs quaked. Phatties plied the streets, rounded up clientage as cowpokes would cattle, wagged their tails like whelps, pounded the pavement in platforms, went whichever way the winds of currency blew. Firmament echoed with blue. Dissipating drizzle. She was higher than train smoke. Almost home ...

The crescentiform moon hung over the earth as a flamingo's foot suspended above water. Lorina felt like she was losing control of her life, as a trolley's wheel slipping off the wire. Chaffinches flew suicidally. Oxygen throbbed like a bird's heart. In the blistering heat, she had the sensation of being a liquefying papier-mâché doll. Her existence was a gift she didn't want. Tawdry establishment glared with bad taste. The surrounding environment resembled a bombed burg. She fought the impulse to snort coke like a key fights with a lock. People of hail ticked as pacemakers. Mine car, filled with surgical implements, was left in the middle of an intersection. Algal ovarian cysts. A clod optically drilled holes in her back. His freckled, oviform frontage was not unlike a speckled egg. Lo and behold, there were geese galore. Her cardiac organ resounded as a vacant theater. Pensive chrysanthemums. Miasma of discarded matter. Mist jiggled cellulitically. Brood of chicks. Her vesture had the odor of a funeral parlor. Her metalliferous arms were like those of cranes. Eye of the sun was clouded over with a cataract. Fragrance of flowers. She was tied to Edith as a goat fastened to a post. Bevy of bureaucrats in fancy suits and sleek shoes. Cocky trollops strutted. Her colitis flared and her pancreas griped. She purchased a pair of tiger print pompom slippers on a whim. Lovey-dovey Romeo and Juliet cuddled and kissed on the chaotic corner in an exhibition of affection and devotion. Reaching to pluck a bud from a bough, it looked like Lorina was handing a coin to an elephant's extended trunk. The encompassing din made her fillings rattle, the sound as pans, hung on nails, banging together when an express rushes by. Panting, her mouth was pursed, like to receive lipstick. Her cheekbones protruded as shields. Her hair, windblown, was like a cockatiel's crest. Gin had her tipsy. Gullied pineapple of her tush. Her tits were outthrust as pointing daggers. A scarecrow with deviant eyes and an evangelical expression quoted Moliere, shook like he was on the verge of keeling over from an aneurysm. Lorina wished to rest, as the deceased in a morgue's drawer. False teeth of hope sank into her fair skin. Squall was a shout of fright. Her chops slammed shut like a cuckoo clock's door. A firetruck, screaming at all and sundry, hurried to a conflagrational calamity. The croissant she got from the cafe was a paperweight in her gut. Torrid summer. She was motionless as a chiseled, ligniform figure on a prow. Whale bones of scaffolding. Rowboat slid like a swan, the oars its wings. Her cumbrous patent leather beige booties. Surfeit of colors of the arcing rainbow. Her mouth scattered mutterings as an acacia does its pollen. She thirsted for anise lacquer. Policemen were on horseback. She was blood in veinous streets. Charcoal cloudlets. Her molars clacked like billiard balls struck by cue sticks. Calvary charge of schoolchildren. All that was missing - bugleblasts and drumbeats. Her arteries were hardened. Scent of camellia. Sun dilated. Starfish weathervane. Tide had the static sonances of walk-ie-talkies. Sultriness persisted. Her hot flashes were as if from menopause. Perhaps she should go out with a bang! Maybe. Hooray!Fulgor's relentlessness. Halo of flour in a bakery searched for a surface to deposit itself upon, the morbidly obese proprietor, dressed in a hussar's jacket and olivaceous apron and wearing a poodle toupee, jab-bered like a parrot to his male and female employees, and leaned on a cane, it as a shepherd's staff. He was not unlike a landlord threatening the tenants with evic-tion. A plane whistled akin to a cannonball. Aroma of dahlias mingled with pot roast. She was embalmed by body odor. She was irritated by her own idiosyncrasies, connected to craziness as a bat to darkness.

Edith's encephalon in her skull fermented like a fly in vinegar. She wanted to crawl under a boulder as a mole going into the ground. Sleet sounded like an MD's rubberoid hammer tapping knees. She stood in the downpour, settled as a stone lodged in a ureter. Excremental gush exploded from the sewer in a volcanic torrent. Fecal spattering. Granite chips of the rains. Her oral pores were puckered. It felt like her heron-belly was as a cement mixer. Her hand, put into a pocket, was like an X-ray stuck into quadratic frosted glass. Loud pops of her flatus had the sonancies of a backfiring, broken exhaust pipe. Aquatic exhalations in her ears. Collapsible cinema was turned into a bathing hut. Incredible images jelled in her noggin. The crick in her back hated and defeated her. Intensity of the coruscation diminished exponentially. Lighthouse beacon was as a miner's helmet-lamp. She sparrow-hopped over a brackish puddle. Fact scrambled her fiction. Exaggerated illumination. Her tresses were not unlike tousled wheat. Her grey matter's cerebrations: low-tide flotsam and jetsam, waves of confidence receding. She was stealing a passage on the boat of self-delusion. Repressing a sneeze. She concluded she didn't know diddly about living life correctly. She was planted by nature and fertilized by experience. Army green verdure. The sun dematerialized as a helium balloon. It was a cinch for the starlings to follow suit. She was feeling like she was an inadequately-dubbed screen starlet, mouthing words whose modulation manifested audibly a moment later. Her panties were high as treetops. And her footfalls were out of sync with the sound of the steps. Strain of her career was heavy on her, like a crucifix on a cadaver. Her fantasy submitted itself to the authority of actuality. She soaked herself in nonfulfillment as a biscuit in joe. Refracting, overlapping layers of lies she told herself. Lacrimal froth ran down the facial cheeks of rocks. Her aspirations retreated from her mind like the bubbles of a carbonated beverage breaking away from the glass. She staggered, sozzled, the asphalt elusive. She was cramped and uncomfortable, as if she spent a decade locked in a trunk. Her initial nonsuccess had sprouted like fruit on the branch of her occupation. There was significant pressure on her, mainly from Lorina. Hers was not a gratifying job. She swam in the dewiness as though she were a frogman, the boulevard with coral barrels and reef meters. Her wooziness worsened. Kitschy garland of those streetlights. Junior cuties, crestfallen, quibbled. Slammed, she was semicomatose, neck stiffened, like calcium crystals were developing. Threshing cement. Golden emanation gilded her entirety. Her reflection was smeared in polished surfaces. A chocolate lab chased an ornate butterfly. A millstone sank in her stomach. This corpulent country singer, with a woodcock's lamps and wilted lids, tied a turban round his head as a bandage to staunch the bleeding of a wound.

After the heinous murders, the victims' replacements established, it was time to send out the units. The troops were officially rallied. Lorina, not exactly fresh as a daisy, flew backward like a hummingbird. She tried to be too palsy-walsy with Edith, as if nothing horrific had happened. It wasn't a pragmatic approach. She'd do anything for peace and quiet! Nondescript detectives barged in on Edith, flinging around this, shoving aside that, rooting through drawers, rummaging in closets, rifling through papers, ransacking the desk and cupboards, searching for clues, forensic evidence, connecting her to the barbaric killings. She was a "person of interest." Canine excrement islands described an unbalanced explorer's map on the curb. Edith: the black sheep of the family. The party girl. Why did Lorina put up with her poppycock? Out of love for her. Brain in her head - lard in a barrel. She would straighten her out! She is not a problem that can be solved in a jiffy! Scintillation gleamed like saliva.

She tried to flag down a cab, futilely. Mosquitoes murmured sweet nothings in her ear. Cops raiding Edith's property, with its mortuary atmosphere, she paced nervously back and forth, her breathing with the sonance of a vaporizer, swayed as a ship at sea, expression not unlike a caged fox's. It was so hot it withered flowers. She cursed, sounded as a frog croaking in a reedy marsh, stared ahead blankly, like from a daguerreotype, and imagined Edith as being a sphinx, cityscape a backdrop of Egyptian pyramids. Cuckoo clock, springs snapping, went haywire, announcing the time. She cussed, audibly reminiscent of a worn-out needle stuck in a record's groove, repeating the same song of madness with excruciating determination. Chalk-scraping sonancies in her cranium. Lorina was in no rush to return home, her sinister flat all polished oak and drawn curtains. Wiping her eyes as though drying tears. Her spine was feeling like a wilted stem, vascular organ as the head of Jesus, wearing a crown of thorns. Milky Way of skyline. Constellations of members of the community. Zits on her back were the size of EKG suction cups. Fireflies' silent Morse code. Pollen was like the talc trapeze artists use. Her bladder and bowels felt as if they were filled with shards of glass. Cawing boobies and noddies. Irrigation channel. Snack bar. She got a whiff of clover and onion. Tomato patch. Cabbages of clouds. Sun was a dot. She froze. Because of the seizure she spawned, it looked like she was turning the crank of a gramophone. She internally predicted her demise. Her back was cutlass-curved. She screamed as an ambulance. She preached the Gospel in Latin to the finches that had alighted upon the iron grating on the barren bluff tinged with teal by the refraction of welkin. Her language was preserved in her cupped palms. Hillsides. Rooftops. She puttered as though this was some leisurely outing. Fishermen. Sailboats. Coral broach of the moon. She emerged from her reverie like a shape from shadow. The segment of the city reeked of a fish cannery. Cirri were solicitous corollas. In her life she felt as though she were a chunk of meat which hung from a butcher's hook. Branches throbbed like arteries. Veins on her hands were as road meanders on a map. Her nares were flared like a cadaver's on a marble table. She glided as water's reflections on cement. She wanted people to believe her existence was one of composure, sobriety, devoid of despair. An Arab patted a poodle and gave her a glower. Exterior sound had an interior silence. It was difficult to distinguish between ocean and azure. She was feeling like she had metalline joints that were corroded, and that she was a clock whose pendulum no longer swung. She sank under the extreme weight of resentment and resignation. Her peers leaned over her as if she were a morose convalescent. She wanted to escape from the caricature of herself. Milky indifference of the moon's eye. Raindrops fell on the megapolis like tears on an onion. Sickly atmosphere. Ozoniferous conundrums. Dealing with Edith, for her, it was as though being an earthworm, tunneling through clay. Occasionally, with her, she felt hung out to dry, like a bathing suit. A motor roared. Her owlish claws were chafed and cranky. Sauntering, her gait was as if she were pedaling a sewing machine. In her vagaries she had the sensation of some-one going in and out of a coma. Her muteness was a wraith of a voice. Her nerves were united in a rebellion against her health. She was bowed low, like a withered hyacinth. Her person was a land of exile for her essence.

Lorina respired as a refrigerator. Nervousness closed on top of her as a tomb's lid. Canvas canopy of the terra cotta Buddha-building was reminiscent of an eyebrow arced in astoundment. Her sparrowy, sweaty feet had the smell of sweet earth. She trod in high heels like a deep-sea diver on a ship's deck. Urinary stink of the wet weather. Her flesh had the color of gravel. Her buttocks looked as two pieces of a puzzle that didn't quite fit together. Vociferant inflections ran through her ears like hot wires. Her thoughts danced and dissipated as dust motes in a film projector's beam. Her throat was bone-dry. She felt useless like the dead. Day withdrew to make way for night. She imagined she was an angel in the missal of her misery. And her coconut was a child-hood house with its surplus of echoes and quietness. She forced an aurora borealic smile, wished to crow as a rooster at forenoon. A church bell rang the heartless hour. Seagulls screeched not unlike streetcars. Cocottes pranced. Smooth-talking hoodwinker of a hulking pimp bragged he could tear a phone book in half, and bend a crowbar over his knee. Stockades of barrels. Booming clientele of johns. Her migraine headache made her grey matter feel split in two, as a volunteer subject on stage, her body sawn in half by a malignant magician. She wore the expression of a drowning woman. Her vulpine strut, neck dwindled to tendons, sulfuric air of sadness and anger. Sorrow spread slowly in her being like mildew on a wall. Spritz pattered the pavement.

Exhaust fumes coagulated on brick, glass and steel. Cirri gray as winter's grass. Stuttering spate. Structures were suggestive of shipwrecks. Shadow conspired with light. She held onto reality like a chimney sweep a brush, or a gable. Torturous storm interrogated her as if to facilitate a confession. She groaned like a rocking chair on floorboards, attempted to fix her hair as a fisherman mends his net. Insectoid planes rumbled. Sparkling stars were like boats' lanterns. Commuters, with transportation down, milled as vagrants. She scratched her itchy armpits like a macaque picking lice from itself. Her epileptic shaking was evocative of a duck coming out of a pond. Confusion in her bean was as a typhoon in the tropics. Her heart galloped like an elephant. Her brain went batty! She felt as if she were carrying some contagious mental illness. Brumal brimstone. Pollution proliferated in the claggy oxygen. Stalks of Satan's flailing, water-starved florets swam in aqueous air like eels. Cracks in her cosmetic foundation as ones on a ceiling caused by rushing trains. She required an injection of the insulin of sanity. She was doily-whitish. Pools as caramel custard. She was dressed like a Spanish doll. She held her pocketbook as an offering. With Edith hiring her as manager, she was feeling like a bum taken in by charity. Her mind was shattered, as a window blasted by a shotgun. Heart in her chest stirred like a bird in its nest. Traffic whined as a tango. Folks lurked as though they were buzzards, lingering, waiting for a thing to perish, then devouring the creature. Lightning lacerated the sky. It shredded the city. Amputated aspens. Her expression was empty like the footwear of the homeless. Heat and humidity depleted her energy reserves, which were running low to begin with. Could she liberate herself from Edith? Edith was the sow and she was the suckling piglet. She wanted to smash her face into a pulp! In this life she was feeling as a stain on the suit of the world and the cosmic dry cleaner could not get it out. Her wrinkled neck shrunk into her blouse like a turtle into its shell. She stood, arms akimbo, statuesque in stillness.

Seashell-echoing sounds of showers sissing. Store signs sprayed garish neon. Cumuli moved as breathing gills belonging to the leviathanic sky. She advanced like an automaton down the whitewashed hallway lined with unclad mannequins, these androgynous dummies as sexless people, to her, creepy, inexpressive creatures assuming dissimilar poses with reptilian lassitude. Lorina's arterial estuaries flowed. She groped her way towards the exit she didn't remember entering. She had the celestial innocence of a cherub. Her forehead was harrowed by worry-wrinkles. She perspired teardrops. She was coming unglued, not unlike dentures. Vermiform moon was breaking through its tissuey cloud. She hiccoughed as a crab, felt frozen like prey. Buggy seraphim swarmed around her in a winged halation, as if she were a suffering martyr in some obscure church painting, instantaneously animated. Her sigh drowned in serous air. Her glycerinic (nervous) giggle. Heaven darkened with latent wrath. Her insanity ostracized her from others. She disrobed a banana. Her lunar lexicon was spat. Her funerary musky perfume. Her distinctly avian movements. She essayed to return to herself, like a dog goes back to its old spots to sniff its own essence. Balled-up napkin was a crumpled dove. She cried as an albatross. Pause. She hissed as a puffin, inwardly opined she was losing her marbles, was destined for the nuthouse. Tide hushed. Was that perverted Beelzebub beating off to her, going berserk, in the bushes? Was she flattering herself? Acorns chattered like teeth. She dreaded going back to that solemn joint. She was perplexed by the episodes leading up to this point, as though she wandered into the middle of a movie and was confounded by the story and characters. Her nerves were feeling pecked at by chickens. Her agitation made her feel stripped, vulnerable. She was uneasy and frail. Her eyes were scarlet as embers. She was empty, vacuous, like an edifice following a fire. Boom of her heart and bovine breath. Her pallor as crepe paper. Mucus rattling in her throat was like bones were driven into her larynx. Her cerebrum was a broken engine which needed fixing. Rain was a clicking cataract, soon settled to sprinkles. Wind whined as a teething baby. Nameless trees gesticulated mockingly. Her thoughts weren't aligned, like differently positioned bodies of a carcrash pileup. To distract herself from her distress, she daydreamed of spiderwebs and silverware. Her totality had a secret register. Her features fit badly, were disfigured in the splendor. Lorina wept, yanked an infinity of tissues from her purse, and wondered: am I going stark raving crazy?

A panic-stricken Edith, piddling, under investigation by the secret police, identified as a prime suspect, aimed to contact Lorina, but changed her mind. Unbeknownst to her, she was dead, having been strangled and left in the shower, discovered by a concerned elderly neighbor. Edith over time noticed a number of alterations to her apartment's furnishings and realized she was actually in a different residence, decorated to resemble hers. Without warning, Alice appeared, wearing dirty 'Wonderland' wardrobe, caught in a psychotic break, beleaguered Edith, believing she was the only Alice of import, impelled to preserve her image by "bumping off" the "fake" Alice Liddell, said that Edith, a "filthy imposter," had been ruining her image, and confessed that she had committed the killings, including dispatching Lorina, who was blatantly interfering with everything. Edith blinded Alice with a flashlight, Alice mistaking it for a spotlight, and pushed her through the mullioned window. A broken bird on the sidewalk, a bloodied Alice gazed up at Edith and sniggered, putting her blond wig back on, and crookedly. Her head was cracked open like a spoiled egg. She sounded as a wounded animal. Her squeaky lamentation mutated into a seashell song. Her split-open temple made Edith   sick. Alice managed somehow to regain her balance, footing complicated, looking not unlike some hambone thespian in melodramatic mode, intonation fluidic, teeth clacking as a skeleton in biology class, and hit the trash compactor like a moth flying into a pane. Her head was critically cut into a gaping yawn. She was runny- nosed and weepy, accused Edith of "taunting" her without the "slightest justification." They were as heated sibling rivals in a bad dream. She claimed hormones spurred her "dispositional crudity." Her bitter rant, comely countenance uglified by resentment. Hissy fit. Unbelievable animosity. She considered herself a precocious anarchist. She basked in introspective petulance.

Her existence was expressed through her barebones upbringing. She was excluded and persecuted by society. She was caught in a whirlpool whilst life flowed forward. Family, to her was akin to scabrous acne flaking off. Their household was so dispiriting even the pets had nervous breakdowns, needed shrink-vet therapy. Another temper tantrum. She, neuroses and phobias firmly intact, wobbly, crouched and micturated on wood chips, the pee sounding as a kerchinging cash register. She was a lightning rod for trouble. A nearby building was ostensibly despondent and neglected. Illumination was as track lighting. Edith's tepid responses transmogrified into the nastily brutish. And Alice slumped onto a stone step. She was still, like in the aftermath of a natural disaster. Geranium down on her nuque. Pocked, chromic moon. Can of sky was sealed by a lid of cloud.

Gracile, gorgeous Edith, now a major successful player in Hollywood, visited a neo-Gothic sanatarium to see Alice, bound to the grody bed, who eagerly received the bouquet from her youngest sister, believing they were from an adoring fan. She was glamorous and graceful, a de facto stunner, at the institutional epicenter of a dense thicket wherein the barking mad resided. Fe-fi-fo-fum of her flatulency. Customarily, if she wasn't invading your personal space, she, mesmerizing, was drawing you into hers, and magnetically. Her curvy, petaline lips and flaxen single stroke of eyebrow. Her brain was a bee in the hive of her head. She was hell- bent on destroying herself, systematically turning her reputation to rubbish, was afraid Edith, plain and predictable as far as she was concerned, would become stratospherically famous, feared she would enjoy a vertical, not horizontal, career trajectory, and that she herself would remain a B-grade actress, slumming in low-budget pictures. She was, to Edith, a sinister sylph with cheese-whitish derma layer, a willowy specter out of a folk tale. Her sham magniloquence was delivered with characteristic chutzpah. She was a radical Rabelaisian character. Edith's latent hatred of her was coming to the fore. With vigor. One time, Alice threw her entire wardrobe, taken from the steamer trunk, the choffonier a vacuum, onto the sidewalk, and it looked like the strewn clothes belonged to plane-crash victims, and, undeliberately, she knocked the original daguerreotype of a landscape, with its faux-gilt frame, off the hessian partition. For Edith, seeing her skimpy smalls, it was embarrassing. Mucousy moisture from burst boils of cirri. Sculptured sun on the plinth of sky. Superstructure was seemingly a warship. Flotilla of factories were in flanking position. Burger World joint was next to a derelict synagogue. Edith, chawing on a twisted pizzle of beef jerky, had a clear memory of the two of them trampolining in the sunken garden, circumscribed by blooming cherry blossoms, and Alice, hunkered as a cyclone, a vicious vortex (Edith taken up into her, a resplendent Rapture), saw fit to boot her off. She was involuntarily immersed in the infantilizing fantasia with her sis, went on tiptoe. Their one-sided confabulation was a vocalic excursion into the unknown ... and went nowhere. Shotgun marriage of sibling rivals. Hadrian's Walls here. Alice, mystical, feisty as ever, punched above her weight, KOing doctors, orderlies and patients alike. Attributable to her Amazonian stature, they were relegated to persons of restricted height. Her existence was punctuated by familial prizefighting. She was always driven. To wit: there was no mountain she wouldn't climb, ocean she could not swim, private property she could resist trespassing upon. She was a Rebel with a Cause. Her lambasting of Edith was a Herculean labor of love. Alice was an anchor dragging her down to the bottom of an abyss. Her insectival eyes, lashes the legs. She, contained in a strait jacket, struggled like Christ agonizing on the Cross, her cries cracking the crystal. Sweat fecundated her with a eucalyptus aroma. She was a humanistic figure on a music box spinning to the song of mental illness. She stared at herself and Edith's reflection in the mirror, and articulated, "you are the real deal."

The packed parking lot was where the Drag Queen of Hearts, painstakingly nudinating, accompanied by his intimidating henchmen, two living playing cards, the mammoth Joker and Trump, proclaimed he never orgasmed, shouted his familiar "Off with her head!" and the bodyguards swarmed all over her. He swore he'd climax. Edith Liddell woke from her dream, or nightmare, brushed what turned out to be dollar bills, not a spray of playing cards, or leaves, from her face. She, neegee, fingered herself on the carpeted floor of a bland studio office in Tinseltown before the rolling cameras on the financially lucrative porno shoot and thought of all the curiouser happenings that had transpired. Her sleeping bag was similar to a body bag.

FIN.

My Grandma With
The Tyrannosaurian Arms

Hellaciously hungover, reader, I, Mackenzie Meatyard (Meathead to my closest compadres), your manfant narrator, so wooden I'm a fire risk, a cardboard cutout, a Ritalin-riddled redneck parttime rodeorider trailertrash sneertastic Svengali of serial couchcrashing in Che Guevara fatigues, a minimumwage slave spaceshot who attitudinally bites the hands I mooch from, in an Abaddonish anteroom between adolescence and adulthood, a washedup playground heartthrob, an iscreen-hooked schlub and lover of uber-cougars who prefers his OJ pulpier than a glass of Mike Hammer, slugging through life like a middleweight boxer hopen to win a heavyweight title bout on points, a walkin wastebasket and humanoid parasite with a hangdog sourpuss, a dorky schmoe with this sheepface, these pleading popeyes in 1970s aviator glasses, designer stubble, mouth an overbloomed blossom, smirk like shaved ice, crooked chiclets, flaxen Oompa-Loompa wig, crazy-quilt abs from crunches uncountable, a hubba-hubba himbo, gawd-awful oil-slick personified, too- smooth-to-be-true, and, whew, inhabitant of a neat name, felt as the corpse of Hector, dragged around the walls of Troy by Achilles; or I was trampled by the Four Horsemen of the Apocalypse. I'd partied animalic at the annual Electric Opalescent Oyster Festeroo, carousing my keister off with Manga-character-appearing Skove Stave, wearing a psychedelic pantsuit outfit Grace Slick would've worn with Jefferson Airplane in her heyday, and pillbox hat, a bespectacled Walmart employee of traffic-stopping radiance, in her moodscape dispensing self-help mantras while I, dressed in a silly shawl, lowrider bell-bottom jeans, and Roman sandals, blazed a hugeous bong and banged a good gong. She clung to the peepers like optical Velcro. She was Perc- peppy, a gung-ho go-getter, sweet as pie, with a Crest Whitestrips smile, an alpha-female born and bred in a hothouse junglescape. She was a deep-throat gagaholic who, in addition, dug hardcore fuckage and facializing. Her humdinger roughdraft performance. I was the matter to her anti-matter. At her side was the menacing, muscular, brown mastiff, Kindred, who apparently wanted to be somewheres cozier, at vet surgery, say. An absolute nerve-fryer! Was a bestial threesome, a ménagerie-a-tois, in the works? Yikes! Jaunty Dixieland jazz. My tall tales' jibber-jabber had Tarzan-style ululations and Promethean thundering. In the port- o-potty I had built an excrementitious epic in the dirty toilet, put on a shitshow (fecal matters), and diligently masturbated, the fantasy emanating like rings rippling in a stream when an insect strikes the surface. Ragtag marchingband playing rackety music on a Navy Yard's drydock. Fireflies flitted round Skov: satellites infinitesimal circling a body heavenly. We drifted as wreckage in floodwater. I'll save ya the shaggy dog story (or the dogged shag story) ... Woe betide the sailor who heeds the siren's song ... She made Pippy Longstocking-esque pigtails duren Duran Duran's lackadaisical set, wore those clothes rather well. She had a charming drawl. I had more balls than a dozen testosterone-fueled gladiators' codpieces. Her klieg-light smirk occupied my cranium like a siege of Huns. Stoned, I sounded as Bela Lugosi and she looked not unlike a Breck girl. We gasped as fishies stranded on shore, banged like there was no to-morrow. She handled my pancake-planate buttocks as if they were dipped in E. coli. She was a cock-draining cum-receptacle who would make a henpecking housewife in some rural yonder, punctuated with churches, gas stations, and mom and pop stores, with a time-lapse-skimming sky. I was the hyper-intense (my intensity set on stun, not kill) Frick to her Frack, Mutt to her Jeff. Her tag-along pals, skanky tweakers, ugloid buds, could have been mistook for extras on the 'Walking Dead' cable series. I was a teller of thigh-slapping one-liners, howled and slobbered like a wolf out of a Tex Avery cartoon. We went round each other as though warriors in the coliseum, and fell to bonelessly embracing and ardently smooching. I was really surprised to find out she was in favor of deforestation, which is on par with a sumo-sized Michelin-Mannish frankfurter-eating champion being an unpaid spokesperson for WeightWatchers. Adam Ant's roadies in actuate. She was polished like marble, Hindu-danced, skinny as an art-deco ornament, rubious chops in a petulant, perverse twist. Her slit-nombril, an exceptional omphalos, peek-a-booed, tulipy nipples erectile. Our amorous osculations and tactions were near-violent. I set the coffee-maker to NASCAR specs. I was I guess a reformed Mephistopheles in myriadcolored pajamas, staring at my anatomic arithmetic angularities in the claustrophobic kitchen, my faden bruises oldpaper-yellow, ladylip-cuts dove-gray and salmon-pink, saggen boy-boobs bearen resemblance to putrescent pomegranates I'd venture. Visual compare. Did I tie one over! Hair of the dog. The empyrean, that sanguinary day, contradicted the earth. Clouds comprised tissue created from the plasm of the firmament. Nah, they were an apparitional armada. And they grew omnidirectionally, like amoebas, stars in them as welders' flames in workshop dust. The oxygen was carpenter-glue-thick-and-sticky. A jargon of oldern jalopies, bereaved of tires, was mummied in woodsmoke troweling on. This terradamnata of homologues of gutsy gunk in a gnawing brook with its metalline redolence, the visceral curiosa, in haphazard, groped toilful in its suck. Brighten sere of gaunted, eldern elms beswirled by poltergeists of fog in a jog. My vision worser than Mr. Magoo's. Skov said I was of the ilk who is in love with the punchline before gettin to the setup. When she smacked me on the choppers it was like being clobbered with paddle-wheels of a steamer of yore. She cavorted as a horse rearen itself on up. She was smoking like a smithy's hole. Her goldice paraphernalia was as dentistical implements, those pertinent tools of the trade. Flying fish porpoised thru white waves. Verdant land. Cinereal soil elevations like elephants lying down. I am a wiseacre given to Owen Meany broad-lettered burstouts and have a Gump-gait, vermiform build, extraterrestrial features, and rat- teeth, my voice plunging headlong (nosediving?) into nasality, hormone-wound, as if in the turbulence of teendom. A retinue of eagles of diverse conformation espaliered the bilious firmament, rather occulted it, forayed into it in contrasting aspects of flight, becoming winged fish in a burning river, delineating the curvature of the hemisphere. Wind sure provoked the shrubs. Redwoods and evergreens was withered effigies of figures from an unfamiliar and forgotten race. Gulls bow-winged cried their oaths, doddered an lapsed off. A long congaline of comicbook cockroaches disbanded on the muculent tiles in winey lambency which brought warmth and clarity. Time dissolved as though winterbreath. Oilcloth-covered, overstuffed armchairs. I agnized my agnail. Noctambulous kindergarteners, scar-pallid and with fresh, faceted physogs, were sequestered on an esparto'd knoll, involved theirselves in a game of cat-and-mousery-type tag. Their nosferatically cadaverous, Caucasic schoolteacher, a gorgeous gorgon, bootylicious and Nordicular, in recondite luminosity, her head, godamighty, fellatially a-nod, Tourette's-spastic, heart-strickenly, heather hair a rampant ruin,

Parkinsonianly spasmic, joined in on the fun. She slank like a tributary. Moose in massivity. Background outraged. Vulturine beak of this mountain peak fed on the Promethean, livery sun in exchange for renewing its genius for breathen effulgent fire. A rainbow overlaid an overcast welkin; a colour filter on a black-and-white photograph. Azure glared as spotless dentures in vastity. I was very perspiry. Varietal species of bird flew; an avian acceptance of air that, with the saturation, smelt of mingled seared fiber and moistened pocketchange. Lush country hazed and dewed with dawn. Remembering Skov, Greenpeace-slash-PETA- dedicated, her desirous, devourous glances, hands crippled into claws, and how I had surprising success with such a glorious honey (divine except for the mangled mitts) in spite of my pick-up cue-card lines that would've embarrassed Lenny and Squiggy. We flailed in unison to Killing Joke's 'Love Like Blood.' If their set was killer, Kajagoogoo was the victim. She was gyren, exhibited me a dogeared, dullen Polaroid of herself in a form-flattering maillot and wedge-shaped high-heels and holding up, victoriously, a nice bouquet, like NFL quarterback Tom Brady the Super Bowl trophy for the New England Patriots, she the winner of the local beauty pageant in a theme park magic kingdom of a hometown. Hey, to be honest here, with all due respect, judging by the golemly, ursoid, gorilline, hippopotamic, pachydermous, hoidenish, and golliwoggy competition there in the shot, it's on the level of bragging you're the tallest midget. Begging pardon. Not to be cruel. Brumal souls raisen from graves, in presentiments of palsy and in suggestions of silentious agony, on a drunkenly crooked trail in tawn and elongate. Clathrate condensation. And sonethin clapt. Poplars were garbled into odd disfigurements by the otherworldly shadows. My countenance I reckon was a haunt of sedge, expression there I expect an enemy-in-wait. Sun was a blistering cyst. Scratches laddered my sallow cheek. The rain began, was conveyed down from a bleak heaven with a rumor of restraint in its repertoire and with an approximation of industrious circumspection and beetle sedulity. I more siphoned and less suspired. Illumination was an insinuation of a slur. Yotes yowled. Weather-beaten, sinewed laurels. The starken vault, eikonically monarchial. Canines lowslung yammered unceasingly. My tootsies, balled, was tarantulas twinned in torment incomprehensible. Olivaceous foliage was lucky not to have got drought as of late. A nasty sunburn scarleted my usually fairskin. An angulose galoot, juvenescent, with a squashy snout, somnambulantly galumphed, palaver exhausting, the gibberish cascading incoherent. His grotesquely sensual slither was reptiloid. He carried a hyaline jar labeled 'hooch.' Lunar landscape. Nymphean hurly-burly. Plethoric illiteracy and illness hereabouts. Adenoid alps, bloodred, seen out of the forever-unWindexed bay window, from my periphery.

Soapscum affronted the aluminum sink. Whisperous refrigerator. Huzzaing (softly) skeeters. Light was a supernal stagger. Typic neighborly hullabaloo. Imagine the heebie-jeebies I had experienced when I blundered into the kinda cramped-camper-incommodious pantry that particular tropic morn in seeing my alutaceous-fleshed, humpbacked grandmother, a Quasimama with a grime-grey, alveated thatch on her dandriffy scalp, she wrinkled as a blouse with a pressing need, scuttling crabwise and fussing with a damnable domestic device, moving like an astronomical ant in anguish, asking herself theological questions she had no answers for, when, suddenly, she spun, an alabaster prune in a continuation of coruscation, and sat yogic on a spic-and-span segment of the otherwise mucoid floor, her tiny, terrifying tyrannosaurian arms sticking out of her grody cotton tee's (it with a Liberacean ruffled collar) sleeves located not on the traditional sides but instead the front. Golly! Her baggy bosoms gone missin. The creeps were sorta given to me. It was raw-nerve, knuckle-suckingly horrific. Her bladdery breadbasket. We was bedeviled by bluebottles bedighten the cookery. My ears rang as bell towers. Sapphire scintillation. My fart sounded like an animal attempting to escape from its cage. Scared, stress was showed in her inflections jumbled. I endured completely awful goshdern sweats, focused on her mutated being. With her whiskers she resembled the Cheshire Cat from the Lewis Carroll story. My face was whiten. My neckfollicles were icicles. I was skeered witless. She was sporadically liverish-spotted. A Baum-bastical "Oz" novel she took out of the library was splayed sexual on the Day-Glo table. Bibliogasm of an orgy of leather-bound reading-material on the cherrywood bookcases. I had the patience of Job in dealing with her. Refulgence mud-brown sprayed diarrhoical. The memories I had of her went to my coconut as pregnant raccoons climbing into an attic to give birth. Phlegm rattled in my throat with the sonancy of loose shutters in a storm, my physiognomy blushed like a warning label on a product. She hurried on her ovaline, hefty haunches as water hastens under the influence of breezes. On the countertop she'd been compulsively potatoes, the pieces piled like Lilliputian bodies. Strips of flypaper. The tyranny of temperature was oppressin us. It violated one's tolerance. The oxygen, cellophanean, sogged with humectation. She sighed, ornery, as a territorial Doberman pinscher guarding private property with a passer- by proximal, her mouth making a tomato-sliver. The vacuum cleaner was a silent sentry. Jesus Christ, what the hell was happenin? My wire-mesh intestines interrogated my gut. Lordy. My cranium, in its disquietude, echoed with an ache. Cobwebby cirri in the corner of the cerulean ceiling. Insectival activity like weirdass tribal animosities. For a moment I distracted myself with Skov's titillating tuchis. We went at it fervid. Two minuses made a plus. I wished to be her lover and mentor - a doggone Don Juan and Obi-Wan. Geeps extravagated. I strived to hammer away at excess as builders did at Notre Dame, to no avail. Gusts gasped I suppose orgasmic. A preggers, pale horizon pusht out infantile cumuli. My orale aperture lollipopped. Grandma's visage was crumpled similar to a cup. Her teensy-weensy, bifurcate-stick, tyrannosauric appendages muthafreaken me out, waved when she rose, not dissimilar to steam from the ground, and rocked like a boat, bigbutt wagging. She reminded me for some reason of a swing tied to an oak no one used anymore. She looked ... ignored. Neglected. Crows croaked. Too noisy. An antique victrola. Dionne Warwick's infectious pop hit, 'Do You Know The Way To San Jose,' played on the dimin radio. Filthy thoughts lancin the boil of my brain. I'm fascinated by lavatorial functions. I suck energy from my surroundings vampirically. To vamose ... Damn Darger-esque/Nabokovian Lolitas, barefooted and in bikinis, burnt sienna-skinned, galloped, squealed, itsy-bitsy tits and tushes wiggling, through an esthetic garden. I scrutinised Grandma's orbicular cranium, globose middle. She was ensconced in her special setting, her safe haven. The house, Bateslike, was the sun she spun round. Homey comfort was critical. Running errands she was a comet. She was confused, changed. Her outthrust tongue recalled a cuckoo left out of its clock. Her flatulence had the sonance of chimps chatterin. Symphonic music heard from clicks distant. Palm-rosy celestial sphere. Vast. My sentences spilled as beans. Pumpkin-hued ottoman. My sanity shook in its boots. Charms on her cheapo necklace were pinned apparent to her chest not unlike an officer's medals. I was mugged by thuggish fear. My midsection lowed as a pig in its sty. Her holey stockings, Bob'sbought, languished at her clayey, Armenoid ankles. Her silhouette, dusk-deepen, was a misshapen Boschian soul. My heart thrummed like an upright acoustic bass. My mind was a womb penetrate by penial dismay. I squiggled, stupid as a slug. My tongue, as I tried to speak, was a key sticking in the piano of my mouth. Her wordulations vociferant. My intonation a vaudevillian ventriloquistic ... I dunno ... She was leaf-veinal, produced a pork-pie like from empty space. Make no mistake: she was no Little Miss Sunshine, with that gravelly, razor-blade, baby-blood voice, rusty-tractor personality, prickly as a cactus, so volatile she made Sam Kinison look like Nelson Mandela. Her porcupine-waddle. Them pterodactylous, discalceate feet. I stork-strutted. Blackbirds were appearingly coils o' smoke. Reeds vibrated as strings of instruments. Chromatic outcry of a closeby bed-and-breakfast. An etiolated Ethiopian in tattery tweed with slapstick timing seemingly did a sendup of religionose supplication, chantry-tolling-chitter-chattering to himself, tying his Adidas sneakers with the queered combination of forensic exactitude and lubricious salacity. Grandma's cheeks custard-jiggled, her respirations expelled like in exhaustion from effort, bacon-fingers impulsively fiddling with esoteric utensils, manila folder derma layer unhealthy. She watched me as a bird-of-prey would a chipmunk. Chrissakes. Skov - Whore of Babbleon. She was jelly-shaken. Her pocketbook was a bottomless bag of tricks from which she brought out items, like it was something out of a Central European folktale, meth impelling, at intervals, her candor, in the hours mildout. She called me a hunkasaurus. Snowslide of luminosity. Clouds curling and uncurling as a snakenest, me casually chronicling in manage to invest this with import, as they went into complicate spiralisations of concentricity, in the profundity of vista. Town-crier sea-gulls cradle-rockin. Grievances of tide. The place, for what it's worth, was in apple pie order. It invited evaluation. A spear of disorientation ran through me. I pictured my parents. They admitted they'd tested the waters of marriage, drowning out their inner voices of doubt (about the commitment), performing, rhythmically in the routine, an intricate, laggard, amateurish minuet: one step forward, two steps back. Foggy revenant gave the impression of possessing a physical character. Drizzle sounded like a librarian's "sssht" and "pssst." A negritic poolside plumper, a thich, slutty sista exhibitionist. There was an eery hush, as prior to a hurricane. Showers effervesced like champagne. Veinlets on Granny's demilune calves was ivy on chimneys. I was drawn to her as liquid to plastic, or a moth to flame. She marched as on parade. I was totally cautious, like I was dealing with a grizzly in the wild. Fright filling my brain as a street with snow during a blizzard. I recognized the phallic vase with its flowers depauperate and the stones testicular. Fantasms of fog. Her gaseous hack. I leakt like a canoe, had a powerful urge to bail pronto. Her hem of gaseity. The portentous mist. Precip beads, lit, was Fruity Pebbles on the winder. Cirri were carnations in a riotous celebration of transformation. She ingested a forkful of veggies and imbibed a glass of Pepsi. Whereupon she put on her letter sweater. I wondered - if all the world's a stage, who/what's waiting in the wings? I cultivated cliches as crops. The cig-stained chaise-lounge on an unwilling porch.

Reality is the Windmill at which unreality Tilts. Fact's the chaos, fiction's the calm. She smacked, for a minute, of a feminine Senator Palpatine from 'Star Wars,' with a grizzled shock, got on a 'French Lieutenant's Woman'- ly hoodie. Insectean clatter. An Akita-finished, masculine African-American arrahed, an afreet-affrayer in the agave. Blood fizzled in these ears of mine. A sotto voce. It has been a hitherto melt of a summer. Zephyrean snivels. Bug whirring. My grandmother started her nightly unsolicited visitations at the family's vacation crumble of a paintlorn cottage of fairy-tale dimensions, situated on volcanic terrain on an isolated island, the joint with its fair share of astrological signs and Da Vinci-esque drawings, leftovers from previous owners, decorating the wainscoting, and a veritable phantas-magoric smorgasbord of odds and ends sardined in the cellar. Initially, with her, I felt irritation, then anger, and, ultimately, despair. I blocked out so much detail, puttin up a dam, psychical, to holdback the flood of shame. The agony, physically and psychologically, was certain intense, and demoralizing. She had vim 'n' vigor, a capable spinstress of excellent, unraveling yarns. She vocalized I was a 'fraidy cat. Discomfort rose like bub-bles in a bath. I pictured the forestal clump of telephone poles and nexus of wires, the sky pulling together cloudy threads into a pleasant pattern ... modified DNA strands ... The shell-sparkling, ivorine-sanded beach, craggy cliffs, overgrown swamp, poorly pruned forsythias, evil-eyes of window-panes with shade-celia examining, spookyly, everthing, outrageous collisions of hotness and dewpoints, crevasses guaranteen to be fallen into, galvanized gallinippers, hollies droopen attributable to disease and years of age, sociopathic, almost ambush-ing mosquitoes, the ocean's wildest waves sweeping as some leviathanic aquatic creature's arms in character-ist puerile temper tantrum, flies in their fervor, keenen seabirds, my tootsie-wootsies feeling like breadcrusts, my humorous trunks sodden in dreadful mugginess, quarrelsome squirrels, tortured partyhats of hills, the weeks and months of events quartered as grapefruit into segments to be savored. Zephyrine enunciates. We looked lost like cast members from 'Little House on the Prairie' and had 'Texas Chainsaw' dysfunction. Can every knot be untied? She got off, Scot-free. I would simmer and she'd buck me up by givin me a Popsicle, communicate in her limp and liquescent articulation. Poontang poppycock. Denial is Duct-tape keeping the fracture of what occurred together. Dungfunk. A feline broadcast it was in heat, advertised this by constantly meowing in dwarven lindens. Grandma was shriveled as a dried worm. Theatrical-spotlight sun. She looped her florid apron and moseyed, flustered conspicuous and flusht. A beaker of rhubarb jam on a whimsic bench. Long ago we had hiked. Her idea. I did not know where we was headed. I jus went. I was a juvie space-craft revolvenround my planetoid grammy. Cloudcover I memorise was a crustish paste, the heavens resultant making mirages of blue augmenting itself from the pal-lidity prevail, the sun, swoll, the dangest thang, goen on up. Branches not unlike burnt bones, remaints from a fire, sacred writ. Wind bore the aroma of chicory. Air as mayo. Our feet, snapping twigs, created sounds of clacking castanets misplayed. She had repaired back her frizzy, stringy strands, otter oculuses becrazed. A glycerinous drencher. My pupils dilated into marvels of magnifying glasses. My lids hurtened. Moonwrought, overclouded brake. Motes of irascible glowflies in rotary motion halved a luscious lane and set us bonkers in the clammy crepuscule, soil-blacken, those lightning bugs the aye-aye eyes of acolytes out of an atavistic vision. Our pace leaden and listen. Sprinkles gloopy sliced o'er us harmless. An amaurotic moon was put onhigh for safekeepen. I was feeling like I was ambling aimless in sleep. Kneedeep fen with gouts of weeds. A lake, viscous and corrugate. The dragonflies and waterspiders bellied thew it on the top. Leaves zephyrously did violinate. Deluge had the sonance of pour'd sugar. Sparse savins. Cumuli floated as though spores sizable. Gunshot thunder. Winks of levin. Viscoid air. Her well- weathered frontage pulled in my gaze like a gravitational field, ye betcha. Scads of beeches and birches. Concussion of gloppy precipitation. Whinnying gales. Skyline unvaguely wintry. A beastly barge neighed, crepitate forth, mouthed the pitchy watercourse infatuate by brilliancy, murmuring, the vessel, as a lunatic in imbecility, and scowling out of the roily miasma in the eventide, the wasting gloam mended by time in advancement. Oily, eddying rivulet had the sonancy of insufflated muck, current palpably quiverous. Celestial sphere in faithful replication of a dimensionless sea, an vice versa. A morbidly obese, maquillaged lady with dusthued dermalayer overfilling a jimdandy, costy onepiece vented torrential invectives when viciously walloped by mean boughs. I vied to set there, um, admired to assess her. She was apparently a gargantuan gagster, boggling up the rear, the monolithic mucker bumbling with the propriety of a seasoned funster. She was pretentious and platitudinous, a pseudo-philosopher. What she verbalized to her peaky yahoo yokel pardner was the melody and harmony to his rhythm section. She seemt blown up by a tire pump. Haggard buzzards gathered gradual on a ridge, mite caulked with brilliance, waxing and waning, making the rock illusorily alivened, and swung away. Hooligans like a pack of hungery jackals, with putty-pigment. Composed mimosas eking oldness swang woodenly in the chinooks, marked out by mincing luminescence. Cloudlets piceous doled out rain. Weather systems complicit in severity. Me percolate on Skov in divagate on Hamilton's Quaternions, Gibbsian vector analysis, Riemann spheres, uh, Prandtl's discovery of the boundary layer, the Hilbert Polya conjecture, Zermelo's Axiom of choice, and the Minkowskian space-time track ... and ... screwit ... A pond enameled with film and spatched with jostlen lilypads. Sourceless avian japin. Heat kindled the day yet. A hiddened whippoorwill proclaimed. Hellward into my historosity. Nacred augment of the diurnal course. Mountainous meridians oblique to the waney empyrean, the glutting cloudlets, curded, a horde of anomalous adherents without much trajection to write about. Weary trudging. I was I admit on the edge of giving out. The atmosphere, right substantial, indicated an impending storm. Grandma ate as a snapping turtle, talked of my granddaddy, slogged like in manure, midge-besieged, and with squint pies because, dislocating as a weaken eidolon in the effluvium, there gave off an odor of stale deadwater. The sun in its habitual fidelity to the firmament was at its fullest. Animal yawling in the vespertine peacefulness.

Vespine pests, undifferentiate, flit and stang remorseless. We stodged sensitively through the stoical bushery. She,

hoarse, intimated with martyred import. Our farcical-
ised silhouettes. Amplitude of vegetation from sumacs
alighted 'pon us. I was feeling buried alive in the copse.
Went thru it regardless. Yessir. In her clung canvas trousers she, threadthin at that point, jaw ajar, mounted the
bile-green and toxic-orange-tinted esker, mantled by
emanation. A-goin, her woreout boots rasped in the
groomed grass, mien quarried from a stoneface. Her tun-
ka-tits. I took a sup outta my vitamined water's bottle.
I had a slumbersome indolence, in the awfullest glary-
hot, off the charts. Fogbank like warsmoke, heralded by
a clump of hillbillies, sweatsoaked, engaged in a to-do
in a cluster of lemon-and-lime trees. I'd thought of her
bucknaked, her upperlegs (with the mucho cellulite)
of worm-bored wood-planks. I stumbled, half-nude,
through the country with its bland placidity and strumming emptiness, with her. Trine of walnuts outlandish.
Colony of kids emaciate, ragamuffins and guttersnipes
galore, denuded stark to our Creator, sprung out of the
coppice, crashed on pranging and violent, smashedup
and splashdowned, speed undiminished, countenances
in contort as they lurched through cherries and apples
in penitent. Prandial rend. Colorful butterflies zigzagged over trump- shaped flowerets. Tzetzeflies in
apoplexy. Hotten heart of the sun that sitteth up there
on the upperearth exploded and beams burst, refinin,
gildin everthin. Interfusing of warmth and humidness
in an ungodly universe, wellnigh intoxicate in which
one could feel naught relief in the weather. Bison-ebon
welkin affrighted the gazer. Bethink thee of an over-
scorning storm in commence. The wondrous wings

of archangelic radiance widen in exiled, holy nature, the aurous plumage in ... divineness, inflicting a certain sorcery that aught to do with my imagination. A manly gal with agatoid blinders bugged and in BVDs, cleft-palated and club-footed, boar-screamed and trotted. A tomboy in jockeys and galoshes, looking gallied, on her tail, waded into the ichorous swamp. Augural anguishes of the afternoon in a lattice of tsking spate. Clearly contaminate waters welled in holes. Branches skewed arcwise. This rabblement, rogueing, hidied an howdied. Ere a gracious, vehement vacancy came over the poignancy of ocean, Africate-melanine, its contrastive, vivacious inhabiters, and ever and anon issuen forth its accustomed hushens. Devilgrinnin skyline, and the waves warwhoopin. Slanted sun, redman-infrared, in abate, and in elucidate of things. A scuzzy beanpole, a sorry species in a velour of rot and tiers of scabs, trinity of them on his revolting integument, adrape in denim damaged, ast about fave grits and to me what's yourn. I didn't reply. Earlyblack in clement and stifling consecration. The vault held the moon sacrificial. A furrowed, tall anthropoid with downtrending shanks hauled a hogget, seeming authentic to be nursing it, doubled no doubt to a stitch in his side. This meanhearted, flaptongued biddy bitched at him, potched and cussed him out. Brief argumentation and they then companied, conversed cordial, in a shadyspot in a precinct of prairie. A dreggy, elfin youngster, goodly diminutive, had a ropy neck and chambered chuckle, in themthere teenager-heighted cattails. Dratted waterlogged woodland in a way warded us off. We did not heed. Hayseeds of no description smoked stogies, made a pall of it. The forest finally admitted us to its verdurous essence. A tubulous, Eskimoid fella flirted with a striking, ruler-built, red-headed nymphet with nifty knockers, taut tokus, and tight, curvy hams, in a skimp two-piece. Nictitating brightness, blinding as brushed teeth. Ballyhoo of barbed, idiosyncratical banter. My eavesdropping can get me into a pickle. Epiphanic splendor. Kept meadow overlaid with phosphorescence, mazes of miscellaneous hedges grubbing out of it, tapped by tempestulent mis-trals. Spinney vivified. In an interregnum of thinking, F-bombing Skov's kisser, in forenoon's luminosities, was like a beautiful Beanie Baby's, rotoscoped by rays, a CGI character, she, ganja-fried and Ecstasied, hys-teric as a Tickle Me Elmo, silverfish-slicking when she went kaput, collapsed, Pieta-posed. I failed to under-stand her screw-loose ranten. I required an explanatory GPS. She did jumping jacks. I was a puddle. Ipso facto. She slaked my thirst. I did not wanna decode the sig-nals her bod was given out. Demonstrative, penumbrine grotesques, extinct and graceless, a shaded populace alienate on the mythical, cowhided terrain, dormant in onerous symmetry. Medusas of chestnuts in a glade. Cirri watersnake-squirmed. A phat pocket rocket left a ginmill hangout. My granddad, Smedley, a rufous, rawboned gonif, a stormypetrel gremlin in his cavern-ous, crudded armyjacket, anatomy gone to cancer, with his fulminating preachifying, gospelarity reverend-ing, was a recovering huckster and smartypants. I can visualize his disastrous lamps, smegma'd lips, Shredded-Wheat goatee, heineous falsies, backfiring, bellpealing whoopen, he a wellspoke, mistried crim, a (dis)reputable crook dure Prohibition, living in a morguey manor, an aristocratic, buckled semisprawl, slate-and-beige, he won in a bet with one of his unrighteous peers. His alky-soaked self-destruction. Granddaddy on nitpicking: 'If there's a nit worth pickin ...' Sun reprieved from the carbonic clouds. Serried moonwort was a ligneous gorgoneion. Ramblen gorse. My cogitations elicited a surcease of perspicuity. I sampled springwater, tasted of iron, whiffed of sulfur. A mistrustful monster of a moose in its preferred segregation regarded me, consulted, methinks, its instincts for advice. I was afeared of it. Yander it plodded. Rundown cabin, chimley MIA. Mayhaps no body resided in it there. A rocker had a lousy witch's wig of mold on it. A dozen mallard ducks in flight, lowered on the ruddied ken. Fixin my moccasins midstep. I coulda been mistaken for some whippersnapper playing Indians. I had a sleight for such feats. My feet were these arachnoid contrites. I spat dryly. Scintillation shone inexpressibly gaily.

Eruption of shrubbery. Swelt an sop in consubstantial intemperance. Pings 'n' pangs in the junction of my heel. Beatup banjo. Our balletic silhouettes. Aft with its weighty fieryness. Manic delegation of downtrod, beggared, rueful riffraff, amassed and zonkers. Sky on the cusp of overcast, sun garlanded in a morass of cumuli. Cutie couple in cupidity and overalls strode on a rutted road toward a hut harried by time, weather, laxity. Clash o' cars in a junkyard. I would've wanted to have had our echoes boomerang to us like carrier pigeons in those canyons stone's throw ways. An Appalachian acreage. My head was a loggy stump axed, split. Me and grandmama bobbled thew an amberous, droning bog. Feculent varmints absently nurtured the noxious palliative they was concocting. They growled as gators, guffawed in the pooling adumbration, and clapped in seal-fashion. I gawpt. A vile weasel with gnashers a dentist called fer, scored with zits, squalled in a vegetative awning. Diaphoresis licked over his whiskered nonchin. Froggyly he sprang. Verdin in the verbenaceous vegetation. My fiddle-physiqued grandmother hurriedly took a pebbled path, partial banded by the nictating luster, internally compassed the tugrik-tinted geography. A numskull sleazoid schnook from Hicksville, USA with a duffelbaggy shape had a looksee at a rangy, roistering heron which rollickingly hopped similar to a circus clown with curious agility and veered upwards. A nitric-greenish freshet was invitational. Tufting tules in an alder patch in shadow indeterminate. She was stern and sonorous. I was sulky and dummied-up. Floundering through the spectrally silent lavender muskeg, careered in android aspens. Azure bequeathed us alas in rain. Leven was a cobalt cognate of the vault's stormy excite. Stupefied scoundrels ceremoniously paralytic, the rascals agibber in their livid limbo of febrile clamor, swarmed not dissimilar to pissedoff armyants. Feathery phenomena. Birdybabble, pronounced. Adeptly we went on, into the shallows, the narrows. My timpanic cardiac organ. I was fevery. Drops drippen. A peewee (premature borned) youngern, frocked in an amethyst dress, she in bedraggle, lightsome and unhoused, and needing fed, worn her garments of rags unwell, moved with clandestine concerns, an endwarfed, enfeebled pitbull, parturiently awaddle, with her, like it was towed, fetched a pail out of a well, took the dipper out, and gandered at the glossy saucer of sun. Clockless hrs in evaporate. Outre herbage, jade, bister an dense. Perspiration laminate my integument. The wasted, disheveled, homeless lass warshed with parodic purpose, her pooch getting a load of her pearly, ball-round bum, untaken, as if she were unaccountable, unmindful of its weightless owner stepping backwards, like a maimed marionette, her wittle pinkpucker apeep out of the propriety of her posterior, flippery toots enbrowned by mulch, deerlegs slathered by mud, a barbarity of surprise flashed on her primate puss in spotting us, her wrenchen rictus witnessed firsthand by me, unbeknownst to Grandma, whose outdoorsy, lived-in-looking pan was evoken Baba Yaga's. She discharged New Age mumbo jumbo. Multitude of pears and peaches in fitful chi-nooks. An ammonially-stinking cloudburster was unaltered, but abated after a longwhile. Ooziest emerald holm. Windbent, sunbleared detonates of bushes, bela-bored by bugs. My vascular organ sounded as though a patron's knuckles drumming on a bar. Florae and faunae cumbered the polder. Teetse flies in a tizzy. My porker's pule of flatus. In a display I chucked pine cones. She threw pennies, dumping them not unlike baggage from a sinking ship. She was knowed to have blowed money. She had a conspic cant to her bearing. I'd've swore. A lanky looby stared at his loof, in exit of an ole outhouse. I hawked the grossest loogy that'd blown mid-air. Sparky orbit of hovery fireflies with their custom uber-bling

bedizen the environment. Furious pantomime of childish commotion. Salad dressing of oxygen. Cicadas
sang in the sedge. Downpour in remonstration. My
cob roller shriek of flatulency. Derelict toolshed of
some age a-topple. Expanse in tranquil. Bigass bull-
frogs catapulted theirselves into a wannish millpond.
Lightstreaks, rosegold, was bestown on us. I wisht to
rest, to have my achin ankle unswole. She shouldered
the mealsack at untenanted plums, hung about as an
unuttered obloquy she did. Clothes on her person - a
snake that is gonna shed its skin at any sec. Garrulous
galloots and ganefs galamphed, galopaded. Aligned
locust trees, scantleaved and a-tower, with sobriety, in
a demesne unknown, demarked by an association of
rooks dement. Dejecta in a dell. I gave it a dekko. In a
min disembodied umbrage processioned in a perimeter
of shiverin scintillation yonder. Tears of these cloudlets
accrued in the wolf-grayen vista, molasses-flowen and
like schooled shoal, given leeway, inaugurate comen
into plain sight, the overcast an advent of wetstuff. A
hunnerd crost it. I was feeling as a spluttering contraption gone haywire. I had the indifferent canter of the
Pink Panther. On the ochreous escarpment a grubby
orphan, a potential trouble-making urchin, the scraggy
imp with a schizoid, satanic presence, a devil's disciple,
maintained he was partialed to prostitutes, umber-
ine tooths in exhibit in a simious mug of incontinent
idiocy. I shrugged, hohum. He fended gnats, utilized
hardest language ineffective. He was stubby, insufficient
furbisht. I figgered he would leave us be. Vale of gloppy-
ing sleet. I had to evacuate afore sunrise. Schlaggy cirri

schismatical in the congou-obsidious heavens. Melees of yaupons and chickasaws and myrtles, cuckoo-wasp-metal-snot-greenly, vines slunk up 'em like elevator cabling. Grass with cullet-frost. Stridence of crickets, spritz parried from the Prussian-blue lid, teakettle- sibilate. Our silhouettes emulations of us. Annuals aromatic. Jungled log cabins, in uncommon cubicity, in increments of illumination. Gibbose hummocks. Indagate hunters, bird-doggen an beaten the bushery. World of womboid dankery. A plow with balded wheels chain-shackled fer snow conditions. Calamities of kudzu. An echelon of shrikes and towhees, flying brokenly, faired on up with ripped screeches, boilt aloft, forsook the land as if ascared of flood, seeking higher ground, sailing centrifugal, in penon pandemonium, blotted off in a keening feathered flume, the parcel, in entirety, rimming the dark, erectile serpentine of a summit in velocious bedlam, and in treble flapping, staining the terra cotta bluff at a shoal-pinken sunset. They was aileron oddments in steerage thew an apricotin aperture of the overall royal horizon. I was in concentrate on Grandma that allelse was constituted like the vectors of a field magnetic. I staved off libidinous considerations as though an Athenian hero keeping the Persians at bay. To a degree I was grateful for the respite that weekend weekend excursion offert me, getten away from my life in its languidity and numben routine, in the dingy shack I shared with my detached folks. My langur-lineaments. Dirty deliberations in persist. I looked I'd wager like a natatory amphibian that came ashore years ago and hadn't bathed since. I talked as you would with an egg yolk in your oral cavity and efforting not to break it.

I was a burnedout firework with a hardon, a swinging schlong with a gnomic cunning and cheetah saunter, besorced by suffering by way of estrangement, my existence dying as a snaketongue of a campfire in a pouring. I sought grace. Burgeoned furor of flowers at their wildest. She toed a stump. I was bent for a breather, my nuque's fur astanding electric. "They's life and they's livin," she said, wheezed like a goddamn doodlesack. Nutzoid younglings, 'The Shining'-ish twins out of a frightmare scarefest at a creaky Victorian fixerupper. Thin clouds curedup inta thickens. Trees malformed wavered inebriant in draughts intoxicant. Cranes a-strut as cocky humans, conceivably, and straight up, like the hanged. One follered the next, solitudes surrendered to company. My heart bonging, I forded branches chinked with a virid mossy substance in crepitant mutations, Grandma herself afoot, squawking as a microphone, like she thowed out her back she was so hunch. Pastoral provinces of the dawnin wherein was a redundant, reticent truculence. This happent. Could anywheres. Drafts incantationed a forfeited invocation, scouted through the nightshade. She trod in jimson, trampled it. I went akin to coaloil in a gutter. I was taken to token a number, had a Rabelaisian wanten for pleasures earthly. With her. It was as if I made a pact with the Devil ... Faust and the Furious ... to secure ... what? I imagined myself fisting my Weeble-constitutioned derrière, rooting around like a break-and-enterer a jewelry drawer for a jowly jailbait ahead. I was a chickenshit, and apprehension ated me as though flame at vellum. Grandma's respirations had the smooth sounds of a latenight DJ. I was a mutt of doom, a hellhound this side of the Baskervilles. Mockingbirds reviled. She loped, chanced her oculi upwards, the gibbous moon open like the yap of a deadman. This was thrilling as an off-kilter carousel ride. Sparrows and finches dispersed. The midsummer rainstorm was rank as rotting contraceptives. Vespertinal lulls. So many words in my vocabulary. I get high on my own supply. Vulpine sopranos. Orthopterous cheepin nigh unto stertorous. My ears rang like buoys knelling. Shrill rodentiform chittering. Lemme pause for this. See, she was an ash- addict, dipping into Granddad's urn, a moonshine jug, to snort lines of him, as ya would cocaine if was inclined. She began cooking and shooting him up like heroin. Disgusting and disturbing habit I grant you. Grandfatherly speedballs. She got hooked. Became a junkie. So. I looked as a bone-white Death from Monty Python with a skin condition, or Orlok down for the Count. Zephyrean harshness. Beetle-reddish, maggot-shaped cirri with incipient condensation. The suprareal skyline with its primarily harlequin hues had a section which was a zone of navy, stretched like a fuckin snake after a meal. I followed her as toilet paper stuck to the sole of her shoe. My clock was slapped by brutal winds as many times as Faye Dunaway in 'China Town.' Jack- and-the-Beanstalk-sized produce. In a sundrained glade, wiping her seamed forehead (reminiscent of a baseball's stitching) with a striped kerchief, she let me know loud and clear my dad was more invested in ale and womanizing than his wife and son. Why their fractious marriage was a frigging travesty, always on the rocks. His head-spinning, beer-swilling and skirt-chasing did not help matters in the least. He was short in stature, could be demanding and dubious, cajole and regale, reserved and grumpy. My hausfrau ma's (she was of German descent) connubial merger was fated from the start. Our hoofing was like bootcamp basic-training. She had a stunned-doll dial and gave out Yoda-esque life-lesson tips that avalanched. I was on hiatus, mentally, betwixt consciousness and co-consciousness. Candescent sun was miscast in boas of cumuli. Gesticulant boughs. Rubberine rings of truck-tires impinged on a dust-dun lawn. My shoulder blades globed with furuncles. Traceries of bramble-scratches on my weaken arms. My shins helt in cotton tourniquets of tubesockage. Perplex of bethorned bracken. Grovy creatures froze taxidermic. Acorns nested in rifflin leavage and breezed-on, balked plants. Jonquil-yellow, douchebaggy moon. Fanwise-flying pigeons. Imponderable, imprecatory, imprecise gusts dry-humped us. A bevy of backwoods race traversed the muten, tawney terrene, luminously fantasticate, the recreants discordant and divorced from direction, to these blinkers, eyes admitted not ideal, risen slumberers waked from a nap and barking as foxes. Stems of pellucid smoke slid out of a beefy caveman's pugilist-planar proboscis. He was in negotiate of the compressed scrub, rammed himself on. A meaty, horrid hominid had branchlets busting on his rugose, villous visage. This demento shambled sloshstewed, speaken inane, in these coronets of fly riffs, his vulvate trap of the damned. Mindless anthropiferous males an females in disregard of us. Catyloid cote. Soil screed with stones. Suicide solitaries of snails. Bridal-whitish celestial sphere. Hurdygurdying ferriswheel. Belting barkers. Crowdcries of the carnival. Diabolism of the sky vexed with trotten cloud over an enlighten civilisation, an indited society. Turbid carcase of boonies. My flesh newborn-tender. Droves' bewailing sounding not unlike the leprotic in epidemic hysteria. Epidendrum-prismatic rainbow. Cathedrals of crags. Amorphic air. Grammaw was monosyllabic, stole thru the fairyrealm quag as a shadow. Dead-to-rights deluge.

Her Tyrannosaurus rex members botched the batch of batter. Our drab decor, the dourest furnishings, were apparently picked from the set of 'Rowan and Martin's Laugh-In.' The Vapors' 'Turning Japanese' was on the transistor. And I listened. The abode was a soot-stygian, gigantesque obelisk ministry, a ginormous, leaning ruinate circumscribed by hobbled honeysuckle, gorged by years. Roaches in make-haste mode, a-scuttle. A vespid vortex. A variance of vehicular deities, gutted and stripped beyond recognize, was propped precarious on plinths of cement blocks on the baring yard delta'd by a recent drencher which slammed slant with enraged rapacity, restitution I accredit for a scriptured dryspell. I heard Debbie Reynolds' 'Tammy.' Insectine helix. On a creviced constellation of asphalt with some surges of crabgrass were foetal condoms semitransparent and ribbed and afreight with semen and incandescenced by effulgence and postcoitally aborted by parental partners alongwith litters of scattered improbable toys, artyfacts I deem postulate to a goneby era, the objects forgot, in thesehere illshaped ruder reaches dreamedup by an

AbsoluteBeing strick by dementia praecox and but lo it survived. The moon, skull-achromic and dissociate, stamped in yon sky. I was a sap, knackered. Lousy linoleum. A tang of disinfectant. Tenacious we troopt. Senseless empyrean composed of sowmilken clouds. A ragman nighthawk, outerspace pitchblack, clacked like a clock's gears, minihead moving as a candleflame, took off, strong and sure, leaving the vestige of a scarp's precipice, it a rockbound chateau containing an archival chattel of allthings Christian. Anothern, preening itself, a creedless, feverine heathen, to me a robed, medieval, Muslim midget, went on aswell, gliding cruciate above a stock, a strain, of men. Bullrush swayed like cobras. Burgeons of lightning. Aneroid sticks. Oxygen of an unguent drear, anointed by microscopic punkies. Grandma's mouf cracked. Her grate-gnashers sawn. Fingernails as boartusks. Her ocelotic pies. Avian threnodies. Mosquitoes dimpled the rhomboid, sluggard rill. A snarling, spangled halation of horseflies was an intransigent, insectile spectra. Speculative sun elliptical with ill-joined clots of coronal cloudlets. Oxidised autos awry on platformiform cinders adorned in the soaker. Lazy nimbus of mayflies as organisms in quixotic scud. The environs in inertia with its crypt-stench coupled with the scent of baken taters and seawater. We broiled in the scorcher. Thunder hammerin foundryishly. Lashes of levin. How long did we stump? Days? Weeks? Months? A runlet rimpled an agog. That cirri reconvened, in forms of theirown contrivance, arrested in the stillborn firmament. I was chockfull of incertitude. Brine in replica of the welkin. I tromped, tentative, my heart tapping timorous. Stars were aguey oculuses of fiends in gauge of us. Sprouts of corkscrews. Nebula diffused like cigarette smoke. Air envacuumed by my shiny lungs. Swifts trilled. Picturebook shoreline suspired as flour in cascade into a glassbowl. I scratched an itch on my flocculent, burnt nape. My silhouette, foreshort, guddered 'neath me on the funky, halfbald esparto, and mutilate. Gulls, or flocks of this genus, mutinied from the turquoise ship of sky in its vastness, the specimen of their blaring suggestion hunger, flew windward o'er leaden aquapura where whitewaves leapt goatlike, those dusken daemons of cumuli of an inexplicit impious disintegrate themselves from the tigeryellowy moon, an eagereye, protrudant, riveted upon a planet of Creation. There was an enigmatic ebonness of penumbrae in deepen. Interblending of torridity and vaporization. I was chapfallen. She flaunted commensurate with a pharaonic priestess in an older thaumaturgic observance. A bell melancholyly toll'd. Spastic passages of chiropteran tweeting. Burgundy battlements of cloistral cliffs. Bluffs ale-brown and rash-carmine. A dumpy, bat-eared rapscallion dervish lunged from a log, downy with lichen, as a bird defecting from a branch. Moisture smelled of barbershop, and sounded approximative to the blip-blip backbeat of a heart monitor. My special bits smarten. Water spurted from a sprinkler not unlike arterial sanguine from a gashed individual. Infinite heaven shone as the back of an orca. Grandma had the malodor of perfumed compost. Twigs we walked on snapped like firecrackers. Skyline and bounding main was hazy: a hexin double-exposure. Enisled tanagers an thrushes. The leatheryn void of twilight. My heart was a thing stirrin in the cave of my chest. Sweat quivered on my beat body. My razor blade breathing. The atmosphere sucked the perspiration from my pores as stories from the cosmos. A lily pondlet was a djinn hallucinate. The redhot ball of moon laid bleeden on it. My Converses felt stiffen like new. My shrunk shorts comic. A flatbed seemed diffidently fixed. Bumblebees humming as wheels on highway blacktop. Doves cooed. I in admission appreciate the enterprise of the environment. Backhome, I fess I was subject to the hazards of humankind. A citizeness with a cavalryman's whiskers, typhoid tinge to her integument, the size of a huge hog, dynamited a primus stove to the Onegin opera. Applebitter windowwasher reeled vertical ondown. Encrusted salt like isinglass granulate. Fugitive geranium-achromatic clouds enlargened in uncoordinate solidarity and solemnity, and vanished abrupt without fanfare. Girls and their granitic gran. Conventional eucalyptuses and lowland firs. Grandma ... If you craved insight into a universal totality you would remark her, eventhough she had the personality traits of a can of pintobeans. Bluejays tweedled, teetered, groggyglazed, I noticed. Morn's grove was ripen to full. Gaslamp-saffron sun. I huffed and puffed, shuddered as a caboose. Parasitic cirri incubated in the indigoid, windless lid. My ticker did whump, an good. Stately savins and cedars right of here. I held my ratty backpack like I'd retrieved it from someone who stole it from me. I clambered over rectilineal slabs of dampen stone, foundation put there, feasibly, by personages from oldendays, the order of the understructure disordered by a destructive tornado, perhaps, the groundwork erased most by forces of nature and left, remnants of plates of rock as remainders of a primordial community hidden heretofore for centuries. Perchance. I complaint I was overtaxed. She observed me like I was an item of curiosity, and she said, with calcified authoritate, I was a sourpuss throwin my own pityparty. In chiaroscuro the futuropolis city below was an unlimited crystal set. Phantasmal flotilla of cumulus. Junipers defiled. Cuntalingus was mulled. As was rectalingus. Her shadow, a secondself, androgyne and a-near. Her buttocks as purses too-supplied, plaguey sphincter a moth in a web; or a deaden, puckery rector on an altar. Her tuningfork, salamandrine tongue, waffled quim and its seareek, labbylip overhang, brewery breath, froggy voice, monk's blinders, basketry of tress, rudimentary encephalon, castiron chompers, swells of breasts and them buoybell nips, flannelfeeling feet and their odor of terminal sickness and germicidal chemicals. She, a shrivelly succubus, a senescent portress of infernal regions, plowed on thew a crucible of boughs. We was in confabulate on 'Smokey and the Bandit,' gotten my twocent vote as a classic, she sayen it was like binge-watching the dying of the human spirit.

I had visions of Kentucky-fried demolition-derby smasheroos and 'Debbie does Dallas.' Irrational, irate bugs. Sun risin dire, would cook yet, soon or late. Unalive mooncalf in steamy crap. Varied trashpapers in plenty of dockweed. My ribcage vised my cardiacorgan. Stickage as digits cautionary and in disembodiment. I belted buttermilk, bolted cornbread. Steel-bluey skyline. We climb-crested on an impressive, dangersome pinnacle with its spurious placidity and implacability in fulgent folds. Monochromic mesas. It was magnificently mildout. A rout of cocoacoloured turkeys shagged like noisecrazed at a quicken carriage thru an agrestic tillage in aridity, distinction, and boundless as forever. My heart pounded like metal at a forge. My soughs sissed as something spit over a fire. I was a dept. store mannequin stiffen. Hail like mortar shells. We made our way as reapers through carp-yellerly reeds, we Siamesed in a pesty parallax of malefic damselflies. We stayed twinned. Goin in conjunction. Mulberries. Locusts. Biennials. I hotched. Malign mounts not without menace. My entirety was feeling Novocain-benumbed. Hortative senilic paranoids with porridge-derma membranaceous-pigmented, indigents ponderously awander, in defecate copious. One, buck-toothed, pug- nosed, and bullet-headed, tandem nares widen (you could drive a septic-truck through each of 'em), was apparently resin solutioned, a glabrate gentleman with a suet-galled gut, in a patchwork outfit. I stewed on my procreators' nearfatal carcrash, by all witness accounts a crashfest dummy sequence, the autogeddon aftermath accident scene sundabbled, the luxury sedan tincanned - a miracle mangle. I felt incomplete: a song cutoff before its final notes. I dog-slinked, a venomose serpent biting my bosom, my brows knitted, eyes fastened to her. The afternoon had heaved itself 'pon us. My originators lived, in critical condition. An eery estuary. Anurae, smooth-skinned, tail-less, and stout-bodied, with suction-cup footsies, their replicants waven in the water glaucousiferous, with its chemic/swampy redolence, amphibian creatures easedup on a lumpen ridge and blinken mesmeric and buttressed 'gainst the day decalescent. Mine locks were feathered in the waftage and awash in the humidness in its heaviness. A vesperal ding-a-linging in the dimming distance. Her husky tones. Looking Glass lakelet. Antics of assorted starlings and lemmings as they accrued outa the stormleached everthing. Her running had a legit thumping to it. Myown had the jitterbugging BugsBunny quicks. I had a galaxy of contusions on me. With the scratches resembling stitches I was a junior Frankenstein's Monster, parts pinched from different burial plots and sewn together in a rush job. Clouds in configurations cryptic. Little 'uns, snips of nippers, shored up the refulgence with their grungy, abrasioned flesh. A mulatto mendicant, overweight and grimestreaked, lagged, lurked like a killer at large, an arrant archaism, a paradigm of a sufferer in damnation in a world of mankind, slewed with lyrically obscene limberness, mimicked buggery with a willing willow in a beadcurtain of precipellets. A wax figurine gamine with a tart smirk and in Daisy Dukes speaken as if it was open mic night slapp'd her apen brow. Covey of swallows. I was like an outboard motor ... speedin spurrin us on howbeit I was an accessory. A Speedo'd twink. The geometry of the geography was recast in rawumber umbrae. Taking a protracted pull from my from my Gatorade, delivering a burp, musing onhow my maritally-challenged progenitors was human being horror shows. She plod as though in a scampy spoof, a faulty mechanical baboon in a deviant carnivale, frown gargoyled in carven stone, leather-padded rear-end crack-riven. Upper atmosphere lithographed with these cirri. Lord amercy my parents were open-and-shut cases of anality and adversarialness. Moms was manipulative to an extent, a Lady Macbeth in our Hopper-esque home silo-leaning, she employing regular reverse-psychology tactics and twisted logic, a foul-mouthed psycho-pixie. Dad was clench-voxed, hard- hearted, absentminded, an obsessive. Them pesky gadflies. Gales pledged in those plants, made my top turnstile on my trunk. Fireflies were ferine lamps, conspirators in the swarting nighttide. Hellaceous amounts of midges. The chill deepened. Jiminy Christmas! Insolvent mademoiselles hopscotched. Grillidae cantillated an arcane doxology. Grass stood as hair electrified. Grandma wenton, and saurianly, me jackal-like. That moon was enamored of the empyrean. Showers sliced surgical, fizzled as police radios. Dirtpoor passel of striplins. Susurrate collisions of orthopaedic branches. Brilliance not unlike duelists' swords. A sprinkler's water-vees. The pouring in deliverance made longish lachryma, failed in the ebonized foliage. Yayo-ish sand. Sheets in create of a gossamer smear. Locks of loco glowflies whizzed cyclonical. Licks of gnats. She was perspired, as if snow had melten on her. I could make out her gauzed chin-whiskers, red-rimmed eyes. She could scare a bulldog off a meat truck. Air gravid with dampness. The gloam found the stand. We scampered across an open orchard, heave-ho'd over this ossein fence, and got into these gyratory convoyerly trees like persons petrified. Cumuli slavered condensate in saporosity and which sifted down as though dust. Surrealistic symbols spraypainted on a brickwall, put there I guesstimate by a demonical cartographer. A carboniferous everglade in simmer. Sputtering course with a mayhem of minnows. Her shaver-nicked lower-leg. Her nicotine-tincted, untrimmed nails. Ravins haunted the firmament like enemy planes. Bemisted bushery. My atonal swansong? My equilibrium lost its impetus. Plantpaws. Magnolias offended by winds. The sun was a Holofernes head hangen from Judith's Heavenly girdle. Cloudy lotuses unfolded and leaves of light burst over an exulting sea, forthwith a cunning duplicate of a malachitean welkin. Thou hast been here, in the unprecedented oceanica. Lively calls of cranes, with skill and energy reckless adhering to the saltiferine oxygen, so true and false to each other, with their intervals of interruptions, fanatically delirious. A succession of capricious waves, incorruptible, rollin and tumblin, assailants deceiving and bedeviling, seethed, foreannounced themselves. Oftener ya can hearken 'em, aye. Optical illusional coast-line. My bleached champers. Dug ground exposed the earth's pipe-viscera; work begun, not finished. Her spluttering delight. The rain accressed out of goo percolate. Chain of lizards shirked not unlike separate segments of a train, in railroad sludge. Hoofcloppin of my vascularorgan. Her throaty modulation, birdnest tresses. She made a farty sound as a squeezed mustard dispenser. I told her of the Carrie-level bullying I withstood at Special Ed, and that, on occasion, I could be faster than 12:15 Mass on the Riviera. A nectarean stickiness an sweetness to the air. Bands of brightness. Purly rindle. Webby, loamgray clouds made the the pale skyline ostensibly into a busted windshield of badglass.

Wildlife, hereto in quietus, bedlammed instantly. Concussions of thunder, snaps of lightning. Sheeeit! Hothouse heat. Drove of paroxysmally wingen ravens. Lumber company. Rankest milkweed. Cuspidine branchlets on the muck becrept by candybar wrappers. Remembering her pastprime physique, unconcealed into natural, the pinchin cavities, those oldin orifices, her wiggly, hoary hindquarters black with fecal matter sos it revived a minstrel's face. Her crown rugged out. Wearied allover I was a gimpen goof. Terrain like from fabled eras. Hen in occlusion. Colt in thrombosis. A thylacine-countenanced kiddo. Cirrus whorlen. Vault choken on them. A hookbacked, sableheaded, rhesus-resemblant ogress in a dress of damask material, she with a seamy mouth and BO of a grave in violate, middlefingerly saluted us, hiking in the carse. Sparver of glimmering boughs. Grandma and me unintentional mimicked the movement of food through the digestive tract, conversing on my folks' free-for-all odd-couple bickering, both going toe-to-toe as block-busting rock 'em sock 'em robots. The atomic vista, partial Hubba Bubba-orange, preparatory to spitting, where cumulus, harboured, were breaths smoking in algor, kalsomimed it, wherein tinny, smallen seagulls, in indications of antecedent, elevate equanimity, and in profound conjugations of time, flewn. Virid plantage hammocked inbetween hirsutulous ferns. A meatless cur titubated and mewled. Her airbrakes-sonanced flatus. Our penumbrous pantomimes in breezes poignant. A yellowbellied stormcloud. Her telephone-rattling breathing. I imagined her magenta, flappy pudendum lowering, in confidence, onto my physog, it lying inwait. I tongued the crepuscular core of her phat azzhole with its cumber of piles, and cleant the lint outa her nauplial bellybutton. She shook spasmodic like a Halloween decoration skeleton, funhouse-warped, my cock on the rise, looking as a molluskan head coming out of its shell. Her unwell pussy was an older, unhealed injury, muff a-grizzle. The perverted spectacle seemed to be a randy RN caretaking of a patient. An excremen-titious cork stoppered her goryglory sphincteral outlet. Her flabby, talcpowdered tochis's pimples like pox. We had bestirred in the matter of entering ourselves in the vicissitudes of the journeying, the aurora waning away, the lambency unsubduable in the unstaked ter-ritory, these fireflies making a sparking celestial spirit, a formless fount of glitter, an unearthly glistery being uprising from the swart soil, a bizarre beacon unbear-ably beckoning, allured us on until it disappeared as if it nevereven existed. Blackbirds companionable con-sorted in a wideopen locality under influences of a hotspell and humectation. The lonesome horizon of a beryloid blandness prevailed everlasting in repose an was attended by cloud put in motion by issues of demo-niac gusts. The ocular sun steadfastly eyeth the remotest range. Her cerisean falsies, vulpine phizz, in my vision. Her flaccidic haunches hung, a prelude to cunnilingus, on the eternal edge of ever. Her liverous, vulvate bivalve swang in a helic course. Her pendular mutant mammies were rotten, rubberoid mangoes in a drainsuckin day-dream. I rimmed her floppy hind's excretal raspberry, orally mesht with it, sampled its crapine backwash-tasting urine, feces. Anatomic abstracts. My passion poised with rue. Her malodor of harbor. Vulpecular and vulturine vulgus. Mine fumblesome mitts on soften hams. Spats of sieving skeeters listing as though a unit in the wellnigh anonymous boscage with its teeming balsams. Clogs o' trout swam not unlike dumpt quarters in the stream iceblue. Ricegrain raindrops peppered and cracked as voltage. Quartziferous moon boring up and blind and suspected to siesta in the blue yonder. In the ashen nitefall you could scarce perceive the chestnuts scalloped like fungus. Nitflies in foment. Processional panoplied cloudlets cast with darken import, a smirchy sleeper's motley, in an outlying vicinity of heaven, came thisaway, in vengeances of gales, segued, cook-white, components of them, into a tail-light red, meniscus part, stalked thataway. Recurrences of jissomy mizzle. Communities of florets vibrant. Progeny of groggy geese hurry-scurried round shambles of shrubs and afterwhile the gaggle swung on up. A herd of gnawin buffalo on the carpet. Catatonical statuary of a suncured lecher with tissuepaper integument rubbernecked us. Okay, branches grappled with theirselves. Deadpanned, slender cuntlets, cadgy, underaged ingenues and purty, with mops matted and eyes sunk, flowerets already wither, aligned in attitudes, drownded in floods of fulgor, shaken with bluebottles, boilt warsh in a vat, they defeated facsimiles of femininity. Skiff alone. Boulders furred with moss jaded. Those cormorants as fluttering pennants. Filaments of lichen on rock. Rags of slime. Cough syrup lagoon. Pacific deeps of the sky. Carbon copy spruces, cypressi. I appeared to be a pubertal pervert I'd opine righthere. Thunderheads Indianfile skirred like waterbugs. Clutches of saplings. Sun eclipsen in a cloud was trained on us. Fog ghosted. Oxygen weighted with swelter. Illumination favored a burly bootlegger in flirtation with a slim, peroxidic-platinum, cherubical whorelet wearin a plungin button-blouse, pencil-skirt, and Dutchy clogs, the post-pubescent lionet prostie brandishin a six-pack. Fancystepping over the cowpats as a filly in skittish. Ligular leaves. Residences rooflorn. Scabrous strays. Shantytown encampment. Swandiving seabirdies into the grackle-marine ocean for aquatic aliment. Squalid denizenry. A lycanthropiform, brawny bumpkin, dresst in burlap, a mondo menial with huridinoid choppers, hist-respiren, an impenitent with a wreckingball potbelly, riflebarrel nostrils, and barbered pageboy with a bombous baldspot, drank from a chromeblue beck, unmaddened by mayflies in incessant circumlocutional bombination and circumvolution; blinken semaphores in noon's glim. He in expatiate prebarbaric to hisself, all tore up, his manhood-pizzle rose lengthen, the detonations of his sobbings resoundful, the gaybull knelt on chalken gravel, the weather in sequential mutate. His spooky, maudlin inflections. The fishes salmoning unordered (to my lamps) thru the ripcurrent. He had maggot-yeller, spongoid growths on his shoulder-blades. A gawken nigga with a gangling Nubian babe. Unfair! A gammy gammoner struggled with a gamp. Boreal wildonion in the glazen midafternoon beams piercing through trees truncate in wasps ravening.

I was a human highlight marker drawing attention to my parents' argumentative batshitery. Grandma and I discussed our family feuds having taken place in a pressure-cooker atmosphere. She was kidfaced an fine-boned in those longago times, fore unsettling caducity, an callous dotage, took hold. Her slain- arachnidan, arthritoid shakers. Her balaustine bottom, a bum to beholden to. Her balanoid, noctule-carmine lips. I was immobilised in the straitjacket of strain. Pelting torrent's rapping on a paltry, second-rate shed sounded as palms bongodrumming on a tabletop. My chiclets clacked like Coleopteran bustle. My heart was a live coal in the fire of my chest. The well of my throat was dried. Mischiefmakers and some toughcustomers of numeral ethnic groups vagabonded. Blood pumped thew my arteries. I had the sensation that communication was broke between us. Skeeters kept snatching themselves around the sedge where a deaden possum layed. They swirlt, frantical, as if they was trappt in a vitreous jar, put in it for fun by delinquents. A fatten skunk rock'd parous. A reedy reprobate. When I did spiel, at was as though an entity in possession of me screed, if that makes anysense. No response was comin forth. I vocalised. Zilch for a rejoinder. Drilling woodpeckers ... a visited rackit ... unwelcome. They skied off. She passed this plastical container with pasta like it was a ceremonial, we akin to chieftains from separate tribes. I perorated. Nothing in return. My oculi were those of a wildling ferocious, in irreclaimable nature. The scissors she used on a chip bag were as sheepshears, she squatten, for a pan, challenging her joints, her ligaments, in variant states of mute ire, struck me as much. Varletry on a vasty dell. Aspic air. She had a turn-on-a-dime demeanor, and a devil-in-the-eyes look, with a foghorn, smoky intonation which belonged to a torchsinger in a jazzclub in the roaren twenties. Courteous maples in postures of benevolence. Migrative orioles, cardinals an robins. Her irides a-glint. Geese beating away. With the braces on my teeth made a slaverous harmonica. Levelly Grandma regarded me. Suspirings repeatedly riflin. Her waterlily-whiten ankle-bone. Moustachioed negrine with a duckbilled visor with his bony, brokedown nag. Nocturnan luminary. Malarial dankness. A scent of hyacinth. The past and present tended to merge for me. This was vibing as fantasy andyet was actuality withal. She mentioned how she invested the house with taste and antiquity. I jus shrugg'd not unlike Atlas. The leven theatric suffused the troublous land with an exceptional vividness of intensity. I poured over the parade of her apparel with its mothball redolence. In the luminosity she was chrysalis-pallid, gooneybird-slim. Larceny of looks took on my part. Where would we go? What would we do? The mortal mind bothered by victim's guilt is capable of playing potent tricks. I'd blocked out powerful, traumatising events with an automatical self- protective mechanism. My lank locks blew and she tidied 'em prompt. Muchas gracias, I said. Memories was mysteries alurk in the decrepit corners of my psyche. She stroked my silken, equine facet. She put the canteen in the satin, serpentiform burn for a refill. Acacia blowsy, midmorning. Insufflating I was in the clearance. Fake foliage, adumbral, interpret out of real. She sucked her breath in. Conceptual greyhoundish silhouettes. Countrified, campestral area covered in pollen as mustard powdered. She acquired a shadow out of the blue. The skew of it was noticeable. We sat in searchin silence. I figured she was taking me far to leave me there to fend for myself, to rid herself of me once and for all; a pet unwant. Anhydrous groan of seethen sonancies of her inhalations, exhalations. Firs flapping like flags of nations outside of a U.N. building. Her pinkie-nail plum- hued. I had the feeling I was being direct to oblivion, the fastlane without a stop at the tollbooth, y'all. She was cool as a cucumber. Pair of frowzy buzzards atop a serious plateau. Severest avian revilen. Slapping a mosquito on my wrist like in a coinflip. Imperial blacken oaks. Dunflies as marauders. Four deers singlefile. I yearnt to remove my undershorts and skinnydip, bared like a lightbulb, in front of her. We were as fencers, preparing at daybreak, the way we behaved, with the ironcurtain and deadair, alltold. She parked herself on a pineboard and swigged tomato juice from a tumbler. Mudhuts of an impaired village at a crossroads. I panted strenuous. Histrionic heretics. Flathatten falcons. A billy browsed in a gully, tugged at vermil grass in develop. I blimped out, gormandising my tacos and tortillas, sating lickety-split, alas! I gestured, and elaborate, for her to dig in, but she waved me off noncommit. I was bleary-eyed and slumpt, weary, worn from wandering. She was tuckered too, widen legs decussate afore her, Gila monster finish grimaced. To sprawl spreadeagle on the hay and cop z's! Yellowjackets bushwhacked us. Lunarly country. Cauterant heavydew. Barren countryside. These birds shelved on treelimbs.

The quartermoon turned horned in the terminal of sky. I felt escorted to my doom. As if to break the ice she told me of her first job, setting up pins in an exotic, erotic bowling alley in the boondocks, attired in only lingerie and stilettos. She was imperfectly goldgrilled like an innercity yomope. Ignescent bugs. Ignes fatui of some migratorial groundclouds. Lotsa loam in an arroyo. Lightning snapped. Thunder pealed. Rains slashed on down, a storm of a type malformed, a better demon in an antagonism, lashed, unleashed itself upon an unsuspecting place. Where were we headed? What was in store for me? Where was she takin me? Where was our destination? Goaties grazed on johnsongrass, a-sprout willynilly. I 'membered Grandma mowen the lambent lawn after raken the leafage in her best ochre finery after church service. I bit my thumb's nail. Dull browns and listless greens of the backwoods. Interplaying luminescence. She, darneded lucid to me, at a juncture was auburn-ringleted, hypnotic-eyed, porcelain-fleshed, figger lusciously long and endowed with perky tits and pert rump-cheeks. Cattalo, beefalo uprooting. I gulped, my sternum sore, as though a bigbroad had plunked herself there for an interim. Variety of featheredfriends. Her slightly wrong face, rusty strands, curvaceous build, in a saturate location with delicate textures myriad. Precip sounded like the short-circuiting of an electric-board. Insect chorus. Doggydin starten up. Zephyrs gabbling as sashes loosed. Sonofagun, was I a nervous nelly! The shade shapin on the sorrel terra firma. Doe feeding on a ridge spectacular. Pewtery breakout of doves skyward. The atmosphere afforded a deal. Aisles of aspen, betula. It was too toasty to tolerate. She relayed we was going for a rocket launch, taking off together, in tandem. Would we crash and burn? I was a thimble of a thing. Brothers in a bromance got lovey-dovey, into hanky-panky. They, supercharged, slipstreamed through a parkinglot, it like an autopocalypse, a carmageddon, them faggots queers in their element of sillyscape. My peepers congruous to those of a buck perishing. In a villatic underregion a jaundiced poacher advented with a viperine virago, in duds drapery and ruptured waders, forded the viola. I thought of our holiday-brochure retreat, an Icelandic, blasted moonscape in its volcanicity, and that Paul Simon golden oldie, 'Fifty Ways To Leave Your Lava.' A boat's engine puttered an chugged. Puddles were congruent to oily pies keeping tabs.

The china-blue aqua pura lemon-colored by the light traversed by uppity swans in perfect progress, as the veriest haughty princesses, such elegant enigmas, their passage smooth, craning their necks, bendable like heatened licorice sticks. One was ebonfaced, mudmade, having, reasonably, chancing its head in muck to get a cameoing fish. I had a chalkyturdy taste in my oralcavity. Stonegrey skyline. Lilac radiance. My rasps leapt from my chapped lips, crackled as an intercom. My visage changed peculiar on me. Evoked in my optics a beige trail slunk in the miasma like a metamorphosed millipede. Fowls snuff-tinged swept, shifted and dipped, thence surmounted the narrows of asperous canyons and crossed the peachening vault as winged comets. I fell to eyeballin them - supplicants of sky. Their flutterings honed away into Grandma's anserine rhapsodise. I post-stood, definitively dumbstruck, in that wonderwood. Horseflies pullulate. Umbilical vinage. Refuse-engorged poison ivy hung with tiny grails of glowflies. Slagdark, goodsized, gruff river. An overalled oldtimer, a woollymammoth, prepped his rod's nylon line, tested it in protocolary sacrament, and sat hisself on a makeshift seat construed I would propose of packingcrates. Swipen at his betruncheoned sneezer. The thicket was proofed for difficulties. Morning glories gutted with a gallimaufry of hubcaps and a collectanea of offal. Overpowering aroma of humus. Smells of perennials. Trumpety datura. Phlox-tincted lagune. Troves of accordioned mosaic of beer and soda cans, with matter and material. Talcose Scotchpine. I funneled down my mineral water. Talcous chicory an hibiscus. Immotile Grandma, reflectin. The sun in suppurate of emanation. Vine-strangulate semi. Herbage trampled under a concrete arch where a rank hermit slept abject like a babybirdy in its nest, his snorts sort of sepulchral. A kind of hellish, desertly pastoral, over yonder. A tramp with acheronian lamps, illspaced chewers, and whelk-whiffer, dredged from the packed chase, in pinched spiffy sneaks. Hornets in motile acerbity. On unused trainrails he, with a netherdank reek, seeped as sewage. Sunpeeled, Grandma mentioned my originators' lovelife, skippering along choppy seas, brought up her own self, a latterday Sisyphus in perpetual fixing the beach house on account of the weather's asperity in assiduity. Gnarly trees. Gnurlt garbage bins with avian-poop accretions. Dang birdlime-hued vista occupied by an organization of squirmen clouds: a blah omen. Bottlecaps winksome in the splendorous beams of brilliancy, bedded in odorous mulch, was, in illusion, artillery cartridges from a forgotten armory. Sorrowing spate. Rooks noiseless. Duckies upflung made a quacky hoopla. Rousties in dishabille, physiques faultless, sculpt from toil and no other, squirreled round, sozzled, in all suspect, in sunfaded, leadtincted sweetpotatoes, in couth. Fleas clove my mane, a strawberry-blond straw-stack. Fact an fiction blurr'd. What was fraudulent, what was genuine? Frazzled-but-flourishing evergreens and redwoods. She apprised them the while, awonder, out on a limb, speculate. Squash-pigmented trees in the unusual brilliance. The roustabout rountineers' cheeks were gravid with gum and/or tobacco, glared like fish, the glozy, columnar beams clung to them and brung to life. Scrape-stigmata. Wildlife hosteled in the forest evident and froze as samples of taxidermy restored to their natural habitat in a morbid exhibition. Brants stunk. Poplars agnate to gigantean puppets, the addled leaves congenerically consistent with hanged leeches. Backhome I was marooned. With her I was a survivor rescued. A hieroglyphical branny gleam in intersect. Sacular moon. Sabulous puffs. StoneAge pike. I'd caught my second wind, saunterin not unlike a jaunted domes-tic cat. Noneventful vespertide. A ferret-countenanced, mascara'd, wasp-waisted, super-slender, mollyhawk tomboy rigged out in a 'do-rag, halter-top, boxsies, and mules, diminished bod waffled in boughs, water moccasin slithered, had a germic celerity and a spider monkey's sprightliness. She was a reveler recuperate, conceived figmental, given my fatigue then. Her young boobies shooken as frying eggs. She had necromantic wales on her tarnished trunk-thighs, those boohoos comparably Mesolithic ecclesiastic symbols, this creatural mallemuck with scabby hickeys on her swoose-cervix in some molecularly dissidence. A humongous log laid a-straddle of an adularescent surge. My aguti-obverse ruddy, pondering Dad's multifarious adulterine relations. Weatherly witcheries. Starkish, blighted blue appropriate by clouds in an imprecise sacerdotal service. Rough-and-ready Vandyke-splendor, complicative and promiscuous. The thoughts in my noggin like illumination refracted thew a prism. 'Twas warm. Her complexionless paint. She was a pucker-scowled bugaboo moving in Matrix-mo, notexactly a javahouse wit from the Restoration era. I searched for perspective, as if I was peering through a viewfinder, a Claude Glass for instance, which is a convex mirror, me yenning to find my lost balance, the sacredest simultaneity of the spatial, the temporal, to gain purchase, the equilibrium of humanistic subjectivity through a necessary objective thingamajig. I was in require of a mental camera obscura, or any perspectival apparatus. I read her like I was vying to grasp an ambiguous allegory. She as though in fabricate. Sapwood. Madness reigned. Her bronto-backside. My manly unit was feeling like a shrunken mummyish pygmoid head with a penile proboscis. I couldn't get rid of the willies-inducing nightmare taking place next to a pastel birthday cake of a candy-colored, Kubla Khanesque Xanadu of a baroque hotel, in a Burroughsian netherworld with elk-pricks whinen and whizzen, sleepwalking, androgynal, faceless forms, Australoid colossi and hirsute homunculi, enceinte-protuberant wainscoting, furry anthropomorphous centipedes, and creepy hermaphrodate chinadolls with testiculate eyes, phallic noses, and cuntal mouths. I assumed she would drop me as a hot potato. She had a sinisterly allosaurian glower. Gadding straydogs scurvy with whimperings made known their starvation. They ceased to sound. Canst thou hearest the silentiousness? The environs esteemeth it, the quietude, with a new-made quiescence of its own. A rockscape was a giant spinal column with misgrown masses of moss on it. Overcast was a parchment unrolling on the yawen horizon proper in reveal of its sapphirous secret consequent upon the absence of cloudcover. Storm commotions retarded it. Sapsuckers ratatatted on the alburnum. Mistrals in chary expedite halloo'd, had their egress. A lubberly lubra with a piratical patch in irate, her imbalancing act leeward increasing, inevitable, her canoe's tendency to sink, the openboat already exhibiting symptoms of capsize. My braining happenings. And anon the distention an contraction of my stomach. Gunk, gook antlered by the branches' shadows. The hightemps makest my topstory go foremost downward, it dangling worn and not given to gravity's dictate. Her Rock of Gibraltarian wrinkles, Pantheon postern, Calpe corporeality. Nay, think ye! A valley was spacious enough in all conscience. A scimitar-shaped, harelipped goon dragged himself like an ox does timber.

I was, now, thoroughly panic-strucken. Was I tripping? Having fuckedup flashbacks? What was I gonna do, dial 911? "Yes, operator, there's been a Kafka-esque Metamorphosis ... my grandmother has T-Rex arms ..."

Mmm, that'll go over like a metalline dirigible. Her sat-elloid, ribald backside belched a calfbawl of flatulence. My intestines were tangled locomotive brakes. Our beloved kitties, well-behaved and loving, black domestic shorthaired siblings, Luisa, the sleek female, and Jose, a stocky male, roamedalong in distinct disinterest in the frighten drama unfolden. Blowed dust on a crookedly path. I buttered a roll. Bloodreddened earlymoon ellip-tic. A brittle and frail screendoor banged as canvas. The skyline in default of stableform because of the agencies of cirri forbade it. A mangy German Shepherd had lain like in state on a lawnchair. Squirrels pilfered birdseed out of feeders. Spots flashin in my eyes was risen as sparks from a fire. Thosethere laundrylines yoked cross yards depilate. Addorsed adumbration in a cropland of plenitude. Swales o' grain. I, perspired, dripped like an oar. Silt ebbed and flowed in those shallows a-shim-mer. Seaweed looked as beached squid I would say, engrailed by daytime's sheen. A hazel osprey gave the impression it was in pursuance of its inumbrated dop-pelgänger, went high and hung, and glid aright abrupt. Others of its genealogy shunted the scruffen earth and its storybook fluke, commended upward, and swooped in unfaltering, unflinching conformity, entrusted theirselves to the spinning empyrean in its glinn. An embayment rife with garbage. Her cargos were snug an lascivious to her anatomy. Hot polder. I attempted not to gawk, plumb quit, pronto. Kelp- octopi. A sepian goshawk on a ledge in a gorge gorgonised goslings. A clarion creek, pret near, scooted, purred its incoherence. Cactoid plantage waved like tipsy orchestral conductors.

I in float shunned force of attraction. The beautifullest bikini'd Barbies, epitomes of beach bunnies, imbued in a game of rage-volleyball, tumbled, oneandall, as Sonic the Hedgehog. Titties jiggled. Behinds bounced. I sipped my Poland Springs. I was feeling not unlike a kamikaze pilot on a collision course. It was fixen to pour - the firmament overtook by cumuli. Ailing halesia and sorbus, boughs benison gesticulate. Dogdays heatwave a Testament curse. Muskeg slime. Her pensive, poetic puss. Greening forest. Deathly blue welkin. Commence of schoolkids wore next-to- nothin. A Charonic ferry-man conveying souls on the Styxian lake for the Hades of shore. Acres bedimmed by vaporous fumes. Glazing pastureland with galore of grass and bovinic convoy and plus our silhouettes in unpremeditate flexion, belated on gambogian ground, inciting ethnological cogni-zance. Galyac-clouds. Ponies in galvanic gallop. We defiled on a hillside, scruffy and declivitous, disem-bogued similar to stool thru a cesspipe. Some filmstrips of rainfall. Leaves dropped as pickedoff bats. My heart, with its valve jangle, caromed. A monotony of mosqui-tos. Chuffs brought on out. Gulls in glissade like sharks. Barrelbulk of Grandma's duff. Her knifegash mush, kissable boody huggable. Her ursine grumbling. Dusky darlings, longlegged negrites, in felonious nubility, Afros wacky, veered into a viaduct, clumpen past, titivated their undershift vestments. Their icecream sandwich tootsie-wootsies (minus the top portion) creeping the dirt. I evaluated them as if there was portent to be founded. Scritches of their gossip. Nubilous lidofblue. They raced on a levee like precip-beads a winder. Zinc

water algally choked and not without botanic surrounds, dew bewept and bug beset, decocted outta the
pea soup. Mosquitoes hummen a refund in melodial
birdsong. Angular anhingas. Staccatic snickering of
orientoid babes burntlooking, mops exceeding bounds,
swimmingsuits apparently painted on, youthy visages
upturned, gibber manic, wonder struck at the glitter
and balm of the MidAmericas on offer, consumed in
the torrid light not dissimilar to torches. A ghoulish,
anguilliform, foul, gabbing, gabardined harridan, with
axcut, gabbroid peepers, vaulted at 'em, in chastigate for
a nebulant wrongdoing. I yearned to punch the ghastly
snatch of a crone in the jaw. What could've motivated the
hag to be such a twat? Breezes herded scraps. Sprinkles
came lukewarm. Rimey cloudlets. Decorticate diesel rig.
My head boomed as a cocksucker! The Albertan layout,
hoarhued in the brume in its obfuscate, lightened palely
in the scintillating shafts, the drear: polarvision of a
soporific crazyperson. A malodor of rancid wool. The
sun impending, oblong and shedding its lances. Slouchy
littoral. Humidity a rheum drainage. Territory inundate
with an iodine volley. Remembrances made their way
through my greymatter like headbeams snow, delivered
there as though a pizza deliverer pies to a frathouse.
Bankside mistletoe. We in peregrination went, paces
purposeful and circumspect, like targets at a shooting
gallery. Perihelial marvel. We'd scarce spoken. I felt as
a deadman walken. Them fenceposts a-loll. Trauma
can distort, destroy. I was like a fugitive captive led to
the gallows. The calidity emerged from the terrain as
from blacktop. Skeeters swarmt not unlike mini-stars.

Castoff innertubes at a waterfront. Plains folded neaten in incandescence woozy an triangulate leaflet fronds. Showers smackin of tin. Yucca-blanched cirri. Baleen-brighten bald eagle in ballismus ballonne'd from a stony projection. I did manducated on my bologna and liverwurst with no enthusiasm, slugged my grape Koolaid. Ailanthic aspens. Angulate albatrosses on a lime- rocky, snaggytoothed aiguille as custodianed lookouts. One in decide quit it. I dunno ... My existence has hitherto been like my senior prom ... disappointing. I wontedly digress. The vault was a sloppy suture. Lunchmeat noisomeness. Atlantis-megapolis in limboid, pestilential smog. Quails gurgled. The squaloid vista which bore the sleazy moon attended by aspectant spanglements of stars. Cockchafers abuzz. Papercups claretcoloured hobbled in the uptempo gusts. An ungendered, buzzardly, snuffling, splay-heron-legged hunchback with a buzz-cut, a geriatric derelict, whiffled fowlwise on a flowered streamside. Bruisy flare of black-and-bluebirds. A ravaged gibbonguy dismantled the caved antiquarian armature of an archaical, antediluvian trolley encoiled in effluvia. A stormic brouhaha. It brewn. Aborticide of the fetal sun in a vaginal heaven by the abortifacient cumuli. Drifting smaze. Grandma's bodily distinction in suggestion of somethin. Pierless waterbed. The trip with her was entertaining as a holding pattern. She disseminate her bad dream was scary as a sock-puppet re-enactment of 'The Exorcist.' The radiance landed invoking to the terrane tormented by the engulphing, direful centralbody of the solarsystem. Gales divulgated themselves. Branches in divergency, divaricate. Weather pardoned and punished equably. Leafage pages of the Book, leaft thew by deitistic winds. Alligator snapper liedby. Cranes in commune. I discerned the kitcats, yerstruly in auscultation of the Righteous Brothers' 'You've Lost That Lovin' Feline.' Horizon furred over with clouds, in sheer usurpation, placidly coasten, most-likely betokening a meteorological system, the rainbow through the bepatching parts, a butterscotch sun in an ominose observance. Crickets in merriment in a pictur-esque field cultivate. Vireos stashed in the scrub scouted, hoisted, an rocketed off. Sultriness held congruate to grim death. A prosperous glebe. Salted zephyrs from the ocean contiguous. That romantic briny expansiveness of mountainspring clarity with wigwam waves in Afric swelter, unawed seabirds exasperate in fullthroat, strug-gling in the ragen squalls, them foundering, a smattering desisted in midair like comets froze, jerking out baleful cries in the fieryred celestialsphere. Blossoming blooms breached up.

I was pustular and attitudinous, sweated as a dang can of Diet Coke, feeling like a medschool casestudy. A toupee'd mechanic, inveterate-lookin, strained himself, with coolness and equanimity, a performing contortion-ist under the hood of a vintageous convertible, in greasy dungarees. He minds you of a person who accom-plishes gymnastic attainments. Ere long, O sir, I saw him tinker, his cogitations nigh incommunicable. A ditzoid, I imagined a high Skov, a you'd-marry-her-in-a-heartbeat hon, so out of my league she was an alien, a sextraterrestrial, the mastiff, Nicorette-masticating, and her schemic musketeer accomplishes, thrill-seeking, seat-of-your-pants, devil-may-care doofi. The darnt sky brighted with cardinal, the approaching clouds slouching away. Our old-fashioned curtains mottled an frayed. Grandma's for real blood-chilling, hackle- raising transmogrification. Sumptuous cakes of enfoamed breakers. Slappings of the beachgoers' flipflopped feet on cooking pavement of the jampacked parkinglot, a-going waterward in the sabbath's extremest incalescence, magic relief of the swell transfixturing, attracting them thither. Humanity and sea wedded, these combers slumbrous as smoke, and sighing. The scores of miles, beyond, in brilliant fervent, having mazy vegetation. Undeviating coruscation in obliterate on the cement. Dromedary hump of dune. Narcissi of bathers, border scandalously ensuited, beholden to their quiverous images given to them by the generose sink, the sunreddish numerous inveigled and sallying with halting steps, and skipping out into the slooshing surf, in foggy sprays, tide's ripcurrents, akin to grasshoppers in a meadow, embarken for the safesand again. What a coast in misten immensity! Weeping an wailing of elemental combat whilst we gnashed our teeth. Skerry. Heapt swimshit. Cay. Crummy commorancies manifested like a bombed district following battle. I was a kidult czar in the thelassic paradise of bewitchin sublim. Space was icebound and crackedup with cirrus, the bilged sun there to see. I fancied nibbling on her gristly clitoral mussel, with me quaked in stimulus. Obstreperous youngsters in tropical tawn in an orgiastic frolic, they clam-size and toothpick-spindle. On the qui vive parents on watch, leanly laughing, smiling as apes, making no ado, anticipants of satisfactory conclusion to the gambol. Thatsun, a resplendent icon in scorchen daze, did its doubleduty as heater and dryer for the chilled and wet after a dip. Maniform plants. I sniffed eggsalad from the unfastened oralcavity of my backpack. What a load! Healthy oxygen. My hamadryad-mane. Cutted reeds laid there. Rank-and-file of light-minded plebeians. Grandma could be kindly and crusty by turns, dealing profundities and banalities. She would have the dulcet, uplifting cadence of a dentist ameliorating an unnerved child who is gonna get a tooth drilled; or the slitherly-sounding tone of the Big Bad Wolf bullshitting Little Red Riding Hood. We pressed on. A Congoid mental manikin, tot-diminutant, hatchet-featured, had a tenpin-cranium, brush-hair, and bosky beard, stood like a wooden idol, growled as a brute, reconciled, I was confident sure, to the fact he was baken. Unanticipate, he spun like a retired primaballerina, romped as Richard Simmons auditioning for the 1980s 'Solid Gold' dancers, sang like in some karaoke competition at an assisted living community. Sundry gaspings of the drink, it a representation of the azure. These sneering, sturdyframed nondescripts were athirst for attention in the hotspell. Congregates of condensed cumulus proffered drizzle. Kelpied billows. Unassuming trees. Fossilized feces. Pneumatic sibilances of outbreaks of influxing whitecaps, micaceously blinksome in muttersome whisks. We went forward. Prepubertal lasses in tankinis hared off into the bush. Cloudlets in demarcate. Phalanx of hussies was ahead. We took a notion to lope thru the unforgiven cane and sassafras and persimmon. Quarteracre of dormant tract

in its finalized doldrums. A Maytag washer and dryer in
the limning blaze at a brokedown farmstead. A limpsy
limmer and a lindying lady in the knotweed. Sphecidae
in a galvanize in a snarling swath outa the pebbly mire
plumed forth in manageable levitate in them fruits and
helter-skeltered. A loafen loadie. Lobeliaceous plantage.
Lobo-hued skyline. I commemorate, subliminal, parting the ruthless brambles, the unmistaken blowups of
grownup conflict, the soundtrack of my youngeryears,
ricocheting through the floorboards. Ma and Da cuddled me as kiddos a pup, but got bored with the care
of the pooch, if this makes any sense to you. I was the
proverb chesspiece in a match each was striven to win
at allcost. I was positioned on the board an manipulate, locked in the middle of their hostility towards
one another. Pops was a smartarse workaholic and
Moms was a functional (barely) prescription pilltaker.
I was a tool in their competition, a prop with which to
gain leverage. The disaccord, disunity, resentment, disdain, was tangible. I was passed back and forth. Hate
is imprisonment. Love is liberation. I needed freedom.
Craved it. I was caught 'twixt 'em in a bitter divorce.
There was a gaping hole in my life, a lack of stability in
my existence. I felt like they were saddled with me. I was
cute as a button, with endearin mannerisms, evenkeel
disposition, saccharoid grin, and had angst to spare. I
was messed up. Falling apart. Torn from pillar to post.
In the familial soap opera their contempt escalated. I
became a lost soul. My folks were egotistical and adversarial, on the destructive hamsterwheel. I absorbed the
spillage like a sponge only to wring it out lateron in

therapy sessions. A rough road. I saw, firsthand, upclose and personal, the lethal toxicity of my parents' "partnership" as it deteriorated. They were so self-involved, invested in their lousy lives. I longed to be their bone of contention. Everything sucked. I wanted to matter. My eyes lit with an animal awareness, my aspect with percipience and without device. Godamighty, I tripped, tried to recapture my footin, grabbed a thorny branchlet, yeowed, my toots sang on the pineneedled floor, and I was feelen like a dolt. My crotch-crickets rankleriled. A freckle-faced, flat-topped, unibrowed, cauliflower-eared, buxom lummix with a rat's rictus in irritate spat into a spittoon, arranged in a hand-me-down panoply with noshape whatsoever, he with thosethere punkin nates and hefty hurdies, natating in the murk, speaking to hisself, took away by the sunshine in the lamps of mine so-so dependable. Rankness of bathless bastards an wetten sawdust. Skeletons of laurels. Gothical harp of deluge. I sported a schizophrenic's asymmetric expression. Segregate lindens. Sun intumescen. The inutterable clamminess. Intortus, intwined clouds. Umbrous shadowy puppety performances played on a soilstage. My windbreaker caped my shoulders. I danced to avoid briar in the hinterland, I speciously a witchdoctor boogeying around the sicken in heal requirement in the welter of brightness. Paupers, as if picked out of the pictures, trooped through, derma layer like dingy panes. The pariahs' facets filth-smeared as guerrillas'. Busty blondie. A wizened, girthy oldster with a bewenned cast budged in the terrestrial sphere's marl like a windup plaything, precarious and proud ya may say, automatous, as though he was mismade, swine-screamed, dukes dug into his forepockets.

Toughen countery. Damn. We wormed thew woods. I was drifting in irreality. I humped up a whale of a steep slope, hauling my rucksack. Arterial spatter of the heavydew. A nambypamby loudmouth had a powwow with a peckdeck of Indians Native. There was more buff mantorsos than you could shake a subscription to 'Men's Health' at. The convict-orange moon. Nobull, brittle Grandma with her glacial poise and tightlipped sangfroid. She was a hotcha hootchie-kootchie number back in the day, dressed to the nines wearing her Sunday best bib and tucker, traipsing through the treacherose wilderness, on our trek to Jesus-knows-where. Spiritin thru a streamlet with our haverbags. Deadcenter of a betterhearted ashen alfalfafield where we ended up at. I halted, friarly vultures sailing in the multicolored sky obligen me to distinguish them. They'd sprung; a flock, flown as one. Here we was. Uncertain whether she had the intention or not. Where we wounded up. Creamy, curdled empyrean quieted like under edictal command. Funnybirds aspired into the sanatory air. A gorbellied goonygunda. Broodful jungle yay wide of us was festooned, in discreet, with flora and fauna. We turned in, flopped shortly after a supper in consist of beans, franks, Jell-O, and joe. I roused first in our tantent. Granulate rain. We were mummified in our rumpled sleeping bags. Testy insects. I unzippered autogenically and unfolded hers surreptitious. She snored waxenly and humorous, in her checkered jamas, laid there comatose in unconscious crucifixion, as laundry to dry out. I spied rumors of her unders. My dick emergent perpendicular. Here's where the assault transpired. Happent automatic it did. I was this robot, programmed to violate her. Gnats gluttonous zipped circular alright. I molested the funbags, fondled that backdoor, a holdalled swinemort, fingered the sandpaperish yinyang, thumbed the excrementic chestnut aperture, you know the one I mean. I received a rush incompare, got a sensation of release like I'd underwent an elaborate exorcisory ceremony, penetrating these precious elder orifices she had on her, bethinken of me in the arcade of her apartment with its aged austerity, its suggestions of former grandeur times, I kneelen repentant, in the bowels of her saggen, springless mattress of the wonky, queenly bed, propped on brickstacks, beatin off as a beast, my pecker in her used pantyhose leg with its overworn stockin stink, to my eyes it not unlike a longate rayon rubber a goliath would utilize. I appraised the room's rococo ceiling, jacken my pud off, in imaginate of her lamplight-pallid, anemic ass, slack and cylindroid, lucent and hex, my respirations amplified in my ears. I whined like a fidobitch needing in emergency to go potty. Whooo, was I fomented! Digitally drilling her, horny, I was going to climax, blow my load all over the joint, goddammit, when her eyes snapped open consistent with an awakening tv zombie's, the dead returning to life. She sat up as a dang vampyre in its coffin, clammed. Methodically she buttoned, meticulously zipped, looked shocked. I was stunned for a moment. Minutes ticked themselves off. I averted my clock, my dial a-profile in shame. I got a whiff of my forefinger; the saddest stench. I was reprehensible. An I was alive. We packed, with diligence, nobody

somuch as emitting a word, and left the site. Lateron,
she confronted me in my crashpad. It was like the entire
sordoid affair had dawned on her in a delayed reaction way. Was I in denial? Was I delusional? Was I the
victim? Was she the perpetrator? Or was she the vic,
me the perp? Was it her idea? Did she have an ulterior motive? Her setup: we were alone. Desirous, I acted
on an impellent influence. Spilling spawn-droplets.
Deeps of her oculars dulled. Her alleymouth reeking
of ashtray compounded by grilledcheese. Slishes of the
soaker. Weather otherwise rancorless. My heart echoed
as mocken sniggertitterin in a cavern. My insides lightened like a pinball machine. She steamed as crockery
on a burner. I seen her from my eyecorner. I held dear
in my mind her stabbing a pickle which squired her
meatloaf sub in a dive chuckwagon, the dinky greasys-
poon with its diversity of clientry, and her sucken on
it like a member. The image gave me a questing boner.
Mishmash hodgepodge of dispatched inconsiderate
litter ferreted into patchwork driveways, scuttering as
useless crabs. John clientage. Scum-pearly clouds gum-
shoed into the starkly firmament. Atheistical asiatics
audienced a gayblade blackman bearing resemblance to
the Cowardly Lion and a faggy fellow (a Homosapien),
lilystalk-scrawn, appearing like Tom Snyder, gladiating
in waiterly unifs, the fairies in the nosegays. I knew them
not. Grandma was in impersonate alleged of a Sammy
Davis Jr. offering. Bold, domineering promontory in
its titanism toweren overthere, the singular spectacle
a correspond to a common skyscraper, commanding

obsequious homage of the ocean in its infantileness. Curven straits. Tralucent bushery of the smother aloft. Welkin ballasted with the refulgent ring o' the sun. Noonday's Isaian illumination. I envisaged eatin her out, puttin anilingus on her. Antiseptic-sharp downpour. Presently, she drank clotted whippingcream from an 'All in the Family' mug, sitting sidesaddle, Stonehenge-solid. I sloshed my peppermint tea that encouraged crackers. Gethsemane glade. Swaths of wheat. Row of gerbera she planted herself. A petaliferous vortex in the wafture. She was reminiscent, corporeally, of an oldern Cabbage Patch Kid; or a geriatrical papoose in mutate. Geraniaceous plants. Gerenuk-russety azure. Craziness came on me as a biblic plague. She was redolent of Raid. Her bedhead-flat beehive, necessitous of perm, was, at a glance, gangsta-braided, crummy corn-coloured gnash-ers gold-capped for street-cred. I received a cerebral cramp. She surveyed her roast beef-and-lettuce sand-wich like a health inspector, calibrated its contents with her tyrannosauric appendages, and munched it, rumi-nant. Her hogshead gut an cylindraceous backend shook. Sedulose manducating. A bobolink, bocor-bounding and singsonging in the highbrush huckleberry and bladderfern. She handled her hankies like ya would the pjs of a patient afflicted with a potentially contagious and deadly virus, tossed 'em into the rubbish. I popped an opioid painkiller. Cosmogonic daguerreotype - tar-black cirri and corpse-white heaven. I envisioned overworked and underpaid Skov, with the doe-pies, chipmunk-cheeks, manhole-sized mouf, buck-toothy over-bite, cycloptic genitalia, drawling on about her sexcapades at meat markets. There was a Death Star-dramatic moon out, careography of gridlock on the neverended interstate, lacquered by light. The drudgery of being an employed drone, for me, was on the level of Solzhenitsyn's Gulag time: the paid work was pushing pixels on screen and punching numbers, me stranded at Gryba, Zerbe Ass. Inc. Co. on a daily basis, dealing with caricatural, carnivalesque Luc Bessonish characters. One such insufferable bozo was a NyQuil-nipping, business-end-broom-enwigged, chummy cockney chap, Gudas, a hypochondriac workerbee slumped as if he was bullied into submission, who, instead of saying "hello" in the hall, would give you the Heimlich maneuver. He was a retired hactivist, a rapey limey who'd served a fraction of his sentence, released early on good behavior. He was infamous for instigating a dance-craze in the clink which took over the prison population, where you would stand like a statue as though you was Gary Numan in the 'Cars' video and repeatedly turn an invisible steering wheel. The company, this sprawling tech bureaucracy, an Orwellian corporate entity, was situate in a decommissioned chapel, Tower of Pisa-like, with dystopian details, managed by garnetiferously pigmentate, gynic Klinkhammer, with his Zorgian hairstyle, Leeloo lingua franca, Karl Lagerfield accent, zebra-striped three- piece, and leopard-print loafers, he firm and fair. Our cubicles were our rabbit-holes, old-school, arcade- fashion video-game consolean, with us strapped into seated stair-climbers, programmers plugged in, cracking codes calculate, with a steady supply of annoyingly inane assignments. When too stressed, I grasped for the first available straw, that is, J-bar. The environment was like a metro station. Crikey! I felt close to being a member of the Rebel Alliance having successfully infiltrated the Death Star; or a Hobbit in Mordor (the merrier!) ... I was docile, pliant. Starin at nothin. Our desks were candy-chromatic organs, teeter-tottering as John Lord's from the rock group Deep Purple, computers Christ-heads with keyboard-Crosses and nailed hands-and-feet modems. The wallpaper was woefully dated Windows 98 ad signage. The workplace was aggressively regressive in its garish design. If your peepers had taste buds it would leave a terrible taste in them. It was a dog-eat-dog domain. The spiral of my misery gained momentum, dimension. When I left everday I'd feel as a jailbird released, temporarily, from Shawshank. There was stacks of files. I went through them with a fine-toothed comb. Grandma sat with a fleshly thud. Rhododendrons and forget-me-nots and lilies got a reprieve from the unfair temperature, in the protection of shade. I snuffed a tang of dank grain and rotten radish. A badboy blowhard and an effeminate milquetoast, blankslates both, were chestthumping and crankblasting upbeat hairmetal in a musclecar on a pigfarm. The scene played out was longer 'n Lent. They were wind-whipped. Tropical greenery. Dusk's devilries. Cumuli disgraced the oranging horizon. Wrens ruptured into accolades of twitters. Them cloudlets spoiled the vault's limpidity, swirled like bats, only slower. My smeller ran as a stein overpoured. Atrabilious Canadian geese in navigational enterprise. Juvenile aberrants cruised like cops, in promote of pisspoor behavior, acted as nutsy foreigners learnen new customs in distant countries, skin marshmallowy, homely and handsome, skinny and stout, sweet and sour of body odor, and foul of (meth) mouth. A mesmeric samesex, eh, younglady couple, intoxicant like whisky, pecked as pigeons at crumbs in a park. The brunette licked the blonde's chin like a stamp and they vamoosed. I wanted to skedaddle! Relentless cumbrous calefaction. My cochlear umbilicus stang. A molderin ham was a disembodied uterus. Erectile penial manufactory in the film in a fade.

Grandma's condition was spine-tingling, goosebumps-making. Aurified, auriform leaves. Shreds of clouds were sperm cells swimming toward fertilization. A confluence of larks visually complemented one another, only had subpar rapport, and went as labmice in startlement. She did a jigsaw puzzle, put away chocolate chip cookies, downed milk out of the carton with missen child photo and information. The vista expectorant. The copious verdure ticked and spattered. Her posture acquired a cant. Her comportment was ... well ... Carrionbirdies got theirselves acquainted with the upper atmosphere. She fought a losing battle with her alliaceous-smellen terrycloth bathrobe which hadn't been laundered in an eon. AllHalloweven-autumnal breezes. Antemeridian antelopean auroral phosphore atremble, sluiced out of the vaginal sun, in quiverous placentary oxygen, ran before walking. She gaped at me like a landlord her tenant (confronting, alas, the inconvenient consequence of eviction) who is late with the rent. My innards knotten as socks. She was sourgrapes, but strove to take her changeover in stride. Hell's bells!

The transformation bothered both of us. Naturally. New Age meditational music came from the trusty transistor radio. I was stonestill, kept my yap shut. She bungled weather-warped vanilla wafers into her trap. I glimpsed our modest furnishings (she a benefactress of persons kindhearted), to divert my gazen at my distinctly dinosaurianly transmutationed gran, staren at the oxidised and marred radiator that usual spurnt ever solicitation made of it. Hit-or-miss brilliance. Heinous henna wallpaper unscrolled in fronds in select corners, and pled its case in most areas. The placentate air. In the horrendous steaminess I was feeling not unlike a fruitcake marinate in sherry. Was I losing my marbles? Was I out to lunch? Cerebrations multiplied as rabbits. Fear stuck me like a roasting pig. My brain was a blown bomb. Her bridged back arched in plausible eroticism. An her Poseidon-posterior honked as she toddled into the dining room in disarray. Trepidation arrived in me like a guest unbidden. A cuddlesome, carrot-topped cutey, petite as you please, juvenescent and sausage-succulent, contain in a one- piece bathing-costume, darted as a bunny for the Nautilus-voyaging ice-cream van playing shuddersome tinkly tunes. Gunge-precip shortlived. An emptyhanded rustic. Worry lingered around me like a housepet. Sheesh. Celestial sphere as silk. Aqueous element like flesh. I was, verily, bough-rigid. Sleet fell as spat tangerine seeds. Our hail-grey and dumpling-brown oldwest-saloon swinging-door opened and closed like a trap. The lop-sided garage in a juncture of deteriorate. Spate had a soda-fizzy sonance. The moles on her shoulders cited projectiles on doughnut-doughy sand after wartime fracasin 'tween forces. Oxygen as beeswax. My skull was a porcelain plate shattered by a rock. Her dermis in relate to onions creamt. She coughed like a hardtop hatchback heap. Apprehension passed over me as the shadow of an aryplane flyen o'er an orchard. She, in a jauk, obtained a jaundiced pallor. She baby-chortled in the undulant flare, its progress unimpede by the tore pterosaur-wing drapes. She sport a luminose moue, it like a strip of unnatural satin splendor under a door in the gloom. I was spoiled (in a negative not positive sense) as fruit. She was partly to blame. She'd deny it, insisted she wasn't at fault. Jays in a jaunt. Kooky cadre. Her voice was a crackly croon when she said, in particular peppy jollity, absorbing a Jeff Davis pie, in uncharacteristic articulate, years ago, my bedroom was our mutual sanctuary, that it offered us ... mmm ... opportunities. Her actions were musical solos accompanied by instruments of different approaches in a ritualised performance in a secretive formality. Reason and unreason was locked in mortal combat. Her glare was an arrow released from a bow, directed at me. Her goggled oculi. Her cat-eye rims. Fruit flies aimless spinning. I slurpt brewskis, in a state of seemingly permanent disequilibrium. It was den-darkened, became dismally dreary. A fetid mephitis, from the entombment of the kitchen, with a little luck getten befriended by relief, me feelen like a bug enveloped in the chrysalis of dread. A villain polarbear of Hogarthian humungousness in reprimand of a bantamine lively lad in the vernacular. I shan't ere long get into the details of the tumult, in its cuttin clamor. Opal moon. Abnormous coconut trees. I endeavored to regulate my breathing. I was a mess, in my Bagger Vance-esque golfing knickers. My heart was as a kitten in its carrier, taken to the vet. In my cranium I worked the situation as a comedian the crowd for yucks at a club. My head was split akin to an an aspirin underfoot. A buildup of cushions and an emaciate assortment of tabloid mags on a wicker basket. She shuffled, hindered, considerable, by arthritis. Grunting guttural, in vacillitate, in the meter of a dripping tap. My pulse rate revved up. My killin belfry. My spittle like broth. My oblate buttocks ached. Sultry as sitting-to-season stew. I glanced at her hound's jowls in their sphericity. Sponge flies did circulate themselves. Her gait was an inept impression of a debilitated sway. Was I swooning, dizzied thus! She shambled, oscillating. With my tuatara-blinders I zeroed inon the wholeslew of collateral she had collected like filmed American Indians cowboys' scalps, and the quaint cookbook volumes on the seesawing shelving. Skov, save me, for I am drowning! We'd gone on a wellattended whalewatch. She was so saturnine and silent she should've been an integral part of an art installation, trunk tornadoed by purring insects, in her nosebleed heels. I was a pious Solomon with my fav concubine. An outermost herd of sperm whales, frisky as common household cats, schools of monsters in their leviathanism, in their sleepy world of water, were submissives of sea, yea, inscrutable creatures, proportions testimony to their bullish, full-grown magnitude. They to'd and fro'd, bade usall adieu, moving like they was chain-and-balled, flexible tails flailing, creating successive concentric circles in the enchanted ocean becharmed by the emanation. Cloud was surf gnawin at the shore of sky. On land, eely-limbed pecan trees, charcoaled, scorched by a wildfire. Bunches of posies. Aggregaten desperadoes on horse-back. Okay, Grandma's googoo blinkers were round an sloe as the sockets of a deadskull. I was unshaven, the stubble drastic. She bent over. Her bulbiform butt. Tubule nips. She tsked. The tyrannosaurus arms. She was never remotely loving, caring, or supportive of her kin. Ever. Was not her way to be. She was unapologetically selfish. Sun was beating on the skyline like a carbuncle on integument from a heart pounding. Everything was not A-ok. Hardly hunky-dory. Her pterodonic tootsies. Her brachiosaurian bulk. A gust coerced the acacias to prance in place. Insectival applause. Winds in abate of their velocity. Gimongous crags. Their enormity was prime. I was gonna collapse as a leadthrown hambone in them quieted oldtime pic-tureshows. Cocks heckle- crowed. Hyperactive finches. Feta cloudlets sailedon. Sis-boom-bah of the boiler was driving me batsoid. Fiction was carved from fact, in my mixedup mind, like a side of beef from its carcass. She had advanced on me, back aways, and I pushed her as I would an antagonizer at recess. She shrieked and recoiled, her li'l' appendages curled like Margaret Hamilton's when she tried to intimidate Judy Garland in 'The Wizard of Oz.' She was a conked shitbox. She leant, as if kowtowing, obeisant, stalled middle-step, the loathly, prominent leer a domesticant chimpanzee's. I threw a rainbow of Starburst candies at her and she ducked a tad. Ramentaceous gnats. Her ramiform appendages. Thoroughgoing agony. My scream was my pain, it at a worthy level. She cringed, astonished, and unexpectedly shot out as though she was a bullet. My glower, in its vacancy, was on my 'Jurassic Park' poster, the one with the ferociously attacking, amazingly CGI'd T-Rex (the tyrannosaurid limbs!), so real it was unreal ... Cocksucker ... Impossible to believe this beast once existed on our planet here. It did. It's extinct. From that point on, Grandma looked at me like I wasn't there. Which was fine. The invisible boy. Our domicile had rooms that were catacombs of desolation. My adolescence didn't achieve its age. I felt the bite of anguish comparable to a wintry wind's feisty nip. I was not a dot on any map. I was off the chart. I was treated with mistreatment. I was usedup by misuse. Captain and Tennille's 'Love Will Keep Us Together' was on. Her enchubbed boody made Jaba the Hut look as Bettie Page. Bruteforce poppymusic ... assailen the listener as an aggravator at Julia's. Deliberations was wove through the loom of my medulla oblongata. Scent of thyme. Fragrance of oregano. Filled my olfactory. She desquamate a banana not unlike it were the wetsuit of a deceased diver. I'd betaken myself to the spice rack, a timorous, inglorious, torpid doughboy. I whewed, whigged. Our silhouettes satirized. Her turkey-wattled chin smacked of cheddar cheese; unpalatable withal. A dedicate druggist, I longed for my stash upstairs ... Nay ... My viscera serpentined, spiralised, in my gut. Inexpressible infiltration of illumination. Mongolian rug bestreaked with it. I was frazzled. I lived in our century, motherfucker, in the crosshairs, it a Trojan Horse, smuggling shite to drown the human being; an arsehole corked with the thumb of man; a wooden steeple burning, its bronzebell, the center, a moltenmass, ringing, the structure of years blazen, the supports of lives cracken, the whole shebang fallen into misshapen pile of wreck that is history. And when in scarifying Sinatroid tones she began singing Frank's 'Summer Wind' song (I wished she would've changed her tune), I bolted. I was bidding bye-bye to her. Sleep's a cow slaughtered in the abattoir of wake. Until this day I feel Grandma is gaining ground. I think of that Erasmus dude and the coolcrap he wrote, something along the lines of - 'Man's mind is much more taken with appearances than with reality.' Tale's been told. I was Lazarus following his resurrection. I had wanted to bring my story into the light and for me to stay in the shade where I belong. Lord. I ran from my grandmother with a rapidity respectable, me a godless chimera, a wayward dreambeing, into the universal twilight, tenebrous and voltaic, the shapen verge of a nameless, unfamiliar cosmos, the one knowed, filled with all living things, mainly mighty mortals. I'll be seein yins. If you all don't care. If ya can identify with any of it, Jesus Christ help ye. By an by, damn me, this came to pass.

End here.

Acknowledgments

Eric, Nina, Harriet, Julianna,
MaryLynn, Paula, Sammy, and Vic.

About the Author

Christopher S. Peterson has been seriously dreaming since he was a bambino, immersing himself in Icarusian flights of fancy. He enjoys film, music, animals, working out, football, hockey, and living in nerdvana. He has been published in several lit mags few people have read. He was properly educated at Wildwood Elementary School in Burlington, Massachusetts and currently lives in Atlanta, Georgia with his black cats.

Fomite

More story collections from Fomite

MaryEllen Beveridge — *After the Hunger*
MaryEllen Beveridge — *Permeable Boundaries*
Jay Boyer — *Flight*
L. M Brown — *Treading the Uneven Road*
L. M Brown — *Were We Awake*
Michael Cocchiarale — *Here Is Ware*
Michael Cocchiarale — *Still Time*
Neil Connelly — *In the Wake of Our Vows*
Catherine Zobal Dent — *Unfinished Stories of Girls*
Zdravka Evtimova —*Carts and Other Stories*
John Michael Flynn — *Off to the Next Wherever*
Derek Furr — *Semitones*
Derek Furr — *Suite for Three Voices*
Elizabeth Genovise — *Where There Are Two or More*
Andrei Guriuanu — *Body of Work*
Zeke Jarvis — *In A Family Way*
Arya Jenkins — *Blue Songs in an Open Key*
Jan English Leary — *Skating on the Vertical*
Marjorie Maddox — *What She Was Saying*
William Marquess — *Badtime Stories*
William Marquess — *Because Because Because Because Because*
William Marquess — *Boom-shacka-lacka*
William Marquess — *Things I Want You to Do*
Gary Miller — *Museum of the Americas*
Jennifer Anne Moses — *Visiting Hours*
Martin Ott — *Interrogations*
Christopher Peterson — *Amoebic Simulacra*
Christopher Peterson — *Scratch the Itchy Teeth*
Charles Phillips — *Dead South*
Jack Pulaski — *Love's Labours*
Charles Rafferty — *Saturday Night at Magellan's*
Ron Savage — *What We Do For Love*
Fred Skolnik— *Americans and Other Stories*
Lynn Sloan — *This Far Is Not Far Enough*
L.E. Smith — *Views Cost Extra*
Caitlin Hamilton Summie — *To Lay To Rest Our Ghosts*
Susan Thomas — *Among Angelic Orders*
Tom Walker — *Signed Confessions*
Silas Dent Zobal — *The Inconvenience of the Wings*

For more information or to order any of our books, visit:
http://www.fomitepress.com/our-books.html

Writing a review on Amazon, Good Reads, Shelfari, Library Thing or other social media sites for readers will help the progress of independent publishing. To submit a review, go to the book page on any of the sites and follow the links for reviews. Books from independent presses rely on reader-to-reader communications.